Mike Ashley is a full-time writer, editor and researcher with almost a hundred books to his credit. He has compiled fifty Mammoth books including *The Mammoth Book of Extreme Science Fiction*, *The Mammoth Book of Extreme Fantasy* and *The Mammoth Book of Perfect Crimes and Impossible Mysteries*. He has also written the biography of Algernon Blackwood, *Starlight Man*, and a comprehensive study *The Mammoth Book of King Arthur*. He lives in Kent with his wife and three cats and when he gets the time he likes to go for long walks.

THE MAMMOTH BOOK OF
MERLIN

EDITED BY MIKE ASHLEY

ROBINSON

RUNNING PRESS
PHILADELPHIA · LONDON

Constable & Robinson Ltd
3 The Lanchesters
162 Fulham Palace Road
London W6 9ER
www.constablerobinson.com

This book was originally published as *The Merlin
Chronicles*, copyright © 1995 Mike Ashley.
This expanded compilation and all additional material is copyright
© Mike Ashley, 2009 (unless otherwise indicated).

All rights reserved. This book is sold subject to the condition
that it shall not, by way of trade or otherwise, be lent, re-sold,
hired out or otherwise circulated in any form of binding or cover
other than that in which it is published and without a similar condition
including this condition being imposed on the subsequent purchaser.

A copy of the British Library Cataloguing in Publication
Data is available from the British Library

UK ISBN 978-1-84901-111-2

1 3 5 7 9 10 8 6 4 2

First published in the United States in 2009 by Running Press Book Publishers
All rights reserved under the Pan-American and International Copyright Conventions

*This book may not be reproduced in whole or in part, in any form or by any means, electronic
or mechanical, including photocopying, recording, or by any information storage and retrieval
system now known or hereafter invented, without written permission from the publisher.*

9   8   7   6   5   4   3   2   1
Digit on the right indicates the number of this printing

US Library of Congress number: 2009923257
US ISBN 978-0-7624-3830-3

Running Press Book Publishers
2300 Chestnut Street
Philadelphia, PA 19103-4371

Visit us on the web!

www.runningpress.com

Printed and bound in the EU

CONTENTS

Contents

ACKNOWLEDGMENTS

My thanks to Larry Mandelsburg for his help in the compilation of this volume. The following stories are copyright and are reprinted with permission as stated.

"Dream Reader" © 1986 by Jane Yolen. First published in *Merlin's Booke* (New York: Ace Books, 1986). Reprinted by permission of the author and the author's agent, Curtis Brown Ltd.

"The Temptations of Merlin" © 1995 by Peter Tremayne. Original story, first published in this anthology. Printed by permission of the author and the author's agent, A. M. Heath & Co.

"Infantasm" © 1995 by Robert Holdstock. Original story, first published in this anthology. Printed by permission of the author.

"The Pledged Word" © 1995 by Marion Zimmer Bradley. Freely adapted by the author from chapter 12 of "The King Stag" section of *The Mists of Avalon* (New York: A. A. Knopf, 1982). Printed by permission of the author.

"The Horse Who Would Be King" © 1992 by Jennifer Roberson. First published in *Marion Zimmer Bradley's Fantasy Magazine*, Spring/Summer 1992. Reprinted by permission of the author.

"A Sword for Arthur" © 1995 by Vera Chapman. Original story, extracted from the novel *The Enchantresses*, and first published in this anthology. Printed by permission of the author.

"The Rite of Challenge" © 1995 by Peter Valentine Timlett. Original story, first published in this anthology. Printed by permission of the author.

"Merlin's Dark Mirror" © 1995 by Phyllis Ann Karr. Original story, first published in this anthology. Printed by permission of the author.

"Morte d'Espier" © 1955 by Maxey Brooke. First published in *Ellery Queen's Mystery Magazine*, June 1955. Reprinted by permission of the author's estate.

"King's Mage" © 1995 by Tanith Lee. Original story, first published in this anthology. Printed by permission of the author.

"A Quest Must End" © 1948 by McCall Corporation. First published in *Blue Book Magazine*, April 1948. Reprinted by permission of Mrs Dorothy Roberts Leisner.

"Cauldron of Light" © 1999 by Diana L. Paxson. First published in *Merlin* edited by Martin H. Greenberg (New York: DAW Books, 1999). Reprinted by permission of the author.

"Namer of Beasts, Maker of Souls" © 1995 by Jessica Amanda Salmonson. Original story, first published in this anthology. Printed by permission of the author.

"The Corruption of Perfection" © 2000 by Mike Ashley. First published in *The Doom of Camelot* edited by James Lowder (Oakland: Green Knight Publishing, 2000). Reprinted by permission of the author.

"The Sleeper and the Seer" © 1966 by H. Warner Munn. First published in *Weird Tales*, September 1939 as part of serial *King of the World's Edge*; reprinted New York: Ace Books, 1966. Reprinted by permission of Mr James E. Munn.

"Midwinter" © 1995 by David Sutton. Original story, first published in this anthology. Printed by permission of the author.

"The Death of Nimuë" © 1985 by Esther Friesner. First published in *Fantasy Book*, June 1985. Reprinted by permission of the author.

"The Knight of Pale Countenance" © 1995 by Darrell Schweitzer. Original story, first published in this anthology. Printed by permission of the author.

"Merlin Dreams in the Mondream Wood" © 1990 by Charles de Lint. First published in *Pulphouse* #7, Spring 1990. Reprinted by permission of the author.

"The Dragon Line" © 1989 by Michael Swanwick. First published in *Isaac Asimov's Science Fiction Magazine* 1 June 1989. Reprinted by permission of the author.

DRAMATIS PERSONAE

A GUIDE TO ARTHURIAN CHARACTERS

The following is a short guide to the Arthurian characters and names you are likely to encounter in this anthology. There are so many names in Arthurian lore that it's not always easy to know whether you've encountered someone of significance or not, and when those names can be subjected to so many alternative spellings, it can become very confusing. I hope the following helps. It does not include minor characters or those invented by the writers.

Agravaine. Son of King Lot and Morgause of Orkney, and brother of Gawain, Gaheris and Gareth. Sided with Mordred in the plot to reveal the adultery between Lancelot and Guinevere.

Ambrosius Aurelianus, also known as **Emrys.** Historically "the Last of the Romans", he governed Britain in the last half of the fifth century and helped stem the tide of Saxon advance in the days immediately prior to Arthur. In Arthurian legend he is sometimes depicted as Arthur's uncle. It was during his reign that Merlin raised Stonehenge.

Arthur/Artorius/Artos. High-King of Britain, son of Uther Pendragon and Igraine, raised as foster-son of Ector of the Forest Sauvage and foster-brother of Sir Kay. Founded the Fellowship of the Round Table, married Guinevere. By his half-sister Morgause he fathered Mordred who later waged war against him, resulting in the final battle at Camlann where both Arthur and Mordred fell.

Aurelianius, see Ambrosius.

Balin. A Northumbrian knight who was imprisoned by Arthur for killing the king's cousin. He also angered the king by beheading the Lady of the Lake.

Bedivere/Bedvir/Bedwyr. One of Arthur's earliest and most trusted knights who served him as his aide. It was he who restored Excalibur to the Lady of the Lake upon Arthur's Death.

Blaise. A hermit monk to whom Merlin's mother went for her confession. He became Merlin's tutor.

Bors. Son of King Bors and cousin to Sir Lancelot. In one tale he is amongst the successful knights in the search for the Holy Grail.

Cae/Cei, see Kay.

Cerdic. A Saxon invader (though his name is Celtic) who landed with his son Cynric near Southampton in AD 495. He is claimed by the annalists as the first king of Wessex, though little is known about him.

Cissa. Son of Aelle, king of Sussex, and his companion in his battles against the British.

Constans. The elder brother (or in some stories father) of Ambrosius Aurelianus and Uther Pendragon, who was raised to the High Kingship of Britain by Vortigern only to be murdered.

Constantine. Son of Cador, duke of Cornwall and the successor to Arthur as High King. He took revenge upon Mordred by killing the usurper's children.

Culhwch. See Kilhugh.

Cynric. Son of Cerdic and king of Wessex from around AD 534–560.

Drustan, see Tristan.

Dubric/Dubricius/Dyfrig. Celtic bishop of Caerleon (or Carlisle) who crowned Arthur.

Ector. Sir Ector was the foster-father of Arthur and the father of Sir Kay.

Elaine. There are three Elaines in the Arthurian cycle: **Elaine of Garlot** the half-sister of King Arthur; **Elaine de Astolat**, a maiden who fell in love with Sir Lancelot; and **Elaine of Corbenic,** daughter of King Pelles and, by Lancelot, the mother of Sir Galahad.

Emrys, see Ambrosius Aurelianus.

Ewaine, see Owain.

Gaheris. Third son of King Lot and brother to Agravaine, Gareth and Gawain. Half-brother of Mordred.

Galahad. Son of Sir Lancelot and Elaine of Corbenic and the purest of all the Knights of the Round Table. With Sir Bors and Sir Percevale, he was one of the successful Grail Knights. He was the only knight able to sit at the "Siege Perilous" seat of the Round Table.

Gareth. The youngest son of King Lot of Orkney and brother of Gawain, Gaheris and Agravaine. He first arrived anonymously at Camelot and was given the nickname "Beaumains" by Sir Kay, owing to his fine hands.

Gawain/Gwalchmai. The eldest son of King Lot of Orkney and brother of Gareth, Gaheris and Agravaine. He was one of the strongest knights of the Round Table. He features in the earliest legends of Arthur and appears in the Celtic texts as Gwalchmai, meaning the Hawk of May. He undertook the challenge of the Green Knight, Sir Bertilak.

Gorlas/Gorlois/Gorlodubnus. Duke of Cornwall, husband of Igraine, and father of Morgan le Fay, Morgause and Elaine of Garlot.

Grainne. See Igraine.

Guinevere/Gwynhwfar. Daughter of Leodegrance, King of Cameliard, and wife of King Arthur. Her adultery with Sir Lancelot caused the downfall of the Fellowship of the Round Table. She was condemned to death by Arthur but rescued by Lancelot and ended her days in a nunnery.

Gwalchmai, see Gawain.

Gwenddolau. A British chieftain who died at the battle of Arfderydd in around AD 573. Merlin was believed to be his bard and adviser.

Igraine/Igerna/Ygraine. Wife of Duke Gorlois of Cornwall and, by him, mother of Morgan le Fay, Morgause and Elaine. Seduced by Uther Pendragon and became mother of Arthur. Later married Uther.

Iseult/Isolde/Isolt/Yseult/Ysolt. Wife of King Mark of Cornwall but lover of her husband's nephew, Tristan of Lyonesse.

Not to be confused with **Iseult of Brittany** whom Tristan married after his banishment from Cornwall.

Kay/Kai/Cai/Cei/Caius. Son of Sir Ector and foster-brother of Arthur. He becomes the king's High Seneschal and is noted for his sour temperament. In the earliest legends Kay is an heroic knight, but in later versions he becomes Arthur's irascible steward.

Kilhugh/Culhwch. A cousin of Arthur who was under an obligation to marry Olwen. Olwen's father, the giant Yspadaddan (or Thornogre Thistlehair) would only grant her hand if Kilhugh could complete a set of impossible tasks. The story is told in the *Mabinogion*.

Lamorack of Gaul. Son of King Pellinore and one of the strongest knights of the Round Table. He became the lover of Morgause after the death of King Lot and was killed by Gawain and his brothers.

Lancelot/Lancelet/Launcelot/Lancot. Son of King Ban and greatest of the Knights of the Round Table. His castle was called the Joyous Gard. His love for Guinevere led to the downfall of the Fellowship of the Round Table. After the deaths of Arthur and Guinevere he became a hermit.

Lanval/Launfal. One of the Knights of the Round Table who is beloved by Guinevere. When rebuffed she beseeches Arthur to punish him. He is saved by his beloved lady of Avalon.

Leodegrance/Lodegreaunce. King of Cameliard and father of Guinevere.

Linet, see Lunetta.

Lot. King of Orkney who opposed Arthur for the crown of Britain. He was the husband of Arthur's half-sister Morgause and father of Gawain, Agravaine, Gaheris and Gareth. He was killed by King Pellinore and his sons.

Lunetta/Lynette/Linet/Lunet. Sister of Lady Lyonesse and Sir Gringamore of the Castle Perilous. She led Sir Gareth on his first quest. Although she later fell in love with Gareth she was given in marriage to his brother Gaheris. In Celtic myth she is the mistress of the lady of the Fountain.

Margawse/Margause, see Morgause.

Mark/Marc. King of Cornwall and husband of Iseult.

Medraut, see Mordred.

Merlin/Merrillin/Merdyn/Myrddin. Magician and adviser of King Arthur. He was the offspring of a girl and demon of the air and was raised in a nunnery. His prophecies began in the last days of King Vortigern. He later raised Stonehenge. He put a glamour on Igraine so that she mistook Uther Pendragon for her husband Gorlois. Merlin became guardian to the young Arthur and later contrived the episode of the sword in the stone so that Arthur was recognized as the future High-King. He created the Round Table. He became enamoured of the enchantress Nimuë/Niniane, who imprisoned him in a cave.

Mordred/Medraut/Modred/Modreuant. The incestuous child of Arthur and his half-sister Morgause. He later attempted to seduce Guinevere and claimed the throne of Britain. He met in mortal battle with Arthur at Camlann.

Morgan le Fay/Morgana/Morgaine. Daughter of Gorlois and Igraine and half-sister of King Arthur. She was educated in the sorcerous arts and became Arthur's major enemy, forever seeking the downfall of the Round Table. By hiding the scabbard of Excalibur, which had previously protected Arthur, she rendered him mortal. She was the mother of Owain.

Morgause/Margawse. Daughter of Gorlois, sister of Morgan le Fay, wife of Lot of Orkney, and mother by him of Gawain, Agravaine, Gaheris and Gareth. She was also the mother of Mordred by Arthur, her half-brother.

Nimuë/Niniane/Viviane/Vivienne. An enchantress who is perceived in a number of roles in the Arthurian legend. She is called the Lady of the Lake, the foster mother of Lancelot, who gave Excalibur to Arthur. She also became the lover of Merlin whom she imprisoned in a cave. She is seen by some as a sister to Morgause and Morgan and thus equated with Elaine of Garlot.

Ogier. A Danish knight in the service of King Charlemagne in the eighth century but whose adventures have become linked to Avalon and the magic of Morgan le Fay.

Olwen. Welsh princess, the daughter of a giant, for whom Kilhugh must perform a series of impossible tasks in order to win her hand.

Owain/Ewen/Uwaine/Yvain. Historical king of Rheged who lived at the end of the sixth century, and is remembered in the poems of Taliesin. In Celtic and Arthurian legend, becomes the son of Morgan le Fay and King Urien.

Palomides/Palamides. A Saracen who became one of the greatest Knights of the Round Table. A suitor for Queen Iseult he later became involved in the ceaseless search for the Questing Beast.

Parsival, see Percivale.

Pelles/Pelleas. The King of the Grail Castle and possibly synonymous with the Fisher King. He was the grandfather of Sir Galahad and is sometimes named as the brother of King Pellinore.

Pellinore. King of the Isles and one of the mightiest of the Knights of the Round Table who, in an early episode, overpowered Arthur and would have killed him had he not been enchanted by Merlin. He was involved in the search for the Questing Beast. He was the father of Sir Lamorack and, in some versions, also of Sir Percivale. He killed King Lot and was, in turn, killed by Sir Gawain.

Percivale/Parsival/Parzival/Peredur. The knight most closely associated with the quest for the Holy Grail. Early legends have him raised in the wilds of Wales, but later legends link him with King Pellinore.

Peredur, see Percivale.

Reinwen/Renwein. Daughter of Hengist, the Saxon invader and first King of Kent, who married Vortigern.

Rhydderch. A historical king of Strathclyde who ruled AD 580–612. Rhydderch fought with Urien against the Saxons.

Riothamus. A British king who ruled about AD 470 who has been linked with Arthur. He assisted the Romans against the Visigoths.

Taliesin. A legendary bard and prophet who has become closely linked with Merlin, though belongs to a later generation.

Tom Thumb. The dwarf son of Thomas the ploughman who becomes famous at the court of King Arthur.

Tristan/Tristram/Drustan. Son of King Melodias of Lyonesse and nephew of King Mark of Cornwall, whose wife, Iseult, he fell in love with. Banished from Cornwall he entered King Arthur's court as one of the mightiest knights, until forced to flee to Brittany, where he married another Iseult.

Urien. King of Rheged in Cumbria at the end of the sixth century, and the father of Owain. He became enmeshed in Arthurian legend as the husband of Morgan le Fay.

Uther Pendragon/Uverian. The brother of Ambrosius Aurelianus whom he succeeded as High-King of Britain. He was the father of Arthur, by Igraine.

Vivian/Vivienne. see Nimuë/Niniane.

Vortigern. King of Britain whose reign preceded Ambrosius in the mid-fifth century. He invited Hengist to Britain to rid the land of Saxons, but Hengist in turn conquered Kent. Merlin first appears in Vortigern's reign.

Ygraine, see Igraine.

Yseult, see Iseult.

Yvain, see Owain.

Introduction

Mike Ashley

Merlin ... the very name conjures up images of magic and mystery. And what a mystery. Perhaps even more than King Arthur, the real character and person of Merlin remains obscure, lost in fifteen centuries of tales retold. But as a creature of the imagination Merlin lives on, and will forever. We all love to dream, and in Merlin we have the forefather of all our dreams, the master of enchantments, the prophet and kingmaker. To Merlin, the all-seeing, the all-knowing, nothing was impossible. Merlin is the root and branch of all that is magic and wonder in the world.

This volume looks at both the life and character of Merlin and the world of magic and enchantment that surrounded him. Merlin was not the only being possessed of magic. The Arthurian world also brings us Morgan le Fay, the half-sister of Arthur, who learned her magic skills from Merlin, and who was the queen who ferried Arthur away to Avalon after the Battle of Camlann. There was also Vivienne, sometimes called Nimuë, who became the lover of Merlin and learned his magical craft, and at length imprisoned him in a cave or tomb where he remains trapped to this day. Some link both Vivienne and Morgan le Fay with the Lady of the Lake. To me there is no more glorious image in the whole of Arthurian literature, perhaps even the whole of fantasy, than when, after the battle of Camlann, Sir Bedivere is charged with throwing Excalibur back into the lake. He twice refuses, but the third time throws it far into the lake where an arm rises from the water, catches the sword, brandishes it three times, and then sinks into the lake. Pure magic. This anthology considers all of that mystery and magic from the earliest days of Merlin to his fate ... and beyond. For magic never dies, and the influence of

Merlin and Morgan le Fay lives on in other tales and legends down through the centuries.

I was delighted at the response from authors when I first sent out word of this anthology. My early researches had shown that whilst Merlin features heavily in many Arthurian stories, few have him as their central character. I wanted writers to explore Merlin's life and character a little more deeply. The response was marvellous, the authors demonstrating their own fascination for Merlin and his influence on the Arthurian world. Marion Zimmer Bradley, author of *The Mists of Avalon*, reworked an extract from that book to present a story about the childhood of Nimuë. The Celtic scholar Peter Berresford Ellis, who writes fiction under the name Peter Tremayne, recreated Merlin in the historical world of ancient Britain, and considered his early life. Robert Holdstock, who has been developing the myths of the Matter of Britain in his books *Mythago Wood*, *Lavondyss* and *Merlin's Wood*, brings us his own interpretation of the scheming, artful Merlin, and of the origins of Arthur. Tanith Lee was the first to respond to my enquiries with a story which considers Merlin's involvement in the quest for the Holy Grail. This raises some of the mystical aspects of Merlin's world, which are further explored by Darrell Schweitzer, who tackled the thorny problem of the very nature of Merlin's existence; Peter Valentine Timlett, who considers the mystical import of the Round Table; and Jessica Amanda Salmonson, who explores the enduring myth of the Dark Lady Nimuë. And that's only half the contents. Inevitably some incidents arise in more than one story, each author developing their own interpretation. This is most true of how Arthur first received Excalibur, and it is fascinating to see the different variations on that theme, all seeking to explore and explain the significance of that episode. And there are similar twice-told tales about Merlin and Nimuë and Merlin's passing. The result is an intriguing exploration of the Merlin myth.

If that's whetted your appetite, let me not detain you, but move on and I hope you enjoy the stories. You can always return here later. But if you wish to stay, I want to explore the literary and historical background to Merlin, partly to help set these stories in the context of the legend, but also for the sheer delight of trying to draw back the veils of time and see if we can catch some glimpse of the real Merlin.

The Origins of Merlin

Merlin's appearance in the ancient writings is patchy, for although some events later ascribed to him are referred to by Nennius in the ninth century, Merlin himself is not named. The Merlin we know was born fully fledged in the writings of Geoffrey of Monmouth. Geoffrey was a cleric and teacher who lived from about 1090 to 1155, for most of that time being resident in Oxford. He tells us that he was fascinated with the ancient tales of the kings of Britain but was unable to learn much about them until a friend of his, Walter, the Archdeacon of Oxford, gave him an ancient little book written in Welsh which gave a complete history of the kings of Britain. This Geoffrey chose to translate into Latin. Unfortunately this original book has vanished over the years and it is impossible to know how much Geoffrey derived from that source and how much was either of his own muddled research or the product of his own imagination. He started his translation around the year 1130. This was a period of much interest in the early tales and legends. A few years earlier William of Malmesbury had produced his *Gesta Regum Anglorum*, another history of the kings of Britain, which mentioned the deeds of King Arthur, and at the same time Caradoc of Llancarfan was writing his *Vita Gildae*, the life of St Gildas, a monk and contemporary of Merlin. This biography mentions Arthur and Guinevere and makes the first links between Arthur and Glastonbury.

Geoffrey found himself pressured to complete his book, but he was determined to be thorough. In order to satisfy demand, in particular that of Alexander, bishop of Lincoln, Geoffrey hurriedly completed a translation of another text he was consulting, the *Prophetiae Merlini*, or the *Prophecies of Merlin*, which he issued in 1134. This text he later incorporated into his major work, the *Historia Regum Britanniae*, or the *History of the Kings of Britain*, which was eventually completed in 1136. It proved instantly popular with a couple of hundred known copies (and probably many more now lost) in circulation before the end of the century.

This book, which seeks to give the kings of Britain a pedigree going back as far as 1200 BC and the Fall of Troy, devotes much of its space to the story of King Arthur, which is itself presaged by the story of Merlin. Although throughout the book history and imagination fight for supremacy, the appearance of Merlin seems to have allowed Geoffrey to pull out all the stops and deliver a tale for the telling.

We are in fifth-century Britain. The British king Vortigern, whose name was synonymous with evil and corruption, had invited the armies of the Saxon king Hengist to Britain to help fight the Picts. The Saxons took advantage of the situation and Vortigern soon found his kingdom under threat. He fled to the Welsh mountains where he attempted to build a fortress, but no matter how hard he tried the fortress kept crumbling. He consulted his advisers who told him to seek out a boy with no father who should be killed and his blood sprinkled over the site. Vortigern's soldiers sought high and low and eventually, at Carmarthen, found Merlin, a boy of about eight or nine. Vortigern learned that Merlin's mother, though herself of royal birth, was a nun who had been visited by demons or incubi, leading to the birth of Merlin. Merlin was aware of the threats against him, but he not only revealed to Vortigern the reason why his tower could not be built, but also issued his prophecies of the future of Britain.

Thus Merlin appears as a supernatural agent, the offspring of demons. This episode had also appeared in the *Historia Brittonum* of Nennius, but there the character of Merlin is called Ambrosius, presumed to be Ambrosius Aurelianus, the general or leader of the British. This anomaly has been reconciled by some by referring to Merlin as Merlin Ambrosius, or Merlin the Divine.

The French poet, Robert de Boron, who was the first to convert the so-called history of Merlin into genuine romance in the 1190s, made more of this background. He suggested that the demons were seeking to place an anti-Christ on earth, a being of total evil to combat the good that was spreading with Christianity. Their plans were thwarted, though, when they impregnated a nun. This resulted in Merlin being a mixture of old-world paganism and modern Christianity, which perfectly depicts the anguish and turbulence of the Arthurian world.

Merlin remains, thereafter, a schemer. His prophecies begin to come true. Vortigern had previously usurped the throne from King Constantine whose sons, Uther and Aurelianus, had fled to safety in France. Now mature, they return to Britain, besiege Vortigern in his fortress which is set on fire, and the usurper perishes. In celebration Aurelianus, now king, seeks to establish a monument. Uther is despatched to Ireland with Merlin to bring back a massive stone circle. Through his magical arts, Merlin dismantles the circle, transports it to Britain and resurrects it on Salisbury Plain – Stonehenge.

Aurelianus dies after a short reign and his brother, Uther, becomes king. Merlin now schemes to arrange the birth of Arthur. Uther desires Ygraine, the wife of Gorlois, duke of Cornwall. Merlin conjures up a glamour which transforms Uther into Gorlois and Ygraine, so deceived, welcomes him to her chamber. Thus Arthur is conceived. In making this arrangement with Uther, Merlin had ordained that he would raise the child. It is Arthur's boyhood with Merlin that forms the basis of T. H. White's humorous and beguiling novel *The Sword in the Stone*.

During Uther's reign the Saxons recommence their incursions into Britain. After Uther's death, the nobles clamour to have Arthur declared king of Britain for, despite his youth, they believe that he is the man to save the island. Geoffrey of Monmouth makes no mention of the incident of the sword in the stone. That appears to be the invention of Robert de Boron who describes how Merlin magically embeds a sword in an anvil which is set upon a stone (not in the stone itself) and challenges the nobles to remove it. He who succeeds shall be king. Needless to say, Merlin's magic ensures that Arthur alone succeeds.

This sword is not the same as Excalibur. Merlin later introduces Arthur to Vivienne, the Lady of the Lake, who gives Arthur the sword. She advises him that the scabbard is more important than the sword, and that provided the scabbard is safe, Arthur will not be defeated. The later plotting of Morgan le Fay ensures that the scabbard is lost and thereafter Arthur's fate is sealed.

Throughout the early part of Arthur's reign Merlin is always there, behind the scenes, twisting and shaping events, perhaps to his own advantage, perhaps to Arthur's. Interestingly, the creation of this role was the job of the later romancers, starting from Robert de Boron, and not Geoffrey of Monmouth. After Arthur has become king, Merlin does not feature again in Geoffrey's *History*. However, after he had completed that work, Geoffrey discovered more about Merlin, or Myrddin in his own language, and in about 1150 published the *Vita Merlini*, or *Life of Merlin*. This is a different Merlin from the one described in the

History, and Geoffrey may have regretted his haste in completing the earlier work. His later researches had unearthed the story of the British bard, Myrddin, whose name Geoffrey had taken and linked with other legends. Did Geoffrey realize what he had done, or was he just careless in his research? Rather than contradict his earlier work, Geoffrey fudged some of the facts and timescales, and consequently gave us two different portrayals of the character Merlin: one of the kingmaker and magician, the other the poet who descends into madness. The result amongst his readers, though, was not confusion but fascination.

For this later tale, Geoffrey drew upon various poems attributed to sixth-century bards, Aneirin and Talieson, though purported to be by Merlin himself. These tell of a Merlin living a century after the death of Arthur. He became allied to King Gwenddolau and, after that king's death at the battle of Arderydd, Merlin, feeling guilty for not saving his king, suffers bouts of madness and flees to the Caledonian forest where he lives like a Wild Man.

In the work of the romancers, Merlin's fate is much more exciting. He falls in love with the beguiling Vivienne, the Lady of the Lake. Having learned his magical craft she lures him to a cave (in other legends a tower or a forest) and there imprisons him. Undying, his spirit remains ensnared down through the centuries.

That, then, is the story of Merlin in its simplest outline. We have a magician, born of demons, who shapes the fate of kings but who falls, himself, for the love of a young girl, and is ensnared by his own magic. Perhaps he lives on, but racked by guilt he flees into the forests where he lives like an animal and becomes mad.

Merlin appears as both friend and foe, as representative of good and evil, of paganism and Christianity. He may be wise but he is not someone to be trusted, and in the end he becomes a victim of his own schemes.

Such is the fabric of legend and romance. But was Merlin purely the invention of Geoffrey of Monmouth and Robert de Boron, or was there a real man, or men, behind the tales?

The Real Merlin?

Like Arthur's, Merlin's story becomes entwined with a number of recorded historical events that may at least give us a starting point to identify when he lived. We are told that he was about eight or nine when Vortigern's soldiers found him, and this followed the Saxon invasion of Britain under Hengist. Hengist's arrival in Britain is usually dated to about AD 449.

Just to set it in context, it might be useful to check out how that date relates to others who were living near or at that time, and who are likely to be better known. To be honest there aren't many. We are really at the dawn of the Dark Ages. There was, though, St Patrick. Although his dates are uncertain it is probable that he arrived in Ireland sometime around 432 on his mission to convert the Irish to Christianity. He at length established a bishopric at Armagh around the year 454 and died around 461. If Merlin existed, Patrick may well have known him or known of him. Attila the Hun was also alive. He had become king of the Huns in 434, and after ravaging most of eastern Europe he invaded France in 451. The following year he invaded Italy and Rome itself was only saved by the intercession of the pope, Leo I, regarded as one of the greatest of the early popes.

This then was the period of Vortigern and Hengist. On Hengist's arrival all at first went well. The Saxons aided Vortigern in the repulsion of the Picts and for a short period there was peace. Vortigern even married Hengist's daughter, Reinwen, to form an alliance. But Hengist now had a toe-hold on Britain and, in 455, he sent for further reinforcements. It would be at this time that Vortigern fled. How long he remained in the Welsh hills is uncertain, but we can imagine there were a few years before his death. The likely date for the first appearance of Merlin, therefore, is around AD 457 or 458, which would place his birth at about the year 450.

Geoffrey's chronology becomes a little truncated over the next events. Aurelianus and Uther return from Gaul almost immediately; Vortigern and Hengist are killed. This is at variance to the traditional story. The *Anglo-Saxon Chronicle* records the death of Hengist in the year 488, thirty years later. In place of Geoffrey's record we can envisage that Aurelianus fought back the Saxons from overrunning Britain and established an uneasy peace with Hengist's men remaining in Kent, and Aurelianus having lordship over the rest of southern Britain.

Not much is known about Aurelianus, or Ambrosius Aurelianus (Aurelian the Divine) as he is sometimes called. He is believed to have been a descendant of a Roman family who sought to uphold the last vestiges of Roman civilization in Britain. He may well have been from a noble British family with Roman sympathies. He was certainly alive around AD 437 when he was involved in a battle at Guoloph, or Wallop, in Hampshire. The date of his death is uncertain but it was probably around the year 473, because it was then that the Saxons began again their incursions, which suggests that opposition to them had weakened.

Geoffrey, of course, now records Uther, called the Pendragon (or chief dragon or ruler), as king, and no doubt there was a successor to Aurelianus who sought to hold back the Saxons, though less successfully than his predecessor. It is possible that there was a second Ambrosius, the son of the first, because some records suggest Ambrosius survived until perhaps AD 500.

Uther must have ruled a few years before he succumbed to the beauty of Ygraine, though that period is not identified in Geoffrey. Allowing for some uncertainty over the dating of the death of Aurelianus, we could place Arthur's conception at around AD 470.

Geoffrey tells us that Arthur was fifteen years old when Uther died, which would bring us to about the year 485, by which time Merlin would be approaching forty. Although a boy king may sustain the support of his people, he would still require a wise counsellor to help him in his judgements, and that would be an obvious role for Merlin.

If Merlin held such an important role, it would seem that there should be some record of him somewhere. It is strange that Geoffrey makes no record of this. But there is something in Geoffrey that may give us a clue. When Uther dies the noblemen of Britain implored to "Dubricius, Archbishop of the City of the Legions, that as their king he should crown Arthur". Here was someone with clear authority and the power to anoint kings. Who was Dubricius?

Dubricius is an acknowledged historical person, who in later years was raised to the sainthood. He is claimed to have founded the bishopric at Llandaff, and to have ordained Samson, late Bishop of Dol in Brittany. Some of the recorded dates conflict here. According to the *Dictionary of National Biography*, Dubricius died in about AD 612 (his entry states that the date of his death is "the most authentic information we have about him"). However, Samson's life is recorded as 480–565. Something is wrong. It may be that because of his later fame, Dubricius's life became entangled with other great names of history. However, other studies assign different dates to Dubricius, such as *The Oxford Dictionary of Saints* which gives his death as about AD 550, whilst other sources date him even earlier living from about 465 to 530. These dates would not only accord with the dates for Samson, but are remarkably close to Merlin's supposed life.

It does seem strange that once Arthur becomes king, Merlin does not appear again in Geoffrey's history. When we come to the all-important battle of Mount Badon, where Arthur convincingly defeats the Saxons and establishes a peace that lasts for forty years, we find that it is Dubricius who speaks to the troops from the Mount. You might think, considering the reputation that Geoffrey has been building for Merlin, that it would have been he who delivered the speech. It is as if Dubricius had supplanted Merlin – the Christian bishop replacing the Druid mage. If so, what had become of Merlin?

There could, of course, be plenty of explanations. In real life, Merlin and Dubricius may have been enemies. Dubricius represented the church whereas Merlin, because of his dubious birth and magical arts, represented a pagan culture, synonymous with the Druids. For Arthur to be a Christian king, it would have been impossible for Merlin to crown him or, for that matter, to remain his principal adviser.

There is another interesting point. Tales and legends about Dubricius were abundant at the time that Geoffrey was researching his *History*. Dubricius's remains had purportedly been discovered on the Isle of Bardsey and transported to the abbey at Llandaff in the year 1120, the same year that a book about him, *Lectiones de vita Sancti Dubricii*, appeared. This book, and other writings, gave Dubricius a miraculous birth. Apparently he had no father, but was the son of a nun, herself a granddaughter of King Constantine and thus second cousin to King Arthur. This accords entirely with the supposed origins of Merlin, and it is more than tempting to think that Geoffrey either confused or linked the stories of Dubricius and Merlin.

In Book 8 of his *History*, Geoffrey mentions Dubricius and Merlin in almost the same sentence. He notes the raising of Dubricius to the see of Caerleon, and he then goes on to describe how Merlin raises the memorial of Stonehenge as a "sepulchre".

It does seem strange that within almost one breath Geoffrey would favour a Christian and then a pagan act. In fact Merlin would seem to be performing a Christian ceremony. However, in Book 9, when describing the members of Arthur's court, Geoffrey makes no reference to Merlin but not only mentions Dubricius as "Primate of Britain", but attributes to him miraculous powers of healing. The last reference to Dubricius tells us that the saintly man had resigned his archbishopric in order to become a hermit, and presumably to devote his final years to solace and prayer.

However you consider it, there are several similarities between the roles of Merlin and Dubricius, both as Arthur's mentor and adviser. This even extends to their names. They could easily be the same person, regardless of the legends that grew around them in later years.

Dubricius is, of course, a Latin name and not the original Welsh, which was Dyfrig. Dyfrig, in Welsh, means "waterman", which might be likened to "baptist", although in Latin it became confused with "merman". By a coincidence one translation of the name Merlin was "mermaid", although the real meaning of the word "mermaid" is maid, or lady, of the mere, or lake!

Merlin was also a Latin name, the original Welsh being Myrddin, a name which is believed to mean "fortress". It was, in fact, an ancient and much revered name, possibly attributable to a god. In ancient days, the island of Britain was referred to as the Fortress Isle, or Myrddin's Isle. It would be no surprise, therefore, to want to link the legendary status of Merlin, as Arthur's protector, with that of the very matter and origin of Britain itself. And if Dubricius was recognized in his day as the Primate of Britain he may have been termed Dubricius of Myrddin.

Either way there is some substance here which could untangle the tales. It seems possible that Geoffrey, knowing the stories and legends of Dubricius, and knowing the other names by which he was called, interlaced these with tales he read in his "little book" and developed the story of Merlin, as Britain's kingmaker, out of the original tales of Dubricius. Although the actions of one were pagan and of the other Christian, six centuries after their existence these events had become impossibly entwined.

There is one other matter to resolve, though, which may provide an additional explanation, and that is the later life of Merlin, or Myrddin, and his relationship to King Gwenddolau.

Here we really run into problems with dates. Gwenddolau died at the battle of Arderydd, which is assigned to the year AD 573. The Merlin of Vortigern would have been over 120 by then. Our image of Merlin as a white-haired, white-bearded old mage, rather like the near-immortal Gandalf in *The Lord of the Rings*, might fit that dating, but in all seriousness it is pushing credibility, even with all of the accepted anachronisms.

In his book *The Quest for Merlin*, Nikolai Tolstoy establishes that this Merlin or Myrddin is a later and distinctly historical person, recognized in the *Dictionary of National Biography* as Myrddin Wyllt, or Merlin the Wild. Myrddin was a bard and adviser at the court of King Gwenddolau. He was known to the Strathclyde bishop of Glasgow, Kentigern, who lived from 550 to 612. Kentigern was appointed bishop by Riderch, the new king of Strathclyde who had defeated Gwenddolau at Arderydd and was, apparently, threatening to hunt Myrddin down – probably because of propaganda Myrddin had been spreading against him. It was for this reason that Myrddin fled into the forest, having already almost lost his reason because both his king and his brothers had been killed in the battle.

Perhaps of most significance is that this later Myrddin, who lived from perhaps 520 to 590, was a contemporary of the Scottish prince Artúir, son of Aedan, king of Dalriada. This Artúir never became king because he was killed in battle against the Picts in 596. Although Myrddin was not his counsellor or mentor, Myrddin was active in the neighbouring kingdom of Strathclyde so there is little doubt that they would have known each other. Moreover, Myrddin was the contemporary of another Artúir who ruled Dyfed sometime around the end of the sixth century and start of the seventh. Dyfed was a small kingdom in the west of Wales though it is unlikely, but not impossible, that Myrddin ventured that far south. The point here is that this later Myrddin/Merlin lived at a time when two warlords called Artúir/Arthur were active, suggesting that Geoffrey had found details about a genuine Merlin but in his *History* transplanted him in error a century earlier.

Although Geoffrey in his *Life of Merlin* sought to reconcile these two legends, clearly they cannot be. What is more likely is that in his research for the *History of the Kings of Britain*, Geoffrey had come across the Prophecies of Myrddin (the sixth-century bard) and had worked them into his story of Dubricius, either because they seemed to fit well with the story of Vortigern, which he had copied from Nennius, or because he genuinely confused Myrddin with an earlier Merlin. As a result, over the centuries, some of the writings and stories associated with the later bard have been grafted on to the story of the earlier enchanter and kingmaker.

This is all, of course, supposition, although it's fairly convincing. If we start from the viewpoint that King Arthur existed, it is not difficult to believe that he would have had a senior adviser, and that that adviser could have been Dubricius. It could also follow that Dubricius became confused with a man of equivalent miraculous powers whom Geoffrey called Merlin, a name he possibly confused with the later bard Myrddin.

It is not surprising that because of, not despite, this confusion, Merlin has become such a fascinating character, with a blending of so many facets: wisdom, madness, good and evil, adviser and schemer. The Arthurian world would be fascinating enough without Merlin: all of those chivalrous and heroic adventures, but add the dimension of magic and mischief provided by Merlin, and you have the greatest fantasy on Earth. For near nine hundred years, since Geoffrey unleashed the story of Merlin and Arthur, writers, poets and artists have been fascinated with the life and the legend.

The Literary Merlin

I will not dwell long on the medieval romancers. We have already seen that the legend of Merlin evolved after Geoffrey through the work of Robert de Boron. He wrote at least three Arthurian ballads, *Joseph d'Arimathie, Merlin* and *Perceval*, though none of the last-named survives. All were composed sometime between the period 1190 and 1202, and between them would have provided contemporary and later troubadours with enough of a basis for the Merlin story to embellish it continually from court to court. At length the tales were incorporated in *Le Morte D'Arthur* by Sir Thomas Malory, writing around 1470, from where it passed into the very fabric of literature.

With the rebirth of the romantic age in literature in the early nineteenth century the poets and artists focused more on the heroic and tragic aspects of the Arthurian legends, and though Merlin featured he did not have a central role. The writers tended to repeat only the basic legends.

Merlin did not return to centre stage until T. H. White's *The Sword in the Stone* in 1938. Typical of the literature of the day, White's Arthurian world is somewhat anachronistic with modern-day elements as visible as the elder world, and the whole book having an air of general amusement. Merlin, or Merlyn as White chooses to spell the name, is already old, with a long white beard, and is rather scruffy and dirty – "some large bird seemed to have been nesting in his hair". His wizard's den included, amongst its paraphernalia, the fourteenth edition of the *Encyclopaedia Britannica* and a complete set of cigarette cards featuring wild fowl by Peter Scott! He wears spectacles and knits. Clearly this is no historical Merlin, certainly not from the fifth century. White has set his story closer to the period of Malory, but lumped in whatever anachronisms he wanted. What makes White's book so enjoyable is that he uses enough of the legend to make it familiar and acceptable, but blends it with a light-hearted dig at contemporary society and morals. White wasn't the first to do this. Mark Twain had created the concept in *A Connecticut Yankee at King Arthur's Court* in 1889, but White went much further in developing his own character of Merlyn, so much so that it's the one we've come to accept, without thinking, today. Merlyn appears throughout the four books of *The Once and Future King*, though he's not central to the later ones. Toward the end of the Second World War White added a fifth book, *The Book of Merlyn*, which was not published until 1977. It sits uneasily with the earlier books, and reflects the mood in Britain during the war years. Some of the humour remains, but it is less successful.

It was up to the American pulp magazines to give further consideration to Merlin. Some were deliberately humorous fantasies, like "The Enchanted Week End" by John MacCormac (*Unknown*, October 1939). Here, Merlin is released from his tomb by an American scholar who then seeks the wizard's assistance in making him an all-rounder on the local sports day. This story was apparently very popular at the time, but it's rather too shallow and contemporary for my liking.

Much better was H. Warner Munn's "King of the World's Edge" (*Weird Tales*, September–December 1939). Munn brought much originality to the legend. He considers a Roman commander who had remained in Britain and fought with Arthur. After Arthur's death, the commander writes a letter back to Rome which tells of Merlin's plans to leave Britain and explore the lands to the West, ultimately settling in America. An extract from this work is included in this anthology.

Other stories at this time were essentially retellings of the original legends, although Theodore Goodridge Roberts, writing in *Blue Book*, at least brought some verve and excitement to his embellished tales, one of which is also reprinted in this anthology.

A major step forward was made by John Cowper Powys in his long and detailed novel *Porius* (1951). Set in the year AD 499, it tells of a young lad, Porius, who determines to join Arthur's cause. Porius, though, must experience the rites of passage to prove himself. This includes taking upon himself the demands of Merlin, here called Myrddin Wyllt. Merlin is given a strong mystical aura – he is called a "creature of earth". He has a long black beard and wears sheepskin clothes. He is depicted as sinister, but forgetful, something of a shaman with shape-changing powers but finding this harder to achieve in his later years. Powys injects some humour into what is otherwise a bleak novel seeking to depict as accurately as possible Britain at the end of the fifth century. It was the first honest portrayal of Merlin to appear in fiction. Powys's achievement was further advanced by Henry Treece in three novels, but especially *The Green Man* (1966), which also depicted the historical world of Arthur and sought to rationalize the Merlin of legend with the known mystical and religious beliefs of the day.

Merlin moved centre stage with a vengeance in the trilogy by Mary Stewart which began with *The Crystal Cave* in 1970, and continued with *The Hollow Hills* (1973) and *The Last Enchantment* (1979). *The Crystal Cave* remains the most complete novel about Merlin's youth, and ends with the conception of Arthur. It is one of the few to consider the legend of the creation of Stonehenge, and Mary Stewart brings a most satisfactory logic to the tale. *The Hollow Hills* follows the same time-frame as White's *The Sword in the Stone*, but is deliberately less facile in its treatment. Merlin supervises Arthur's upbringing from a distance but is still seen as engineering his future. Since these novels are related in the first person we see little of Merlin's physical appearance but get to know much about his thoughts and motives. *The Last Enchantment* is the most powerful of the novels and considers Merlin's own fate. In all three of these books Mary Stewart draws from a basis of legend but applies her own interpretation. She was the first to consider Merlin's whole life seriously and place him, not in an historical context, but in a legitimate interpretation of the legend.

Mary Stewart's novels set the standard for later works, and were a difficult act to follow. Most Arthurian novels since then have continued to focus on the tragic life of Arthur, his knights or his queen, and only a few have looked in depth at Merlin. Robert Nye brought an erotic and bawdy interpretation to the legend in *Merlin* (1978), a book which nevertheless pumps life into the old man, and develops the links between Merlin and the source of life. Some of these mystical aspects also emerged in Marion Zimmer Bradley's brilliant *The Mists of Avalon* (1982), which sought to blend history, legend and the religious beliefs of the day. It depicts Merlin, or *the* Merlin as he is here (recognizing the name as a title not a personal name), as a victim more than a vehicle of fate as Christianity seeks to blend with pagan beliefs in sustaining the elder world of ancient Britain.

Jane Yolen cleverly took different aspects of Merlin's life and blended them in a series of stories which made up *Merlin's Booke* (1986). Because they are distinct stories she is able to explore various forms of Merlin's character without being restricted, and though it makes the book uneven as a single read, the individual stories are ever refreshing, and one of them is reprinted here.

Stephen Lawhead's *Merlin* (1988), the second volume in his Pendragon Cycle, is set in the same time as Mary Stewart's *The Crystal Cave*, following Merlin's life from youth to the events of the sword in the stone. Merlin is less scheming, finding himself as much a victim of fate as the world unravels in the violent days before Arthur.

Then there is Nikolai Tolstoy's *The Coming of the King* (1988), the most complete book to look at the bard and mystic Myrddin. Tolstoy provides another first-person narrative of Merlin's life, but this time set in a post-Arthurian world, showing Merlin's role in uniting the successor kings of Britain in an attempt to protect Britain.

There are plenty of other recent Arthurian series which feature Merlin even if he is not always centre stage. Of special merit are the Guinevere trilogy by Persia Woolley: *Child of the Northern Spring* (1987), *Queen of the Summer Stars* (1990) and *Legend in Autumn* (1991). Merlin's role is most prominent in the first volume where he is seen as a wise man and seer who somehow gets involved in events mightier than he had reckoned. There is also the Daughter of Tintagel sequence by Fay Sampson which focuses more on Morgan le Fay, but is a detailed interpretation of the clash of magic and power. The influence of Merlyn (as he is here) is evident throughout but especially in the third novel *Black Smith's Telling*, though the image remains more romantic than realistic. The series runs *Wise Woman's Telling* (1989), *White Nun's Telling* (1989), *Black Smith's Telling* (1990), *Taliesin's Telling* (1991) and the rather idiosyncratic and personalized *Herself* (1992).

Merlin has also been depicted in films and on television, notably in the film *Excalibur* (1981), where he was portrayed by Nicol Williamson, the American TV mini-series *Merlin* (1997) with Sam Neill, and the British TV series *Merlin* (2008) where Colin Morgan plays him as a young man. Even if you've read other books about Merlin I am sure you will discover something new here. Now, for those who have waited patiently, I hope you feel you have learned something about Merlin's life and world. Let us now hand the centre stage over to him. Merlin . . . your world awaits you.

DREAM READER

JANE YOLEN

Jane Yolen (b. 1939) is an extremely prolific writer of fantasy fiction for both adults and young readers. I still regard her early book for children, The Magic Three of Soldatia *(1974), as one of her best, though several other offerings, such as* Sister Light, Sister Dark *(1988) and* Briar Rose *(1992), are equally memorable. Jane Yolen has won several awards including a Special World Fantasy Award in 1987 for her contribution to the field. She has written several Arthurian stories including the young Merlin trilogy* Passager *(1996),* Holsby *(1996) and* Merlin *(1997). The following, which sets us on the road by taking us to Merlin's childhood, comes from* Merlin's Booke *(1986).*

Once upon a time – which is how stories about magic and wizardry are supposed to begin – on a fall morning a boy stood longingly in front of a barrow piled high with apples. It was in the town of Gwethern, the day of the market fair.

The boy was almost a man and he did not complain about his empty stomach. His back still hurt from the flogging he had received just a week past, but he did not complain about that either. He had been beaten and sent away for lying. He was always being sent away from place to place for lying. The problem was, he never lied. He simply saw truth differently from other folk. On the slant.

His name was Merrillin but he called himself Hawk, another kind of lie because he was nothing at all like a hawk, being cowering and small from his many beatings and lack of steady food. Still he dreamed of becoming a hawk, fiercely independent and no man's prey, and the naming was his first small step toward what seemed an unobtainable goal.

But that was the other thing about Merrillin the Hawk. Not only did he see the truth slantwise, but he dreamed. And his dreams, in strange, uncounted ways, seemed to come true.

So Merrillin stood in front of the barrow on a late fall day and told himself a lie; that the apple would fall into his hand of its own accord as if the barrow were a tree letting loose its fruit. He even reached over and touched the apple he wanted, a rosy round one that promised to be full of sweet juices and crisp meat. And just in case, he touched a second apple as well, one that was slightly wormy and a bit yellow with age.

"You boy," came a shout from behind the barrow, and a face as yellow and sunken as the second apple, with veins as large as worm runnels across the nose, popped into view.

Merrillin stepped back, startled.

A stick came down on his hand, sharp and painful as a firebrand. "If you do not mean to buy, you cannot touch."

"How do you know he does not mean to buy?" asked a voice from behind Merrillin.

It took all his concentration not to turn. He feared the man behind him might have a stick as well, though his voice seemed devoid of the kind of anger that always preceded a beating.

"A rag of cloth hung on bones, that's all he is," said the cart man, wiping a dirty rag across his mouth. "No one in Gwethern has seen him before. He's no mother's son, by the dirt on him. So where would such a one find coins to pay, cheeky beggar?"

There was a short bark of laughter from the man behind. "Cheeky beggar is it?"

Merrillin dared a glance at the shadow the man cast at his feet. The shadow was cloaked. That was a good sign, for he would be a stranger to Gwethern. No one here affected such dress. Courage flooded through him and he almost turned around when the man's hand touched his mouth.

"You are right, he is a cheeky beggar. And that is where he keeps his coin – in his cheek." The cloaked man laughed again, the same sharp, yipping sound, drawing an appreciative echo from the crowd that was just starting to gather. Entertainment was rare in Gwethern. "Open your mouth, boy, and give the man his coin."

Merrillin was so surprised, his mouth dropped open on its own, and a coin fell from his lips into the cloaked man's hand.

"Here," the man said, his hand now on Merrillin's shoulder. He flipped the coin into the air, it turned twice over before the cart man grabbed it out of the air, bit it, grunted, and shoved it into his purse.

The cloaked man's hand left Merrillin's shoulder and picked up the yellowing apple, dropping it neatly into Merrillin's hand. Then his voice whispered into the boy's ear. "If you wish to repay me, look for the green wagon, the castle on wheels."

When Merrillin turned to stutter out his thanks, the man had vanished into the crowd. That was just as well, though, since it was hardly thanks Merrillin was thinking of. Rather he wanted to tell the cloaked man that he had done only what was expected and that another lie had come true for Merrillin, on the slant.

After eating every bit of the apple, his first meal in two days, and setting the little green worm that had been in it on a stone, Merrillin looked for the wagon. It was not hard to find.

Parked under a chestnut tree whose leaves were spotted with brown and gold, the wagon was as green as Mab's gown, as green as the first early shoots of spring. It was indeed a castle on wheels, for the top of the wagon was vaulted over. There were three windows, four walls, and a door as well. Two docile drab-colored mules were hitched to it and were nibbling on a few brown blades of grass beneath the tree. Along the wagon's sides was writing, but as Merrillin could not read, he could only guess at it. There were pictures, too: a tall, amber-eyed mage with a conical hat was dancing across a starry night, a dark-haired princess in rainbow robes played on a harp with thirteen strings. Merrillin could not read – but he could count. He walked toward the wagon.

"So, boy, have you come to pay what you owe?" asked a soft voice, followed by the trill of a mistle thrush.

At first Merrillin could not see who was speaking, but then something moved at one of the windows, a pale moon of a face. It was right where the face of the painted princess should have been. Until it moved, Merrillin had thought it part of the painting. With a bang, the window was slammed shut and then he saw the painted face on the glass. It resembled the other face only slightly.

A woman stepped through the door and stared at him. He thought her the most beautiful person he had ever seen. Her long dark hair was unbound and fell to her waist. She wore a dress of scarlet wool and jewels in her ears. A yellow purse hung from a braided belt and jangled as she moved, as if it were covered with tiny bells. As he watched, she bound up her hair with a single swift motion into a net of scarlet linen.

She smiled. "Ding-dang-dong, cat's got your tongue, then?"

When he didn't answer, she laughed and sat down on the top step of the wagon. Then she reached back behind her and pulled out a harp exactly like the one painted on the wagon's side. Strumming, she began to sing:

> *"A boy with eyes a somber blue*
> *Will never ever come to rue,*
> *A boy with …"*

"Are you singing about me?" asked Merrillin.

"Do you think I am singing about you?" the woman asked and then hummed another line.

"If not now, you will some day," Merrillin said.

"I believe you," said the woman, but she was busy tuning her harp at the same time. It was as if Merrillin did not really exist for her except as an audience.

"Most people do not," Merrillin said, walking over. He put his hand on the top step, next to her bare foot. "Believe me, I mean. But I never tell lies."

She looked up at that and stared at him as if really seeing him for the first time. "People who never tell lies are a wonder. All people lie sometime." She strummed a discordant chord.

Merrillin looked at the ground. "I am not *all people*."

She began picking a quick, bright tune, singing:

> *"If you never ever lie*
> *You are a better soul than I …"*

Then she stood and held up the harp behind her. It disappeared into the wagon. "But you did not answer my question, boy."

"What question?"

"Have you come to pay what you owe?"

Puzzled Merrillin said: "I did not answer because I did not know you were talking to me. I owe nothing to you."

"Ah, but you owe it me," came a lower voice from inside the wagon where it was dark. A man emerged and even though he was not wearing the cloak, Merrillin knew him at once. The voice was the same, gentle and ironic. He was the mage on the wagon's side; the slate gray hair was the same – and the amber eyes.

"I do not owe you either, sir."

"What of the apple, boy?"

Merrillin started to cringe, thought better of it, and looked straightaway into the man's eyes. "The apple was *meant* to come to me, sir."

"Then why came you to the wagon?" asked the woman, smoothing her hands across the red dress. "If not to pay."

"As the apple was meant to come into my hands, so I was meant to come into yours."

The woman laughed. "Only you hoped the mage would not eat you up and put your little green worm on a rock for some passing scavenger."

Merrillin's mouth dropped open. "How did you know?"

"Bards *know* everything," she said.

"And *tell* everything as well," said the mage. He clapped her on the shoulder and she went, laughing, through the door.

Merrillin nodded to himself. "It was the window," he whispered.

"Of course it was the window," said the mage. "And if you wish to talk to yourself, make it *sotto voce*, under the breath. A whisper is no guarantee of secrets."

"Sotto voce," Merrillin said.

"The soldiers brought the phrase, but it rides the market roads now," said the mage.

"Sotto voce," Merrillin said again, punctuating his memory.

"I like you, boy," said the mage. "I collect oddities."

"Did you collect the bard, sir?"

Looking quickly over his shoulder, the mage said, "Her?"

"Yes, sir."

"I did."

"How is she an oddity?" asked Merrillin. "I think she is –" he took a gulp, "—wonderful."

"That she is; quite, quite wonderful, my Viviane, and she well knows it," the mage replied. "She has a range of four octaves and can mimic any bird or beast I name." He paused. "And a few I cannot."

"Viviane," whispered Merrillin. Then he said the name without making a sound.

The mage laughed heartily. "You are an oddity, too, boy. I thought so at the first when you walked into the market fair with nothing to sell and no purse with which to buy. I asked, and no one knew you. Yet you stood in front of the barrow as if you owned the apples. When the stick fell, you did not protest; when the coin dropped from your lips, you said not a word. But I could feel your anger and surprise and – something more. You are an oddity. I sniffed it out with my nose from the first and my nose—" he tapped it with his forefinger, managing to look both wise and ominous at once "—my nose, like you, never lies. Do you think yourself odd?"

Merrillin closed his eyes for a moment, a gesture the mage would come to know well. When he opened them again, his eyes were no longer the somber blue that Viviane had sung about but were the blue of a bleached out winter sky. "I have dreams," he said.

The mage held his breath, his wisdom being as often in silence as in words.

"I dreamed of a wizard and a woman who lived in a castle green as early spring grass. Hawks flew about the turrets and a bear squatted on the throne. I do not know what it all means, but now that I have seen the green wagon, I am sure you are the wizard and the woman, Viviane."

"Do you dream often?" asked the mage, slowly coming down the steps of the wagon and sitting on the lowest stair.

Merrillin nodded.

"And do your dreams often come true?" he asked. Then he added, quickly, "No, you do not have to answer that."

Merrillin nodded again.

"Always?"

Merrillin closed his eyes, then opened them.

"Tell me," said the mage.

"I dare not. When I tell, I am called a liar or hit. Or both. I do not think I want to be hit anymore."

The mage laughed again, this time with his head back. When he finished, he narrowed his eyes and looked at the boy. "I have never hit anyone in my life. And telling lies is an essential part of magic. You lie with your hands like this." And so saying, he reached behind Merrillin's ear and pulled out a bouquet of meadowsweet, wintergreen, and a single blue aster. "You see, my hands told the lie that flowers grow in the dirt behind your ear. And your eyes took it in."

Merrillin laughed, a funny crackling sound, as if he were not much used to laughter.

"But do not let Viviane know you tell lies," said the mage, leaning forward and whispering. "She is as practiced in her anger as she is on the harp. I may never swat a liar, but she is the very devil when her temper's aroused."

"I will not," said Merrillin solemnly. They shook hands on it, only when Merrillin drew away his grasp, he had a small copper coin in his palm.

"Buy yourself a meat pie, boy," said the mage. "And then come along with us. I think you will be a very fine addition to our collection."

"Thank you, sir," gasped Merrillin.

"Not *sir*. My name is Ambrosius, because of my amber eyes. Did you notice them? Ambrosius the Wandering Mage. And what is your name? I cannot keep calling you 'boy'."

"My name is Merrillin but . . ." he hesitated and looked down.

"I will not hit you and you may keep the coin whatever you say," Ambrosius said.

"But I would like to be called Hawk."

"Hawk, is it?" The mage laughed again. "Perhaps you will grow into that name, but it seems to me that you are mighty small and a bit thin for a hawk."

A strange sharp cackling sound came from the interior of the wagon, a high *ki-ki-ki-ki*.

The mage looked in and back. "Viviane says you *are* a hawk, but a small one – the merlin. And that is, quite happily, close to your Christian name as well. Will it suit?"

"Merlin," whispered Merrillin, his hand clutched tightly around the coin. Then he looked up, his eyes gone the blue of the aster. "That was the hawk in my dream, Ambrosius. That was the sound he made. A merlin. It has to be my true name."

"Good. Then it is settled," said the mage standing. "Fly off to your pie, Hawk Merlin, and then fly quickly back to me. We go tomorrow to Carmarthen. There's to be a great holy day fair. Viviane will sing. I will do my magic. And you – well, we shall have to figure out what you can do. But it will be something quite worthy, I am sure. I tell you, young Merlin, there are fortunes to be made on the road if you can sing in four voices and pluck flowers out of the air."

The road was a gentle winding path through valleys and alongside streams. The trees were still gold in most places, but on the far ridges the forests were already bare.

As the wagon bounced along, Viviane sang songs about Robin of the Wood in a high, sweet voice and the Battle of the Trees in a voice deep as thunder. And in a middle voice she sang a lusty ballad about a bold warrior that made Merlin's cheeks turn pink and hot.

Ambrosius shortened the journey with his wonder tales. And as he talked, he made coins walk across his knuckles and found two quail's eggs behind Viviane's left ear. Once he pulled a turtledove out of Merlin's shirt, which surprised the dove more than the boy. The bird flew off onto a low branch of an ash tree and plucked its breast feathers furiously until the wagon had passed by.

They were two days traveling and one day resting by a lovely bright pond rimmed with willows.

"Carmarthen is over that small hill," pointed out the mage. "But it will wait on us. The fair does not begin until tomorrow. Besides, we have fishing to do. And a man – whether mage or murderer – always can find time to fish!" He took Merlin down to the pond where he quickly proved himself a bad angler but a merry companion, telling fish stories late into the night. All he caught was a turtle. It was Merlin who pulled up the one small spotted trout they roasted over the fire that night and shared three ways.

Theirs was not the only wagon on the road before dawn, but it was the gaudiest by far. Peddlers' children leaped off their own wagons to run alongside and beg the magician for a trick. He did one for each child and asked for no coins at all, even though Viviane chided him.

"Do not scold, Viviane. Each child will bring another to our wagon once we are in the town. They will be our best criers," Ambrosius said, as he made a periwinkle appear from under the chin of a dirty-faced tinker lass. She giggled and ran off with the flower.

At first each trick made Merlin gasp with delight. But partway through the trip, he began to notice from where the flowers and coins and scarves and eggs really appeared – out of the vast sleeves of the mage's robe. He started watching Ambrosius' hands carefully through slitted eyes, and unconsciously his own hands began to imitate them.

Viviane reached over and, holding the reins with one hand, slapped his fingers so hard they burned. "Do not do that. It is bad enough he does the tricks for free on the road, but you would beggar us for sure if you give them away forever. Idiot!"

After the scolding, Merlin sat sullenly inside the darkened wagon practicing his sotto voce with curses he had heard but had never dared repeat aloud. Embarrassment rather than anger sent a kind of ague to his limbs. Eventually, though, he wore himself out and fell asleep. He dreamed a wicked little dream about Viviane, in which a whitethorn tree fell upon her. When he woke, he was ashamed of the dream and afraid of it as well, but he did not know how to change it. His only comfort was that his dreams did not come true literally. *On the slant*, he reminded himself, which lent him small comfort.

He was still puzzling this out when the mules slowed and he became aware of a growing noise. Moving to the window, he stared out past the painted face.

If Gwethern had been a bustling little market town, Carmarthen had to be the very center of the commercial world. Merlin saw gardens and orchards outside the towering city walls though he also noted that the gardens were laid out in a strange pattern and some of the trees along the northern edges were ruined and the ground around them was raw and wounded. There were many spotty pastures where sheep and kine grazed on the late fall stubble. The city walls were made up of large blocks of limestone. How anyone could have moved such giant stones was a mystery to him. Above the walls he could glimpse crenellated towers from which red and white banners waved gaudily in the shifting fall winds, first north, then west.

Merlin could contain himself no longer and scrambled through the wagon door, squeezing in between Ambrosius and Viviane.

"Look, oh look!" he cried.

Viviane smiled at the childish outburst, but the mage touched his hand.

"It is not enough just to look, Merlin. You must look – and remember."

"Remember – what?" asked Merlin.

"The eyes and ears are different listeners," said the mage. "But both feed into magecraft. Listen. What do you hear?"

Merlin strained, tried to sort out the many sounds, and said at last, "It is very noisy."

Viviane laughed. "*I* hear carts growling along, and voices, many different tongues. A bit of Norman, some Saxon, Welsh, and Frankish. There is a hawk screaming in the sky behind us. And a loud, heavy clatter coming from behind the walls. Something being built, I would guess."

Merlin listened again. He could hear the carts and voices easily. The hawk was either silent now or beyond his ken. But because she mentioned it, he could hear the heavy rhythmic pounding of building like a bass note, grounding the entire song of Carmarthen. "Yes," he said, with a final exhalation.

"And what do you see?" asked Ambrosius.

Determined to match Viviane's ears with his eyes, Merlin began a litany of wagons and wagoners, beasts straining to pull, and birds restrained in cages. He described jongleurs and farmers and weavers and all their wares. As they passed through the gates of the city and under the portcullis, he described it as well.

"Good," said Ambrosius. "And what of those soldiers over there." He nodded his head slightly to the left.

Merlin turned to stare at them.

"No, never look directly on soldiers, highwaymen, or kings. Look through the slant of your eyes," whispered Viviane, reining in the mules.

Merlin did as she instructed, delighted to be once more in her good graces. "There are ten of them," he said.

"And what do they wear?" prompted Ambrosius.

"Why, their uniforms. And helms."

"What color helms?" Viviane asked.

"Silver, as helms are wont. But six have red plumes, four white." Then as an afterthought, he added, "And they all carry swords."

"The swords are not important," said Ambrosius, "but note the helms. Ask yourself why some should be sporting red plumes, some white. Ask yourself if these are two different armies of two different lords. And if so, why are they both here?"

"I do not know," answered Merlin. "Why?"

Ambrosius laughed. "I do not know either. Yet. But it is something odd to be tucked away. And remember – I collect oddities."

Viviane clicked to the mules with her tongue and slapped their backs with the reins. They started forward again.

"Once around the square, Viviane, then we will choose our spot. Things are already well begun," said the mage. "There are a juggler and a pair of acrobats and several strolling players, though none – I wager – with anything near your range. But I see no other masters of magic. We shall do well here."

In a suit of green and gold – the gold a cotte of the mage's that Viviane had tailored to fit him, the green his old hose sewn over with gold patches and bells – Merlin strode through the crowd with a tambourine. It was his job to collect the coins after each performance. On the first day folk were liable to be the most generous, afterward husbanding their coins for the final hours of the fair, at least that was what Viviane had told him. Still he was surprised by the waterfall of copper pennies that cascaded into his tambourine.

"Our boy Merlin will pass amongst you, a small hawk in the pigeons," Ambrosius had announced before completing his final trick, the one in which Viviane was shut up in a box and subsequently disappeared into the wagon.

Merlin had glowed at the name pronounced so casually aloud, and at the claim of possession. *Our* boy, Ambrosius had said. Merlin repeated the phrase sotte voce to himself and smiled. The infectious smile brought even more coins, though he was unaware of it.

It was after their evening performance when Viviane had sung in three different voices, including a love song about a shepherd and the ewe lamb that turned into a lovely maiden who fled from him over a cliff, that a broad-faced soldier with a red plume in his helm parted the teary-eyed crowd. Coming up to the wagon stage, he announced, "The Lady Renwein would have you come tomorrow evening to the old palace and sends this as way of a promise. There will be more after a satisfactory performance. It is in honor of her upcoming wedding." He dropped a purse into Ambrosius' hand.

The mage bowed low and then, with a wink, began drawing a series of colored scarves from behind the soldier's ear. They were all shades of red: crimson, pink, vermilion, flame, scarlet, carmine, and rose.

"For your lady," Ambrosius said, holding out the scarves.

The soldier laughed aloud and took them. "The lady's colors. She will be pleased. Though not, I think, his lordship."

"The white soldiers, then, are his?" asked Ambrosius.

Ignoring the question, the soldier said, "Be in the kitchen by nones. We ring the bells here. The duke is most particular."

"Is dinner included?" asked Viviane.

"Yes, mistress," the soldier replied. "You shall eat what the cook eats." He turned and left.

"Then let us hope," said Viviane to his retreating back, "that we like what the cook likes."

Merlin dreamed that night and woke screaming but could not recall exactly what he had dreamed. The mage's hand was on his brow and Viviane wrung out cool water onto a cloth for him.

"Too much excitement for one day," she said, making a clucking sound with her tongue.

"And too many meat pies," added the mage, nodding.

The morning of the second day of the holy day fair came much too soon. And noisily. When Merlin went to don his green-and-gold suit, Ambrosius stayed him.

"Save that for the lady's performance. I need you in your old cotte to go around the fair. And remember – use your ears and eyes."

Nodding, Merlin scrambled into his old clothes. They had been tidied up by Viviane, but he was aware, for the first time, of how really shabby and threadbare they were. Ambrosius slipped him a coin.

"You earned this. Spend it as you will. But not on food, boy. We will feast enough at the duke's expense."

Clutching the coin, Merlin escaped into the early morning crowds. In his old clothes, he was unremarked, just another poor lad eyeing the wonders at the holy day fair.

At first he was seduced by the stalls. The variety of foods and cloth and toys and entertainments were beyond anything he had ever imagined. But halfway around the second time, he remembered his charge. *Eyes and ears.* He did not know exactly what Ambrosius would find useful but he was determined to uncover something.

"It was between the Meadowlands Jugglers and a stall of spinach pies," he told Ambrosius later, wrinkling his nose at the thought of spinach baked in a flakey crust. "A white plumed soldier and a red were quarreling. It began with name calling. Red called white, 'Dirty men of a dirty duke,' and white countered with 'Spittle of the Lady Cock.' And they would have fallen to, but a ball from the jugglers landed at their feet and the crowd surged over to collect it."

"So there is no love lost between the two armies," mused Ambrosius. "I wonder if they were the cause of the twisted earth around the city walls."

"And after that I watched carefully for pairs of soldiers. They were everywhere matched, one red and one white. And the names between them bounced back and forth like an apple between boys."

The mage pulled on his beard thoughtfully. "What other names did you hear?"

"She was called Dragonlady, Lady Death, and the Open Way."

Ambrosius laughed. "Colorful. And one must wonder how accurate."

"And the duke was called Pieless, the Ewe's Own Lover, and Draco," said Merlin, warming to his task.

"Scurrilous and the Lord knows how well-founded. But two dragons quarreling in a single nest? It will make an unsettling performance at best. One can only wonder why two such creatures decided to wed." Ambrosius worked a coin across his knuckles, back and forth, back and forth. It was a sign he was thinking.

"Surely, for love?" whispered Merlin.

Viviane, who had been sitting quietly, darning a colorful petticoat, laughed. "Princes never marry for love, little hawk. For money, for lands, for power – yes. Love they find elsewhere or not at all. That is why I would never be a prince."

Ambrosius seemed not to hear her, but Merlin took in every word and savored the promise he thought he heard.

They arrived at the old castle as the bells chimed nones. And the castle was indeed old; its keep from the days of the Romans was mottled and pocked but was still the most solid part of the building. Even Merlin, unused as he was to the ways of builders, could see that the rest was of shoddy material and worse workmanship.

"The sounds of building we heard from far off must be a brand-new manor being constructed," said Ambrosius. "For the new-wedded pair."

And indeed the cook, whose taste in supper clearly matched Viviane's, agreed. "The duke's father fair beggared our province fighting off imagined invaders, and his son seems bent on finishing the job. He even invited the bloody-minded Saxons in to help." He held up his right hand and made the sign of horns and spat through it. "Once, though you'd hardly credit it, this was a countryside of lucid fountains and transparent rivers. Now it's often dry as dust, though it was one of the prettiest places in all Britain. And if the countryside is in tatters, the duke's coffers are worse. That is why he has made up his mind to marry the Lady Renwein. She has as much money as she has had lovers, so they say, and that is not the British way. But the duke is besotted with both her counte and her coinage. And even I must admit she has made a difference. Why, they are building a great new house upon the site of the old Roman barracks. The duke is having it constructed on the promise of her goods."

Viviane made no comment but kept eating. Ambrosius, who always ate sparingly before a performance, listened intently, urging the cook on with well-placed questions. Following Viviane's actions, Merlin stuffed himself and almost made himself sick again. He curled up in a corner near the heath to sleep. The last thing he heard was the cook's continuing complaint.

"I know not when we shall move into the new house. I long for the larger hearth promised, for now with the red guards to feed as well as the duke's white – *and* the Saxon retainers – I need more. But the building goes poorly."

"Is that so?" interjected Ambrosius.

"Aye. The foundation does not hold. What is built up by day falls down by night. There is talk of witchcraft."

"Is there?" Ambrosius asked smoothly.

"Aye, the Saxons claim it against us. British witches, they cry. And they want blood to cleanse it."

"Do they?"

★　　★　　★

A hand on his shoulder roused Merlin, but he was still partially within the vivid dream.

"The dragons . . ." he murmured and opened his eyes.

"Hush," came Ambrosius' voice. "Hush – and remember. You called out many times in your sleep: dragons and castles, water and blood, but what it all means you kept to yourself. So remember the dream, all of it. And I will tell you when to spin out the tale to catch the conscience of Carmarthen in its web. If I am right . . ." He touched his nose.

Merlin closed his eyes again and nodded. He did not open them again until Viviane began fussing with his hair, running a comb through the worst tangles and pulling at his cotte. She tied a lover's knot of red and white ribands around his sleeve, then moved back.

"Open your eyes, boy. You are a sight." She laughed and pinched one cheek.

The touch of her hand made his cheeks burn. He opened his eyes and saw the kitchen abustle with servants. The cook, now too busy to chat with them further, was working at the hearth, basting and stirring and calling out a string of instructions to his overworked crew. "Here, Stephen, more juice. Wine up to the tables and hurry, Mag – they are pounding their feet upon the floor. The soup is hot enough, the tureens must be run up, and mind the handles. Use a cloth, Nan, stupid girl. And where are the sharp knives? These be dull as Saxon wit. Come, Stephen, step lively; the pies must come out the oast or they burn. Now!"

Merlin wondered that he could keep it all straight.

The while Ambrosius in one corner limbered up his fingers, having already checked out his apparatus and Viviane, sitting down at the table, began to tune her harp. Holding it on her lap, her head cocked to one side, she sang a note then tuned each string to it. It was a wonder she could hear in all that noise – the cook shouting, Stephen clumping around and bumping into things, Nan whining, and Mag cursing back at the cook – but she did not seem to mind, her face drawn up with passionate intensity.

Into the busyness strode a soldier. When he came up to the hearth, Merlin could see it was the same one who had first tendered them the invitation to perform. His broad, homey face was split by a smile, wine and plenty of hot food having worked their own magic.

"Come, mage. And you, singer. We are ready when you are."

Ambrosius gestured to three large boxes. "Will you lend a hand?"

The soldier grunted.

"And my boy comes, too," said Ambrosius.

Putting his head to one side as if considering, the soldier asked, "Is he strong enough to carry these? He looks small and puling."

"He can carry if he has to, but he is more than that to us."

The soldier laughed. "You will have no need of a tambourine boy to pass among the gentlefolk and soldiers. Her ladyship will see that you are well enough paid."

Ambrosius stood very tall and dropped his voice to a deep, harsh whisper. "I have performed in higher courts than this. I know what is fit for fairs and what is fit for a great hall. You know not to whom you speak."

The soldier drew back.

Viviane smiled but carefully, so that the soldier could not see it, and played three low notes on the harp.

Merlin did not move. It was as if for a moment the entire kitchen had turned to stone.

Then the soldier gave a short, barking laugh, but his face was wary. "Do not mock me, mage. I saw him do nothing but pick up coins."

"That is because he only proffers his gifts for people of station. I am but a mage, a man of small magics and tricks that fool the eye. But the boy is something more." He walked toward Merlin slowly, his hand outstretched.

Still Merlin did not move, though imperceptibly he stood taller. Ambrosius put his hand on Merlin's shoulders.

"The boy is a reader of dreams," said the mage. "What he dreams comes true."

"Is that so?" asked the soldier, looking around.

"It is so," said Viviane.

Merlin closed his eyes for a moment, and when he opened them, they were the color of an ocean swell, blue-green washed with gray. "It is so," he said at last.

From the hearth where he was basting the joints of meat, the cook called out, "It is true that the boy dreamed here today. About two dragons. I heard him cry out in his sleep."

The soldier, who had hopes of a captaincy, thought a moment, then said, "Very well, all three of you come with me. Up the stairs. Now." He cornered young Stephen to carry the mage's boxes, and marched smartly out the door.

The others followed quickly, though Merlin hung back long enough to give the other boy a hand.

Viviane sang first, a medley of love songs that favored the duke and his lady in turn. With the skill of a seasoned entertainer, she inserted the Lady Renwein's name into her rhyme, but called the duke in the songs merely "The Duke of Carmarthen town." (Later she explained to Merlin that the only rhymes she had for the duke's name were either scurrilous or treasonous, and sang a couple of verses to prove it.) Such was her ability, each took the songs as flattering, though Merlin thought he detected a nasty undertone in them that made him uncomfortable. But Viviane was roundly applauded and at the end of her songs, two young soldiers picked her up between them and set her upon their table for an encore. She smiled prettily at them, but Merlin knew she hated their touch, for the smile was one she reserved for particularly messy children, drunken old men – and swine.

Deftly beginning his own performance at the moment Viviane ended hers, Ambrosius was able to cover any unpleasantness that might occur if one of the soldiers dared take liberties with Viviane as she climbed down from the tabletop. He began with silly tricks – eggs, baskets, even a turtle was plucked from the air or from behind an unsuspecting soldier's ear. The turtle was the one the mage had found when they had been fishing.

Then Ambrosius moved on to finer tricks, guessing the name of a soldier's sweetheart, finding the red queen in a deck of cards missing yet discovering it under the Lady Renwein's plate, and finally making Viviane disappear and reappear in a series of boxes through which he had the soldiers thrust their swords.

The last trick brought great consternation to the guards, especially when blood appeared to leak from the boxes, blood which when examined later proved to be juices from the meat which Viviane had kept in a flask. And when she reappeared, whole, unharmed, and smiling once the swords had been withdrawn from the box, the great hall resounded with huzzahs.

The duke smiled and whispered to the Lady Renwein. She covered his hand with hers. When he withdrew his hand, the duke held out a plump purse. He jangled it loudly.

"We are pleased to offer you this, Ambrosius."

"Thank you, my lord. But we are not done yet," said the mage with a bow which, had it been a little less florid, would have been an insult. "I would introduce you to Merlin, our dream reader, who will tell you of a singular dream he had this day in your house."

Merlin came to the center of the room. He could feel his legs trembling. Ambrosius walked over to him and, turning his back to the duke, whispered to the boy. "Do not be afraid. Tell the dream and I will say what it means."

"Will you know?"

"My eyes and ears know what needs be said here," said Ambrosius, "whatever the dream. You must trust me."

Merlin nodded and Ambrosius moved aside. The boy stood with his eyes closed and began to speak.

"I dreamed a tower of snow that in the day reached high up into the sky but at night melted to the ground. And there was much weeping and wailing in the country because the tower would not stand."

"*The castle!*" the duke gasped, but Lady Renwein placed her hand gently on his mouth.

"Hush, my lord," she whispered urgently. "Listen. Do not speak yet. This may be merely a magician's trick. After all, they have been in Carmarthen for two days already and surely there is talk of the building in the town."

Merlin, his eyes still closed, seemed not to hear them, but continued. "And then one man arose, a mage, who advised that the tower of icy water be drained in the morning instead of building atop it. It was done as he wished, though the soldiers complained bitterly of it. But at last the pool was drained and lo! there in the mud lay two great hollow stones as round and speckled and veined as gray eggs.

"Then the mage draw a sword and struck open the eggs. In the one was a dragon the color of wine, its eyes faceted as jewels. In the other a dragon the color of maggots, with eyes as tarnished as old coins.

"And when the two dragons saw that they were revealed, they turned not on the soldiers nor the mage but upon one another. At first the white dragon had the best of it and pushed the red to the very edge of the dry pool, but it so blooded its opponent that a new pool was formed, the color of the ocean beyond the waves. But then the red rallied and pushed the white back, and it slipped into the bloody pool and disappeared, never to be seen again whole.

"And the man who advised began to speak once more, but I awoke."

At that, Merlin opened his eyes and they were the blue of speedwells on a summer morn.

The Lady Renwein's face was dark and disturbed. In a low voice she said, "Mage, ask him what the dream means."

Ambrosius bowed very low this time, for he saw that while the duke might be easily cozened, the Lady Renwein was no fool. When he stood straight again, he said, "The boy dreams, my lady, but he leaves it to me to make sense of what he dreams. Just as did his dear, dead mother before him."

Merlin, startled, looked at Viviane. She rolled her eyes up to stare at the broad beams of the ceiling and held her mouth still.

"His mother was a dream reader, too?" asked the duke.

"She was; though being a woman, dreamed of more homey things: the names of babes and whether they be boys or girls, and when to plant, and so forth."

The Lady Renwein leaned forward. "Then say, mage, what this dream of towers and dragons means."

"I will, my lady. It is not unknown to us that you have a house that will not stand. However, what young Merlin has dreamed is the reason for this. The house or tower of snow sinks every day into the ground; in the image of the dream, it melts. That is because there is a pool beneath it. Most likely the Romans built the conduits for their baths there. With the construction, there has been a leakage underground. The natural outflow has been damaged further by armies fighting. And so there has been a pooling under the foundation. Open up the work, drain the pool, remove or reconstruct the Roman pipes, and the building will stand."

"Is that all?" asked the duke, disappointment in his voice. "I thought that you might say the red was the Lady Renwein's soldiers, the white mine or some such."

"Dreams are never quite so obvious, my lord. They are devious messages to us, truth ..." he paused for a moment and put his hands on Merlin's shoulders, "truth on the slant."

Lady Renwein was nodding. "Yes, that would make sense. About the drains and the Roman pipes, I mean. Not the dream. You need not have used so much folderol in order to give us good advice."

Ambrosius smiled and stepped away from Merlin and made another deep bow. "But my lady, who would have listened to a traveling magician on matters of . . . shall we say . . . state?"

She smiled back.

"And besides," Ambrosius added, "I had not heard this dream until this very moment. I had given no thought before it to your palace or anything else of Carmarthen excepting the fair. It is the boy's dream that tells us what to do. And, unlike his mother of blessed memory, I could never guess a baby's sex before it was born lest she dreamed it. And she, the minx, never mentioned that she was carrying a boy to me, nor did she dream of him till after he was born when she, dying, spoke of him once. 'He will be a hawk among princes,' she said. So I named him Merlin."

It was two days later when a special messenger came to the green wagon with a small casket filled with coins and a small gold dragon with a faceted red jewel for an eye.

"Her ladyship sends these with her compliments," said the soldier who brought the casket. "There was indeed a hidden pool beneath the foundation. And the pipes, which were as gray and speckled and grained as eggs, were rotted through. In some places they were gnawed on, too, by some small underground beasts. Her lady begs you to stay or at least send the boy back to her for yet another dream."

Ambrosius accepted the casket solemnly, but shook his head. "Tell her ladyship that – alas – there is but one dream per prince. And we must away. The fair here is done and there is another holy day fair in Londinium, many days' journey from here. Even with such a prize as her lady has gifted us, Ambrosius the Wandering Mage and his company can never be still long." He bowed.

But Ambrosius did not proffer the real reason they were away: that a kind of restless fear drove him on, for after the performance when they were back in the wagon, Merlin had cried out against him. "But that was not the true meaning of the dream. There *will* be fighting here – the red dragon of the Britons and the Saxon white will fight again. The tower is only a small part – of the dream, of the whole."

And Ambrosius had sighed loudly then, partly for effect, and said, "My dear son, for as I claimed you, now you are mine forever, magecraft is a thing of the eye and ear. You tell me that what you dream comes true – but on the slant. And I say that to tell a prince to his face that you have dreamed of his doom invites the dreamer's doom as well. And, as you yourself reminded me, it may not be *all* of the truth. The greatest wisdom of any dreamer is to survive in order to dream again. Besides, how do you really know if what you dream is true or if, in the telling of it, you make it come true? We are men, not beasts, because we can dream and because we can make those dreams come true."

Merlin had closed his eyes then, and when he opened them again, they were the clear vacant blue of a newborn babe. "Father," he had said, and it was a child's voice speaking.

Ambrosius had shivered with the sound of it, for he knew that sons in the natural order of things o'erthrew their fathers when they came of age. And Merlin, it was clear, was very quick to learn and quicker to grow.

THE TEMPTATIONS OF MERLIN

PETER TREMAYNE

Peter Tremayne is no stranger to the Arthurian world. Under his real name of Peter Berresford Ellis (b. 1943) he has written over a dozen books on Celtic history and mythology, including the definitive The Celtic Empire *(1990) and* Celt and Saxon *(1993), plus* A Dictionary of Celtic Mythology *(1992). Under the Tremayne alias he has written nearly thirty books, including two excellent collections of Irish horror and fantasy stories,* My Lady of Hy-Brasil *(1987) and* Aisling *(1992). He has more recently found fame with his novels about Sister Fidelma, a seventh-century advocate and investigator of the Brehon Court, whose adventures are set to rival Brother Cadfael's. The series begins with* Absolution By Murder *(1994) and* Shroud for an Archbishop *(1995). The following long story endeavours to present the historical Celtic world of Merlin.*

I

The tall man paused in mid-stride. He stood head to one side in a listening attitude. A frown disfigured the ugly features of his black bearded face. Then he scowled, making his expression even more hideous.

He was a heavily built man, a warrior by the cut of his clothes, his breastplate and helmet. He carried his double-edged sword in his right hand while a small rounded shield protected his other side, hanging from his left shoulder. Great muscles rippled under the bronzed skin of the giant, for he stood not short of seven feet in height. His features were marred by a grim and repulsive countenance accentuated with a white weal of a scar running from the corner of his left eye across his cheek before disappearing into his bushy beard. Even in repose, as he stood listening, his whole appearance was threatening.

He waited a moment in the narrow defile of a forest path, hemmed in by towering oaks and closely growing undergrowth. It was dark among the trees although, beyond the flickering branches above him, there was an impression of sunshine and blue skies.

The big warrior sniffed the air suspiciously, inhaling the musty smells of the dank forest.

To his ears came the sound of rushing water, the babbling of a fast flowing stream, not too far away.

He grimaced again and eased the weapon in his grip before continuing his forward movement along the path. In spite of his big frame and his heavy build, the warrior moved quietly. His feet seemed to meet the earth so lightly that no twig snapped nor leaf rustled under their impact.

He came upon the bank of the stream with an abruptness, moving from the darkness of the forest into an area of bright noonday light where the broader defile of a swift flowing mountain stream snaked its way through the tightly growing trees. The stream gushed and bubbled in its downward path over grey granite rocks, heading down the slopes of the mountain towards the valley below.

The big warrior smiled, dropped to one knee and, swiftly moving his sword from right to left hand, placed his hand into the water. It was icy cold to his touch. His smile broadened and he looked carefully about him, transferring his weapon back to his sword hand again. Rising to his full height again, he began to move cautiously downstream.

He had not gone many yards before he saw the figure.

Seated with his back to him in the middle of that icy stream was a naked youth. The cold waters pounded against him, the white foam gushed over his pale skin and the youth's long, silver-blond hair, which fell over his shoulders, sparkled with the droplets of its spray. The youth was seated alone in the middle of the surging current, crossed legs, hands resting loosely in his lap. His age could have been no more than a score of years.

The giant warrior's grim smile widened now and he carefully picked his way along the bank. Hardly a sound came from his stealthy movement. And if a sound were made, surely it would have been silenced by the surge of the mountain current?

Yet, suddenly, the body of the youth, still with his back to the oncoming warrior, stiffened almost imperceptibly and then relaxed again.

"I hear you, Mawr," the youth called. His voice was strong, belying the fragility of his slight frame.

The warrior halted and blinked. A slight look of annoyance crossed his features. He let out a soft exhalation of breath.

"Then come out and defend yourself, Plentyn-Maeth," he commanded.

The youth rose from his sitting position in the cold waters which now came up to just above his knees. Slowly he turned to face the giant warrior.

The youth's body was white-skinned and not well-muscled. At first glance, it seemed frail-looking, but the sinews were stringy and disguised a toughness. It was a lean body, perhaps a little too thin. But it was not the body that attracted the attention so much as the hard, angular face of the youth. The features were not handsome but they were commanding. The long silver-blond hair was striking and enhanced the eyes which, initially, seemed deep blue but on a closer look were orbs of near sapphire without pupils. They flickered with a strange light. The mouth was thin, the lips unusually red, as if the effect were achieved by artificial means.

It was clear that the youth was deathly cold from sitting in meditation in the icy current, yet he held his body easily and made no attempt to move his limbs to restore his stunted circulation.

"Well, Mawr?"

In spite of the fact that the youth had no weapon and was naked, the giant warrior fell into a fighting crouch, the tip of his sword started to describe wicked little circles in the air.

With deliberate slowness of motion, the youth moved to the bank of the stream and emerged to stand a few feet away from the menacing warrior.

He stood still, no emotion showing on his features.

Suddenly the warrior gave a roar, undoubtedly meant to freeze his prey, for surely the naked youth was no opponent, and rushed forward, his sword swinging.

It was difficult to see what happened exactly. One second it seemed that the youth was about to be spitted on the end of the mighty blade of the warrior, the next the warrior was sprawling on the ground and the youth was standing staring down at him with folded arms. There was no expression on the angular face.

The warrior leapt to his feet with a swiftness that belied his huge bulk.

The sword swung again.

The youth moved with a precipitance that no eye could follow. He rushed in under the sword arm, twisting slightly as his hands caught at the wrist of the giant. There was a rapid motion, and the warrior was sprawling on his back again, staring stupidly up at the youth.

Again, with an alacrity that was scarcely credible for his bulk, the warrior was on his feet once more, roaring in battle fury and striking out left, right and centre.

The naked youth responded to the strokes as if he were engaged in some awesome dance, playing with death itself. The grim dance ended with the great warrior sprawled against a tree, gasping for breath, for the youth had kicked out with both feet into the tall man's solar plexus in a two-footed blow that sent the warrior flying.

The youth stood, hands on hips, frowning down at the tall man.

"Well, Mawr?" he asked laconically.

The giant warrior shook his head as if to clear his confused thoughts. Then he lifted it back and gave a great roar. This time it was not a roar of battle anger but a great guffaw of laughter that set his giant frame quivering. He stabbed his sword into the ground and reached forward an outsized hand to the boy.

"You have done well, Plentyn-Maeth! Now the pupil has become the master."

For the first time, the youth addressed as Plentyn-Maeth allowed a small smile to align his thin lips.

"Is it truly said, Mawr?"

The great warrior, called Mawr, clapped the youth on the back.

"Truly said, Plentyn-Maeth. Now let us collect your clothes for the Venerable Fychan wishes to see you." The warrior picked up his sword and sheathed it. "Never has anyone bested me in all three passes after the water test. Indeed, it was truly said. One day you may become a Master even as the Venerable Fychan."

II

"Mawr tells me that you have done well, Plentyn-Maeth."

The old man sat shrouded in a heavy white lambswool cloak in the darkness of the room. He sat on a tripod stool before a smoky fire. On the walls of the room a few burning brand torches gave out a flickering and unsatisfactory light.

The youth, now dressed in warm plaid trousers and a linen tunic, over which a sleeveless lambswool coat was belted at the waist, stood silently before him.

The old man, the Venerable Fychan, chief Druid of the Isle of the Mighty, gazed at the youth with brightly sparkling grey eyes which burnt curiously in the reflected light of the torches.

"You do not speak, Plentyn-Maeth?"

"There is nothing to say. If Mawr says I have done well, that is his opinion and does not need my opinion to balance it."

The Venerable Fychan gave a wheezy cough as he stifled a laugh.

"You are correct, Plentyn-Maeth. Yet I will confirm that you have done well. You are now at the age of choice and your learning here is done. You have succeeded in every test that is allowed. You have shown that you are the master of all the skills which a 'man of oak wisdom' should have before he goes forth into this theatening world of ours."

The old man suddenly raised a skeletal arm and beckoned the youth to approach him.

"Come, boy, and sit at my feet for a while. There are some things I must tell you before you leave this place."

Frowning slightly, the youth addressed as Plentyn-Maeth moved forward and settled himself in a cross-legged posture before the old master.

"You know well, my boy, that there is a new religion taking over this land of ours; this land of Britain which was once known as the Isle of the Mighty. Alas, we are no longer mighty. First the Romans came and occupied our shores for over three centuries before they departed. By the time we Britons emerged again as free and independent, most of our people had accepted the new religion which the Romans spread in their wake."

The youth nodded slowly. Surely everyone knew these facts?

"But, Venerable Fychan, some of us still retained the old ways, the old religion and knowledge," he pointed out.

"This is so. But I have seen the beginning of the end, for the old ways will eventually pass. What concerns me more is that two generations ago, after the Romans had left, new would-be conquerors came to our shores."

The youth grimaced.

"The Saxons! Who does not know this?"

"Indeed, the Saxons who are without religion other than the desire to destroy and conquer. Vortigern, our High King, learnt the cost of trusting a Saxon's word. Emrys then united our people and, for a while, he drove the Saxon invaders into the extremities of this island, back to the shores of the land of the Cantii, but they regrouped and came on again. Now the battle raven is continually flying out of the east in this struggle and not from the west."

"Is there no hope of defeating the Saxons, master?"

"Just one hope. I have seen a vision that there will come a bear from the west and drive all before him and his name will be spoken of down the centuries. Indeed, over a thousand years from now, even the descendants of his enemies will acclaim him as a great hero."

Plentyn-Maeth stared curiously at the old Druid.

"A bear from the west?"

"Even so. And for him we must keep the old faith and the old knowledge alive for it will only be through the old knowledge that he will triumph over his enemies, both the enemies of his own race as well as the Saxon foemen."

"When will this saviour of Britain appear, master?"

Fychan smiled and shook his white locks gently.

"I know that he already walks our land, but it is not given me to foretell the exact date of his victories. I see the green fields redden with the blood of heroes, and ... after ... there will be a golden age for our people."

"This is great knowledge, master," breathed the youth.

The old man gazed down with his twinkling grey eyes.

"It will come to pass, Plentyn-Maeth. It will come to pass so long as there are some among us that cleave to the old knowledge, the old religion which took our forefathers on the raven's wing to breach the walls of Rome, to defeat the generals of the Macedonian emperors and to come through the gorges of Parnassos to sack the shrine of Delphi and defy the gods of the Greeks. It is the same religion which spread the raven's wing into the east and into the west and from north to south. We walked upright once and so shall we walk upright again."

There was a silence in the room of Fychan.

"Why do you tell me this, master?" asked Plentyn-Maeth after a while.

The old man coughed a little. Then he sighed.

"Your destiny is woven in the destiny of our people, Plentyn-Maeth. Beware of the new religion. Beware of the followers of Christ for their creed is weakening our people. While the Saxons strike us down, these followers of Christ tell us that to take arms against them even in our defence is wrong. They say that we must forgive them; that we must love them; that to fight them is more evil than the wrong they do to us."

Plentyn-Maeth pursed his thin red lips in disapproval.

"I know their teachings well enough."

"They would weaken us and allow the Saxons to overwhelm us. Soon you will go out into this unhappy world. When you do so, beware of these Christians. Never reveal that you are a Druid except to those you would trust your life to; never reveal your power to any save only those same people."

"That I will do, master."

"Many of our brethren have been persecuted unjustly by these Christians, Plentyn-Maeth. Trust them not."

"It shall be so."

"Are you ready to face the outside world, Plentyn-Maeth?" the old man suddenly asked after a pause.

The youth sat for a while in silence while he contemplated the prospect.

"Yes."

The old man smiled sadly.

"You are not fearful about the unknown?"

"Have you not taught, of all passions fear weakens judgement most?"

The Venerable Fychan nodded slowly.

"Yet, I have also taught, danger breeds best on too much confidence."

The youth's features betrayed a slight conceit.

"I am ready to face the outside world, master."

"If you say so, it shall be so. Yet remember this, the knowledge which stops at what it does not know, is the highest knowledge."

The youth frowned slightly, hesitated and then said: "Well, I would know more about myself, master."

"More? Is there more to know?"

"I don't know who I am."

"That can only be decided by you."

"I meant, I do not know who my parents were."

The old man, seeing the expression on the youth's face, suddenly relented.

"I did not mean to mock you. Truly, my son, there is little I can tell you except that you were a foundling. You were six months old when you were found at the house of Dolwar, my steward. None ever knew nor discovered who you were. You were wrapped in a single blanket and on that blanket was embroidered the symbol of a curious knot."

"A knot, Venerable Fychan?"

The old Druid turned to a box, opened it and drew forth a piece of blanket.

"I knew you might ask about this one day. I have kept it safe. Here is that same blanket. Take it with you and you might come to know your destiny."

The youth glanced down and saw, indeed, a curious patterned knot had been embroidered on the section of blanket. "It is richly worked," he observed.

"You were fostered by us and brought up in the knowledge of the old ways. This is why we named you Plentyn-Maeth, the foster-child.

"When you set out now, it will be the start of your journey to discover your self and your destiny. I can only tell you this; your journey lies east. Travel east until you find the symbol of the knot. That is your quest, Plentyn-Maeth."

"It is little enough to know of oneself."

Fychan grinned at the youth.

"Look into your mind, Plentyn-Maeth. You know everything there is to know about yourself. What you are asking is merely the superficial."

"But," protested the youth, "how do you know that the symbol of this knot can be found east of here?"

Fychan raised his eyebrows in marked censure.

"You question your master? Ah, truly you have come of age. Tell me, my foster-son, what will the weather be like this evening?"

Plentyn-Maeth wondered why the old master was changing the subject.

"It will be raining."

"How do you know this? Beyond these walls it is a fine, bright day."

"Easy to say. To the south-west there are many round-topped clouds with their bases flattened. The wind is from that direction and so they will bring rain, sudden and short lived."

Fychan nodded amiably.

"And as you know this, which many will find beyond their understanding, allow me to know what I know."

Plentyn-Maeth sighed deeply but he said no more and rose to his feet.

"You have said that I have passed all the tests required of me, master. When may I become an adept of the ancient knowledge? When may I be of the ancient order?"

The Venerable Fychan's face was expressionless.

"It will require no words of mine to make you so. You will become an adept once you have discovered the purpose of your quest in life."

Plentyn-Maeth nearly forgot himself by raising his eyebrows in surprise. The grin of delight was stilled on his face.

"But I know that quest now. Does that mean that I may set forth from here now?"

"If you believe that you know this purpose, you may do so. We have nothing more to teach you. You can now only instruct yourself. If you do not know now, then you will surely learn as you go. There is nothing more to bind you to this place. Remember, though, it is only when you leave this place that you will start to accrue the true knowledge. Be humble and learn well."

Yet the youth's face was also filled with pride.

"You now have only yourself to rely on," insisted the Venerable Fychan. "Remember this, knowledge without thought is toil wasted. Thought without knowledge is a perilous path."

The youth's face was a picture of excitement. He began to rise. The old master held up a thin, bony hand to stay him.

"But one thing more; since Dolwar found you at the portal of our house, we have simply called you Plentyn-Maeth, which means 'the foster-child'. Once you step out into the world you will no longer be a foster-child but, having reached the age of choice, you will be fully in charge of your own destiny. You will need a new name."

The youth looked puzzled.

"But what name shall I have?"

The Venerable Fychan smiled gently.

"It is as your foster father that I have the right to name you. In all your tests you have excelled. In every art you have shown your abilities. In no area were you lacking. Therefore I shall name you Myrddin, or 'many', signifying the many talents which you possess."

The youth blinked a little.

"Myrddin." He carefully enunciated the name. "Myrddin. I shall like that name."

The old master, Fychan, rose unsteadily and moved forward to embrace the youth now standing before him.

"Go, then, Myrddin. Set out on your quest to find yourself, to find your destiny. Remember all that I have told you and all that you have learned in these mountains that are sacred to our order. But I urge you again to guard against the evil of vanity. You are still young in years and no one, not even I, am possessed of all knowledge. We are constantly learning even at the hour of our death. Should the time come when you have need of advice, then we shall be here."

Only when he had left the house of the Venerable Fychan did the youth, Myrddin, allow a tear to stain his cheek. But his face was set and he walked with a firm and steady gait away from the only world that he could truly call "home". At the same time as the regret of parting, some inner part of him tingled with excitement and happiness. It was a curious contradiction but he did not want to analyse his feelings now. Above all his confused and contradictory emotions he had a sense of . . . of destiny. If he had admitted it, he also had a sense of youthful pride for knowledge of things may not necessarily be a knowledge of self-awareness.

III

Myrddin had been riding for two days across the broad mountains of the west of the Isle of the Mighty and down among the foothills, moving ever eastward. He did not know why he had taken this route, only that he was following the suggestion of the Venerable Fychan. In truth, he had never been beyond the Island of the Druids before, the small island which lay just west of the mainland. He had set forth eagerly, purchasing a horse on the way. The regret at leaving Fychan and Mawr and all his fellow students and teachers was still tempered by the exhilaration of a sense of freedom, of the purpose of questing.

He rode his black mare with a feeling of relaxation yet his eyes were never still, they were aware of everything around him, taking in the new sights and memorizing the paths. Yet as wary as he was, he had a youth's exuberance of independence, of being special in this new, exciting world which lay before him.

He had come to a knoll and from its bare top he halted and surveyed the countryside before him. The small, rounded hill rose, bald except for heather and brush, in the middle of a forest land. He saw that three trails met and divided again at the foot of the hill. There was the trail by which he had come to that place, a trail to the east and a well-worn track which ran on a north to south axis, or south to north, depending on the prospect of the traveller.

Myrddin paused a while in the warming rays of the midday sun, leaning forward in the saddle, resting on its pommel, and wondering if he should deflect his path from due east, turning north or south.

It was then he became aware of the approach of two horsemen from the south. He noticed immediately that one of the approaching riders was elderly, for the man was stooped forward in the saddle, his body frail. His long white hair could be seen wisping from his burnished helmet. Myrddin's eyes narrowed as he saw that the elderly man was clad not only in warrior's armour but that he wore a rich cloak and his horse was well accoutred.

The second rider was a younger man, a youth whose age Myrddin guessed was not many years either side of his own. He rode erect and he, too, was well armed and dressed. He kept glancing towards his companion and concern showed in his body language as now and then he leant towards the elderly man, touching him as if in reassurance. Myrddin presumed that the elderly man must be ailing.

Neither of the two riders glanced up the knoll and so did not perceive Myrddin sitting astride his horse there. Myrddin mentally criticized their sense of awareness for he could easily have been an enemy, waiting to ambush them.

Myrddin was about to call out a greeting when his ears detected a sound; his training caused his senses to tense. There was danger somewhere in the woods. He had scarce drawn the conclusion when, out of the woods, sprang four horsemen. Four armed warriors who, with yells and cries of triumph, rode down on the elderly man and his young companion, waving their swords.

Myrddin could not fault the reaction of the pair. The elderly man, as old and frail as he was, had his sword out and spurred forward to meet the first blows that fell from the leading assailant. A split second later his young companion had joined the fray. The scene that had been so peaceful a moment before was now a mêlée of men intent on bloodshed, horses stamping and whinnying, blades clashing on blades, accompanied by the hoarse shouting and cries of the combatants.

Myrddin sat astonished at the sudden change of the peaceful scene.

The newcomers, four warriors, were strangely dressed. Two of them wore great bushy flaxen-coloured beards and conical metal helmets. Their shields carried alien designs to those carried by the Britons. The two others were more richly dressed. One seemed younger than the other. The other, a dark, swarthy figure. Myrddin suddenly realized that he was seeing, for the first time, the feared Saxon warriors. He had heard stories of their fierceness, their invincibility. He examined them with new interest and found that they seemed to be only men and not mighty, indomitable beings.

Years ago, so the story went, scarcely two generations before, the High King Vortigern had invited the ancestors of these Saxons into the Isle of the Mighty to serve him as paid soldiers. They had mutinied and attempted to seize the kingdom for themselves. Thus had begun a war between them and the Britons. Soon more of these Saxons, in bands of thousands, were landing along the eastern and southern coasts of Britain and pushing the Britons slowly westward.

Eventually, Vortigern, to save his own power, made a treaty with them, marrying his daughter to one of their leaders, to the disgust of his people. Constans, a rival claimant to the High Kingship of Britain, rallied the opposition to Vortigern so that the Britons could unite and drive out the invaders. Vortigern had Constans murdered. But Constans had two sons, Emrys and Uther who, being children, were smuggled to Armorica in Gaul, where they had grown to manhood. They had returned to overthrow the elderly Vortigern. Then they led a renewed war against the Saxon kingdoms. But the Saxons, having gained their hold on the eastern seaboard of Britain, would not be shaken loose and as Emrys had grown older, the slow, inexorable tide of the Saxons resumed its westward flow. Now almost a quarter of the Isle of the Mighty was settled by them and the Britons driven westward.

Briton and Saxon were now enemies of blood.

It was with these thoughts, therefore, that Myrddin, seeing the four Saxons attacking the two Britons, unsheathed his own sword and, giving a wild yell, rode down the hill to the swirling battle. He rode forward at full pelt, scattering the scrimmage. With surprise on his side, he was able to disarm one of the Saxons with a swift sword blow which sent the weapon flying from the man's hand.

He turned swiftly to fend off the attack of another warrior who was the first to recover from his surprise and hastened to defend the man who had been disarmed. The younger Briton was also pressing the attack on another of the assailants but, to Myrddin's dismay, he saw that the elderly man had been wounded. He was slumped forward in his saddle with blood staining his cloak. His sword had already fallen from his nerveless hand. Myrddin perceived this in no more than a split second before he closed up with his opponent and metal rang against metal.

There came a scream from another Saxon and Myrddin saw that the young Briton had struck the man's sword arm, almost severing it. The scream distracted his own opponent allowing Myrddin to knock aside the man's weapon and plunge his own fully into the undefended stomach.

One of the two remaining Saxons gave a cry of rage and would have renewed the attack. He was a young man, not much older than Myrddin himself. He had been the warrior whom Myrddin had been able to disarm but he had now retrieved his sword. However, his companion, a hawk-faced warrior of more mature years, yelled at him.

"Back, my lord, Cynric! Back for your life! We cannot succeed here."

Then the two were fleeing back into the cover of the forest.

The third man, with the wounded arm, was left to escape after them as best he could.

Without a word, the young Briton had leapt from his horse and helped the elderly man from his mount, laying him gently on the ground.

Myrddin waited a moment, watching intently, in case the attackers regrouped and came back. Only when he was sure that the signs of danger were no longer there did Myrddin sheathe his sword and slide from his horse.

"Is the old man hurt bad?" he demanded. "I have some knowledge of healing."

The young man glanced up at Myrddin.

Myrddin took an immediate liking to him. He was lithe in form but muscular. His features were even, the blue eyes wide and without guile and the hair was golden under his war helmet. His face, though anxiety was creasing it now, seemed more accustomed to smiling than to anger. Handsome was a word that seemed inadequate. Almost immediately, Myrddin felt a quiet charisma emanating from the natural command of the youth.

"He is hurt badly," the youth replied. "See for yourself."

Myrddin bent to one knee and examined the old man's wound.

The old man stirred and gazed up at Myrddin with deepset, dark eyes. His features were strangely serene.

"I am dying," he whispered.

Myrddin attempted a smile of reassurance.

"You still live."

"Do not be an optimist, Druid," replied the old man with a wan smile.

Myrddin allowed an eyebrow to rise in momentary surprise.

"How do you know who I am?"

The old man sniffed.

"Am I so senile that I do not recognize a 'man of oak wisdom'? Come, I am dying. I was dying before the Saxon steel bit into my shoulder."

"You cannot die, my lord!" It was an agonized cry from the younger man.

"Everyone has to die, Artio. That is the only thing we can be sure of in this world. Lowly servant and high-born noble, it all comes to the same thing in the end."

Myrddin made a quick examination while the old man spoke.

"Well, young Druid?" demanded the old one. "Will I have until sundown?"

Myrddin grimaced. The old man expected honesty.

"No longer than that," he admitted reluctantly.

The old man sighed.

"Then help Artio here secure me on my horse for I wish to die in my own fortress of Dinas Emrys this night."

"Dinas Emrys?" Myrddin frowned, wondering why the name seemed so familiar.

The old man grinned wryly.

"This night shall pass the soul of Emrys, High King of the Isle of the Mighty . . ."

He groaned a little in pain.

"Is there nothing you can do?" demanded the young man who had been addressed as Artio.

Myrddin shook his head, trying to quell his astonishment at the identity of the old man. He had known about Emrys but had always pictured him as a strong, young warrior, not allowing for the passage of the years.

"If he was not so old, if the wound were an inch to the right . . . he will not see sunrise, of that I am sure."

Artio suppressed a sob.

"Then help me secure him to his horse. I will take him back to Dinas Emrys to die."

In silence, Myrddin helped the young man lift the elderly High King on to his horse. By use of leather thongs they secured him so that he would not fall and Myrddin picked up his sword and replaced it in its scabbard. He stood silently as Artio swung into his own saddle.

"Where are you going?" Artio demanded.

"To the east," Myrddin pointed.

"That way lies Saxons," frowned the youth. "Did you hear the name that passed the lips of one of our attackers?"

Myrddin, who had learnt many languages from the lips of his tutor, Fychan, nodded, for he understood well the Saxon tongue.

"The man called the youth Cynric."

"And Cynric is newly anointed king of the West Saxons. There must be a strong raiding party nearby. I would have a care and avoid going further east."

"But that way lies my destiny," replied Myrddin, undeterred.

The young man, called Artio, frowned and gazed closely at him.

"Is it true what my lord said – are you of the old faith, a 'man of oak wisdom'?"

Myrddin bowed his head.

"I am a Druid," he admitted with pride, quite forgetting the Venerable Fychan's counsel.

"Then tell no one of what has passed on this road, Druid. We were already on our journey to Dinas Emrys to meet the princes and chieftains of the Isle of the Mighty so that Emrys, who felt himself too feeble to continue to hold office, could appoint his successor as High King. Unless he can do so before his death, I fear that anarchy and despair will stalk this land."

"No one shall hear of his passing from my lips," Myrddin vowed.

The young warrior gazed at the young Druid for a moment or two. Then he smiled and reached forth his hand.

"I thank you for your assistance. Say a prayer to your gods, Druid," he said. "For this night at the fortress of Emrys the soul of the last High King of the Isle of the Mighty will pass on into the Otherworld. Who then will protect us against the Saxons?"

"Another will come," replied Myrddin.

But the two riders were already moving away with the young warrior leading the old man's mount by the reins. They moved north-westward towards the distant mountains.

"Another will come," Myrddin said again firmly, though half to himself, as he mounted his own horse. "The Venerable Fychan has said so." He paused a moment to look after the disappearing pair of riders. Then he turned his horse and nudged it gently along the eastward trail.

V

The moon was rising to its zenith.

Myrddin threw a few more sticks onto the fire which he had set to warm him for the night was chilly. He stretched languidly before it and yawned deeply. It had been a long and tiring day. In the distance, he heard wolves baying at the moon. They did not trouble him. He knew enough of the behaviour of wolves to know that they would ignore him unless he annoyed them. They were hunting in a pack and looking for bigger game such as the deer herd he had passed in a forest clearing shortly before dusk.

He had tethered his horse nearby and unrolled his blanket and cloak before the fire. Now he lay at his ease, hands clasped behind his head, staring through the swaying branches of the canopy of the trees, beyond to the dark blue sky, the white smudged face of the round moon with the myriad of twinkling silver stars around it. A new moon. The start of new beginnings.

He was about to close his eyes when something attracted his attention. He frowned and sat up. Through the trees he caught sight of a luminescent glow, a light which seemed to pulsate, flickering between the trees.

Myrddin was curious. What manner of phenomenon was this? It was not another camp fire nor was it the light from a lantern. He had never seen such a light before.

He rose to his feet and made sure his sword was in his hand. Then he glanced at his horse which stood unperturbed and at ease. Myrddin was reassured by this for if there were danger threatening from nearby then his horse would be showing signs of distress and skittishness.

Inquisitively, Myrddin walked slowly towards the pulsating glow, moving quietly between the trees and skirting the undergrowth so that it might not rustle and give warning of his approach.

The forest ended abruptly after a hundred yards or so, at the base of a sudden outcrop of rocks which constituted a small cliff face. It was a precipitous thrust of granite breaking aside the surrounding trees of the forest and creating a small hill. Myrddin's eyes grew rounded as he gazed up for there, some twenty feet or more above his head, came the pulsating light. It seemed to shine out of a small aperture, an opening in the rock.

Sheathing his sword, Myrddin moved to the rock face. He did not question the fact that it was dark and even with the bright, new moon, hanging low in the sky, he could hardly see any prospective foothold. Some instinct, perhaps the training of his senses – for a Druid was taught to use his senses just as much as his reason – caused him to run his hands over the dark granite and then launch himself upwards.

It took him a while, with one or two false moves which grazed his shins and arms. Myrddin found himself heaving his body over the edge of the rock and into the aperture. It was tall and narrow, just big enough to take a moderately sized man. Myrddin found himself grinning in reflection; in no way would Mawr the giant warrior have been able to pass through it.

Myrddin moved forward towards the pulsing light which began to respond more rapidly until it pulsed in time to his very heartbeat, its light growing stronger, brighter with each footstep he took towards its source.

He could not count how long it took him to move along that small confining passage for time seemed immeasurable. Then he stood in a great cave, but so strong was the pulsing light that he had to close his eyes to prevent himself from being blinded.

"Name yourself, stranger!"

The voice was a thin, reedy wail.

Myrddin tried to locate its owner but the light was too strong.

"I am Myrddin, foster son of Fychan," he replied.

"The Venerable Fychan?" demanded the voice.

"The same."

"Then answer three questions, Myrddin, and then you may enter here. What is the depth of a river?"

Myrddin frowned.

"The depth of a river?" he echoed stupidly.

"Yes, yes, yes!" The voice was annoyed. "Can a foster son of the Venerable Fychan be so stupid?"

Myrddin suddenly realized what was expected of him and he suppressed a smile, for he was well practised in such riddles.

"The distance from its surface to the river bed."

"What trees are there in this forest?"

"Two kinds; the green and the withered."

"What is sharper than the point of the sword you carry?"

"Understanding."

Suddenly the light dimmed and Myrddin blinked rapidly. He was in a large cave, and in the middle of this cave was a huge granite slab whose surface was encrusted with curious stones of milky-white substance that glowed with a soft light. Myrddin realized that these stones must have been the source of the strong, pulsating light for even now they still pulsed and glowed.

Yet it was the object which stuck out of the top of the granite block which caused him to stare in surprise. It was the hilt of a sword. The hilt was attached to a blade which seemed to be buried in the granite block. The hilt itself was encrusted with precious metals and stones.

Myrddin swallowed hard.

"What manner of place is this?"

The voice cackled with laughter.

Myrddin became aware of a figure seated on a chair which was placed on a dais just behind the granite block. The figure was clothed in a white robe, with a silver half-moon necklet of the Druidic brotherhood hanging around his shoulders, stretching down to his chest. The man was old, the face so lined and creased that it was not possible to say how old; it might have been centuries which witnessed the furrowing of such lines. The hair was long and as white as snow.

"You seem startled, Myrddin."

"I am . . . puzzled."

The cackle of laughter came again.

"Then let me give you knowledge. You are in the Cave of the Sword. For centuries, no, for eons, this sword has awaited a rightful claimant. It was shaped by Gofannon, the smith-god, and brought to this land by the mighty Lleu Llaw Gyffes from the mystical city of Gorias, where the ancient gods and goddesses once dwelt. The sword is named Caladfwlch, which means the hard dinter, the sword of gods and heroes. Centuries ago Lleu plunged that sword into the living molten rock when this world was forming and decreed that only a great hero could pluck it forth in the cause of truth and justice for his people."

"What has this to do with me?" demanded Myrddin, feeling some awe in spite of himself as he gazed upon the great slab of granite.

"Easy to say; when it felt your presence the jewel-encrusted granite began to pulse with light and send out its emissions to attract you to this spot."

"Why? Am I to be such a hero? Is the sword mine to have?"

The old man gave a wheezy laugh and shook his head.

"That is not your destiny, Myrddin."

"What then?"

"You will set the path for the hero to come. That is your destiny, son of the divine waters. You have gazed on this magical sword, Caladfwlch, you know its purpose. The hero is coming soon. He is the bear that will come out of the west to save his people at their time of greatest peril. He must pluck the sword from this stone and by its possession he will become invincible."

"I do not understand this, old man. Our people have stood in as great a peril before this day. Why did Lleu Llaw Gyffes not bestow this gift on the heroes of the past, on the great Vercingetorix, on Cassivelaunos, on Caradog, or Bouddica or on Emrys? All were mighty heroes at a time of great peril for our people."

"It was not their time. It was not their destiny. Go now, son of the divine waters, you have learnt what you must learn. That is enough. But tell the bear, whom you must bring here, that once he plucks the sword, it will serve him and bring him strength only while there is sincerity in his heart and goodness towards those of his kin. Once jealousy, desire or hate, the progenitors of injustice, enter his heart then the sword will no longer serve him. What the gods can bestow they can also take away."

Myrddin shook his head in bewilderment. He was about to question the old man further when he realized, to his astonishment, that the old man had vanished. Gone also were the dais and the seat on which the old man had sat; gone as if they had all been some illusion, a phantasm from the past.

Yet the sword and the stone were still there. That was no illusion.

Myrddin walked slowly around it, examining the softly glowing milky-white stones set in the sides of the granite block.

Then the temptation came on him, an inquisitive desire which he could not refuse. He stepped swiftly to the block and seized the handle and tugged. The sword was set fast in the granite. He tugged again. Then, as he was about to tug a third time, a terrible pain seized his hands and arms. There came a blinding flash and Myrddin found himself being thrown backwards across the cave.

"Do you doubt my word, Myrddin?" came a hollow voice. "You are only the conduit for he that follows. Now leave this place and do not tempt the anger of the gods again."

Rubbing his hands and arms to restore some circulation, for they were quite numb, Myrddin reluctantly retreated from the cave. By the time he had traversed the narrow defile of a passage back to the entrance onto the cliff face, he was feeling strong enough to attempt the climb down again. His mind was a-tumble with thoughts but he finally exerted his Druidic training to still them.

He had been told all that he should know at this time. Only when the time came would he know more. Only when the time came would he recognize the one for whom this sacred artifact was destined.

When he awoke by his dying, smoky fire, in the early morning light, the episode seemed like some curious distant dream.

V

By the following afternoon, Myrddin had traversed the great expanse of forest which separated the foothills of the mountains of the west from the low-lying plains to the east. He had followed the Venerable Fychan's suggestion, keeping to the eastward paths which would, he had been assured, lead him to a revelation of self and destiny. But Myrddin was growing irritable at the endless and boring journey. He was lonely and longed for the company of people, and even the excitement of the curious incident in the cave had waned. Myrddin now considered it a strange, hallucinatory dream. The young man even questioned the purpose of his journey, so bored with it had he become. He was, after all, a free man. Had he not passed the rigours of training and become a "man of oak wisdom", as the Druids were euphemistically called? He could go anywhere and do anything. He no longer had to obey the solemn warnings of the Venerable Fychan.

He paused on the edge of a rolling plain of cultivated fields, with lips pursed, as he considered the position. Yes; he would return to more familiar territory, to the shores of the westward seas. It was futile moving eastward for there was naught but Saxons there.

Having made his decision, he glanced up at the sky and decided it lacked an hour or two to dusk and therefore it was better to make a camp on the edge of the forest than try to move on now. He was about to dismount when his eye caught a glimpse of a wisp of smoke rising in the distance. He stood in his stirrups and narrowed his eyes. Some way away, across the rolling cultivated fields, he saw signs of a habitation of sorts. Why trouble to build a camp when he could ask hospitality and perhaps sleep in a dry bed rather than on the floor of the forest? The thought made the youth cheerful again.

He urged his horse forward along a path that skirted the fields and came to a small copse beyond which granite buildings rose and from which a growing pillar of smoke ascended. Myrddin recognized the grey austerity of the building at once. It was a Christian abbey. Before it stood a high granite cross, a cross surrounded by a circle, marking the intermix of the new faith with the old, for the Druids held to the eternal circle of life and such was their symbol.

He rode up to the great wooden doors and, without dismounting, he tugged at a rope, sending the clamour of a bell echoing beyond the walls.

There was a pause. Then a small aperture in the door swung open, no bigger than that necessary to frame a pair of eyes which examined him curiously.

"What is it you seek, stranger?"

"Hospitality and shelter for this night," replied Myrddin.

"Are you Briton or Saxon?"

Myrddin raised an eyebrow.

"Is it not the custom of our people, and therefore Christians, to offer hospitality to all?"

The person behind the door sniffed.

"You must be a stranger to these parts to think so, warrior. You are in the kingdom of Gereint of Dumnonia and Dumnonia is assailed by the warriors of Cynric of the West Saxons. Never a day goes by without news of some devastation on our borders. Though you be a stranger, however, you have the accent of a Briton."

"I am from . . ." He hesitated as he remembered the Venerable Fychan had warned him not to reveal his ancient faith to any Christian. "From beyond the western mountains. I am not a Saxon, that I assure you."

"Then you may freely enter and be welcome."

The aperture slammed shut and a moment later the gate opened allowing him to nudge his horse forward into a courtyard. The gate slammed shut behind him as he swung off his horse. A stable-boy came to him and took the reins while Myrddin turned to the gatekeeper. She stood revealed as a middle-aged woman, clad in the robes of a religieuse, and wearing a silver crucifix around her neck.

"What place is this, good sister?" Myrddin asked, remembering how one addressed those of the Christian orders.

"This is a house dedicated to the blessed Elen and is known as Llanelen, in Dumnonia. It was the blessed Elen who brought the

True Faith to the people of these western lands. Come, I will take you to our Mother Abbess."

Myrddin did not protest. Apart from some boys and a few men, who were performing such tasks as were unsuited for the hands of women, he could see no other men about the courtyard. There were, however, many religieuses in their robes. He deduced that the abbey was a Christian religious house for women only. He had heard of such places.

The female gatekeeper led the way through the towering building, along a cloister, to a door upon which she knocked. A voice bade her enter.

"A stranger has appeared asking for asylum, Mother," announced his guide, standing in the doorway so that he could not peer into the room beyond.

"Briton or Saxon?" demanded a woman's voice.

"Briton."

"Bid him enter."

Myrddin found himself in a small dark room lit by a burning brand torch. A woman was seated in a chair and beckoned him to approach.

"Who are you?"

"I am named Myrddin from behind the western mountains."

"You are welcome to Llanelen. I am the Abbess Aldan. Do you seek refuge for the night?"

"I do." Myrddin took a pace forward, so that he stood by the light of a torch.

He became aware of a soft intake of breath from the woman called Abbess Aldan. She leaned forward in her chair and seemed to be examining his features closely.

"Is there anything wrong?" he demanded.

The abbess seemed to catch herself and then shook her head.

"No. No." Her voice was slightly breathless. "I thought ... you reminded me of someone I knew long ago. No matter. Sister Rhinwedd here will show you to your room. We dine within the hour."

When Myrddin left the Abbess Aldan he had the impression that she was in a state of some consternation but he could not fathom a reason why.

He was shown to a small room, a *cubiculum*, so Sister Rhinwedd called it, where he washed and took the dust and fatigue of travel from his person and his clothes. Then a distant bell started to chime and he reasoned it was the summons to the evening meal. Outside his *cubiculum* he merely followed the religieuses who were heading towards a single point which was surely the refectory room of the abbey.

Inside the room were two long wooden tables before which the sisters of Llanelen stood. At the far end of the room at a cross angle to the two long tables was another table at which the Abbess Aldan and a young girl were seated. Sister Rhinwedd came bustling forward and led him to this table.

"You are a guest," she whispered, "and may be seated next to our abbess at her table."

Yet it was not the abbess, nor her acolytes, who caught Myrddin's attention as he made his way to the seat which Sister Rhinwedd indicated he should take. It was the young girl, perhaps a year or two younger than himself, who was seated on the other side of the Abbess Aldan. She was clearly not of the sisterhood but clad in clothes that denoted a woman of rank. Myrddin drew in his breath sharply.

The torchlight made her hair seem on fire. It glistened red and gold in the light and was braided into four plaits which hung behind her almost to waist level. Her face was fair, the cheek tinged red as if by the foxglove of the moor. The eyebrows were blackened and the eyes were deep pools of blue. Her tunic was of green silk, embroidered with a myriad of reds, golds and blues, while at her throat was a circlet of red gold. Her skirt was long and of deep blue and was again embroidered with many symbols in varied colours. She held her head high as one used to commanding and being obeyed.

As Myrddin took his place, she caught his gaze and returned it for a moment or so before the foxglove of her cheeks contrasted with the natural red of her blush and she lowered her eyes.

The Abbess Aldan uttered a Christian *Gratias* in the tongue of the Romans and motioned everyone to sit and commence their meal.

"What do you seek in this area of the world, Myrddin from beyond the western mountains?" the Abbess Aldan asked as they fell to eating. It was a meal of good meats and mead.

"What does any man seek," countered Myrddin, "but his destiny?"

"And do you know your destiny, warrior?" the young girl intervened from the other side of the abbess.

Myrddin grinned at her.

"What makes you so sure that I am a warrior?" he countered.

The girl pouted.

"You do not have the look of a farmer or a fisherman. Your hands are too well tended to be an artisan, a smith, a cobbler or stone mason. And you are no member of the religious."

Myrddin's smile broadened.

"You are perceptive in your youth, lady. And since we fall to guessing games, you, I would say, are a chieftain's daughter?"

The girl's chin came up.

"I am, Gwen . . ."

"Lady!" interrupted the Abbess Aldan, her voice edged in warning.

"Mother Abbess," replied the girl, her voice sounding bored, "I do not think we need fear harm from this young man. He is a Briton."

"Even so. The Saxons have been reported close to and . . ."

As she hesitated, Myrddin laughed and finished her sentence.

"And Britons have been known to accept Saxon gold to betray their fellows before now? I can say that the Saxons are nothing to me, Abbess Aldan, excepting that I have crossed swords with them."

"They should be enemies to the blood of all true Britons," snapped the girl.

"As they are to you, lady?" inquired Myrddin with an indulgent smile.

"As they are to me," confirmed the girl, her tone serious. "For they have killed my mother and father and my three brothers. They have dispersed my people who once dwelt on Ynys Wyth. These Saxon murderers now live in my island, live in the prosperity my people once enjoyed while we now starve and perish in the countryside. We should not rest until all the Saxons lay dead or are driven from this land."

Abbess Aldan looked shocked.

"That is not in keeping with the teachings of Our Lord, Lady Gwendoloena."

Myrddin caught the name. It meant nothing to him.

"Gwendoloena?" The abbess glanced at him but was clearly annoyed at herself for having betrayed the girl's identity. "Well, Gwendoloena, you speak like a true Briton keeping faith with the spirit of our ancestors. It is not good to offer an aggressor the other cheek, he will merely seize the opportunity to do further injury. Better to punish him for his aggression so that he may be dissuaded from the assault."

The Abbess Aldan looked outraged.

"I cannot have such heresy spoken of before my sisters, Myrddin."

But the young girl was smiling.

"You know that he is right, Mother Abbess." She glanced to Myrddin. "You *are* a warrior, are you not?"

Myrddin gave way to the temptation of pride before the admiring gaze of the young girl.

"I am not a warrior, although I am versed in arms. In deference to the Mother Abbess, I can only say that I follow a different path."

Abbess Aldan closed her eyes, swayed a little and moaned softly.

The Lady Gwendoloena's face grew astonished.

"Then you are a . . .?"

"Hush, daughter," hissed the abbess. "We will talk of such things later."

She glanced quickly round the room but the sisters did not seem to have overheard their conversation.

They resumed their meal in silence but during it Myrddin was aware of the blue eyes of the girl appraising him now and then and they were full of interest. As for his own feelings, he felt a strange attraction to the girl. Even though they had exchanged only a few words, Myrddin felt that he had known this girl before, perhaps in other lives, for it was the ancient belief that the souls of men and women lived countless existences; countless beyond time. There was this world and there was the Otherworld and when a soul passed from this world, it was reborn in the Otherworld. When it passed from the Otherworld, it was reborn in this world. Thus a constant exchange of souls took place time without ending.

Perhaps there was some compatibility, an inner spark, which brought down the reserves that most people erected when trying to communicate with each other. Whatever it was, Myrddin felt a closeness to the girl.

After the meal, and after the Abbess Aldan had uttered another *Gratias* and dispersed the gathering, she turned to Myrddin.

"Now, Myrddin from beyond the western mountains, I need an oath from you."

"An oath?" he queried. "Why so?"

"You have learnt of the presence of the Lady Gwendoloena in this house. For that knowledge you might be well rewarded."

"By Saxons," intervened Gwendoloena, standing behind the abbess. "I do not think this young man would betray me to the Saxons."

"Even so, a whisper in the wrong quarter . . ."

"You have my solemn oath, I would not say anything to harm you," said Myrddin speaking directly to the young girl. "But why would the Saxons be seeking you? You say they have killed your family, dispossessed your people and driven you away from Ynys Wyth. What harm could you do them now?"

Gwendoloena pulled a face.

"The Saxon king, Cynric, desires me. I have hidden from him these last three months and now found sanctuary in the abbey of Llanelen. We have heard that Cynric leads a raiding party of his warriors in an attempt to find me and take me to his fortress. If they find me . . ."

She shrugged eloquently.

"Then you may count on me not only to keep my own counsel but to stand ready to protect you . . . always."

The girl blushed but smiled happily at the vehemence in Myrddin's voice.

A bell tolled in the distance.

"The hour grows late," chided the Abbess Aldan. "It is past the hour for retiring. I trust, Myrddin, you will be continuing your journey tomorrow? It is not seemly that a . . . a pagan should seek sanctuary in the House of God."

Myrddin smiled sadly.

"Is this God of yours so fastidious that he will turn those seeking hospitality away simply because they might not know nor acknowledge Him? Have no fear, though, Mother Abbess. Tomorrow, I shall depart."

The night was spent in restlessness for Myrddin. His waking

dreams were of the young girl, Gwendoloena. He began to regret promising the abbess that he would depart so soon. Was this to be his destiny? He realized that some powerful emotion stirred within him every time he thought of her. Was it love? If so, it was the love of a salmon for the river and not of a dog for the sheep. Of that he was sure. He wondered what excuse he could give to stay further in the abbey of Llanelen.

When he finally dropped off to sleep, in that curious hour which stands between the darkness of the night and the onset of dawn, when small birds here and there, pre-empting the coming of the light, began to call awkwardly from their nests, it was a sleep of tired exhaustion. Yet hardly had he descended into it than something jerked him awake.

He lay for a moment or so, listening and trying to sort out the mêlée of sounds that assaulted his ears.

A woman's voice was screaming. He finally made out the words.

"Saxons! The Saxons are attacking!"

There came the sound of wood crashing against wood, of the crackle of flames, the clash of metal upon metal, the screams of women and the ferocious yelling of men.

Myrddin grabbed his sword and, without putting on his clothes, he dashed into the courtyard.

The gates of the abbey were smashed open and a dozen fierce-looking warriors had spilled in. Some of the boys and the male workers lay sprawled on the ground; the blood on their bodies and the positions in which they lay told Myrddin they were beyond earthly help. Here and there the body of a sister lay, struck down indiscriminately by Saxon swords.

A rage gripped Myrddin and he sprang forward.

The Saxons were mainly on horseback but a small group had dismounted and, even as he looked, two of them were dragging the struggling Gwendoloena out of one of the abbey doors towards the waiting horses.

As he moved towards them, a Saxon on horseback rode down on him, his blade swinging. Myrddin had to turn to defend himself. The Saxon was no novice and Myrddin was sweating as he parried and thrust to prevent the swinging metal cleaving his head. Skill was with him for he gave an upward thrust which caught the Saxon in his unarmoured side. The man grunted and fell back, toppling slowly from his horse.

Myrddin swung round to where the girl had been. The Saxons were all mounted now and, with the abbey in flames, and smoke billowing across the courtyard, he saw one man had thrown Gwendoloena across his saddle bow and was spurring away with his companions after him. They thundered through the broken gates as, with an inarticulate cry, Myrddin raced vainly after them.

Then, as the riders passed out, Myrddin skidded to a halt in shock. The last rider was the hawk-faced warrior who had been of the party who attacked Emrys and his young companion. But it was not that which caused Myrddin to stand still in astonishment. The Saxon was carrying a battle banner. The banner was fluttering in the morning breeze. On it, Myrddin beheld the curious embroidered elaborate knot. The very same knot which the Venerable Fychan had shown him on the blanket in which he had been found wrapped as a small babe; the symbol which marked his destiny, the only thing which might identify his origins.

He stood paralysed for a moment staring at the disappearing banner.

Then his world exploded into bright lights before he sank down into the dark black, bottomless pit.

VI

Myrddin blinked and tried to focus.

He was lying on his back on the ground. He could still hear the crackle of fire, the cries of people and see the billow of smoke around him. A face was peering anxiously down at his: a woman's face, disfigured by a stream of blood across her forehead and cheek.

He blinked again and finally realized it was the Abbess Aldan.

He tried to raise himself and groaned as the pain shot through the back of his head.

"Lie still a moment, Myrddin," instructed the abbess.

He obeyed, for it was too painful otherwise.

"What happened?" he asked foolishly.

"A Saxon raider smote you from behind. By Christ's miracle, only the flat of his sword struck the back of your head and knocked you unconscious. Otherwise . . ." She shrugged. As she spoke she was bathing his face and his head with a cloth soaked in water.

"I remember. I saw the knot . . . my destiny." He suddenly groaned again. "They took Gwendoloena!"

Abbess Aldan nodded slowly, looking at him with a curious expression.

"You saw the knot?" she asked curiously.

"A symbol on a Saxon battleflag. No matter. They took Gwendoloena. She is in danger."

He tried to sit up and became aware again of the burning buildings and the bodies lying scattered around.

"You paid a heavy price for giving her sanctuary, Mother Abbess."

"There is a price to everything," agreed the abbess dispassionately. She helped him to a sitting position. "Have a care, now. Do you feel dizzy?"

"Somewhat. How did it happen?"

"The Saxons surprised us before dawn, smashed in the gates and killed all who opposed them. They obviously knew that Gwendoloena was here for that was their object, to kidnap her."

"We must get her back."

The abbess smiled thinly.

"We? A party of religieuses, shocked and some badly wounded? That we cannot. The abbey is on fire but we may yet save it if all the sisters work together to douse the flames."

"But what of Gwendoloena?" demanded Myrddin, rubbing his head.

"They say that God moves in mysterious ways. Perhaps he sent you for that purpose. Go after her, my son, and find a way of releasing her from her Saxon captors. There is no one else who is able to do so."

Myrddin gazed around him again and realized that the Abbess Aldan was right. Most of the male workers at the abbey had been slain, as well as several religieuses. The rest were either too shocked or needed to help put out the fires that threatened their monastery.

"Very well," he said. "Did they leave me my horse?"

"They took only the girl."

"How will I find them?"

"They are Cynric's men, and Cynric is king of the West Saxons. He has his fortress to the east."

Myrddin bent to pick up his fallen sword.

"Do you recognize that curious knot symbol, Mother Abbess? Is it the battle banner of Cynric?"

The Abbess Aldan shook her head.

"What makes you so curious about that symbol?" she demanded.

"It has much to do with my destiny. I must know its origins."

"Return here with Gwendoloena, and I may find out its origin. But this I can tell you, it is older than Cynric of the West Saxons."

Myrddin hesitated but a moment more. He would have pressed the abbess. He was sure that she was hiding further knowledge, but he knew every moment counted if he were to catch up with Gwendoloena and her captors. So he hastened back to his smoke-filled *cubiculum* to retrieve his clothes and dress before going to the stable. The stables had been gutted by fire but some of the community had managed to lead all the livestock from it, including his horse which was now tethered just beyond the walls of the abbey of Llanelen. It took him a moment or two to ready the beast and spring into the saddle.

The Abbess Aldan turned from directing her sisters in their slowly succeeding efforts to douse the fires and held up her hand towards him in the Christian blessing.

Myrddin raised a hand in a parting gesture and nudged his steed into an immediate gallop after the trail of the Saxon raiders in the direction of the south-east.

For a day and a night Myrddin had followed the trail left by the Saxon raiders. It was easy. Indeed, they had made no attempt to disguise their passage. Perhaps they were contemptuous of any pursuit for they cleaved their way through Dumnonia, leaving behind burning homesteads, slaughtered farmers and raped women. Myrddin felt a growing hatred for the race. His fears were for the person of Gwendoloena and he took comfort in the rationalization that they would not harm her if the West Saxon king, Cynric, desired her and led his warriors to take her as captive to his fortress. He would undoubtedly ensure that the girl would not be harmed.

It was not until the morning of the second day that Myrddin began to set his mind to wondering what he would do when he caught up with the raiding party. After all, he was but one against many. Perhaps he had been a fool to rush headlong into danger without a thought as to how he would rescue Gwendoloena or extract himself from the situation. Rather, he should have gathered a group of warriors to accompany him. Again he had been tempted by vanity.

The thoughts began to nag at his mind especially now that he had clearly passed from the territory of the Britons, which was the kingdom of Dumnonia, into the lands of the West Saxons. Of course, no boundaries marked the border over which Briton and Saxon had battled for two generations. One year the border would be in one place, another it would be elsewhere depending on the waxing or waning of the fortunes of either side.

What clearly marked his advent into the Saxon kingdom was the sign of the crude Saxon habitations and farmsteads, so unlike the British farms and palatial villas, villas that were the bequest of three centuries of Roman influence.

In older times, Myrddin reflected, this area had once been the kingdom of the Durotriges, "kings of strength" as their name boasted, one of the wealthiest of the tribes of the Isle of the Mighty. They had gone now, disappearing firstly under the might of the conquering Vespasian's II Augusta Legion, then under the assimilating processes of Roman administration, and lastly under the invasion of the West Saxons under Cynric's father, Cerdic. Cerdic was dead and now young Cynric ruled this land.

The sound of a bowstring inadverently loosed before its drawer was ready caused Myrddin to start, and he clasped a hand to his sword.

It was too late.

Fool that he was, he had been so occupied with his own thoughts that he had neglected to keep a careful scrutiny of his surroundings.

Four horsemen surrounded him. Two of them had bows drawn with arrows pointing unerringly at his heart. A third, the man who had loosed the bowstring inadvertently, was now swiftly stringing another arrow with a flustered look on his grim features. The fourth man, obviously their leader, sat astride his horse in front of Myrddin, a grin on his features, a sword held loosely in his hand. Myrddin recognized him at once. He was the hawkfaced man who had taken part in the raid into

Dumnonian territory. The man who had carried the banner bearing the emblem of the knot.

VII

"So what have we here? *A welisc*, by Thunor!"

It was clear that the man did not recognize him at all.

Myrddin found the man's Saxon language was easy to follow. Mentally he thanked the Venerable Fychan for having made him study several languages of which Saxon had been one. Myrddin knew that the word *welisc* was a derogatory term by which the Saxons named all Britons as "foreigners" in their own land.

A swift glance showed Myrddin that he had no immediate means of escape. He sat in a frozen posture, unmoving, lest the arrows fly from their bows.

"Who are you, *welisc*? Do you understand me?" the hawkfaced man was demanding.

"I understand well enough," replied Myrddin, indifferently.

"Then hear me. I am Centwine, thane to Cynric, king of the West Saxons. Who are you who has the appearance of a warrior of the *welisc*?"

"No warrior," replied Myrddin, thinking that some honesty might stand him in better stead with his foes. "I am a shaman of my people."

Centwine's eyebrows shot up.

"A wise man in one so young? Come, I'll not believe it. Besides, the religion of the Britons, who are followers of Christ, has no shamans."

"I believe in the old gods of my people, Centwine, thane to Cynric," Myrddin explained.

The Saxon thane examined him cynically.

"Yet you bear the look of a young warrior. What are you doing in the land of the West Saxons?"

"Looking for someone."

"And that someone is . . .?"

"A fellow Briton."

"No Briton lives here unless they be slaves. I believe you not. You are a spy, warrior, come to plot an invasion of our territory."

"That is not so."

"And you would swear by your god, Christ?" sneered the Saxon.

"No, for one must believe in Christ before one can take an oath on his name. I have told you that I do not. I believe in the old gods of my people. I will swear by them."

Centwine chuckled sourly.

"By Thunor's stroke, now here is a unique excuse for not swearing an oath. You are honey-tongued, *welisc*. I shall discover the truth of this matter in my *tun*."

He moved forward, keeping out of the line of fire from his bowmen, and removed Myrddin's weapons. Then he signalled his men to close in and turned to lead the way along the path.

Myrddin cursed himself many times during that short ride for his inattention. He was escorted a few miles before a grim wooden stockade became visible. The construction housed a small village and this was called a *tun* or fortress by the Saxons. Myrddin saw that it was well defended and at its portals stood gruesome war banners, one bearing a human skull transfixed to a pole beneath which bull's horns stood out with pieces of gaudy coloured clothes. Myrddin looked in vain for a glimpse of the banner carrying the emblem of the knot.

Once inside, he was beset by a group of rough Saxon men who dragged him from his horse, spat, punched and kicked at him before dragging him inside one of the buildings. It was a great hall in which many were gathered around feasting-tables. At one end, large roasts of oxen and sheep were being turned on spits. Men and women with iron collars around their necks hurried to and fro, mostly to keep the vessels, which each man seemed to hold, refilled from large jugs.

Centwine followed his men, grinning sourly, as Myrddin was dragged into the centre of the hall.

The seated warriors stopped their wassail and thumped the table top with the drinking horns, crying out the name of their chief.

Centwine walked to his captive and held up his hand to command silence in the hall.

"We have an extra guest. *A welisc*. He is going to tell us what he is doing in this land of ours."

"I told you truly," replied Myrddin, struggling in the hands of the Saxon warriors.

"Then we must question this *welisc* warrior more closely. Acca, the task falls to you to prise information from our friend."

Myrddin saw a burly, evil-looking man rise from his seat and come forward.

Willing hands tore the clothes from his body and leather thongs strapped him to a wooden pole which seemed to be one of the roof supports.

Centwine's features were suddenly before him.

"You have a chance to speak freely, *welisc*. Is it Gereint of Dumnonia who sends you to spy in this kingdom?"

There came the sound of a horn being blown from outside the hall.

Centwine glanced up in annoyance as a warrior ran in and called loudly to the assembly.

"My lord, it is the king. Cynric is coming."

A few moments passed before a group of men entered. At their head was the youthful Saxon who had been with Centwine in the attack on Emrys. He stood without helmet and Myrddin's eyes widened a little.

Myrddin found himself staring into the face of a youth scarce any older than himself. And, curiously, there was something in the youth's face that seemed familiar to him. It was not simply recognition from the day of the attack on Emrys. He was sure he had never seen Cynric before that day. But then why did he seem so acquainted with Cynric's features?

The king of the West Saxons glanced indifferently at Myrddin and then turned to Centwine.

"What sport is this, kinsman?"

"A Briton, my lord. A spy of Gereint, no doubt."

"No one sends me to spy. I am a wandering shaman," protested Myrddin.

"If so, let us hope that you are a good shaman for you will need to save yourself," Centwine sneered. Then he turned to Cynric. "With your permission, my lord, we were about to question the dog to learn his purpose here."

The Saxon king dropped languidly into a chair and waved a hand.

"Do not let me stop this sport," he said. "I came here merely to rest my horse and take refreshment before returning to my fortress." For the first time his eyes met Myrddin's. A slight look of bewilderment entered his gaze. Myrddin wondered whether the Saxon felt the same recognition that Myrddin had felt for him? Myrddin bit his lip trying to dredge his memories. Yet it was clear that, like Centwine, Cynric did not recognize him from the previous encounter.

"Acca," Centwine was saying, "the ritual by burning iron."

Myrddin turned his mind from the problem of Cynric as he saw Acca walk to the fire. Someone had already placed a branding iron in its hungry flames. He went cold as he realized what was coming. He tried to clear his mind of all thoughts and began to chant softly beneath his breath in an effort to invoke the process of meditation. He had often done it during his long years of training but it took time to reach the highest point of the meditative process called the act of peace.

He was aware of his surroundings but somehow they were no longer part of him.

He was aware of the evil, grinning face of the churl called Acca, approaching with the hot branding iron, but he felt none of its heat. He was aware of the branding iron moving towards his chest.

"Speak, *welisc*, and your pain may yet be avoided. Who sent you to spy here?"

"I am no spy!" Myrddin replied tightly.

He was aware of the branding iron touching his flesh, yet it was cold upon his skin. There came the sound of sizzling to his ears and the faint smell of roasting pork. He felt no other sensation than coldness.

The grins and cheers of the assembly suddenly died away as Myrddin still stood, eyes wide, simply chanting softly under his breath.

Centwine came forward, glancing at the seared and mangled flesh, and then at Myrddin. His expression was filled with sudden awe.

"By Woden's light! The man must be a shaman, how else can he stand the pain of such a wound?"

Still chanting in his mind, Myrddin gazed beyond Centwine to where Cynric sat, leaning forward in his chair to share his thane's wonder at Myrddin's reaction to the branding iron.

"By the dark and viewless powers, whom the storms and seas obey, I will curse your people to extinction, Cynric, king of the West Saxons, unless you release me now. I have spoken truly and you did not believe. Take this as a token of my power."

He lowered his head and beads of sweat stood out from his brow as his mind probed towards his horse which was being held outside the building. It was an old Druidic discipline, the sending of one's thoughts into the mind of a susceptible subject. Myrddin's horse reared up, striking out with his forelegs, catching the man who had been holding its reins a powerful kick on the side of the head. Then, released, the beast burst into the hall, crashing through the wicker gate, and rearing up in the confined space.

The Saxons yelled in fright as the beast approached and they hurried to the sides of the hall, away from the threatening animal. Only Cynric continued to sit in his chair without concern. Centwine backed behind Myrddin for protection.

One Saxon warrior, bolder than the rest, ran forward to catch its reins, but the beast reared again, knocking the man back across the hall with a blow of its powerful hooves.

Then the horse trotted docilely up to Myrddin and stood snorting and pawing at the ground before him.

Myrddin relaxed a moment from his efforts and heaved a sigh.

"Release me and let me depart, Saxons, and no further harm shall come to you. Keep me or try to kill me and you shall be cursed even to the seventh generation."

Centwine was white-faced now. He turned to Cynric. The young king rose slowly to his feet.

Even Acca, ashamed of having left his king and thane undefended, returned to stand trembling a little before them.

"Best do as he says, my lords. He must be a powerful wizard to withstand the pain of the iron," he urged.

Cynric's lips compressed tightly a moment and then he said: "For one so young, you appear a powerful enemy to have, *welisc*. What is your name?"

"Mark well my name, Cynric; it is Myrddin from beyond the western mountains."

"I shall remember it. Cut him free, Centwine. He may depart this *tun* in peace."

The Saxon thane suddenly leant forward and cut the thongs with a knife.

Myrddin staggered forward a little but quickly regained his balance.

"You may leave here in safety," Cynric told him. "But if you are found still within my kingdom at sunset then my warriors shall slaughter you, as they would a wild dog, and they will slaughter you on sight."

Myrddin walked in as dignified manner as he could summon to his horse and, slowly hauling himself painfully into the saddle, he turned and rode out of the hall, through the sullen yet quiet throng outside and out of the gates. Then he put his heels against the beast and sent it into a furious gallop.

Only when he had gone several miles did he draw rein and halt. The pain was beginning to prick at his mind in spite of his meditation. The branding iron had left a wound which would have caused the death by shock of the pain to many another.

He looked around and saw a small stream nearby. Edging his horse near it, he almost tumbled off and threw his aching body in its cold, bubbling waters. Then exhaustion overcame his mind control. The pain hit him like the points of several knives all at once. In his mind he thought he screamed out loud. In reality, a low moan came from his lips and he blacked out.

VIII

Myrddin awoke in darkness.

He was lying in a bed between cool sheets of linen, his head resting on a feather pillow. While the wound on his chest burned and irritated, it was not painful. Someone had dressed it with oils or lotions and placed strips of linen over it. His mind felt strangely peaceful, relaxed and untroubled.

He frowned but could derive no memory to suggest how he had come to this place, whatever place it was.

He was in a large room. Outside he realized that it was night for he could see the twinkle of stars in the sky. Wolves howled in the distance. In the gloom he realized that he was in a well-built house of the type the Romans had once built in Britain. There were frescoes on the wall and pillars supporting the high ceiling while, beyond the windows, he could hear a fountain playing. That part of the floor which he could discern was carpeted in mosaic.

He tried again to dredge up some memory, some explanation of what had happened.

His mind was sluggish.

He thought that he must have been drugged.

The door opened abruptly and a shadowy figure passed into the room and came to stand at his bedside.

"Who are you? Where am I?" were the questions that sprang to his lips. Slow, hesitant questions.

The answer came back in Saxon from a woman's voice.

"Do not be afraid, Myrddin. You are quite safe here."

Myrddin frowned.

"Who are you?" he demanded again, this time in Saxon.

"My name is Lowri. I am sister to Centwine, the thane of Cynric."

Myrddin groaned as the implication registered in his mind.

"Am I Centwine's prisoner again?"

"No. You are no one's prisoner. I followed you from Centwine's *tun* and found you drowning in the waters of a stream. I pulled you out and brought you here."

"Where is here?"

"This is my palace. I am told that it was built long ago by the Romans. Here I live. We are many miles from Centwine's *tun*. You are safe from recapture for the time being."

"Why?"

"I do not understand."

"Why have you helped me? You are Centwine's sister and a Saxon."

"Shall we say it is because I admire a brave man."

Myrddin shook his head. "I still do not understand," he said.

The woman moved closer and lit a torch.

"Have no fear, Myrddin, for I am a healer among my people. You have nothing to be alarmed about."

"You dressed my wound?" he asked.

"It will heal soon, but it will leave a scar."

Myrddin gazed up, still bewildered.

Although the light from the flickering brand torch was not good, he could see that the woman, Lowri, was handsome. More voluptuous than pretty. Her features were heavier than Gwendoloena's. He found the comparison came naturally. The features had a slight grossness that was more sensual. Lascivious was the word that eventually came to mind. Her features were dark and rounded, the lips pouting enticingly. Her figure was full but not unattractive.

She smiled down at him and her hands removed the strips of linen on his chest.

"Ah," she nodded approvingly. "The wound is healing well. I will anoint it with more balm to quicken the process."

"You have also given me some compound to sedate my mind, haven't you?"

Lowri looked quickly at him.

"You are, indeed, a wise man. You were in need of tranquillity of the mind to bear the pain of the wound. I shall give you nothing more if you do not wish the sedation. But balm you must have to heal your wound."

Myrddin felt no anxiety.

"Do what you can, healer, for I can do nothing until I am healed."

Lowri nodded, then bent to her task, pouring a cooling balm over his chest. She poured a drink from a flagon and left it by his bedside.

"You may take this if the irritation grows strong in the night. It is up to you. By dawn the pain of the wound may bring a fever. I shall be here and help you. But, if my prediction holds true, you will be quite well by dusk tomorrow."

"I still do not know why you are doing this," Myrddin said. "Especially if Centwine is your brother."

Lowri shook her head.

"We may talk about that when you are better. Now try to rest. By dawn the fever will come."

Lowri was right.

Myrddin awoke from his sleep, or, at least, he thought he had. One part of his mind told him he was in a hot, sweating fever, yet shivering in bed. Another part awoke him in a dark cavern and as he moved towards its interior he saw Gwendoloena smiling at him, imploring him to come to her arms. Yet when he did so, he saw that her head was attached to a long scaly neck, the neck of a huge reptilian dragon. A sword was in his hand and, crying in terror, he hacked and hewed at the beast, while all the time, the head of Gwendoloena implored him to help her.

He started from the bed screaming, one hand stretched out before him as if to fend off danger.

Firm hands on his shoulders pressed him back to the pillows.

"Quiet now! You have been dreaming."

He stared about him and then focused on the face of Lowri.

He saw that there was a twilight outside the room. He was still lying in a sweat-sodden bed, hot and sticky from the hours of his fever.

"I thirst," were his first words.

The woman Lowri reached forward and brought a cup to his lips. It was water, ice cold and refreshing. She allowed him only a few swallows.

"It is not good to drink so much at once," she reproved, reaching out to dab at his perspiration-coated brow with a cooling cloth.

Myrddin heaved a deep sigh.

"The fever came as you said it would."

Lowri grinned.

"And the wound has begun to heal without infection, as I said. Tomorrow, after a night's sleep, you will be able to get up and walk about."

"Then I shall need to know why you have helped me," he murmured, allowing himself to fall back into the bed. A deep natural sleep overcame him even as she replied.

"You will know . . . tomorrow."

In the bright, morning light, he felt refreshed, strong, and his mind was clear and sharp. A slave came with water for him to wash while another brought him food and drink to break his fast. He indulged freely and then a third slave arrived with fresh clothes to replace the ones that had been torn off his back at Centwine's *tun*. He dressed and they fitted him well.

His chest, though he was conscious of the healing wound, did not trouble him at all.

This Lowri was a good healer, he admitted.

The door opened and another slave, or perhaps it was the same one, bowed low:

"My lady requests your attendance if you are ready, my lord."

Myrddin sniffed, for he disapproved of such subservience. He had heard of the Saxon institution of slaves and knew that those who wore iron collars on their neck had no freedom at all among the Saxons but could be bought and sold at the whim of their owners.

"Lead me to her, man."

The slave bowed obsequiously.

Myrddin was astonished by the affluence and beauty of the villa as he was led from the chamber across an elegant courtyard, with a marble fountain, into a set of more private chambers and out into a small sun-filled but secluded courtyard.

Stretched on a couch was the woman, Lowri.

She gazed up languidly and smiled.

"You are better, Myrddin from beyond the western mountains."

Myrddin returned her smile and inclined his head.

"Thanks to you, Lowri of the West Saxons."

She waved her hand for him to be seated on the couch next to her.

"You put fear into my brother's heart," she chided, as he obeyed. "You are young to be so well trained as a shaman."

"I studied under the adepts since I was a baby. It is not by age that one is judged but by knowledge."

"Truly spoken. Nevertheless, my brother was fearful. Be warned that out of fear is born hate and it is my suspicion that the next time you meet he will kill you."

"Will there be a next time?"

Lowri pouted and looked uncomfortable.

"If you are wise, Myrddin, as wise as you have shown yourself knowledgeable and unafraid, you will avoid Centwine."

"I have little intention to renew our relationship," grinned Myrddin. "But it may be, if we do meet again, that it will be I who will kill him."

Lowri leant forward a little and gestured to a jug of mead which a slave carried forward.

Myrddin shook his head.

"Mead is not for drinking this early in the morning for it causes men to lose their senses or sleep to overcome them. And there is much I should know."

Lowri waved the slave to depart.

"There is much that I should know also, Myrddin," replied the woman. "I risk my life to save you from drowning and healed your wound. Tell me, truly, are you Gereint of Dumnonia's spy? Did you come into this land to spy for our enemy, Gereint?"

Myrddin shook his head.

"I know nothing of the king of Dumnonia. I came here for . . . for my own reasons."

"Your own reasons?" She frowned.

"I spoke the truth to your brother, lady. I came seeking someone."

"A Briton, you said."

"Indeed. A Briton."

Myrddin eased himself in his chair and, in shifting his position, he suddenly caught sight of a banner decorating the wall of a room, whose open doors led onto the courtyard. In surprise he sprang up.

"What is it?" demanded Lowri, alarmed.

Myrddin took a pace or two towards the room.

There was no mistaking it. It was the banner with the embroidered knot that he had last seen carried by Centwine as the raiders left Llanelen.

"What banner is that?" Myrddin demanded, reseating himself. "I think that it is familiar to me."

Lowri followed his gaze and shrugged.

"As thane to Cynric, my brother, Centwine, often carries that battle banner. It was carried for Cerdic, Cynric's father, years ago."

"It is Cynric's battle banner?"

"Yes."

"Ah!" Myrddin breathed out slowly. He felt confusion. Questions tumbled into his mind and yet he could not articulate them.

"Tell me something of yourself, Myrddin, and of this person whom you seek in our kingdom," pressed Lowri.

"Of me there is little to say. I came to this kingdom with no intent to harm it but merely to recover something."

"Even more mysterious," Lowri said. "You are a handsome and mysterious man, Myrddin. I have become attracted to you."

She reached out and laid a cool hand on his cheek.

Myrddin tried to shake off the thoughts of the mysterious banner, and concentrate on Lowri. She was being deliberately provocative, her sensuous lips pouting, the expression one of promising excitement.

"You are a handsome woman, Lowri," he conceded absently. "Tell me, your brother is close to your king Cynric?"

She frowned, unused to her advances being deflected.

"Centwine is Cynric's thane and right-hand man. Why?"

"I would go to Cynric's court. Where does it lie from here?"

Lowri laughed a little falsely.

"Truly, I think you are here to spy on Cynric to wish to hurry to his court and dismiss a more promising dalliance here. Cynric's fortress lies over the next hill but I would have a care of going there. Any Briton found wandering about on his own would be cut down within half a mile of it. Cynric does not love Britons."

"I hear the opposite," Myrddin threw out the bait.

Lowri frowned.

"How so?"

"I hear that Cynric is enamoured of a British princess."

The woman gave a dismissive sniff.

"The daughter of the former king of the Isle of Wight."

"Just so. Gwendoloena of Ynys Wyth."

Suddenly Lowri was suspicious.

"What do you know of this?" Her eyes widened in sudden realization. "Is it for this Gwendoloena that you have come to this kingdom? Is it for her that you seek?"

Myrddin hastily shook his head but he had not fooled the Saxon princess.

Lowri smiled softly in satisfaction.

"So? It is true that Cynric is enamoured of this Gwendoloena. If you seek her, then you may rest assured that you will never see her again. She is beyond your powers of rescue. She is now safely lodged in the fortress of Cynric, beyond the hills there. Do you desire her yourself or has Gereint sent you to test out the land for a stronger force to come and attempt a rescue?"

Myrddin stood up. He tried to keep the irritation from his face. He had let his own arrogance lead him into admitting more than he should have done to this strange Saxon woman.

"I do not seek her, lady," he denied. "I was curious about the stories that I had heard. That was all. I am no spy, nor am I enamoured of her."

Lowri rose and stretched languidly.

She looked at him appraisingly under lowered lids.

"If that is so, it is not hard to disprove. I have a strange attraction to you, Myrddin from beyond the western mountains. Come and prove to me that you do not care aught for this Gwendoloena."

She turned with slow, languorous movements, and walked into one of the darkened side rooms which surrounded the courtyard.

Myrddin glanced round quickly.

The only exit was barred by an armed slave. The only thing he could do was play along with Lowri and wait until he had a chance to leave without suspicion. He could not deny that his youthful male vanity was flattered by the Saxon woman's overt erotic ardour. What man could deny such sensual adulation?

He hesitated but a fraction before he turned and followed Lowri into the bedchamber.

IX

When he awoke, Centwine was bending over him with a knife held at his throat.

Behind Centwine's shoulder stood Lowri. She was combing her hair and smiling absently.

"I told you that it would be easy to discover his secret, brother. Where you waste time in torture, often physical gratification will bring better results."

Myrddin silently cursed himself for a fool. He had been a fool all along, falling prey to temptation that any novitiate of the order would have spurned. And he was supposed to be a "man of oak wisdom". He deserved to die at the hands of these Saxons for his stupid folly. He cursed his youth and his stupid vanity. Truly had the Venerable Fychan taught that danger breeds best on too much confidence. Vanity had led him into overconfidence. His expression told Centwine the truth of what his sister was saying.

The Saxon thane chuckled grimly.

"So? You are come to our land in search of the lady Gwendoloena? So either you come as a spy for Gereint or you are come to rescue her because you are in love with her yourself? Yes, I think the latter reason is the one. How noble! Never did I think the *welisc* were possessed of such nobility."

He spat on the floor to emphasize his cynicism.

"Yet it is true, brother," Lowri said indifferently. "His love-making was like lying with a tree trunk, so indifferent to my body was he, his mind was clearly on thoughts of his *welisc* bitch."

Centwine's hand came up and he hit Myrddin hard across the mouth.

"How were you going to effect a rescue?" he snarled. "Are there others waiting nearby to aid you?"

Myrddin blinked but did not reply.

"Where are your warriors?" demanded Centwine.

The hand struck again.

"I do not think he has any warriors," interposed Lowri, dispassionately. "I think this poor moon-struck calf came of his own accord. He must have followed you from Llanelen for he recognized the battle banner."

"Llanelen?"

Centwine peered forward and then swore.

"By Thunor's stroke! I recall you now! You are the warrior who was fighting with our men in the courtyard of that abbey. So? You have done well, my sister. Now we know the dog."

Myrddin moistened his lips.

"If I am to die, Saxon, tell me what your battle banner means. What is the symbol of the knot?"

Centwine raised a quizzical eyebrow.

"The banner? It was a trophy, a prize of war, taken in the time of Cerdic. We use it to remind the *welisc* of our conquest."

"From where did you seize it?"

"Why would you want to know?" demanded Lowri, interested for once.

"I told you, I think I recognize it."

"Well, before you die, *welisc*, I will tell you," sneered Centwine. "And that death will be very soon. Get to your feet."

Centwine backed off the bed.

Myrddin knew he had little choice. He made to rise, pretended to fall back, seizing the hand of the Saxon thane, and then exerting such pressure that, with the momentum of his backward fall, he heaved the surprised Saxon over his head. It took but a split second. His hand grabbed for the knife. Even before Lowri had uttered her scream, he had seized the knife and buried it in Centwine's heart.

Then he was up, grabbing the woman and swinging her round to act as a shield before him as several slaves burst through the door to investigate the sounds of the commotion.

"Tell them to back off," hissed Myrddin, "or you will be the next to die, lady."

"Leave us!" screamed Lowri in terror. "Leave, or he will surely kill me."

Reluctantly, the slaves edged out of the door.

"Now," whispered Myrddin, savagely, for he still nursed an anger that he had been so fooled by this voluptuous woman for her own ends, "we shall walk slowly to the front of this villa.

Order your slaves to have my horse saddled and my weapons waiting for me."

Again, Lowri saw no alternative but to obey him. But after she had given the instructions she snarled at him: "It will avail you nothing, Myrddin. You may have killed Centwine but I also know your purpose. You are going to Cynric's fortress to get the *welisc* bitch. Have no fear, for I will ensure that Cynric will be waiting for you."

Myrddin bit his lip.

"Then if you are to warn Cynric, 'twere best I kill you now."

Lowri had regained her composure now. He would kill her to save himself or for any one of a number of life-threatening reasons, but she knew he would not kill her in cold blood merely to silence her.

"I know about you 'men of oak wisdom'. You have a code of honour which will not allow you to kill a defenceless woman, even a woman of an enemy race, just to silence them."

Myrddin smiled thinly.

"This is true but . . ."

He spun her round quickly and stared deeply into her wide, surprised eyes, giving all his concentration to the ancient art which the Venerable Fychan had shown him.

"Your mind to my mind, Lowri," he whispered intently. "Your soul to my soul. Concentrate, concentrate and sleep, sleep and in your sleep you will forget, forget . . ."

He saw her eyes glazing, the eyelids drooping, in spite of herself.

"Forget all about Myrddin, about Gwendoloena, forget about all this . . . Now, walk with me slowly to the gate where I will mount my horse and ride away. And you will then sleep. You will dismiss your servants, go to your bed and sleep, sleep for a day and a night and nothing will awake you until you arise refreshed but still in forgetfulness about what has happened. Do you understand?"

"I . . . understand," she whispered.

Turning her again, he walked slowly with her through the courtyards of the villa, while slaves stood watching and scowling at him. Someone had brought his saddled horse, another handed him his weapons. Lowri stood passively, staring into the middle distance, while he buckled on his sword belt and clambered into his saddle.

"Sleep and forget!" he called and then he had kicked at his steed and sent it bounding away from the villa. But no cries of alarm came to his ears. The slaves seemed to be awaiting orders from Lowri, the sister of Centwine, but no orders appeared forthcoming.

Bending low along his horse's neck, Myrddin determined to put as much distance as he could between himself and the villa. There was no knowing whether his mesmerizing of Lowri would work and for how long. He had attempted the accomplishment only once or twice before and then on fellow students for short periods. He hardly believed that it worked at all. This he knew: that he had to effect the rescue of Gwendoloena from the fortress of Cynric immediately. The sooner he attempted it the better, for even the sight of her slain brother might awaken the memories in Lowri's mind. If she was right, and the fortress of Cynric was not far distant, he had little time before the alarm was raised.

The one thing he wished he could have pressed further with Centwine and Lowri was the matter of the mysterious banner, the banner with the same embroidered knot emblem that had been on the blanket in which he had been found as a babe. Where had it come from? From whom had it been stolen? And did it mean that he was a scion of the house who used it as their symbol? Yet there was no time to consider the matter now.

He urged his horse to increase its stride, eventually turning from the main path that ran to the villa in order to conceal himself amidst the forest tracks.

X

Myrddin had concealed his horse in a small grove of oaks on the edge of a sprawling forest which surrounded the approaches to Cynric's fortress. The fortress was a tall grey stone fortress which stood on top of a great rolling earthwork which crowned a large hill and dominated the plain below. A river pushed sedately by, just skirting the edge of the hill at one point. It had obviously been built in the olden days by the Britons to defend themselves against Roman attack, then vacated during the days of their occupation but reoccupied at the time of the Saxon invasion. Now the Britons, the former occupants of the fortress, had been forced away and the Saxons commanded the heights and reinforced the walls and vantage points of the fortress.

To Myrddin, as he lay hidden in the gorse and bracken of a nearby hill and examined the mighty gates, the patrolling warriors, the earth bank heights, it seemed an impossible task to infiltrate Cynric's fortress and find Gwendoloena. He lay flat on his stomach, propping himself a little on his elbows, as he scanned the battlements with growing dismay. No wonder Cynric had decided not to destroy this fortress but occupy it in turn as his stronghold. The Britons had built it to withstand the storms of ages. And they had built it well.

Myrddin's eyes narrowed and he sighed.

But then, he reminded himself, the fortress had fallen firstly to the Romans and then to the Saxons. Therefore, it was not impregnable. He simply had to find a way inside and . . .

His ears detected the rustle of the gorse a split second before he felt hands pinning his arms behind him, a gag thrust into his mouth to prevent him crying out, and a rope expertly used to bind him. Then a cloth was placed around his eyes and he was dragged to his feet.

He felt that there was more than one assailant around him but no one spoke. He had the impression that he was being dragged down a hill. There was a pause and, with a jerk, he realized that he had been thrown over the broad shoulders of a powerful man who carried his slight form as easily as a babe.

Once more Myrddin had cause to curse himself for his stupidity. A "man of oak wisdom"! He was but a silly, vain child, without knowledge. He was a mere boy let loose in the world whose years of training had counted as naught against the cunning and wiles of his enemies.

He had trained with Mawr, the warrior; had learnt the art of forest craft with Fychan, yet twice his concentration and concern about the rescue of Gwendoloena had blinded him to the very basic principle of survival. For the second time he had allowed the Saxons to catch him. He'd better start using his store of knowledge to better effect.

He wondered whether his mesmerism of Lowri had been insufficient and she had raised the alarm as to his purpose and plan.

With Centwine's death, the Saxons would show him little mercy now, if mercy was ever a word in their vocabulary.

He dragged his mind away from his self-reproach, realizing that self-reproach was also an immature luxury he could not afford.

He realized, with some surprise, that he was being carried away from the Saxon fortress. The subconscious part of his mind had registered that his captors had taken him down the hill from his spypoint, but away from the fortress, and into the surrounding forest. Were they Lowri's men intent on vengeance?

With a sudden abruptness, the man carrying him halted and flung him unceremoniously onto the earth, knocking the breath from his body.

Someone grasped his tunic and dragged him upright, thrusting him backwards, so that his back encountered the bole of a tree.

"Sit up!" hissed a voice in Saxon.

Myrddin presumed that he had been seated with his back against a tree. He felt puzzled.

A familiar voice came from a distance.

"What is it, Carannog?"

"A Saxon lookout. We found him near Cynric's fortress. We might persuade him to tell us how to get inside."

Myrddin was astonished.

The voices spoke in his own language. They were Britons. And why was the first speaker's voice so familiar?

He struggled against his bonds.

"I doubt any Saxon would betray Cynric, even if his own life depended on it," came another voice. "Better to kill him now, Carannog, and save us trouble."

"No, wait!" It was the first voice. "The thing a Saxon warrior fears most is a death which is not in battle and without a sword in his hand. They believe that their god Woden will only allow them entry in their Otherworld, their Hall of Heroes . . . they call it *Wael-haell*. If they die bound and without a sword, then they have no after life."

"A stupid belief," sneered the unnamed third speaker.

"Stupid or not, Cadell, we will try to persuade our Saxon friend here that he will die bound and gagged and obtain no after life unless he shows us the way into Cynric's fortress. Carannog!"

Myrddin felt a hand close on the cloth that had been placed over his head and it was wrenched away. Then someone loosened his gag.

He gasped as he sought to regulate his breathing.

"Now, Saxon, we have a proposition for you ..." began Carannog.

"I am no Saxon. I am a Briton, like you!" Myrddin managed to say between his gasps for breath.

"What?" There was a gasp of astonishment from half a dozen throats.

Myrddin gazed up and focused on a burly, red-haired British warrior bending over him in surprise.

"Have you no eyes to recognize a Briton from a Saxon?" demanded Myrddin, recovering himself. "Untie me."

"What trick is this?" returned Carannog. "What would a Briton be doing at Cynric's fortress?"

"The same as you, seeking a way in," snapped Myrddin.

"How can we believe you ...?"

"We can believe him, for I have seen this man before."

It was the owner of the first voice who spoke again.

A young man crossed the small forest clearing in which the group of British warriors were apparently resting.

Myrddin raised his eyes to meet the grim features of a young man, the young man named Artio whom he had encountered with the elderly Emrys, the dying High King of the Isle of the Mighty.

"This is the man who helped Emrys and I when we were attacked by Saxons. Your name is ...?"

"Myrddin."

"Just so. Release him, Carannog."

The red-haired warrior, with a muttered curse, bent forward and cut Myrddin's bonds. Myrddin came to his feet rubbing his chafed wrists.

"Now, Myrddin," the young warrior said, "you have some explaining to do. What are you doing at Cynric's fortress here in this kingdom of the West Saxons?"

Myrddin made a gesture of irritation.

"I have no more explaining to do than you, my friend," he countered. "I left you with a dying man heading west to Dinas Emrys. Now I find you here in the land of Cynric."

Artio looked annoyed, as if he were about to argue, and then he shrugged.

"We shall both swap tales. Mine is simple. Emrys, God be merciful to his soul, died before I had gone far. His bodyguard had just joined us, having come to seek us on the road, and so it was decided that some of them would escort his body on to Dinas Emrys. A dozen of us, those you see here, decided to return the Saxon raid before they learnt of the tragedy."

"Why would you need to return the raid before they learnt of Emrys' death?" asked Myrddin.

"Easy to tell. Once Cynric learns that Emrys is dead, and the Britons are without their High King, he will raise the West Saxons, indeed, he will raise all the kingdoms of the Angles and the Saxons to unite in a fresh attempt to annihilate the Britons. My aim is to forestall this with these chosen warriors. We planned to enter Cynric's fortress and slay him and so balance the scales."

"But with Emrys dead, is it not better to elect a new High King as soon as possible and prepare a defence?"

Artio grinned sourly.

"Alas, my friend Myrddin, you know little of the politics of our land. Emrys held the Britons together by the force of his personality, by the victories he won against the Saxons. It is only because of the unity that Emrys forced on them that the Britons have been able to keep the Saxons in check these last forty years. With Emrys gone, until a new strong leader emerges, the Britons will become a series of petty kingdoms, with their kings and chieftains arguing amongst each other. Hywel of Cornwall demands that he be recognized as the equal to Gereint of Dumnonia, Gwid of Elmet demands precedence over Padarn of Gwynedd; Tryffin of Dyfed believes he is superior to Cyngar of Powys and so on ... each squabbling with each other over inconsequential considerations while the enemy is at their gates."

Myrddin shook his head in sadness.

"Is there no one who can unite them?"

Artio shrugged.

"At this time, I can see no one person capable of such a deed. So, while the arguing goes on, I believe that a swift raid on Cynric's fortress and his death would redress the balance and throw the Saxons into disarray, giving us time to mend our differences and restore the balance of power."

Myrddin could see the logic of the plan.

"And now, your story, Myrddin. How came you here?"

"I was staying at the abbey at Llanelen when Cynric's men stormed and burnt the abbey and killed many there."

The youth named Artio looked concerned.

"And the Mother Abbess, the Abbess Aldan, was she killed?"

"No. But they kidnapped the lady Gwendoloena, daughter of the king of Ynys Wyth. I was there, though they knocked the senses from me. When I recovered, I tracked the raiders here."

"What made you recognize Cynric's men? Was Cynric their leader?"

"Not that I saw. But I recognized Centwine."

Artio brought a fist into the palm of his other hand.

"By the Living God! This Centwine shall pay for his sacrilege."

Myrddin's lips thinned.

"He already has. But a few hours ago, I slew him. But not before I discovered that Cynric has Gwendoloena imprisoned in his fortress."

Artio stared at Myrddin.

"You told me that you were no warrior, yet you act and think as a warrior."

Myrddin shrugged.

"You know that I am a 'man of oak wisdom', Artio. I am a believer in the old gods."

"Let each man honour his conscience. I care not which path you take so long as it leads by the parallel morality to the same place. Give me your hand, Myrddin, for I honour you."

"The time to honour each other is when we have succeeded in our plan. Yours is to kill Cynric while mine must be to rescue Gwendoloena. However, in these plans we may join together for part of the way."

Carannog stirred and sighed.

"You have seen Cynric's fortress, Myrddin. It is impossible to scale the walls."

Myrddin nodded and then grinned sharply.

"If it is impossible, then why attempt it?"

Artio frowned.

"What do you mean, Myrddin?"

"There are other ways into the fortress which are not impossible. For example, why not walk through the gates?"

Carannog laughed loudly.

"Because the Saxon warriors might object to a band of British warriors riding up to their king's fortress and asking for entrance."

"Then why go riding up as British warriors? You are in the land of the Saxons. Are there not enough Saxon garments about for the taking?"

Artio began to smile gently.

"I see what you are about, my friend. But, in fact, we do have another plan but we are not sure of it. That is why we have been seeking other ways."

"What plan?"

Artio motioned to another of the warriors, a swarthy man with thin features.

"Cadell here was the son of Idwal whose home was once in that very fortress before the Saxons drove the Britons from it. Come here, Cadell, and tell your story."

The thin man approached.

"Little to tell," he said. "I was born in the west of Dumnonia where my father fled as a young man following the fall of the fortress yonder which Cynric now makes his own."

"Go on," pressed Artio when Cadell paused.

"I do not vouch for the truth of this," he hesitated. "When I was young I used to listen to my father speak of the impregnable fortress of his people. He told me that the only reason that the fortress fell was because the Saxons had forced a local farmer, curses on his name, to reveal the existence of a tunnel which leads up from the river that skirts the hill. This is a passageway into the centre of the fortress. By this means, a band of Saxon warriors infiltrated the fortress and opened the gates to allow their fellows inside."

"A tunnel? What sort of tunnel?"

"It was built to take effluence away from the fortress and into the river. A conduit. But that is the only information I have. I have no knowledge where such a secret tunnel starts or where it comes out."

Myrddin thought for a moment.

"That may be enough for our purpose. If Cadell's father was correct, then there is only a short stretch of river where the conduit can exit into. What Saxon warriors have done, we Britons can do."

"You mean, we will climb into the fortress through the conduit?" asked Carannog.

"Certainly. If it leads to the river then there is only an area of one hundred yards on the far bank to search. We should soon find it, if it exists. Let us draw up a plan. How many speak the tongue of the Saxon?"

Artio glanced about at his men.

"We have a company of eleven, plus myself and now you. Thirteen all told, of which five of us speak the Saxon language."

"Do you include me?" asked Myrddin. "For I also have knowledge of it."

"Then six of us."

"Very well. We must ensure that those who do not speak Saxon are always in the company of one of us who does, in case we need to bluff our way out of danger."

"A good stratagem," nodded Carannog.

"And it augurs well," smiled Myrddin confidently. "For we have a leader and twelve to follow and that reflects good fortune for it is written that twelve followers constitutes a magical force."

"Christ had twelve followers," interposed Carannog.

"Which is why his influence was great," agreed Myrddin, "for he must have known the significance of numerology to choose them and no more."

"Very well," Artio was a little impatient. "What now?" It was clear that he was not happy that Myrddin had assumed the authority of planning strategy.

"We must leave some men outside when we enter. A total of four, I think. Two men to guard the entrance of the conduit, for we may wish to make our exit through it, if all goes well. And two to place themselves on the hill where Carannog found me to watch the main gates. It will be the purpose of these men that, if we exit with the Saxons in pursuit, they must ensure our horses are available. We can tether them in the oak copse behind the hillock where I tethered my own."

Artio nodded in agreement.

"That means nine of us shall enter the fortress."

Myrddin grinned.

"Another number signifying good fortune. Nine is the sacred number of our people for the ancient heroes went in companies of nine."

Artio was impatient.

"I know the ancient stories, Myrddin. And will this good fortune show us the way to the entrance of the conduit?"

"Let us hope so, my friend." He glanced at the sky. "Dusk will soon be here. We will use its darkness to examine the river bank for sign of the conduit. Now who comes into the fortress and who remains outside?"

It was Artio who took over and made the necessary appointments.

"Once inside," Artio added, "we must go quickly in search of Cynric."

"And of Gwendoloena," Myrddin pointed out.

Artio bit his lip as he considered.

"Agreed. We may have to split up for the task. You, Myrddin, may take Carannog and Cadell and search for her. I and the rest will look for Cynric. Each party will make their own way in case of trouble. And each party must place the success of its own task before any other consideration. If one party gets into trouble, the other must continue. We must have no useless sacrifices."

"Agreed," Myrddin said.

"Then," Artio glanced up at the darkening sky, "let us be about this work."

XI

They crossed the river just after dusk. There was a brisk current to it and Cadell recalled that in his father's day it was called Fram, which meant "briskly flowing". All Artio's men were good swimmers and there was no problem to the crossing. Once on the far side, they divided into the two parties, the quicker to traverse the river bank in search of the entrance to the conduit.

It was Cadell, appropriately enough, who found it. A tunnel opening straight into the river under a small outcrop of rocks. The only way one could gain entrance was to climb into the river and swim into its dark, cavernous maw. The entrance was not large; indeed, it was only big enough to take two men abreast.

Myrddin and Cadell went first to make a reconnaissance.

The smell from the effluence was putrid and almost took away their breath.

"We need a light," muttered Myrddin as he tried to peer into the black depths of the entrance.

Cadell offered to swim back and see if there was something which could be used.

He returned after what seemed an eternity to Myrddin, who was waiting in the darkness, waist high in cold water.

"I have a brand torch," Cadell whispered, "Artio had several made in case they were needed. I am holding it above my head. Round my neck, to keep it out of the water, is a bag of flints and tinder. Do you think you can strike a light?"

Myrddin, his eyes having grown accustomed to the gloom, waded across to the man and took the bag. He had seen some sort of ledge to the side of the entrance, just above the water level, and he waded towards it and felt its surface. It was dry enough and so he placed the flints and tinder on it and managed to strike a light quite easily. He enkindled the brand torch and held it up high.

It was the conduit right enough. A channel had been cut through the rock and earth leading upwards towards the fortress on the top of the hill. It was no bigger than four feet wide and the same measurement in height. The incline was steep. To one side, a deeply grooved channel showed where the waste was pushed down into the river, while to the other side, on a slightly raised area above the channel, was a paved way whose incline was softened by steps every so often.

"Perfect," breathed Myrddin. "All we have to do is follow this path upwards. Cadell, fetch the others, and tell them to bring the other brand torches in case they are needed."

Myrddin heaved himself out of the river water and onto the dry path.

He was suddenly aware of a squeaking noise and of black shapes darting hither and thither along the pathway. He held up the torch and shivered. Rats. He might have known. He hoped that the light would scare them from the path.

It was a few moments before Artio and the others came crowding behind Cadell.

"There is only room for one man at a time to move up the path," Myrddin said. "So we must go in single file. I propose that I go first, next Cadell, and then you, Artio, and your men."

The young warrior hesitated as if to object but Myrddin was already moving upwards and Cadell was hauling himself out of the water behind him.

There was a pause while another torch was lit and then the file of Britons were moving up the ancient conduit towards the heart of the fortress.

It seemed a long and tiring journey. Every so often they were forced to pause, so steep, and sometimes so slippery, was the pathway. The conduit was evil-smelling and nearly choked them with its foul odours.

Eventually, Myrddin signalled a halt.

"I think the entrance is just above," he whispered to Cadell, telling him to pass the information back to Artio and the others.

Myrddin moved forward carefully. The conduit had reached its starting point. It was a cold, granite-slabbed room without light and full of refuse and waste of all kinds. Myrddin moved across to the entrance of the room. It gave on to a corridor, lit with flickering torches.

He turned back as Artio joined him.

"We'll extinguish our own torches now. This is a main corridor within the heart of the fortress. We will have to find our separate ways from here."

Artio compressed his lips.

It had sounded all right in the planning, but now it seemed an impossible task. How were they to find Cynric's chamber or, indeed, where Gwendoloena was imprisoned, from here? How were they to make their way through the complex corridors of the fortress, to find the right rooms, without raising the alarm?

However, Artio was not a man to change his mind without good cause.

"Very well. Remember, each man for himself. If either party be discovered, it is up to the other one to succeed in their task. Is that understood?"

Myrddin signified his agreement.

"Good. You, Cadell and Carannog go first. Which way will you go?"

Myrddin shrugged.

"One way is as good as another. We'll take the left branch of the corridor."

He extinguished the torch and signalled to Carannog and Cadell to follow him.

Cautiously, with swords drawn, they moved away from the conduit room. Myrddin made careful mental notes of which way they went in relation to the room for soon they might have to return there in a hurry and make good their escape.

The area of the fortress they were in was obviously used for storage, and soon cooking smells came to Myrddin's senses. Wherever Cynric's apartments were they would surely not be placed too near the kitchens. He gently tugged on his lower lip as he tried to consider what best to do.

There came the sound of a footfall.

It was Cadell who seized his sleeve and pulled him back into a darkened alcove off the passageway.

An elderly man, weighed down under the weight of a full side of beef, which he carried on his shoulders, came shuffling along the corridor. The man was clearly a slave for he wore an iron collar around his neck.

Myrddin pressed back into the shadows as the old man passed by and entered a doorway a few yards away.

Luckily the old one was too absorbed in his task to notice the three armed men shielding themselves in the dark recess. Or perhaps he did not care?

A thought suddenly occurred to Myrddin. He turned to the others and whispered: "I mean to question the slave when he comes back. Help me."

He turned back to the corridor.

The old man, divested of his side of beef, had left the room and was shuffling back along the corridor, eyes downcast and without apparent interest other than placing one foot in front of the other.

Myrddin decided to gamble on the attitude of the other. The man was a slave and his instinct was to obey. Myrddin stepped into the path of the old man and said in harsh Saxon: "Come with me!"

The old man hesitated, but he did not even raise his eyes to Myrddin. He obediently shuffled after him.

Cadell and Carannog fell in behind, not believing the simplicity of the situation.

Myrddin turned into an empty room which he had previously noticed further down the corridor. The old man followed with Cadell and Carannog on his heels. Carannog swung the door shut behind them.

"I want you to answer me some question, old one," snapped Myrddin, still speaking in Saxon.

The slave coughed nervously, but did not raise his eyes.

"At your command, my lord," he mumbled.

"Where does Cynric keep his prisoners? I mean the prisoners he has recently taken in raids?"

"He does not, my lord. They are either sold as slaves, like me, or else slain."

"Then do you know of a female prisoner recently brought to this place? She was recently taken and is a Briton."

The old one shrugged.

"I have heard nothing of such matters."

Myrddin swore softly.

"Then we must go and ask Cynric personally," he muttered, half to himself. "Tell me, old one, where are Cynric's apartments?"

"On the floor above this one, lord."

"You must take us there."

"I am a kitchen churl. I am not allowed out of the kitchens, lord."

"I am ordering you, slave!" snapped Myrddin.

"I can only obey the overseer of the kitchen slaves, lord. It is more than my life is worth to leave this level."

Myrddin gave an exasperated sigh.

"Very well, how do we reach the floor above?"

"There are stairs at the end of this corridor, lord."

"Listen, slave. You will remain here until someone releases you. If you cry out then I will return and kill you."

"Yes, lord." There was no emotion to the old man's voice, just a quiet resignation.

They found the stairs easily enough but the corridor above was not so deserted as the one below. Warriors strolled up and down it with weapons drawn. Cynric was a careful monarch.

Myrddin crouched with Cadell and Carannog in the shadow of the stairwell wondering what to do.

As if in answer to his thoughts a door along the passageway opened and an imperious but familiar voice called out.

"Guard! Bring the girl to me. I will see her now!"

Myrddin had no difficulty recognizing the voice of Cynric.

A guard jerked to attention and then went hurrying away, his leather-soled shoes slapping on the stone flags of the corridor as he sped to his task.

Myrddin exchanged glances with Cadell and Carannog.

There was still another guard standing outside the door from which the man had called. But if they were quick they could cross the corridor and get into the room facing them. Perhaps there was a way through to Cynric's chamber from there. Myrddin conveyed this idea to the others tersely. They nodded agreement.

Myrddin went first, swung open the door and prayed there was no one inside. There was not. It was an empty room. He turned and waved the others across and closed the door behind them.

Cadell had crossed to the window.

"A sheer drop to the valley below," he muttered. "We are deceptively high up here. But . . ." he suddenly leaned out of the window and peered along, "come and see. There is a small ledge which runs from this window along to the other rooms. It might be just big enough for a man to edge his way along."

Myrddin glanced out and saw that Cadell was right. Nevertheless, one false step and there would be no reprieve. It was certain death to fall from the wall of the fortress down into the valley below.

There was a noise in the corridor outside.

Myrddin crossed swiftly back and inched the door open only a fraction.

His heart skipped a beat.

The dishevelled figure of Gwendoloena was being dragged along by two grinning Saxon warriors. Her dress was torn, her hair in disarray and there was a smudge of blood on her cheek. Yet she held her chin defiantly and there was no hint of tears on her face. Myrddin's heart went out to her.

Then she was gone from his sight.

He turned back to the others.

"There is no choice but to go along the ledge. I am not asking you to do so. I will do it and, when you hear that I am in need of you, try to fight your way along the corridor to me."

Carannog grinned and shook his head.

"Where you go, Myrddin, we will follow. I have never felt such confidence in a leader before, unless it be young Artio. You have not only led us safely into Cynric's fortress but we stand yards from Cynric himself."

Myrddin laid a hand momentarily on his shoulder.

"Then let us not waste time."

He sheathed his weapon and climbed out on the ledge. It was twelve inches in width and to move along it one had to stand, back to the wall, and ease along. The wind whispered and whipped at his clothing and hair. It was Myrddin's gift that he had never known a fear of heights, even as a small boy when the Venerable Fychan used to take him up to the inaccessible mountain peaks of the west, the better they might commune with the ancient powers and the gods and goddesses which peopled the purple peaks of the Gwynedd.

He moved cautiously only because moss and other growths made the ledge a little slippery.

He paused when they came to a window and listened for a moment, wondering if anyone was in that room. There was a silence and so he moved on. A second window and a second room was passed. Thankfully, these were also empty.

Myrddin heard a sudden gasp to his right, a scrabbling noise and the falling of stones. He turned his head, fearing the worst.

Indeed, Cadell, following him, was hanging by one hand on the ledge. Carannog was not far away and even as Myrddin looked, the man had sprung into the room over the window ledge and was reaching out to drag Cadell by the one arm upwards and into it safely. Had Cadell slipped in any other position along the ledge there would have been no way that Carannog could have aided him.

Myrddin let out a sigh of relief as he saw Cadell's legs disappear over the ledge into the room.

He eased himself back to the spot and followed.

Cadell was standing trying to recover his breath, panting as he realized just how close to death he had been.

"Sorry," he muttered.

Myrddin did not respond.

"I think Cynric is in the next chamber," he said, "But it might be hard to surprise him coming in from the window."

He saw Carannog grin and he raised his eyebrow in silent interrogation. The warrior pointed.

"Then why not use a door?" whispered the warrior.

Myrddin turned towards the wall that he had indicated.

Indeed, there was a wooden door separating this chamber from the next one. Myrddin realized that this was probably Cynric's sleeping chamber for there was a richly tapestried bed in one corner and a few other items of furniture as well as rugs which indicated what use the room was put to.

Myrddin went to the door and pressed his ear against it. The door was of thick oak and while he could hear voices rising and falling he could make no sense of the words.

He glanced down at the iron ring which secured the latch, gave a warning glance to the others and then carefully turned it. It turned silently and he gently drew it open a fraction.

So concentrating was he on opening the door without noise that he let the latch fall with a clatter.

It seemed an eternity in which there was a deathly silence in the room beyond.

Everyone must have heard the door being opened.

Then there was shouting. A door crashed open in the room beyond.

"My lord, my lord, we have cornered a band of armed slaves by the gates!"

"Slaves?"

"Yes, lord. Who else could they be but slaves in revolt? But we have them. They are not a large force."

Myrddin gave a startled glance to Cadell and Carannog.

Artio and his party must have been discovered and mistaken for rebellious slaves. He felt the urge to run to their aid. But it was each man to his own task. Artio had said so.

"Send the guards there and disarm them," cried a voice. "I do not want them killed. Bring them to me. How can my fortress be threatened by armed slaves? I shall want explanations. The commander of my guards will suffer for this indignity to my honour!"

Cynric's voice was almost hysterical with rage.

"Yes, lord! The girl, lord? Shall we take her back to her dungeon?"

"No! I am man enough for a girl. Go, go quickly and rouse all the guards! Let no one escape and let no one be killed. They say all die slowly! Go! Go!"

The door beyond slammed.

Myrddin was unable to believe the service which Artio had unwittingly paid him.

"Now, you stubborn bitch," Cynric was saying, "my patience is at an end. You have spent several days in my dungeons refusing food. The choice whether you now live or die is yours. I offer you the honour to be my concubine and you spit at me. Either you come willingly to my bed or I shall turn you over to the male slaves to occupy themselves with. Speak!"

Drawing his sword, Myrddin motioned to the others and they pushed into the room.

In a split second Myrddin's eye took in the entire scene.

This was undoubtedly the reception room of Cynric of the West Saxons. Cynric believed in pampering himself. Soft draperies covered the walls, and fine upholstered chairs and couches graced the rug-strewn room. A fire blazed in a hearth before which, sprawled on a rug on the floor, was the figure of Gwendoloena.

A man stood above her, feet astride, hands on hips. He held a short whip in his hand and had obviously been ill-treating her. It was Cynric.

Now he glanced up in surprise as Myrddin and his comrades entered; his mouth opened, but Myrddin simply presented the point of his sword towards his throat and the cry for help was stillborn.

"Cadell, secure the door. Carannog, stay by the other one."

Gwendoloena raised her head at the sound of his voice and a mixture of expressions chased each other across her features.

"Myrddin!"

Myrddin reached down with one arm and drew the girl to him. She did not resist the intimacy of his embrace but clung joyously to him.

"Thanks be, you have come!"

"So?" There was a sneer in the Saxon's voice. "We meet again, Myrddin. You are, indeed, a skilful enemy. How came you here?"

He did not seem alarmed, merely surprised. Cynric was confident in his own fortress.

"Easy enough." Myrddin's smile held no mirth. "Has he abused your honour, Gwendoloena?"

The girl blushed but shook her head.

"Thanks be, no. But he has harmed my dignity right enough. Him and that Centwine . . ."

"Have no fear of Centwine," interrupted Myrddin. "He is already dead."

Cynric's eyes widened, for the first time there was a tinge of fear in them.

"You have murdered Centwine?" he breathed as if unable to believe his ears.

"I objected to Centwine holding a knife at my throat. So I slew him. There was also the matter of his branding iron to take into account."

Cynric glanced around quickly as if expecting his guards to come to his aid.

"You will never get out of this fortress alive, Briton."

"As we entered it, so shall we exit," Myrddin assured him without humour.

"We should hurry, Myrddin," warned Carannog. "His guards may come back any moment."

"Indeed, and when they do we will use you as a roast upon the spit," threatened Cynric.

"We must do as Artio planned as well as rescue the girl," Cadell said. "Let me do this, Myrddin."

Myrddin bit his lip. He had little stomach for it. Yet he had promised Artio.

"No, it is my responsibility."

He motioned to Cadell to take the trembling girl from him.

Cynric was watching Myrddin's eyes and read what was in his mind.

With a wild cry like an animal, he leapt across the room and seized a lance from the wall, whirling it over his head so that Myrddin was forced to back away.

"Now, dog of a Briton, you will pay for this affront!" he cried.

Myrddin had stopped. He was staring at the silken flag which was fluttering from the lance. It bore the embroidered knot that was haunting his life.

"For God's sake!" yelled Carannog, leaping across the room and giving Myrddin a shove.

The lance split the air where Myrddin had been transfixed and grazed Carannog's shoulder, causing him to wince in pain and swing backwards.

The jolt brought Myrddin to his senses.

Cynric was rushing forward again, lance point at the ready. Myrddin dropped under the point, shouldering it upwards, and thrust out with the tip of his sword. It entered Cynric's body in an upward stroke just below his breastbone. With a quick twist, Myrddin brought it out, so that Cynric jerked back with a terrible cry and dropped the lance from his hands.

The young Saxon king fell to his knees, his two arms cradling his upper stomach where the entry wound had been made. Blood began to dribble from his mouth.

Wrenching the lance away, Myrddin dropped to his knees beside the Saxon.

"Tell me, you must tell me, where did you get that banner? What does that knot signify?"

Cynric's eyes were already glazing but even in his dying moments he forced a tight smile.

"Rot in hell . . . Briton!"

With the death rattle in his throat, he fell to the floor and lay still.

"Myrddin, we must hurry!"

Myrddin was aware of Carannog crying in anxiety to him.

He took up his sword, rose and hurried to the door into the passageway.

"Are you all right, Carannog?" he asked, noticing the spreading stain of blood on the other's shoulder.

"I have had worse pinpricks, Myrddin," Carannog grinned. "A flesh wound, nothing more."

"Very well. I plan to get back to the conduit and escape that way."

"What of Artio?" demanded Cadell.

"You know what was agreed," Carannog rebuked him. "Time to think of him when the lady is safe."

"Let's go then!"

They opened the door cautiously onto the passage. The guards were gone on the orders of Cynric. They hurried to the stairwell and moved down the stairs to the floor below. As before, the kitchen corridor seemed empty. Swiftly, Myrddin led the way along it. The girl kept up with them without complaint.

"Lady," Myrddin turned to her, as they entered the refuse room, "the way is not a nice path but it is a safe one. Will you trust us?"

Gwendoloena smiled confidently at Myrddin.

"I have trusted you ever since I first saw you at Llanelen," she replied fervently.

Myrddin found himself blushing. To disguise his embarrassment he bent to light the brand torch which he had discarded when they first arrived in the fortress.

"I'll go first. You will follow. Carannog and Cadell will come behind."

Gwendoloena nodded and made no complaint as he climbed into the foul-smelling tunnel and motioned for her to follow.

They had gone about halfway down the conduit when Cadell gave an urgent whisper.

"We are being followed, Myrddin."

Myrddin raised his hand to halt the company, listening. The sounds of several people coming after them down the inclining tunnel were clear. Without a word Myrddin waved them on again, increasing the pace slightly to keep ahead of their pursuers. There was only one thing to do. He would have to order Carannog and Cadell to push on to the rendezvous with the horses, taking Gwendoloena with them. One man could stop the pursuit for a while by placing himself at the tunnel entrance where there was only room for one to swing a blade.

As they reached the bottom of the tunnelway and plunged into the cold river water which filled the tunnel entrance, Myrddin, in terse tones, told them of his plan.

Gwendoloena would have protested but Cadell and Carannog realized it was the only chance for some of them to escape.

The sounds of pursuit were close now.

They simply seized Gwendoloena and drew her out into the river where the two men Artio had placed on guard came forward to aid them across the brisk river current towards the forest where the horses were tethered.

Myrddin drew his sword and extinguished the brand torch, positioning himself ready to withstand the assault of the Saxon warriors.

They came sliding and slipping along the tunnel.

"Here's the entrance, Artio," the leading figure called as Myrddin was about to raise his sword and plunge it into the dark shadow. "Where's the brand torch?"

The third figure appeared, carrying the torch.

Myrddin swallowed hard.

"Is that you, Artio?"

"Myrddin!" came the young warrior's surprised tones. "We thought you had been captured!"

The warriors of Artio came spilling from the tunnel, voices raised in excitement.

"Hush! We are not out of danger yet," snapped Artio as he came wading into the water and facing Myrddin. "What happened? Where are Cadell and Carannog?"

"With the lady Gwendoloena, hopefully on the other side of the river. We thought you and your men were trapped by the main gates of the fortress."

Artio grinned in the flickering light.

"So did the Saxons. We were looking for Cynric's chambers when we were spotted."

"How did you escape? I hear no sounds of pursuit."

"Easy to tell. We found some Saxon prisoners awaiting execution. We released them, gave them weapons, and many of them preferred to fight than go willingly to a ritual death. I think they are still fighting Cynric's guards now. Alas, we did not find Cynric's chambers and, with the guards alerted for us, we decided a withdrawal was the best policy until we can devise a new plan. What of you?"

"As I say, Gwendoloena is safe and you need have no worries for Cynric," Myrddin said grimly.

"Why so?"

"Cynric is dead. I slew him."

Artio stared at him, astounded.

"You are truly a great warrior, Myrddin," he breathed in reluctant admiration. But he was unable to keep the slight tinge of envy from his tone. He had set himself the task of slaying the Saxon king and now he found himself robbed of the deed.

Myrddin grimaced.

"I have said before that I am no warrior."

"Then I would like to be by your side if you ever decide to become a warrior," Artio chuckled, recovering his humour.

"We best move across the river and get away from this accursed land," muttered one of Artio's band, for they were standing shivering in the cold waters of the tiny cavern.

"Indeed," agreed Artio fervently. "Let us make our withdrawal."

XII

The sun was high in the sky when the column of horsemen entered the foothills of eastern Dumnonia, across the broad river which provided the current main border between the war-stricken kingdom and its neighbour. The young warrior Artio rode at their head while behind him came Myrddin and Gwendoloena. They had been almost inseparable during the two days of travel through the darkened forests of the land of the West Saxons. There was no need to tell the rest of the company who came on behind them what the two felt for each other. Romance was clearly in the air.

When they stopped to rest at midday, by a small stream, Artio came and seated himself beside them.

"Do you plan to take the lady Gwendoloena back to Llanelen Abbey?"

Myrddin stared at him a moment. In fact, for the first time since his departure from Cynric's fortress, he realized that he had been travelling without purpose, merely allowing himself to follow the tide, content to be only in the company of Gwendoloena. It was the girl who answered for him.

"Yes. The abbess is my guardian, my foster-mother, since the Saxons slew my family. It is my duty to return to her."

"And you, Myrddin? You will go to Llanelen?" pressed Artio.

"I shall," said Myrddin, so ardently that Artio could not suppress a grin while Gwendoloena had the grace to blush.

"But then? What are your plans? For I have witnessed your mettle. The Isle of the Mighty needs such men as you in these perilous times. Even though Cynric is dead, the Saxons will soon gather strength again and contest the supremacy of this island with us. They will try and drive us out of this land. We will need every man we have."

Myrddin nodded.

"When that time comes, I shall not be wanting, Artio. But after Llanelen, though much depends on the lady Gwendoloena here, there are other quests I must fulfil."

"Quests?" Artio asked, interested.

Myrddin smiled softly.

"Alas, they are of a nature that I cannot speak more of them. But they are of importance to me."

Artio sighed in disappointment.

"Then, my friends, it seems our paths diverge once we reach the edge of that forest yonder," he pointed with outstretched hand. "I must go back to Dinas Emrys with the news of the success of our raid and I can assure you that the name of Myrddin will soon be on the tongues of the bards of Dinas Emrys."

Myrddin shook his head. He was aware of his faults and knew how guilty he was of the very fault which the Venerable Fychan had warned him against.

"There is little enough to sing about Myrddin. He was a youth who thought he knew all things and found he knew little; he was tempted in self-delusion, in vanity and in desire. He has since learnt many things; above all he has learnt of the depth of the emotion of love. But of the things he thought he had set out to learn, he learnt nothing. Myrddin is no one to sing about."

Gwendoloena reached forward and touched his hand.

"Admitting that you have learnt nothing is the start of learning."

Myrddin grimaced.

"You are wise in your youth, Gwendoloena," he said.

Artio chuckled softly.

"One thing you have learnt is humility. But beware of false humility, Myrddin, my friend. Learn to know your assets as well as your faults. But still the bards of Dinas Emrys shall sing of your deeds. The death of Cynric has bought us time. Let us hope that the squabbling of the petty chieftains will be overcome and they can agree on a new High King who will unite them and strengthen them against the war that is to come out of the east. For too long the black raven of death and battles has swooped on our defenceless people out of the eastern skies. Would the raven will fly from the west now."

Myrddin stirred as he remembered what the old master, Fychan, had said.

"All I can say, Artio, is that I once heard a prophecy that the raven will soon fly from the west," Myrddin assured him. "The time will be soon."

Artio snorted in disgust.

"We need no more prophecies, my friend. We need a sign and a strong leader."

"He will surely come," Gwendoloena said. "If he does not then the people of the Isle of the Mighty will go down into the abyss and be no more."

It was two hours later, beyond the edge of the forest, that Myrddin and Artio embraced as if they had been brothers. He embraced Carannog and Cadell also, his companions in adventure, and received warm hand clasps from the rest of Artio's men. Then he and Gwendoloena sat on their horses watching the column of riders turn north-west through the foothills which led to the mountains of the west. Only when they had vanished did he and Gwendoloena turn south-west through the rolling hills of western Dumnonia towards the abbey of Llanelen.

It was another full day before they came to Llanelen again. The abbey still stood fairly intact, with its grey granite scorched and blackened, but it seemed that the sisters of the community had managed to douse the flames before they could destroy the towering buildings.

Someone must have seen their approach along the road for suddenly a group of sisters came crowding to the gates. A hubbub of sounds arose from them. Myrddin recognized Sister Rhinwedd, the gatekeeper, trying to chide her fellow religieuses for their unseemly display of excitement. But she, too, was pleased to see them.

Myrddin halted his horse and dismounted, turning to help a smiling Gwendoloena down.

As they turned, the Abbess Aldan came striding forward. She said nothing, her face wreathed with smiles, as she held out her arms to the girl who went running forward to embrace her.

Abbess Aldan gazed across the girl's shoulder at Myrddin.

"You have done well, my son. If one man could succeed in this task, I knew it would be you."

Myrddin gestured deprecatingly. "I could not accomplish Gwendoloena's rescue on my own. I had help."

The abbess glanced at him in interrogation.

"A young warrior named Artio and his men helped me enter Cynric's fortress."

"Artio? Artio son of Uther, nephew to Emrys?"

"I knew only that he was Artio and one time companion to Emrys."

Abbess Aldan turned back to Gwendoloena and held her at arm's length.

"And you, my child, are you hurt? Has any harm or dishonour been done to you?"

Gwendoloena smiled happily.

"None that lasts in my memory, Mother Abbess."

Abbess Aldan was wise and she saw the happy glances that were exchanged between Gwendoloena and Myrddin. It would have taken someone less sensitive to ignore what they meant.

"Come. I am forgetting my etiquette and keeping you standing before our gates. Come to my chambers so that you may tell me all while we drink mulled wine together."

As she led the way she asked over her shoulder:

"And where is the young bear now?"

"Young bear?" Myrddin was puzzled.

"Why, young Artio, of course."

"Artio? Why, he has gone to Dinas Emrys. But why do you call him 'young bear'?"

Abbess Aldan laughed softly.

"I thought you were possessed of all knowledge, Myrddin," she chided. "What does the name Artio signify . . .?"

Myrddin's eyes widened.

He had thought of the name as no more than a name. But its meaning, in the ancient tongue of their forefathers, was "bear". Artio was an ancient deity among the old gods; the hunter, protector of the forests and guardian of the bear people which dwelt within their darker recesses. Artio the Bear.

He halted in mid-stride. He felt suddenly foolish, stupid and blind and not worthy at all to call himself a brother of the oak wisdom. He was but a child playing without understanding. Time and time again in this questing he had made such mistakes as only a fool would make. He was a conceited fool.

To his mind came the voice of the Venerable Fychan.

"I have seen a vision that there will come a bear from the west and drive all before him and his name will be spoken of down the centuries."

And then the strange and ancient guardian of the Cave of the Sword.

"You will set the path for the hero to come. That is your destiny, son of the divine water. You have gazed upon the magical sword, Caladfwlch, you know its purpose. The hero is coming soon. He is the bear that will come out of the west to save his people at the time of greatest peril. He must pluck the sword from the stone and become invincible."

Myrddin groaned and hit his balled fist in the palm of his hand.

He was aware of Gwendoloena's troubled gaze and her soft hand gently on his cheek.

"What troubles you, my love?" she asked, anxiety tingeing her voice.

Myrddin grimaced in annoyance.

"I am a stupid knave, that is all. I have been vain and my vanity has made me blind. I still have a quest to fulfil."

The Abbess Aldan smiled thinly.

"Your quest can wait an hour or so, Myrddin. I think there are other things that you would wish to learn before you set forth again. Come."

She turned into her chamber and gave instructions to a sister to prepare wine for them while she sought the details of their adventure.

At the point where Myrddin recounted the finding of the banner with its embroidered knot, the abbess interrupted him with excitement in her eyes.

"And this banner was in the house of Centwine?"

"Rather Centwine's sister, Lowri," admitted Myrddin, wishing, in the presence of Gwendoloena, to gloss over that encounter. Yet he desired to know the meaning of that banner.

"I see," the abbess breathed. "Cynric was not possessed of it?"

"Yes," Myrddin admitted. "He had a lance with a smaller version of the banner attached to it. What does this symbol mean? They said it was Cynric's battle banner, a banner to remind the Britons that the Saxons were conquerors. I do not understand."

Abbess Aldan rose and paced before their puzzled gazes, pressing her hands together for a while. Then she halted.

"You deserve the truth," she said, at last. Then she looked from Myrddin to Gwendoloena and back again. "You both deserve the truth for you both wish to marry each other, is that not so?"

Gwendoloena coloured a little and nodded.

"Is it so apparent, Mother Abbess?"

"You shout it from the hilltops, my child," smiled the religieuse.

"It is true enough."

Abbess Aldan turned her gaze to Myrddin.

"And you, my son? Do you love Gwendoloena?"

Myrddin nodded emphatically.

"Then you deserve the truth. The banner and its symbol was the emblem of a noble family of Britons who dwelt in the south-east of Dumnonia a generation ago. One day Cerdic, the father of Cynric, and his Saxons came raiding. The story is, alas, one that is all too common in these sad times. The Saxons massacred the family apart from a young daughter of the house. She was a comely maiden who had never known a man. Cerdic took her for his plaything. I need not go into details.

"One day, the girl became heavy with Cerdic's child. This girl escaped from the Saxon camp and crawled off into the cold snowstorms. She wanted more than anything to die. To kill herself and that child of Cerdic's within her womb. But God did not let her die. She gave birth, the snow reddened with her blood. Her first thought was to throw that crying child into the icy stream by which she had given it birth. Yet something stayed her hand. Even as she gazed upon it, she realized the innocence in that child. We enter this earth innocent and it is only what we are taught that guides our destinies."

The abbess paused.

Gwendoloena reached out and grasped Myrddin's hand firmly.

"What happened to that innocent babe and his mother?" the girl demanded.

"The mother wandered many weeks with that baby to the west until she came to the house of the steward to a wise teacher, one who still followed the old ways. She left the child wrapped in a piece of blanket on which that noble symbol of her ancestors was inscribed. It broke her heart to abandon him. But she knew that it was her destiny and his destiny that it be so. She left him and went forth into the world and joined a community of religieuses, where she prospered."

The Abbess Aldan raised her head and gazed into the eyes of Myrddin.

"She often asked herself if the child prospered. And she came to know he did . . . His destiny is a great one and now she has no regrets that she had to do what she had to do."

Myrddin's face showed a conflict of emotions as he realized the truth of his background. He used every effort of his training to control the tempest of emotion within him, knowing that the abbess's manner precluded any familiarity. Her emotions were held in check by a lifetime of self-denial. Myrddin deflected his thoughts by asking:

"And the West Saxons use this emblem on their battle banner to stress their victory over the Britons? The emblem of their defeated enemy?"

"That is so."

"And the baby you speak of grew to manhood believing himself to be a Briton yet all the while base Saxon blood flowed in his veins?"

"Hardly base. He was of the seed of Cerdic and of Saxon kings. There is some nobility in that. But even more, he is more his mother's child. Do not our cousins, the Picts of the north, appoint our kings from the line of the mother? Their reasoning is that one may not necessarily know who a person's father is, but one is always sure to know the mother. And the child's mother's line was Briton and noble. He was raised by the best intellects of the Britons and in him rests the hope of the Britons."

"But he is half Saxon," Myrddin pointed out stubbornly.

"By blood only. And blood is of little consequence. It spills and is diminished. The intellect is beyond blood for by intellect a man or woman may become anything they choose and transcend all man-made boundaries and prejudice. You are what you believe you are and what you are capable of doing."

Myrddin sat awhile in thought. Then, finally, he gave a long exhalation of his breath. He had matured a lot during these last few days. When he had left the house of the Venerable Fychan, he had thought he knew all there was to know in preparation for his life. What he had come to realize was his ignorance. He had learnt much recently but the more his self-knowledge increased the more his ignorance had unfolded. He was contrite as he realized what the Venerable Fychan had tried to warn him of. Well, one thing he had realized: the desire of knowledge, like the thirst for riches, ever increased with the acquisition of it.

"It would make me happy, Mother Abbess, and it would ease my anxiety if you could continue to give sanctuary to Gwendoloena while I am away."

Gwendoloena turned in surprise.

"Where are you going, Myrddin? I will come with you."

Myrddin turned to her and sadly shook his head.

"Gwendoloena, I have come to love and need you as I do the air that I breathe. But I cannot marry yet for I have realized that I am not prepared. Hear me," he continued quickly, as he saw the reaction in her face, "I do not mean to hurt you. I will return for you, that is certain. But first I must return beyond the western mountains to fulfil my quest for self-knowledge. For only when

I have that self-knowledge will I be able to come to the maturity necessary for my purpose in life."

The girl was trying hard to understand.

"What purpose do you speak of, Myrddin?"

"There is a task I must perform. As I have said, I must find Artio again and set him on the path for his great destiny. I cannot do that unless I am capable of doing it."

The girl was puzzled.

"Artio? What destiny, Myrddin? What is Artio's destiny?"

"His is the right to hold the sword called Caladfwlch, the sacred sword of gods and champions, and be acclaimed our High King. Only he can lead our people to shelter from the gathering Saxon storm. I have finally realized the goal of my own quest. And must prepare for that quest."

The Abbess Aldan smiled softly.

"We shall take care of Gwendoloena. I know you shall return, my son, even as she knows it. And it shall be even as you say. Whenever the name of Artio is mentioned by future generations, then shall the name of Myrddin, his counsellor, also be spoken."

Myrddin reached forward and took the hands of the abbess in both of his.

"Then I am contented with my destiny, *mother* ..." he whispered in final acknowledgement. "I will spend a moment or two with Gwendoloena before I depart."

Then, as he was about to turn away, his mouth suddenly slackened and he stared at her in horror as a new realization came to him.

"Tell me, if Cerdic was my true father then ... then Cynric ... ?"

She met his troubled eyes and nodded slowly in sympathy.

"Yes, my son. Cynric was your half-brother."

INFANTASM

ROBERT HOLDSTOCK

Robert Holdstock (b. 1948) first achieved recognition for his science fiction, especially the novels Eye Among the Blind *(1976) and* Earthwind *(1977). At that time he was also producing a variety of fantasy novels under different pseudonyms, including the Berserker series as Chris Carlsen, some of the Raven the Swordsmistress series as Richard Kirk, and most interestingly the Night Hunter series of occult novels as Robert Faulcon. Then, in 1984, he achieved major recognition for* Mythago Wood, *a fascinating study of the Matter of Britain permeating through to today. The book shared the World Fantasy Award for best novel in 1985. He has since explored this concept further in* Lavondyss *(1988), "The Bone Forest" (1991),* The Hollowing *(1993),* Merlin's Wood *(1994),* Gate of Ivory, Gate of Horn *(1997) and* Avilion *(2009). He has also completed the* Merlin Codex *series of novels,* Celtika *(2001),* The Iron Grail *(2002) and* The Broken Kings *(2007). Holdstock doesn't feel he's finished with the character of Merlin yet; in fact, Merlin's rather started to warm to him.*

It takes time and a great deal of concentration to fabricate even a single *infantasm*. It is always necessary to draw on time in the long-gone, and often essential to reach as far into the long-to-come as is possible, depending on the imaginary talents one wishes to give the child. It is not a process, then, that I initiate lightly, and when the Chief Dragon rounded me up from my forest dance and stated bluntly that he wished to talk to me about *infantasm*, I was more alarmed at the prospect of the magic he might require than irritated by the way his ruffians prodded me at spear-point back to the great fort.

When the winding forest track left the tangle of wood behind and joined the old Roman road, I abandoned all thought of escape and trudged the smoothed stone between the snorting horses of my captors, huddled in my wool cape, aware that Uverian, as he pompously called himself (in reflection of the forgotten Legions, whose weapons he and his mercenaries still used) was watching me smugly as he rode behind me.

Now that we were on the open path, I concerned myself quickly with how in the name of Mabon – locally, a powerful and perceptive deity to the ignorant fools who served, for bellyfuls of bread, meat and mead, the needs of the Chief Dragon – how in That One's name Uverian had found me. I was certain that I had closed the forest around my shrine. I was certain that my dancing had been silent in this time, although the forest music, the thunder of the drums, might have echoed a thousand years behind me (or perhaps ahead of me?). But silent *now*, my grove quite scentless. Senseless! And yet the Dragon Bastard had spotted me, as an eagle spots the sudden tension of a leveret in its form and swoops to take the helpless hare.

After abandoning my self-rebuke, I explained at great length to the amused and determined man on his sleek, roan mare that *infantasm* was not a magic that could be simply summoned. I shall not concern you here with my argument, which mainly explained in as much tedious detail as I could summon from truth and lie the process of drawing the bones from the wood, the flesh from the wormy soil where a body lies undergoing decay, the skin from leaves, the bloom from flowers, the blood from water where a wounded man has bathed, the bowels and other internals from animals killed with stone – hares for their essence and spirit, of course, polecats for durability, boars for aggression, birds for many other things.

"Whatever you need you shall have," Uverian said sharply. "Now stop talking. My head is ringing with your whining."

Good! *My* head was ringing with apprehension.

For what purpose, foul or cunning, could he wish the making of a child from another time?

Instants after I had passed through the three gates of his fortress, my legs aching from the steepness of the winding road that led between the defensive walls, I was besieged by the *infirm*. Some of these had unhealed wounds, or breaks in bone, or the aches and pains of age, all curable if I so chose; but most were infirm of *spirit*. These ever-hopefuls, longing for marriage, for visions of the great God Llug (or lesser Mabon, Brigga and all the rest), or for successful quests for lost talismans (as if they'd be effective when found!), or for strength to their sword-arms against the raiders, reivers and neighbours who took arms against them, these were a blight to my life, a bane to my magic.

They had all been told I would be *fetched* from the forest – a realization that further insulted my talent at disguise – and had gathered to line the road to the Dragon Bastard's house, where the three shields of the clan hung in silent, mocking tribute to me (I had helped the man in the three deeds that had earned him the shields, but the shields reflected only the deeds of the man!)

Uverian's knights (I hardly dignify them with the name, but at least they were on horseback, and knew how to ride) pushed the crowds back to the inside walls of the fort and their ragged houses, where forges, bakeries and tanneries burned, crisped and stank the outer town. In the centre, among the tree shrines and stone sanctuaries, and next to the oak-branch cage that covered the well, Uverian's house was a long, smokeless hall, divided several times by heavy woollen curtains, dyed in the colours of forgotten Rome.

He had clawed up with his own hands the mosaic tiles of a Roman house, four days' ride east of this fortification, and reassembled the horned face of that Roman deity on the hard floor in front of his chair. The chair was made from the marrowbones of elk, an odd allusion to a long-forgotten Warlord dynasty – all priests, warriors, skystones in circles and green-edge bronze – that I suspect I might have mentioned inadvertently to him:* in any case, he had created and adopted the foul chair, with its marrowbone frame, its carved oak panels and duck-feather cushion, and rested there now, legs spread, britches loosened to ease his saddle bruising, belly hard and scarred and hideously gaping from his untied leather shirt.

* Merlin is known to have been active during the so-called Wessex period of the Bronze Age, *ca.* 2500 BC, when the major formations at Stonehenge, Woodhenge and Badon's Ring were constructed. Many talismanic objects survive from this period, including the carved and patterned long (or marrow) bones of elk.

"I didn't expect you to be so popular," he said quietly, scratching his ragged beard, not a happy man, but watching me with interest rather than with the beetling scowl that usually meant he would soon get drunk and violent.

His reference to my popularity was meant to be pointed, but in fact I had been surprised myself.

The last time I had occupied this wind-swept, hilltop hell-hole I had failed to predict the attack by Gorlodubnus, the Bastard Blackwolf of the Dumnonii,★ who occupied land in the southern part of Albion, and whose precocious child-bride, Grainne, so haunted Uverian's lustful dreams.

Although the slaughter had been restricted to the death of two champions from each side, my failure had led me to expect to be arrow-shot rather than welcomed should I ever have returned.

(What fools! To think that prediction is guaranteed. Otherwise, why would the world ever progress in any way other than round about and round about, all things singing, all things known? What fools!)

However, now that I was welcomed outside, at least, there would be wealth to be made in my short stay, since there's nothing quite like a charm, an insight and a breath of promise to bring out the hidden silver from these mountain idiots, and the vibrant, willing flesh of those idiots' strong-limbed daughters.

I had gone short of many pleasures in the last few years; it was time to catch up.

And then, as I sat smugly (but expressionless) on the rough matting, facing the shattered mosaic of Bacchus and the slumped, indulgent form of the Chief Dragon, I remembered what I was here for. My heart shifted position and the movement was heavy.

Infantasms.

So hard to create!

"Didn't you once tell me," Uverian said quietly, "that in your youth you fashioned a girl, pretty as a lark's song, blushing pink as an apple, from the gathered petals of flowers?"

I nodded casually; was the fool confusing the flower girl with an *infantasm?* I hadn't created her myself, in fact, but had

---

★ The reference is clearly to Cornwall, in the south-west of the island, but "Gorlodubnos" (Gorlois of familiar legend) is a strange appellation for this part of post-Roman Britain. "Blackwolf" was the tribal sign.

gathered the flowers for an older man, a charmer of little, though creative, talent, who had made the creature. This was so long ago that the sound of metal striking metal hadn't yet begun to disturb the sleep of those who lived upon the land. Stone weapons are much duller, and very effective. I had often used flowers to create mannikins – for amusement – and gave them names and stories for each part of the world I was visiting, but such creatures have nothing but blushes and instincts, no mind to speak of. Rather like the child-thing Grainne, really.

"Could you make me a lithe, lucky and lovable boy in the same way? Out of flowers, or twigs, or anything? You name it, you shall have it to work with."

"It would have no wits."

"Why would it have no wits?"

"Because it would have no life. It would be vital, not vibrant. It would sing, but like the wind rather than the lark. There would be no purpose to it. Why do you want such a thing?"

My objection was based not so much on the possible relief of his having confused two magical traditions and would in fact ask me to perform a trick so easy that I could teach you here and now, should I wish, but rather that he would strip my skin when he realized his mistake (something I've seen him do to warlords stronger by far than him, and to enchanters every bit the equal of me. Men such as Uverian can turn charm against the user, making enchanters helpless, even though they have no talent for charm themselves).

"I don't understand why it would have no wits. You have told me before that these children of time can live for years, and even mate and give rise to bastards."

I sighed and in irritation reached out and lifted two tiles from the mosaic, tossing them at the sprawling fool, who slapped the stone away and began to roar and rise from his chair.

I remained quite still, staring up, and when gaze met gaze he calmed a lot, sank back, sat down and scowled at his damaged treasure.

"You're just a boy," he said grimly. "I ought to skin you from neck to groin."

"I'm older than you by ten thousand times your father's life-time," I said to him, as I had often said to him before. He had once tried to work out the actual number of seasons this monstrous age involved, but had given up. Ten thousand was a favourite number of Uverian's, though essentially meaningless. He could cope with a hundred – he owned that many horses – and four times a hundred was easy too, since he could visualize four squadrons of a hundred men on four hilltops waiting to descend in attack upon the enemy in the valley. But after that, his numeracy was shrouded in a fug of enormity. Ten thousand was to him all of time itself, all of the stars, and all of the number of blades of grass.

That I looked like a wisp-bearded youth annoyed him, since he knew this was simply my guise. I do believe he would have preferred – and been more respectful to – an old man, bent-backed and grey-haired, hazel-staffed and charm-tattooed. But an enchanter lives in the body he chooses, and is restricted like all men by the ability and energy of the flesh that is chosen, and therefore the relative importance of the acts of feasting, running and making love will *dictate* the choice of body.

I would always sacrifice the illusion of sagacity for the reality of virility!

"*What* exactly do you wish this child to *achieve*?" I asked with transparent frustration, and clear, controlled impatience.

"I need it to sneak through Gorlodubnus's reeking legs and enter the stone maze at Tintagel fort."

I had thought as much, though I had repressed the notion in the slim hope that I was wrong. Uverian, of course, would be the mind inside the child! The small hands that stroked the girl would be Uverian's own sword-calloused leatherfingers.

"You want the child to come close to Queen Grainne, wife of Gorlodubnus."

"Closer than close," he said, leaning forward with a wild, lascivious look. "As close as two heaving bodies, groin-locked, writhing, fused together by the sweat of—"

"Yes, yes! I think I understand what you have in mind. So you wish the child to be quite . . . grown, then. Very *capable* in certain areas."

Clearly, the problem of the prowess of this *infantasm* hadn't occurred to the Chief Dragon in his wild dreams of conquest of the child bride. He frowned and shook his head. "A boy several years younger than her. It must be that. How else will he gain entry?"

"But don't you think that a boy several years younger than her, even a boy of her own age, would be very *disappointing* compared to . . . say . . . just for the sake of argument, you understand . . . Gorlodubnus, her husband?"

"She can't stand the sight of him!"

"*What?*"

Not what I had heard . . . !

"She can't stand the sight of him," he repeated with self-certainty, and I smiled reassuringly.

There could be no question about the beauty of Gorlodubnus's young queen. I had heard from a reliable source that she was born with an arm's length of golden hair around a face already serene and aware, and the shadow of a torque around her throat. Her breasts even then were perfectly formed, and within an hour of her birth she had uttered the name of the man she wished to marry: Gorlodubnus.

The reliable source, of course, was the local enchanter, adept at illusion, a woman of great strength, sly look, and an adept at finding uses for the useless, such as the leaves of oak, which seem to me to have no power at all. I forget the woman's name (she inhabited a sea cave, or so she said). And of course, the nature of the child at birth and the so-called first word, were an illusion, part of her own ruse to gain more authority in the fortress of the King.

Gorlodubnus, as witless in certain ways as my own dear Uverian, had fallen for it, spear, shield and leather britches.

Nevertheless, Grainne's beauty, as I say, was not in dispute, nor her own prowess on the straw-filled palliasse, and I could well understand Uverian's lustful longing; my failure as any sort of adviser was in not explaining to him that it was all in the anticipation; that the reality would be a swiftly swivelling focus of his wretched *single eye* towards some other young and unattainable beauty, immediately after the conquest.

The great test of a true enchanter is to know when to predict well, when to predict nothing (looking suitably humble at the failure of vision rather than amused at the vision one has experienced), when to advise because one can support that advice. When to keep quiet!

I kept quiet.

Gorlodubnus had built a vast stone maze in the centre of his cliff-top stronghold. At the heart of the maze was a garden, a house, and a temple, all of them exquisitely appointed, all of them to service the needs and pleasures of Grainne, his Queen.* Only children were allowed into the maze, and only a few of them found their way to the garden, and to the company of the Queen herself.

Any adult man found inside the stone walls was strapped to his horse and sent galloping across the forested hills, his head tied to the horse's rump. Any woman found inside, without Grainne's express approval, discovered the perils of flight from the top of the sea cliff.

It was this very natural protectiveness that Uverian was determined to subvert, by penetrating the maze in the body of a child and seducing the fair Grainne in disguise.

All of what I have told you had occurred in the privacy of Uverian's private room in the long hall, his knights having been sent away out of the sight of eyes, if not the sound of ears. Hungry now, Uverian called for simple food, and four of his men came in, crouching around the Bacchus table, watching me suspiciously, talking quietly about horses, raids, the collapse of the stronghold's walls where rain had weakened the earth, the reported sight of the great god Llug at dawn, sailing down the nearby river, golden-helmeted and distant-visioned.

If the latter experience had in fact been true, then it would suggest a second *charmer* in the region. I had detected no such presence, but then I had been dancing, and by dancing had closed the world around me.

Nevertheless . . . a vision of Llug, Uverian's discovery of me through the veil of forest darkness . . . if another charmer *was* around, and was helping the Bastard Dragon, then several things could be explained: but not necessarily his reasons for needing *me* and not the other!

Who was spying on me?

* There are numerous locations claimed for "Igraine's Maze" – from Tintagel in Cornwall to Vercovicium on Hadrian's Wall. The labyrinthine structure is likely to have been of drystone walls erected along a turf-maze pattern, without foundations, and would have been easily dismantled by local farmers in the Middle Ages.

The food, when it came, was in a wide copper bowl filled to overflowing with the roasted cuts of fowl, swan and pig. The aroma was as haunting as any I had experienced and I, like the knights, scrabbled for the richest meat, chewing down to the succulence close to the hot bones, sucking the marrow then teasing the dogs – also allowed to enter the room – by waving the scraps at them.

These dogs were typical of Uverian's possessions, doing nothing until they were told, bolting scraps thrown to them, but never daring to approach the Bacchus table and the diminishing dish of bloody flesh.

All the while the Chief Dragon watched me, even when he wiped the fat from his beard, even when he cracked the bone. Eventually he sat back and called for drink. His two daughters brought elegant clay flagons for the knights and their father, a tall copper flask of honeyed ale, and an exquisite glass cup for me.

"Pick it up," Uverian commanded and I did so without hesitation. Two layers of fine, crystalline glass enclosed scenes, inscribed on the inside of the glass itself, of strange animals, dancing women, and the enjoyment of Avilion, or however the world of Bright Shadows – the *otherworld* – was envisioned by foreign Kings. It was a world contained within the very translucency of the cup and I drank the sweet ale from it with heightened pleasure.

"What do you think of the glass?"

"Radiant," I said. "Remarkable."

"Clever bastards, those Romans. Could you make such a cup?"

He was always trying it on! He wanted me to say yes, then he would test me, either by asking for such a cup to be made anew, or by suggesting that I was insulting something that had been given to him by the gods. I knew instinctively that this was a cup from some trader, and was originally part of the spoils from a skirmish against an elegant settlement of the forgotten Roman people. I also knew that I could *echo* this cup in no more than a day, but that is all I could do. A piece of beauty, like this, was the work of a craftsman, and an enchanter is no craftsman of that ilk. We can copy, mimic, give short life in illusion; but in no way could I summon such beauty without foreknowing it.

"Could I make such a cup? I wouldn't want to. I'm glad enough of the one already made."

Uverian looked disgruntled by my simple answer.

"It came from Verulamium.★ It was dug out of the ashes of the fire by a dog, a great red-furred dog, which carried it from the east to these hills and left it at the gates of the fort. Who do you think was in that dog. Eh?"

I could think of several answers to this question: The great god Llug – marking Uverian as someone special. Uverian himself – flattery; Grainne, the answer I suspected he wanted. I said teasingly, "From before Rome, a hero, a man of great courage, red of hair, who touched the shores of this land more than twenty of your father's lifetimes ago—" (what a satisfying frown on the Bastard Dragon's face as he tried to work out the figure!) "—and marked the site of a great stronghold, possibly this one."

Uverian and his knights leaned towards me, gape-mouthed, grease-stained, wide-eyed, eager to hear account of their favourite subject, the forgotten hero, the hidden land.

"Do you have a name for this man?"

"Not yet. Give me time."

Time to think a bit, to work out a good story.

"The cup is yours, you young-old man." Said with sincerity and just a hint of sarcasm.

Astonished – the glass was of great value, a very rare possession – I could only say, "Thank you. I shall treasure it."

"Now come and sit beside me."

I moved around the knights and sat awkwardly beside the marrowbone chair. As I reached for more mead, it was Uverian himself who refilled the cup for me, and I drank the sweet brew, aware of the cool, smooth glass and the echoes of the past that imbued the inner world of dancers and strange beasts, caught between the crystal layers.

Eventually the knights lay down, ludicrously in the Roman style, stretched around the Bacchus table, and fell gently into the

★ St Albans, north of London, UK. The Roman town was sacked and burned by the huge army of the Celtic Queen Boudicca (Boadicea) in AD 60. After her defeat by the Romans, under Suetonius, Boudicca is reputed to have been interred alive with her two daughters on the hill above the burned town, where the Abbey now stands.

sleep of war, hands caressing the horn-carved heroes on their iron knives, their faces, behind the beards, like children; children dreaming of midwinter fire.

"Can you make me what I need? A handsome boy child, sturdy, vital, innocent enough to enter the maze, witty enough to find the key to the maze, to get to the heart of the stone wall and its precious secret, eloquent enough to strip the lady, to tumble on the straw with her, to kick leg with her, press belly to belly, to turn her over, backside up; to lick the salt from her. Can you do it? Can you *do* it?"

I looked up at Uverian and saw that his doubts now fed his lust, desperation brewing a heady mix of anxiousness and guilelessness. I spoke without hesitation.

"No."

"No?" he roared.

"No."

"I don't accept no."

"No is all I offer."

"You can offer more than that. Give me back the cup."

"The cup is mine. Take it back at your peril."

"Horse's breath! The cup is worth a champion's head."

"I know. And it's mine. You gave it to me. I can't do what you ask, not under the terms you impose upon the deed."

"So the *no* is not wholehearted . . . ?"

"It's a qualified no. Yes."

"Yes?"

"Yes."

"Qualified by what?"

"By the nature of your intentions. By what you want to achieve. I can make the child, but the child cannot make the Queen. Do you have no idea at all how fornication is practised?"

He rightly slapped my face, but I held the glass before me, licking its cool surface, reminding him with my impertinence of the red-haired hero who had carried the cup in antiquity. (An idea was beginning to form to embellish my account.) He frowned, curious, irritated, then pacified.

"I know *everything* about fornication."

"I'm sure you do."

He stared at me hard. He was wondering if he was missing something. I laughed and said lightly, "Truly! You do! You know everything you need to know."

And before he had time to think on those words, I added, "But an *infantasm* cannot do the bidding you request."

"Then give me another idea."

I outlined to him, then, what I believed quite truly was the perfect way for Uverian, Dragon Lord of the Ordovices, to enter the stronghold and the stone maze of Gorlodubnus, Seagull Shit and weed-brained lord of Castle Tintagel, husband of Grainne, owner of sea, cliff and rank moorland in the western extremities of a vile and valueless country so steeped in lore and mist and hazard, that not even the forgotten Romans had bothered to march its hunt-trails.

But if he wanted to go there, I could get him there.

"I will *form* you. The effect will last long enough for your long ride in, your long ride there! Your long ride out. I will make you look like the Seagull Bastard himself."

"Who?"

"Gorlodubnus."

"Gorlodubnus?"

"Exactly. Set up a raid on his eastern border. While he's away fighting, you enter the maze."

Uverian was staring at me, a man watching a moron, head shaking. I felt a prickle of discomfort. He clearly was about to explode, but I pressed on.

"You appear as Gorlobdubnus, but it seems you have been *wounded*. And so, you have returned from the skirmish. You perform the dance of healing on the naked, nubile Grainne." I winked at him. He stared at me blankly. "You shred straw mattresses; you crack roof poles. You tear wool blankets. You muddy your backs until you are both the colour of earth." (I knew the Bastard Dragon's taste for romping in the dirt.) "Then you leave, and no one will be the wiser. It's foolproof."

His hands gripped my throat, shook the fool; his teeth (well kept, I thought, as they ground and gnashed in my eyesight) bit back the words I should always have remembered.

"She! Doesn't! Like! Her! Bastard! *Husband*!"

With my various lives gathering in my vision as death began to throw them out, urging me to use charm to escape the murderous grasp, I tried to think of some way to convince the Irate Dragon that actually Grainne liked her husband *very much indeed*, so much, in fact, that when he was away she had certain of the younger knights dress in his clothes, talk in his voice, and come and pay attention to her, kicking legs, shredding straw mattresses etc.

How could one man, one warlord, one magnificent fighter, a strategist of immense cunning, the inheritor of Roman wisdom, the practitioner of a Rule of Law so carefully conceived, so considerate in its aims, that all who lived within a horn's call, or a fire's call of his fort, respected and felt safe under the raised hand, sword and shield of its perpetrator (even bowing to the leather britches as he rode by on horseback, hence his affectionate nickname) ... how could this great man be possessed of such *ignorance* in the way of love?

If all he wished was to mount the mare, if he desired no more than simple gratification, then he need do no more than imitate the enemy. Good Mabon! how many times had he imitated the enemy on the field of slaughter, *tricking* them into submission and thus bringing them to the moment of single combat, lopping head and leaving with bloody, bearded honour gaping from his spear point?

Imitate the enemy!

But he wouldn't hear of it.

"*Infantasm!*" he bellowed. "If nothing else, I'll at least get to see her. You can put sight in such a creation. Can't you? I'll be able to see, to touch, to rest in her arms ..."

"If she touches you. Yes."

"Llug's Balls! Do it, then. Tell me what you need for the magic. I *have* to see her."

Wearily, I took my glass treasure and went away to think.

It's so very hard working with great men.

I shall spare the full details of the fabrication.

Like cooking over an open fire, the use of magic depends very much on inspiration, chance, and experimenting with ingredients for an unusual end effect.

In other words, I can't now remember precisely what I did.

Uverian had built a stone and wood lodge for me, well away from the forges and tanneries, and away from the sound of children. It was comfortable enough, with curtains to soften the cold of the stone walls, a rush-mat floor, covered with rugs, and a table shaped from the local, blue-tinged stone that he knew spoke to my senses. Food came by the dishful, despite my insistence that I needed to fast. Two of his horsethugs had been deputized to be my running hounds and do my slightest bidding, and they fetched me the creatures, plants, clays and bones that I needed, never showing disgruntlement until they had left my presence, at which point they exploded with oath and obscenity, cursing Uverian's as yet undug grave for being made to fetch vegetables for a crazy youth!

For the *infantasm* itself I drew on the memory of a boy from the Labyrinth that had once sprawled below an island in the southern sea.* I had visited the place twice, first in the long-long-gone, when the earth itself was still being burrowed to shape the maze, then later when a king had constructed a megalithic tomb to contain the subterranean passageways. Here, he had imprisoned a man-bull, claimed by his enemies to be his son. The Labyrinth was cunningly hidden in the centre of the island. False echoes – imitations of the maze – were built in the north and south of the land, though only that in the north remains now.

To run the *infantasm* through the maze that protected Grainne, I had to give it the instinct to seek beyond the shadows, to make sight into smell and heat into touch. And thus the boy took shape, a dear thing as he grew, his skin tanned, his eyes dark, his hair a mass of tight black curls. He was cheeky, this one, always slipping out of the lodge to play with the other children; because he was a stranger to them, he often got into fights, but his bruises healed as fast as he grew, which was as fast as a spring flower. To give him the wit he needed I sacrificed wit of my own, and felt increasingly angry at my complacent acceptance of Uverian's command.

When the child of time could have passed easily for a grown boy, though not yet a man, I sent him to sleep, then summoned

* The reference is to Knossos on Crete. The true Labyrinth, of Minotaur fame, seems to be located below Phaistos, in central Crete, and is as yet unexcavated. The present-day Knossos (by Iraklion) is one of several "false labyrinths", built during the fifth millennium BC, but is likely to have been the site used by King Minos (*ca.* 1450 BC) to imprison the inventor Daedalus, well away from the imprisoned Minotaur at Phaistos. Elsewhere, Merlin refers to "four echoes" of the Labyrinth on Crete.

Uverian to give his blood, his skin, his kiss, his tears . . . other things . . . to the charming vehicle of his passion.

"She'll adore him," Uverian announced, staring down at the lad as he staunched the blood from his arm. "You look very thin," he added, staring at me in genuine concern.

"It's a hard business," I said. "I warned you. There is a lot of my own spirit in this boy as well as yours, as well as Time's."

And I want it back.

"How long will he live?"

"As many years as I give him," I murmured, and a shiver passed through me, not because of the lie involved – I had limited control over the lifespan of any illusion or fabrication – but because the boy was so beautiful, and would have to be killed so brutally. The more life I gave the *infantasm*, the less life would remain to me. I had no intention of letting Minoxus, as we had named him, see out a full cycle of seasons, but I could anticipate all too easily the sorrow of returning him to the earth.

It was time to go, and we crossed the water to a landing place in the territory of the Durotriges, who were insular and unwelcoming, but more inclined to help us on our way than challenge us. By sailing to this sandy bay we had saved fourteen days or more riding round the wide inlet of the sea into the land of Albion. Now we faced a ride of similar duration to the west, through forested valley and over stinking moorland, ancient territory that would welcome us with all the enthusiasm of a cygnet welcoming the eagle.

Before too long we were lost, and though all four of Uverian's retinue scoured the animal tracks and hunter's trails for a way through the tanglewood, we eventually gathered near grey rocks, in an unnatural clearing, completely adrift in the forest.

Minoxus rode suddenly through the greenwood, laughing at us, calling to us, and we followed him round the twisting trails, watching his small form bent to the side of his horse as he studied the ground, brushed at low branches, and eventually brought us to the open road, where the impressions of chariot wheels, and the broader wheels of carts, told us that this was a thoroughfare to the west and east.

How easily my maze-reader had read the labyrinth of the forest. Could I have done it myself? Perhaps. But with Minoxus carrying a part of my spirit, and part of Uverian's, a brief life in full, abundant vibrancy, it seemed easier to let the natural talents of the youth guide us to safety.

"I feel I know this forest," the boy said to me as we crouched, comfortable, around the fire that night. "I can see the patterns. I see how the tracks of hare, pig and deer mix and mingle. I see how there are ways in and ways out of every thicket. The tracks themselves are full of signs of who has been here, where they've come from. I feel at home here."

"You should do," I said to him quietly. He snuggled closer to me, stretching his toes before the fire to warm them as the night deepened and the dew began to form. "You were born to follow hidden paths, to enter forbidden realms."

"Are we all born for something or the other?" he asked. "I mean . . . is there always something in our birth that marks our life? Could I have been born to chase hares? Or to carry stones from the quarry?"

I remembered that one of his friends from the fort was already, at a tender age, being taught to cut, split and fashion stone, his father's occupation. The other, with whom Minoxus had been extremely close, was a hare-chaser, a witless child, let loose on the sacred beasts since he knew no better. For the short while they had been friends, the two of them had talked in nonsense language, and made pacts, signs and promises, using hands, gestures and the marking of earth.

Hare-chaser had been distraught when Minoxus had left the stronghold. I could still see his scrawny shape, standing on the hill over the valley, one hand raised, a living statue desperate at his loss, following our small group out of sight. I had thought Minoxus unaware of the boy, but there were tears in his eyes and he kept looking back, surreptitiously, from below his cowl.

"Of course. We are always born with an end in sight. But there are no rules that say we can't bend the years to our own design."

"I want to run mazes," he said. "I dream of them. Mazes in grass, in wood, in stone. I dreamt last night of a maze stretching from here to the Moon. White horses galloped round the paths and I was running with them, following them as they galloped. But the dream turned bad, because a bull came up behind me. That's when I woke up."

I stroked the boy's hair and sang him to sleep. As he hovered between this world and the other I quickly glanced at the noisy part of his mind, and saw a bull like none I have ever seen, save in the sanctuary on that distant island. Hideous, wide-horned, malevolent. It was waiting to be released at the moment of the boy's death, though whether in celebration or in vengeance I could not say.

I was angry with myself for forgetting how *much* of the long-gone is dragged to the *infantasm* during its creation; my earlier words to Uverian – concerning witlessness and lifelessness – were arrogant, and substantially wrong. It is impossible to mould a creature without pressing memory, and therefore true life, into the clay.

A day or so later we had come into the shadow of the cliff fortress, and Uverian disguised himself crudely as an old knight, battle-worn, foreign, and unthreatening, in search of a bed, some food and conversation before his joyous journey to Avilion, the beautiful Isle. I came in as the wild man I was, the boy a waif we had encountered nearby and brought to the fort for protection. Minoxus was led away by one of the guards, to the safe-keeping of the nursery, though he was a tall boy, on the edge of manhood, and would probably be looked after in one of the bigger houses, close to the War Chief's hold.

Uverian was billeted with a knight of his own supposed age, a man so lost in the reverie and uncertainty of reality caused by drink that he fell upon my companion gratefully, with stories, recollections, wistful reminiscences, and at no time seemed suspicious of the irritation, arrogance and regal bearing that Uverian was hard-pressed to conceal.

I, of course, slept with the chained hounds, though the accommodation was straw-lined, weatherproofed and more comfortable by far than my own forest dwelling. I was given food by one of the ironworkers, who sat with me in the heat of his dying fire, a long day's work completed. His wife laughed all the time as she talked, despite the constant squabbling of their three children. When the ironworker went to sit with the other men of his neighbourhood, around a brazier, talking and drinking from clay flagons, I was summarily dismissed by the wife and set loose to prowl the paths between the sheds and houses of the fort.

I soon found the stone maze and walked around its inward-leaning walls, head low, avoiding lingering as this might have aroused the suspicion of the four guards, each standing beside a flaming torch. There were temples, chariot-housings and stables close to the maze, and I lurked in the deeper of the shadows until, at last! Gorlodubnus swaggered from the nearby hall, shirt undone below his kingly cloak, preening his moustaches, staggering slightly from drink and food. He entered the labyrinth, to follow the spiral path to his fair Grainne.

He was there for a short while, then returned to the hall, and now I went in search of Minoxus, calling him from his slumber in the corner of the nursery. "Of you go. Into the maze."

And as soon as I had seen him walk to the guard and be waved into the winding passage, I sought Uverian, and this time put the Dragon into the slumber that would unite him with the boy. From the moment Uverian's eyes were closed, he was running the maze in the form of Minoxus; and at length, entering the sanctum of the Queen he loved.

As I waited, I could tell from the laughter of the sleeping man, the cooing, chortling, hand-waving gestures of delight, that all was going well. His host slept deeply in his own bed and murmured in his own world, and I cast a scant glance at him – and was shocked!

For the first time since I had come to the fort I realized that this was Gawain! He was aged, now, although his exploits were still recounted along the length and breadth of the crow's flight across the land. He was maudlin and mead-crazed, but still so strong in all his limbs, and so proud in his face! I had once fought alongside this man, and he was one of the few of the noble breed who had had genuine vision of the land as it had once been fit for heroes, and who had declaimed that the times to come should again be times of the nobility of iron.

He had made no great fuss about the gods, and no great fuss about his wounds. He was an honourable and delightful man, and he had saved my life at the time of that battle, and then slipped away into a mist that was redolent with the stench of swordbane.

How could such a knight have come to this? I felt sad and kissed him on his withered lips. I whispered a certain promise, to help him in a certain way, although that promise, my deed of thanks to Gawain, is for another story.

Soon, Uverian was belly down and demonstrating the familiar Dance of Spring. I could have attached a rope to his belt, slung it over a beam, attached it to a wooden paddle and used the motion of his body to churn milk to cheese.

I was soon weary of watching and listening to the simple game he played. At dawn he was still going strong – remarkable for a man his age, although it occurred to me that he might be dead, by now, with only the energy of the *infantasm* keeping the corpse in rhythm – and I went outside to greet the day, particularly avoiding the crowing cock (since I saw Uverian's grinning jowls in everything from its swollen cock's-comb, gaping beak and loose, red wattle!).

I couldn't avoid the Dragon Bastard, of course, and he was soon breathlessly embracing me, promising me bronze so pure – he knew how much I valued it – that not even the forgotten Roman could have fashioned it in less than a full turning of the moon. Whatever I wanted I would have. Someone, somewhere would make it. He'd see to it.

Oh, and by the way: "I like Minoxus! He's a young man after my own heart! He's going back tonight. Grainne can't wait! Nor can I . . . It felt so *real*."

I left the fort, hid in the woods, survived on the memory of the long gone, shedding water, shedding weight, thinning, hardening, becoming ready for the deed that would return Minoxus to the litter of the forest, and my broken wit to my breaking heart.

I was confused. The image of the cheeky boy, of his brown eyes, his grin, his trickery, kept him so much alive in me that I weakened on two occasions, joined him in sleep, journeyed in his dreams as he curled against the soft feather pillow of the Queen's bed.

Uverian was there, the beast, raging at the edges of the flesh, but pacified by action, subdued by intercourse, prowling in the shadows as Minoxus himself consumed the scents and sounds of the hidden palace, felt the down-like touch of the woman, responded to her tears, her fears, her kisses and her confidences. In Minoxus she had found an unexpected lover (little realizing the potency of the Dragon behind the youthful energy of the boy) and an unexpected friend. Raised on a diet of Gorlodubnus, only now was she aware of the extent of her imprisonment. I had misjudged her, maligned her; only through Minoxus's eyes and ears could the full extent of this wretched woman's condition be revealed, to contrast with the slaggard gossip of those knights who rode between the strongholds, and whose lies could win them favour and their meat and drink.

I had been such a fool!

It had certainly been my intention to kill the boy. Now, though, I was torn between killing him and nurturing him. If I could keep him close to me, I could keep my wits about me. Literally! It would be imperative to hold him close, and to make him understand the nature of his being. But for the first time in my life – and it had been a long life to say the least – I felt the presence of a companion who could enrich me as much as I could enrich him, a boy who could grow, learn and live a full life until a death in the normal course of things. I had denied myself children from the moment of my birth. (Certainly! The possibility was there as I opened my eyes for the first time! I had other things in mind . . .). Uverian, for all his transgressions, had at least served me well by encouraging me to bring to life the son of the Labyrinth.

I listened to the talk between the Queen and the boy I would take with me into the forest.

I should have paid more heed to the scratching, fuming shadow of the king.

"Get up, you young-old fool."

I stirred from the saturated earth, stared up at the shadowy form of the man above me.

"Who are you?"

"Open your eyes, you trickster."

It was Uverian; his voice was hoarse, as if he had been shouting, or maybe crying.

"What are you doing here?" I asked.

"Minoxus needs you. He's dying. Quickly: to the fort!"

Bemused, my youthful body betraying my older mind, I staggered from the glade, staff dragging behind me, pushing the lank hair from my eyes. I ran towards the winding road that led between the massive walls of earth and wood, but stopped at the sound of a horse and a man's laughter behind me.

Turning, I saw Uverian with the boy in his arms, mounted on a tall stallion, cloak wrapped tightly. The king was smiling.

I shouted: "Give him to me. You have no right to him."

"Take him from me if you can. The boy is mine, now. Grainne was fun, but with this young bear I can conquer nations. You created well, you young-old man."

"He'll die. You *must* let me have him."

"He'll outlive me. Great Llug, your power is quite amazing! There's something from all corners of the earth in this young bear! Minoxus no more. He's Artorius from now! I'll cherish him, and raise him, and one day he'll ride in honour, carrying the emblem of our clan. Thankyou for that."

"Give him back!" I cried. Minoxus looked calm, indifferent, watching me through those dark eyes, his mouth moist. There was something hungry about him. He was finding life, feeding on the life of the Dragon who twisted and turned on the snorting horse, then turned away and rode away, back to the forest and the gloom beyond.

"This will turn out badly," I whispered to the boy.

"Worse than you think," the answer came, "when Grainne gives birth."

Beyond the walls, behind me, a woman was screaming.

Not for the first time in my life I wondered what I had started!

THE PLEDGED WORD

MARION ZIMMER BRADLEY

Although there's hardly been a dearth of Arthurian novels in recent decades, Marion Zimmer Bradley's The Mists of Avalon *(1983), through its breadth and quality, captured the public imagination and catapulted the genre onto another plane, ushering in a new generation of writing. The book was the first to consider seriously the relationship between the spread of Christianity through Britain and its impact on the old religion, which was as much a conflict as the physical one between Saxon and Briton. Bradley (1930–99) had hitherto been better known for her science fiction, which she had been writing and selling since 1953, especially her long series of Darkover novels, which began with* The Sword of Aldones *in 1962 and which gradually shifted in treatment away from science fiction to fantasy. Today Bradley is best remembered for her historical, or perhaps more accurately her mythological fantasies, such as the blockbuster novels* The Firebrand *(1987), set at the time of the Trojan War, and* The Forest House *(1994), set during the Roman invasion of Britain.*

The following story is a reworking of part of The Mists of Avalon. *We move briefly away from Merlin to consider the childhood of Nimuë, whose life will later entwine with Merlin's.*

It had been a long time since Morgaine had been to Avalon; she was not entirely sure that she could find her way back through the mists. But now it was time for her to make the attempt.

Her first step was to go to Pellinore's castle, sent by Lancelet to bear his greetings to his wife and children. And then, when she was alone with Elaine, she came to her true purpose.

"Remember you made me a vow once – that if I helped you win Lancelet, you would give me what I asked of you. Nimuë is past five years old now, old enough for fostering. I ride tomorrow for Avalon. You must make her ready to accompany me."

"No!" It was a long cry, almost a shriek. "No, Morgaine, you cannot mean it!"

Morgaine had feared this. She spoke sharply. "Elaine, you pledged your word."

"She is a Christian child – how can I send her from her mother into – into a world of pagan sorceries . . . ?"

"I am, after all, her kinswoman," Morgaine said gently. "How long have you known me, Elaine? Have you ever known me do anything so dishonourable or so wicked that you would hesitate to entrust a child to me? I do not, after all, want her for the dragon, and the days are long, long past when even criminals were burnt on altars of sacrifice."

"What will befall her, then, in Avalon?" asked Elaine, so fearfully that Morgaine wondered if Elaine, after all, had harbored some such notions.

"She will be a priestess, trained in all the wisdom of Avalon," said Morgaine. "One day she will read the stars and know all the wisdom of the world and the heavens." She found herself smiling. "Her brother told me that she wished to learn to read and write and to play the harp – and in Avalon no one will forbid her this. Her life will be less harsh than if you had put her to school in some nunnery. We will surely ask less of her in the way of fasting and penance before she is grown."

"But – but what shall I say to Lancelet?" wavered Elaine.

"What you will," said Morgaine. "It would be best to tell him the truth, that you sent her to fosterage in Avalon, that she might fill the place left empty there. But I care not whether you perjure yourself to him – you may tell him that she was drowned in the lake or taken by the ghost of old Pellinore's dragon, for all I care."

"And what of the priest? When Father Griffin hears that I have sent my daughter to become a sorceress in the heathen lands—"

"I care even less what you tell him," Morgaine said. "If you choose to tell him that you put your soul in pawn for my sorceries to win yourself a husband, and pledged your first daughter in return – no? I thought not."

"You are hard, Morgaine," said Elaine, tears falling from her eyes. "Cannot I have a few days to prepare her to go from me, to pack such things as she will need—"

"She needs not much," said Morgaine. "A change of shift if you will, and warm things for riding, a thick cloak and stout shoes, no more than that. In Avalon they will give her the dress of a novice priestess. Believe me," she added kindly, "she will be treated with love and reverence as the granddaughter of the greatest of priestesses. And they will – what is it your priests say? – they will temper the wind to the shorn lamb. She will not be forced to austerities until she is of an age to endure them. I think she will be happy there."

"Happy? In that place of evil sorcery?"

Morgaine answered with conviction, "I vow to you – I was happy in Avalon, and every day since I left I have longed, early and late, to return thither. Have you ever heard me lie? Come – let me see the child."

"I bade her stay in her room and spin in solitude till sunset. She was rude to the priest and is being punished," said Elaine.

"But I remit the punishment," said Morgaine. "I am now her guardian and foster-mother, and there is no longer any reason for her to show courtesy to that priest. Take me to her."

They rode forth the next day at dawn. Nimuë had wept at parting with her mother, but even before they were gone an hour, she had begun to peer forth curiously at Morgaine from under the hood of her cloak. She was tall for her age, less like Lancelet's mother, Viviane, than like Morgause or Igraine; fair-haired, but with enough copper in the golden strands that Morgaine thought her hair would be red when she was older. And her eyes were almost the color of the small wood violets which grew by the brooks.

They had had only a little wine and water before setting out, so Morgaine asked, "Are you hungry, Nimuë? We can stop and break our fast as soon as we find a clearing, if you wish."

"Yes, Aunt."

"Very well." And soon she dismounted and lifted the little girl from her pony.

"I have to—" The child cast down her eyes and squirmed.

"If you have to pass water, go behind that tree with the serving-woman," said Morgaine, "and never be ashamed again to speak of what God has made."

"Father Griffin says it is not modest—"

"And never speak to me again of anything Father Griffin said to you," Morgaine said gently, but with a hint of iron behind the mild words. "That is past, Nimuë."

When the child came back she said, with a wide-eyed look of wonder, "I saw someone very small peering out at me from behind a tree. My brother said you were called Morgaine of the Fairies – was it a fairy, Aunt?"

Morgaine shook her head and said, "No, it was one of the Old People of the hills – they are as real as you or I. It is better not to speak of them, Nimuë, or take any notice. They are very shy, and afraid of men who live in villages and farms."

"Where do they live, then?"

"In the hills and forests," Morgaine said. "They cannot bear to see the earth, who is their mother, raped by the plow and forced to bear, and they do not live in villages."

"If they do not plow and reap, Aunt, what do they eat?"

"Only such things as the earth gives them of her free will," said Morgaine. "Root, berry and herb, fruit and seeds – meat they taste only at the great festivals. As I told you, it is better not to speak of them, but you may leave them some bread at the edge of the clearing, there is plenty for us all." She broke off a piece of a loaf and let Nimuë take it to the edge of the woods. Elaine had, indeed, given them enough food for ten days' ride, instead of the brief journey to Avalon.

She ate little herself, but she let the child have all she wanted, and spread honey herself on Nimuë's bread; time enough to train her, and after all, she was still growing very fast.

"You are eating no meat, Aunt," said Nimuë. "Is it a fast day?"

Morgaine suddenly remembered how she had questioned Viviane. "No, I do not often eat it."

"Don't you like it? I do."

"Well, eat it then, if you wish. The priestesses do not have meat very often, but it is not forbidden, certainly not to a child your age."

"Are they like the nuns? Do they fast all the time? Father Griffin says—" She stopped, remembering she had been told not to quote what he said, and Morgaine was pleased; the child learned quickly.

She said, "I meant you are not to take what he says as a guide for your own conduct. But you may tell me what he says, and one day you will learn to separate for yourself what is right in what he says, and what is folly or worse."

"He says that men and women must fast for their sins. Is that why?"

Morgaine shook her head. "The people of Avalon fast, sometimes, to teach their bodies to do what they are told without making demands it is inconvenient to satisfy – there are times when one must do without food, or water, or sleep, and the body must be the servant of the mind, not the master. The mind cannot be set on holy things, or wisdom, or stilled for the long meditation which opens the mind to other realms, when the body cries out 'Feed me!' or 'I thirst!' So we teach ourselves to still its clamoring. Do you understand?"

"N-not really," said the child doubtfully.

"You will understand when you are older, then. For now, eat your bread, and make ready to ride again."

Nimuë finished her bread and honey and wiped her hands tidily on a clump of grass. "I never understood Father Griffin either, but he was angry when I did not. I was punished when I asked him why we must fast and pray for our sins when Christ had already forgiven them, and he said I had been taught heathendom and made Mother send me to my room. What is heathendom, Aunt?"

"It is anything a priest does not like," said Morgaine. "Father Griffin is a fool. Even the best of the Christian priests do not trouble little ones like you, who can do no sin, with much talk about it. Time enough to talk about sin, Nimuë, when you are capable of doing it, of making choices between good and evil."

Nimuë got on her pony obediently, but after a time she said, "Aunt Morgaine – I am not such a good girl, though. I sin all the time. I am always doing wicked things. I am not at all surprised that Mother wanted to send me away. That is why she is sending me to a wicked place, because I am a wicked girl."

Morgaine felt her throat close with something like agony. She had been about to mount her own horse, but she hurried to Nimuë's pony and caught the girl in a great hug, holding her tight and kissing her again and again. She said, breathlessly, "Never say that again, Nimuë! Never! It is not true, I vow to you it is not! Your mother did not want to send you away at all, and if she had thought Avalon a wicked place she would not have sent you, no matter what I threatened!"

Nimuë said in a small voice, "Why am I being sent away, then?"

Morgaine still held her tight with all the strength of her arms. "Because you were pledged to Avalon before you were born, my child. Because your grandmother was a priestess, and because I have no daughter for the Goddess, and you are being sent to Avalon that you may learn wisdom and serve the Goddess." She noted that her tears were falling, unheeded, on Nimuë's fair hair. "Who let you believe it was punishment?"

"One of the women – while she packed my shift—" Nimuë faltered. "I heard her say Mother should not have sent me to that wicked place – and Father Griffin has told me often that I am a wicked girl—"

Morgaine sank to the ground, holding Nimuë in her lap, rocking her back and forth. "No, no," she said gently, "no, darling, no. You are a good girl. If you are naughty or lazy or disobedient, that is not sin, it is only that you are not old enough to know any better, and when you are taught to do what is right, then you will do so."

And then, because she thought this conversation had gone far for a child so young, she said, "Look at that butterfly! I have not seen one that color before! Come, Nimuë, let me lift you on your pony now," she said, and listened attentively as the little girl chattered on about butterflies.

Alone she could have ridden to Avalon in a single day, but the short legs of Nimuë's little pony could not make that distance, so they slept that night in a clearing. Nimuë had never slept out of doors before, and the darkness frightened her when they put out the fire, so Morgaine let the child creep into the circle of her arms and lay pointing out one star after another to her.

The little girl was tired with riding and soon slept, but Morgaine lay awake, Nimuë's head heavy on her arm, feeling fear stealing upon her. She had been so long away from Avalon. Step by slow step, she had retraced all her training, or what she could remember; but would she forget some vital thing? Would they even want her back?

I bring them Viviane's granddaughter, she thought. *But if they let me return only for her sake it will be more bitter than death. Has the Goddess cast me out forever?*

*   *   *

No, for when she summoned the barge to take them to Avalon, it came at her call. Nimuë was wide-eyed and confused during the brief journey to the island and her presentation to the priestesses.

"Well, Nimuë," the priestess Niniane asked, "have you come to be a priestess here?"

Nimuë looked around at the sunset landscape. "That is what my aunt Morgaine told me. I would like to learn to read and write and play the harp, and know about the stars and all kinds of things as she does. Are you really evil sorceresses here? I thought a sorceress would be old and ugly, and you are very pretty." She bit her lip. "I am being rude again."

Niniane laughed. "Always speak out the truth, child. Yes, I am a sorceress. I do not think I am ugly, but you must decide for yourself whether I am good or evil. I try to do the will of the Goddess, and that is all anyone can do."

"I will try to do that," Nimuë said, "if you will tell me how."

THE HORSE WHO WOULD BE KING

JENNIFER ROBERSON

Perhaps it is timely to inject some humour into the proceedings. It was inevitable that somewhere in this anthology there needed to be a story about the sword in the stone. I didn't want to reprint the episode as it is treated in the standard tales, and because of the later more mystical treatment of the sword Excalibur, I wanted something that looked at the incident of the sword in the stone in a more refreshing light. I was thus delighted to encounter Jennifer Roberson's "Never Look at a Gift Sword in the Horse's Mouth" published in Marion Zimmer Bradley's Fantasy Magazine. *I've reprinted the story here under its subtitle, "The Horse Who Would Be King". Roberson has brought the T. H. White treatment to Merlin and Arthur in a delightful way.*

Jennifer Roberson (b. 1953) is probably best known for her eight-book sequence about the Cheysuli, which began with Shape-changers *(1984) and ran through to* A Tapestry of Lions *(1992). She has also turned her attention to the Matter of Britain, though not so much the Arthurian world as that of Robin Hood, with* Lady of the Forest *(1992).*

My master had a problem. He knew it. I knew it. But nobody else knew it. And we needed to keep it that way.

"You're a magician," I told him comfortingly. "Use some smoke and mirrors, a little sleight of hand, a pinch of razzle-dazzle – no one will even notice."

The morning, for Britain, was bright: the half-hearted sun was a tarnished, brass-colored splotch in the haze of reluctant day. Birds chirped. Bees buzzed. Mice rustled. Down the hill, a camp dog barked.

My master slumped disconsolately against the broken tree stump in the hollow of the hill, rump planted precariously near an anthill. The ants, as yet, were oblivious; unfortunately, so was he.

"Magician," he muttered disgustedly. "I'm bloody Merlin, you fool!" I considered polite ways of pointing out the anthill and the potential consequences of taking up residence, however temporary, in its immediate environs, but decided the topic at hand was more immediate. My master was touchily proud of his position as the most exalted, learned, and powerful magician Britain had ever known, and protected that reputation with a fervor verging on obsession . . . any challenges to his authority, intended or no, required delicate attention.

"I know that," I reminded him, implying mild reproof; a long and peculiar acquaintanceship allowed me great latitude in familiarity. "You've taken great pains for some years now to establish exactly who you are, with commensurate reputation. No one in all of Britain doesn't know who you are."

He cast me a baleful glance from dark, brooding eyes overshadowed with thick untidy dark hair only infrequently combed or cut. "And there's the rub," he complained. "I'm a victim of my own success. I'm left no room for failure."

I snorted. "There's no reason you shouldn't be successful this time."

"No reason!" The baleful glare reasserted itself as affronted outrage. "I'm supposed to supply Britain with the greatest hero-king she's ever known, and you say, ever so blithely—" with the soft-spoken, icy precision that cut the legs out from lesser souls, "—there's no reason I shouldn't be successful."

I ignored the ice and derision. "No reason at all. Trust me."

Merlin glared, surrendering verbal acrobatics; none of them worked, with me. "Trust you."

"Yes."

With elegant precision, my master said distinctly: "You are a horse."

A moot point, and unworthy of discussion. I tossed my head, flopping my dark gray forelock eloquently between upstanding ears. "I'm confident you'll find someone for the job."

Merlin ground his teeth, spitting out his commentary with a repressed passion that underscored his frustration. "It can't be just anyone, don't you see? It must be someone very special. Someone unique in all respects. Someone perfectly suited to unite all the warring tribes so Britain can fend off foreign invaders."

I looked down my nose, a posture better suited to me than to him, as my nose was considerably longer. "You just need someone who can kiss a lot of ass," I told him, "although why anyone would want an ass when there's a perfectly presentable horse available, I don't know."

"Don't be so arrogant," Merlin sniffed. "After all, I made you."

"And I'll be the making of you." I gazed back at the encampment some distance away. Smoke clogged the trees, drifting hither and yon. I heard the sounds of laughter, raillery, arguments, mock fighting, weapons practice. The air stank of smoke, burned meat, and unwashed human bodies. "We haven't failed yet. We'll come up with a plan."

Merlin heaved a sigh, picking idly at a snag in his second-best enchanter's robe. "Not just any plan. It has to be very delicate. Very selective, so there's no question as to the outcome. I can't just point at a fellow and say: 'That's the man there, don't you know, rightwise born king of all England.' "

I cocked a hoof, standing hipshot. "Why not?"

"It smacks of dictatorship. They won't like it, from me. These people like signs, and portents, and omens . . . they're a superstitious lot, bound up by ritualistic gobbledygook – never mind such things are as easy to arrange as buying a girl for the night." He glowered at me. "Not that I can buy one, mind you . . . whose idea was it that Merlin had to be chaste?"

"You had to be something," I reminded him. "You needed a gimmick. Nobody cares if you sing, or tell stories, or swill wine with the best of them – what sets a man apart in these immoral times is his chastity."

He flapped a hand at a bee. "You might have picked something easier on me. Or at least let me geld you, so we suffer equally."

I pointedly ignored the suggestion. "As to signs and portents and ritualistic gobbledygook, you've been the one arranging those very things for years, now."

He snapped a loose thread free of his robe, inspecting it morosely. If he kept at it, part of the robe would unravel and hence become third-best. "I have to make them think they've something to do with it . . . or else make it so obvious there's only one conclusion."

"Tests are good for that. They weed out the inappropriate."

The line of his mouth crimped. "I hate to make the kingship of all Britain contingent upon a test."

"Why? Makes as much sense as drawing names out of a pot."

I pawed at damp turf, digging an idle hole. We all have our bad habits. "After all, it's you who'll be running the realm."

Merlin thought about it. "I need the right sort of man. A very particular type of man. Stupid enough to be malleable, but wise enough to know his limits. Young enough to be suitably idealistic, big enough to be impressive."

I plucked a succulent clot of turf from the damp ground, shook it free of mud, ground it to bits between my teeth.

"There's always Artie."

Truly taken aback, Merlin gazed at me in horror. "You can't be serious!"

"He's pretty good at carrying your baggage around, and he always feeds me on time."

"Artie's thick in the head."

"All the better for you." I smiled, displaying teeth. "He's young enough, big enough, certainly stupid enough – and he listens to you."

"Because he knows if he doesn't I'll turn him into a frog."

"No, you wouldn't. Artie's an innocent. You'd never hurt him like that."

Merlin just scowled; he hates it whenever I remind him he's not the tyrant he pretends to be.

I switched my tail. "It's a good idea, and you know it. He's been quiet since we arrived, so no one knows much about him. He looks enough like Uther to qualify as his bastard; and anyway, Uther's dead. He won't care."

Merlin grunted. "Who's his mother, then?"

I ruminated a moment. "What about that women living out on the edge of nowhere in Cornwall? At Tintagel. She's supposed to be a trifle touched in the head, too."

"Gorlois's widow?" Dark brows lanced down. "That's Ygraine. No one's seen her for years. She lives out there with a couple of servants and a castle full of cats."

"That's what I mean. She won't put up much of a fuss. And

if she does, just keep sending her merchants with wagons full of wares. Shopping will keep her mind off things."

"Uther's bastard, got on Ygraine."

Merlin chewed a lip. "It could work."

"Of course it could."

"I'll have to concoct some bizarre tale full of supposed magic and superstitious nonsense to account for the bedding."

"Uther bedded half the woman in Britain."

"But he's allergic to cats. He'd never have bedded Ygraine, or he'd have sneezed for a month."

I waggled dark-tipped ears. "You'll think of something. You've done it before." With my help, of course, but we don't always mention that.

"And something to prove Artie's worthy." Merlin chewed a ragged fingernail. Very bad habit. "That will be the hard part."

I disagreed. "Just figure out a straightforward test with all the right sort of bells and whistles, then contrive the thing so Artie passes when no one else can."

"Ants!" Merlin cried, leaping to his feet. In a frenzy of activity unbecoming to the most exalted enchanter Britain had ever known, he beat off the ants with both hands. "Begone!" he thundered.

I winced, wondering if England would keep her ants. The last time Merlin had been so irritated, we'd been in Ireland, with snakes.

Though someone else got the credit for that.

Artie came up to see me at midday. All the other horses were picketed at tents or elsewhere in the trees, but everyone had learned very quickly that the big gray horse with the sword-shaped blaze on his face was not to be bothered.

I nickered a greeting as he made his way up the hill, using horse language in case anyone else was around. Only Artie and Merlin knew I could talk, and we'd decided it was better left that way. Actually, I think it was because Merlin didn't like sharing his notoriety; a talking horse would siphon some of the attention from him.

Artie wore that distant, slack-jawed expression that others took for stupidity, including my master. In truth, Artie wasn't that stupid. He just daydreamed a lot.

I'd asked him once what he thought about when he turned himself sideways to the day and wandered the dreaming lands that separated waking life from sleep. He'd just hunched his big shoulders and answered "things," in that infuriatingly unspecific way that said everything he needed to say, and nothing at all of what I wanted to hear.

But that's Artie, God love him.

For a man as big as Artie, he knew how to walk quietly. I heard nary a crackle of underbrush and deadfall as he climbed the hill to me. I smelled the oatcake before he dug it out of his tunic, expanding nostrils to breathe heavily at him.

"All right, all right . . ." Smiling widely, Artie unknotted the corner of his tunic and caught most of the crumbs before they fell. His hands were huge and gentle, cupping my muzzle tenderly as I lipped up the oatcake.

Once finished, I put one large nostril up against his face. We traded breaths a moment, reasserting our bond, and then Artie patted me firmly on one shoulder, smacking palm audibly.

"More swordplay today," he told me. "Kay will have his turn."

"What about you?" I asked.

Artie shook his head, hitching one shoulder. "Not for me."

"Why not? Ector'd let you."

"Kay would complain."

"Let him. Merlin paid enough coin for your fosterage – let it buy you a chance, too."

But Artie just shrugged again. "Doesn't matter."

I eyed him thoughtfully. "They've been at you again, haven't they?"

Another shrug as he stroked the underside of my jaw.

"You're big enough to beat them all at their own game, Artie."

"That's what they want me to do."

"So, you'll let them call you names without trying to make them stop."

"They'll say whatever they want, anyway."

"If you learned some of the skills—"

"No." Wrinkles marred his forehead beneath the lank of light-brown hair. "I'm good at what I do. I don't need to be like them."

"You could be better than them."

Artie just shook his head.

I rested my chin on his shoulder and leaned. "There's more to life than fetching and carrying for Merlin."

He laughed. "I could say the same to you."

"But I'm a horse, Artie. That's what horses do."

"And I'm just Artie. It's good enough for me."

I snorted damply at him. He just wiped his face clean and cast me a reproachful glance.

The trouble with people like Artie is you can never reason with them. Especially when they're right.

Merlin, hunched over his grimoire, looked up crossly as I stuck my head inside the flaps of his tent. His expression cleared as he saw me. "What is it?"

"Have you made any progress on your plans for Artie's test?"

He scowled. He had changed from his second-best robe to his third-best, which meant he'd probably unravelled enough of his second-best to make it the new third-best, thereby elevating the former third to second.

"No," he said shortly.

"I think I may have the answer."

"Oh?" He shut the grimoire and placed it back on its tripod, rising to stand before me. "Pray tell me, horse, what Britain's greatest magician can do to deliver a king?"

"I told you. There's Artie—"

Merlin made a rude sound. "It's a stupid idea."

"Why? Would you rather have someone like Kay make a play for the realm?"

Merlin snorted. "Kay's a hotheaded, braying fool."

"While Artie's a kind man who wants the best for everyone."

"Kind men don't make good kings."

"With your attitude, you could make up the difference."

We glared at one another. Merlin broke it off. "All right, enough already. What do you suggest?"

"This," I said, and told him.

The night was cool, crisp, very dark, save for the spill of argent moonlight glinting through leaves and branches. Merlin slid off my back, muttering under his breath of foolish ideas and superstitious nonsense. The grimoire, wrapped in pure black silk, was tucked under an arm; he hitched it more securely between elbow and hip, and stalked ahead of me through the darkness.

"Over there," I told. "On the other side of that tree."

He went around the designated tree and stopped at the huddled rock formation. Not large, not small; kind of medium, worn smooth by time and dampness. "This?"

"That." I plodded onward and stopped beside him. "Appropriately unique, wouldn't you say?"

"It's a rock."

"Not just a rock. The rock. Have you no imagination?"

Merlin grunted. "I suppose it will do."

"It had better, if you're to maintain your reputation." I ignored the sideways scowl. "You said there was a spell for what we need."

"Oh, I can melt the rock with no real difficulty, and even fuse it back. I just don't understand why I should."

"Leave that to me."

Merlin stared at me fixedly. "Look here," he said finally, "you've given me a lot of good ideas over the years, but you can't deny the fact you're a horse. How do I know this trick of yours will work?"

"It won't cost either of us anything to find out."

Merlin heaved a sigh. "You're being obtuse, as always."

I reached out a forehoof and banged it off the rock. "If it's to be done by dawn, we'd better get busy."

"All this just for Artie."

"All this just for England – and your reputation."

Merlin sat down, opened the grimoire and began to page through it.

"Here," he rasped at last. "This one should do it."

It was nearly dawn. I blinked myself awake, peered blurrily at the rock, then blew out a blade of grass that had lodged itself in one nostril as I'd grazed earlier. "Now for the sword," I murmured.

Merlin was alarmed. "Sword? What sword? You said nothing about a sword. I didn't bring one with me."

"That's my part," I told him. "All right. Close your eyes. Sit very still. Don't move until I say so."

"Are you sure this is going to work?"

"I'm sure it won't work if you don't do as I tell you."

Merlin gritted his teeth. Closed his eyes. Sat very still.

"No peeking," I warned. "This is very delicate magic."

"I'm the magician," he muttered. "I know a little about such things."

"Shhh."

Merlin held his tongue.

It wasn't so bad, after all: just a small piece of myself, made over into something else. My head ached a little, and my knees were a bit wobbly, but in the end the task was accomplished with little fanfare. I bent, put my head down close to his lap, and let the sword fall.

"Now," I told Merlin.

He caught it, clasped it, gazed in awe up it. "A sword," he whispered. Hands caressed the weapon, wary of the blade. "A sword," he said again.

I saw the acquisitive glint in dark eyes. "Artie's sword," I told him.

"Artie's . . ." He looked up at me. From his posture on the ground, I loomed over him.

"Artie's," I said pointedly. "Now it's your turn."

"My turn?"

I thrust my nose toward the rock. "Melt it. Put the blade in it, with the hilt left standing upright. Fuse the stone back."

Merlin was aghast. "You want me to seal it up?"

"For now."

"What good is it, then? How will it ever be used?"

"It will be used to determine a king."

Merlin made an inelegant sound in the back of his throat. "That'll be the day."

"Tomorrow," I said. Then, reconsidering, "Sometime today, that is."

"This is the most ridiculous thing I ever heard—"

"Just do it," I told him. "There's a lot riding on this."

Merlin sighed and set the grimoire aside, heaving himself up with the sword clasped in both hands. He strode to the stone, shut his eyes, held the sword above his head, and hissed the incantation.

The air crackled and turned blue. All the hair on my body rose. Stone parted, then flowed aside. It swallowed the naked blade as Merlin thrust it downward. Then it flowed back, cradling the blade, and remained completely liquefied until Merlin spoke once more. A single, sibilant word made it stone again. The blue light went away. The crackle died out.

"There," he rasped hoarsely. "Stuck in the rock, forever."

Splay-legged, I shook my entire body as violently as I could to rid myself of the itch left by all the magic. "Give it a few hours." He scooped up the grimoire, wrapped it in silk again, gazed wearily at me out of bloodshot eyes. "This will determine a king?"

"Signs and portents," I told him. "Ritualistic gobbledygook. But I think it will do the trick."

"What do we do next?"

"You wake everybody up at dawn and parade them up here. Tell them it's been revealed to you that Whosoever Pulleth This Sword From The Stone Shall Be Rightwise Born King of All England."

"What?" Merlin croaked.

"Trust me," I told him.

Merlin, being Merlin, enticed everyone to the rock by dawn, promising them who knows what in the elegant, eloquent pomposity of language that impresses those mere mortals who can't decipher it.

Artie, being Artie, meandered up through morning mist and stopped next to me, rooting through his tunic for an oatcake.

"Go down with the others," I murmured from the side of my mouth, pitching my voice so no one else could hear.

"What for?" Artie untied knots.

"Just do what I say. Listen to Merlin."

Artie squinted through the dawn haze and listened briefly as Merlin harangued the gathering. "He's just going on again," Artie said finally. "He does that sometimes."

"You're supposed to be down there with the others."

"Here." He held out a crumbled oatcake.

I shoved his hand aside, knocking the cake to the ground in a shower of crumbs. "I don't want the bloody thing! Just go down with the others and take your turn!"

"My turn?" Artie, squatting to gather up the largest of the crumbs, peered up at me. "What am I supposed to do?"

"Have a shot at the sword," I told him.

"What sword –? – oh, that sword." He straightened, frowning. "How did that get there?"

"Magic," I hissed. "Go get in line, will you?"

Artie stared at the sword thrusting boldly upright in the stone. "Seems to me if someone went to all the trouble to put that sword in the rock, we ought to leave it there."

I tucked my nose into the small of his back and shoved him down the hill. He staggered a few steps, caught his balance, looked aggrievedly back at me. I glared at him ominously.

Merlin, seeing this, cut off his exhortation. He motioned curtly at Artie. "Get in line. Get in line. Everyone has his chance."

Kay's voice rose above the murmurs. "Come on, Artie! Afraid to fail in front of everybody?"

I scowled down at him. Artie just shrugged his shoulders, scratching at lank brown hair.

It took a while, as expected. Each man had his pull, then stepped aside, muttering, and waited with the others to watch the next attempt. So far, all had failed. I nodded across at Merlin, who orchestrated the trial. But it wasn't until I saw the wild glint in his eyes that I realized Artie was missing.

I trotted over to Merlin. "Where is he?" I hissed.

"I thought you were with him?" Merlin waved his hands in an approximation of a spell, just to keep the crowd distracted.

"I sent him down to stand in line."

"This is the end of the line. Artie isn't in it."

Trust Artie – never mind. "I'll find him," I said grimly. "Just send everyone back to bashing at one another to find out who's the best swordsman."

"I just went through this whole rigmarole about finding the Rightwise-Born-King-Of-All-England," Merlin growled. "What do I tell them now?"

I swung away from him. "You'll think of something. I've got to look for Artie."

Eventually, Artie found me. In a black mood I grazed the hilltop near the sword in the stone, tearing up clumps of turf. I wasn't really hungry, but it was something to do.

"I need a sword," he said.

I lifted my head and glared at him. "Where have you been?"

He hitched slabbed shoulders. "I went for a walk."

"You were supposed to try to pull the sword from the stone, like everybody else."

He toed a stone out of its bed. "I didn't feel like it."

"But now you need a sword."

"Not that one. One for Kay. He broke his."

I reached out and grabbed a hunk of tunic with my teeth, then dragged him ungently over to the rock. "Try this one, Artie."

"It's in a rock. I can't."

"Trust me," I suggested. "Kay won't mind."

Artie heaved a sigh and wrapped one big hand around the grip. He tugged.

Nothing happened.

"Try both hands," I said.

Artie did. Nothing happened. "See?" he said. "It's supposed to stay in the rock."

Alarums sounded. "No, no. Try again. Harder, this time."

He did. Then gave it up as a bad job. "I'll go see if I can borrow a sword for Kay."

"Wait—" I grabbed the back of his tunic. "Humor me, will you? Look … you just grab it and pull—" I locked my teeth around the hilt and dragged the thing from the stone.

Artie just blinked at me.

"Take it." My words were warped by the grip in my mouth. "Take the thing, will you?"

Obligingly, Artie took the sword.

"Quick like a bunny," I told him, "run down the hill to Merlin and show him what you've got."

"But – Kay needs it."

"Don't give it to Kay. Take it to Merlin."

"Why?"

I leaned my chin on his shoulder. "Have I ever steered you wrong?"

Artie, being Artie, didn't argue with the obvious.

Smugly, I waited on the hilltop for Merlin's Voice of Pronouncements to roll throughout the forest, setting leaves and saplings to shaking. But I didn't hear anything at all out of Merlin until he came racing up the hill, stumbling over rocks. Mostly, he just panted.

"What did you do?" he demanded. "By God, I ought to sell you off to Welsh archers. They shoot horses, don't they?"

"Now, now," I said mildly, "things can't be that bad. Did Artie bring you the sword?"

"He wandered by with a sword, said something about Kay, then wandered off again. By the time I figured out just exactly what sword he had – I never did see it – he'd given the thing to Kay!"

"Oh, God. And now Kay's—"

"—spouting off to everyone with ears that he's Rightwise-Born-King-Of-All-England," Merlin finished, panting a little. "Couldn't you have come up with a shorter title?"

My mind raced. "But you didn't announce it, did you? As Merlin?"

"Not officially, no. I haven't said anything."

Relief bubbled. "Then we're safe."

Merlin's expression was crazed. "How can we be safe, blast you? Kay's got the bloody thing, and Artie's out looking for baby rabbits."

"Out looking—? Never mind." I thought a moment. "Go get it back."

"Get what back – the sword? On what pretext?"

"Tell Kay he's got to draw the sword from the stone again. That it doesn't count unless everyone witnesses it. That's fair, isn't it?"

"Oh, God," he murmured. "Why do I ever let you get me into these things?"

"Just go round up Kay and everyone else and take them to the stone. I'll see if I can flush Artie."

"You didn't have much luck last time."

"Kay," I said firmly.

Gnashing his teeth, Merlin dragged up the trailing hem of his third-best – no, his second-best – robe and went back down the hill.

"Rabbits," I murmured thoughtfully, and went off in the other direction.

I found Artie sprawled face-down in front of a burrow. His expression was rapt. "You gave him the sword," I said.

Artie jumped, rolling to his side, then clapped a hand to his heart. "You scared me to death!"

"I'll do more than that if you don't get your rump up from the ground and come with me back to the stone."

Artie got up slowly, picking grass and leaves from hair and clothing. "Kay needed it."

"I told you to take it to Merlin."

"I did."

"You took it near Merlin. There's a difference."

"He would have used his Voice of Pronouncement. It hurts my head when he does that."

"It's supposed to. It's so you'll realize what he's saying is something important."

On cue, Merlin's bellow worked its way through the trees. Artie winced. "See?"

I nudged his shoulder. "You'll have time for rabbits later. Right now there's work to be done."

By the time I got Artie back to the stone, Merlin was looking a little frazzled. He saw us coming, stopped waving his arms, and glared balefully at Artie. Kay, I saw, stood in a belligerent posture at the front of the crowd. The sword hung from one hand.

I dropped my head down to Artie's shoulder, leaning weight into it. "Promise me one thing," I said. "Try the sword, this time."

"I tried before. It didn't work."

"Artie – please. If you love me, give it a try."

Artie stopped short, swung on his heels, slung both arms around my neck. "But of course I love you."

The watching crowd snickered. Kay said something snide, but I couldn't quite catch it.

"All right," I hissed, "that's enough. Don't make a scene – yet."

Artie disentangled his arms from neck and mane. His eyes were suspiciously bright and his cheeks were damp.

A soft-hearted fool, our Artie.

"Go stand with the others," I murmured.

Obligingly, Artie went off to stand at the edge of the throng. As usual, people made comments.

Merlin turned back and thrust his arms into the air. The Voice of Pronouncement bellowed forth once more. "So there can be no doubt as to who shall rule Britain, I pledge to you that Whosoever Pulleth This Sword From The Stone Shall Be Rightwise Born King Of All England!"

A voice from the back of the crowd: "We did this once, already."

Merlin glared at them all. "Do it AGAIN!"

Kay didn't move.

Merlin scowled at him. "Put the sword back."

He didn't so much as twitch.

"Put the sword back."

Kay's eyes narrowed. "Make me."

A single massive indrawn breath nearly sucked the leaves from the trees. Expectancy abounded.

Merlin took two steps to Kay. He leaned forward slightly. No one dared to breathe.

Very softly, Merlin said, "Put. The sword. BACK."

Everyone on the hillside clapped hands over ears as the final word crashed through the forest. Trees fell. Lightning flashed. Camp dogs barked, while picketed horses squealed.

I, of course, didn't, though I had to unpin my ears with effort.

Somewhat hurriedly, Kay went over and stuffed the blade into the rock. But his intransigence remained firm. "I get first crack."

"Fine," Merlin gritted. "First Kay, then everyone else."

He stabbed a look at Artie. "You too, this time!"

Artie nodded glumly.

England's greatest magician waved impatient hands. "All right. Let's get going. We don't have all day."

Kay tried, and failed. Three times, in all, grunting and straining, sweat running from his red face. Then two of his friends caught him by either elbow and pulled him bodily away.

"Next!" Merlin called.

Everyone had a try. Lastly came Artie.

"It won't work," he muttered to us. "I tried this already."

Merlin stuck his face into Artie's. "Just DO it!"

Sighing, Artie wrapped both hands around the grip and yanked.

Nothing happened.

"Oh God," Merlin breathed. "I'm ruined. I'm finished. It's over. It's done with. Finis—"

"Shut up," I hissed. "He's not done yet."

But he was. Artie tried twice more. The sword didn't budge.

"Keep your hands on the grip," I said quickly. Then, to Merlin: "Your Voice of Pronouncement! Now!"

"What am I supposed to Pronounce?"

"And make some fog. Hurry!"

"Hell, fog's easy."

It was. Almost instantly, the forest was choking in fog.

"Hey!" someone called. "What's all this, then?"

I shut my teeth on the grip and dragged the sword yet again out of the stone. "Here," I mumbled to Artie. "Hold the blasted thing."

"Again?" he asked wonderingly.

"The Voice!" I hissed at Merlin. "Britain has a king!"

Merlin began Pronouncing.

"For God's sake," I said desperately, "make the fog disappear! No one can see anything!"

In mid-syllable the fog winked out, leaving Merlin Pronouncing enthusiastically, me blinking owl-eyed, and Artie – dear, sweet Artie – clutching the sword.

"Whosoever-Pulleth-This-Sword-From-The-Stone—"

"Here," someone said, "I didn't see anything!"

"—Is-Rightwise-Born-King—"

"Not Artie!" Kay shouted. "My God, not ARTIE!"

"—Of-All-England!" Merlin finished. "The End."

"Not yet," I said aggrievedly.

"For me, it is," he rasped. "I need a drink."

"Artie didn't do it!" Kay shouted. "It wasn't Artie at all! I was standing right here – I saw—" He dragged in a wheezing breath. "Merlin's HORSE did it!"

Heavy silence ensued. And Kay, who is not entirely a fool, realized what he'd said, what it sounded like, and what it might do for his future.

I selected that moment to bestow upon the earth my undeniably horsey essence in a noisy, lengthy stream.

Glumly Kay looked at Artie. "Long live the king."

Very quietly.

As I knew he would, Artie came up to see me later. I stood hipshot in the moonlight, whuffing a greeting. I smelled oatcakes.

Artie untied a knot and held it out. I lipped it up gingerly. "Where's the sword?" I asked, once I'd finished the cake.

"Merlin's got it. He says he doesn't trust me with it yet. He says I'd probably give it to Kay, or somebody equally unsuitable."

"Well, you did once."

"But don't you see? I'm not suitable, either!"

"The sword says you are."

"That sword says nothing at all! You pulled it out!"

I didn't answer at once.

Artie nodded firmly. "Twice, you pulled it out."

"Yes, well . . . you can't very well expect a horse to be King-of-All-England."

"You can't expect me to be, either!"

"Too late, Artie. Merlin's done his Pronouncing."

"But I can't be Whosoever-Pulleth," he insisted. "It wouldn't be right."

"Rightwise," I murmured. "And Artie – it doesn't really matter that much. This is how things are done."

"What things?"

"Important things. They happen the way people make them happen, and then other people sing songs and tell stories and write about them the way they wished they'd happened." I twitched a shoulder. "It's just the way life is."

"I never wanted to be king."

"Maybe that's why you'll be a good one."

"Will I?" He brightened. "Are you sure?"

"Leave it to Merlin. He'll see it comes out all right."

Artie hooked an arm over my withers. "You're the finest horse I've ever known."

"Thank you."

"I'd like to do something for you. Something grand and wise and kingly, so no one will ever forget you."

"They'll forget me, Artie. I'm only a horse, after all."

Artie looked worried. "But you're sort of the glue that holds us all together!"

I winced. "Let's not mention glue, shall we?"

"All right." He brightened. "I'll name my firstborn son after you!"

I snorted. "After a horse? That's not very kingly – and the son might object, once he's old enough."

"But I have to do something."

It wasn't worth arguing over. Besides, it would hurt nothing. Part of me was already on permanent loan. "Do as you will, then," I said. "It's Excalibur."

"Your name?"

"Yes."

Artie grinned. "I'll see you're never forgotten! I'll see to it the name lives on forever and ever!"

"Artie . . ." But I let it go. "Thanks, Artie. I appreciate it."

He hugged my neck tightly. "Excalibur," he whispered. "A good name for a horse."

"Go to bed," I suggested. "You've got a full day ahead tomorrow."

"I suppose." He slapped me in farewell. "I'll bring you an oakcake in the morning."

He meant it, I knew. I also knew he'd already fed me the last of the oatcakes. "Go on," I said, and nudged him very gently.

Waving goodnight, Artie went back to the camp.

"All right," I said. "You can come out now."

He came, drifting out of the darkness like a nightwraith. "So," he said. "Excalibur, is it?"

"Yes."

Faint accusation: "You never told me."

"True Names contain magic. You know better than that."

"But Artie intends to let everyone know it. It won't be you, anymore."

I twitched an ear. "It doesn't matter, now. I have no part in the story. Let him use it as he will."

Merlin stroked my nose. "We've made England a king, old friend."

"Artie will do fine."

Fingers drifted up beneath the forelock, then brushed it aside. The dark eyes so full of magic were bright in the moonlight as he studied my forehead. "So that's where it came from."

I twitched a shoulder dismissively.

"Powerful magic, that. More than I'd risk."

I shook the forelock back into place. "Doesn't matter, does it? It's over and done with."

"I suppose so." He patted me on the shoulder. "A good plan, old friend. Most assuredly, my reputation will survive."

"And your name." I swished my tail. "Artie – and England – will need you."

"And Excalibur." Which was no longer me.

Another pat, and then Merlin, who knew, was gone. I shook my head again, aware of a vague tingle in the place beneath my forelock where the sword-shaped blaze had been.

I gazed up at the waning moon. "A kingdom for a horse?"

No. I rephrased it.

A SWORD FOR ARTHUR

VERA CHAPMAN

There is no doubt that if there is one aspect of the Arthurian legend that captures everyone's imagination then it is Arthur receiving his sword Excalibur from the Lady of the Lake. Arthurian legend sometimes links the sword in the stone with that of Excalibur. I have even seen one interpretation of the name being ex-caliburn, i.e. out-of-the-stone. Whether the two swords were one and the same or different adds to the fascination of the tale. Even Malory got them confused. You will find differing interpretations of the event in several stories in this volume. Here is the first, taken from Vera Chapman's novel The Enchantresses *(1998). Vera Chapman (1898–1996) was no stranger to Arthurian fiction although she was a latecomer, producing her first novel,* The Green Knight, *when she was already into her seventies. That and its two related novels were issued in a single volume as* The Three Damosels *in 1978.*

Merlin came rowing the boat over the loch, on a calm sunny morning. He rowed in the way the southerners do, standing and facing the way he went, with the oars crossed before him, so he could see the lake-island of Nimuë coming into sight, and the gleam of the white walls of the little castle.

An older Merlin by some fifteen years, his thick black hair was now well powdered with silver, and glittered in the sunlight; his beard, still black, was now bushy and spade-shaped, his hair falling over his neck to meet it smoothly. His teeth flashed out sound and white, and his dark blue eyes were as bright as ever. But there was a look of stress about him, as if he was never free from thoughts of anxiety.

The approach to the island showed many changes since the morning when he had first brought Vivian there with the baby Arthur. Trees had been cleared away, others planted. Flower beds, bright with colour, bordered the marble walkway. All along the water's edge, roses overflowed and shed sweet petals on the water; the rose briars made a thick screen, and quite hid the strong fence that ran along the water-line, not so much to keep intruders out, as to keep childish feet from slipping into the lake. A strong gate closed the landing place, but it was standing open now.

As he brought the boat alongside, a lovely little girl, about nine years old, ran down to meet him. Her black curls were like his own, but her eyes were green.

"Father! Father!" she cried in her clear shrill voice. "Oh, Mother – Father's come!"

Behind her at the top of the steps were Mae, now grown fat and matronly, and Mari, Mae's daughter, a sturdy lass of fifteen. Behind them came Vivian, the sunlight touching her red hair, slim and light-footed as ever. But the little dark-haired girl was more light-footed still. She had bounded up the stairs, and back down them again to Merlin, before her mother could so much as look below and smile at Merlin coming up to her. The little girl was dragging him up by the arm now, and babbling to him.

"Now you're back we'll have fireworks, and stories, and magic – Did you see Arthur? How is he?"

"Certainly I saw Arthur," he said, chuckling at her. "Considering I spent the last six months teaching him—"

"Teaching him what? Magic?"

"Well, no, not *much* magic. Not more than he will need. You see, he isn't going to be a magic man."

"Not a magic man? What then?"

"Something very different – something better perhaps—"

"A knight? Oh, he's to be knighted, then?"

"Why no – not a knight, or not yet. He couldn't be that until he's eighteen, you know. His foster-brother Kay is to be made a knight at Christmas. But Arthur – perhaps he's to be something else—"

"I know! I know!" She jumped up and down in her excitement. "A king!"

At that moment they reached the top of the steps and were

caught in Vivian's embrace. Merlin was drawn into the welcome of his little household.

Blaisine, his only child – he gathered her into one arm and Vivian into the other. Blaisine – he had christened her so, after his old master Blaise, the great magician of Brittany. From her very earliest days she had shown herself full of strange powers. How could she fail to be gifted, with such parents? She had everything in her small way – the clear-sight, the instinctive control of the weather, the remarkable sympathy with animals, the healing hands – if Vivian had a headache, or Merlin himself, it was Blaisine's cool little hands that soothed it away. She was a quick learner, picking up a great deal of the magical technique without really trying. Merlin, in spite of all misgivings, and his desire that she should be a normal happy child, could not refuse to teach her.

She was not really a solitary child, although she had never yet set foot outside her little island. There was Mae's Mari, and there had been Arthur, the adored big brother. But now, since he was eight, Arthur had gone away to live with Sir Ector and Sir Ector's two brothers, and his kind wife; and though he often came back on visits, the time between them seemed very long to Blaisine. Mae, though good-natured, could not share Blaisine's thoughts, and more and more she drew in upon herself. Vivian watched her with understanding.

Blaisine chattered on to Merlin as they went up towards the house. "Father, look, there's the place where the Little People were last night. They're here most nights when the moon's full. Do you know, Mae can't see them at all, nor can Mari – aren't they stupid? Arthur could always see them – can he still?"

"I daresay he can, my love," Merlin replied, "but I don't think they come around much where he now is – too many people. But there's other things he'll be able to see, in time."

"Is he coming back to us soon?"

"Not yet. I'm afraid he's going to be very busy. But we'll all go up to see him at Christmas, when Kay is to be knighted."

Blaisine clapped her hands and capered. "Oh, lovely, lovely! But I wish Arthur was to be made a knight as well."

"You wait and see, my dear. Arthur's turn will come . . . We want a sword for Arthur."

"A sword? Oh, that's easy. There's plenty here hanging on the walls. There's the one he used to play with."

"Too small for him now! – No, we want a special sword for him – a very special sword – But here we are. Oh, by the Powers, here's all the dogs – My slippers – oh, thank you, sweetheart, and you can take my cloak. It's good to be home again."

After supper, Blaisine recognized preparations that she was familiar with.

"Oh Father, you're going to make magic tonight. Can I come in too?"

He put his hand caressingly on her head.

"I'm afraid not, sweetheart. Your mother and I are going to make magic, but it's a not very nice magic. Not for you."

"How do you mean – not very nice? You don't mean – Black?"

"No, no – only rather frightening."

It was dark as Merlin led Vivian along, into the depths of the castle.

"Take a candle," he said, and his voice was deep and solemn, "and follow me."

"Where are we going?" she said, and the candle in her hand shook a little.

"Down – a very long way down." And he led the way down a stone stairway she had never descended before.

Although the little castle, above its foundations, was very compact, yet underneath there were cellars and vaults of unknown depth, extending down through the mount on which the house was built, and into the rock of the island – possibly deeper . . . In the fifteen years that Vivian had lived on the Island of Nimuë there were some of these into which she had never ventured. Of course there were wine-cellars and wash-houses and storerooms – this was Mae's department, and Vivian did not go there much. But further down, she knew, were places where Mae did not go, nor anybody else. The entrance to them was enough for Vivian – she did not like the look, nor the sound, nor the smell, nor the feel of them. But here it was that he was inexorably leading her.

He halted for a moment, and set down his candle.

"We are going into a very dangerous place," he said.

"Is it Morgan again?"

"No, not Morgan. For the moment the stars are against her, and so we must work fast, before the stars pass. I must have a sword for Arthur, and the keeper of the sword will not give it up easily."

"Who is he, then?"

"You have heard people speak of Old Nick?"

"Why, yes – Old Nick – that is what some call the Prince of Darkness," and she crossed herself.

"And yet they are mistaken. Some that have heard that name bestow it on the Evil One, almost in a jest. But there is Old Nekr, or Neckar, that the Northerners know. Some, far up in the northern isles, call him Shony, or Jonas. It is he that lives in the utter deeps, in darkness and slime, where everything goes that drowns and is decayed. He is not Neptune, nor Poseidon, whom the Greeks knew as the ruler of the waters, Jove's brother, that shakes the earth. Neckar, or old Shony, is darker and more deadly. He should be subject to Poseidon, but he is a disobedient subject. Away down there in the slippery residue of drowned worlds Shony can evade all rule. His daughters are the Nixies, beautiful but deceitful. Shony himself has something of Proteus, for he changes and slips away and eludes those who would bind him. But we must go and seek him now."

"Why must we?" She whispered as if afraid to disturb the silence down there.

"Because it is to him that all the lost treasures go that men cast into the sea, or lose in shipwreck. He hoards them, down there. And his treasure of all treasures is the sword that I must have for Arthur. The sword Caliburn."

Picking up his candle again, he led on, down into the darkness and clamminess.

"We are below the water now," he whispered to Vivian. The walls each side of them were damp and slimy, the roof dripped above them – black shreds of some dark growth hung down like wet rags. The smell of decay was overpowering. On they went into the darkness.

Then they halted in front of a door, blank and black. Vivian saw Merlin's hand wave, tracing figures, and heard him muttering strange words. Then, his candle grasped in his left hand, he thrust firmly against the door, and it opened.

Inside was a chamber no larger than a closet, and all its walls were inlaid with shells. They caught the light of the candles and gleamed back against the darkness – a mosaic of shells, disposed in geometric forms. Right in front, as the door was opened, a central panel bore a crude figure, depicted with larger and more luminous shells. The figure of a man with a fish's tail – or, one might say, half man, half fish. The clumsily drawn tail curved round below the figure. Its human arms spread out to right and left, and the face was round and doll-like, but a doll's face that was both stupid and malignant – a grinning mouth showed a row of saw-like teeth. There was nothing else in the little room and no light save that of the candles Merlin and Vivian carried.

Merlin stood at the doorway, and raised his candle. Then he called, on a low and resonant note:

"Shony – Shony, Shony, Shony. Neckar also I call you, and Deva Jonas. Shony, Shony, Shony. Dweller in the inmost dark, in the place where drowned things go and are decayed – Shony, by the Ruler of the Element of Water, I call you."

And from the black wall before them, as it would seem from the white figure on the wall, came a voice – rusty and grating, as if from between those jagged teeth:

"Shony, Shony, Shony. I am here. What would you?"

"I require your treasure of treasures, the sword Caliburn."

There seemed to be a hiss as of indrawn breath.

"What I have I hold."

"Then I adjure you in the name of the Earth-Shaker, Poseidon the Mighty, the Brother of the Sky – I require the sword Caliburn."

"What will you give me in return for it?" The voice took on a note of cunning.

"No, you creature of the slime, you devourer of dead men's bones, I do not make bargains with you. I command you in the Name . . ."

The word he spoke could not be heard clearly in Vivian's terrified ears – it was too thunderous and resonant – three syllables, or maybe four, echoing on and on, shaking the earth above.

"As you say, Master," the spirit voice assented, more soft and meek now. "But it is a long way off – far down at the bottom of the Great Ocean."

"Then send your slaves to fetch it. Now!"

Lights seemed to flicker across the shells that made up the crude figure of the ugly merman. The surface seemed to shake.

"Master, I have it here."

"Then give it to me."

"No – no – not to you. Only to the right one. To a woman. To the Lady of the Lake. To herself."

"She is here. Nimuë, the Lady of the Lake. Now give it up to her."

"Not so. You are on dry land, and I am in the water. She must come and take it. Let her row a boat to the head of the Loch, and I myself will come up from the waters, and give her that sword."

Vivian listened with sinking heart.

"Then I will come with her."

"You will not. If you are in the boat I will drown you, and her also, and the sword will go back. She must come alone. I will not harm her."

"You had better not harm her, or by the Name I have invoked, I will send the Fires Below to destroy your secret place. By THAT NAME, submit to me now, and yield up the sword to the Lady of the Lake."

"I will do so, but she must come *now* – not wait for daylight – and she must come alone. I have said all that I will say." And the voice was suddenly still.

"Depart in peace," came Merlin's voice, as he stepped backwards out of the little chamber, and closed the door. He held the candle above Vivian's head.

"Dare you, my dear—? Of course I know you dare, but God forgive me for sending you into this!"

They went quietly and quickly up the stone passages and stairs. It was night above, but the faint moonlight seemed dazzling after the darkness below. Merlin led the way down to the water's edge.

The roses, exuberant over the edge of the loch, gave a sweet scent as they passed. Vivian breathed it deeply and gratefully after the dead smells of the underground place. It was a still and overcast summer night, the moon's light diffused behind the clouds, showing the paleness of the gleaming water between the dark trees. Vivian fetched out the little light boat they used for crossing the lake, and seated herself in it, facing astern to row. With a few strokes she sent the boat moving smoothly away from the steps – she had to look backwards over her shoulder to see the way she was going, but after one look she kept her eyes fixed on the tall white form of Merlin as he receded from her.

The loch opened into the sea, and all its seaward extent was tidal – the water rose and fell, not much but perceptibly, once a day, making a fresh interchange between fresh and salt water; but at the head of the loch was a stagnant creek, where all the floating rubbish and refuse drifted and stayed, and sank into the black ooze. Dark, sour plants grew there, and yew trees and black alders overhung the bank; by the day the air was full of pestilent midges, and at night, stealthy creatures moved between the dark bank and the dark waters. No one went there. But that was where Vivian had to row her boat, softly in the darkness.

Presently she could feel the boat scraping upon the mud and the mess of broken branches below. She shipped her oars.

"Shony," she called, her heart beating.

From the bottom of the boat, where Merlin had placed it for her, she picked up a black cockerel, bound up by the feet. A knife lay beside it. Shuddering, she lifted the bird by the feet, hanging its head over the side of the boat, and with one single movement sliced off the cockerel's head. The bird struggled and fluttered horribly in its dead reflex, and the blood gushed out into the lake. She held it for a minute, and then dropped it into the bloodstained water.

"Shony," she cried again. And then she saw him.

In the dim light he came up out of the water – first a smooth hump, like a thick black bubble, then it became his head, then head and shoulders – greenish-black, streaming wet, the long slimy hair straight down over the featureless face, but through it a gleam of cruel eyes and teeth – and with it came a horrible stench of fermenting vapours.

"Now," she said, trying to keep her voice from shaking, "Shony, give me the sword Caliburn."

The apparition spoke from under its streeling hair.

"Are you Nimuë, the Lady of the Lake?"

"I am Nimuë, the Lady of the Lake."

"Then come and get it!" – and the creature gave a harsh, barking laugh, and held out, with black shrivelled hands, a long sheath-like shape. Still seated in the boat she turned half round, keeping a grip on the thwart with her left hand, and with her right reached out and seized the shape. Undoubtedly it was a scabbard, which she held by the point end. Shony, laughing again, pulled back and wrenched out the sword within, leaving her with the empty scabbard in her hand.

"There it is then – swim for it if you want it!" he croaked, and flung the sword, in a shining arc, far over his head and out into the lake. Then the baleful presence was gone down into the water.

After a minute's utter dismay and loss, Vivian grasped the scabbard in both hands – an ancient thing it was, slippery with the mud of the sea bottom, but discernible as a piece of leather-work overlaid with bronze – more by touch than by sight she made out the runes on it, and pronounced the words written there, aloud over the water. Then pointing the open end of the scabbard out over the water, she spoke the sword's name.

"Caliburn – the blade of destiny. Arthur's time has come, I Nimuë, Lady of the Lake, call you – in the NAME which Merlin has pronounced."

The words echoed off the surface of the water.

And the sword floated and came towards her, skimming over the surface as if a lodestone drew it. Straight to the boat's side and she put out her hand into the water (still afraid of feeling Shony's slimy touch) and drew it in and placed it back in the scabbard. Then all in one movement, not staying for one instant, she picked up the oars and struck out for the Island, all the time, as she rowed, her eyes on the dark creek where Shony had risen. But when she turned her head to see her way, there was Merlin, white and straight on the steps, and his arms received her safely, and took the sword from her. His hand traced the banishing pentagram against the black water of the other shore.

"By the grace of the Mighty One," he said, "Arthur has a sword."

In the firelit hall of the little castle, they examined the sword. Merlin laid it on the table, having first carefully placed a cloth lest any fragments of the scabbard should fall. For both sword and scabbard were blackened, and corroded, and crumbling. With great care, Merlin drew the sword from the scabbard, and laid it by its side. The blade appeared to be of some dark brown metal; the hilt was of a strangely beautiful shape, cross-formed but curving; the quillets, or side-pieces, were outlined in garnets and agates, which even in its decayed state caught the light; and the pommel was one round, perfect, white crystal, now clouded grey like the moon. The scabbard, now that the blade was withdrawn, was ready to fall to pieces, for it was made of many small metal parts, set upon leather, now shrivelled and cracking like so much rotten wood. He lit a lamp, such as they had, and looked long at it.

"This is very old," he said, "Oh, very, very old. It was made in the days when all weapons were made of bronze, and yet it is not all of bronze. It is made of a subtle mixture of all the seven metals: gold, silver, iron, quicksilver, tin, copper and lead, by an art long ago lost to man. I knew the man who made it – in another life. By strange and cunning ways he made it – some of the metals he melted and mangled, others he interwove into the inscription on the blade – there were other skills as well. So, by the interchanging of the natures of the seven metals, a powerful magic was put upon the sword. Although it was made in the days when men had only bronze, yet there is a power upon it that could cut through steel. Therefore it is called "Caliburn" – "Cut-Steel" in one of the old languages. I know a man that can restore it, both blade, hilt and scabbard. Tomorrow I will go in search of him."

"But Shony?" Vivian said, still trembling.

"Ah, Shony cannot harm you now. You have paid him his proper due, and he dare not ask for more. Never fear Shony."

"All the same, I'll keep away from the head of the loch, and – can we seal up that place underground?"

"We will do so, dear. But have no fear! From now onward, Arthur's star is rising."

THE RITE OF CHALLENGE

PETER VALENTINE TIMLETT

Peter Valentine Timlett (b. 1933) erstwhile student of the occult, is the author of the Seedbearers trilogy: The Seedbearers *(1974),* The Power of the Serpent *(1976) and* The Twilight of the Serpent *(1977). These novels follow the fall and destruction of Atlantis and the survival of the Atlanteans in ancient Britain. The story includes a more authentic rationale for the construction of Stonehenge than Geoffrey of Monmouth's. Timlett has also written an extensive Athurian novel,* Merlin and the Sword of Avalon, *published in 2003. It is a detailed consideration of the mystical aspects of Merlin and his influence upon the Arthurian age. Along with Mary Stewart's trilogy and Nikolai Tolstoy's* The Coming of the King *it is the most complete work written about Merlin. Judge for yourself. The following is an extract from the novel which has been completely revised and expanded by Timlett to form a self-standing novella. Timlett's other Athurian novels may be found at www.imaginationforum.co.uk*

A dark barge towed by twelve bearded and fierce-eyed knights crept down the west coast of Britain from Caledonia in the far north. Down through the Sound of Jura it came, hugging the coast which knew of ancient Ardifuir, Duntroon, and Druim an Duin, down past Kintyre and across open sea past dour Crammag Head and down past the dreaded Isle of Manx to skirt the coast of Wales. Ever southward it grimly came, past the Isle of Mona which bore within its bosom the whitened bones of slaughtered Druids, round Bardsley Isle and across the fierce-watered bay to South Wales, round Skomer Island, and at last turned east into the wide channel whose southern shore was the wild sea marshes of south-west Britain, and nosed cautiously up the sluggish marsh river that led to Wearyall Hill, the outlying buttress of Avalon near to Glastonbury Tor.

For the most part of that wild journey a woman had stood grimly silent in the prow of the boat, her black hair and cloak blowing about her as the wind sought to drag her into the merciless sea. When the barge finally came to the jetty at Ponter's Ball she bade the sailor-knights make camp and wait for her return. She then left them and skirted Wearyall Hill until she came to the ancient chalybeate well close to Glastonbury Tor. There, in a cluster of crude stone-built hermit cells, she greeted the twelve who had waited her coming.

"Welcome, Mistress," said the senior of the twelve priestesses. "You have come more quickly than we had dared hoped."

The woman nodded. "Fortunately I was able to leave immediately. Is the prisoner still safely held?"

The priestess nodded towards one of the cells. "Naked and bound, but we have neither questioned him further, nor harmed him, but waited your coming."

"Good." The woman stared briefly at the sky. "It will be dark soon. Light the fire. We will talk after supper."

As the priestesses busied themselves with their task the woman walked across to the well. She cast forth her cloak and other garments and stood for a moment staring down at the reflection of her nakedness. Then from her bull's-hide carrying-bag she drew forth a heavy, all-enveloping, midnight blue ritual robe and drew it about herself. She then took out a garter of red eastern silk, a symbol recognized throughout the land as the insignia of a high priestess of the Elder Faith, and fastened it around her left thigh beneath her robe. This finished she joined her companions at supper. During the meal itself she forbade any serious talk but when they had finished she commanded the fire to be replenished, and the flames leapt high in the evening darkness and illuminated the thirteen faces in an eerie glow.

"Firstly, what news of the black-robes?"

On the far side of the Tor was the tiny Christian church of Glastonbury whose priests wore robes of black. For nearly five centuries an uneasy truce had existed between the newly emerged church of Christ and the ancient Elder Faith, both of whom were determined to hold their place at Glastonbury. The enmity would have been expressed openly long ago had it not been for the fact that of the five centuries four had been lived under Roman occupation when both Christian and Elder Faith alike had to pay lip service to Mithraism and the Roman Imperial Cult. But on the departure of the Romans the enforced truce had been growing more and more uneasy.

The senior priestess spread her hands. "Nothing has changed since your last visit. They go about their business and studiously ignore us. It is as though they seek to convince themselves that we do not even exist."

"And the prisoner?"

"In a ritual some weeks ago, using the well as a mirror, we saw him coming in this direction. We recognized him as Silvanus from Merlin's group, and since you asked us to keep watch on the wizard's activities in this area we watched him closely."

"And?"

The woman shrugged. "Priests after the Order of Merlin are difficult to read, as you know. We knew that he was coming to see the Christian monks but we could not tell why. His purpose was deliberately hidden within his mind, and guarded. On the grounds that only the valuable is specially guarded we decided to detain him and put him to the question. He arrived two days later and we were able to capture him before he could announce his arrival."

"So the monks do not know we have him?"

"Correct. Obviously his arrival was not expected."

"Did you seek outside help to capture him?"

"No, he is no longer young and we are twelve."

The High Priestess relaxed a trifle and even smiled. "You have done well," she said softly. "So what is the purpose of his visit?"

The woman hesitated. The others of the twelve stared at the ground and could not meet their Mistress's eyes. "We do not know," the senior confessed.

The High Priestess frowned. "You put the question?" she said sharply.

"Repeatedly – for a week – but he remained obdurate, and so we sent for you."

The Pythoness pursed her lips thoughtfully. There were few indeed who could withstand the ritual question of the Elder Faith. "From whence does he draw his strength to resist?" she said suddenly.

The twelve visibly relaxed. They had feared her anger but were now reassured. "We do not know but we suspect from Merlin himself."

"Does the wizard know we have him?"

"No, not as far as we can tell."

The High Priestess was silent, lost in thought. "You have done well," she said suddenly. "No blame attaches to you. Tend the fire and bring the prisoner here."

Two of the juniors leapt to feed the fire and stir it into fresh life, and the senior priestess and two others went to fetch the prisoner.

Naked, his hands tied behind him, Silvanus was brought stumbling into the firelight. His grey, almost white, hair was matted and his wrists were dark with dried blood from the chafing of the thongs.

"Unbind him, bring water to bathe him, and give him his cloak," the Pythoness commanded.

The senior priestess slipped a knife beneath the thongs and cut them, and Silvanus grimaced with pain as the blood began to circulate. The two juniors brought a bowl and washed his face and wrists, and covered his nakedness with his robe. All this while Silvanus kept his eyes lowered and uttered no word.

"My handmaidens were over-zealous in their guardianship," the High Priestess said, "but we intend you no cruelty. All we need to know, indeed will know, is the purpose of your visit."

The monk did not reply and still kept his eyes lowered. Ever since his capture he had known that his best chance lay in saying as little as possible, and above all not to look at their eyes. He had not even given a single glance to this new arrival, but there was something in the voice that was familiar.

"You may safely look upon my face, Silvanus," the voice said. "I will not beguile you. I have other methods of making men talk."

Curiosity, and the utter confidence in the woman's voice, made him risk a glance, and as he recognized her his heart sank.

"Yes, you are right," said the woman, "I am Morgan le Fay, wife to King Uryens of Gore, half-sister to King Arthur, Pythoness in the Order of Theutates, High Priestess of the Elder Faith. Many a time when I was a girl I sat in your teaching circle to learn your philosophies, but it has been many a year since Morgan le Fay graced your meetings."

"Witch-Queen!" he burst out. "You will learn naught from me. I will die first!"

The woman shrugged. "Having knowledge of the Elder Faith you know perfectly well that one of senior grade such as myself can read the mind of a man as his soul leaves his body at the moment of death. So you can either tell me now and live, or reveal it all as you die. It matters little to me either way."

Silvanus knew that such a thing was certainly claimed, but he had no way of knowing whether it was true or merely a ploy to frighten the gullible. "I do not believe that you can do any such thing," he said slowly.

Morgan le Fay smiled a horribly ominous smile. "You now have the opportunity to put the matter to the test," she said confidently. She rose and gathered her robe about her. "You have the night hours to ponder your dilemma. At dawn you will tell me, one way or the other." She turned to the senior priestess. "Bind him and guard him. Have all in readiness an hour before dawn," and she turned and walked away into the darkness towards the hermit cells.

Within minutes the fire had been doused and Silvanus had been returned, bound, to his cell, two priestesses set to guard his door, and all grew quiet, a silence wherein his thoughts raced frantically seeking an avenue of escape from his predicament.

The matter was simple of definition but not so simple of solution. If Morgan le Fay could really do what she claimed then there was no point in throwing his life away. He might just as well tell her voluntarily and live. But could she? He had no fear of death itself, though he was apprehensive about the manner of dying, but neither was he prepared to end this incarnation without good reason.

Time and again during that long night he tried to contact Merlin on the inner, but failed. Presumably he and Arthur were already on their way to Avalon, travelling at night, in which case it was nearly too late for Morgan le Fay to interfere anyway.

The settlement was astir before first light. They came for him a little before dawn and took him to the chalybeate well at the foot of the Tor; the well whose iron-laden waters rose from the oldest rocks and whose flow never altered, summer or winter, flood or drought. On the surface of the water, and indeed below it, floated a misty mass of rare red water-fungus that some said gave rise to the name of Blood Spring, though others said the name sprang from a darker, more gruesome reason.

Above the well-head was built a chamber of great blocks of stone such as were used at Stonehenge, the great stone circle some few miles away. A single block of stone formed three sides of the well-mouth, a stone whose masonry filled with the closest accuracy, true square and perfectly perpendicular. The round well-shaft led down some fifteen feet to a bed of blue lias gravel through which rose the powerful and never-failing spring.

Opening out of the well-shaft just below the surface of the water was a large chamber of finely hewn stone. In one wall of that chamber was a recess in which a man could just stand. To one side was a sluice which enabled the water to be run off so that the inner chamber could be entered. When the sluice was closed the well would rapidly refill so that once more the chamber and its recess would be below the surface. Into the wall of the recess were set four huge iron staples to which a man or a woman might be bound. As Silvanus was brought to the well he could see that the sluice was open and that the well was rapidly emptying.

"As you probably know," said Morgan le Fay calmly, "at dawn today, Midsummer's Day, as the sun rounds the shoulder of the Tor a shaft of light shines straight into that inner chamber. Let us hope that it illumines your mind as well as your face so that you may make the right decision."

"And if my decision does not please you," said Silvanus drily, "no doubt you will then close the sluice and allow the well to refill with me still bound within it."

The High Priestess shrugged. "The choice is yours." She looked at him with some compassion. "You are a good man, Silvanus, one who is sympathetic to the Elder Faith, and I do not wish to see you die. Tell me the purpose of your visit, and live." He shook his head and said nothing. Morgan le Fay sighed and turned to her senior priestess. "Take him and tie him in the recess."

The well was now empty and the priestess led their prisoner down the rough-hewn ancient stone steps into the well itself, into the inner chamber, and fastened him by thongs to the iron staples in the recess. This done she looked up at Morgan le Fay for instructions. The High Priestess glanced at the sky. "Don't be a martyr, Silvanus. Tell me now before it is too late," but again Silvanus shook his head.

Morgan le Fay reluctantly gave the sign and the senior priestess pulled on the lever that let fall the wedge-shaped piece of stone that blocked the sluice-way, and immediately the water began to rise. Hastily the senior and two junior priestesses scrambled up the stone steps to safety, the hems of their robes already soaking wet from the rapidly rising water. As they scrambled clear the sun's first ray lanced from behind the Tor and struck into the inner chamber and into the recess and lit up the monk's face, but the water was already swirling about his knees and rapidly rising higher.

Silvanus had made his decision some time earlier. Merlin must already be well into his dawn ritual at Avalon. By delaying matters until now he had successfully thwarted the Witch-Queen's plans. It was now time to save himself.

"Very well, Witch-Queen," he cried out, the water now to his waist. "You win. I will tell you all you wish to know. Release me!"

Morgan le Fay leant over the well-head. "Tell me first, then I will release you," she said calmly.

"It will be too late."

"Then die, monk," she said.

The water was now halfway between his waist and his chest. "All right, all right. I came to inform the Christian monks that Merlin is planning to place the sword Excalibur in the hand of the Christian king, Arthur Pendragon."

So that was it! She leaned further over. "When?"

"Today – now – at dawn. You are already too late, Witch-Queen. Now I hold you to your vow. Release me."

For a fleeting moment Morgan le Fay was tempted to let him drown, but she rose and said: "Release him, quickly."

Three of the junior priestesses plunged into the well and swam into the inner chamber to the recess. By the time they arrived the water was up above his chest and reaching for his chin. Two of them dived beneath the surface to free the thongs that bound his ankles, and the third trod water and supported his head.

"Quickly!" he gasped. "Quickly!" He felt one leg go free but the other remained fast. The swirling water reached above his chin and he strained his head upwards.

"Take a deep breath," the priestess cried, "and don't struggle."

One of the two below the surface came up for air. "We cannot free the other one!" she gasped. "The thongs are too tight."

In that moment Silvanus took a last despairing breath as the water came up over his mouth and covered his head completely, reaching the roof of the actual recess itself and within a foot of the ceiling of the entire inner chamber.

The second priestess came up for air and handed the knife to the first who now dived below the surface again. The body of the monk was thrashing wildly, making it difficult for her to reach the trapped leg. Several of the thongs were cut but there were still two to go. Suddenly the body gave a final lunge and then was still. Frantically she sawed at the thongs regardless of whether she was cutting through flesh or not, and at last they parted. She gathered her feet to the floor and thrust herself to the surface.

In the meantime the other two priestesses had released his arms but in his last paroxysm he had grasped hold of both of them and they could not release his grip no matter how frantically they struggled. By this time the water had reached so high that as the third priestess shot to the surface she smashed her head a sickening blow against the rock ceiling of the inner chamber, driving the breath from her body. In her dazed state she tried to breathe but took in more water than air, and in those last few seconds the water reached the ceiling. She turned towards the opening of the large chamber and the open surface beyond but the struggling group were in her way, and as she tried to squeeze past she became caught up in their furious thrashing. For a further full half-minute the four danced a macabre dance of death below the surface – and then they danced no more.

At the well-head the others had seen the terrible predicament but had not dared at first to interfere lest they add to the confusion. When the surfacing priestess smashed her head Morgan le Fay snapped her fingers and three more priestesses plunged into the well, but by the time they had dived and reached the inner chamber the group had already become still. But there was still time to save them if they could get them out quickly.

The doomed four were now floating hard up against the rough-hewn ceiling of the inner chamber, and as the rescuers tried to pull them those few precious feet to the open surface their robes caught against spurs of rock and held them fast. Furiously the rescuers struggled to free them, but then had to desist and return for air. Three times they dived and three times they struggled but all to no avail, and Morgan le Fay signalled for them to abandon the attempt lest they too became snagged, and they came dripping out of the well, their robes flattened wetly against their bodies, their hair matted into thick wet ropes.

The well was now full and the water was quiet and peaceful. Fifteen feet below the surface they could see see the bed of blue lias gravel, and in the water and on the surface lazily floated the misty clouds of red water-fungus. The sun's rays, stronger now, lanced into the inner chamber and lit up with motes of gold the four who now floated serenely, clasped together below the surface of Chalybeate Well.

Merlin deplored the enmity between the old and the new, for to him Christianity was but an extension of the Elder Faith into the new age, both were stretches of the same river of spiritual thought and thus sprang from the same source and were headed in the same direction for the same reason. But each considered the other to be a blasphemy and in such a climate it was impossible for the seed of co-operation to take root.

The great symbol of the Christian Church at Glastonbury was the Cup that Joseph had brought to Britain, the very one that Jesus had used at the last meal with his disciples. Monks then hid it deep within the Tor in a secret chamber guarded by three pure maidens to prevent it being profaned by the Romans or blasphemed by the Elder Faith. This was the Cup of Avalon.

The great symbol of the Elder Faith at Glastonbury was the sword of Excalibur, secreted below the lake in the halls of the Lady of Avalon, the Lady of the Lake, and there it was guarded by the three goddess-queens. This was the Sword of Avalon.

Merlin was neither Christian nor of the Elder Faith, for he was of that company that transcends both and knew that both the Sword and the Cup were archetypal symbols of the same spiritual power and that if they could be used in conjunction with one another then the way could be gloriously opened for the Most Holy Grail of God to descend to earth and remain there permanently for all men to see for all time. But the Elder Faith was dying because it refused to recognize and accept the Cup, and Christianity was already sterile and would last but a short impotent time in the evolution of mankind because it refused to accept and wield the Sword.

"What *is* Avalon?" said Arthur as he and Merlin rode through the night. "It is a strange place. I have been there several times and each time my dreams are filled with the most curious imagery."

Merlin patted the horse's neck as he rode. "It is the holiest earth in Britain. It is many things to many different types of soul. It is that part of your realm where the veil to the inner is thinnest. There has not been a phase in the spiritual story of our race that did not involve Glastonbury and Avalon. Its influence twines like a golden thread throughout the story of these islands. Even the most ancient of the folk-stories, those that are full of deep spiritual significance to those whose hearts are tuned to their key, are linked to the spiritual pulse of Glastonbury."

"But what of Stonehenge? I thought that was the sacred centre of our race."

Merlin nodded. "Cor Gaur, to give it its ancient time, has been the sacred centre of the outward religious life of the people for some four thousand years, but Glastonbury was always its secret heart. One of the secret Green Roads of the soul, the mystic way, leads through the hidden door of Avalon into a land known only to the eye of vision. There is the Avalon of the Cup and the Avalon of the Sword, as I have told you, but this mystic way is known as the Avalon of the Heart. This mystic Avalon lives her hidden life, invisible save to those who have the key to the gates of vision. Glastonbury is a gateway to the unseen. It has been a holy place from time immemorial, and to this day it sends its ancient call into the heart of the race it guards, and still we answer to its inner voice. Since you are the true king, Arthur, then your heart already knows all there is to know of Avalon."

The trackway wound its ancient way, worn by wandering feet and hooves that sought firm ground. In the east the sky had already begun to lighten as king and priest breasted the last barrier of hills and descended towards the alluvial salt-marshes. Ahead of them the wide flat land stretched out in the early grey light to the sea beyond, hidden in the mist of distance. One side of the plain was guarded by the Polden Hills, and the other by the Mendips. Here and there on the plain itself rose sudden hills called "islands" by the local peasantry, for much of the plain was often below water. As Merlin and Arthur descended the slopes to the lower levels they could see that in the middle of the plain rose the grey pyramidal hill crowned by a tower, the Tor of Glastonbury itself, and beside the Tor rose the dreaming green hill called Chalice Hill, and beyond it, they knew, lay the magical Lake of Avalon.

"The Christian monks have their settlement at the foot of the Tor," said Merlin, "and Morgan le Fay, your half-sister, leads a cult of the Elder Faith upon the slopes of Chalice Hill, but we will avoid both until we have done what we came to do."

They descended onto the plain and picked their way along the ancient trackway that wound across the salt-marsh levels, skirting both Tor and Chalice Hill until they came to the reed-banked Lake of Avalon beyond. There they wearily tethered their horses and waited by the water's edge for the coming of the sun.

"It seems deserted," said Arthur presently.

Merlin smiled. "The Lady of the Lake knows that we are here, and why. She will come to us."

Arthur said nothing but his heart was full of doubt. He tethered his horse and sat on the grassy bank, his back propped against a wind-stunted bush. His body shivered in the chill air, and he pulled his cloak more closely around him. There were times when he wished himself back with his foster-father Sir Hector, to be as he used to be, a carefree youth, squire to his foster-brother Sir Kay. As king he had expected to be in command of all around him, but with this priestly magic and ritual he felt as a dry leaf blown by strange winds into strange lands that he did not understand.

He sighed and closed his eyes for a few moments and saw himself as he had been at the castle, working in the kitchen, tending the horses in the great stables, or polishing Kay's armour. As a boy he had been at everyone's beck and call from dawn to dusk – aye, and beyond dusk when the great hall rang to the drunken laughter of visiting knights and squires when he had been required to serve mead to the great table – and yet in a strange way he had felt in control of his life and had understood his small world and his place in it. But then had come that fateful journey to London when magic had first invaded his soul. There were times when he bitterly regretted ever having seen that sword in the stone. From that moment his life had become no longer his own.

He opened his eyes, and as the sun rounded the Tor behind them and lit up the surface of the lake he saw to his astonishment that across his lap lay a finely jewelled sword and scabbard of surpassing beauty and craftsmanship. He took the hilt in his hand and immediately he was as one with the sword and felt its strength flowing through him. He looked up. "But what is . . ." he began, but Merlin was already gathering his horse.

"Come," said the wizard sternly, "we may not delay."

"But the sword? What . . ."

"That," said Merlin, springing to saddle with an agility surprising in one no longer young, "is Excalibur. It is given into your keeping for a little while by the Lady of the Lake," and he swung the horse's head and cantered away.

Arthur struggled to his feet and girdled the scabbard about his waist. For a moment he paused, gazing at the sword, hefting its balance and scything it around him in a practice swing – and nodded in wonder. As king he had fine swords a-plenty, but nothing like this – a king among swords, fit for a king.

By the time he gathered his horse Merlin was already a good distance away and Arthur galloped after him. "Merlin," he shouted, "Merlin!" but the wizard paid no heed. Arthur urged his horse to full gallop and came up behind the wizard and pulled to a stop in a flurry of stamping hooves. "MERLIN!" he bellowed with as much authority as the tone of his young voice could muster.

The wizard pulled his horse around and stood waiting, eyeing the youth. For some long moments king and wizard stared at each other, and then Merlin smiled inwardly and came trotting back. "Sometimes," said Arthur coldly, "you forget who is king here."

Merlin shook his head. "I forget nothing. What is it you wish of me . . . your majesty?"

Arthur patted Excalibur's hilt. "Explain."

Merlin shrugged. "What profit me to explain what you already know?"

"I know nothing," snapped Arthur. "I closed my eyes for a few moments and when I opened them the sword was there – explain."

"They were merely your physical eyes, your outer eyes. You must learn, Arthur, to hear with your inner ears and see with your inner eyes, for there are things to hear and see that are not of this plane of existence."

Arthur sighed irritably. "I have but one pair of eyes and they saw nothing."

The wizard brought his horse closer to Arthur's. "If you cannot veil the physical world with your own effort of will then close your outer eyes so that you may see," and he reached across and drew his hand down the young king's eyes, closing the lids. "Picture the scene as you saw it, Arthur," he whispered. "See the lake, see the reeds bend and sway in the dawn wind. Do you see, Arthur, do you see?"

And Arthur strove to see through the mist that veiled the inner. "Yes, yes, I seem to see – the lake, the water rippling."

"Do you not see the dark barge creeping towards us, towards the shore where we stood?"

"Yes, yes," whispered Arthur, "I see it," and for a moment he really did see the barge, dark and sombre, gliding silently towards them.

"Whom do you see in the barge, Arthur?" said Merlin softly. "How many?" He saw the young king's brow furrow as he strained to see. "Relax, do not strain – let the images rise, do not force them. Relax, Arthur, and tell me what you see."

"There are two figures in the barge," and Merlin's countenance darkened sadly, "no, three, I see three," and Merlin nodded.

"Describe them," he said sternly.

"They are dark," whispered Arthur, "three dark queens."

"Why do you call them queenly?"

"Because they wear ancient crowns upon their heads."

Merlin nodded, knowing now that Arthur saw truly. "Aye, ancient crowns they are, older then time, for they are the three goddess-queens who guard Excalibur." He placed his hands on either side of the king's head. "Look now beyond the queens, do you not see, there across the water, towards the middle of the lake – do you see? – do you see the arm rising from the water?"

And Arthur stared, and in wonderment saw that an arm clad in white samite had risen above the surface, the hand grasping a finely jewelled sword and scabbard.

"And that is the sword Excalibur," said Merlin calmly, "and here comes the Lady of the Lake and her sister queens," and Arthur saw the dark barge come to rest gently on the reedy bank where the mortal men were waiting, and saw three dark queens come ashore.

"Tell me what you see," whispered Merlin.

"I see . . . I see one of the queens step forward and address you in sombre tones."

"And what does she say?"

And Arthur, king, sat on his horse, his eyes tight shut, and saw and heard the matters that few dream of. "She says 'Who is this who crosses the portal of the mysteries of Avalon?' "

"And what do I reply?"

And in his vision Arthur saw Merlin bow low and answer in grave manner. "One who seeks the sword Excalibur in order to be the better equipped to serve God and Man."

"By what right does that one so seek?"

"By right of being the true Christian king of all Britain."

"And who shall vouch that his claim is true and just?"

Then Arthur saw the wizard draw himself up and his voice was vibrantly powerful. "I, Merlin, Arch-Mage of all Britain, Priest after the Order of Melchisadek, do so solemnly swear and vouch that his claim is true and just."

The Lady of the Lake acknowledged Merlin with a slight bow and turned to the fearful king. "Arthur Pendragon," the vision said, "why do you seek to know the Sword?"

And Arthur tore his eyes open. "No, no!" he cried, and his horse shied and skittered away. "These things are images, dreams, strange scenes that wizards put in the minds of men for their own purpose."

Merlin came after him and gentled the nervous horse – and king. "It is not so," he said softly. "You shied away because you suddenly saw that it was so, that what you saw was true. Shhhhh, hush now, close your eyes, Arthur Pendragon, and see again. Look now and see yourself as you answered the Lady of the Lake," and Merlin closed the king's eyes.

And Arthur saw the Lady and heard again the question, and saw himself answer her. "I desire to know in order to serve," he whispered, using ritual words that he had not known he knew.

"Worthily answered, King of all Britain," said the goddess-queen, "you may safely embark upon the Lake of Avalon, for where the heart is pure and single no evil can enter. Excalibur shall be yours for a time if you vow that it shall be returned from whence it came when you can no longer wield it truly, or no longer wield it at all in earthly life."

"I do so swear," said Arthur.

"Then take thou my barge and cross the waters of Avalon and take the most ancient of swords."

Again Arthur wrenched his eyes open. "It is not true. This way lies madness – madness!"

Merlin gripped him fiercely. "It is the truest experience of your life. Do not deny it – do not deny. Do you not remember how I led you onto the barge and sat you in the prow? And do you not remember how the vessel moved across the water under its own power and drew alongside the mysterious arm?"

"And I drew back in fear," whispered Arthur. "I remember, I remember. You laid your hand on my shoulder and I took heart and grasped the sword and the scabbard firmly, and immediately the strange and eerie arm, clad in white samite, disappeared below the surface, and the barge returned gently to the shore."

"And we stepped ashore together, you and I, king and priest," said Merlin, "but there was no sign of the three dark queens, and when we turned we saw that the barge too had vanished, leaving the lake as still and empty as when we had first arrived. Do you remember, Arthur, do you remember?"

And Arthur Pendragon, King of All Britain, remembered and his heart was uplifted by joy and wonderment.

"But *was* it real?" said Arthur. "Or was it a dream?"

Merlin grunted sourly as they turned the horses away. "Sometimes I despair of this world."

Arthur brought his horse alongside as they made their way up the trackway. "Well, was it?"

"Each plane has its own reality," grunted Merlin. "To the uninitiated it is the physical plane that seems to be the only reality, all else being a dream, imagination, a vision. When he moves upon another plane then the events that occur on that plane are equally real to him. Only when he returns to the physical plane does he begin to doubt and question the reality of his experience."

"Yes, but . . ."

"No, no 'buts'," said Merlin firmly. "Did you not see the dark queens? Did you not hear the Lady of the Lake when she spoke to you? Did you not smell the incense that lingered on the barge? Did you not taste the salt spray that blew in your face as we moved across the water? And did you not feel the touch of that mysterious hand as you took the sword from its grasp?"

"Yes, all these things seemed real at the time."

"Then they *were* real. If a watcher had been hidden in the reeds he would have seen us arrive, sit for a few minutes, and then ride away again. He would not have seen the three queens, the barge, or the arm, and certainly he wouldn't have seen us cross the water."

"He would have seen the sword," said Arthur shrewdly.

Merlin nodded. "Yes, he would have seen the sword in your hand as you stood at the water's edge and perhaps wondered why he had not noticed it before – that is all." He shook his head warningly. "Try not to reject the reality of this experience, or you will be the poorer for its loss."

"But I am not a priest or a wizard," said Arthur. "To me these things are dreams, visions. It is natural that I should question their reality."

"Very well," said Merlin sourly, "if you must question the truest experience of your life, then ask yourself this – if it was all unreal, untrue, mere imagination, then where did the sword come from?" and he spurred his horse and cantered on ahead.

As Merlin breasted the rise he saw on a further ridge at the foot of Chalice Hill a figure standing motionless. Although it was too far for recognition the wizard knew that it was Morgan le Fay, looking for him, and that she was the bearer of no good tidings. He waited for Arthur to catch up with him and then said shortly: "I must leave you for a while. Return to Cadbury. I will join you there as soon as I can."

Arthur looked at the distant figure but asked no questions. He had had enough of the priestly world for one day. "So be it, then," he said, and with the wondrous sword and scabbard at his waist he rode away.

Merlin waited until he was out of sight and then set his horse towards the distant ridge. When he drew near he reined the horse and leant forward in the saddle. "Greetings, Morgan le Fay," he said grimly. "Our paths have crossed many times on the inner, but this is the first that we have met on the outer for twenty years, not since a small girl threatened me in the courtyard of Cadbury Castle."

"Things might have been different, Merlin, had you heeded me then," she retorted.

"Perhaps. Who can say? But what of now? I fear you have grim news for me, if I read the signs correctly."

She looked up at him and nodded. "Though not of my choosing, or my intent, nevertheless I am responsible for the death of your priest, Silvanus, and of three of my own priestesses," and she told him of the tragically ironic accident that had occurred at dawn that very morning.

When she had finished they both remained silent for some time. Presently Merlin said heavily: "You owe a debt to the souls of the dead which you will have to repay in full measure, Morgan le Fay, and your act of murder is also a crime against the life-force itself."

"Not so. I acknowledge the debt to those who died, but not to the life-force, for their deaths were an accident, not murder, indeed three gave their lives in an attempt to rescue the priest."

"Yes, to rescue him from the predicament in which you had placed him."

"His obstinacy was of his own choosing. Tragically he delayed too long. I am the cause of his death but I am not guilty of his murder."

Merlin shook his head grimly. "You argue a fine point, Morgan le Fay, but it is not for me to lay judgement upon you. You are answerable to the One, as indeed are we all, and you will find that the scales will not fall in your favour. But that judgement will come to you at another time and in another place. In the meantime I have lost a friend and a priest, and you have lost three priestesses, four lives utterly wasted for no good reason, for even if you had known of my purpose there was nothing that you could have done about it."

"Don't underestimate my powers, Merlin."

"I don't, but neither do I rate them as highly as you do yourself. You are the High Priestess of the Elder Faith and as such you owe allegiance to the Lady of the Lake whose powers are infinitely greater than yours. I can scarce believe that you would have had the temerity to oppose your own goddess in this matter. Since the Lady of Avalon was willing to hand the Sword to Arthur what on earth do you think you could have done to stop it?"

"I only know this, Merlin," said Morgan le Fay calmly, "that I will do anything and everything in my small power to prevent the Sword remaining in the hands of a Christian king, for to me it is the ultimate blasphemy. We of the Elder Faith have served the One faithfully for thousands of years, but these so-called Christians call us evil and thus blaspheme the Great One. I wish that they could be plunged into the fires of the inner earth and be thus wiped from the face of the earth and all their blasphemy with them."

"Do you then oppose the Christ?" cried Merlin.

"No. He is of the Star Logoi, a great one from beyond the Veils of Limitless Light. I do not oppose the manifestation of the One, but I do oppose with all my being these so-called Christians who are no true servants of the Christ."

They both fell silent for some time, and then presently Merlin said quietly and sadly: "For all my perception I can see no resolution to this confrontation. The Cup and the Sword should be as one, for Christianity and the Elder Faith are but two different parts of the same path to the Throne of God. But one will destroy the other and in so doing the destroyer will sow the seeds of its own ultimate destruction. There is opportunity *now* for the Most Holy Grail of God to descend into earth itself for all men to behold and be uplifted by its glory, but it cannot descend while such confrontation exists."

Morgan le Fay shook her head. "You are wrong, Merlin. The time has not yet come for such a manifestation, and you blaspheme in attempting to bring it to pass before its allotted time."

"There is no allotted time. All that is needed is for men's hearts to cry out for its coming and it will surely come, but for as long as you and those like you oppose its coming then it will not be perceived except by the very few. Your intentions are good, Morgan le Fay, for you do but seek to serve the One, but you are so very wrong in your assessment of these matters."

The High Priestess gathered her robe more closely about her. "It is not I who is wrong, Merlin, but yourself, but you are too blind to see it."

Merlin sighed wearily knowing that nothing more could be said, and an hour later he rode away with the body of Silvanus across his saddle, leaving Morgan le Fay to bury her own dead.

A full moon rode high over Chalice Hill. A few wisps of wind-driven cloud scurried across its face. Dark trees rustled their leaves and black bushes crouched in the shadows. The night was foreboding, ominous, the shadows made more menacing by contrast to the silver radiance of the moon.

In the hollow at the foot of the hill Morgan le Fay, robed in blue, stood with arms upraised to the night sky. Her eyes were closed and her lips moved soundlessly. For a long time she remained thus, unmoving save for the silent words of prayer, and then she lowered her arms, made a deep obeisance to the moon, and then moved gracefully and soft-footed to the ancient and most holy well that nestled at the foot of the sacred hill.

Another woman rose to meet her, she too robed as a priestess. The High Priestess knelt by the rim of the well and motioned the woman to kneel by her side. Together, silently they gazed into the still waters which reflected the Queen herself and the far-riding stars, but the two priestesses did not see the earthly images for with an ease born of long practice they had adjusted their eyes slightly out of focus, creating as it were a cloudy mirror in which the inner images could rise.

"O Queen of the Night," murmured the High Priestess, "Daughter of the Lord of All, hearken to me, thy Priestess in Earth. Uncloud my eyes that I may see the foul deed of thine enemies that I may strike them down in the midst of their blasphemy."

The cloudy surface moved as though stirred from within. Morgan le Fay bent a little closer, her brow furrowed to a frown at what she saw. The day was clear and bright, the sky a summer blue, the trees and grass that vivid green that comes from bursting life, and there in the image, winding its way between the hills, was an ancient trackway along which a score of men and six great horses struggled with some monstrous object in tow. Two knights directed the labours and by their helms she knew them to be from the court of King Lodegreaunce, long-time friend to King Arthur. The peasants struggled and cursed, and the horses' flanks steamed with sweat, their eyes rolling and their nostrils flaring. Strapped and roped to the great cart was a massive wooden flat-topped contraption which she could not at first identify, and then when recognition finally dawned the vision faded and vanished.

For a long time the two priestesses remained silent. "What did you see?" said the second woman.

The High Priestess looked at her sharply and then pursed her lips in dissatisfaction. "I would have been happier had you seen it too, then I would have known that it was a true vision."

"But what was it you saw?"

"Two of King Lodegreaunce's knights and a score of peasants and six great horses struggling along a trackway with a monstrous great round table."

"Ah," said her companion, "I know about that table. I heard the tale from a master craftsman who was but lately at Castle

Camylarde. Lodegreaunce commissioned the table as a wedding gift to Arthur. It is similar to one that used to belong to Arthur's father, Uthr Pendragon, before it was destroyed by fire. The present one, I hear, is based on the same design but far larger."

"But why round?"

The woman shrugged. "Who knows? The original table was designed by Merlin, I believe, who also suggested this present model to Lodegreaunce."

Morgan le Fay frowned even more deeply. "If that arch-fiend is involved then there is mischief afoot that bodes no good for the Elder Faith. But why . . ." She broke off sharply as a sudden revelation burst within her mind. "Oh, of course – the Table Round!"

"The what?"

Morgan le Fay snapped her fingers impatiently. "The Round Table of Glory. It was a concept known to the early Druids though there were no rituals based on it. It was considered far too early in human evolution to attempt to manifest such a concept in earth, even by having a physical plane symbol of it." She rose to her feet suddenly. "The Company of Just Men Made Perfect. It is one of the great inner plane symbols of a time in the far future when mankind will have reached the zenith of its evolution. At each seat at that table is a figure representing the perfected example of each type of human soul, and collectively they represent the totality of God's concept of humanity. And from the centre of that table springs the living essence of the godhead itself, overflowing a great golden chalice from which all at the Table may drink to thus achieve fusion with the living God – and another name for that Chalice is the Holy Grail. *Now* I understand the whole of Merlin's dream, the fool!"

"*I* don't understand."

"It is simple. He is having that great round table installed at Camelot, and at it will sit the very best of Arthur's knights. Because it is a symbol of the inner Table he hopes that the knights will be inspired to emulate the great archetypal figures who sit at the real Table on the inner. If contact is established between symbol and that which it symbolizes then the power will begin to flow, and if that flow is maintained without corruption it is possible that the Holy Grail itself will be drawn into the earth sphere and will appear in the centre of the Round Table for all the knights to see. The fool, he knows not the power with which he meddles!"

Her companion frowned. "Forgive me, Mistress, but it sounds like a worthy enough ambition to me."

Morgan le Fay grunted irritably. "You of all people, Netzah, should understand the danger, for you are responsible for the ritual training of all the junior seeresses and priestesses in the Elder Faith. You know better than most that a priestess, or a priest for that matter, makes of herself a vessel to hold the power that she invokes, and if she is untrained or too junior for that particular ritual then the flow of power will shatter the vessel."

"Ah, yes, sometimes death, though more usually a form of insanity."

"Yes, insanity, that type of insanity that causes a schism between the soul and the personality. Imagine the power involved in an invocation of the Round Table of Glory and the Holy Grail itself – it would be colossal – and those invoking the power would not be doing so for themselves alone. If I know Merlin he will attempt to use the Knights of the Round Table as being representative of the entire British race, perhaps even of the whole of humanity. He is certainly vain enough for that."

"And if it fails?"

Morgan le Fay shook her head. "I shudder to think. A form of racial insanity probably, a gigantic abyss between the Group Soul and the Group Mind of the race. Such a failure could herald a dark age that could last for centuries. It might even permanently prevent the Holy Grail from ever being able to manifest in earth. It is too early, far too early. The irresponsible old fool may cause untold damage to the spiritual life of the race."

"But what can we do?"

"In the long term, sow the seeds of corruption amongst Arthur's knights to prevent any contact between the symbol and the inner reality. Bring about the death of Arthur, or get rid of Merlin, or both."

"And in the short term?"

"Destroy that table, for without the symbol the work cannot even begin."

"How?"

Morgan le Fay mused for a moment. "Are you familiar with the rituals of the Tenth and Fourteenth Keys?"

The woman frowned. "To invoke wrath and violence, yes, but those rituals are rarely used."

"There is rarely good purpose, but there is now. If we are not too late we must destroy the table before it reaches Camelot."

"Hold that wheel! Hold the wheel, you dolt!" Sir Agrinore spurred his horse back up the treacherous slope. "Put a stone under it. Quickly, quickly! Oh God, it's going to run away! Hold the wheel!"

One wheel spinning free, the other momentarily lodged against a stone, the whole contraption, the giant cart and its cumbersome load, lurched sickeningly and threatened to veer off the track and plunge out of control down the side of the hill. Two peasants leapt to the wheel and hung on, and two more grabbed a large stone from the side of the trackway and raced to place it beneath the wheel. The horses reared in panic, their eyes rolling and their nostrils flaring. The man who had been holding the head of the lead horse was lifted clear off his feet and dragged into the mêlée of the panic-stricken animals. Those who were desperately clinging onto the cart felt their feet sliding away from them in the mud. Two of them left the cart and raced to control the horses. One of them scrambled between the animals to rescue his friend. A flailing hoof smashed his head and he disappeared beneath the jumble of thrashing bodies. With the stone in place the cart came to a sudden halt and the horses began to quieten down.

Sir Margryn galloped back up the slope. "What happened?" he shouted.

"Nearly went over the side," said Agrinore. "It's safe enough now but I don't think we should attempt any more today. These fellows are exhausted."

"We can't camp on the side of a hill."

"And we can't go on either. If we do the whole thing will likely capsize. We might damage the table or lose it altogether, and you know what Lodegreaunce would say about that."

"God's curse on this wretched table!"

"Aye," said Agrinore gloomily, "So it would seem."

The two knights looked at the sky. Though barely mid-afternoon in early summer the day was already dark and chill. The rain teemed down, the fierce wind driving it almost horizontally into their faces. Margryn threw up his hands in exasperation. "Bright sunshine not two hours ago, and now this. It's not natural."

Agrinore shivered and looked about him cautiously. "I saw three ravens this morning. I knew it was an ill day." He patted his horse's neck soothingly. "This is Merlin's table, and anything to do with that hell-spawned wizard bodes no good for the likes of you and I."

"It's the wrong shape," said Margryn. "It's not natural for a table to be round." He looked again to the sky. "I say again that God's curse is on this thing, and on us for being involved with it."

"What do you suggest?"

"What else," said Margryn irritably, "except to get this cursed thing to Camelot as quickly as possible and so be rid of it."

At that moment one of the peasants came up to them, a huge fellow naked to the waist, by trade a stone-mason. His skin glistened with water and his eyes glowed redly with a sullen anger. "Aidan, the ostler, is dead," he growled briefly. "Head cracked open like an egg. Hywell's leg is broken."

The two knights looked at each other. "And there's the proof," said Margryn grimly. "One death already. How many more to come?"

Agrinore looked up the hill. "We'll camp under that over-hanging bluff. That'll shelter us from the worst of the rain." He turned to the stone-mason. "When the horses are tethered and fed you can bury the fellow."

"There's no priest to say the words," said the man sullenly.

"Priest? What d'you want a priest for, he's only an ostler. Just dig a hole and drop him in. Don't waste my time with stupid questions." He turned back to Margryn. "Did you hear that? A priest he wants, as if he was a knight. By God he'll be asking for a tomb next."

It took them an hour to unhitch the six great draft-horses and get them up the slope to shelter, and to prepare such evening meal as they could in the rain-sodden conditions. After the meal the peasant buried the dead ostler on the hill-side and marked the place with a pile of stones.

"Do you see that?" said Agrinore. "A cairn no less. Lode-greaunce has been too easy with these dolts."

The huge stone-mason, Glyndwr by name, came up to the two knights. "We have set Hywell's leg as best we can," he growled, "but we are no healers."

Agrinore shrugged. "He will have to take his chance. He can travel on the cart."

"It will kill him," the man said simply. "It is still five days to Camelot, even if we make good time. As well as the broken bone the leg is split open from knee to crotch. If we do not get him to a healer the rotting disease will set in and he will die."

"I can't help that. It was his own fault. He was careless."

"He was trying to rescue his friend."

"That makes him a fool as well as careless."

"There is a village near here, and the cell of a hermit healer. If we leave at first light six of us could get him there in a litter by noon and be back here by mid-afternoon."

"And waste a day? Certainly not. He can take his chance on the cart."

"But he will die."

Agrinore sprang to his feet. "Great God in heaven, must I stand and argue with a peasant dolt like you! He will take his chance on the cart, I say, or stay here and rot, and if I hear one more word of argument you will taste my sword. Now get about your business and don't bother me again."

Glyndwr's eyes glowed redly but he turned and strode back to his companions. Agrinore slumped back to the ground and leant back against a rock. "All this and insolent peasants too."

Margryn looked at his friend closely. "You are nervous. I have never heard you speak like that before, particularly to one like Glyndwr. He's the finest stone-mason for three days' march in any direction. I always thought you liked him."

"As a stone-mason, yes, but a few words of praise have obviously gone to his head if he thinks he can argue with his betters."

"Hywell is a friend of his. We have been a week on this journey already, and another week to go. One more day will not matter and it might give a chance for the weather to clear."

"What weather? Did you not say yourself that this was God's curse? Make up your mind what you believe – bad weather or a curse."

"Aye, God's curse, and likely to grow heavier if we leave a man to die."

Agrinore sprang to his feet again. "By all the demons in hell," he shouted, his face suddenly flushed to a blotched and ugly red, "are *you* going to argue as well!" He glared down at his friend. "The table is going to Camelot without a moment's delay despite every insolent peasant and stupid knight in Christendom, and if you wish to say otherwise then say it with your sword!"

For a brief second Margryn's face was a portrait of astonishment, but then the expression changed to a sudden and uncontrollable laughter. "I have tolerated your peevishness enough for one day," he roared, struggling to his feet and pulling at his sword.

Agrinore raised his own sword high above his head in a two-handed grip, and before Margryn was even properly on his feet he swung the blade down with all his strength and split his companion's head from crown to neck as easily as slicing an apple in half. For one half-second of horrible suspense the mutilated body remained on its feet and then crashed heavily down amongst the rocks.

The peasants sat huddled round their fire. For a long time Agrinore remained unmoving, and then he turned and saw the men staring at him. "And the same goes for anyone else who wishes to argue," he growled, and sheathing his sword he stamped angrily away to the far end of the rock shelf.

At first the men were silent, heads down, not looking at one another. Presently one of them stirred the fire to new life. "Sir Margryn was right," he said shortly. "There's an evil curse on this work."

One of the men, older than the others, pulled his sodden tunic more closely around his body and spread his hands to the fire. "I have known Agrinore and Margryn since they were infants together. I was a body servant to Agrinore's father. Never have I heard them speak even an angry word to each other until today."

"It was a cowardly blow," said one of the others.

Suddenly Glyndwr held up his hand for silence, his head cocked to one side. His sharp ear had caught a sound from further down the hill, and as he rose to his feet they saw a rider coming up the slope towards them.

"It's Merlin," one of them whispered.

"It's his doing," whispered another angrily. "Wherever there is evil, there is Merlin."

The Arch-Mage reined his horse and slid from the saddle. He stared at the sky, the rain beating on his face and beard, knowing that elsewhere not half a mile thence in any direction the sun still shone in a bright summer's evening. He looked back down the trackway to where the cart and its contents lay drunkenly askew, and at the muddy hoofmarks where the great horses had been brought up the slope to shelter.

He then walked a few paces and stared down at the mutilated body of Sir Margryn, then moved along the rock shelf to where Sir Agrinore lay. The sword was by its owner's side and Merlin saw the blood on its blade. The knight made no move nor any sound. The wizard gently grasped the shoulder and turned him over, and from behind him a dozen voices gasped their surprise. Sir Agrinore was quite dead. There was no mark of a wound, but the face was mottled to so dark a colour as to be almost black. The eyes were wide open and staring, the expression frozen into a glaze of terror, the mouth horribly agape.

Merlin sighed and closed the dead knight's eyes. He then retraced his steps back along the rock shelf, noting the mound and cairn of stones where Aidan the ostler had been buried, and then knelt by the injured Hywell and examined the broken and split leg.

Finally he walked over to the group by the fire. "All this," he said grimly, "has been the work of sorcery. Don't blame Sir Agrinore for he was its victim, but now there will be no further incident." He pointed to the injured man. "Your friend must be taken to a healer, and soon."

Glyndwr stepped forward. "I tried to tell Sir Agrinore that there is a hermit healer near here. Six of us could have him there by noon tomorrow and be back here by mid-afternoon."

"Good, then I leave that to you, Glyndwr. We will wait your return, and then we must continue the journey, but this time I will travel with you. That table must reach Camelot. More than you can appreciate rests upon its doing so."

For the next hour they busied themselves digging a double grave for Agrinore and Margryn. "They were friends together in life," said Merlin, "and so shall it be in death." Then all save Merlin rolled out their skins of fur and under a rapidly darkening sky fell thankfully to sleep.

Merlin retired to the other end of the natural shelf and sat down with his back to the rock wall. He shut his eyes and slipped from his body and rose high above the scene. For half a mile around, centred on the human encampment, was a great black writing cloud of evil-looking vapour. The disgusting cloud trailed off to a thin black line that disappeared into the distance to the south-west. He rose a little higher and moved to each cardinal point in turn, drawing a line of force. He then, as it were, drew the ends together and set up a vibration that soon broke up the foul vapour into smaller and smaller pockets of miasma until only the thin black line was left.

Then, grimly, he faced the south-west and projected his image into the distance to the point where the vapour had originated, and there, below him, in the great stone circle, was the source of their trouble. Cor Gaur, Stonehenge: the circle had borne many a name in its four-thousand-year history, but ever it had been the great sacred centre of the Elder Faith. Ignored to their detriment by the Christian monks, feared by them if the truth were known, it was the very centre of the great web of force that radiated throughout the land. Other stone circles there were, smaller circles, hundreds of them, who knows but perhaps a thousand spread throughout the petty kingdoms that would be Arthur's realm, all part of the great web of the earth-force that found its upwelling source at Cor Gaur. And there below him, at the centre of the web, spinning her magic, was Morgan le Fay and her twelve witch-maidens, grouped around the Hele stone, chanting one of the Elder rites.

His image drifted lower, and lower still, until it came to hover at the eastern portal. The thin line of black vapour still writhed upwards from the centre of the Hele stone, but Merlin snuffed it out at its source, and as he did so the chanting stopped and all was still.

Morgan le Fay remained still, every sense both inner and outer alert, seeking the intruder. The priestesses also neither moved nor spoke, their eyes on her – waiting. Never in her lifetime had any outsider ever broken into any ritual of hers, though occasionally a few had tried in the early years of her stewardship. She moved to the East and faced outwards, and then, pointing her long taloned finger at shoulder height in front of her, arm rigidly straight, she drew the five-pointed pentacle and uttered the ritual phrase of sealing in a vibrantly powerful voice – and then, with arms and finger still extended, she moved deosil round the Hele stone to each of the cardinal points in turn, South, West, and finally the Northern portal, effectively sealing the area. Then, returning to the centre, to the Hele stone, she intoned: "The Seals are in place. The Officers and members will keep vigil until the High Priestess returns." She then spread herself full length up the stone and with an ease born of long practice she slipped from her body and rose on the inner.

Grim-faced, Merlin waited her coming, and when she stood before him, cold-eyed yet regal and powerful, he said sternly: "You are a stubborn woman, Morgan le Fay, with a closed mind. Two more have died because of your plots and I say that enough is enough."

She smiled thinly, her expression as grim as his. "If we continue as we are then many more will die before this struggle is over, but the root cause of it lies with you, Merlin, not I."

He sighed heavily. "I wish you no ill whatsoever, indeed it is my fervent wish that you abandon your opposition and join us in the quest of the Holy Grail."

"That I will never do for the reasons I have already stated. I will continue to oppose you with every breath in my body and with every power at my disposal, for I believe with all my heart and mind that what you are doing constitutes the most colossal blunder in the whole history of human endeavour. You will fail of your ambition, Merlin, and your failure is likely to plunge humanity into a Dark Age that will cause an abyss between God and Man so vast that it may never be bridged again."

"If that were true," said Merlin, "then I would be the most damned human soul of all time."

"And there at last you speak the truth," she retorted. "But I, too, say enough is enough. Let there be an ending to our struggle. I challenge you, Merlin, by that most ancient of rituals – The Rite of Challenge. Do you accept?"

Merlin was taken aback. It was an ancient rite of the Elder Faith known only in legend. He looked across at the defiant figure before him. "That Challenge has not been issued for untold centuries," he said slowly. "Legend has it that it was only ever issued when it was believed that the High Priestess had succumbed to being a pawn of the dark forces. It was always issued by the priestess next in order of seniority. It was a challenge as to who should control the Elder Faith – the loser would withdraw from office – or die."

"How appropriate to our present situation," she said coldly.

"The terms?"

She leaned forward. "If I win – and I will win, Merlin – then you will abandon your plans to manifest the Grail in Earth, you will return Excalibur to the Lady of the Lake, and you will withdraw all support from Arthur and let him find his own level."

"And if you lose?" said the Arch-Mage softly.

She shrugged. "I will not lose, but for the record let it be known that if you triumph then I will withdraw all opposition to your plans and allow the Elder Faith to gradually sink into oblivion to henceforth be known only in the race-memory."

Merlin nodded to himself. It was a tempting offer. His work so far had involved the coarse and vulgar path of blood and battles, but soon now, when the Round Table was established with the Knights of Honour in their places, then would begin the Quest of the Grail and matters would march with a more delicate balance. It would be of immense value to have nullified the opposition of the Elder Faith; indeed, without Morgan le Fay it might even be possible to bring Christianity and the Elder Faith together into a synthesis – the old and the new together – the Cup and Sword as one. Oh, what mystical magic could then be woven.

"I accept," he said simply.

Morgan le Fay could scarce believe it, but quickly she said: "As challenger I have the right to choose the place of the testing."

Merlin nodded. "So be it – choose."

She smiled her dark smile and said softly: "Then I choose the dark caverns beyond and below the realm of the Dweller on the Threshold." She threw up her arms in triumph. "There you will find me, Merlin – if you dare!" and she became as a mist, a wraith, a cloud of smoke that streamed downwards, downwards to the utter depths of existence.

Merlin hovered for a few minutes, and then gathering himself together he turned and created in his imagination the scene that he would need. On his left the bare rock of the mountain slopes gave way to patches of thin tough grass and wild flowers, and on his right the precipitous cliff gradually levelled out as he came down into a great plain. The beaten track ran on before him across the plain and ahead he could see the great Tau arch and beside it the moon and sickle symbol of Saturn, the Great One of the Night of Time – and there, just before the arch, set to one side of the path, was the Well.

On the well-head itself, wedged into the great stones, was an iron bowl and a skin of freshly drawn water. Merlin took the cup and raised it to his lips. The water was fresh and pure and tasted as nectar. Then he mounted the well and made his way down inside. The great slabs of stone that formed the stairway spiralled steeply downwards. There was no guard-rail, only the stygian emptiness of the central void of the well. The walls were dank and dripped moisture. Soon it was too dark to see the steps and he could only continue by sliding his foot forward to find the next stair. But below him he began to see a dim yellow light and he knew that he had passed the first of the tests. Emboldened now he stepped with more confidence, downwards, ever downwards, until he came to a tunnel opening to his left – and there, set high on the wall, was an ancient carved cresset containing a lighted flambeau. He took it and held it high, and by its light he could see below him the tunnel that led off to his left down to the cavern of the Dweller.

All was as it should be. He had trodden this ritual path many, many times and knew that the Witch-Queen would try no tricks this side of the abyss. Stepping firmly he descended and turned into the tunnel. The walls were dank and dripped moisture, and his footfall echoed eerily.

The tunnel twisted and turned its serpentine path, but ever downwards, sometimes broad and high-ceilinged, and sometimes narrow, barely the width of a man so that he had to turn and shuffle sideways, the rock ceiling pressing down upon him. Then, at last, the tunnel opened out into a vast cavern a hundred feet wide, or more, split by a gigantic chasm left to right, and from the abyss there came the far-off sounds of rumbling and groaning as though the rock itself was in such pain.

Across the abyss there stretched a rock bridge to the far side, and there in the centre of the bridge was a swirling, writhing cloud of dark grey vapour waiting to take form, the Dweller on the Threshold, the symbol of the atavistic levels far below even the subconscious; levels of consciousness that were formed and used long aeons ago in the dawn of human evolution.

Formless now – waiting – it needed but one pace upon the rocky span to give the vapour form and life, to cause it to shape itself into a symbol, often a dread symbol, to reflect the state of the subconscious of the one who would cross, the embodiment of all good and all evil committed through all the incarnations of that soul to date.

Dread deeds, evil deeds, lie in the past of all who take the human form, and for those who refuse to accept the truth of their own history the shape that stands athwart the bridge becomes the living essence of all that they fear, the embodiment of terror, the horror of their own inner self – and for them the Dweller is a dread figure to be feared; for them there is no path across the bridge.

Merlin had long since accepted and absorbed the Dweller, and for him the swirling shape was usually of a young boy at the threshold, an eager apprentice, a bold youth at the gate of learning, or some similar symbol – but now, as he advanced upon the bridge the swirling grey most rose up high above him, and in its depth there formed two eyes of red, baleful and terrible, and above those eyes there gradually formed a hideous face, hooknosed, pocked and scarred, the skin riven by open sores that wept a foul-smelling ooze.

The Arch-Mage stepped onto the rock-bridge and then stood grimly, feet apart, his staff in his left hand, planted firmly, his right arm extended, finger pointing commandingly at the foul apparition before him. "Get thee gone," he cried, "back to whatever foul lair whelped thee. Thou hast no authority to be at this place, nor power to wreak thy will."

The figure swirled, the grey mist grew dark, and the red eyes glinted evilly. "I am thy Dweller," it hissed. "If thou wouldst secure thy safety thou shouldst pay me homage."

Merlin shook his head. "Thou art no Dweller, and in claiming thus thou dost blaspheme. Get thee gone, I say," and firmly he advanced, pace by pace, his staff thrust before him as a sword.

The miasmatic creature from the abyss, given hideous life by Morgan le Fay, rose high above him, its jaws agape, its fangs dripping a foul and corrosive ooze that hissed and babbled as it fell to the rocky floor. A great screeching roar filled the air and the creature gathered itself and flung itself upon the tiny figure below.

As the foul mist fell on him Merlin could feel the hot stench of its breath, but he stood firm. The creature, he knew, was from a lower plane, dredged up by the Witch-Queen, and it had no reality upon *this* plane unless his own fear gave it form. With the foul vapour swirling all about him, Merlin's words rang with power throughout the cavern: "Get thee gone, I say. Thou hast no dominion here!" and the creature's roar rose to a screech, its hideous features dissolving, the vapour shrinking, falling away until it was all quite gone.

The Arch-Mage took a further pace upon the bridge, and there was the true Dweller in the shape of an eager boy, a youth, and Merlin bowed in acknowledgement and passed in safety across the abyss. But his heart was grim, troubled even. Never had he known anyone, Mage or Pythoness, that could supplant the Dweller with a form of their own summoning. Morgan le Fay was a mistress of her art, a more powerful priestess than any he had hitherto encountered.

The tunnel through the solid rock led to the left and sloped downwards, ever downwards to the lower levels, twisting and turning so that Merlin lost all sense of direction. Here there were cressets every few yards, and finally, by the light of their flambeaux, Merlin saw that the tunnel ended by an iron-studded oaken door. There were no signs or sygils upon the door, no runes or symbols of any kind – and the door stood ajar.

Merlin stood for a moment upon its threshold, and then resolutely stepped within, and found himself in a bleak and windswept forest. Winter gripped the land. The snow lay deep and flurries of it blew in his face – and then with a shock he realized that he was loping swiftly through the trees, a wolf, running with others in a pack hunt. Only when he tried to veer away did he realize that he was not the wolf, merely within it, his consciousness sharing the body but unable to affect its actions. He could feel the mind of the wolf, primitive, instinct-driven, but he could neither contact nor influence it. Helplessly he stared from its eyes and saw that there ahead of them the great elk that they had driven through the forest had now run into deep snow and had turned at bay, exhausted – and the pack fell on the great animal and began tearing it to pieces, Merlin's wolf no less than the others.

He could feel his own mind slipping, fading, of his own node of awareness becoming that of the wolf's. He resisted it, summoning all his power, for he knew that if he became that wolf there was the danger that he would not be able to return and would run as a wolf for the rest of his incarnation and all his plans for the Holy Grail would come to naught. How Morgan le Fay had brought this about he did not know, and as he fought to stay as Merlin within the wolf he was grimly appalled that obviously there was much about the Elder Faith rituals that he did not know – and for a fleeting moment the thought that he might lose the challenge sped through his mind.

Tearing the flesh of the great elk in a frenzy of feeding, lips drooling saliva, there issued from his throat a savage bestial snarl as he fought for space on the carcass with others of the pack.

Finally, the frenzy abating, many of the wolf-pack, including his own, withdrew and sat nearby licking their front paws and grooming themselves. The snowstorm blew across the desolate landscape, rippling the fur along their backs, but the wolves were full-fed now and if necessary could run for a week before the next meal.

Now that the frenzy was over his own wolf had become aware that something was wrong. It could not reason, could not grasp concepts beyond its own instincts, it knew only that something was wrong, that it was impaired in some way, damaged, and it began to run round in circles, snapping and snarling, trying to bite itself.

The other wolves gathered swiftly around, and one big male edged forward, snarling, cautious, and then suddenly dropped into a menacing crouch. His own wolf, realizing its danger but not knowing why, turned and ran from the clearing as swiftly as only a wolf can run. There was no baying behind them, for a wolf does not waste breath on a hunt, just a soft swishing sound as the entire pack gave silent chase through the trees. His own wolf had perhaps ten yards' start, but it was not enough, and when it streamed into another clearing it spun round, its back to a huge tree, snarling hideously, ready to do battle, but the pack did not wait for the ritual encircling but just fell on it, this thing that looked like one of theirs but wasn't – and as his consciousness burst clear Merlin knew now what it felt like to be torn to pieces, to have a predator tearing your flesh, its snout burrowing into your still living entrails.

There then came a fleeting moment when Merlin felt that he had triumphed and that Morgan le Fay had lost, for he had retained his own awareness throughout – but the scene shimmered, melted, changed . . .

. . . the shaman danced in the centre of the circle of swaying bodies, arms whirling, feet stamping, his jackal head-dress swaying. The drums were pounding, the flames of the fire leaping high into the night sky. The whole village was there, the tribal elders, the goatherds, the hunters, even the women were allowed to watch, for this was the dance of the jackal, and everyone swayed to the rhythm, hypnotized, transported. Faster and faster the drums beat, changing their rhythm to an incessant pounding, and the shaman whirled faster and faster, his head thrown back, his eyes glazed, and from his throat there rose the spine-tingling high-pitched screams of a jackal in rut. Again and again he screamed, whirling his body in a frenzied ecstasy, and then fell to the ground inert as a log.

Merlin was within the body of a young girl, a nubile girl, her body swaying, stamping, her mouth agape, her breasts glistening with sweat, her loins on fire. What little primitive intelligence she had was set aside in the frenzy of the dance. Merlin could feel the passion sweeping her, the desire, and despite himself he began to share her excitement, for desire is of both mind and body.

Then from beyond the firelight he came leaping towards her, the one the girl wanted. He grabbed her hand and together they leaped over the heads of the swaying watchers into the clearing, feet stamping, head swaying, her loins thrust forward, wanting him, demanding him. Then the leaping figure before them was no longer a man but a jackal, and the girl turned, her fur glistening, her haunches ready for him, her jaws dripping the rutting saliva – and Merlin's mind within the girl-jackal was ablaze with lust, desiring, wanting no less than she. A lifetime of celibacy, of suppression, was exacting its price, and Merlin felt himself slipping, wanting to abandon all control, eager to experience all that he had denied himself – but some part of him, that part of him trained during life after life as an initiate of the mysteries, that part strained to hold him back, fighting the power of the rut that would engulf him – and as the man-jackal leaped upon them the consciousness that was Merlin burst from the girl's body, and he found himself full-length on the cave floor back across the rock-bridge, scrabbling at the stone, gasping and crying, his body afire.

Gradually, through the tremors that racked him, he became aware of a pair of sandalled feet in front of him and the hem of a robe, and looking up he saw Morgan le Fay standing over him. "Well, well," she sneered, "the Arch-Mage of all Britain, trembling like a lust-sick boy!" He scrambled to his feet, unable for the moment to speak at all. "By the Lady," she cried, "I do believe that if I were to cast aside my robe you would leap upon me here and now. There is your Grail, Merlin, the Grail before which all men worship."

"Do not blaspheme!" he cried. "You failed of the Challenge for I did not submit, I did not merge with your foul creations."

She paused for a moment. "Yes," she said slowly, "I did not win, but then neither did I lose. Acknowledge, Merlin, as an initiate of the truth, acknowledge that you did not win either."

He remembered, and in remembering he knew that he had won the first encounter with the wolf, but with the second he felt the fire of passion that had swept through him, the desire he could still feel even now, and knew that he had not won.

He sighed. "I acknowledge," he admitted.

She moved away along the tunnel to the Well. "You should be grateful, Merlin, for I have shown you your weakness." She turned back for a moment. "The time will come when Arthur must stand alone, as all men must when they face the truth of themselves, and at that time the mantle of Arch-Mage of All Britain will be withdrawn from you by those on the inner." She smiled. "Then, Merlin, wizard, then will come one who will renew the fires you just have experienced, and they will be your death," and she turned and vanished into the tunnel opening.

Merlin remained for a moment, and on the rock-bridge his Dweller reappeared and smiled at him compassionately, and Merlin sighed and turned away. Wearily he retraced his steps from the Well and closed the ritual and returned to his body.

It was dark now. The rain had stopped and the sky was rapidly clearing of cloud. Merlin gathered his own skins of fur and wrapped them around him. The Table at least would get to Camelot and the Knights of Honour would be established. As to the rest . . . For a moment he stared towards the eastern sky. That was a prophecy if ever he had heard one. Was that his fate? Would it be lust that would cause his death?

He sighed and settled himself down to sleep. Let come what may. He would deal with matters as they arose – that's all any man or wizard could do.

But that girl. The way she . . . forget it, sleep, Merlin, you old goat, sleep.

MERLIN'S DARK MIRROR

PHYLLIS ANN KARR

Although her husband continues to urge her to write "serious" novels, it is to our delight that Phyllis Ann Karr (b. 1944) still produces the occasional Arthurian short story. In fact she generously provided me with three manuscripts to choose from, each as good as the other, which allowed me some flexibility in minimizing any overlap between themes and incidents. Phyllis's best-known Arthurian work is the delightful murder mystery The Idylls of the Queen *(1982), and she has also written* The King Arthur Companion *(1983).*

Merlin told his dark mirror: "Last night our young king had a troubling dream. He woke from it shrieking like a little child."

The mage cast his message in as favorable an aspect as possible. Arthur had heard his counsel through and seemingly been much swayed; but at last he had commanded even Merlin, with shouts and tears, to leave him pondering alone for a while. Pondering and, the necromancer feared, praying. The boy suffered from an inconvenient milky streak.

Merlin could scry in any clear or shiny surface. Even now he had a basin of water ready at his elbow for watching his boy king. But the dark mirror – a hand's-breadth of polished jet enframed in gold – was meant for no ordinary scrying. Wherever Merlin went, whether alone or with the king's court, his first act after choosing the place for his secret study was to install the dark mirror in a shrine of honor where it sat with a black candle and a little incense burning before it, untouched by the surrounding clutter, while the mage watched and waited, hoping to see his father's face therein, like a hermit hoping someday to see the face of Christ appear in sacred host or chalice.

Merlin's father was the Devil. All knew how Merlin had been engendered. Most folk supposed that, in so far as he adhered to any creed, it was a personal blending of Christianity and the Old Religion. Few, if any, guessed how loyally the mage kept faith with his true sire.

Yet perhaps even his great faith was imperfect. Today, as always, the mirror remained dark.

Sighing, the mage turned to his basin and spoke the words that would let him see young Arthur's dream for himself. Laying the king's description together with the motions and twitching of the imagery, Merlin was able not only to see, but almost to feel, what the dreamer had felt.

The water's surface showed the scene as through the dreamer's vision, as if a lad newly burgeoned from childhood to manhood gazed down along his own proud and lusty young body as it lay naked on a silken-covered bed. But something moved at the right side of the belly. A tiny pink thing wiggled up, like the tip of a finger protruding out of the warm flesh. For a moment he watched it with a calm and delightful quickening of the heart, wondering if God was treating him as another Adam, fashioning him a bedfellow out of one of his own ribs. He felt just enough pain to know that whatever the thing was, it was indeed piercing through his own skin.

But something was not as it should have been. His bedfellow was not to become one whom he would have chosen. Like the bulbous root of some scabrous plant, the pink worm crawled forth, waving its little head, and somehow grew within the space of a few heartbeats to monstrous size – a dragon, a beast with gaping jaws and bulging eyes. It snapped at the king – once, twice, and again. He lay shuddering, unsure whether he were frozen with fear or with some mortal wound. Blood smeared everything in the chamber. Was it his own blood?

The monster reared up, swelled to even greater size, and burst the walls. They lay in ruins about the king's bed, while the sky opened a tempest upon him. By turning his head this way and that, he could see his entire realm of Britain stretching out to every side; and he watched, weeping as the monstrous worm tore through city and hamlet, ravaging everything, dividing the land with raging rivers of blood on which bodies and bits of bodies bobbed like helpless gobbets of foam.

Merlin snapped his fingers to end the review, and sat back. "Yes. The worm was indeed myself. So something in the boy's soul thinks of me as a danger."

Turning, he addressed the dark mirror. "But young Arthur's mind still belongs to me, to mold as Thou, Father, willest. How easily – indeed, how eagerly! – he swallowed my reading of that worm as a child of his own begetting." The mage chuckled. "Even though it seemed to issue from the side of his flank, and in no way from that proud new procreative member. There lay my ally, in the vanity of flowering lust romping like a young stallion among his subjects' fields, taking mare after mare, whether commoner or gentlewoman, wherever his fancy may light, and reading every acceptance, no matter how trembling, as joy in finding herself the king's chosen. Uther's son, indeed!" Merlin had always encouraged that lust, knowing well how much he could make of it. "The difficulty," he mused, "ought to have lain in persuading him that the worm truly issued from his own insides, that it did not simply pierce the skin to wax fat for its work upon his blood. Again, his pride helped me. Each man is the center of his own universe – how much easier for my boy king to see everything as issuing from himself than to see me as anything other than his wise old mentor and truest counselor!

"And see, Father, what I have made of this in Thy honor. Have I not put it into our little king's mind, believing the dragon of his dream to be his own seed, to forestall the danger by putting to death every babe that *might* be of his planting? And how tell them apart?" The mage's heart swelled in happy anticipation of some reward for a task well done. "At most, Arthur has not yet actually lain with more than a score of gentlewomen and perhaps thrice that number of commoners. But he does not remember half, even of the gentlewomen, by name, nor could he recognize most of them by face, scattered as they are throughout his lands and the lands of his allies. Thus, to be safe, he has no other choice but to have them all slain – all children born since first he began to exercise his manhood!"

Merlin laughed aloud for pure joy. "The realm will be rent! Strife and blood unending to Thy honor! Is not the martyrdom of a few years' worth of holy innocents small price to pay for the wars of vengeance they will bring? For war it will be indeed. My arts will keep enough men loyal to Arthur for a balance of forces as long as we desire it, and then, with Thy help, we shall end it by crowning him anew as high king of all Britain.

"And more, far more. Even beyond the short delights of war, we will have our king's very soul! The story of Oedipus he has never heard, but that of King Herod he knows well. What Christian does not? Now see: by slaughtering all these babes, he makes himself a second Herod – he commits the most mortal of mortal sins, saving only that one which cannot be named – he damns his own soul into Thy keeping forever! Father, does this not redeem me for my errors with Le Fay? As soon as Arthur becomes Herod, even if Dame Morgan should succeed in robbing us of his earthly services, we have still gained his soul for Thy eternity!"

Trembling slightly from the pure depth of his emotion, the mage sat back and gazed steadily into his mirror for many minutes. It remained blank, unmoving and seemingly unmoved.

At last, with a sigh, he turned and looked again into his bowl of water. This time, seeing the king's present condition, the mage sprang to his feet in alarm. Arthur had three with him – he must have sent for them in Merlin's absence – his foster-father Sir Ector, foster-brother and seneschal Sir Kay, and, most dangerous of all, his "high saint," Bishop Dubric.

To seek their advice – did the boy think of throwing so grave a matter as this before his full council in open session? Merlin lost no time in making his way back up to the king's chamber.

Pressing through the ever-crowded antechamber, opening the king's door and striding in, as none save Mage Merlin could ever do, he found them arguing hotly. "Father!" thought Merlin. "I should not have left him alone long enough to summon them. At least he is arguing against all three of them – but why, therefore, did he summon them? I give Thee thanks that Arthur's High Saint is never likely to ally his heavenly powers with Dame Morgan's earthly ones."

Even as this thought formed itself in his brain, he heard the bishop urge the boy king, "Before you commit any such sin against God and nature, send for your good queen mother and consult with her."

The queen mother – Ygraine, Morgan's mother as well as Arthur's. "My liege Lord," the necromancer said quickly.

Arthur looked up, relief spreading over his face, which was

haggard beyond its years, as he saw Merlin. "I will speak again with my mage," he declared. "Alone!"

"Artus!" Sir Kay exclaimed. "For the love of God, listen to *us* for once! Send for—"

"I am the king!" Arthur shouted, standing up and hurling his wine goblet across the room to smash against the far wall. "All of you, go! I am the king! I will consult with my great mage! *Alone!* GO!"

Mournfully, old Sir Ector laid one hand on his son Kay's shoulder and drew him from the room. Dubric followed, turning at the door to lock his gaze with that of his adversary.

Merlin did not flinch. Let the high saint suspect what he would, he could prove nothing against the mage.

Sighing, Dubric made the Sign of the Cross at Arthur and Merlin, uttering a prayer that God guide their deliberations. Long practised in outward appearances, Merlin bowed his head, rejecting the blessing only in his heart. Any stranger glancing upon the scene would have named Arthur alone, by the doubt and turmoil in his face, as a potential rebel against his bishop.

Dubric left. At a gesture from Arthur, one of the servitors outside pulled the heavy door shut.

Alone with his mage, the king slumped down into his chair and buried his face in his hands. "Merlin, Merlin, what am I to do? All of them – *all* of them – stand against what you say must be done."

"Beware of Kay. Has he not tried once already to wrest the throne from you, falsely claiming that he himself had drawn the sword from its anvil and rock? And Sir Ector is Kay's father by blood, yours only by fostering."

"No! They love me as true father, true brother. And Bishop Dubric says the sin of it would outweigh any earthly gain."

"Your Grace. For all intents and purposes, our holy bishop dwells already in the other world. He scatters his counsels abroad as if he were advising angels how to prosper among angels, not as if he understood what men must do to survive among men."

"They call me Herod. Merlin, I *am* Herod!"

"My liege, there is no comparison. Herod tried to murder God's son and true anointed, rebelling against God's will. But you are your God's anointed king of Britain, seeking only to preserve your true realm from a serpent of your own illicit begetting."

Folding his arms upon the table, Arthur laid his head down on them and sobbed.

Merlin pressed what he hoped was his best advantage. "Your Grace knows how the realm suffered when folk thought that Uther Pendragon had died without leaving an heir. How they rent the land, every petty king and duke gathering his little alliances and waging war upon all the others, how among them they crushed and bled the common people. Would you wish such another storm to break upon us through your own weakness? To see a child unworthy to have sprung from your loins rise up and attempt to wrest the realm from you, unlawfully, disloyally, and unfilially, loosing upon your hapless realm all the horrors of your evil dream?"

"I will . . . I *will* send for Dame Ygraine!"

"Your mother," said the mage, "is a great and noble lady. But she is still woman, and thinks rather with her heart than with her head."

"I WILL send for my mother! I am the king!"

"We know without summoning her what she will advise, and that her advice, if followed, will result in the dread fulfilment of Your Grace's dream."

"Nevertheless, I *will* send for her."

Seeing the collapse of his plan if the godly Dame Ygraine, who had every reason to hate Mage Merlin, should add her voice to those of Dubric, Ector, and Kay, the necromancer risked a dangerous stroke. "Did she not refuse to hear of harming her babe, even at that time when she mistakenly but sincerely believed you to be the very seed of Hell, the offspring of an incubus? No, my liege, if we would save your realm, we must think as strong and politic statesmen, not as worldly-foolish clerks or weak and heartbound women."

"Leave me," said Arthur. When Merlin did not at once obey him, the young man stood, struck the table with his fist, and repeated his words in a shout. "LEAVE ME! I will weigh these things in my own soul and give you my decision when I am ready. I AM THE KING!"

Merlin left him, returning to the antechamber but waiting apart from Ector, Kay, and Dubric, as befit his ancient, solitary, mystic, and powerful wisdom. From time to time he glanced at them, as if in sad and beneficent patience. The servitors who came to offer refreshment to the other three kept well distant from Mage

Merlin, but he scarcely noticed them, wrapped as he was in his own deep thoughts.

He could not have allowed Dame Ygraine near her son, any more than he could have allowed her youngest daughter Morgan, whose name he had so resplendently blackened at court as to erase – he hoped – his early mistakes of first leaving her alive and later actually teaching her magic in hopes of winning her for his father. Either of those two women, his enemies both, might have guessed that he himself was the serpent of Arthur's dream. He wondered if any of the three men yonder could have suggested it to the boy . . . but Dubric, caught up in the ideals of glorious celibacy, seemed unlikely to see beyond Merlin's own earthier explanation; Dubric would simply have denied that the dream had any true meaning at all, not sought for an alternative explanation to Merlin's. And the necromancer judged that the imaginations of Ector and his son were limited.

Nevertheless, those two had done nothing to stifle their fosterling's troublesome native goodness. Merlin wondered if he might have found a more suitable foster father, some richly wicked baron . . . but such a man might either have struck the child dead in rage or malice, or else hardened him beyond Merlin's own molding. No: already past his prime, Sir Ector had asked few questions; and Arthur had had, not a whole household of healthy Christian brothers and sisters, but only the single foster-sibling to influence his youth. A sheltered, unambitious, and familial upbringing, carefully selected to leave the boy king malleable to Merlin's kindly counsel.

True, Kay had unexpectedly given some slight trouble, whether truly hoping for the crown himself, or longsightedly attempting to shield a silly little brother, or caught in the human muddle of both motivations at once. Merlin had turned that neatly to his advantage, painting young Arthur in saintly colors while at the same time discrediting Kay and limiting his influence over the new king. And, meanwhile, even High Saint Dubric appeared to accept the plausible lie that Merlin had done all this for Arthur's own safety, as if High King Uther had lacked power to protect his own child, as if it were not among the foremost duties of any king to give his people an acknowledged and visible heir, as if a half-grown boy, all unprepared and untaught in kingcraft, could unite a torn realm by being thrust suddenly, by dint of a disputed miracle, upon the throne . . .

For two years and more Merlin had held sway over his new little king. But still he feared that unfortunate milky strain in the lad. Until now, the work of quelling the inevitable rebellions of those who refused to accept Merlin's sword-in-the-stone test and the delights of discovering manhood had occupied Arthur's time. This evil dream provided the necromancer his first real opportunity to test the lad's suitability as a tool for the Devil's work.

Sirs Ector and Kay fretted. High Saint Dubric for the most part kept his eyes closed in prayer. Secretly as anxious as any of them could be, yet allowing none of it to show, Merlin waited, outwardly calm as stone.

At last Arthur shouted for the door to be opened and one page to come in. After a moment, the page returned with a summons for Bishop Dubric, Mage Merlin, Sir Ector, and Sir Kay, those four alone, to enter the king's presence. They went, Merlin smoothly maneuvering himself to take the lead even over Dubric.

If Arthur had looked haggard two hours ago, he looked even more so now – pale, drawn, and old with an age void of wisdom. Merlin's heart rejoiced.

Bishop Dubric opened his mouth, but Arthur raised one hand.

"I am the king," he said. "You are but my advisers. I have already listened to all of you, and I have made my decision, Now hear it in silence.

"For the safety and welfare of my people," the king went on quickly, "the monster of my dream must be destroyed. Yet it is unheard of that a commoner should challenge a throne, so no baby whose mother is below the rank of gentlewoman shall be touched. Also, weighing all your advice, I have decided that we need fear no female, so sons only shall be taken. Thirdly, my dream fell on the eve of May Day, and I interpret this as meaning that I have nothing to fear from any son born in any other month than May. Lastly, this dream must surely refer to a danger already in existence, so no child to be born after the month of May in this present year shall be concerned.

"Thus, every son born during the month of May to any gentlewoman or noblewoman presents the gravest danger to my kingdom. But we ourselves must not shed their blood. Therefore,

I am sending my loyal men out to every corner of the realm to gather up these children. They will all be put into a ship, and it shall be treated as a Ship of Fools, set adrift upon the sea . . . and if, in God's great mercy, it should find its way to any city on the coast, wherein I hold court, the babies shall be my wards and prisoners for the rest of their lives. And if it fails to find port, may God have mercy on their poor little souls."

"God have mercy upon *thy* soul!" cried Bishop Dubric. "For the moment you issue any such foul command, you risk your own eternal damnation."

Strangely calm in his grief, the young man gazed back at the bishop. "I have already risked it. Knowing that you would still raise your protests, I have sent the order secretly by my loyal knight Sir Ulfius, through secret passages. On the first day of June, holy Father, I will shrive myself and attempt to cleanse my soul with whatever penances you think good. But the people of my realm must be spared the horrors my dream warned me of."

By the first day of June, Merlin comforted himself, the realm would already be in revolt, suffering some of those very horrors, and Arthur laying aside his promise of confession and penance in the press of putting down that new rebellion. Nevertheless, the mage knew his victory for partial at best. As soon as he decently could, he retired from the royal presence to seek his own secret chamber.

There, closeted once again with the dark mirror, he sought out how to make the best of matters. "Even as our Divine Enemy must make use of imperfect human clay, Father, so must Thou. In large part, I have failed. The lad has excluded as many as he could find excuses to exclude, and he has given all the rest some very slight chance. This chance I can destroy with a word to Sir Ulfius, my tool since Uther's days. He will soon see the need for holes in the hull of Arthur's Ship of Fools. But Arthur's own intention gives them a chance.

"Yet for all that he has made himself Herod in his own eyes, as in the eyes of every good Christian in his realm, even of those who remain loyal to him. There is still hope that I can do somewhat with this boy to Thy honor.

"And, while he knows the story of Herod, he does not know that of Oedipus. I will take steps at once to ensure that at least one child survives the shipwreck to come. The latest child born to Morgawse, King Lot's wife . . . Yes, perfect! Arthur may have fathered it as easily as Lot, and Dame Morgawse is Morgan le Fay's own sister and therefore Arthur's, though neither of them knew it when they tumbled together, thanks to my longsightedness in delaying the revelation of Arthur's parentage. The ideal son to carry out his Oedipal destiny and work his father's downfall in spite of all Arthur's precautions! Yes . . . Lot and Morgawse must not know at once that their son survives, or Lot might hesitate to join the rebels. But I will take steps to insure that son's corruption to our cause, even should I not be able to sow the final seeds myself. Father . . . Father, are you pleased with my efforts?"

Earnestly the mage gazed into his mirror.

For the first time, faintly and briefly, he descried a red gleam. That night, he slept comforted.

MERLIN AND TOM THUMB

DINAH MARIA MULOCK

After some of the more sinister aspects of Merlin's life, it's time for some lighter diversions. The English fairy tale of Tom Thumb goes far back into history, so far that its roots are unknown. References to the character of Tom Thumb may be found in books written during the days of Elizabeth I, especially in the work of the great debunker Reginald Scot (1538–99). He refers to Tom Thumbe amongst a long list of "bogies" in his Discoverie of Witchcraft *(1584), suggesting that he was already by then a well-known character in stories told to frighten the young or the gullible. The first to record the tale of Tom Thumb in print was probably the pamphleteer Richard Johnson (1573–1659). An edition of his* The History of Tom Thumbe the Little, for his small stature surnamed King Arthur's Dwarfe, *dated 1621, survives, though there were probably earlier printings. The story would have fitted in with the then vogue for tales of fairies, including Spenser's* The Faerie Queene *(1590) and Shakespeare's* A Midsummer Night's Dream *(1596). Indeed, Johnson's version bears some comparison with* The Faerie Queene *with its depiction of knights and deeds of chivalry. Quite where and when the links with King Arthur and Merlin began we just don't know. Johnson's version makes reference to the giant Gargantua. He had featured in an anonymous volume* The Great and Inestimable Chronicles of the Grand and Enormous Giant Gargantua *which appeared in France in 1532, and which was instantly picked up and rendered anew by François Rabelais who produced his own sequels* Pantagruel *(1532) and* Gargantua *(1534), both of which had an enormous success throughout Europe. The giant motif as represented by Gargantua had been popular in tales and ballads for centuries, and there are links with King Arthur's battle against*

*the giant at St Michael's Mount. The popularity of Rabelais' works
coming so soon after Malory's* Morte d'Arthur, *may have led to a
conflation of the tales in their telling and the Tom Thumb story as
we now know it coming into its final form some time in the mid-
sixteenth century.*

*The story rapidly passed into the language and was equally
rapidly embellished and then adapted for children. The character
of Tom Thumb was so well known by the eighteenth century that
his name was used on the earliest known collection of British
nursery rhymes,* Tommy Thumb's Song Book, *in 1744. With the
increased popularity of fairy tales in the mid-nineteenth century,
following translation into English of the works of Charles Perrault,
the Brothers Grimm and Hans Christian Andersen, the tale of
Tom Thumb was again revived. The version reprinted here is that
by Dinah Maria Mulock from* The Fairy Book *(1863). Dinah
Mulock (1826–87) is much better known under her married name
of Mrs Craik, under which name most of her books were reprinted,
although all of her best work was written before her marriage,
including the most popular,* John Halifax, Gentleman *(1856). In*
The Fairy Book *Dinah Mulock revised and rewrote nearly forty
stories from a variety of sources. It became a standard children's
book in Victorian times and is often the source of the best-known
versions of our favourite fairy tales. Dinah Mulock deleted some of
the Arthurian references from the earlier versions but maintained
the strong link with Merlin.*

In the days of King Arthur, Merlin, the most learned enchanter
of his time, was on a journey; and being very weary, stopped one
day at the cottage of an honest ploughman to ask for refreshment.
The ploughman's wife, with great civility, immediately brought
him some milk in a wooden bowl, and some brown bread on a
wooden platter. Merlin could not help observing, that although
everything within the cottage was particularly neat and clean,
and in good order, the ploughman and his wife had the most
sorrowful air imaginable; so he questioned them on the cause
of their melancholy, and learned that they were very miserable
because they had no children. The poor woman declared with
tears in her eyes, that she should be the happiest creature in
the world, if she had a son, although he were no bigger than his
father's thumb. Merlin was much amused with the notion of a

boy no bigger than a man's thumb; and as soon as he returned home, he sent for the queen of the fairies (with whom he was very intimate), and related to her the desire of the ploughman and his wife to have a son the size of his father's thumb. She liked the plan exceedingly, and declared their wish should be speedily granted. Accordingly, the ploughman's wife had a son, who in a few minutes grew as tall as his father's thumb. The queen of the fairies came in at the window as the mother was sitting up in bed admiring the child. Her majesty kissed the infant, and, giving it the name of Tom Thumb, immediately summoned several fairies from Fairyland, to clothe her new little favourite:

> "*An oak-leaf hat he had for his crown,*
> *His shirt it was by spiders spun:*
> *With doublet wove of thistledown,*
> *His trousers up with points were done;*
> *His stockings, of apple-rind, they tie*
> *With eye-lash pluck'd from his mother's eye;*
> *His shoes were made of a mouse's skin,*
> *Nicely tann'd with hair within.*"

Tom was never any bigger than his father's thumb, which was not a large thumb neither; but as he grew older, he became very cunning, for which his mother did not sufficiently correct him: and by this ill quality he was often brought into difficulties. For instance, when he had learned to play with other boys for cherry-stones, and had lost all his own, he used to creep into the boys' bags, fill his pockets, and come out again to play. But one day as he was getting out of a bag of cherry-stones, the boy to whom it belonged chanced to see him.

"Ah, ha, my little Tom Thumb!" said he, "have I caught you at your bad tricks at last? Now I will reward you for thieving." Then drawing the string tight round his neck, and shaking the bag, the cherry-stones bruised Tom's legs, thighs, and body sadly; which made him beg to be let out, and promise never to be guilty of such things any more.

Shortly afterwards, Tom's mother was making a batter-pudding, and that he might see how she mixed it, he climbed on the edge of the bowl; but his foot happening to slip, he fell over head and ears into the batter, and his mother, not observing him, stirred him into the pudding, and popped him into the pot to boil. The hot water made Tom kick and struggle; and his mother, seeing the pudding jump up and down in such a furious manner, thought it was bewitched; and a tinker coming by just at the time, she quickly gave him the pudding; he put it into his budget, and walked on.

As soon as Tom could get the batter out of his mouth, he began to cry aloud, which so frightened the poor tinker, that he flung the pudding over the hedge, and ran away from it as fast as he could. The pudding being broken to pieces by the fall, Tom was released, and walked home to his mother, who gave him a kiss and put him to bed.

Tom Thumb's mother once took him with her when she went to milk the cow; and it being a very windy day, she tied him with a needleful of thread to a thistle, that he might not be blown away. The cow, liking his oak-leaf hat, took him and the thistle up at one mouthful. While the cow chewed the thistle, Tom, terrified at her great teeth, which seemed ready to crush him to pieces, roared, "Mother, mother!" as loud as he could bawl.

"Where are you, Tommy, my dear Tommy?" said the mother.

"Here, mother, here in the red cow's mouth."

The mother began to cry and wring her hands; but the cow, surprised at such odd noises in her throat, opened her mouth and let him drop out. His mother clapped him into her apron, and ran home with him. Tom's father made him a whip of a barley straw to drive the cattle with, and being one day in the field he slipped into a deep furrow. A raven flying over picked him up with a grain of corn, and flew with him to the top of a giant's castle by the seaside, where he left him; and old Grumbo, the giant, coming soon after to walk upon his terrace, swallowed Tom like a pill, clothes and all. Tom presently made the giant very uncomfortable, and he threw him up into the sea. A great fish then swallowed him. This fish was soon after caught, and sent as a present to King Arthur. When it was cut open, everybody was delighted with little Tom Thumb. The king made him his dwarf; he was the favourite of the whole court; and, by his merry pranks, often amused the queen and the knights of the Round Table. The king, when he rode on horseback, frequently took Tom in his hand; and if a shower of rain came on, he used to creep into the king's waistcoat-pocket, and sleep till the rain was over. The king also sometimes questioned Tom concerning his parents; and when Tom informed his majesty they were very poor people, the king led him into his treasury, and told him he should pay his friends a visit, and take with him as much money as he could carry. Tom procured a little purse, and putting a threepenny piece into it, with much labour and difficulty got it upon his back; and, after travelling two days and nights, arrived at his father's house. His mother met him at the door, almost tired to death, having in forty-eight hours travelled almost half a mile with a huge silver threepence upon his back. Both his parents were glad to see him, especially when he had brought such an amazing sum of money with him. They placed him in a walnut-shell by the fireside, and feasted him for three days upon a hazel-nut, which made him sick, for a whole nut usually served him for a month. Tom got well, but could not travel because it had rained: therefore his mother took him in her hand, and with one puff blew him into King Arthur's court; where Tom entertained the king, queen, and nobility at tilts and tournaments, at which he exerted himself so much that he brought on a fit of sickness, and his life was despaired of. At this juncture the queen of the fairies came in a chariot, drawn by flying mice, placed Tom by her side, and drove through the air, without stopping till they arrived at her palace; when, after restoring him to health and permitting him to enjoy all the gay diversions of Fairyland, she commanded a fair wind, and, placing Tom before it, blew him straight to the court of King Arthur. But just as Tom should have alighted in the courtyard of the palace, the cook happened to pass along with the king's great bowl of furmenty (King Arthur loved furmenty), and poor Tom Thumb fell plump into the middle of it, and splashed the hot furmenty into the cook's eyes. Down went the bowl.

"Oh dear! oh dear!" cried Tom.

"Murder! murder!" bellowed the cook; and away poured the king's nice furmenty into the kennel.

The cook was a red-faced, cross fellow, and swore to the king that Tom had done it out of mere mischief; so he was taken up, tried, and sentenced to be beheaded. Tom hearing this dreadful sentence, and seeing a miller stand by with his mouth wide open, he took a good spring, and jumped down the miller's throat, unperceived by all, even by the miller himself.

Tom being lost, the court broke up, and away went the miller to his mill. But Tom did not leave him long at rest: he began to roll and tumble about, so that the miller thought himself bewitched, and sent for a doctor. When the doctor came, Tom began to dance and sing; the doctor was as much frightened as the miller, and sent in great haste for five more doctors and twenty learned men. While all these were debating upon the affair, the miller (for they were very tedious) happened to yawn, and Tom, taking the opportunity, made another jump, and alighted on his feet in the middle of the table. The miller, provoked to be thus tormented by such a little creature, fell into a great passion, caught hold of Tom, and threw him out of the window into the river. A large salmon swimming by snapped him up in a minute. The salmon was soon caught and sold in the market to a steward of a lord. The lord, thinking it an uncommon fine fish, made a present of it to the king, who ordered it to be dressed immediately. When the cook cut open the salmon, he found poor Tom, and ran with him directly to the king; but the king, being busy with state affairs, desired that he might be brought another day. The cook resolving to keep him safely this time, as he had so lately given him the slip, clapped him into a mouse-trap, and left him to amuse himself by peeping through the wires for a whole week; when the king sent for him, he forgave him for throwing down the furmenty, ordered him new clothes, and knighted him:

> "*His shirt was made of butterflies' wings,*
> *His boots were made of chicken skins;*
> *His coat and breeches were made with pride:*
> *A tailor's needle hung by his side;*
> *A mouse for a horse he used to ride.*"

Thus dressed and mounted, he rode a-hunting with the king and nobility, who all laughed heartily at Tom and his fine prancing steed. As they rode by a farmhouse one day, a cat jumped from behind the door, seized the mouse and little Tom, and began to devour the mouse; however, Tom boldly drew his sword and attacked the cat, who then let him fall. The king and his nobles, seeing Tom falling, went to his assistance, and one of the lords caught him in his hat; but poor Tom was sadly scratched, and his clothes were torn by the claws of the cat. In this condition he was carried home, when a bed of down was made for him in a little ivory cabinet. The queen of the fairies came and took him again to Fairyland, where she kept him for some years; and then, dressing him in bright green, sent him flying once more through the air to the earth, in the days of King Thunstone. The people flocked far and near to look at him; and the king, before whom he was carried, asked him who he was, whence he came, and where he lived? Tom answered:

> *"My name is Tom Thumb,*
> *From the Fairies I come;*
> *When King Arthur shone,*
> *This court was my home,*
> *In me he delighted,*
> *By him I was knighted;*
> *Did you never hear of*
> *Sir Thomas Thumb?"*

The king was so charmed with this address, that he ordered a little chair to be made, in order that Tom might sit on his table, and also a palace of gold a span high, with a door an inch wide, for little Tom to live in. He also gave him a coach drawn by six small mice. This made the queen angry, because she had not a new coach too: therefore, resolving to ruin Tom, she complained to the king that he had behaved very insolently to her. The king sent for him in a rage. Tom, to escape his fury, crept into an empty snail-shell, and there lay till he was almost starved; when, peeping out of the hole, he saw a fine butterfly settle on the ground: he now ventured out, and, getting astride, the butterfly took wing, and mounted into the air with little Tom on his back. Away he flew from field to field, from tree to tree, till at last he flew to the king's court. The king, queen, and nobles, all strove to catch the butterfly, but could not. At length poor Tom, having neither bridle nor saddle, slipped from his seat, and fell into a watering-pot, where he was found almost drowned. The queen vowed he should be guillotined; but while the guillotine was getting ready, he was secured once more in a mouse-trap; when the cat, seeing something stir, and supposing it to be a mouse, patted the trap about till she broke it, and set Tom at liberty. Soon afterwards a spider, taking him for a fly, made at him. Tom drew his sword and fought valiantly, but the spider's poisonous breath overcame him:

"*He fell dead on the ground where late he had stood,*
And the spider suck'd up the last drop of his blood."

King Thunstone and his whole court went into mourning for little Tom Thumb. They buried him under a rosebush, and raised a nice white marble monument over his grave, with the following epitaph:

"*Here lies Tom Thumb, King Arthur's knight,*
Who died by a spider's cruel bite.
He was well known in Arthur's court,
Where he afforded gallant sport;
He rode at tilt and tournament,
And on a mouse a-hunting went;
Alive he fill'd the court with mirth,
His death to sorrow soon gave birth,
Wipe, wipe your eyes, and shake your head,
And cry, 'Alas! Tom Thumb is dead.'"

THE SEVEN CHAMPIONS

E. M. WILMOT-BUXTON

The turn of the twentieth century saw a massive increase in the study of British folklore, due in part to the efforts of Andrew Lang and Joseph Jacobs. In the wake of this came several books collecting together famous British legends, often rewritten for younger readers. One of the best of these was Britain Long Ago *(1906) by Etheldreda Wilmot-Buxton. With a name like Etheldreda, in honour of one of the greatest of the Anglo-Saxon saints, the queen of Northumbria and foundress of the abbey of Ely, it is not surprising that Miss Wilmot-Buxton found fascination in the tales of early Britain. Her story of "The Quest of the Seven Champions" has all the elements of the Arthurian heroic romance and shows a different portrayal of Merlin as one of the Arthurian heroes.*

In the days of King Arthur there lived a noble young prince named Kilhugh, to whom it had been foretold that he should never marry until he could win for his wife the maiden Olwen, daughter of Thornogre Thistlehair, the Chief of the Giants. But, though he was full of love towards the very name of the unknown maid, he could not find out where she lived, nor could anyone tell him anything about her.

He was not cast down, however, but set off upon his steed of dappled grey to seek help from his kinsman Arthur. A fine sight he was, indeed, as he rode along on his prancing horse. His bridle was made of golden chains, his saddle-cloth of fine purple, from the corners of which hung four golden apples of great value.

His slung war horn was of ivory, his sword of gold, inlaid with a cross that shone like the lightning of heaven; his stirrups also were of pure gold. Two spears with silver shafts were in his hand, and two beautiful greyhounds, wearing collars set with rubies, sprang before him "like two sea-swallows sporting." So lightly did his charger step that the blades of grass did not bend beneath his tread.

At length he came to Arthur's castle, and having with much difficulty satisfied the Chief of the Porters of the Gate, a sturdy warrior known as the Dusky Hero with the Mighty Grasp, he made his way into Arthur's presence and told the King his story.

"This one boon I crave of thee, O King," he ended, "that thou wilt obtain for me Olwen, the daughter of Thornogre Thistlehair, Chief of the Giants, to be my bride. I ask it of thee and of all thy valiant knights, for the sake of of all the fair ladies who have ever lived in this land."

Then Arthur said: "My Prince, I never heard of this maiden, nor of her kindred, but messengers shall at once set forth to seek her if thou wilt give them time."

So it was agreed that, this being New Year's Day, they should be given until the last day of the year for their quest.

The messengers of Arthur set forth in haste, each taking a different way. They travelled throughout all the land of Britain, the "Island of the Mighty," and then to foreign lands, asking as they went: "Dost thou know aught of Olwen, the daughter of Thornogre Thistlehair, Chief of the Giants?"

But everyone said "No."

At length came the end of the year, and on the appointed day the messengers appeared in the wide White Hall of Arthur's castle, and all alike declared that they had no news whatever to declare concerning the maiden Olwen.

Then Kilhugh was very angry, and said in hasty words: "I alone am denied by my lord the gift I ask. I will depart from hence at once, and take with me the honour of Arthur, whom men call the most honourable King." But Kai, one of the knights, reproved him for his angry speech, and offered to go forth with him and any others who would accompany them, saying:

"We will not part till we have found the maiden, or till thou art forced to own she is not among those who dwell on this earth."

So Arthur chose six of his knights to go forth with Prince Kilhugh upon his quest.

First came Kai, whose offer had but just been spoken. An excellent spy and sentinel was he, for he could make himself as tall as the tallest tree in the forest, and so scan all the country round. He could hide himself under water, and lie hidden in lake or river for nine days and nights if need be. Such fire was in his nature that when they needed warmth his companions had but to kindle the piled wood at his finger; he could walk through torrents of rain as dry as on a summer's day; he could go for nine days and nights without sleep, and no doctor could heal the wound made by his sword.

Next came Sir Bedivere, close brother-in-arms to Kai, the swiftest runner, save Arthur himself and one other, in all the land. One-handed was he, yet he could give more wounds in battle than any three warriors together.

Then followed Uriel, who understood the speech of all men and all beasts; and Gawain, who was called the "Hawk of May," because he never returned from any undertaking until it had been performed by him.

The fifth to answer Arthur's call was Merlin, a master of magic, who knew how to put a spell upon the knights that would render them invisible.

Last came Peregrine the Guide, who knew how to find the way as well in a strange country as in his own.

"Go forth, O Chieftains," said the King, "and follow the Prince upon his quest; and great shall be the fame of your adventure."

So the Seven Champions rode forth through the great gates of the palace, and set out with high hearts to seek for Olwen, daughter of Thornogre Thistlehair, Chief of the Giants.

Onward and onward rode Kilhugh and the six knights until they came at length to a vast plain, stretching in every direction farther than the eye could reach. Over it they rode, and at length perceived through the misty air the towers and battlements of a great castle far away on the borders of the moorland. They rode towards this castle all day long, but yet they never seemed to get any nearer.

All the next day they went on riding, and still the castle seemed as far away as ever. The third evening brought them no nearer. At length Sir Gawain exclaimed: "This must be Fleeting Castle, which can always be seen from a distance, but can never be actually reached."

Now, on the fourth day, to their surprise, the castle no longer advanced before them as they approached, and soon they were able to draw rein before it, and to wonder in amazement at the thousands of sheep which fed upon the plains surrounding its massive walls. Near by sat the shepherd with his dog, tending his enormous flock. The shepherd was a giant in size, and was dressed in the skins of wild beasts. The dog was larger than a full-grown horse; he had the shaggiest of coats, and, though an excellent sheep-dog, was destructive enough elsewhere, for with his fiery breath he would burn up all the dry bushes and dead trees in that region.

The Champions looked somewhat doubtfully at this great animal, and Kai suggested to Uriel that as he knew all tongues, he had better go and speak to the shepherd.

"Not I," answered Uriel. "I agreed when we set out to go just as far as thou, and no farther."

But Merlin came to them, and explained that he had cast a spell over the dog, so that he could not hurt them. So Kilhugh and Kai and Uriel went together to the shepherd, and asked him very politely who owned that countless flock of sheep, and who lived in yonder castle.

"Where have ye lived not to know that?" cried the shepherd. "Everyone in the world ought to know that this is the Castle of Thornogre Thistlehair, Chief of the Giants."

"And who art thou?" they asked.

"I am Constantine, the brother of Thornogre Thistlehair," replied the man, with an angry look. "A fine brother indeed has he been to me! He has taken from me all my lands and possessions, and now I am obliged to earn a living by feeding his sheep."

Then he asked them why they came, and when they replied that they were seeking for Olwen, daughter of Thornogre Thistlehair, he sadly shook his head.

"Alas!" he said, "no one ever tried to find her, and returned from this place alive. Go back at once, lest ye all perish also."

"That will we never do!" cried Kilhugh; and the Champions echoed his words.

Then Constantine inquired who Kilhugh was, and when he heard, he cried out that he was his own nephew, and begged that he and his comrades would spend a night at his house, and to this they readily agreed. And as a mark of affection Kilhugh gave his uncle a golden ring; but it was much too small for the giant, who put it forthwith into the finger of one of the gloves which hung from his belt as a sign of his rank as chieftain. Then he signalled to his dog, who immediately began to drive the sheep towards home.

When they reached the house the giant entered first, and gave his wife his gloves to hold. She soon pulled out the ring, and at once began to question him about it; so he told her that their nephew Kilhugh, with six comrades, was even then dismounting at the door. Then the shepherd's wife was glad, and ran forth with hands outstretched to clasp him in her arms; but so big and strong was she that, as Kai quickly saw, no knight could survive her embrace. So as she threw her arms round Kilhugh's neck, he snatched up a log of firewood, and pushed it into her arms instead of the young prince; and when she unloosed it, it was twisted out of all shape. It was somewhat to their relief, therefore, when she took them into the house without further embracing, and set them down to supper. This was a very frugal meal, and served with great simplicity, for Thornogre had not left his brother so much as a silver goblet or a single chair in his barren hall.

When they had supped, the shepherd's wife asked Kai and Uriel to stay behind after the rest had gone out to the courtyard, and, taking them to the chimney-corner, she opened a great stone box. As she lifted the lid, to their amazement a beautiful boy with golden, curly hair rose up from within.

"Pity indeed," exclaimed Uriel, "to keep so handsome a child shut up here. What hath he done?"

Then the lady wept, and answered: "All my three and twenty sons have been killed by Thornogre Thistlehair, Chief of the Giants; and now my only hope of keeping him alive is to hide him in this chest, where he has lived ever since he was born." And she wept to think that her boy would never have a chance of doing valiant deeds and of becoming a great knight. Then Kai bade her be of good cheer and let the lad come with them, promising that he should not be slain unless he, Kai, were killed as well.

She agreed to this very gladly, and asked them why they had come to that region. But when she knew they had come to seek for Olwen, she advised them strongly to go home, since in that very quest all her three and twenty sons had perished.

They laughed at her fears, however, and asked if the maiden ever came to the shepherd's house.

"Yes," said the shepherd's wife; "she comes every Saturday to wash her hair. She leaves behind her all her jewels and rings in the water which she uses, and never asks for them again."

Then they begged her to ask fair Olwen to visit her at once, and she agreed, on condition that they would not carry her off against her will.

To this the Champions agreed, and sat waiting in a hall for the coming of the maiden.

Very fair she looked as she approached, dressed in a robe of flame-coloured silk, and wearing a jewelled collar of gold round her neck.

More yellow was her hair than the flower of the broom, and her skin was whiter than the foam of the wave; and fairer were her hands and fingers than the blossoms of the wood-anemone amidst the spray of the meadow fountain. The eye of the trained hawk, the glance of the falcon were not brighter than hers. Her bosom was more snowy than the breasts of the white swan; her cheek was redder than the reddest roses. Who so beheld her was filled with love of her. Four white trefoils sprang up wherever she trod; therefore was she called Olwen of the White Footprints.

Having entered the house she sat down by Kilhugh, who at once loved her greatly, and began to pray her to come away with him, and be his wife. But Olwen, though she returned his affection, answered that she had promised her father not to go away without his leave. She also told him that Thornogre knew that her bridal day was fated to be the day of his death, so that he would withhold his leave as long as possible. She advised him, however, to go to her father, and to grant him everything he demanded, and so in time he should win her hand; but if he denied the giant's least request, he would lose both her and his own life.

When she had said this, she returned to the castle.

The Seven Champions now determined to make their way to the castle, and force an entrance to the hall of Thornogre Thistlehair, Chief of the Giants. It was very dark when they set out, but they easily found their way by the trail of white trefoils which the footprints of Olwen had left.

The castle was guarded by nine warders at the gate and nine watch-dogs along the road which led up to it; but a strange silence had fallen upon both men and beasts, and the Champions slew them all without a sound being heard.

Then they passed through the great door, and entered the hall of the castle.

Just opposite the entrance sat Thornogre Thistlehair upon a high wide throne. He was terrible to look upon. His eyebrows were so long and bushy that they fell over his eyes like a curtain, and he was taller and broader than three other giants put together. Close by his hand lay three poisoned darts.

After they had greeted him courteously, he asked who they were; and they replied that they were come from Arthur's Court to ask that Olwen, his daughter, should marry Kilhugh the Prince. Then the giant roared for his pages to come and prop up his eyebrows, that he might see what sort of son-in-law was proposed for him.

So when they had propped up his eyebrows he looked angrily at Kilhugh, and bade him come the next day for his answer.

But as they went out of the hall, the giant threw one of his poisoned darts at them. Sir Bedivere caught it just in time and threw it back so neatly that it caught the giant in the knee. Then they laughed, and withdrew, leaving him to storm at them, declaring that the great wound hurt as much as the sting of a gadfly, and that he might never be able to walk quite so well again.

At dawn the next day they returned to the castle, and again demanded the hand of fair Olwen in marriage. But the giant replied: "I can do naught in this matter till I have consulted her four great-grandmothers and her four great-grandfathers. Come again for my answer."

So they turned to leave the hall; but as they went the giant snatched up the second of his poisoned darts, and flung it after them. Merlin caught it deftly, however, and threw it back with such force that it entered his chest, and stuck out through his back. This left him grumbling that never again would he be able to climb a hill without losing breath, and fearing lest he now might sometimes suffer from pains in the chest.

The third time they visited the giant he was on his guard, and shouted to them not to dare throw any more darts on pain of death. Then he roared to his pages to lift up his eyebrows, and when they had done it, he snatched up the third poisoned dart, and flung it at them without more ado.

But Kilhugh caught it this time, and cast it back at him, so that it pierced one of his eyes. Then, while he grumbled that now his sight would not be so good as before, they went out to dine.

These events made the giant treat his visitors on their next arrival with more civility; besides, he had no more poisoned darts. He once more inquired why they had come, and when he realized that Kilhugh was determined to marry Olwen, he made him promise that he would do all that he required of him in return for his agreement to the marriage. Kilhugh, mindful of Olwen's warning that he was to agree to perform whatever her father proposed, gave a ready promise, and bade him ask away.

Then did Thornogre Thistlehair propound to him forty Impossible Things, of which these seven are the chief:

Firstly, he must gather nine bushels of flax sown hundreds of years ago in a field of red earth, of which never a seed had sprouted. Not one grain of the measure must be missing, and they must be sown again in a freshly ploughed field to make flax for Olwen's wedding veil.

Secondly, he must find Mabon, the son of Modron, who was stolen from his mother when three days old, and had not since been heard of.

Thirdly, he must find the Cauldron of Cruseward the Cauldron-Keeper, in which, if one tries to cook food for a coward, one may wait for ever for the water to boil but if for a brave man the meal is ready directly it is placed therein. In this cauldron must all the food for the wedding feast be prepared.

Fourthly, since the giant must shave for the wedding, he must obtain for a razor the tusk of the Boar-headed Branch-breaker, which to be of any use must be taken from his skull while he yet lived.

Fifthly, since the giant must wash his hair, all matted together as it was, for the wedding, he must bring to him the Charmed Balsam kept by the Jet-Black Sorceress, daughter of the Snow-White Sorceress, from the Source of the Brook of Sorrow, at the edge of the Twilight Land.

Sixthly, that the giant's hair might be smoothed and combed he must bring the scissors and the comb that are found between the ears of Burstingboar, the Wide-Waster, since they alone would perform the operation without breaking.

Seventhly, he must obtain the sword of Garnard the Giant, since that alone would kill the Wide-Waster, from whom, unless he were killed, the comb and scissors could never be obtained.

When he had made an end of speaking, the giant jeered at the Prince, who, unless he could do all these impossible things, might never wed his daughter. But Kilhugh answered with a high heart: "I have knights for my companions, horses and hounds, and Arthur is my kinsman. I shall do all that thou requirest, thou wicked giant, and shall win thy daughter, but thou shalt lose thy life."

Scarcely had the Seven Champions left the castle of Thornogre Thistlehair when they were joined by the fair-haired son of the shepherd, who had lived all his life in the chest. Eager to make a great name for himself he implored them to let him accompany them, which accordingly they did. Then they turned their faces towards Arthur's castle.

At evening-time they reached the gates of a very great castle, the largest in the world, and as they pulled up their horses before it, an enormous black giant came out of the gate, and looked at them very hard. They greeted him politely, and asked whose castle this was.

" 'Tis the castle of Garnard the Giant," he answered.

They looked at each other with glee, for one of the appointed tasks was to obtain the sword of this very giant. Then they asked if he were used to treat strangers courteously.

The black man shook his head. "No stranger ever entered that castle and came out alive," said he; "but ye have little chance of entrance, for no traveller is permitted to enter who knows no handicraft."

The Seven Champions on hearing this rode on to the entrance gate, and called for admittance. The porter refused, however, saying that there was revelry within, and that no man set foot inside who did not bring his craft with him. But Kai declared that he was a burnisher of swords, and that no man could excel him at that trade, whereupon the porter went to report the matter to Garnard the Giant. Now, it so happened that Garnard had long wished for one who could brighten and clean his sword, so he bade the porter to admit him.

So Kai entered alone, and was brought before the giant, who ordered his sword to be brought to him. Then Kai drew out his whetstone, and, first asking if he required it to glitter with a blue or a white lustre, he polished half the blade, and returned it to the giant, saying: "How is that?"

The giant was highly pleased. "If the rest of my sword can be made to look like that," said he, "I shall value it above all my treasures. But how comes it that so clever a craftsman is wandering about alone without a companion?"

"But I have a companion," said Kai – "a cunning craftsman, too, though not at this work. Send, I pray you, and admit him. And the porter shall know him by this sign: the head of his lance shall spring into the air, draw blood from the wind, and return to its place again."

Then the porter opened the gate, and Bedivere marched into the hall, ready for what might befall, and stood watching Kai as he went on polishing the sword. This being done, to gain more time he asked for the sheath, and he fell to mending it and putting in new sides of wood.

Meantime, as he had hoped, while all the porters and followers of the giant stood gaping round him, the young son of the herdsman had managed to climb over the castle hall, and to help his companions over also, whereupon they were able to make their way to hiding-places behind doors and pillars, from which they could see the company in the hall without being seen themselves.

By this time Kai had finished both sword and scabbard, and, stepping up to the giant's great chair, pretended to hand them to him. But, as the giant was off his guard, he lifted the sword and brought it down on Garnard's neck, so that he cut off his head. Before his followers could lay hands on Kai and Bedivere, the knights rushed out upon them, and slew them all. Then, having loaded themselves with gold and jewels, but above all with the precious sword, they set forth again for Arthur's palace.

This time they reached it in safety, and, having told their story, asked the advice of the King as to which of the six remaining quests they should first undertake. To seek out Mabon, the son of Modron, was Arthur's decision; and for this undertaking he chose Uriel because he could understand the speech of both animals and birds, as well as that of all strange men; and Idwel, because he was Mabon's kinsman, with Kai and Bedivere, because they were known never to turn back from any adventure until it was accomplished.

So these four set out upon their quest.

Now, Mabon had been lost so long ago that not the oldest man on the earth, nor their great-grandfathers before them, had ever heard anything at all about him. But Idwel remembered that many birds and beasts live much longer than the oldest man, so they determined to seek out the oldest of these.

"And who," said they, "could be older than the Ousel of Deepdell? Let us seek her help."

So they made their way through a great forest till they came to a shadowy place, where on a small stone sat the Ousel of Deepdell; and her they implored to tell them if she knew anything of Mabon, son of Modron, who was taken from between his mother and the wall when he was only three days old.

"When I first came here," answered the Ousel gravely, "I was but a fledgling. On this spot where I now sit stood a smith's stone anvil. Since then no hand has touched it, but every evening I have pecked at it with my beak as I smoothed my feathers before sleeping. Now all that remains of it is this little pebble upon which I sit. Yet through all the years that have passed while this change took place I have never heard of Mabon, the son of Modron. But do not despair: I will take you to a race of creatures who were made before me, and them ye shall inquire of again."

Then she took them to a place where, at the foot of an ancient oak, lay the Stag of the Fern Brake. Of him they once more asked the question: "Dost thou know anything of Mabon, son of Modron, parted from his mother when three days old?"

The Stag answered: "When first I came here this great forest was a vast plain, in which grew one little oak sapling. This sapling became in time an oak-tree, and after its long lifetime gradually decayed until it became this stump. Now, an oak-tree is three hundred years in growing, three hundred years in its full strength, and three hundred years in its decay. Yet in all this time I have never heard aught of Mabon, son of Modron. But, since ye are Arthur's knights, I will take you to one who was made before my time." Then he led them to the Owl of Darkdingle.

"When first I came here," said the Owl from his dark cavernous home when he heard their question, "this valley was covered with a vast wood. It decayed away, and another grew up, and after that had withered away, a third, which now ye see. But never have I heard of the man whom ye seek. Yet, since ye are Arthur's knights, I will take ye to the oldest creature in the world – to the Eagle of the Aldergrove."

So thither they went, and when he heard their question the Eagle answered: "When I first arrived, there was a rock in this place so high that I could perch on its top and peck at the stars, and so long have I been here that now it is but a few inches high. Never have I heard of this man save once, and that was when I visited the Lone Lake. There I stuck my claws into a salmon, hoping to kill him for my supper; but he dragged me into deep water, so that I barely escaped with my life. But when I went with all my band to slay him, he sent ambassadors, and made good peace with me, and came and begged me to take fifty fish-spears out of his back. He, if anyone can, will tell you what you want to know, and I will be your guide to him."

So they journeyed on till they reached a great blue lake, hidden in the depths of the forest, and there they found the Salmon of the Lone Lake. He heard their question, and looking at them very wisely replied: "Such wrong as I have never found elsewhere have I found under the walls of Gloucester Castle, on the River Severn, up which I travel with every tide. And that ye may know it is so, come, two of ye, and travel thither upon my shoulders."

Then Kai and Uriel came down to the water, and stood upon the shoulders of the Salmon of Lone Lake, who swam with them down the Severn, and brought them under the walls of Gloucester Castle.

"Hark!" said the Salmon; and as they listened, a voice was heard from the dungeon wall wailing in deepest sorrow and woe. Then Uriel cried: "Whose voice is this that moans within this gloomy cell?"

"Alas!" wailed the voice, "'tis that of Mabon, the son of Modron, shut up eternally in the prison of Gwyn, son of Nith, King of Faerie. Here I, the Elfin Huntsman, ever young, am shut out eternally from the sight of wood and fell and the joyful chase which is my birthright."

"Canst thou be ransomed with silver and gold?" asked Uriel.

"No," answered Mabon; "if ever I am rescued from this cruel place it must be by battle and strife."

Then Uriel and Kai returned to their companions.

Seeing that this was the kind of adventure that Arthur loved, they journeyed back to the King, and told him all. So he prepared a great army, and marched by land to attack Gloucester Castle. But while he fought before the gates, Kai and Bedivere had sailed down the river on the shoulders of the Salmon of Lone Lake, and finding the water-side portion of the Castle unprotected, they broke through the wall, and carried off Mobon, the son of Modron, and he returned with them to Arthur's Court.

While Arthur and his knights were discussing which of the Impossible Tasks should next be undertaken, it so happened that a certain prince, named Gwyther, who was also one of Arthur's knights, was walking over a mountain in his own country, the Land of the Dawn.

And as he walked, deep in thought, he heard a sad little cry. Up and down he looked, but nothing could he see that could explain such mournful cry. But presently it came again from under his very feet, and there he saw an ant-hill. Inside the ant-hill the little creatures were wailing piteously, for the heath on the mountain-side was afire, and in a short time their kingdom would be all in a blaze.

Then Prince Gwyther drew his sword, and cut off the ant-hill at a blow, and threw it into a place of safety.

"Our grateful thanks are thine," cried the ants. "Now tell us what we can do for thee in return, Prince Gwyther of the Land of the Dawn."

The Prince pondered a moment, and then replied: "All the world knows that Kilhugh, one of the Companions of Arthur, seeking the hand of the fair Olwen, is required by her father to bring him the nine bushels of flax seed sown in his field to make the wedding veil for his bride. If one grain is missing the marriage will be forbidden; and, though we are Arthur's knights, not one of us can find these tiny seeds. Now, can ye do this task for me?"

"That will we joyfully," cried the ants, and they made their way in haste to the field of Thornogre Thistlehair, Chief of the Giants.

When evening began to fall they returned to the Land of the Dawn, where Prince Gwyther had set up a bushel measure. Up its sides they climbed, each with a seed in its mouth; and nine times they filled the measure, until only one seed was wanting. "'Tis well," they cried; "the lame emmet has not yet come home." And before nightfall the lame emmet toiled up to the bushel measure, and dropped in the last seed.

So the nine bushels of flax seed were taken to the castle of Arthur, and given to Prince Kilhugh.

Then said King Arthur: "Let us now go to Ireland to seek for the Cauldron of Cruseward the Steward of Odgar, the Irish King."

Now, this cauldron, as you will remember, was of such a kind that when food for a coward was cooked in it the food remained as it was at first, but if for a brave man, it was ready for eating directly it was placed in the pot. So it was very precious; and when Arthur's request for it was received by Odgar, Cruseward replied in wrath: "Not a glimpse of my cauldron shall he obtain, even if it would give him all the blessings in the world; much less will I give it him altogether."

Then Arthur called together his men of war, and sailed over the stormy seas to Ireland. When the people saw him in battle array, they were afraid, and counselled Odgar to receive him peacefully. So Odgar sent friendly messages, and invited him to a banquet in his palace.

Now when the banquet was over, Odgar was about to give presents to his guests, but Arthur would take nothing. He wanted naught, he said, but the Cauldron of Cruseward. When Cruseward heard this, he thundered out: "Nay, King Arthur, I will never give it to thee. If thou couldst have it for the asking it would have been given at the bidding of King Odgar, not at thine."

When Bedivere heard this rude reply he was very angry, and, rushing upon him, seized the cauldron, and set it on the shoulders of Arthur's Cauldron-Bearer. Then swords were drawn, and the men of Arthur's host fell upon Cruseward and his followers, and slew them. Thus they carried off the cauldron, and bore it, full of Irish gold, back to the Island of the Mighty.

After this adventure they set forth to obtain the Charmed Balsam that was guarded by the Jet-Black Sorceress, daughter of the Snow-White Sorceress, at the Brook of Sorrow, on the edge of the Twilight Land. And when they approached the dismal cavern where she dwelt, King Arthur was joined by Gwyn of the Twilight Land, and Gwyther from the Land of the Dawn, who, knowing the Sorceress and her power, advised that two of his attendants should first be sent into the cave. Directly the first appeared the Sorceress seized him by the hair, and threw him down, and trampled on him. The second dragged her away from him, but could do nothing against her, for she kicked them and beat them and thrust them forth again.

Then Arthur would have gone in himself; but Prince Gwyn and Prince Gwyther prevented him, saying it would not be a fitting adventure for so great a king, and persuaded him to send in the two Tall Brothers. But these two were so ill treated by the Sorceress that they came out more dead than alive, and had to be lifted on to their horses. Then, when he saw his followers so ill used, nothing could keep Arthur back. He rushed into the cave, and with one stroke of his dagger, killed the wicked Sorceress, while Kai carried off the Charmed Balsam.

They next set out to hunt the Boar-headed Branch-breaker; but soon they heard that no man could pluck out the tusk from the living head of this terrible animal but Odgar, King of Ireland.

With some difficulty they persuaded him to accompany them; but at length the huntsmen gathered together, with him at their head, and a great hunt for the boar began. The swiftest dogs could not bring the animal to bay, until at length Arthur's own hound, Cavall, brought him to the ground, and Odgar rushed up to pull out the tusk; but he would have been killed, had not Kai been there to strike the Branch-breaker down directly Odgar had plucked it out.

There yet remained to seek out the jewelled scissors and comb that were between the ears of Burstingboar, the Wide-Waster.

Now, this Burstingboar had laid waste a great part of Ireland, so that all men went in terror of him; and, that the heroes might not be misled about the curious things said to lie between his ears, Merlin was sent to Ireland to seek him out and see if it were as the giant had said.

So Merlin tracked Burstingboar to his den on Cold Blast Ridge, and, having changed himself into a bird, flew down into a thicket close by. From thence he could see the creature lying on the ground, with his seven young boars at his side, and between his ears twinkled the jewels of the scissors and the comb. Then Merlin thought it was a sad thing that the heroes should lose their lives for such things, and determined to try to carry them off himself. So he flew upon the head of Burstingboar, and tried to snatch up the razor; but all he really got was a great bristle. Then Burstingboar rose up in a great rage, foaming at the mouth. He could see no one; but a fleck of the poisonous foam fell upon Merlin, and hurt him so that he never quite recovered.

When he heard this news, Arthur gathered together such a number of brave knights and squires that the Irish feared he was about to attack their land, but when he told them he had come to deliver them from the dreaded Burstingboar, their joy knew no bounds. And so it was arranged that those Irish who had joined his host should first attack the boar; then, if he still lived, he should be attacked by Arthur's own knights; and if by that time he were not slain, Arthur should himself hunt him on the third day.

But the first day and the second saw the boar triumphant; and when Arthur took his turn he fought for nine days and nights without even wounding the creature or one of his cubs. At the end of that time all the knights besought Arthur to tell them the secret about the boar, which all this time he had kept.

Then Arthur told them that the creature had once been a king, but for his sins and his great pride had been changed into a boar. And he sent Uriel to confer with him concerning the jewelled comb and scissors. But when Uriel spoke gently to him, bidding him deliver these up at the request of Arthur, the boar grew very fierce, and said: "Not only shall Arthur never even see these jewels, but I with my young ones will go forthwith and harry the land of Arthur, doing all the hurt to it that we can."

When they heard this news all the host arose at dawn to prevent them leaving Ireland; but when they looked towards the sea, there was the boar with his young ones swimming far away to the coast of Britain. And before the King could cross the Irish Sea, the boars had landed at Milford Haven, and destroyed every living thing in the neighbourhood.

Then terror fell on the land, and eagerly men looked for Arthur to come to their aid, who, when he arrived, set out at once with a crowd of mighty huntsmen to kill the beasts. But it was exceeding hard to find the boar, though his tracks were well marked by the ruin of flocks and men; and when they did come up with him, he slew with his mighty tusks a full half-dozen of Arthur's followers, and dashed off to a mountain-top, where they lost all sign of him: neither man nor dog could tell whither he had disappeared.

At last they heard that the boars were ravaging a valley some miles away. Thither they followed, and after a hard struggle they killed the young boars one by one. But after a long pursuit Burstingboar vanished again, so completely this time that the host returned to Cornwall, thinking he must have left the land.

Scarcely had Arthur entered his palace when a breathless messenger rushed into the hall.

"Arise!" he cried. "The boar is ruining thy domain, trampling down towers and towns, uprooting trees, and killing men and cattle on all sides, and he is now coming over the mountains to do the same in Cornwall.

Then Arthur made this speech to his followers:

"Men of the Island of the Mighty, Burstingboar, the Wide-Waster, has slain many of our bravest men, but he shall never enter Cornwall while I live. You may do as you please; but for me, I will no longer hunt him, but shall meet him face to face."

Forthwith he posted men at various spots to prevent the creature from landing, and then rode up to the river's brink. As he arrived, suddenly with a great rush, Burstingboar sprang out of the forest, and tried to cross on his way to Cornwall. But Arthur and his companions drove their horses into the water, and followed him, and somehow or other seized him by his fore feet as he scrambled up the bank, and flung him back into the river; and as he fell, Mabon, the son of Modron, caught the razor from behind one of his ears, and Kenneder the Wild snatched the scissors from behind the other.

Yet, even while they did this, Burstingboar upreared himself from the water, dashed up the river-bank, and disappeared. Then all the host followed, but they only came up to him when he had got well into Cornwall. Then a desperate fight began. By harassing him all day they managed to keep him from ravaging the land, and when he tried to get into Devon they were too many for him. Over the moors, down the coombs, up the hills, they chased him, till at length, being desperate, he turned, and made for the sea. In he plunged, but, though the pursuing horses stayed their feet at the water's edge, those two good hounds, Raceapace and Boundoft, who had followed him so long, could not hold themselves back, but plunged in after him into the waves. For long the heroes watched his course, with those two fierce dogs close behind him; but from that day to this nothing more has ever been heard of either Burstingboar or the two hounds.

Now, all the Impossible Tasks had been fulfilled, and joyfully did Prince Kilhugh ride to the giant's castle to claim his bride. But Thornogre Thistlehair looked on in gloomy silence as the marvels were spread out before him; he allowed himself to be shaven and combed; but though he could not refuse to give the Prince his daughter's hand, he openly said that he did it with no good will. Then the herdsman's son stood forth, and cried: "O giant, three and twenty of my brothers thou hast foully slain, and defrauded my father of his heritage. For these things thou shalt surely die by my hand to-day."

So he dragged him by his hair to the castle battlements, and, being very strong, he slew him there, and cut off his head. And the castle was given to the herdsman; but Kilhugh married fair Olwen, and they were happy ever after as long as they both lived.

MORTE D'ESPIER

MAXEY BROOKE

Maxey Brooke (1913–1994) was a qualified research chemist but was perhaps best known for his books of puzzles and mathematical problems, such as 150 Puzzles in Crypt-Arithmetic *(1963). He used this lateral thinking to write several stories featuring Merlin as a proto-detective, starting with "Morte d'Alain" (*Ellery Queen's Mystery Magazine, *December 1952), which I reprinted in* The Pendragon Chronicles. *Here's the second of them.*

And now at long last war had come to the realm. The court was in a turmoil. Many a knight, having waxed fat from five years of good living, found himself scarce able to don his cuirass. All night the fires of the armourer and the smith burned. All day provender was brought to the castle and packed in the battle-wains. And amidst the hustle and bustle I stood by useless. *Wouldst that my father had apprenticed me to a knight, or even to a craftsman, rather than a sorcerer,* I thought bitterly.

"Nay, my son," quoth my master Merlin whom I had not heard approach. "Your time will come. And soon."

I looked at him, taken aback. "Then you can read thoughts as 'tis rumoured."

"Nay. I had but to look at your face. 'Twas written there as in great runes."

"Oh." Sorcery always seems so simple after my master Merlin explains it. "And when will that be?"

"Alas, I cannot read the future, although there are those who are convinced I can. I can only predict how future events are influenced by the past. Ere this conflicts ends, every man's special talents will be used. Come, even now your skills are needed in the Council Chamber."

The Council Chamber! 'Twould be the first time I had accompanied my master to his closetings with our King. And there was no man prouder than I in the length and breadth of England. My skills indeed! I would show my master that he did not err in having me accompany him.

We crossed the courtyard together, through the Great Hall of the Round Table and to a small chamber adjoining. Seated there was our King, his captains and chief stewards. King Arthur smiled when he saw us.

"Ah, my good Merlin and his young pupil. We were about to begin. Enter and be seated. There and there."

We bowed gravely as befits magicians, and sat as ordered – my master at our King's right hand and I behind him at a small table whereon were quills, paper, and ink – ink of my own making, from nut-galls and iron rust, though there are those who believe that I conjure it from a familiar.

'Twas then I learned I was not to be consulted on the conduct of the war but rather to keep an account of what transpired. For the knights, great men and brawny though they were, and full courageous and skilled in all arms, could scarce tell one letter from another. Even our good King could read and write but haltingly. As my master explained to me later, a king need not be scribe or magician when he can command the skills of those who are. Thus he can keep his mind free for the duties of state – even as I handled many of the details of his sorcery so that my master could concentrate on its use.

And though my council was not required I learned much about the conduct of a war. Scarce had I realized how many details were needed.

Nor was it the last council I attended and kept records thereof. But when the army marched off and quiet once again settled on the court, no longer were the captains and stewards present – but only our King, my master, and I who listened each day to the reports from runners and thus followed the battle from afar.

Far to the north was the wall built across Britain by the Romans. Even though King Arthur's domain extended beyond the wall, few sons of the nobles of that part of the realm were sent to the Court to become Knights of the Round Table. Clannish they were, and harsher of speech and darker of skin than was becoming an Englishman. And they were banded together under the leadership of one Sir Brian, who now called himself King Brian, and were challenging the authority of King Arthur, Ruler of Britain by the Grace of God.

For some days the reports were neither good nor bad. Our army had established itself near the great wall. Sorties had been made to seek out the enemy and try his strength. But as the day passed, the reports became increasingly bad. Our sorties were ambushed. Outposts were ridden against in force. And always when our forces made contact, 'twas against superior numbers though 'twas known that they did not have as great an army as we. And at last our King could contain himself no longer. His great red beard bristled and his mighty fist crashed down on the table. He roared in a voice of thunder.

"By the Almighty! Do we have an army or a rabble! Why do they not move on that infernal Brian and crush him once and for all? Why, I ask you? Why?"

My master faced him calmly as I did try, though I confess I was quaking inside.

"They have moved time and again, Sire, but always Brian eludes them."

"That I know. But how? Is he a greater warrior than my knights? Is he a greater warrior then I?"

"Nay, Sire, nay. But long have I studied the reports and at last I think I see a pattern."

"Speak on, man. Speak!"

"No matter where we move in strength, there he is not. But where we leave a weak garrison, there he attacks. He could do that only if he knew our plans."

"Mean you there is a traitor in our midst?" The King's words were low and intense – more frightening even than his roar.

"That I doubt. Your men are trusted. But a spy . . ."

"A spy! How like that black-hearted scoundrel to use so un-British a device." His anger quieted and he toyed with his beard. "But how, Merlin? How could a spy learn our secret plans?"

"That too, I think I know. Were I but with the army I could seek him out."

"Then you shall be with the army. Come, Merlin. Come, Alaric. We ride at dawn."

And at dawn we rode. Our King, my master with full saddle-bags, a dozen squires and men-at-arms. Hard we rode, and fast and long. At night I could scarce sit to eat my meal. And at last we reached the army unannounced as night was falling.

Our King strode into the great tent where the captains were assembled. He pushed up his visor and glared at them.

"What manner of knights are you? Unable to crush an army half your strength."

They leaped to their feet, looking for all the world like a group of stable-boys caught gaming at dice.

Sir Launcelot spoke: "Your Majesty, if there be fault it is ours. The men are full brave and eager. But fighting this Brian is like fighting a flea. Where you strike, there he is not."

"So," roared our King, "I must travel across half of Britain to teach you how to catch a flea."

"Nay, Sire, I did not mean . . ."

"Enough! If we cannot win by force, then we must win by sorcery. Merlin, take charge."

Dark were the flushes on the cheeks of the fighting men. For in the past most of them had matched wits with my master, and had always been the loser. But ere long their resentment died, for Merlin spoke to them softly and reasonably. And they were men of great courage who could listen to reason.

"In this tent you plan your campaigns?"

"Aye."

"And 'tis well guarded that none may eavesdrop?"

"Aye. 'Tis not well that our men know of the plans too early."

"Do these plannings last long?"

"Surely, good Merlin. One does not map out a battle in a moment."

"Then during these plannings you must need refreshment?"

"Aye. 'Tis a dry business."

"Who, then, furnishes the refreshment?"

"Why, the serving-men, of course."

"Then others *are* present while the battles are being talked of?"

The light of understanding came into their eyes. Our King spoke softly.

"The serving-men. By the Saints, 'tis one of the serving-men who betrayed us." Then in his great voice, "Ho! The guards! Fetch in the serving-men. And the chief steward!"

And in a trice they were brought. Six lads clad in leather jerkins, with the white napkin which was the symbol of their rank at their belts, and behind them a little fat man whose belly was enough to denote him chief steward.

They lined up before our King with eyes downcast. He looked at them full long.

"One of you has betrayed me. One of you has eaten my salt and betrayed me to my enemy. Speak! Which of you is the Judas?"

There was a tremor in the line, but none spoke. King Arthur turned to the chief steward.

"Bare their backs. A taste of my riding crop and we shall know the guilty one."

Merlin touched his elbow.

"Sire, under pain they will all confess. And we will be none the wiser."

"Then hang them all! We will rid this camp of vermin."

"And you will carry to your grave the killing of five innocent men."

Our King sat down heavily. He put his hand to his eyes.

"Then how? How will we know which to hang?"

"Allow me, Sire. Alaric, my saddlebags."

I brought them to him with haste. He took therefrom a jar, in the likes of which good wives store treacle. He poured from it on the ground, forming a circle about the six serving-men.

"And now, remove the torches."

When this was done, the tent became not dark as would be expected. But the circle about the serving-men glowed green, filling the tent with a fearsome light. I could see fear on the faces of all. But they could not know, as did I, that the magic circle was but foxfire mixed with honey.

My master said slowly, in deep tones, "There you stand within a circle of fire. And the spirit of fire will seek out the guilty one . . . Hold out your right hands!"

Six trembling hands were extended. Into each Merlin dropped a white stone the size of two thumbs.

"Clasp the stone tightly. If you are innocent you have nothing to fear. But the spirit of fire will have no mercy on the guilty one. Tightly, I say, more tightly!"

For full a hundred heartbeats they stood clasping the stones.

Then great drops of sweat began to form on the forehead of one. He clenched his teeth as in pain. The fingers of his hand slowly opened, as though against his will. The stone fell to the ground and there in the palm of his hand was a great blister, as though he had been holding a red-hot coal.

"Bring in the torches," cried my master.

This was done. The lad stood there staring at his hand in disbelief.

"Who is this wretch?" asked our King of the chief steward.

"He is one Richard Dale, Your Majesty."

"And where did he come from?"

"He was assigned me by Sir Marvin."

"Then call Sir Marvin and let him explain."

"That he cannot do. Sir Marvin was killed in the first day of fighting."

"Then you know not that Sir Marvin truly assigned him?"

"He came to me saying that. I was in sore need of serving-men and took him."

"You could not know," said our King. Then wearily, "Take the lad to the hangsman."

Then for the first time the lad spoke. He squared his shoulders and looked our King full in the eyes.

"Nay, Sire. Condemn not Robert dhu Brian to so base a death."

"Robert dhu Brian? Sir Brian's nephew. Very well, then. Execute him with honor at dawn."

They took him away. Could I but say that after his death the war was quickly over! But 'twould not be so. True, Sir Brian's army met with defeat, and soon, but many weary months were to pass ere all his followers were searched out and found.

On the way home, naught was spoken of the events that had transpired. 'Tis not well for sorcerers to discuss their art before those not versed in magical lore. But at last we were alone in our chambers. Merlin was leaning back in his great chair, staring at the ceiling.

"Master, you have not taught me to control the spirit of fire."

He looked at me.

"There is no spirit of fire." He thought a moment. "No, I am wrong. There is a spirit of fire, but not a supernatural one. You know the natural spirit full well."

"I do?"

I tried to remember all he had taught me, but I remembered not that. He reached into a box beside him and tossed me a white stone.

"Hold that in your hand. Tightly."

I grasped the stone. In a moment I felt it becoming warm. Then hot. In alarm, I dropped it. My palm was already red.

"Examine it."

I picked up the stone carefully. It was now cool but my palm was still hot. 'Twas but a piece of sandstone. I smelled it and understanding came.

"Mustard," I exclaimed. "The spirit of fire is naught but the spirit of mustard which burns the skin even as fire."

"Aye. One stone was soaked in oil of mustard and I had but to drop it into the hand of the guilty one."

I smiled to myself at having been able to riddle the secret. And 'twas minutes before I realized that I had not riddled the full secret.

"The guilty one, Master? How could you tell to which servingman to give the stone?"

Merlin smiled.

"As I gave the stones, I examined their hands. That of a serf or even a freedman is horny with toil. Only a noble could have had a hand as soft as that of Robert dhu Brian."

KING'S MAGE

TANITH LEE

Tanith Lee (b. 1947) is one of Britain's most accomplished and most respected writers of fantastic fiction. Ever since her first adult novel, The Birthgrave *(1975), Tanith has developed a formidable body of work. In some she creates her own world of legends, such as her Tales from the Flat Earth sequence, starting with* Night's Master *(1978), drawn from the* Arabian Nights, *whilst in others, like* Red as Blood *(1983), she offers her own rewrite of folk and fairy tales. Surprisingly she has written few Arthurian stories, although many of her tales of doomed knights reflect the Arthurian paradox. You will find her "The Minstrel's Tale" in Parke Godwin's anthology* Invitation to Camelot *(1988), and the beautifully Arthurianesque "The Kingdoms of the Air" in the special Tanith Lee issue of* Weird Tales *(Summer 1988).*

He looked down from his dark tower, and saw the land as he had seen it, changing only with seasons and weather, times of day, for almost two decades. The familiarity of the view did not reassure. It bored him, oppressed him and, on bad days, made him fearful. But then, he had everything to fear. They thought, those golden young men and silvery girls, they thought his fears were of sombre terrors and Hellish acts they could never, even in their high and incredible and stupid, blind courage, dare to contemplate. Only he was brave enough to stare into the mirror and beyond the veil. But he knew such things were only shadows, or lies. What he truly feared was they themselves, the knights and ladies, the beautiful ones. And, obviously, himself.

The view was, though, quite pleasing. The rolling plain with its fields now bronze and green, the soft hills rising away to bluer taller heights beyond. The river. The walled castle-city, with its stone towers and streaming pennants. And, westward, the forest, haunt of wolves and bears and lynxes. Useful, the forest. They went there, of course, the young men and girls, they went Maying and hunting and sometimes trysting, under the green summer boughs. But he knew the forest in winter, and moonlight glades and caves, the rare plants and herbal secrets. Here, at the tower top in the room to which, very seldom, any of them intruded, rested polished skulls he had found, collections of feathers, mossy stones. At these they looked askance and with reverence. They imbued his childish treasures with romantic power: they were his.

He rubbed his shoulders. Today both were sore. There was a herb for that, or a bee-sting might be better, but he did not like to kill bees just to ease himself for a month or so. He must expect discomfort. He was very old, in his fifty-second year, an age few others would reach. Even the king, goldenmost of them all, even Artur would probably not live into his forties, let alone any longer. His pale beautiful queen would doubtless die of childbearing, as half the women did. Then again, they had been married a while, and she showed no signs. She might be barren. Or Artur was impotent, another possibility. He was a man for men, liked his knights about him, fighting and jousting and gaming, even praying in the chapel. The company of women made Artur uneasy. He held them at a distance, wanting them to be icons. Gweneva was fitted for that, with her long flaxen hair, her pale skin and cool, moated eyes.

The old man had never had much taste for women either. In his youth they had frightened him, one especially, whose image, like a bright hot yellow flame, had never left him. By thirty he had lost all inclination, and Artur's laws finally, which put women upon pedestals and left them there, made casual lust difficult, and the old man was not displeased. The young managed as they could, but mostly they did everything but lie together – or they did so with a sword between them, trembling with need, until one or both was released by a spasm less pleasure than exasperation.

Those who fell knew better than to come to the mage for assistance. There was a village witch who could do as much as he, in any case. Old Thistle it had been, once, though who had the function now he did not know. She too kept clear of him.

Merlinus sighed. He must go on with the grinding of the pestle and mortar, hurtful to his joints though it was. He had been out before dawn, out in that forest. Foxes were still playing under the trees, slender amber creatures that fled without much fright, more from scorn, at his arrival. He had plucked the funguses, recognizing them by their Satanic shape. He knew well the places where they grew.

Over the plain below the castle, rooks cawed, and Merlinus peered to see what disturbed them. His sight was not as sharp as it had been, but at a distance he could make out things quite well. He saw a mailed and armoured figure, fiery in the early sunlight, a plume of dull red floating from his helm. A knight, and on the track to the tower. Wanting something very much, or he would not have dared to trouble the king's mage.

Merlinus shook out his sleeves. He went to the carved chair at the stone table, and sat down to wait. All around, the things which were his silent accomplices, the huge books brought, at such expense, out of the East, and from Rome, books which they, in their ignorance, did not know he could read, or barely, tracing the script with one finger, saying aloud things he had memorized in his youth, or – those things forgotten – new, invented things. And the human skull, on which sometimes he laid a possessive hand. The phials of liquids, the bronze balance, scribblings in a Latin he himself had made up.

He glanced at his own hands as he sat there. Claws like an ancient eagle. Rings of gold and silver grown into the thin pouched flesh. A wristlet of iron that they believed had powers, but which he had found in his childhood, on a rubbish dump.

Presently, he heard the knight at the threshold below. The door to the tower of Merlinus was always ajar. There were guardians, of course, unseen – unreal – revered. He heard the knight greet them politely, and ask leave to ascend. Then, since nothing stayed him, he came up. The mailed feet scraped the stair.

Merlinus wondered if he would remember the name of the knight. But, as the young man appeared, stooping in the low doorway, Merlinus knew he had not recalled. And so he gave the knight a fresh name, a mystical name. "Greetings, Knight of the Morning. I have been awaiting you."

The knight was serious and stern, his eyes enlarged. He would be about eighteen, the age of most of them, the flower of Artur's men. His hair was cropped, in the Arturian fashion, his skin brown and clear, his body wide with muscle and good food.

He licked his lips, a little nervous at being in the close private presence of the king's mage, a man said to be many hundreds of years old, who perhaps even lived backwards, who had seen the past, the future too, who had abilities greater than those of sword and lance, darker talents, brighter.

"You knew that I was coming, sir?"

"Naturally," said Merlinus.

They did not seem to understand he could, anyway, see them for miles from his high tower.

"Then, sir, my reason for seeking you—"

Merlinus divined that the young man, thinking the mage could read minds, supposed there was no need to enlighten him.

Merlinus said, quietly, "You must speak aloud your mission to me. How else am I to judge if your mind and heart are in agreement?"

The knight faltered. What was his name? Perivalle? Gwern? No, it would not come. Merlinus recollected seeing him joust, knocking others from their horses, flaunting a lady's favour with tiny pearls that were shaken off as he rode.

"I long to do the work of my king," said the knight. "Some task—"

Merlinus grasped the facts easily now. The young man was dissatisfied. He wanted a quest. It was continual, this hunger. Fighting and singing and praying and eating were not enough, hungering after a woman's white body, constantly chastely denied, wore them down. Really, he need not have bade the knight speak out. Merlinus could have guessed it all, and, ten years before, he would have risked a pronouncement. No matter. The knight had not fluctuated from his urgent awe.

"Perhaps," said Merlinus, "some deed awaits you." He put his hand upon the skull, and the knight's eyes flickered to it, and away. "If you will vaunt with death. If you dread nothing save dishonour."

The knight knelt before the mage. Probably it was more comfortable, the young man was tall and the tower ceiling low.

"I am pledged. To my God, my king, and my lady."

"Then you have only to wait," said Merlinus.

"How long?"

It was a cry, nearly anguished. Travel was what they wanted most, to move away from the safe castle-city where every ritual was prescribed. To wander oceans, lands, to take a chance, trusting only their strength and the might of Heaven, which was on their side.

Merlinus, in his youth, had never been like that. He had been forced to wander, wishing only to be safe. He had felt no sure protection, and learned the little he had of herbs and conjuring tricks from old outcasts, witch-women who had fancied him, unwise priests. His small knowledge served him where he had no fighting skills. At eighteen, this one's age, the hair of Merlinus had already turned white from constant worry and under-nourishment. A young old man. People began to respect this curious apparition, who had the wit, by then, to stare them down, promise ill in exchange for bad treatment, and good for good.

By the time Merlinus had spied Artur, a peasant's son, but so handsome, so bold and strong, like a crown of gold, Merlinus had had the wit, too, to put his fortune in with Artur's. And as Artur swung and hacked and roared his glorious way up the staircase of Britannia, Merlinus had trodden at his back, a shadow with glowing eyes. He could poison also, and that had been handy. And, once, Merlinus had had a wonderful voice. Actor's gifts. Murderer's gifts. And luck. Lucky to have fallen in with the golden bear who ruled like a sun in the high stone house.

"Not long," Merlinus said to the Knight of the Morning. "Go and pray. Pray to God. Something is moving towards the castle-city. Perhaps it is for you it comes."

The knight seized his free hand and kissed it. Merlinus knew he reeked of medicines and dusts, proper sorcerous things.

As the boy went down the stair again, Merlinus took up the pestle and mortar and began once more on the fungus.

They were all of them so hungry. For adventure, for life. Was this what could make their days so short? And was it his aversion to and terror of life that had rendered him extended years?

There would come a time, he would need to find some quest that could encompass them all. He foresaw that, as if by sorcery, indeed. Their restlessness, no wars any longer to entertain them. Some huge enterprise must be found.

The bronze ground on the bone, and the strong-smelling muck squashed between. The kiss the knight had given his fingers might have anointed the young lips. Already maybe, he would be enjoying some notion of fate.

Merlinus saw the yellow sunlight had reached his table, and for a moment, she was there. Only a moment. Morgan, with her hanks of yellow hair, her smooth yellow dresses, her yellow cat's eyes.

There were stories of her still, her vast genius with magic, her wickedness. There was some tale she had seduced Artur, or was his sister, or something like that. Merlinus remembered her better than the knight he had spoken with ten minutes before. He had seen her draw a saffron snake out of her bosom, and feed it back. This was a clever conjuring trick, like some of those he had mastered. But she had grown old, as he had. The fox hair went to grey, and the firm serpent body to rolls of fat.

She was no more a sorceress than he was a mage. And both of them were famous. How strange.

Every night they feasted in the castle, but on certain nights, times of religious or military significance, the feast was of a sensational nature. Tonight was such a time, and Merlinus was to go to the castle. He would sit on the king's right hand.

The afternoon was turning over, the rooks circling the plain, winging above the fields between the villages.

The king's mage walked, as was his custom, in his rook-dark robe, leaning on his staff, from whose top, if he had said the fearsome word, lightnings might shoot.

In the villages they stole out to look. The women curtseyed and the men touched their foreheads. A child brought the old man a stoop of cool milk. He said kind words to them and they rejoiced.

The road sloped up, and as it came towards the castle-city, grew steep, and Merlinus heard the breath rasp in his lungs, despite the infusion he had given himself.

In the end, he would die. It must come. How then to protect them, these trusting people, the equally trusting, glittering, dangerous lords of the citadel, the king himself? Some fantasy would need to be woven. He should think of preparing it. He could not simply go away.

He climbed, and his ears rushed like the sea. Some of them would go over the sea, after tonight. He had decided, it should be a great quest, now. Not only for the one young knight, for whoever responded. But what, what should it be? Was his invention deserting him? Perhaps one of them would cry out something, as had happened those other several times – the image of the white hart crowned with stars racing into the hall, or the giant with the green beard – a pagan totem that they had passed, for they were Christians, and paganism among them was unthinkable.

The gates stood open, and he had paused in a grove of trees to breathe, so that he went in lightly. Artur's guards saluted him, and on the street they swayed aside to let the mighty magician pass.

At the high place too he was saluted and motioned courteously on. Long ago, it had amused him, amused him alongside his fear that they would find him out. But now, now he was only glad. It seemed to him that, mingled in their reverence, their whispers of his name, was a gentleness that would not let them see – it never had – the truth, the elderly bent man in his ruinous dark robe stinking of nightshade and wolfsbane and cloves and mushrooms.

The castle was beautiful. Towers and walls. A wide stair led from a courtyard ripe with banners, up into a hall of massive pillars, with a painted floor. Beyond lay the Chamber of the Round Table, where Artur sat in council with his knights. That table was a wonder, brought from far off, some Eastern land, a great wheel of pale greenish stone, made like the antique temple to the south, by ancient craftsmen whose skills mysteriously exceeded modern ones.

Flags dripped from the walls of the hall, and weapons were put up there, and trophies taken in war and tournaments. But the tables were draped with white embroidered Eastern cloth and the chairs were carved, unlike the plain stone benches of the Table Chamber.

Already the musicians played warbling tunes, and the knights and the women went to and fro, and the vast wolfhounds padded about in their collars of gold and silver. Perfumes burnt in trays, but overall there was the smell of the coming dinner, enormous roasts of boar and venison, and little ones of hare and chicken, rich malty breads, dishes of beans and cabbage, pastries, while on the boards already balanced castles of marzipan, and platters heaped with red and green summer fruit.

When Merlinus entered, they applauded him, calling his name. They were really happy that he had come, and he knew that if he had not done so, due possibly to the inertia of old age, they would have been afraid. He was their talisman. None had a mage like Merlinus, as none had a king like Artur.

And next Artur was there, walking between his court in a blood-red garment trimmed with gold, and, with her pale hand on his arm, that pale woman Gweneva, her white greyhound stalking on its jewelled leash at her side. Artur held the mage in his arms, and the crowd applauded again, that their king could be so familiar with the sorcerer.

Merlinus presented his gift, an alabaster vessel filled with choice Roman wine.

"For the most sumptuous course," said Artur. "And tonight, my queen shall drink it too."

Gweneva lowered her protective, primitive eyes. "It is too strong for me, my lord."

"She always says this," said Artur. He invited, by some glint of his expression, that those who heard should see Gweneva referred also to him: *He is too strong for me.* His kisses had burned her, his seed scorched. For this reason she did not conceive.

He drew Merlinus aside, and three knights came chastely to woo Gweneva. She fed her dog apples.

"My mage, I must talk to you, about the queen."

Merlinus said, softly, "You are the sun and she the moon. Two such lights cannot always be as one."

"No riddles," said Artur. He added quickly, "I beg you, sir."

"Artur," said Merlinus, "something comes towards this place. I think that tonight it will be among us. It is greater and more valid than any earthly love, however sweet, or wish, however needful."

Artur tensed a little. He knew, secretly, that it was his fault he had no heir. Merlinus could work miracles, but not such a miracle as that. Only God could do that, and had done so. To be distracted was a fine escape.

"Is this a prophecy, sir?"

"A feeling, merely. We must see."

They went to their seats, everyone sat down, and the dogs lay under the tables. The food came on silver inlaid with gold.

Merlinus ate sparingly, which they thought ascetic. In his youth he had gorged himself whenever – rarely – he had had the occasion. Would have done so now, his mouth watered. But his digestion would not allow him greed. He must always be careful. He plied his silver knife and skewer cautiously, and in the windows the light ran thick honey, and then blue crystal, and the pages lit ranks of candles like tall white girls with heads of rippling flame.

And Merlinus pondered if he would think of her again. Morgan, the witch girl in her yellow dress. Soon the roasted stag would be brought in, clad in antlers and wreathed by roses. Artur would pass around the alabaster flask of sorcerous wine.

Generally Merlinus pretended that he drank from it. Tonight – tonight should he do so? He glanced about. The golden young men and the silver girls. They laughed and toyed together, twined fingers and sometimes, daringly, a kiss was put upon a peach or piece of bread, and given over. Under the Eastern cloth, the brush of feet. They must do no more.

But now the knights were eager for other sustenance. Their eyes blazed. That one, the Knight of the Morning, he had murmured of the mage's words. Something came towards them – only the king had not heard, Merlinus had had to tell him himself.

The doors opened wide, and in staggered the servers with the stag. They brought it to the carving place, and split it open. The dogs, so well-trained, even they could not quite resist now, and stood up. The knights strained forward.

They did not know what he put into their wine. And yet, they understood that it was always at this point of the feast that magic or wonder occurred – the maiden on her milky horse pleading for justice, the giant, the hart—

The alabaster flask began to move. Each poured a drop into his cup, into his lady's cup. And Merlinus too. But never before had he drunk.

He was so old now, perhaps it would kill him. What would they do if he died before them here? Think some enemy had struck him down by an evil spell, and go back to war?

No, it would not kill. A mild dose in the heady wine. The fungus anyway was benign. Did not the birds sometimes eat it, and the rabbits?

Merlinus watched until all were served. They raised their goblets high. They drank deep. It was the mage's gift. His blessing.

And Merlinus allowed himself one sip.

Too little, it must be. For nothing at all – he must wait, as in the past, for their cries to begin, the images of their brains appearing before them. And then he must direct them.

And yet. Ah, but he saw. All the tall candles *were* girls. Their intoxicating heat spread to envelop him, like high noon in July. Not uncomfortable, soporific. Soothing. Merlinus stared, and suddenly the closer vision of his youth seemd to have come back to him. Through the doors, as if through a curtain of mist, he saw them come, the white girls with their flaming hair. But she walked before them, Morgan, young, in her primrose gown and tresses, her wild eyes like a cat's, fox's, veiled. The women held the things of war, lances, swords, but she, she held a cup of gold under a golden cloth. Was it for him, this drink, at last the wine to end all fear – and was it death, and would he take it, abandon them, let them think what they wanted as he fell dead in their midst? An end to responsibility.

But she did not bring that, and he was still responsible. It was not fear, he did not fear them any more. He had made them give him safety, and now he must repay their – what? – their reverence, their respect? Or was it – was it love they had given? Oh, how to repay their love.

He stood. Merlinus raised his voice, and it was marvellous again, as once it had been. He said, "Three women bearing the weapons of death, and also the Cup of Life. Do you see?"

And they saw. In wonder they sat, their faces pale as the tablecloths, their eyes bright as the silver and the gold. They did not visualize terrible, lovely Morgan, the enchantress. They saw a holy Christian vision, born of some mushrooms in wine, and some words he had said.

"God, God," muttered Artur, his white wife forgotten, as Merlinus had forgotten the name of the young knight. "It is the Cup of the Christ."

The hall was full of burning exquisite light, and there the cup floated. Merlinus looked at it, and knew that he had done the nicest and the best thing of his life. He had given them an ultimate hope and beauty, better than sex or castles, better then mere existence.

He sat down quietly and realized that even if he did nothing, for his death some wonderful story would suggest itself to them. For in his way he had deserved it. In his way he was a true mage, a maker, a sorcerer.

The women were crying, tears like pearls, and the men crossed themselves and never had they looked so strong and valiant, so mighty. And there the Morning Knight – yes, his name was Percival. His eyes were like stars. His soul showed through his body like a gem.

Merlinus sat, and pushed away the sorcerous wine, tenderly, without complaint.

As his sigh dimmed back into the ability of an old, old man, he watched gorgeous Morgan, and her retinue of angels, bear from the hall of the castle the golden Cup of Christ's blood, the Grail.

A Quest Must End

Theodore Goodridge Roberts

Theodore Goodridge Roberts (1877–1953) was one of the few writers to produce a regular flow of Arthurian stories in the years after the Second World War when fantasy fiction generally dropped out of favour. At that time he was writing chiefly for the men's adventure magazine Blue Book *which contained a wealth of fantastic and historical adventures. These included a series of Arthurian stories which I had the pleasure of collecting together as* The Merriest Knight *(2002), and which included the following story.*

The Forge in the Wilderness

Quests ridden on, and sweated and bled for, and peradventure perished in, are as multitudinous as the stars. They have been of dreams, vanities, love, ambition, hate, whiffs of temper and idle whimsy; for the Fountain of Youth, the Phoenix' nest, unicorns with golden horns, dryads and nymphs and yet more elusive beauties, the Questing Beast which ran with a noise in its belly as of a pack of baying hounds, and was chased by King Pellinore and others of renown; and latterly the Holy Grail, which was sought by many and achieved – quite obviously with the assistance of the celestial hierarchy – by exemplary Sir Galahad.

Almost all questers rode singly, and won their places in song and story as solitary champions, but a few shared their quests and went in couples, and of these were old King Torrice of Har and his young Irish grandson Sir Lorn Geraldine. Once met, only death could break that fellowship or divide its mad adventures.

For more than a sennight they had followed tracks which had

come to nothing, day after day, save narrower and rougher tracks. It was fifteen days since their last dealings with a farrier or any other kind of smith; and now, what with broken shoes or no hoof-iron at all, every horse was lame; and every man, whatever his degree, was on his own two feet. King Torrice was in a fretful humor, for pedestrianism was as foreign to his spirit as it was to his feet, and irked his soul equally with his corns. But young Sir Lorn maintained his habitual air and appearance of baffled thought and pensive abstraction, walking equably and unconcernedly. In truth, it was only when violently employed with spear or sword that he seemed to know or care how many legs were under him and at his service. Ah, but he knew then, never fear, and made the most of whatever number it happened to be!

"We'll be carrying them on our backs before we can win clear of this cursed wilderness," complained the King.

Next moment, one of the squires cried out and pointed a hand.

"A smithy! Look there under the great oak. Forge and anvil complete, by Judas!"

All came to a dead stop and looked, like one man and one horse: and there it was, sure enough – a rustic hut with an open front disclosing forge and bellows and anvil.

"But no smith, of course," said the King. "He's gone off in despair – and small blame to him! A fool he must be to look for trade where there's no population – unless he counted on the patronage of unicorns and wild cattle."

"Nay, sire, look again!" cried the same squire. "At the forge. Stirring the fire. But I'll swear there was no blink of fire a moment ago!"

All except Sir Lorn gasped and gaped in astonishment, and even he looked interested; for there, for all to see, was a human figure where naught but wood and iron and the leather bellows had been visible a moment before. A lively figure, at that, with the right hand busy at the red glow in the blackness of the forge, and the left raised high to the upper beam of the bellows: and while the travelers still stared as if at a warlock, the bellows creaked and exhaled gustily, and the fiery heart amid the black coals pulsed and expanded. A piece of white-hot metal was withdrawn in the grip of long pincers and laid on the anvil and smitten with a hammer, and sparks spurted and flew.

* * *

Then King Torrice bestirred himself; with a mutter in which irritability was somewhat tempered by awe, he turned left into the ferns and brambles, and advanced upon the smithy stiffly but resolutely, with his hoof-sore charger stumbling after, and did not halt until his whiskers were threatened by the sparks. Then he spoke in a loud voice, but the tone was constrainedly affable.

"Greetings, good Master Smith! Well met, my fine fellow!"

After six more hammer-clangs of cold iron on hot, the din and sparks ceased and the smith looked up from the anvil. He too was of venerable appearance and whiskery, but most of his snowy beard was tucked out of view and danger into the top of his leather apron, whereas Torrice's luxuriant appendage flowed broadly down his breastplate even to his belt.

"So here you are!" said the smith. "Well and good! One score and three completed, and this one will fill the tally." He nodded toward clusters of horseshoes of various sizes dangling from spikes in a wall, then thrust the cooling iron in his pincers back into the heart of fire.

"What d'ye say?" the old King-errant gasped. "Irons ready for six horses? Even so – and I don't believe it! – they'll not fit my six!"

"I'll attend to you in a minute," mumbled the smith.

The bellows creaked and snored, and the fire glowed; and soon that piece of iron, again white as noonday sun, was back on the ringing anvil, and the sparks were flying again like golden bees. King Torrice stood silent, gawking like a boy, until the iron was beaten exactly to the smith's fancy, and pierced for nails, and finally plunged into a tub of water with a hiss and jet of steam. Now the smith was at his horse, and old nails and fragments of old shoes and hoof-parings fell simultaneously.

"He must have six hands!" muttered the King.

Now a little hammer went tapping as fast as the sedate charger could lift and lower his feet.

"Next!" cried the smith

Sir Lorn's great white horse came next, then the squires' hackneys, and last the two packhorses led by grooms, but all so fast – for every ready shoe fitted – that the King and the squires began a suspicious inspection. The smith straightened his back, tossed his apron aside and uttered a cackle of laughter.

"You are wasting your time," he said, and fell to combing his whiskers with a golden comb that appeared in his hand as if by magic. "All is as it seems, if not more so," he added, and cackled again.

"In all my life I never saw anything like it," said the King.

"You could forget a few things in that length of time," said the smith.

Torrice stiffened and asked loftily: "What do I owe you, my good fellow?"

"I'll name you a special fee, a mere token price, having taken a fancy to Your Worship," replied the smith. "What d'ye say to paying for the nails only, and never mind the shoes and the labor? One farthing for the first nail, a ha'penny for the second, a penny for the third, and so on?"

"I can afford to pay what I owe," said Torrice, with a royal air, "and am accustomed to paying more, so you will oblige me by stating your charge and having done with it."

"Not so fast!" cried the squire who had spotted the forge. "What d'ye mean by 'and so on,' old man? Tuppence for the fourth nail and fourpence for the fifth, is that it?"

The King exclaimed fretfully: "Enough of this vulgar talk of farthings and pennies! Pay him what he asks, good Peter."

"Nay, sir, mauger my head!" cried the squire. "I learned that manner of computation from a farrier at St Audrey's Fair, in my youth, an' would still be in his debt – and I had but one beast, mark ye! – if I hadn't settled the score with my stout cudgel, there an' then."

The smith laughed heartily, patted Squire Peter's shoulder and chuckled: "Spare the cudgel, friend, and I'll be content with a horn of ale."

"I don't get it," muttered Torrice. "All this jabber about nails. But let it pass." His voice and brow cleared. "But ale you shall have, worthy smith, and a share of our supper, and three silver crowns for your pouch."

"Gramercy," said the smith.

The horses, all firm of foot now, were soon unsaddled, unloaded and hobbled in a nearby glade of sweet grasses to which the smith had led the way. But now the sun was behind the westward tree-tops. A small pavilion was pitched; a small keg was broached; and a fire was made of deadwood from thickets of underbrush. By the time the black pots were boiling, the smith's horn had been replenished twice, and a white star was glinting in the east.

It was a simple supper of boiled corned beef and bacon and wheaten dumplings, barley scones and cheese and honey; and for drink there was malt ale for all, and mead and usquebaugh too for the knights and squires and thirsty guest. The smith ate and drank more than anyone else, and at the same time, did most of the talking. The King, who had been taught never to drink with food in his mouth, and never to speak with his mouth full, was horrified at the simultaneous flouting of both rules of behavior: and at last he cried out a protest:

"There's plenty of time, friend! Have a care, or you'll choke!"

The smith laughed, and said: "I apologize for offending your quality, of which I cannot pretend ignorance, for this is not our first meeting. I would know you anywhere and at any time for what you are, no matter how small your retinue and how restricted your commissariat at the moment. But don't misunderstand me. Your present company makes up in character and promise what it lacks in strength. This young knight is suffering from a misadventure, but the fact that he survived it with nothing more serious than a gap in his memory and a grievous void in his heart is proof that he is destined for great things."

"What do you know of that?" Torrice interrupted, loudly and with a violent gesture.

"What I see," replied the smith coolly.

"And what's that? There's nothing to see!"

"Nothing for dull eyes, you mean. But as I was saying, this is the first time I have known the munificent Torrice of Har to lack a few flasks, at least, of French or Spanish wine."

"So you know me?" the King cried, "But I was never in this forest before!"

"Nor was I," the smith chuckled; and while all save Sir Lorn gaped in wonder, he added: "Are you so old, my friend, that you no longer recognize the master-touch?"

The King clapped a hand to his head, and sighed and muttered:

"Merlin! I should have known it at the forge! But you were not so helpful at our last meeting – on the contrary! But that was long ago." He stood up and did the correct thing, though still dazedly. "Duke Merlin, this is my grandson Lorn Geraldine – an Irish grandson. And these two gentlemen are our squires Peter and Gervis."

Sir Lorn stood up and louted low, cap in hand, but no slightest flicker of eye or twitch of lip paid the tribute of recognition to that potent name. But the squires' reaction was entirely flattering. Standing bare-headed and bowed double, Peter and Gervis regarded with awestruck eyes and blanched faces the person who had so lately shod their horses; and the uncouth fellows at the far side of the fire sat with podding eyes and hanging jaws, powerless to stir a muscle. The great magician looked around with a gratified smirk.

"Gramercy, friends," he said. "You have heard of me, it seems – and only good, I'm sure. But sit down, gentlemen, I pray you. Let us be at ease together again."

King Torrice said to his squire: "Peter, be so good as to fetch that flask of green glass you wot of."

"Good Master Peter, by fetching all four flasks you wot of, two green and two brown, you will spare yourself a deal of footing to and fro," said Merlin dryly.

"Quite," said the King resignedly; whereupon Peter moved off hastily toward the stacked baggage.

Those treasured flasks contained potent foreign cordials, and not wine at all. The squires took their shares of the first one, then slept where they lay. The young knight went on to his share of the second flask, then retired to the pavilion on wavering legs but with unabated dignity. This left the two ancients tête-à-tête; and the talk, which had been anecdotal, changed in its character.

"A fine young man, your grandson, despite what happened to him," said Merlin. "Bewitched, of course! His case suggests the fine and merciless art of – but why name her? She goes by more names than Satan, and has done so since before Stonehenge was set up, like as not: *Lilith, Circe, Queen Mab, la Belle Dame sans Merci, the Maid of Tintagel, the Lost Lady of Caer Loyw, Fair Fiona, Dark Essylit, Weeping Rosamund, the Damosel of the Tower* and as many more as I have fingers and toes, but all one and the same perilous and indestructible witch, in my opinion. There are other and lesser enchantresses abroad; and as one can never be quite sure of one's ground in such matters, a man is well advised – aye, even such a man as myself – to avoid them all. I have taken chances, naturally – but as you see, without serious consequences.

"But my case is beside the point, considering the fact that my power of wisdom – call it magic, if you like – is greater than that of any known or recorded wizard or witch, and I doubt that I would have suffered more than a slight and temporary emotional disturbance even if I had ever fallen into the clutches of Lilith herself, under whatever guise or name. But your case, friend Torrice, is different; and I must confess that your respectable mentality – I say respectable for want of a more precise term – surprises me somewhat, after all your years of errantry. I am sure it has been by good fortune rather than by good management that you have escaped the attentions of one or more of those mischievous ladies."

"I am not so sure of that," said the King, unstoppering the third flask and replenishing both cups. "In my quest of Beauty, which I have followed devotedly, save for occasional domestic interludes, ever since winning my spurs, I have had many contacts with ladies, many of whom were mischievous; and I am not at all sure that some of them were not witches. I have never consciously avoided that sort of thing, but in the interests of my high quest have sought it, and even now I would not avoid the most disastrous of them all."

"Stout fellow!" exclaimed Merlin merrily, but on a note of derision.

He laughed, but briefly. He leaned toward his companion in sudden gravity and wagged a finger at him.

"Have a care, my friend," he cautioned. "Don't be too cock-a-hoop about your powers of resistance and survival. You've been lucky, that's all. I admit that your luck has held a long time, but I warn you that it will not last forever. That you have encountered many enchantresses in your long and comprehensive quest I'll not deny, but I tell you – and I'll stake my reputation on it – that every one of them has been entirely human. There wasn't a witch in the lot. Just daughters of Eve, all of them; and even they have caused numerous deviations from your quest, and not a few considerable delays.

"Don't think I don't know what I am talking about, old friend, for I have followed your extraordinary course with interest ever since chance first brought you to my attention, though you have been blissfully ignorant of my surveillance most of the time. And

I'll tell you now when that was. It was a great day with you, poor Torrice – young Torrice, then – the day an old woman in a red cloak gave you a little crystal vial containing two ounces of what she claimed to be the Elixir of Life. You have not forgotten it, I see."

"Certainly not!" cried the King. "Why should I forget it?" he demanded, with a defiant gesture in the course of which he drained and refilled his cup. "I drank it, didn't I? And it was a long, long time ago, wasn't it? And here I am!"

"True, my friend, here you are, and a marvel of spirit and physical fitness for a man of your age. Aye, or for one of a quarter your age. But what you swallowed that day was not the real thing – not the magical liquor you believed it to be. It was but an experimental step in the development of the true, the pure, the perfected elixir. But even so, it was not without merit, as you have proved. It has served you well so far, my friend: but it is my duty to warn you that the virtue of the stuff you drank on that May morning of the first year of your – ah, if you'll forgive the expression, your delightfully latitudinous quest – cannot be depended upon indefinitely."

"It was the Elixir of Life! And I am as good as I ever was!"

"Nay, not quite."

"Not quite? What do you mean by that?"

"Calm yourself, old friend. I speak for your own comfort and guidance. I mean that the old woman in the red cloak gave you a liquor that was not the perfected article, and that you are showing signs of—"

"Not so! I'll prove it on your person with spear or sword, horsed or afoot, if you promise to keep your unholy magic out of it! And what the devil do you know of my traffic with that old hag?"

"I abstain from all armed encounters, for the very reason that I could not keep my advantage of magic out of them even if I would: and my answer to your question is: *I was that old woman.*"

Sobered as if by a bucketful of cold water, Torrice hung his head in silence. Merlin also was in no mood for further speech at the moment, but refilled his cup and sipped with a contemplative and compassionate air.

The King was the first to resume the conversation.

"But what of you? You have drunk of it."

"Yes, when I had perfected it, I drank it," said Merlin.

"Then I may still drink of it," said Torrice hopefully.

"Nay, old friend, or you would live forever," Merlin replied gently.

"Why not? You will live forever. Then why not both of us?"

"I have my wisdom to support me – magic, to you, but the greatest in the world, by any name – to strengthen and console me. You have none of it."

"I could learn it."

"Nay, good Torrice of Har, not in a century. Nor in a millennium, for that matter. You lack the necessary – ah! – you are not the type for that sort of thing, dear old friend."

"Never mind the magic, then, but give me the elixir."

"No. I don't want to be the object of your curses throughout the ages. You have discovered a grandson and companion-at-arms. Do you want to outlive him? Consider that prospect, my friend."

The King considered it, sighed deeply and shook his head. He stared and sat blinking at the red embers of the fire.

"How long have I left to go?" he whispered.

"Long enough," said Merlin cheerfully. "I can't be more exact than that," he added: and the lie was cheerful too.

"And the end?" whispered the King anxiously.

Before replying to that, the magician pressed a hand to his brow as if in an extraordinary effort of foresight.

"I see it. Hah! Well done! Nobly done! . . . Ah, old friend, I envy you."

"Gramercy! And the lad? What of his – How fares he – at the last?"

"Nay, I cannot see so far."

The Smith is Gone but They Hear of a Pilgrim

The squire named Peter was the first of that company to awake to the new day. The sun was still behind the eastward wall of the forest when he opened his eyes. Having lain out all night, he was damp with dew from head to foot. He sat up and blinked at slumbering Gervis, at four overturned flasks of rare outlandish glass on the dew-gemmed sward, and at the black and gray of the fallen fire. The events of the previous evening flashed on his mind, confusedly yet vividly, and painfully, for his brain felt tender and his eyes too big and hot for their sockets.

"Honest ale will be good enough for me from now on," he muttered.

He made his stumbling way to a brook which skirted the glade, knelt there and immersed arms and head in the cool water. Vastly refreshed, he went back and stirred Gervis and the grooms to action; and all four, without a word but as if by spoken agreement, began rounding up the horses and examining their hooves.

"So it wasn't a dream!" cried Gervis; and he called all the saints whose names he could remember to bear witness that the episode of the forge had been sober fact. "I never thought to have that old warlock shoe a horse for me," he added.

"When you have served good old Torrice as long as I have, nothing will surprise you," Peter answered with a superior air.

"A search of the smithy now might be worth our while," suggested Gervis. "The secret of that trick would be useful, and it might even win a battle under certain circumstances."

So the two squires left the glade by the way they had come into it less than twelve hours before, in the hope of wresting a hint at least of Merlin's formula for horseshoeing from the deserted smithy while the magician continued to sleep off his potions in the pavilion. They had not far to go; and the back-tracking of the passage of six horses and seven men over fat moss and through lush fern was a simple matter. And there they were. There was the great oak, anyway – the identical old forest patriarch bearing scars of thunderbolts, a herons' nest and three bushes of mistletoe, and doubtless, a hamadryad in its wide and soaring world of greenery. The squires stood and stared. They moved their lips, but no sound came forth. Gervis' tongue was the first to thaw.

"Not here," he whispered. "Not the same tree. This isn't the place."

But he knew better. This was a unique tree. And here were the two ancient thorns, that had crowded one end of the smithy, and the hollies that had crowded the other end of it. This was the place, certainly. A fool would recognize it. Everything was here, just as it had been – except the smithy.

Peter shivered and found his tongue and said: "We'll go back and take another look at the horses' feet."

They returned to the glade and inspected all twenty-four hooves again. The new shoes were still in their places.

"I feared they had flown away after the smithy, forge, anvil and bellows," muttered Gervis.

"They may yet," said Peter grimly.

"But he seems to be a merry old gentleman and a true friend to King Torrice," said Gervis.

"There's more to that old warlock than meets the eye," Peter answered. "As for his friendship – well, from all I've heard, I'd liefer have him with me than against me, but it would suit me best to be entirely free of his attentions. He has a queer sense of humor, and a devilish odd idea of a joke, by old wives' tales I've heard here and there. Take King Arthur Pendragon's birth, for instance: You know about that, of course! Well, was that a decent trick to play on a lady? For all his high blood – he was born a duke, no doubt of that – the mighty wizard Merlin is no gentleman. He doesn't think like one – not like our Torrice, nor like our Lorn, nor like you who can boast an honorable knight for a father, nor even like me, stable-born and stable-bred. Aye, though my gentility be scarce a year old, I'm a better gentleman than Duke Merlin, by my halidom!"

"I agree with you, Peter – but not so loud, for here they come from the pavilion," warned Gervis.

King Torrice, in a kingly long robe of red silk, issued from the pavilion and looked to his front and right and left with an inquiring air. Sir Lorn, in an equally fine robe, appeared and stood beside his grandfather, yawning and blinking. And that was all. The guest, the great Merlin, did not come forth. The squires ran and halted and uncapped before their knights.

"How are the horses' feet?" asked the King.

"We have inspected them twice this morning, sir, and found all in order and every shoe in its place," Peter replied, and after a moment's hesitation, added: "But the smithy is gone, sir."

King Torrice nodded. He looked thoughtful, but not surprised.

"So is the smith," he said. "Let us hope and pray that his handiwork does not follow him."

"Every iron is tight and true, sir," Gervis assured him.

Peter spoke hesitantly.

"Sir, may I suggest that it might happen? His handiwork might follow him – the twenty-four iron shoes – even on the hooves of Your Honor's horses – if all I've heard of that old warlock's magic be true."

The venerable quester blinked and asked: "How so, lad? D'ye suggest that their potency could, and might, pull the hooves off the horses? And why not, come to think of it? It smacks of the Merlin touch, by Judas!"

"Yes sir – but I did not mean it just in that way. I meant to suggest that he might, if in a tricky mood, bid the twenty-four shoes to follow him – horses and all."

"Hah!" the King exclaimed; and he swore by half a dozen saints. "That's his game, depend upon it! And I was simple enough to think he had done us a good turn out of pure good will! The master touch, indeed! But what does he want of us? What devilment is he up to now? 'A horn of ale will settle my score,' said he. And he leaves an empty cask, empty bottles and four empty flasks of Araby. But he is welcome to all that, and would be welcome to a hundred silver crowns besides if I knew that the score was settled. But forewarned is forearmed; and we'll see to it that our horses go our way, not Wizard Merlin's, even if we have to unshoe them and lead them afoot again."

Breakfast was eaten; packhorses were loaded; the squires harnessed the knights and then each the other; and all four mounted into their high saddles. It was in all their minds that the march would be resumed in the same direction from which it had been diverted by the discovery of the smithy; so when all the horses wheeled to the right and plunged from the track as if by a common and irresistible impulse, King Torrice cried "Halt!" and pulled mightily on his reins. The squires pulled too, and the grooms pushed manfully against the thrusting heads of the packhorses; but Sir Lorn, up on mighty Bahram and with his thoughts elsewhere – probably in Faeryland – neither drew rein nor cried halt, but crashed onward through fern and underbrush. The pulling and pushing and protesting of the others was of no avail. Where Lorn's great white warhorse led, the King's old charger, the squires' hackneys and the stubborn beasts of burden would follow.

"Sir, this is what I meant!" cried Peter, coming up on the King's left.

"Gramercy!" gasped Torrice, who seldom forgot his manners, especially to his inferiors in rank.

Now they were beneath great oaks, with fallow deer bounding before them through netted sunshine and shadow, and tawny wild swine scattering right and left. Now charger and hackneys and ponies took their own heads for it, and ran as if possessed by devils. At the same moment Lorn drew rein and turned his head and waved a hand. The King and squires were soon up with him. He pointed through a screen of saplings.

"A good track," he said. "A wide and beaten track."

They all looked. There below them lay a better track than they had seen in a sennight, sure enough.

"It must go to some fine town, sir!" Gervis cried.

"I don't like it," said the King. " 'Tis not of our own choosing."

" 'Twill lead us out of the wilderness, sir, wherever to," Peter said: and in his eagerness to see a market and a tavern again, and houses with ladies and damosels looking down from windows, his distrust of Merlin was almost forgotten.

"Still I don't like it!" Torrice muttered. "Nor what brought us to it against our wills. I have gone my own way since first donning gold spurs. I'm a knight-errant, and baron and king. I acknowledge no human overlord save Arthur Pendragon – and I might defy even him at a pinch, as I have defied his father King Uther upon occasion. And now am I to jink this way and that at the whim of a tricky old magic-monger and the itch of bedeviled horseshoes? Nay, by my halidom!"

Just then the white stallion and Sir Lorn went through the saplings and down the short bank, turned left on the track and trotted purposefully; and the King's charger and the King followed, willy-nilly; and the hackneys and the squires; and the grooms and their charges, clanking and running and eating dust.

"Hold! Hold!" King Torrice bawled, worked up by now to a fury of defiance that was foreign to his naturally placid though restless spirit – but all he got for it was a bitten tongue.

But that flurry of advance took the little cavalcade no farther than around the next curve in the track. There Lorn pulled up, and all the others at his stirrups and his tail. Then all saw that which he had seen first. It was a dwarf standing fairly in the middle of the way and louting low.

"What now, my good manikin?" asked Torrice suspiciously: and he stared searchingly at the little fellow, looking for Merlin in yet another disguise.

Clearly and briefly the dwarf revealed his business. His mistress, Dame Clara, a defenceless widow, begged their lordships' protection from a cruel oppressor who had confined her within her manor house, beaten her stewards, driven off a full half of her flocks and herds, and was even now collecting her rents into his own pouch and demanding her hand in marriage.

"A widow," said the King reflectively, stroking his beard and wagging his head. "A beautiful widow, I presume – and as virtuous as beautiful, of course."

"The most beautiful lady in the land, Sir King!" cried the dwarf.

"Sir King?" queried Torrice. "Hah! So you know me, my friend! We have met before, is that it?"

"Nay, Your Kingship, but a poor old palmer home from a pilgrimage to Jerusalem visited us but a few hours since, and informed my mistress of the approach of the great King Torrice of Har and his noble Irish grandson Sir Lorn, and assured her that now her troubles were ended," replied the manikin.

Torrice looked at Lorn in consternation. He placed a shaking hand on the other's mailed thigh.

"You hear that, dear lad? Merlin – just as I expected! But he'll not make monkeys of us – to pluck his chestnuts out of fires. I'll wrench off those cursed shoes with my bare hands first! We'll turn now, and ride hard the other way."

The young knight said, "Yes sir," but immediately acted contrarily. Instead of wheeling Bahram, he stooped from his saddle and extended a hand downward to the dwarf, who seized it and was up behind him quick as a wink; and next moment all six horses were trotting forward again, with the great white stallion leading, but the King's tall gray – despite the King's protests – pressing him close.

The forest fell back on either hand, and they rode between ditches and hedges, green meadows and fields of young wheat and barley.

"Not so fast, young lord," cautioned the messenger. "Your great horse may need all his wind in a little while."

Lorn slowed the stallion's pace to a walk, and the rest slowed as well.

"I fear we'll pay dearly yet for our new shoes," said the King.

"But this is in the true spirit of our quest, sir – to succor distressed ladies and damosels," Lorn answered, with unusual animation in voice and eye. "How better can we discover what we are questing for, dear sir – whatever that is?"

"The soul of Beauty," said his grandfather. "In her true and imperishable shape! But at that time I believed myself to be imperishable too. But never mind that now. You are right, dear lad – the quest is the thing; and the higher and harder it is, the more honor to the quester, win or lose. But I'd feel happier about this if Merlin hadn't a finger in it."

They came to the brow of a hill and looked down upon a wide and verdant vale. There was a little river with a red mill, a great water-wheel and a pond lively with fat ducks. There were cornlands and grasslands; orchards of apple, pear and plum; hop-gardens which foretold brown ale, and little gardens of sage and thyme and savory foretelling well-stuffed ducks and capons and Michaelmas geese spitted and roasting to a turn; thatched roofs of farmsteads, and in the midst of all, the slated roofs, timber walls and stone tower of a great manor house. They drew rein and gazed at the fair prospect.

"What is it called?" asked King Torrice.

"Joyous Vale," the dwarf replied in a pathetic voice. "It was named in a happier time than now. Your Kingship," he added with a sigh.

"And where is your grievous tyrant?" asked the King.

"His pavilion is behind that screen of willows beyond the ford there; but he will show himself at the sound of a horn," said the dwarf.

Torrice stroked his beard and said: "As we have come thus far at Merlin's whim, we may as well see this thing through of our own will and in our own way. Peter, you have a horn. But just a moment, if you please. Lorn, the fellow is yours. If there is another, I'll attend to him. If there are more" – he smiled kindly at each of the squires in turn – "we'll have a proper ding-dong set-to, all for one and one for all. And now the horn, friend Peter."

It was already at Peter's lips; and he blew as if he would split it and his cheeks too. The echoes were still flying when a tall and wide figure in a blue robe appeared from behind the willows, stared, shook a fist and retreated from view.

"This is Sir Drecker, the false knight," said the dwarf. "He has a comrade as knavish as himself, but not so large, called Sir Barl, and four stout fellows who are readier with knives than swords. If they are all in camp now, Sir Drecker will soon reappear in full force; but if his rogues are tax-collecting and looting cupboards around-about, Your Kingship will not have to do with him yet awhile, for he will avoid contact until he has a sure advantage."

"D'ye say so, Master Manikin!" cried the King, snapping his eyes and bristling his whiskers. "Then you don't know me and my grandson, nor these two gentlemen our squires, nor, for that matter, these two grooms neither! We'll hunt him like a red pig! We'll exterminate him and his dirty marauders like rats in a granary!"

The dwarf smiled slyly, well pleased with the old King's temper. Sir Lorn, gazing fixedly at the willows beyond the little river, did not speak, but his nostrils quivered and his lips were parted expectantly. The horses stood with tossing heads and pricking ears.

"Here they come!" cried the dwarf.

Two knights on great black horses came slowly into view from the screen of willows. Their visors were closed and their shields dressed before them, but their spears were still at the carry, cocked straight up. They wheeled and drew rein above the ford.

"They have chosen their ground," said the dwarf.

"And very prettily – if they think we are fools enough to go charging down and through and up at them like mad bulls," jeered the King. "But where are the others?" he asked.

"Hiding under the bank, sir, among the osiers, depend upon it, Sir King – just in case their knives are needed," said the little man in green.

Torrice jeered again.

"In silk and fur-lined slippers I am one of the world's most artless fools, but in leather and iron I am quite another person," he told them. "Just as I have acquired all the skills of knightly combat, even so have I learned all the answers to the cowardly tricks of such scoundrels as these: by the hard way. Now give me your attention."

Five Die, but One Rides Away

Torrice and Lorn rode down to the ford at a hand-gallop, with closed visors, dressed shields and leveled spears; and the oppressors of the lady of the manor laughed derisively within their helmets, for now they would have nothing to do but push the witless intruders back into the river, men and horses together, as they scrambled, blown and off balance, to the top of the bank. But it did not happen just so. The false knights moved forward easily to the sounds of splashing and the clanging of iron on stones down there below their line of vision; but when nothing appeared at the top of the bank – no head of horse, no plume-topped casque, no wobbling spear-point – they drew rein. Now all was silent down there. And now the two squires of the intrusive knights came on at a hand-gallop, and clattered down to the ford and so from view; and silence reigned again.

Sir Drecker felt a chill of misgiving. He cursed, but uncertainly, and ordered his companion to advance until he could see what was going on under the bank. Instead of obeying, Sir Barl uttered a warning cry and pointed a hand. Drecker looked and saw a dismounted knight straightening himself at the top of the bank some ten spear-lengths to his left. Drecker laughed, for the advantage of horse and spear and shield was all his. He wheeled his great charger; but not even a good horse can be jumped to full gallop from a standing start, however deep the spurring. In this case, the spurring was too deep. The horse came on crookedly, with rebellious plunges. Sir Lorn moved suddenly in every muscle, and his sword whirled and bit the shaft of the spear clean through. Lorn dropped his sword then, and laid hold of the tyrant with both hands and dragged him from the lurching saddle. He knelt to unlatch the tyrant's helmet.

"Mercy!" screamed Drecker; and he straightway made a prayer pitiful enough to soften a heart of stone.

Lorn stayed his hand, but the weakening of his purpose was due to disgust, not pity.

"Faugh!" he cried; and he rose from his knees and booted Drecker's iron-clad ribs with an iron toe.

He stood straight and looked around him. He saw King Torrice come up from the ford on his venerable gray, moving slowly but with leveled lance, and ride at Sir Barl, who was ready and riding hard. Lorn's heart misgave him for a moment, but recovered as quickly when Barl's horse went clean out from under its master and galloped away, leaving that unhandy rogue grassed beneath a split shield and a punctured breastplate. Now he remembered the rogue Drecker, but only to see him up and running and already ten yards off. And now his white stallion Bahram topped the bank within a few paces of him, swung his great head and glowing eyes to survey the field, snorted like a dragon and went in thunderous pursuit of Sir Drecker.

After one backward glance, the tyrant went faster than any knight in full harness had ever before gone on his own unaided legs. He fled toward his own horse, which stood at no great distance. He would make it, even though the white stallion should continue to gain a yard on him at every earth-jarring bound. He would just make it, with nothing to spare – but once in his saddle, he would beat the devil off with his mace. He saw the mace, short-hafted and spike-headed, where it awaited his hand on the saddlebow; and it held his agonized gaze, and spurred him to the utmost cruel fury of effort, like a bright star of salvation. Now! One more wrench of muscles, nerves and heart, and he would be safe! He flung himself at the saddle, touched it with outflung hands – *and the black horse swerved*. Screaming like a snared rabbit, he fell flat on his vizored face.

Sir Lorn, who had stood staring like one entranced, shook off a mailed glove, thrust two fingers into his mouth and whistled like a kelpie. The great stallion clamped all four hooves to earth, tearing and uprolling the sod before him, and stayed his course a hand's-breadth short of his quarry. He stood uncertain, tossing and swinging his head and clashing bared teeth; but at a second shrill blast, he wheeled and trotted back to his master. Lorn patted his neck and was about to mount, but was checked by King Torrice.

"Too late," said Torrice, pointing.

Sir Lorn looked and saw the scoundrel whom he had spared twice up on his strong horse and in full flight, across meadow and cornland, toward the nearest edge of forest.

"Why did you let him go, dear lad?"

Lorn looked apologetically at his grandfather, who was afoot only a pace away, with the old gray's reins in his hand.

"A false knight," continued Torrice mildly. "Murderer, torturer, infanticide, seducer, traducer and common thief, according to the manikin Joseph. He would be better dead."

"I'm sorry," Lorn muttered with a red face. "Had he cursed me, or had he turned on Bahram – but no, he squealed for mercy. Mice have more manhood. I stayed my hand, and Bahram's hooves, for very shame – shame of all creatures made by Almighty God in His own image."

The old man was startled, distressed and confused. For all his ding-dong years of unconventional, even crazy questing, and his competence in the making of romaunts and rondels, he was still, at heart and head, a gentleman of the old school rather than a philosopher.

"Never mind it, dear lad!" he cried hurriedly. "There's no great harm done, I dare say. But your squire could have used that big horse very well. We have five remounts, however; and the least of them is bigger than a hackney. All proper warhorses. I shall shift my saddle to the late Sir Barl's big courser, and so let faithful old Clarence here travel light from now on. We have done very well. Five dead rogues and five quick horses, and not a scratch taken."

"And the blackest rogue and the biggest horse gone clean away!" moaned Sir Lorn. "But never again – no matter how so he may squeal and pray like a soul in torment!" he cried.

They crossed the little river and went behind the willows and took possession of the pavilions and everything else that they found there. The false knight who had fallen to King Torrice's spear, and the four knaves who had fallen to the swords and knives of squires Peter and Gervis and grooms Goggin and Billikin, were buried deep, and without benefit of clergy, by a party of rejoicing yokels.

The dwarf, whose name was Joseph, ran forth and back between manor house and camp, whistling in high spirits. He was a lively little man of uncertain age, flickering eyes and a sly smile. He fetched wine and cakes, with the Lady Clara's compliments and thanks, and took back King Torrice's poetical expressions of devotion. He fetched jellies and sweetmeats, and a pretty message from the lady to the import that she had made them with her own hands of the very last of her store of honey and other such ingredients: whereupon the King sent back to her, by the two squires in their best suits of velvet and Turky leather, his last crock of brandied peaches, a cup of silver gilt and a necklace of French workmanship.

The squires went side by side, with Joseph strutting importantly before. Master Peter carried the crock, which was considered by King Torrice as the senior gift, and Master Gervis carried the cup and necklace. Peter did not like the mission.

"Much more of this tomfoolery, and by Sir Michael and Sir George, I cast my new gentility like a snake his old skin and go back to my currycombs!" he muttered to his companion, as they marched along the most direct path to the great house.

Gervis laughed at him. Gervis had been born and bred to this sort of thing, and liked it.

"Then the more fool you, my Peterkin!" replied Gervis. "There would be no gentility but for the thing this mission of ours is a token of. Without it, chivalry would be naught but dust and sweat and spilled blood and broken teeth; and if bruises and empty bellies and foundered horses were the only rewards for questing, how long would knights-errant continue to mount and ride? Our royal old Torrice prates of the Spirit of Beauty, but it's the soft eyes and red lips which beset his ways that have withheld him all these years from the softest armchair in the biggest castle of Har. As for young Lorn – do you think he rides only for love of weary marches and hard knocks? Nay, nay, my Peterkin! He seeks that which he can neither remember nor forget. The Spirit of Beauty? Not so! The eyes and lips and hands and tender breast of a damosel he knew are his quest: and that she happened to be a heartless witch as well as an enchanting companion is his sad misfortune."

"I've had neither time nor opportunity for such plays, and no more acquaintance with elegant damosels than with luring witches," said Peter gruffly.

"But you have bussed goosegirls behind haycocks," said Gervis, and as Peter ignored this, he added: "Goosegirl or damosel or Queen Mab herself, the only differences between them are rosewater and moonshine. They all ply the same arts: otherwise, there would be no more chivalry in the courts of Camelot and Carleon than in forests of red swine."

"A pox on it!" muttered Peter.

People of all ages and several conditions gathered about their path from every direction. There were wobbly gaffers and gammers, and able-bodied men and women, and youths and wenches and toddlers and babes in arms. Only a few wore the bronze collars of serfs, but all appeared to be of the humblest sorts of peasantry – plowmen and herdsmen and ditchers, without a yeoman or steward among them, nor even a smith. All stared curiously and hopefully, yet fearfully, at the two squires, though these bore gifts in their hands and had only short ornamental daggers at their belts.

"Bah!" exclaimed Peter; whereat the nearer members of the crowd cringed backward as if from a whip.

"Are they sheep?" he continued, but less emphatically. "The tyrants were but six – and right here I see enough brawn to overcome a dozen such."

Joseph turned his head and replied, with a rueful grimace:

"You say truth, fair sir: but lacking a master, muscly brawn has no more fight in it than clods of earth. Sir Gayling and his squire were long past their physical prime; nor had they ever been notable cavaliers, but bookmen and stargazers and alchemists. They were murdered in my lady's rose-garden by the base knight Drecker – spitted like larks, and as easily; and the high steward and Tom Bowman the head forester – old gentlemen both – were waylaid and done to death in the North Wood; and the miller, a masterful man, was slain trickily in his mill by the other dastard knight; and their six knaves set upon Ned Smith working late at his anvil, and slew him; and after that, the four that had come alive out of the smithy, murdered three farmers and a master cheesewright in their beds."

"Weren't there any men about the house – butlers and the like?" asked Peter. "Scullions? Grooms and gardeners?"

"All too old," said Joseph. "Boyhood companions of poor Sir Gayling, most of them."

"A dozen old men hobbling on sticks, or old women even, would have served to chase off Drecker and his rogues," said Gervis. "Better still, a mixed force. I can see it in my mind's eye: the old lady herself, up on her palfrey, leading a host armed with crutches and distaffs against the invaders. That would have confounded them, and saved us the trouble of killing them."

He chuckled at the conceit, then sighed. Being young and romantic, he had hoped for something more amusing than the relict and household of a doddering old philosopher. The dwarf's only answer was a slow, peculiar smile. And so they passed through the wide gate and were met in the courtyard by an ancient major-domo and two old lackeys. After having names and style and mission shouted into his left ear by Joseph, the major-domo, leaning on his staff of office, led the squires into the great hall.

Dame Clara Entertains her Champions

The squires were gone a long time on that errand: fully two hours, by King Torrice's impatient reckoning.

"So here you are at last!" the King exclaimed with a poor effort at severity. "I began to fear that Merlin had waylaid you in the guise of a distressed damosel. Now what of your visit, lads? Were my poor gifts well received? And what is your opinion of the poor lady, and of the situation generally? The late Sir Gayling, I gather, devoted his time to stargazing and kindred impractical pursuits, with the result that his affairs were in a sad way even before his foul murder. The manikin has hinted as much, at least, in his own elusive manner. But even so, we have no time to administer the estate of every distressed person who receives our chivalrous services. We are knights-errant, not lawyers or magistrates. Have I neglected my own earthy interests all my life – the one score baronies and five score manors of my Kingdom of Har – to concern myself, at this late day, with a stranger's petty problems of lost rents and ravished cheeselofts? Not so, by my halidom!

"I am sorry for the poor old dame, of course; but we have already done our knightly duty by her. If she will accept a few hundred crowns, she is welcome to them. But we must be on our way again by noon tomorrow, without fail. Now tell me your opinion of this Lady Clara, my lads. Her messages have been prettily worded – but her manikin Joseph is a clever fellow, I suspect."

Gervis slanted a glance at Peter, but the senior squire continued to look straight to his front.

"Yes sir," said Gervis. "Very clever. I mean very pretty. That's to say, the lady was very polite. And she sent another message to Your Highness – and Sir Lorn – and it includes Peter and me too. It is an invitation to supper this evening."

Torrice sighed.

"Supper with a mourning widow." he muttered. "Do you know, dear lads," he went on in a better voice, "I fear I took a strain in the spitting of that rogue Barl. It looked easy – but the fact is, I'm a shade past my physical prime. A wrench when the full weight of man and horse was arrested by my point, you understand. A wrench of the back, which has already extended upward to the neck – a thing not to be disregarded, especially at my age. I have seen young knights incapacitated for days by just such wrenches. I shall stop here and rub my neck with tallow. See – I can hardly turn my head. And I am sure that my company would be of no more comfort to the bereaved chatelaine than her tears and moans would be to me. With a grandson and two squires to represent me at the supper table, I shall rest here on my cot with an easy conscience, no matter how uneasy a neck."

Again Gervis slanted a glance at Peter; and this time it was returned.

"Then we may go, sir?" cried Gervis, joyously.

Torrice regarded him with raised brows.

"It is the wine, sir," said Peter. "Gervis enjoys his cup. Dame Clara is very hospitable. We have tasted her wine already, sir. Wines, I should say – various but all rare. The despoilers did not get into the cellar. Old Sir Gayling's father was a collector of vintages from many lands, but Sir Gayling drank only milk and whey, it seems. And the lady said that she would produce even rarer vintages at supper than those already tasted by Gervis and me. And the butler told me there will be a lark-and-pigeon pie for supper."

"And strawberries and a sillabub," said Gervis.

"Say you so?" murmured the King; and he bent his brows and stroked his whiskers consideringly. "Poor lady! She might take it to heart, as an affront – my refusal of her hospitality. I don't want to hurt her feelings, but neither do I want her or any woman to think me discourteous, which she might if I excused myself on the plea of a crick in the neck. So, on second thoughts and for our common credit in the poor dame's eyes, I shall go, and grin and bear it."

Sir Lorn, who had lain flat and motionless and silent on a cot throughout the conversation, now swung his feet to the ground and sat up and spoke in a dull voice.

"I'll stay here. The poor lady owes me nothing at all – neither supper nor thanks."

"Nonsense!" his grandfather protested. "You pulled down the biggest of them all – and you afoot! No champion in Arthur Pendragon's train could have done it better, my dear boy."

"And to what end, sir?" Lorn muttered. "I pulled down the biggest rogue from the biggest horse – and they are gone unscathed, man and horse! But your rogue, and all the rest of them, are buried deep, and their good horses are ours. Peter and Gervis bloodied their swords, and the grooms their knives. Only I failed in duty. I'll stop right here, sir, by your leave."

But after half an hour of argument – in which Gervis was almost as voluble as the King, and even Peter grumbled and swore in support of the majority argument – Sir Lorn gave in.

Joseph reappeared at the pavilion to escort the guests to the manor house. The dwarf was still in green, but now of silk and velvet instead of wool. The knights and squires were sumptuously garbed. Having arrayed himself as if for a royal feast at Westminster or the court of Camelot, the King had insisted that Lorn and the squires should help themselves to what remained of his extensive wardrobe. Sir Lorn and Peter had accepted no more of this additional finery than could be politely avoided, but young Gervis had taken full advantage of the opportunity. They made the short passage from pavilion to great house on foot, with Joseph strutting before. People came running.

"Mark His Kingship's mortal great whiskers with more hair in them than three horses' tails!" cackled a toothless gaffer.

"I vum they be all kings an' princes," shrilled a woman.

A young man cried: "It was him – the old gentleman – as run a spear through Sir Barl – through shield an' mail an' breastbone – like skewer through duckling."

Another cried: "And I see the big young prince there pull Sir Drecker to earth like a sack of corn an' set dagger to gullet – an' Sir Drecker get up an' run an' ride away with his head half cut off."

"Not so!" cried the first. "I see that too, but not like that, Dickon Cowherd. I was up in the pollard willow. I see the prince spare his gullet, an' kick his ribs, an'—"

"Mind your manners, you louts!" screamed the dwarf, with a baleful glare around and a hand at his belt.

*   *   *

It was still daylight without, but the torches flared and smoked in the great hall. The tottering major-domo met King Torrice and his companions at the threshold and led them within. Joseph ran ahead and disappeared. The guests advanced slowly on the heels of the house-steward. The King looked about him alertly, narrowing his eyes against the wavering reds and blacks of flames and shadows. He observed trophies of arms and the chase on the walls – weapons of chivalry and venery of an earlier time, and moth-eaten boars' heads with upthrust tusks, and pale skulls and horns of stags and wild bulls, and one even of a unicorn; and toothy masks of wolves, badgers, wildcats, otters and a dragon; but though he gave the green fangs and leathery forked tongue of the dragon a second glance – an inferior specimen, in his opinion, obviously – his concern was for the weapons.

He stepped twice from his place in the slow procession to jiggle antique swords in their sheaths, and nodded at finding that they would come clear easily, despite the dust of idle years. He glanced and smiled meaningly at his grandson and over a shoulder at the squires. Peter and Gervis grinned and nodded back at him. Good old Torrice! Always the gentleman! He would as lief and as likely be seen consorting with murderers as wearing arms and armor – little begemmed daggers are but table-gear – when supping with ladies; but to ascertain the whereabouts of the nearest weapons, just in case of accident, was no breach of etiquette.

The major-domo drew aside a curtain of arras and stood aside with it, bowed low. The King and Sir Lorn halted and blinked, and the squires halted at their heels and blinked past their shoulders. For a moment, all their eyes were dazed by the shimmer and shine of tapers. For a moment it seemed to them that the place was full of slender, pointed yellow flames, and gleams and sparkles of fire from metal and crystal.

"Welcome, King Torrice," said a lilting voice. "Welcome, Sir Lorn. Welcome again, friends Peter and Gervis."

And now they saw her, but vaguely and glimmeringly at first, like a face and form materializing from the sheen and soft radiance about her, but more clearly as she approached, and definitely when she stood within a small step of the King and extended a hand.

"This – forgive me, my dear! Your Ladyship must try to excuse me – forgive me – my confusion – surprise," he stammered.

"You are forgiven," she murmured, and laughed softly.

He sank on one knee, took the proffered hand lightly and pressed his lips gallantly to the bejeweled fingers, while his twirling wits cried a warning between his ears:

"This isn't real – nor right! More devilment of Merlin's, this – or worse! Have a care, old fool!"

But he was smiling blandly when he straightened his knees and released her hand, though he staggered slightly and blinked again.

Now the lady gazed at Lorn, and he stared back at her. She smiled a little with her bright, soft mouth; and her eyes – whatever their color in honest sunlight – were black and warm and limpid. But his eyes were clouded strangely, and his lips unsmiling. She put out her hand shyly and uttered a shy, tender whisper of soft laughter. Then he knelt lightly, took and kissed her fingers and rose lightly to his feet again – but to sway and stagger for a moment, and steady himself with a fumbling hand on the King's shoulder. Squire Peter saluted the lady's hand without kneeling to it, but his face and the back of his leathery neck were red as fire. Squire Gervis put even the King's courtly gesture to shame, and kept his lips on the jeweled and scented fingers so long that he might well have been testing the pearls in the rings.

The guests found themselves at table: but how this came about, not one of the four could have told you. It was a round table, and not large. It was spread with damask as white and bright as snow, and illuminated by scores of beeswax tapers in tall, branched sticks of silver; and there were other clusters of tapers in sconces on the walls. Stemmed cups of foreign crystal as fragile as bubbles to the eye, and vessels of gold and silver, some of them studded with gems, glowed and glinted like flowers and stars. Behind one chair stood the major-domo in his robes of office, with the manikin beside him, and behind each of the others stood an ancient footman in a livery of murrey and pea-green laced with tarnished silver. There were only five chairs. There was but the one lady present. The King and Peter were on her right, and Sir Lorn and Gervis on her left – but thanks to the smallness and shape of the table, none was far removed from her. In fact, the squires could gaze at their ease, whereas their masters had to turn their heads slightly to look at her.

"My companion, the damosel Mary, is indisposed, but hopes to join us later, with her harp," the lady informed them all, but with her gaze and smile on the King.

Torrice acknowledged the information with a feeble smirk. He was still mazed. He had braced himself to meet the lachrymose gratitude of a bereaved dame of advanced age, and heartbreaking pleas for further relief. And what had he met? Could this be the widow of a doddering old stargazer? He had seen, and had to do with, beauties in every court in Christendom, and dames and damosels of devastating charms in many sylvan bowers and remote castles, and – or was this but vain thinking? – ladies whose enchantments were more than human, without losing his freedom for long at a time. And to lose it now! His very soul, at last! Nay, it could not be! Not his free and questing soul! He would not believe it. He glanced past her, at his grandson. Lorn was staring fixedly to his front, with a pale face. Torrice glanced farther, at young Gervis, who was regarding their hostess with bright-eyed, pink-faced and rapturous ardor. He looked at Peter, hoping that his practical, unvisionary, tough ex-groom at least would be unaffected by this thing which had already enmeshed his gentler companions. But not so! That matter-of-fact young man was gaping even more ardently than Gervis.

Yellow wine was poured. It made giant topazes of the cups of crystal. The lark-and-pigeon pie was served. The King had set out with a fine appetite, but where was it now? He had only a thirst now. He drained his cup. It was refilled, and so he emptied it again. The squires also had lost their appetites and retained their thirsts. But the young knight, it seemed, had lost both. Of the five, only the lady comported herself without sign of mental or emotional disturbance. She sipped the yellow wine occasionally and composedly, but not – so Torrice observed excitedly – from a bubble of rare glass, but from the little silver-gilt cup of his giving.

And when he saw, at that incomparable white throat, the modest necklace which he had sent to her, a confusion of shame and exultation all but suffocated him. Why had he not sent his finest remaining string of emeralds, or of diamonds or rubies, or brought it in his pouch? Why had he ever distributed such things – priceless treasures all from the secret and immemorial treasure-chest of Har – to the right and the left up and down the world and over the years? He moaned at the thought of the wasted expenditures of his lifelong quest. No exception could be taken to the quest itself, as he had proved on the bodies of hundreds with spear and sword: but it graveled him now to recall, however mistily in most instances, the innumerable necks and bosoms of beauties – aye, and the wrists and fingers – adorned by him on his long and crooked road to Beauty herself.

For he could not doubt he had found her – Beauty herself, soul and body in one – though this astounding realization was tinged with a fearful reluctance and a sense of weariness that was almost of despair. His crystal cup was shining like a topaz again. He drained it once more and sighed profoundly. So this was the end of the high quest! And the achievement was as dust and ashes in his heart and mouth – in the heart and mouth of an old man. For Merlin had destroyed his dream of immortal manhood. Now he mourned the fact that his quest had not lasted out his mortal life. Now he knew that, however far he might ride in the months or years remaining to him, the marvel he had sought would lie behind him, found by him, but not for him to grasp.

His crystal cup glowed again, but now redly like a great ruby. He drained it. He turned his head and met her questioning gaze. Or was it questioning? Or telling? Whichever – whatever – it held his own gaze fast.

"Who are you?" he asked; and his voice sounded strange to him, and from far away.

She whispered, leaning a little to him and smiling: "I am the lady of the manor."

He said: "You are very young, and Sir Gayling was old – but not so old as I."

She veiled her eyes and unveiled them instantly, even brighter, and deeper, and kinder than before.

"You are not old like poor Gayling. He was so old that only the stars were old enough for him to love. But I know about you, King Torrice of Har, who have kept a young heart without the help of sorcery, on a high quest. Oh, a mad quest – of pleasure and excitement and change: but you called it noble, and by a noble name – the Quest of the Soul of Beauty."

"It is noble," he protested, but weakly. He tried to avoid her gaze, but in vain.

"I am a poet too – not only a knight-at-arms, not only a lord of lands," he went on confusedly. "Beauty! I have sought her at peril of limb and life, at cost of blood and treasure. The Soul of Beauty. I have made songs to her: the best in all Christendom. They have been stolen and sung by generations of jinking troubadours. But I am not the Lord God, nor Archangel Michael, nor even a sneaking wizard, to know soul from body at a glance. There was Lorn's grandmother. There was nothing of beauty there deeper than her skin. And the Princess of Castile, with – but what matter now? It was long ago."

"And now you have given up," she sighed, and withdrew her gaze.

He saw that the cup of crystal had become a glowing ruby again; and again he turned it back to a bubble of air.

"No, I have found you," he muttered. "Beauty! Soul and body in one. And mortal. And I am mortal – but old – as old as Merlin; but not ageless, like that warlock. There is nothing now – the quest ended – only the hope for a quick end left – and God's mercy!"

She looked at him. His head drooped, and he stared down at his trencher with unseeing, desolated eyes. She glanced to her left. The young knight, staring fixedly at a candle-flame, paid no heed. She smiled at the squires, both of whom were regarding her ardently. She turned back to the old King.

"I know all about you and your quest, and the Irish grandson and the trick Merlin played you, long ago, in the guise of a hag in a red cloak," she said.

"The old palmer told you," he muttered. "He was Merlin."

She laughed softly.

"Yes, he was that warlock, that poor palmer. Do you think I did not know? Or that I did not know about you without any help from him? Look at me."

He looked at her. She smiled and touched his nearer wrist with light finger-tips.

"Do you see that for which you have quested and bled, and kissed and ridden away from, all your long, mad life?"

He nodded and moaned.

"Nay, do not grieve, dear Torrice. You are old, 'tis true – but the beauty you quested for is old too. And I am old too."

"Are you? What are you?" he gasped.

"Are you afraid of me – even if I am a sorceress?" she sighed.

Was It Sorcery or Inspiration?

It was late when the Lady Clara's guests returned to the pavilion beside the river and the willows. Joseph, who had guided them with a lanthorn, stopped only long enough to light a few tapers for them. King Torrice sat down heavily on the first couch he chanced to stumble against, and held his head with both hands. Peter and Gervis did likewise. Only Sir Lorn appeared to have the complete mastery of his legs.

"It was the wines – yellow and red and green," moaned the King.

"And pink," moaned Gervis.

"Pink? Nay, I saw no pink. What did you see, Lorn? Did you see a pink wine?"

"No sir, only yellow – and I drank but two cups," mumbled the young knight, who stood steadily enough, but with a hand to his brow and his eyes burning in his pallid face.

"There were wines of every color," said Peter thickly, "and I drank them all – like one bewitched."

"And you're drunk!" Torrice cried fretfully. "You too, Gervis! Me too! But you, dear lad? You must be sober – on two cups."

"I don't know," muttered Lorn.

"You can't be otherwise, dear lad. Two cups. Tell me what you saw. Tell me of this Dame Clara. She looked very young to me. How did she look to you?"

"Yes sir. Very young."

"And – ah! – comely?"

"Beautiful!" cried Gervis, springing to his feet, only to reseat himself as suddenly and clasp his head again.

Lorn nodded.

"And *you* found her beautiful, dear lad?"

Lorn nodded again. Squire Peter uttered a short, harsh note of despairing laughter.

"Why don't you say it?" he cried. "Drunk or sober, you could see she's beautiful! I could see she's beautiful, and I'm not afraid to say so – tell the world – mauger my head! Me, stable-born! That lady's beautiful, I say! Rose of the world! Who says she isn't?"

"You are drunk, good Peter," said the King. "Calm yourself. My poor brains are jangled enough without your unmannerly howls. Nobody says she's not beautiful. I asked for a sober man's opinion, that's all."

Peter muttered an apology and hung his head.

"Sir, I'm not sober, but I want to say that I think as you do, Your Highness – Your Majesty," said young Gervis, speaking with care and a look of profound deliberation. "I think – my studied opinion, sir – she is everything you named her in your wonderful song."

"What's that?" cried King Torrice. "What song?"

"Your latest, sir – and most wonderful, in my humble opinion. The one you sang tonight."

"You're mad! I did not sing tonight. But hold! Or did I? Now that you mention it, I seem to – but no, I'd remember it – unless I was bewitched!"

"Gervis speaks truth," said Sir Lorn, gravely and sadly. "You sang tonight, sir; and it was a song I had never heard before, and the best I have ever heard. It was after the Damosel Mary played her harp and sang a few ditties."

The King protested that he knew nothing of it.

"Then you were bewitched in very truth," said his grandson. "For she made a great to-do with the biggest harp I ever saw."

"And a voice to match it," said Peter.

Torrice protested ignorance again, but uncertainly.

"And yet you left your seat and went to her and took the harp from her," said Gervis. "You must remember that, sir! Your eyes were wide open. And Lady Clara said to the damosel, who tried to push you away – and she was old enough to be Lady Clara's grandmother: 'Let him have it, Mary.' So she let Your Majesty have it, but with a scowl on her face. Then you made a song to Lady Clara. You sang like a flute, sir, and now and again like a trumpet, but mostly like a flute; all the while the harp sobbed and sighed and hummed like little breezes in a forest of pines. You called her Beauty and Desire, sunshine and moonlight and star-shine, saint and enchantress, Love and Life and Immortality, goddess and witch, a rose and a dew-drop and a star, and by some heathenish names I had not heard before. And Lady Clara wept but did not hide her face, and smiled through her tears. And the ancient damosel covered her face with her hands, and so did Sir Lorn, and even Peter had to wipe his eyes."

The King turned a troubled, inquiring face to his grandson.

"It is the truth," said Sir Lorn grimly.

The King looked at Peter.

"It is Christ's truth," honest Peter told him, gruffly. "Nay, Satan's, more likely! You were bewitched and bedeviled, sir. No mortal man – not the best poet in the world – could make such a song else – nor any drink from this side heaven or hell!"

"Inspiration!" cried Torrice fretfully. "Must you bawl witchcraft and deviltry just because I make a good song? I'm a poet. Pure inspiration. But as I cannot recall it – song nor incident – not clearly. . . . The wine may have something to do with it. But enough of this! Let me sleep now. We all need sleep."

"May I suggest, sir, that Duke Merlin bedeviled the wine?" ventured Gervis.

"Hah – that old trickster!" the King exclaimed. "What more likely – since he brought us here on his bedeviled horseshoes? He doesn't love me, that warlock! He first tricked me long ago, in the matter of an elixir. And today he stayed Lorn's dagger from Drecker's throat. And tonight those wines! We must be on our guard every moment, at every step. But now let me sleep!"

After a little while of grumbling and uneasy tossing, the dark pavilion was silent save for the old King's fitful and uneven snores, and the occasional sighs and moans of his companions. Every one of them suffered strange dreams. Torrice fought with a knight in black armor, both of them afoot in dry sand, until arms and legs ached with weariness; and his sword broke on the black helmet, but that same stroke brought the sable knight groveling in the sand; and when Torrice tore away the helmet – behold, the thing disclosed was a fleshless, eyeless skull! He had done battle with a dead man.

And Sir Lorn wandered about the margins of autumnal tarns and in desolate mountain gorges with red sunsets flaring at their far ends. And the squires pursued damosels who turned into hags in red cloaks, and creatures of mist and moonshine, and hedge-goblins and young dragons, between their hands. All were dreams of ill omen, according to the best authorities; so it was fortunate that only illusive and elusive fragments remained with the dreamers when they woke . . .

It was another fine summer morning. Sir Lorn, who had taken only two cups of the Lady Clara's yellow wine, was the first of the four cavaliers to wake. He went out from the pavilion softly and into a new world of level sunshine and dew-washed greenery. His eyes were clear, but his mind and heart were darkened by dream-shadows. As he looked about him, the shadows withdrew.

He saw Goggin and Billikin busy among the horses; and he heard them too, for the lively fellows were whistling to match the birds in the willows and orchards. Observing the increase of the herd by the five big black chargers, yesterday flashed on his mind like pictures:

Five strange horses? Five instead of six! He alone had failed to contribute a good beast to the herd and a dead rogue to the common grave! Again he saw Drecker galloping off unscathed; and he blushed with shame. To blame the warlock Merlin did not occur to his honest mind. He blamed his own faint heart. To slay a man horsed and spear in hand, or afoot and sword in hand on even terms, had never distressed him greatly, for he had never – unless in that time of which he had no clear memory? – engaged to the death with any save tyrants and murderers and false knights of sorts; but to kill one beaten and disarmed and squealing for mercy, he lacked the required hardihood. He knew this, and felt guilt and shame. And then he thought of that old questing king-errant his grandfather, asleep there in the pavilion behind him. He had seen that champion in six mortal combats, but never had he seen him put a disarmed and beaten foe to death.

So he thought less shamefully now of having spared that false knight.

Young Gervis issued from the pavilion and greeted his master with a merry face. Sir Lorn regarded him with surprise, having expected to see pallid cheeks and bleary eyes.

"It was faery wine of a certainty, sir, for even if I had drunk as little last night as you did, I swear I'd feel no brighter than I do," babbled the squire. "And I pray the same for the King and Peter. I suffered some horrid dreams – but they have fled already, glory be to the holy saints! And now to bathe and shave, sir."

"Shave what?" Lorn asked gravely.

"I have numerous sprouts, sir," Gervis informed him proudly; "and 'tis a full sennight since I last laid steel to them. And may I venture to suggest that a touch of the razor might become you as well, sir; for I seem to remember having noticed something last night – and that by the dazzle of tapers. We may meet her again – the lady of the manor, that is to say! – at any moment; and in broad daylight, I hope. That's to say, I hope the King doesn't intend to ride away without seeing her again."

Lorn fingered his chin and cheeks thoughtfully, and puckered his brow, before he replied:

"I hope not. He can't do that. She – these defenceless people – are still in peril. It is my fault, for letting Drecker escape. So it is my duty to remain till all danger from Drecker is past. He will see that, at a word from me – my grandfather will. And I think you are right about my face. But my razor is duller than a hedger's hook."

"You may use mine. It is of Damascus steel and honed to a whisper. Come down to the river, sir, and we'll both use it."

So they went down to a screened pool in the river and bathed and shaved. They were joined there by Peter, who raised his eyebrows for a moment in acknowledgement of their smooth faces, but reported matter-of-factly that he had inspected the horse-lines and found all correct.

"The shoes?" murmured Lorn.

"Every shoe still firm in its place," Peter assured him.

"Is the King awake yet?" asked Lorn.

"He was combing essence of lavender into his beard when I saw him last," said Peter.

Gervis laughed and said: "A dash of the same, and a touch of the razor, would not be amiss with you, my Peterkin."

Peter nodded, stepped close to his fellow squire, took the razor of Damascus from unresisting fingers, and a little vial of crystal from Gervis' wallet with his other hand, and knelt and stooped to the mirror of the pool – all without a word or a smile. Merry young Gervis laughed again.

"But that's not lavender, my Peterkin! 'Tis essence of laylock."

"Anything will serve but essence of horse," muttered Peter.

Gervis winked at Sir Lorn.

"There's sorcery in it, by my halidom!" he cried, and laughed again. "And sorcery more potent than any of old Duke Merlin's hocus-pocus. When did our Peterkin ever before prefer lavender or laylock to honest horse?"

"I don't agree with you," Lorn said gravely. "I think all this babbling of witchcraft is childish – in this case. It is all quite human and natural – especially for Peter to become more particular about his toilet, no matter how suddenly. As for your faery wine – it was good wine, pure and old, that's all. There's no sorcery here."

"I but joked, sir," Gervis replied. "But you cannot deny enchantment. There was enchantment last night of more than the juice of earthy grapes, else how did the King come to make that song, and sing it like an angel, without knowing anything about it?"

"Inspiration – as he told us himself," said the knight; but his tone was more troubled than assured. "He is, in truth, a great poet. I admit that the wine he drank made him forget the performance when we told him of it last night – but I think we shall find that he can recall it now, and even the words and air of the song."

They returned to the pavilion, leaving Peter still splashing and scraping.

"Look there!" gasped Gervis, gripping his master's arm.

They stood and looked. The curtains of the pavilion's doorway were drawn back to right and left, and King Torrice sat smiling out at them across a table bright with napery and silver dishes and polished horns and flagons. Behind him stood the manikin Jospeh and one of the ancient footmen.

"Fried trout and hot scones!" he cried. "Strawberries and clotted cream. Brown ale and dandelion wine. Lady Clara sent it over. Come and eat, dear lads. No time to spare. Where's Peter?"

"No time to spare?" Lorn echoed. "What d'ye mean, sir? You cannot possibly intend to take the road today, dear sir – and that parlous rogue I spared, foul Drecker, still at large?"

"Certainly not!" retorted the King, fretfully, with a quick change of countenance for the worse. "We recognize our responsibilities, I hope. I said nothing of taking to the road again." His merry smile flashed again. "We are to attend Lady Clara on a tour of inspection of her demesne, to see what damage it has suffered. She sent word of it with our breakfasts. Half-armor and swords. All six of us mounted."

Both Sir Lorn and Gervis looked their relief. They took their places at the table and ate and drank as if for a wager. Peter arrived, smelling like a spring garden, and with his face shining like a summer apple; and upon hearing the King's news, he sat down and fairly gobbled and guzzled.

They paraded in the forecourt of the great house within the hour. Sir Lorn was up on his white stallion, but the King rode the black charger from which he had so recently hurled the late Sir Barl. The squires were on black warhorses too, and the grooms Goggin and Billikin forked the squires' lively hackneys. All six wore breastplates and long swords, but there was not a helmet among them. The King's, Lorn's, Peter's and Gervis' caps were of crimson velvet, and the grooms' were of leather. The gentlemen sported long feathers in theirs, the knights' fastened with gold brooches and the squires' with silver. The Lady Clara appeared from the gloom within and paused under the arch of the doorway, with the Damosel Mary, seemingly old enough to be her grandmother, blinking over her shoulder. The King and Sir Lorn and the squires came to earth and louted low, caps in hand, like one man. The lady blushed like a rose and curtseyed like a blowing daffodil. She was encased in samite of white and gold, and from the white wimple which framed her face soared a pointed hat like a steeple with veils of golden gauze floating about it like morning clouds.

"Our jennets were stabled beyond the wall – and carried off to the forest, saddles and all; so Mary and I must go afoot," she cried in pretty distress.

"Nay, our horses are at your service," the King told her. "Choose any two that take your fancy, my dear."

"Gramercy!" she laughed. "But the saddles?"

"Hah!" Torrice exclaimed; and he regarded the great war saddles with baffled looks.

Then Gervis spoke up, in dulcet tones.

"If I may venture a suggestion, Your Majesty and Your Ladyship, I suggest pillions. And may I add that this newly acquired steed of mine is as gentle and easy-gaited as a jennet for all his size and strength, and is therefore peculiarly suited to the task of carrying double."

Torrice eyed him dubiously, then turned a glance of doting inquiry upon Dame Clara.

"The very thing!" she cried, with a swift widening and half-veiling of her multi-colored eyes; and she turned her head and called for two pillions.

(Lorn thought: "*I can't make out their color, even by daylight; and they are not always black by candlelight.*" Something with a sharp, hot edge stirred in his brain. Memory? A thin splinter of it from that lost time by which he was haunted night and day, and yet of which nothing remained to him save the sense of loss? He tried, fearfully yet hopefully, to remember. He racked brain and heart cruelly but in vain. He sighed.)

Two of the ancient footmen brought two pillions and followed their mistress and the Damosel Mary down the steps. Dame Clara, moving very slowly because of the attentions of King Torrice and the squires, inspected and seemed to consider each of the four chargers, and spared gentle glances even for the hackneys upon which Goggin and Billikin sat like seasoned men-at-arms.

"May I sit behind you?" she asked the King.

His eyes shone, and his lavender-scented whiskers rippled. He strapped a pillion to the back of his saddle with his own hands, mounted with but little apparent effort, leaned and held down his right hand. A hand touched his, a foot touched his stirruped foot, and she came up to the pillion like a white bird. From that soft perch she pointed at Sir Lorn's saddle with her left hand, while holding fast to the King's belt with her right. And so it was that the Damosel Mary had a higher seat than the lady of the manor, by half a hand. Lorn's face wore a polite smile which was entirely muscular. His eyes were blank. Gervis looked dismally dashed, and Peter grinned derisively. As the little cavalcade moved off, the manikin Joseph leaped up behind Peter.

"What else would happen to me?" Peter grumbled.

"Worse might have happened to you, my friend," said the dwarf. "Would you liefer it was the big damosel gripping you about the middle, as she even now grips the young knight? You might do far worse than ride double with poor Joseph."

"I am glad to hear it, since I seem to have no choice in the matter," said the squire. "But will you be so kind as to tell me why?" he added.

"There are many reasons why," the dwarf replied. "One is, I was born with seven wits, whereas you and your grand friends have only five – and those somewhat deranged in the cases of your old King and your young knight. But I was born with seven, but at a sad cost to flesh and bone. If I had your stature, King Arthur Pendragon would be taking his orders from me."

"I believe it," said Peter, with mock solemnity. "I feel your power and see it in your eye, but I don't quite understand it. I never before met a person possessed with seven wits. Is it the power of knowledge or wisdom or cunning?"

"Of all three," the dwarf answered, complacently. "I know everything; I understand everything; and I can think as quick and crooked as any witch or wizard."

"In that case, you would know Duke Merlin if you saw him."

"Yes, it was that old warlock brought you here, though he pretended to be a holy palmer. But he didn't fool me. He drank two quarts of wine and took the road to Camelot. He said he was going to Tintagel, but I knew better.'

"You are wonderful, Master Joseph. Now tell me why you and Merlin brought us to this place?"

"To rid the lady of her oppressors."

"So they are friends – your mistress and Merlin?"

After a moment's hesitation, Joseph said: "No, it was old Sir Gayling, the stargazer, who was Merlin's friend."

"And yet Sir Gayling was stabbed to death in a rose-garden, while his friend the powerful magician played his hocus-pocus elsewhere," sneered Peter.

"As to that, my friend, I could enlighten you if I would, but I know without trying that it would be too much for your five poor wits," the dwarf replied, in a voice so insufferably supercilious that Peter was hard put to it to control an impulse to reach a hand behind him and brush the little man to the ground. "However," Joseph resumed, "I shall satisfy your curiosity concerning the Dame Clara."

But, at that very moment, King Torrice drew rein at a word from his passenger; whereupon Sir Lord drew rein, and Peter drew rein, and the dwarf slid to the ground, and every rider drew rein. Peter and Gervis fairly flung themselves from their saddles in desperate competition for the honor of dismounting Dame Clara from the King's pillion. Gervis won. The lady descended to earth like a feather, and the King followed her down smartly.

All were down now save Sir Lorn and his passenger from the back of the mighty Bahram. The knight could not dismount in the orthodox manner while Damosel Mary remained up behind him; and he was not in the mood to sacrifice his own dignity, not to mention proud Bahram's, by quitting the saddle with a forward, instead of a backward, swing of the right leg. His grandfather and the squires were too intent upon Lady Clara to perceive his difficulty; and it was not until the dwarf had pinched both the squires, and Peter had come – however ungraciously – to his rescue, that he dismounted.

Afoot, they inspected a farmstead in which the farmer had been murdered and from which five beeves had been driven into the forest by the Drecker gang and there handed over to confederate but less daring outlaws, and a bag of silver pieces taken and pouched by that rogue knight himself; a second farm from which a dairymaid and cheeses and barrels of ale had been carried off after the murder of a stubborn cowherd; and a third in which the master had been tickled with knives – he was still in bandages – until he had handed over all his life's hoardings of ducats and crowns. And all this was no more than a representative fraction of the villainies perpetrated by the scoundrel Drecker.

"I don't understand this," said King Torrice, who had suffered more footwork and more emotional strain than he could endure with manly resignation. "Are your people mice? Nay, for mice will fight. Then why didn't the rogues make a job of it, instead of only killing and thieving a little every here and there? Why didn't he put your own house and household to the torch and sword? Hah! – now I recall what the manikin told me – that the foul Drecker aspired to your hand!"

He leaned against his horse and clapped a hand to his brow. The lady hung her head and touched a very small handkerchief to her eyes. Sir Lorn moved close to her; and if he thought, it was sub-consciously. Without a word, and with a dazed, far-away look in his eyes, he laid a hand on her nearer arm and propelled and guided her, gently but firmly a few paces aside to where his great white stallion stood watching them. King Torrice lowered his hand from his fretful brow and blinked after them, but before he could utter a word of inquiry or protest, his squire Peter spoke at his shoulder.

"Sir, I've but now heard it all from her dwarf. Let us mount and ride into the fields, and I'll tell you the whole story.'

There was no argument. The King mounted with alacrity, though a trifle stiffly. He was eager to hear what trusty Peter had heard from the lady's dwarf, and even more eager to get his weight off his poor feet.

The Dwarf Told Peter and Peter Told the King

The Dame Clara (so Peter told King Torrice) was one of four daughters of a gentleman of remote kinship with the late rich and star-struck old philosopher of Joyous Vale. The father, when young and single, had cut a dash in the train of old King Uther Pendragon for a few years, but had been cheated out of all his patrimony by certain fashionable companions; and too hot of head to retire from court gracefully, he had brawled with, and mortally wounded, one of the cheaters in the King's own hall; and so he had fled for his very life and not stayed his flight save to sleep, and to eat when he could find food, until he was across the Marches of Wales.

A Welsh chieftain of the lesser and wilder sort – not one of the nine princes – had befriended and practically adopted him; and so, in due course, he had married a beautiful daughter of the chieftain. Married, as single, they had continued to live with her family in her parental home, which was a confusion of stone and timber towers and halls, and bowers and byres, overlooking a glen of crofts and huts, and itself overhung by a great forest of oaks. Strange to say, the life had suited him better than it had his mountain-bred wife. This had not been so in the first year, but with the arrival of the first daughter, and increasingly so with the arrival of each of the following three, the mother had bemoaned the lack of social opportunities for young ladies in those parts. But the exiled courtier had laughed at her – for he preferred his present to his past and looked to the future with gusto. In hunting wolves and bears and wild boars, in occasional armed clashes with encroaching neighbors or invading savages, and in less frequent but even more exciting raids into the Marches under the banneret of his father-in-law and the banner of Prince Powys, he had found life very much to his taste and nothing to worry about. But he had died in the course of one of those battles of the disputed Marches, leaving hundreds of mourners, chief of whom were his widow and four daughters.

Now for a jump of time and space to Sir Gayling of Joyous Vale. Hearing from a wandering soothsayer that the most knowledgeable of all living stargazers, and the one possessed of the finest astrolabe and cross-staff in the world, inhabited a high tower atop the highest mountain of Wales, Sir Gayling had set out to find him, accompanied by his squire and lifelong friend Master John of Yarrow (who was as old and almost as stargazy as himself) and a few servants. It was a most other-worldly and untraveled company, for the gentlemen had never before been farther afield than Salisbury, where both of them, as youths, had studied astrology and kindred sciences under the famous Friar Gammish; and the servants had never been out of the Vale.

But they went unmolested, day and night, league after league. Some took them for holy men, others for mental cases (and so equally under divine protection), and yet others for magicians or worse. Their innocence was their armor. Jinking thieves and all manner of roving, masterless knaves, shared the best of their stolen meats and drinks with them, and honest farmers and lords of castles alike entertained them honorably. They came into Wales in due course, unscathed and in good health, and Sir Gayling and Master John still keen in their pursuit of knowledge.

There they asked the way to the highest mountain in the world of everyone they met, and at every door, but the answers were mostly conflicting. One point which all their informants agreed upon, however, was that it was somewhere in Wales. In most cases, the person questioned simply pointed to the highest summit within his range of vision. Up and down, up and down and around, toiled the questers after stellar wisdom. They found the people hospitable but inconveniently scattered. They were glad when they came at last, after weeks of fruitless mountaineering, upon a narrow valley full of crofts. The crofters regaled them with strange and potent liquors and collops of venison, but it was not long before a little man in green came to them and requested them to follow him to his master.

It was the manikin Joseph himself; and his master was the father of the widow with four beautiful daughters. The chieftain was an old man by then, and the widowed daughter had silver in her black hair, and only one of the beautiful girls remained unmarried and at home. She was the youngest and the most beautiful – and, as you may have guessed, her name was Clara. The travelers were so well treated that they almost lost sight of their reason for being so far from home; and when the mountain lord himself had assured them, after mental searchings, that he had never heard of an outstanding Welsh stargazer in all his life, nor of an astrolabe, whatever that might be, but could name the world's twenty greatest bards and harpers and ten greatest warriors, and all of them Welshmen, Sir Gayling decided to let the matter rest – and himself with it – for a few days. The cushion of the chair he sat in was softer than his saddle, and the bearskins underfoot did not cut and bruise like rocky mountain tracks.

Lapped in comfort, he drowsed while the widow told her romantic story, which was always in her heart and never far from her tongue. She began by telling him that her husband had been an English fugitive like himself, only larger and much younger. He protested sleepily that he was not a fugitive. She continued with a glowing description of her lamented partner, and a dramatic account of his career at King Uther's court, his justifiable slaying of a false friend in the royal presence, and his subsequent flight. Sir Gayling, who had heard rumors of an affair of the kind a long time ago, bestirred himself sufficiently to inquire as to the gentleman's name and style.

"Roland of Fenchurch, the Earl of Fenland's third son," the lady informed him proudly.

"I heard something of it at the time," he replied; and he went on, though reluctantly, for he was still drowsy, to say that the Fenland family was distantly related to him on the spindle side.

As the lady accepted this information in silence (a very busy silence, but he didn't know that), he thought no more of it till the following morning, when Master John told him that the widow had questioned him, John, exhaustively concerning Sir Gayling's life, condition, affairs and establishment; and he confessed that he had answered her fully, though against his better judgment. The old squire was suspicious and uneasy, but the old knight laughed at him, saying that the lady's curiosity was perfectly natural. Even when his anxious friend suggested that she was contemplating a second English marriage, he refused to be alarmed. Days and nights passed and ran into weeks – days of ease and good cheer, and nights in feather beds – so peacefully that Master John forgot his suspicions of the dame's intentions and both old stargazers forgot their mission. Nothing in the place was too good for them, and their servants and horses grew fat and frisky with idleness and high living.

But this idyllic time came to an end. One morning the widowed daughter of the chieftain and mother of the beautiful damosel requested an astonishing service of the knight. Addressing him as Cousin Gayling, and with a hand on his shoulder and a compelling gleam in her eyes, she advised him to set out for home within the week, so as to establish Clara comfortably before the first hard frosts. The stargazer could only gape, at that: but when she added that Clara would prove to be the ideal wife for him, he cried out in agonized protest. She laughed at him kindly, even affectionately, and made known her plans to him patiently and with the utmost good humor, as if to a dull but beloved child. His continued protests became feebler and feebler, though no less agonized. The damosel herself was of no help to him. When he protested to her that she could not possibly want him for a husband, she contradicted him, politely but firmly.

Well, they were married by the domestic chaplain of Prince Powys before many witnesses. The bride and her mother were radiant, the company was merry; but Sir Gayling and Master John were dazed beyond words. They set out for home with a formidable escort, to which the prince and neighboring chiefs had contributed generously to assure them a safe passage of the Marches. Twenty leagues south of the border, the bulk of the escort turned about and withdrew. Only the bride and her grandfather, her mother, her harpist ex-governess the Damosel Mary, the family counselor Joseph and a score of clansmen on mountain ponies remained in addition to the original English party. Forty leagues farther on, every Welsh heart save Dame Clara's, Damosel Mary's and Joseph's was seized by irresistible and unreasoning nostalgia for the mountains and airs of home; and in a fit of mob panic, the old chief and the widow and their highland cavalry wheeled about and headed back on the long road to Wales.

The ladies were somewhat dashed by that, but Sir Gayling, who had feared that his mother-in-law intended to make of Joyous Vale her permanent abode, congratulated himself and Master John . . . Two days later, they were joined by two cavaliers who introduced themselves as Sir Drecker and Sir Barl, knights-errant from King Arthur's court. Their manners were excellent, and they made themselves very entertaining; especially Sir Drecker, and he very particularly to Sir Gayling and Master John, to whom he declared a keen interest in astrology – and a lamentable ignorance of it.

From then onward all the way to Joyous Vale, the two old stargazers belabored their pupil's ears with stellar truths and mysteries. But the dwarf noted the furtive rovings and oblique glances of Drecker's small but lively eyes. Trust Joseph – by his own telling! He warned his mistress against the stranger, and received in return an enigmatic smile. His warning to Sir Gayling won a promise of consideration upon the proper drawing up and study of Sir Drecker's horoscope, which would require at least ten days. But Joseph continued to watch and suspect, wore a shirt of chain-mail under his tunic, and added a short sword to his armament of daggers.

They reached Joyous Vale in safety, however, and found all as the astrologers had left it five months before, save for a few natural deaths and those mostly of old age. Dame Clara established herself and her ex-governess in the best bedroom, and Sir Gayling and Master John returned thankfully to their old quarters and neglected telescope at the top of the tower and set to work on Sir Drecker's horoscope. What might have happened if that task had been completed is anybody's guess, for upon the departure of the self-styled knights-errant within the week, the astrologers laid it aside and forgot it in the pursuit of more abstruse stellar secrets.

Winter came and passed uneventfully. Sir Gayling and Master John were happy with their books and arguments, and since philosophically accepting the rumored Welsh astrologer and his peerless instrument as mere myths, with their telescope too. Also, they became aware of improvements in food and service, and the whole economy and atmosphere of the place; and each confessed to himself, though neither to the other, that the adventure into Wales had been nothing worse than a loss of time. April brought back Sir Drecker and Sir Barl. Drecker's original intention was (by Joseph's reckoning) to carry off Lady Clara and the old knight's treasure-chests, but he changed it for the more ambitious plan of marrying the lady and settling down as a lord of lands. The first step toward his goal – the transforming of a wife to a widow – was mere child's play for him, but then difficulties developed. The gates of the great house were closed and barred against him. Accepting that as a purely provocative gesture on the lady's part, he subdued the tenantry, murdering and robbing and despoiling just enough to show her who was master, and bided his time.

That is the story, as told (rather more than less) by the Welsh manikin Joseph to the squire Peter and by the said Peter to King Torrice.

"It's a queer tale, but I've heard queerer," said the King. "How old did you say she is?"

"I didn't say, but Joseph told me she will be eighteen very soon," Peter answered.

"Eighteen or eight hundred," the King muttered. "If but eighteen, how can she be what I believe her to be – the achievement and the end of my quest?" He looked at Peter keenly and added: "If that is the whole story, why has Merlin dragged us into the affair? He is not one to take all the trouble of conjuring up a forge and shoeing our horses just to save a distressed lady from a tyrant. But whatever and whoever she is, and whatever that old fox's game may be, we are committed to her protection."

He looked back at the farmyard from which he and his squire had come away and saw it empty. He turned the other way then, and looking widely over meadows and cornlands and orchards, saw the little cavalcade enter the outer court of the great house; and he sighed. Peter, who looked too and also saw that Lady Clara rode pillion with Sir Lorn, chuckled to see that Damosel Mary rode pillion with Gervis.

"This is no laughing matter," the King reproved mildly; and he added: "Have you forgotten that the rogue Drecker is at large?"

Peter replied that he had not forgotten Drecker's escape.

"Has it occurred to you that he will return some day, any day now, with all the cut-throats and robbers from forty leagues around at his heels?" demanded Torrice.

"It has, sir; but, knowing that you would bring the subject up in plenty of time for us to do something about it, I haven't worried over it, sir," replied Peter.

The King looked embarrassed and muttered: "I hope you are right, but I must confess that I had quite forgotten the peril we are in – not the rogue, but the menace of him – until now, God forgive me!"

The Lady Rides with a Hand on Sir Lorn's Sword-Belt

The Lady Clara rode home on Sir Lorn's pillion, up on the great white stallion Bahram.

"King Torrice told me of your quest," she murmured.

He neither spoke in reply nor did he turn his head to glance at her. She murmured again, leaning a little closer to his apparently unresponsive back.

"But how can it be one and the same quest, if he searches for that which he has never known, and you for something you have known and lost?"

Lorn continued to gaze straight to his front in silence. The great warhorse's advance was very slow, despite much showy action. He tossed his head and plumed his silver tail; but high though he lifted each massive hoof in turn, it was only to set it down softly on practically the same spot of ground.

"You heard his song?" she murmured. "The things he called me? Poor old man! – it must have been the wine he drank. If I am a wicked old witch, how can I be the end of his quest? And yet he truly believes me to be both, it seems – poor me! – and he is unhappy and afraid now for his quest's end."

"Not afraid," he said. "Whatever he may believe, he is not afraid of it. He has never feared anything – neither its end nor its beginning."

"Do you too take me for a witch?"

He let that pass.

She sighed: "You do not take me for the end of your quest, that is sure."

Her right hand, which grasped his sword-belt, transmitted a slight quiver to her heart.

"He is mad, I fear, for how else could he think me beautiful? And now he is unhappy because of me, in his new madness, and you are still unhappy in your old madness. So your unhappiness is my fault too, for if I were actually as your dear grandfather sees me in his madness, you might forget your loss or mistake me for the lost one. But I am not, and you do not; and so two brave knights are unhappy because of me – one in the foolish belief that his quest is ended, and the other because he knows that he has not found what he seeks."

Again her hand transmitted a quiver from his sword-belt to

her heart. He spoke a word; but it was to Bahram, who instantly stopped his shilly-shallying and went forward at a purposeful walk. But not for long.

"I fear I'll be shaken right off, at this pace," the lady whispered.

At another word from Lorn, Bahram resumed his dilatory posturings.

"If I were a witch," she said, "I would make myself appear to the king as you see me, and to you as he sees me."

Though the only response she received was by way of the telltale belt, she smiled quite contentedly at the knowledge that, no matter how he might pretend to ignore her, she could make him tremble like a leaf . . .

Later, Dame Clara told one of the ancient servitors to find Joseph and send him to her. It took four of the old men the better part of an hour to carry out the order.

"Take my compliments to King Torrice, and remind him that I am expecting him and Sir Lorn and their gentlemen to supper," she instructed the manikin. "And don't take all night about it," she admonished gently.

"They won't come," he said, consequentially. "Too busy. Even Sir Lorn is busy. And why shouldn't he be busy now – that moon-struck quester! – since 'tis all the fault of his fuddling?"

Before Dame Clara could speak, for astonishment and indignation, Damosel Mary spoke.

"How now, little man? If you have forgotten my teachings of ten years ago, I shall have to take your education in hand again."

Joseph had not forgotten. Sadly deflated, he recalled to mind the matter and the occasions referred to by the gray-haired damosel. That stalwart and learned governess had not confined her instructions to little Clara, but had given the household dwarf and mascot a course in manners that, being much needed and long overdue, had proved extremely painful to the recipient. Now he ducked and turned to slip out by the way he had swaggered in; but Lady Clara was upon him like a falcon on a partridge.

"No, you don't!" she cried. "Oh, you saucy knave, how dare you speak so? For a pin, I'd send you back where you came from! Fuddling? What d'ye mean by that, you jackanapes? How dare you speak so of that – of your betters? For a pin – at one more word – I'll shake you out of your boots, you wicked Joseph!"

She had him in both hands. Her face was pink; her eyes shot

fire and her lofty head-dress was askew. She shook him like a clout.

"And quite rightly too," said the old ex-governess judicially. "The silly rascal has outgrown his boots anyhow. But stay your hand, my dear, I beg you, so that he may tell us more of this business that's afoot – unless he invented it to puff up his own importance – before he loses the power of speech, which might happen if he bit off his tongue."

Clara complied instantly, but kept a grip on Joseph with one hand while straightening her headdress with the other.

"Now then, out with it!" she demanded, but in a softer and reasonable tone of voice. "Tell us what it is they are all so busy about."

He hung limp and gasping in the grip of the small white hand and rolled his eyes piteously. Never before had he been treated with violence, or angry words even, by his beautiful young mistress.

"He needs wine, poor fellow!" she cried.

The damosel thought so too, and brought it quickly. He drained the cup and recovered his breath and something of his assurance.

"It's the rogue Drecker," he said.

"Drecker? But he's gone," the ladies protested.

"That's it," he said. "He's gone, whole and horsed. Would they fear him now if he were dead and buried with the others? They'd not give him a thought. But now they must guard against his return."

"But he dare not come back!" Clara cried.

The dwarf shot an oblique glance at Mary; and as she was not watching him, but gazing thoughtfully at nothing, he risked a sneer.

"Dare not?" he questioned, with curling lips. But he kept the curl out of his voice. "With all the outlaws of the forest at his heels? And this time it will be with fire and sword. This time he will take what he wants – and that will be what brought him here the first time, and everything else he can carry off – and hot torches and cold iron for the rest."

"But our defenders?" she whispered. "They'll not desert us!"

"Six," Joseph said contemptuously. "They were enough against six – enough to slay five, anyway. But against sixty or eighty or a hundred? That will be another story."

"Not so fast, little man," the governess interrupted. "Why not a thousand, while you are about it? But tell me first, does Drecker's army grow on trees?"

"You can say that," the dwarf answered, with more than a hint of his old impudence. "On the ground under the trees, anyhow. Runaway serfs and all manner of masterless knaves, and Gypsies and thieving packmen and renegade warders and archers, and first of all, the band that has been receiving and marketing our beeves and cheeses all the while."

"And just what have our defenders become so suddenly so busy about?" asked Damosel Mary.

"Bringing the people closer in, with their livestock and goods and gear, and setting them to work on walls and ditches, and making men-at-arms of clodhoppers," Joseph told her, civilly enough.

"We must get busy too!" Clara cried. "We're both good bowmen, Mary. We'll teach the old men to shoot. My grandfather Cadwalledar made me a little bow when I was only four years old; and when I was six, I could pick his cap clean off his head without waking him up, at ten paces. I hit him only once, and that was only a scratch; but after that he always retired to his chamber for his naps. There must be scores of old bows and arrows somewhere about here. We'll look high and low; and we'll have new ones made, if need be. I know that one of the cooks used to be a bowyer. We'll start now. Where has Joseph gone?"

"You let go of him, my dear," said the damosel resignedly.

"Good riddance to him!" the dame cried. "He would only tell us where to look and then what to do and how. He will be much happier advising the King and Sir Lorn. Now to work!"

When Two Men Look out of One Man's Eyes

There was little rest in Joyous Vale that night, either within or without the manor house. Lady Clara permitted only the oldest and shakiest members of the household to retire to their couches at the customary hour. As for the old ex-bowyer Tomkyn, it was long past midnight when he was allowed to creep off to bed; and as for the dame and the damosel, they heard the false dawn saluted by sleepy roosters. And so it was without, abroad over the whole manor to the edges of the forest on every side. By sunrise, every farmstead and croft had been warned and set astir by one or another of the King's party, or by Joseph up on one of the King's ponies: and when the chatelaine, wakened from a short sleep by the hubbub without, looked out from her high window, she rubbed her eyes and looked again. For the inner court was gay with the colored pavilions which Drecker and his rogues had pitched, and left perforce, under the willows beside the river. The chivalry had moved in. The outer courtyard was not so gay, but was far livelier. Here were tents of hide, makeshift shelters of spars and thatch, heaps of country provisions and household gear, pens of swine and poultry, excited women jabbering and gesticulating, gaffers seated on bundles of bedding, and barking dogs and shouting children dashing around.

The home orchard and paddocks also had undergone a startling change. The latter were alive with horned cattle and sheep, all in confusion and many in violent disagreement, and herds and woolly sheep-dogs trying to restore order and keep the peace with sticks and teeth. Through the orchard greenery appeared the tops of hastily constructed stacks of last year's hay and straw, and arose the bellows, moos and bleats of more displaced livestock. Beyond all this moved wains and wheelless drags, horse-drawn and ox-drawn, the loaded approaching and the empty departing; and groups of rustics coming and going; and here and there a cavalier in half-armor riding this way or that.

Dame and damosel were back at their self-appointed tasks when King Torrice presented himself. He had been in the saddle sixteen hours, with two changes of horses, and yet looked fresh as a daisy. It was only leg and footwork, or sitting on chairs, that fatigued him.

"Lady, I crave your indulgence for the liberties I have taken with your people and property, and shall continue to take, for your own and their good – but all with due respect to your title and lordship, madam," he pronounced.

Lady Clara dropped what she was about and jumped up and toward him, and extended both hands to him. Still regarding her gravely, he received her hands in his own, then blinked and started slightly and looked down curiously at the little hands in his big ones, at the right and at the left, then turned the right palm-upward and fairly stared at it, then the left and stared at it.

"Blisters!" he exclaimed.

"We have been making arrows, Mary and I," she answered, gently and shyly. "And splicing old bows. And twisting and waxing bowstrings."

He looked her in the eyes, then stooped over her hands again and touched his lips lightly to each of the blistered palms in turn, muttered "Gramercy, my dear!" and straightened and backed out by the way he had come in.

Clara returned to her work, but fumblingly. She blinked to clear her vision, and tears sparkled on her cheeks.

Mary eyed her thoughtfully.

"A grand old man," said Mary. "Well, a grand old knight-at-arms, however – and as good a poet as any in Wales, even. But as simple and innocent as a baby, or poor Sir Gayling even, for all his questing and gallivanting; and I'd liefer have him for a battling champion, in the ding-dong of rescue and defence, than for a husband or father."

"Is that so?" cried Clara. "I don't believe it! We don't know anything of him as a father, but we can see that he is a good grandfather to poor Lorn; and I have my own opinion as to what your answer would be if he asked you to marry him."

"Fiddlesticks, my dear! And if you contemplate becoming the Queen of Har yourself – and a crook of your finger is all that's needed – I advise you to be quick about it."

Clara stared at her ex-governess and asked tremulously: "Why do you say that – and look so strange?"

"Because you have no time to lose; and if I look strange, who wouldn't after glimpsing a dead man in a living man's eyes?"

"What d'ye mean by that? Speak out, or I'll shake you!"

"Calm yourself, child. I mean what I say. I saw him dead – that poor old King – just as surely as I foresaw your own grandmother dead while she was still walking and laughing, and just as surely as my grandsire True Thomas foresaw and foretold the death of King David at his marriage feast and was whipped for the telling. It is when you see two pairs of eyes glimmering in the eyeholes of the one head – and one pair of those eyes are cold and blind."

Lady Clara cried out, "To the devil with your soothsaying!" and clapped her hands to her face; and her tears burned and stung the abraded palms. Mary sighed, brushed a furtive hand over her own still face and took up her work again.

★   ★   ★

At noon, Lady Clara told the major-domo to send Joseph to her. That important person received the command in silence, and with a weary shake of the head. He was thinking of the easy and peaceful years before poor dear Sir Gayling's mad expedition into Wales. Those had been the times. There had been no big Welsh damosel then to drive honest men around every day with besoms and mops, in pursuit of honest dirt and dust and cobwebs; and no giddy young dame to demand gleaming crystal and shining plate, and tarts and jellies and custards for every meal till the cooks and scullions were fit to tear out their beards. And now it was worse. Now it was the very devil. Sweeping and scrubbing, and polishing and burnishing and cooking, had been hard enough on the poor fellows, but ferreting out ancient war-gear and repairing it, grinding edges onto rusty swords and axes, splicing old bows and whittling new bows and arrows, and being driven and drilled by Tomkyn the ex-bowyer, was harder.

"The whole world be turned upside-down," grumbled the major-domo; and instead of going on the lady's errand, he went in search of some hole or corner in which he might evade Tomkyns' officious attentions for a little while. Imagine a major-domo hiding from a cook! Such a thing could never have been in the days of Sir Gayling. And so, quite naturally, the dwarf failed to answer his mistress' summons; but Squire Gervis presented himself some three hours later, and quite of his own volition. He was dusty, but in high spirits. When he took Dame Clara's proffered hand, he turned it over tenderly, gazed at it adoringly and said that he had heard about it from the King.

"How fares the dear King?" she asked softly.

"That old wonder-boy is as lively as a grig," he replied enthusiastically. "And as merry too. And even Sir Lorn is companionable. That's the way it always is with those two. The prospect of a fight, and never mind the odds against them, acts like mothers' milk – if you'll forgive the expression – on those mad questers."

"Mad?" she whispered; and Damosel Mary looked up from her work with glue and feathers on a clothyard shaft and said, in the voice of a governess: "It's a very wise man, or a fool, who dares cry 'Mad!' at his fellows."

Unabashed, Gervis replied with unabated good humor:

"A fool, then! And in my folly I repeat that our noble friends are mad. Who but a madman would spend a hundred years and more – some say two hundred – in pursuit of the very thing from which he turns and flees whenever he catches up with it?"

"What thing is that?" murmured Clara.

"He calls it beauty," he laughed.

"Nay, he calls it the soul of beauty," she murmured.

He shrugged a shoulder delicately and winked politely.

"And what have you to say of Sir Lorn's madness?" she asked gently.

"I'll say that is different," he answered, with a touch of gravity. "Who wouldn't be mad, after a year in Færyland with the Maid of Tintagel, or Helen of Troy, or maybe it was Queen Mab herself? But he is mad, our poor Lorn; and it's struck deep, else he would forget her now, whoever she was."

He gazed adoringly into her eyes, and she smiled back very kindly, and a little sadly and with just a flicker of pity.

"It is sometimes difficult to distinguish madness from foolishness," said Damosel Mary.

He turned to her and shook a playful finger, then turned back to Clara.

"I'll tear myself away now, back to my duty, before one of those mad questers appears and drags me away ingloriously by the scruff of the neck – for my folly."

And he was gone as lightly as he had come.

The Invading Horde

Dame Clara told the dwarf Joseph to take post on the tower and keep watch on the edges of the forest from dawn till dark: but he excused himself on the plea that he could not be spared from his duties as galloping aide-de-camp to King Torrice. This was on the night of the second day after the King's and and Gervis' visits. For two days and a night now the lady had been neglected by her champions, save for the verbal message from Torrice, by Joseph, to the effect that she had nothing graver to worry about now than the blisters on her pretty hands, and that he would compose another song to her as soon as the dastard Drecker reappeared and was finally disposed of.

"He sounds very sure," she said to the messenger.

"And with reason," he replied condescendingly. "We are ready and waiting for Master Drecker and his riff-raff. Every stratagem of defence and attack is planned; and we have made more than a score of men-at-arms, all horsed and harnessed and armed, out of your clodhoppers of yesterday."

So Joseph escaped back to his active military duties; and at the first pale gleam of the next dawn, Lady Clara herself took post on the watch-tower, leaving the command and business of the household archery to Damosel Mary and the bowyer Tomkyn.

She peered down at a shadowy world, but not a sleeping one. A few dark figures moved to and fro about the inner court, and more in the outer court, and yet more in the paddocks beyond and about the edges of the home orchard; and her heart swelled wth gentle pride and sweet gratitude and perhaps with even tenderer emotions at the thought that she was the inspiration and first cause of this vigilance and devotion. She wept a little in happy sadness, but soon dried her eyes on the silken lining of one of the hanging sleeves of her green gown. As the clear light increased, rising and flooding, she saw more and more, and farther and farther. Thin feathers of smoke uncurled above the leafy roof of the orchard, the busy human figures increased in number and formless bulks and darkness took shape. Now she saw the abatis of new-felled forest trees which enforced and topped the old wall of tumbled field-stones around the home farm, and four massy clumps of leafy timber far out toward the four nearest screens of the surrounding forest, and each at a point where nothing taller than hay had grown previously.

By now she could see to the forest walls all around, beyond the farthest meadows and cornlands and deserted steadings. The forest edges to the westward, struck full by the level rays, showed leafy boughs and brown boles like a picture on tapestry, but to the eastward they were still gloomed with their own shadows . . . It was from the shadows that the first running figure appeared. It was of a tall man in leather, with a strung bow in his left hand. He checked for a backward look, then ran again. A horn brayed in the shadows and was answered from the right, and then from the left, as if by echoes. A second man in leather appeared, and three more a moment later, all running like partridges from the shadow of a stooping hawk. A leather cap lifted and fell to earth, leaving the shaggy hair of that runner streaming in the wind of his flight. The watcher on the tower could make nothing of that: but after another had stumbled and run on with bowed head and hunched

shoulders and in zig-zagging jumps, and yet another had fallen
flat and then crawled like a snake, she made out little glints and
gleams in the sunshine, and knew them for flying arrows.

Again a horn brayed, but louder and nearer this time. Now
a horseman appeared as if from nowhere, galloping toward the
screen of shadow from which the men in leather were fleeing,
gesticulating and screaming. Four of the runners turned and set
arrows to their bowstrings and shot, hard and fast, into the green
gloom.

The rider drove through them, wheeled, dismounted and laid
hold on the crawler with both hands. The wounded man rose to
his knees, to his feet, and sagged across the horse. It was a small
horse, but hardy; and so the rescue was made, with the pony
running like a dog, the wounded forester draped across like a
half-filled sack and the rescuer running beside and holding him
in place. He was a small rescuer. Boys of nine years have been
taller.

"Joseph!" cried the lady on the tower. "'Tis none other, by my
halidom! Run, Joseph, run!"

All the visible actors in that flurry of action disappeared among
the hedges and walls, and under the thatched roofs, of a steading.
Now, for a long minute, nothing moved in Lady Clara's wide
field of vision – though she looked in every direction – save a
few feathers of smoke and wings of birds and ever-trembling
leaves of tall poplars. No more arrows leaped from shadow to
shine. Nothing moved on the ground. The horns were silent
now, but cocks crowed in the home orchard. She gazed abroad
and down in growing and fearful wonder, peering for some sign
of awareness of danger, listening for a sudden commotion and
shouting of armed men; but the great house below her, and the
bright landscape all about her, were as still and quiet as if they
lay under a spell. Was some wicked magic at work here, to her
undoing? What of her champions?

But no, she had already seen little Joseph and five scouts in
action; and she refused to believe that any spell save death itself
could withhold the hands of that old King and the squires from
her defence. Of Lorn she was not so sure. Even though she had
made him tremble with a touch of her hand on his sword-belt,
she did not blink the fact of his old bewitchment and sojourn in

Færyland. What were her frail enchantments, though exercised with all her heart, against those of ageless sorcery? For that dear knight – for succor from those dear hands – she could but hope and pray.

Now the lightening rim of gloom from which the five vanished foresters had emerged stirred again, and the base of that green obscurity was alive suddenly with a score of men in leather and wool, with strung bows in their hands. They did not dash forward, but extended to right and left and advanced cautiously, setting arrows to strings. As many more invaders now emerged and formed a second line. A few of these were bowmen too, but most of them carried boar-spears, short axes or halberds. Close behind these came a fellow with a burning torch and two with a black kettle slung from a pole between them. The torch smoked blackly and flamed palely in the sunshine, and a thin haze of heat quivered above the kettle.

"The rogues! They mean to set us afire!" cried Clara.

Again she looked all around, and again in vain for any sign of a defender. The skirmishers continued to advance, and with more assurance. A big knight in full armor, on a black horse to match, came into view in rear of the two-score skirmishers, riding at a foot-pace. He signaled with a hand – its mail flashed in the sunlight – and shouted a command, whereupon the fellows in front drew together on the run and headed straight for the steading into which Joseph and the five foresters had disappeared. The knight followed them, but neither fast nor far, and soon drew rein and sat with uneasy shiftings and turnings, as if he too (like the watcher on the tower) was puzzled by the stillness. The two-score raiders halted and sent a flight of arrows into the farmstead, and then a second flight, and three fire-arrows flaming like comets: but no shaft came from hedge or wall in retaliation. They loosed a dozen fire-arrows, one of which struck a thatched roof, stuck there and blossomed like a great poppy. And still the spell was unbroken.

Clara, up on her tower, was as spellbound as the menaced steading and the fields spreading stilly all around from the silent house under her to the still walls of the forest. She wanted to scream, but her throat refused. It seemed to her that the forest watched and waited expectantly, and that everything within its sinister circuit, seen and unseen, would start and cry out in protest but for the same fatal hand that gripped and silenced herself . . . Once more she tried to scream – and for cause, God wot – but with no more success than before. That same span of leafy gloom stirred to life again and spewed forth running men; but this time it was a multitude. It flooded into the sunshine like a dark tide flecked with glinting spear-points and upflung blades and spotted with garments of tattered finery among the jerkins of drab leather and wool. An awesome sound rose from it like the hum and growl of sea surf. It flooded to and around the mounted knight and bore him with it toward the smoking farmstead into which the vanguard continued to shoot fire. It did not check, but in its weight of hundreds, carried the first two score forward with it against the still hedges and silent walls. And then the spell broke.

A hundred arrows darted from hedges and walls and gables; shouts and the braying of horns shook the smoke and were answered by shouts and horns from the right and the left; and more arrows darted forth and struck and stood quivering. From the ambushes of felled trees on either hand came armored men on large horses, shouting and with leveled spears, breaking from the trot to the gallop – a dozen from the right and a dozen from the left. Lorn led one party, up on the mighty Bahram, and in front of the other charged King Torrice under his plume of black-and-white ostrich feathers. The invading flood recoiled; and its front – what remained alive of it – turned upon the pressure from behind, screaming and striking for a way of escape. Now it was every knave for himself, of those murderous hundreds.

They were spitted like partridges. Lorn was among them. He threw his spear aside and hewed with his sword. They were split like fish. The white stallion tore them with his teeth and crushed them under his terrible hooves. Torrice was among them, not charging now but reining his black horse this way and that and using his great spear as a lesser craftsman might use a light sword, prodding here and there. Though a master of every chivalrous combat-tool, he held that the spear was the knight's first weapon. Peter and Gervis were among them. Like Lorn, they too had discarded spears for swords for such infighting as this. Goggin and Billikin were among them, plying their long blades like gentlemen born. Twenty armored rustics on plow-horses were among them, hacking with axes and bashing with spiked maces. And even the big knight who had brought them here with promises of easy rich rapine now took part in the slaughtering of them, cutting them down and riding them down in his frantic efforts to win clear and away. Screaming like trapped beasts, the remnants of the horde broke in every direction – but not all of them to safety, for the dwarf Joseph and the hundred archers from the burning farmstead were on their heels.

The lady on the tower shut her eyes. She cried out, but in the din of triumphant shouts and horns from the house and courts below, her voice was no more than whisper in her own ears. After a little while, she looked again, avoding the motionless shapes on the ground. Footmen still ran in groups and pairs, pursued and pursuing, to the flashes of knives and axes. Some of the horsemen still galloped and struck, but most of them moved more slowly and with an air of aimlessness now.

But King Torrice and all his five men, and Joseph on his running pony, were still in play. And Drecker, clear of the rabble at last, was riding like a madman for the nearest edge of the forest. His spear was gone. His great shield was cast off. He dropped his sword and cast off mace and ax from his saddle-bow. Anything for speed with which to escape a red doom: for that old King and that young knight were after him, converging on him from right and left. But he hadn't a chance. At the very edge of the forest – But the watcher on the tower had closed her eyes again.

Quest's End

King Torrice of Har was dead. The exertions of that last mêlée and the final stroke on Drecker's neck had stilled that long questing forever. He had lived to be carried in by Lorn, and to smile and murmur a few words at the touch of Clara's tears on his face. Now he lay on a couch of silks and furs in the great hall, in full armor, with tall candles at his head and feet. His hands were crossed on his breast, on the cross of the long sword that lay there unsheathed. His helmet, with its proud plume, was at his left elbow. Clara and Lorn knelt on the right of the couch and the squires on the left. At the head of it, a wandering friar read from a great missal, now muttering and now chanting. All the surrounding gloom was full of kneeling people, and over all rang and sighed and sobbed a dirge from the Damosel Mary's harp.

Clara turned her face to Lorn.

"He told me he was happy – in his quest's end," she sighed.

The young knight gazed at her with clear eyes.

She sighed again.

"But what of *your* quest?"

He moved his right hand a little toward her; he found her left hand and clasped it.

"I have forgotten what it was," he answered.

Cauldron of Light

Diana L. Paxson

Diana L. Paxson (b. 1943) is a noted advocate of paganism worship and is a minister of the Fellowship of the Spiral Path. She also edits the journal Idunna *for the Troth (www.thetroth.org), which promotes an understanding of the Germanic polytheistic religion of Asatru. She has written many novels that draw upon Celtic and other folk roots such as her Westria series, which began with* Lady of Light *(1982). Her Hallowed Isle series, which began with* The Book of the Sword *(1999), retells the Arthurian story. When Marion Zimmer Bradley wished to continue her Avalon series she recruited Paxson to work with her on* Priestess of Avalon *(2001) and* Ancestors of Avalon *(2004).*

Light glittered on the water, starry flashes reflecting a shifting glimmer across rock and tree and the face of the man who stood knee-deep in the pool. He blinked once, then stilled, allowing awareness to sink past that shimmering surface, seeking the silver flicker of the fish that drifted, suspended between earth and air, curving with the current of the stream.

He had been a fish once, a great salmon, returning home from the sea. He knew the myriad subtle messages of taste and touch and pressure, more meaningful to him now than the ways of courts and kings. His mind became that of the salmon once more, while his hands, forgotten, drifted against the current like water-weed.

The trout grew still, attention focused on the ceiling of light. The mind of the man floated with it, perceived the ripple as a fly touched the surface. Silver sides flexed; hands flickered, scooping the trout out of its element. It wriggled furiously, protesting the impossible emptiness of the world.

Merlin straightened, his mind snapping free as the trout gasped out its life on the grass. He watched in unwilling sympathy – most of his life he had been out of his element, but Arthur, whom he had counselled and defended, was grown now, and a king. The mage was become a stranger to Camelot, his rightful home the wildwood, where he could be both more, and less, than a man.

He winced as back muscles began to complain against the unnatural angle he had forced them to maintain, and stretched, long arms, pelted with hair whose brown was grizzled now to grey, reaching for the sky. When he was a child, he thought ruefully, he could do this all afternoon. Where once he had been as flexible as a sapling, he was aging like an old tree. How old, he wondered? An oak could live until felled by disease or lightning or the hand of man, growing larger and stronger with each year. He had fortunately ceased to grow when he was a half a head taller than most men, and hair and beard had silvered. But he was still strong.

Merlin looked at the trout, whose colours were dulling already. One small fish was not much of a meal. The day before had been stormy, and he had huddled in his cave, fasting. He wondered if he could manage another fish, and bent once more to the stream.

Wind gusted suddenly, whispering in the trees, lifting the sheltering branches so that light flared blindingly from the surface of the pool. He swayed, all other awareness fleeing as his mind filled with light. The whisper of wind became a woman's voice that pierced the soul—

"*Merlin! The Grail is gone! Merlin, help me!*"

The wind passed; the branches, subsiding, veiled his sight. The vision released him then, and he collapsed gently into the pool.

The shock of the cold water brought Merlin upright, gasping. On her holy isle, the Lady of the Lake guarded the sacred Cauldron which was also called the Grail. He could not believe anyone had breached its wardings, but the Hallows sometimes moved of their own will. When they did so, kingdoms could fall.

He clambered out of the pool, shaking himself like a wet dog. First, he needed food, and then he would be on his way. Skewering the trout on a piece of green wood, he began to kindle a fire.

As Merlin moved south, he heard rumours. They spread across the land like a river in floodtime, murky with silt and choked with debris. Neither the Lady nor the Grail were at the Lake, cupped by its northern mountains. The only certainty was that the Hallow had appeared at Camelot, and now it was gone. Half of Arthur's war band, it was said, had ridden out to search for it.

What brave men might accomplish, they would do. It seemed to Merlin that he would accomplish little by running after them. Better to be still, and wait for wisdom like a fisherman at a weir. In time, he heard that the Cauldron had mysteriously returned to the Isle of Maidens. But men still sought the Grail. To Merlin, its true nature was now an even greater mystery.

As summer faded into fall, he settled finally in the woods near the ruined fortress of Mediolanum, where the road that angled across southern Britannia toward Londinium met the longer tracks that linked the north with the south and west. There he built himself a little hut of branches and heaped stones. Less visible, but stronger, was the net of power that he laid across the roads to catch the fragments of truth and the men who bore them.

On an autumn afternoon Merlin heard a horse approaching. The hoofbeats stopped outside his hut, and someone called for water. He emerged from the hut, head bowed and body hidden by the voluminous white wool of a Druid's robe, a wooden bowl brimming in his hands.

"Holy father, I thank you, in Christ's name—"

Merlin repressed a smile, understanding that the boy had taken him for one of those hermits who sought the wilderness, finding even a monastery too worldly for their needs. No doubt he had joined Arthur's band since the last time Merlin visited the king.

"In the name of the god you serve, you are welcome," he answered gravely. "You look weary. Alight, and share my simple meal, and tell me of your journey."

"I suppose it is no sin to accept the hospitality of a holy man," the boy said, frowning. "My name is Amminius son of Lucius, a warrior of Arthur's Companions, and indeed I am in need of counsel."

"Then you are welcome," Merlin answered him.

"It is not a journey, but a quest that I am on," said Amminius when he had slaked his thirst and they were seated by the hearth. "Perhaps you will have heard?"

Merlin nodded, and put another stick on the fire. "There have been many rumours. What did you see?"

"It was the night of the great storm—" the young man began. "All the folk in Camelot were gathered in the great hall, listening to the timbers groan and the wind whistle through the thatching, and praying to whatever gods they knew. It was close to midnight when the doors were flung open. A woman screamed – we all thought our last hour had come. And then there was a great light, and a stillness, as if we lay in the eye of the storm. The light moved through the hall, and before each one, it paused . . ." He lifted the beaker to his lips and drank.

"And what was it?" asked Merlin then.

"In truth, I do not know," Amminius replied. "I know what I saw and heard, but I have spoken to others, whose experience was quite different. To me," he continued, "it was a chalice, such as the priest uses at the mass. But this one was far richer, and it shone. And there was a Voice that spoke to me," he added, but he did not tell what it had said.

Merlin did not expect it. His own visions had taught him how difficult it was to convey their real meaning in human words.

"I think it was the Cup of Christ's passion that I saw, but on the next day word came that the Cauldron they keep at the Isle of Maidens had been stolen. So I do not know now what it is I am searching for, or why—"

"Do you not? When you spoke, the memory of what you saw shone in your eyes. To deny that truth is to deny yourself!"

Amminius shook his head. "I was brought up in the faith, but I have never been devout. I always meant to be a warrior . . ."

"And now—"

"Now my only desire is to see that vision again! But I know that once I am back at court I will forget, and so I wander—"

"You are not searching for the Grail, you are fleeing the world." Merlin searched his memory for the teachings of the priests he had heard at the court of Vor-Tigernus when he was young. "If you follow this path you will remain in limbo, able to attain neither heaven nor hell."

"But what must I do?"

Merlin shook his head. He could preach Christian doctrine, but he refused to take responsibility for this boy's soul. "You must choose . . ."

For a long moment Amminius sat with head bowed. When he looked up at last, the memory of glory shone in his eyes.

"Oh, good father, thank you!" His voice rang out joyously. "In the hills above my home there is a cave. I will go there, and live on berries and roots and the water from the stream. And perhaps, if I purify my heart and wait patiently, the Grail will come to me . . ."

Merlin stared at him in amazement. "Do not thank me, but the god within you—" he said at last. *He has found his Grail,* he thought, *though he may not yet realize it. But if it is the Chalice of the Christians, what then is the Cauldron?*

On the heels of a winter storm another traveller found his way to Merlin's door. This one was older, a dour, heavyset man called Cunobelin, who had served with Arthur since the Saxon wars. In the old days, the mage had known him well. The mage came upon him as he led a limping horse down the road.

"What are you doing here?" he said as Merlin moved out from among the leafless trees. Cunobelin had never been one of those who made the sign of the Horns if they touched the mage's shadow, nor did he follow the Christians. Indeed, Merlin doubted the man had faith in anything at all.

"Waiting for you—" he answered. "Or someone like you. I have a shelter nearby. Come rest your horse and eat a bowl of soup by my fire."

For a moment Cunobelin considered him, then he nodded. "A friendly face and a little warmth will be welcome. This wind blows chill."

Merlin waited until the man had eaten before he questioned him about the Grail.

"What did I see?" Cunobelin laughed harshly. "A bright light that moved through the hall. So in truth I do not know what we are all seeking, but it is clear that I am not the one to find it. I am returning now to Camelot."

"You speak as one who has failed—"

"Is it not so?" Cunobelin asked bitterly.

"Perhaps you have been looking in the wrong place."

"What do you mean?" The warrior frowned.

"I think that you are one who must be able to see the object of his adoration. It is in this world, not the Other, that you will find what you are looking for."

"The sun and the moon are still in the heavens, as anyone can see, but no one has suggested we search for *them!*"

Merlin shook his head. "Surely the heavens hold wonders, but they do not make your spirit soar. Think back. Is there anything else that has made you feel as you did in the moment when the light passed through the hall? A person, an experience – in the Otherworld, things do not have to be alike to be the same."

"A person?" whispered Cunobelin. He closed his eyes. "Nothing that anyone else would think worth remembering . . ." For a time he was silent. When he spoke again, it was as one in a dream.

"I was very young when I first came to Londinium to serve the king. The lads wormed out of me that I'd never lain with a woman, and they took me to a courtesan. I was ashamed of my ignorance, but she . . . was kind to me. And when she received me into her arms, it was like a great light breaking around me . . ." He shook his head and looked up, an unaccustomed colour in his cheeks. "But surely to remember that is blasphemy, when everyone is talking of a holy thing!"

"For you, her embrace *was* holy," said Merlin. "Why have you never married? You deny your nature."

"What could I offer a wife, when I was always going off to war? But I've dreamed of finding a woman who would come with me to one of those abandoned farms I've seen in my travels and make it bloom again." He stopped short, staring at Merlin. "Have you bespelled me? I have never told anyone these things!"

"I have cast no spells," the mage said softly. "I only point the way—"

Cunobelin was never seen at Arthur's court again. All that winter season, other men came to Merlin's hut in the forest, eager or disillusioned, proud in their strength or feverish with wounds. The weak he nursed and the strong he counselled, and from each one he learned something of the Hallow they were all seeking.

He had heard once an ancient tale of the blind men who were asked to describe an elephant, their reports all different, and all accurate descriptions of the part of the beast each man had found. On the Isle of Maidens, the priestesses guarded a Cauldron. He had seen it, and knew it for a thing of power. But was that the Grail, or only one appearance of something whose true nature could only be known by combining the myriad visions of those to whom it called?

Merlin's last visitor came riding by on a day when spring had drawn her first veil of greenery across the land and the skies were clamorous with returning waterfowl, borne north on the warm breath of the wind. Merlin had thrown off the heavy Druid's robe and donned his garment of skins. The hut where he had spent the winter seemed cramped and odorous, as tattered as the winter pelts the beasts were shedding to make way for the new growth of spring. His muscles twitched with the urge to action, yet still he tarried. When he met the young warrior's dazzled gaze, he understood what he had been waiting for.

"Eliuc—" Softly he called his name, waiting for the wide eyes to track slowly downward, for recognition to focus there.

"It is you . . ." the boy said at last. "I sought you . . . because you might understand . . ."

"Why? Who do you think I am?"

"You are the Wild Man of the Woods, yourself half of faerie," the answer came.

Merlin grunted. This boy was too young to recognize him, but in a way, his words were true.

"Were you not one of those who rode out to seek the Grail? Your face seems to say that you have found it—" he said when the horse had been unsaddled and tethered to graze.

Eliuc sank down on an outcropping of stone. "I found . . . something. It haunts my dreams." His skin was luminous in the dappled shade of the young leaves.

"Tell me—"

Haltingly, the story came – the privations of a quest pursued through winter weather until despair was near. Eliuc had taken refuge at last with a shepherd, earning his keep by guarding the ewes as they dropped their lambs and keeping off the wolves. When the weather warmed, he set off again, letting the horse choose the way.

One night, he had made camp beside a small spring. He woke to the touch of moonlight that glimmered through the branches and reflected from the pool in a haze of light. He sat up, staring, for in that light a figure was forming, slender, luminous, beautiful beyond mortal ken.

"She smiled at me . . . she held out a vessel of pure silver, rimmed with river pearls, and I took it from her hand. It was brimming with what looked like water, but the taste of it overwhelmed my senses. I was lost, to myself, to the world, overcome by joy."

"And then?" asked Merlin, seeing him begin to drown once more in that rapture.

"Then it was morning, and I was alone." The desolation in Eliuc's tone made the mage's eyes prick in sympathy. "For a week I waited, but she did not come again. Since then I have wandered. Food has no savour, even my dreams are pale echoes of what I have seen. Was it in truth the Grail that I found?"

"For you it was," Merlin said gravely. "You have tasted the wine of the Otherworld. Be grateful for what you have seen, and do not seek to recapture it."

"That is cold comfort! How can I live in a world from which the magic is gone?"

"There are many kinds of magic—" Merlin began, but Eliuc shook his head.

"I will go back to the spring. Perhaps if I am patient, one day she will open the door to me once more!" He leapt to his feet, eyes once more afire with remembered glory, and before the mage could speak again, had run to his horse and was gone.

Arthur will not thank me for this day's work, Merlin thought sadly. The king's men had sought the Grail to bring healing to the kingdom, but too many, one way or another, had been lost to king and kin. To each of them, it brought the fulfilment most desired – for one, the Christos, for another, a woman's body, and the ecstasy of the Otherworld for a third.

It was time for the hermit to leave the forest. The lure had become too strong – the Grail had appeared to him, if only through other men's eyes, and he had now no choice but to search for it.

What face, he wondered, *will the Grail wear for me?*

Merlin's way led toward the Lake and the Isle of Maidens. The Grail, it was clear, was not the same as the Cauldron, and yet by taking the Cauldron into the lands of mortal men, a way had been opened for the Grail to appear, establishing a connection between the Hallow and the men who sought it. For all his wizardry, he could take no path but the one the Hallow had already chosen.

He came in the evening, as the light of the setting sun, reflected from the heavens, was filling the Lake with gold.

Merlin had known the Lady since they both were young, and insofar as it was given to him to feel for a mortal woman, loved her. There had always been respect between them, but she faced him with hostility now.

"By blood you are priest of the Sword, and the god of the Saxons has given you his spear. By what right do you claim access to the Cauldron? It is a Woman's Mystery!"

"A woman bears the Grail, but it calls to men and women alike. Arthur is the Defender of Britannia, but I am his mage. When magic touches the land, it is my responsibility, and my right, to understand it. And it is your duty as Guardian of one of the Hallows to assist me."

For a long moment she looked at him, and then she sighed. "Perhaps it is so. Certainly I have not been so secure a custodian as I might wish, though the Goddess brought good from mischance in the end. But your reasoning does not entirely convince me – the lands of men have not seen you for years on end. Men thought you dead, or a legend. Why should the Grail draw you back?"

"Why, indeed? You are right to wonder. I have lived in the forest as a Wild Man, forgetting my humanity. I thought I would die there, but I am still strong. Perhaps the Grail will show me, as it has shown to others, a way I may be released from the world."

And when he had said that, the priestess ceased to argue, and together they waited for night to fall.

"What is it that you expect to see?" asked the Lady of the Lake as she led him to the dell below the cave.

"A vessel, a container, a passage between the worlds . . ."

"And does the greatest mage in Britannia need such devices for his journeying?" Her voice was cool, but in her words he heard echoes of the Otherworld, and the hair on his body stood out as if from cold.

"For this journey, I do."

"I will tell you once more. If it was the Cauldron that passed through Arthur's hall that night, it was borne by no mortal hand."

"Have you lost faith in your own Hallow, Lady?" He shook his head. "This is not the end of Desire, but this is where I must begin."

The opening to the cave was a dark slash in the rough rock that pushed through the turf of the hill. Torches set to either side hissed and flickered, sending ruddy light pooling across the worn stone. Merlin sank down upon the boulder that faced it, keeping his breathing long and slow. But he could not control the pounding of his heart.

The silence deepened until he could hear the whisper of fine linen as the wind stirred the Lady's veil. In the shadows of the cave mouth, something pale was moving. A female form, swathed in white, emerged from the darkness, torchlight flaring across the polished silver surface of the vessel she bore. She came to Merlin and set the Cauldron gently on the slab of stone before him.

It was half-filled with water.

"It is only water from the spring," said the Lady. "What meaning you find there must come from within."

"I know it." Merlin lifted his hands in blessing and invocation. "By fire and water I summon truth to me, by the radiance of the spirit and the darkness of the womb."

He felt, rather than heard, her leaving him. And then he was alone with the ripple of light on water and the surrounding shadows.

He saw, first, his own features, wild hair twining in distorted spirals like some ancient carving. Beneath the heavy brows, his eyes captured light from the torches' flames. Merlin continued to gaze, breath passing in a slow and regular rhythm that barely stirred the hair of his beard, waiting for the water to still, the fires to burn low, until he saw only the shimmer of backlit hair like a halo around a mask of darkness.

Gazing, he allowed his consciousness to sink into those depths, until he no longer saw the Cauldron or his own face within it. Presently new images formed within the shadow – stars in a night sky and the dim shapes of trees, a face framed by the rim of a cauldron.

But the cauldron he looked into was wrought of black iron, and the face reflected from the steaming brew it contained was that of a boy.

"Stir it, Viaun, you wretched chid! Have not I told you the liquid must always be kept moving?" A white hand reachd past his head and cast pungent leaves of mugwort into the cauldron. The hand of Cerituend . . .

His grip tightened convulsively on the ladle and he began to draw it sunwise through the liquid once more. Already the sharp scent of the herb was melding with others – mints and sages, leek, salt and darker, heavier odours he did not want to name. It smelled like magic.

"It will not be long now. Do not fail me! I will be back soon!" Cerituend's voice was like honey, like the scent of her, fading as she moved away. A memory that was not his own made him shiver with mingled fear and desire.

Merlin who was Viaun reached out to the nearby woodpile and slid more sticks beneath the pregnant bulge of the cauldron. Soon the brew was bubbling gently. The roiling of the liquid intensified. He slowed his stirring, trying to calm it. Perhaps he should not have added more fuel to the fire. *She* had said the potion was almost complete – as he stared into the cauldron, its contents heaved as if that last addition had awakened it. The potion was meant to give her son wisdom in compensation for his ugly countenance. No wonder it seemed to have a life of its own.

He looked nervously over his shoulder, involved entirely in the vision now. Black branches netted the dim blue of the evening sky. And in that instant of inattention, he heard the bubbling of the potion intensify. In the next moment it was boiling over, splashing his hand. He squealed with pain and clapped it to his lips.

The concentrated liquid scalded, at once tart and sweet, bland and salty. Then the confusion of flavours became a maelstrom of meaning. He understood *everything*, the movements of the heavens and the growth of herbs, the ways of all beasts and the tongues of men. He comprehended, in that moment, the meaning of the Grail, and beyond that, overwhelming him with terror, knew that he had stolen the magic of the Goddess, and that She would destroy him.

He was Viaun and Merlin, he was every man who has transgressed Women's Mysteries. He dropped the ladle on the grass and began to run.

For a time he ran blindly, but soon enough his new knowledge told him that She was coming after him. He became a hare, coursing swiftly through the undergrowth. But the Goddess had turned herself to a lean hound bitch to run him down. When he leaped skyward as a sparrow, she became a plummeting hawk.

He was the stag that fled the wolf-bitch, the salmon that twisted away from the otter's tooth, the vole that fled the owl. All these he had been, in that other lifetime when he was Merlin. As Viaun, he was pushed from transformation to transformation, fleeing the terrible Mother down the cycles of the years.

In the end he no longer possessed the strength or invention to continue his evasions. His last defence was to turn himself to something insignificant beyond her attention, one grain in a pile of corn. And there he waited, until the huge black hen pecked her way across the farmyard and swallowed him up into the dark.

For a time beyond time the soul that had been Merlin lay cradled in the pregnant womb of the World. And in that darkness came visions. He saw men of Camelot still searching for the Grail, some to give up the quest in despair, some to die, and some, under a dozen different guises, to find what they most desired. The veil of Time swirled, and he saw Arthur facing Mordred upon a bloody field. He struggled then, sure he could stop it if only he were free, and saw an oak tree in the heart of the forest whose trunk had the shape of a man.

"*Have I failed entirely?*" his spirit cried then. "*Shall Camelot fall, and all my wisdom pass with it from the world?*"

"*From whence did that wisdom come?*" asked the Darkness.

After a time, Merlin answered slowly, "*From the Cauldron, which holds the distilled essence of the earth.*"

"*Then how can it be lost? It is men's knowledge of that wisdom that will disappear . . .*"

"*I have lived long, but this body is not immortal—*"

"*Then take a new one. I have taught you the way of transformation.*" The answer, slow and amused, came to him. "*Let your power be rooted in the land, and your spirit pass to the child of prophecy. Your wisdom will never be forgotten, so long as you remember that it came from Me . . .*"

Merlin floated, thinking. The warm darkness that surrounded him was changing, becoming the slow surge of the sea. At last a final question came to him. Other men had asked whom the Grail served, but that was not what he needed to know.

"*Who are you?*"

The attention of that Other intensified. Once more Merlin tried to get away, but how could he flee that which contained him?

"I am the Quest, and I am the Grail. Men seek Me, not knowing that they will gain their desire only when I find them. They flee, not knowing that flight forces the transformation that will bring them to My arms. I am the Divine Darkness and the Light that shines beyond the circles of the world. I am the Truth beyond all goddesses and gods. I am the Mystery ..."

The rhythmic motion grew more violent. Dizzied, Merlin struggled against the membrane that contained him.

"Who—" he cried. *"Who is the Child of Prophecy?"*

He was dying. He was being born. A last convulsion slammed him hard against an unyielding surface. The darkness that surrounded him was torn open and someone lifted him into the air.

"Look!" came a voice. "It is the Radiant Brow!"

When Merlin could think again, he found himself lying tangled in his cloak on the stones before the cave. The Lady of the Lake knelt beside him, but the Cauldron was gone. Had he dreamed its presence? It did not matter, for the vision it had given him still shimmered in memory.

"Are you all right?" she asked, helping him to sit up again. "Did you learn what you needed to know? You began to struggle, and then you cried out and collapsed."

"I think so . . ." he nodded. "Help me to rise and I will tell you what I saw, lest it disappear like a dream."

He finished his story sitting with the Lady on the stone bench on the lakeshore, watching the sky grow bright above the eastern hills.

"I must go back to Arthur's court," Merlin said finally. "I cannot change what is to come, but I can bear witness, and pass to the Child of Prophecy the story. . . ."

"But who is he?" asked the Lady.

"He is Taliesin, the babe with the Radiant Brow. In forty years, he will be born—for the first time. And I will be waiting to teach him, for in body and spirit I will be one with this land. That body will die, but his spirit, my spirit, will come again and again, renewing the ancient magic, rebirthing the old stories into the world . . ."

A fish leaped from the Lake before them, the twisting body flaring gold. In the next moment it fell back again, but the impact sent ripples circling outward across the still water long after the fish itself had disappeared.

"And did you find what you were looking for?"

The mage nodded, gazing out across the shining expanse of water cupped within its sheltering hills. *This is the Grail,* he thought. *The Cauldron and all the other vessels, are but analogues for this precious and lovely world, which is itself a sacrament, given meaning by the life it holds.*

And in that moment the sun lifted above the rim of the hill, and sky and water and Merlin's spirit were filled with light.

NAMER OF BEASTS, MAKER OF SOULS
THE ROMANCE OF SYLVESTER AND NIMUË

JESSICA AMANDA SALMONSON

I wanted Jessica Salmonson (b. 1950) to be in this volume right from the start. Other pressures and commitments meant that, for a while, it might not be possible. But, as a true professional, she came through at the end with a story that fair knocked me asunder. I've read no other Arthurian story like this, and I hope you enjoy it as much as I did. It was no less than I expected from Jessica whose work has always shown not only an originality of treatment but depths of emotional power. Her works have often drawn upon legendary themes, including her earliest, Tomoe Gozen *(1981), set in an alternative reality based on a mythical Japan. Several tales based on legends will be found in her collections* Mystic Women: Their Ancient Tales and Legends *(1991) and* The Mysterious Doom and Other Ghost Stories of the Pacific Northwest *(1993). This story originally grew out of a project to bring together a series of stories tracing the history of Lilith from prehistory to the present. Lilith is the archwitch of Jewish mythology, reckoned as the first wife of Adam, before Eve. Here Jessica translates the character of Lilith into the personality of Nimuë, and sets us on the road to Merlin's fate.*

They are many, and she but One
And I and she, like moon and sun,
So separate ever! Ah,
yet I follow her, follow her.
(Alfred Noyes, "The World's Wedding")

Just as there are two Liliths – Lilith the Elder, and Lilith the Younger called also Naamah – so too there are two Merlins: Merlin Ambrosius, and Merlin Sylvester called also Celidoine. Whoever despises one history of Merlin can say, "But that was *not* Ambrosius, a wonderworker from birth, who saw in the stars the rise of the House of Pendragon; rather, it was Celidonius, who lived always in a forest, and never strayed." Yet such severe dichotomies cannot be fully made, for the two Merlins are One and Immortal, just as the two Liliths are One and Immortal.

Celidoine lived in the manner of Adam before the coming of Eve, when he was a seeker not fully enlightened. Merlin the forest shepherd dwelt in the roots of ash-trees, and was King of Beasts. He knew the True Names of animals, the very names first uttered by the voice of Adam. And beasts obeyed Celidoine with such implicitness that when he went into the meadows as a herdsman, a gigantic lioness that beforetimes belonged to the Great Mother of Tyre walked with him into his fold and lay down by his feet, purring sweetly, molesting neither sheep nor cow.

And this forest-Merlin possessed a living Throne of fiery amber, having a pulsing light within; and the Throne had a voice like unto that of a sweetly loving mother who sings lullabies to her children. The Throne was hemmed in on all sides by dense thickets of hazel; and when Merlin sat thereon, only the most meditative of seekers ever saw him.

From the left side of the Mother Throne issued a fire that joined sunlight and moonlight to every earthly hearth. At the right side of the Throne there arose a silent, shimmering curtain of motionless water that joined all earthly stores of water to the sparkling, celestial river. The Throne existed at that point of vibration where Fire and Water are harmonious lovers, and from whose embrace the Existential Universe first emanated by stages and degrees in the forms of a Crown, a Key, and an Egg.

From this seat Merlin gazed outward at all things, yea, the things of All. And the All was held fast where Merlin sat, even as the spokes of a wheel are sunrays anchored to a hub.

Meanwhile Merlin's bride dwelt in all the rivers of the world, but most especially in a mountainous lake of Celidoine's sacred wood, much as Adam's first wife was the Lilith who dwelt in the Sea of Reeds, from whence she held back the waters for Moses, but not for Pharaoh.

She was called the Lady of the Lake because she was like unto a Well in whose black water all celestial Wisdom is reflected. The pooled gaze of Nimuë is like a concave mirror wherein the vastness of the universe is writ small, and held fast, so that the completeness of All is visible in her merest glance. And if we may suppose God is a Great God, and Merlin a Little God, then Nimuë was the concavity by which the little knew the large. Thereby she boasted, "By Me, God made the universe."

All great and godly consorts are brother and sister, so that Nimuë was the same, though not entirely the same, as Ganicenda, Merlin's twin. And despite that Ganicenda was one and the same with Nimuë the Lady of the Lake, she was at the same time distinct from her.

Ganicenda was mightiest on land, for she was of the fire that dwelt in the hearth and emanated from the left side of the Throne. She did not enter into water, for she was that part of Mother Earth whose hands restrained the Flood. It was said of her that her face was in heaven, while her feet went down to Sheol; that the sun was her Face, and the moon was her Crown; and the Apples of Avillion sprang from her very footsteps.

She was a waystation on the road to Sheol, but she was not of Sheol itself. She prepared banquets and invited evildoers into her house of seven pillars, and insinuated herself upon he that was blind to spiritual treasure. By slow degrees he perceived the way of salvation, saying, "Thou art Wisdom who hast turned my road about." But if still a fool unable to perceive purity, he says, "Thou art a Harlot!" and continues his descent. For Ganicenda was a demoness to fools as wholeheartedly as she was Divine Wisdom to those with open hearts.

In an era when Merlin, wisest of earthly beings, was called Solomon, it was of Ganicenda he sang, "My sister, my bride." Solomon the consort of Divine Wisdom was builder of the Two Temples, the one belonging to Yahweh, and the other to Ashtaroth of Sidon, established at the behest of Naamah the Amoritess, queenmother to Solomon's doomed son, the forerunner of Merlin's fosterling Arthur.

And it was said that Solomon did not build his two temples by any mortal means, but that a demoness of the Danites was bound into Solomon's service. It was she that built the Temple of

Ashtaroth, while her son, a Tyrian architect, built the Temple of Yahweh in accordance with his mother's plan.

This demoness was Solomon's twin; for when Solomon sucked at the left teat of Bathsheba, his sister sucked at the right; and when Solomon sucked at the right, his sister sucked at the left. When she was weaned, Queen Bathsheba sent her to live in Tyre, until Solomon was capable of receiving her in the form of the Temple of Ashtaroth, as Solomon took on the form of Yahweh's Temple.

Now Ganicenda was a huntress whose companion on the chase was Fair Arawn, Lord of Death, called Adonis in the East, otherwise Adonai Sabaoth. And Arawn said to Ganicenda, "Ha ha! Your brother Sylvester is wise, yet he has no palace. He rules beasts but hasn't even a barn to keep them in. How can he be master of the earth when his throne is in a thicket twixt fire and wave? Ha ha! He has no palace!"

Therefore the sister-bride Ganicenda built for her brother-husband a castle out of logs, deep in Sylvester's hidden glade within the Forest of Broceliande. Like Behemoth foraging, Ganicenda rendered bald a thousand hills in Lebanon. She bound the cedars with hazel rope to form spires and minarets and flying buttresses, with vast rooms opening into other rooms which opened into others. She built the castle in a single night, though a thousand workers in a thousand years could never have achieved so much.

The palace surrounded the Mother Throne, before which Ganicenda placed a Globe of Life that was Merlin's footstool. And because her feet went down to Sheol, she caused to be raised from out of the earth a circle of seven pillars and laid upon them a massive, circular stone, whereon grew a shining bush hung about with hazels.

To the eye that looks but does not see, there was no castle, but a mountain that had not been there beforetimes, or an impenetrable mist into which few ventured and fewer returned with mind intact. To anyone of true vision, there it plainly stood, a gargantuan log castle with one hundred doors that opened into Everywhere, yet without windows.

Ganicenda gave no windows to the palace because Death enters through windows. By her trick of architecture, she caused Merlin to be immortal.

Soon thereafter Merlin sat in languid pose, his feet upon the globe, saying to himself, "Mine is the fairest tower in the world!" He leaned back and gazed upward through the smoke-hole in the roof, through which he read the stars. And the stars whispered to him, "Mightiness, mightiness, mightiness," but he was not even then fully enlightened, and pondered careless interpretations by means of wild surmise.

Now Merlin of the Wood was very black, even as Nimuë of the Lake was black but comely. And Nimuë said to him, "Sylvester, Sylvester, come into my rose-petaled bower." Merlin set down his ghastly, enormous axe that was stained with sap and blood; and he removed from himself the visage of a greybeard and cast aside his ragged garment made from skins of wolves. He revealed himself youthful, hairless, and dark as a sapphire lit by starlight from within, a beautiful giant with strength in all his limbs, including that which extended mightily from the center. Nimuë said, "Sylvester, Sylvester, lay your body on this bed of moss and flowers, your head upon my myrrh-scented pillow."

As he lay upon her, she wrapped him in her thousand arms, her thousand legs, that were a radiating energy. He became the axle through the center of the universe. And from their glad repose, Nimuë taught the tawny Merlin all things, yea, the things of All.

She invested him with such an energetic wisdom that when they quit the bed of rose and myrrh, he said, in a voice that caressed, "You are the dancer between two armies. One of your armies is terrifying for its protective righteousness, and the other is terrifying for its unforgiving judgement. Will you continue, O Nimuë, to fill me with the Light of your Instruction, or will you in the end set upon me corrupt minions from underneath the Earth?"

As Merlin spoke, the blackness of the Lady became pale as bone, then paler, until she rushed away from him, having become a sinuous, serpentine river that flowed from out of his hands, leaving him bereft of all but her scent of myrrh, and rose, and hazel.

Then was his love for Nimuë like wormwood in his mouth. "I must rule the whole of the world to impress Nimuë the Daughter of Eve," said Merlin. "I will perform deeds no Son of Adam hath dared before this time."

He repaired to his log castle that had no windows, but only an opening in the roof, through which he read the stars. He saw therein that which he believed his need required, and he said, "I will upraise a barbaric bastard to be king. And through him will I hold planets in the cup of my hand, and be to Arthur like God."

So saying, he stood abruptly, filled with false insight. The Mother Throne sank into the Earth; the glimmering sheet of water dissipated into mist; the wall of glittering fire became a pillar of smoke that rose through the star-hole of his log castle's roof and was no more. Sylvester tore the burning thistle from off the vast stone table, and set it behind him on the ground, where it rooted itself in the place where the Throne had been, and lost its glow. Then lifting the round tabletop from off the circle of stones, he rolled it through an open door, and followed after it, vanishing forever from the forest and the sylvan glade.

Then did the River that was Nimuë became salty as from tears.

In the depths of her lake, Nimuë possessed a crystalline palace, wherein doves with jewel eyes and rose-tint feathers sang and fluttered from room to room. To the random observer on barge or bank, the castle appeared to be only an enormous grey stone. But for the visionary, the castle possessed a clarity of structure that rendered it invisible, so that all within the stone was seen: Nimuë, Queen of Depths, in the guise of Rahab the Dragon, upon her garnet throne; with birds of fire going in and out of her stormy mouth.

She pondered the treachery of the Sylvan Merlin who had turned away from a perfect, loving togetherness in favor of the world of materiality, misusing spiritual powers possessed through her. Nimuë's gift was meant for purposes nobler than power to govern, to conquer, to amass great wealth and fame. Merlin had become a treasonous lover, an abuser of Truth, and Truth abused rises up like a lioness enraged, a cobra no longer charmed, the Dragon-mother leaping from her depths to engulf the earth with boiling floods.

Well she knew that it was not truly Sylvester who set out to upraise the barbaric Arthur. Rather, it was Ambrosius, whom Sylvester, as shapeshifter, so easily became. A true shapeshifter cannot change that which is material in his nature without changing that which is spiritual. Hence Ambrosius, contrary to Sylvester, knew not Nimuë, so was unaware by what means he misguidedly betrayed her. He did not know who or what it was that tugged at mind and heart with vague, uneasy promises of redemptive unifaction, versus threats of destruction and everlasting regret. He mistook this aching, invisible thing that pulled at him as Destiny, and could not imagine he might ever be deprived of godlike power. Poor Ambrosius! Pitiable wizard that was meant to be the living soul of nature!

With every Good that Lilith undertakes, there is a shadow underneath; and for every Evil to which Lilith aspires, a bright truth arises from it.

The two natures of Lilith, that dwelt harmoniously within Nimuë, sought foremost to assist her errant lover, so that Arthur might be illuminated in accordance with Merlin's desire. But this achievement was to be Merlin's greatest failure and undoing, for She simultaneously sought an unrestrained vengeance for Merlin's faithlessness.

Thus pondering in the watery void, Nimuë struck upon a labyrinthine plan, and called forth from her womb a boychild fair and innocent, whom she named Lleminawac, "Whose Hand is Purity." She reared the pale lad to young manliness in a twinkling, though it seemed to him like many years, and this occurred in a chamber of light beneath Loch Corrib. At length she sent him forth in a bewildered state, under numerous compulsions, and he was afterwards called Lancelot of the Lake.

Then she rode forth on a dappled mare, whose form was like smoke, with a small white hound scenting the way through darkness, and thirty long, sleek, black bitches swift upon the mare's heals. And she came in cloudy moonlight to a menhir in a glade, breathing her Breath of Life upon it as she said, "Come forth, Baal Zephon. Come forth from your eons of slumber, bringing with you all that you have learned from the Lord of Death!"

White eyes opened in the stone's grey surface. Moments after he was called forth, there stood a rustic knight, Sir Balin the Savage, He of the Dolorous Stroke, predestined destroyer of Castle Sangrail upon the Glassy Isle.

The white-eyed giant knelt before the Lady of the Lake. She kissed him at the left side of his throat, leaving her mark upon him. Then he strode away toward Camelot, his cloudy mind roiling like a nimbus.

And Nimuë called forth a thoughtful and fearless knight whose name was Pellinore.

He wandered idly through Cornwall and Wales until he came to the lake's shore. He did not suspect he was beckoned, but thought only, "I have found a holy place." He stood leaning upon a spear's haft, the blade of which was a long as a sword, and double-edged.

He sighed in appreciation of the wildness and startling beauty of the lake. His seeker's heart noted first the enormous stone beneath the lake. As his observance grew deeper, the stone became translucent, then transparent to the point of invisibility, so that he saw miraculous subaquatic doves flitting within crystal chambers.

At the heart of the mystic castle, coiled upon a carnelian throne, he saw Nimuë in the form of the Echidna, such as was a dragon from the waist down, and a woman of grave and terrible beauty from the waist up.

As Nimuë uncoiled herself from the throne, her tail split in two, so that she slithered weirdly upon serpentine legs around and around a spiral of crystal stairs, her upper body writhing like a black flame. The water fell away from her, so that she came upon the surface of the lake, a monstrous giantess dwarfing the tall quester.

She roared and bared two long fangs that dripped venom, dashing her head toward Pellinore as though to devour him in one bite. He raised his long-bladed spear and scuttled backward, sorely confused by the vision shifting and wavering before him; for now he perceived an obscene reptilian head turn to mark him with one dark eye. That eye glimmered as with starlight reflected in a deep well. It observed him evilly, swaying back and forth, seeking a means to strike around Pellinore's steady spear.

In that self-same moment Sir Pellinore saw, however briefly, all things from the Beginning of Time, unto the Dissolution, and knew not merely his own destiny, but that of the Universe entire; for Time was a serpent coiled twice upon itself, and Time's name was Nimuë.

No sooner was this known to him than his mind clamped shut over a multitude of scenes, lest a premature enlightenment destroy him as with fire. He was left with only his sense of awe for the creature that swayed before him.

A tongue like a two-tined fork licked forth. Pellinore gasped in horror of that tongue, each part long enough to wrap about him twice. His two-edged spear-blade batted the tongue with eager self-defense. As the blade swung left then right, he was bathed in blood from the gaping mouth. The fangs fell loose in the form of finely scabbarded swords whirling away through air. The twin swords splashed into the midst of the lake; and one was destined for the hand of Arthur, the other for his twin sister, called Cybele, the Morrigu, or Morgan le Faye.

The dragon dwindled until black Nimuë clad in white stood at the lakeside. Her abandoned serpent's skin sank into the watery void; and that skin was Morgan who hid herself in an aquatic forest with one sword in her left hand, one sword in her right, waiting, waiting.

Having been doused with dragon's blood, Pellinore found that his skin acquired a ruddy glow. Bewildered more and more, he threw aside his weapon in horror of his actions, for he saw in Nimuë's apparition something of Stella Meris, Mother of Stars and Sea, known anciently as Ashtaroth, and afterward as Mary.

Pellinore fell to his knees, whispering, "Forgive me, My Lady. I did not know that it was You."

Nimuë took him by his shoulders to raise him from his knees; and still she was taller than he. She bent to his throat, to the right side, and there kissed him, leaving a pale white mark. Pellinore shivered and sighed as he slipped from her embrace, falling weakly to his hands, his brow damp and his golden locks dangling from his head hung low.

Nimuë said, "From this time on, you are my champion, and may never come to harm, for you are sheathed in the blood of Rahab the Dragon-mother. There are numerous compulsions upon you, that over time, one by one, you shall feel unfold. Go forth and do slaughter for My sake, but remember this, there is one you may not slaughter, whose name is Artos of Camelot."

He bowed his head once more in deep devotion. When he lifted his gaze, the moonlit lake was no more, nor yet the sylvan watershed. Rather, he found that he had pitched a pavilion at the ford of a brackish river that wound its way near Camelot.

★   ★   ★

All who tried to cross, Sir Pellinore challenged. He spared nothing of mercy, but seemed to despise all who sought the court of Arthur and his mage, Ambrosius.

A chieftain of a far country came with his squire, and saw Pellinore standing utterly naked on the bank of the ford. The wandering chieftain said, "I seek the Court of the Matchless King, to serve who rules there. I have no time to joust with madmen without armor."

Pellinore whirled his spear three times about his head, declaiming fiercely, "There are madmen ringed everywhere about the Court you seek. No one may see to the heart of the world who cannot first defeat madness."

The spear of the wandering chieftain broke against the ruddy chest of the naked challenger, whereas the chieftain was run through the heart, lifted into the air like a bloody flag, and tossed away as would be a worthless tattered rag. The body was carried away face down in the river, blood tinting the water all about.

The dead knight's tearful squire ran forth with shortsword upraised; and, sobbing like an orphaned child, he strove to avenge his master. Pellinore swung once and disarmed the lad. He swung a second time, and tore open his arm. Now the young squire stopped weeping, and stood ready to be slain, his chin held in defiance.

"What is your name," asked Pellinore.

"Girflet," he replied.

"I will not slay you, Girflet, for you are but a child. I will let you pass, so that Arthur and his mage may learn why it has been that none have come to him by this road for many a day."

Girflet led a horse across the ford, then mounted unsteadily to gallop away.

A champion, mighty of appearance, rode out of Camelot, his lance longer than Pellinore's spear. And he said to the demonic guardian of the ford, "You have done harm to many that I love. Therefore have I come to sweep you from your camp by the river."

"Know you this," said Pellinore haughtily, astride a red roan mare. "I and this spear are baptized in dragon's blood, and may never come to harm in this world."

"And you know this," was his reply. "Within me runs the very blood of dragons!"

He dashed forth upon a stallion. Pellinore met him halfway in the river. The long lance splintered upon Pellinore's naked chest and he was not unseated from his roan. The court's champion, winded by a blow, plunged backward into the river, his armor so heavy he could not rise easily, but might have drowned had not Pellinore gotten down from his steed and lifted the champion's head from out of the water. Pellinore raised the visor of his fallen foe, and drew forth a dagger with which to give a coup de grace.

Swift astride a coal-black mare rode a greybeard in mage's robes, whom Pellinore knew to be Ambrosius. From some distance closing fast, the sorcerer began shouting baleful spells that fell impotently from the ruddy skin of Pellinore. The spells in no way restrained hand or dagger, poised above an opened visor.

Addressing his fallen opponent, Pellinore said, "Before I've killed you, tell me who I slay, that I may pray for the easeful repose of thy spirit."

"I am Arthur Pendragon," said the champion, causing Pellinore to sheathe his knife. With deep chagrin he drew the fallen king to the bank of the river.

Merlin sat by the sickbed of Arthur, whose ribs were crushed. Pellinore was there as well, for Arthur, before he fell to raving, granted a king's absolution, and invited the ruddy knight into the privileged circle.

Now Pellinore coursed about the room, filled with self-recrimination. Seeing Merlin Ambrosius so uncertain in the face of Death, Pellinore decided upon an action. He leaned close to the sweating face and matted hair of Arthur to whisper, "Your spirit must seek Nimuë, My Lady of the Lake." Instantly the body of the injured king grew calm, as his spirit fled away from Camelot by some method Pellinore half-wittingly induced.

"Leave this room at once!" cried Merlin, who left off his murmured spells upon hearing the name of Nimuë, though he knew not why her name roused him to such a passion.

Pellinore bowed before leaving, turning in the doorway to see that Merlin strove ineffectually to rouse Arthur.

It seemed to Arthur as though he came to a beautiful glade under clouded moonlight. From out of a weird dark lake arose a pale arm which upheld the sword Caliburnus. Arthur waded into the waters and took the strange blade from the shy nymph.

He knew that he was dreaming, yet it was not wholly a dream, and he heard himself asking, as from a far place, "Art thou the Lady of the Lake that hath handed me this sword?"

"No," replied a voice behind him. "She is not; but I am Nimuë."

The naiad's arm withdrew below the surface, leaving not the slightest ripple. Arthur turned about and saw a woman upon a smoky mare, with thirty black hounds and one white running close to the ground in figure eights, in and around the legs of the moveless mare.

Arthur waded from the shallows. He stood as near to her as dream allowed. She asked, "Which will you value highest, little dragon? The steel of Caliburnus, or its sheath?"

He drew forth the metal and inspected it in a shaft of moonlight. "The sheath is carved with Celtic whorls and set all about with jewels. It is too gaudy for my liking. But this metal I cannot help but admire, and shall keep it by me always."

"One day, that blade shall break. It is the sheath you should better value. For so long as you possess the sheath, you will be invulnerable, even as you found my champion Sir Pellinore of the Glassy Isle."

"Since you have already a Champion," said Arthur, "what boon is left that I can offer?"

"I *will* ask one gift, although you can give me nothing from your present dream. I will come to you in the world of materiality, although I warrant you shall not give whatever I require."

"I would deny you nothing," protested Arthur.

She smiled when he said that, but there was nothing merry in her smile. She said, "If you possessed sufficient wit to ascertain your moment of crucial and difficult obedience, you would never have preferred hard steel to wisdom, for such is the true nature of the sheath you've dismissed as gaudy. Soon I will send to you the Giant's Daughter to teach you the ways of wisdom. She that is Eve Incarnate will reveal to you the things of All at the halfway-place on the Road of Sheol. If you love her unreservedly, you will come in time to Michael in Heaven to stand beside him in defense of the Spirit. But if you despise your Illuminatrice, you will remain in the world to await the Dissolution, striving uselessly in behalf of Matter."

He meant to swear to her a binding oath never to neglect the spirit nor despise his Illuminatrice. But he woke too soon, his lungs no longer burdened, the bones in his broad chest newly healed. "Such a dream!" he told a startled Ambrosius. Arthur sat up amidst the curtains of his bed, looking about excitedly. "What is that odor?" he cried out to his mage. "Is it not midnight roses, and myrrh from a distant land?"

"No, my ward, it is the scent of hazel," said Merlin, hiding his wonderment when he saw, amidst Arthur's coverlets, the broadsword in its jewel-encrusted sheath.

When the marriage of Arthur and Gwenhwyvar was arranged, Arthur was delighted, for it was politically an advantageous match that would bring him much land. The woman was beautiful in the bargain, and reputedly wise.

Arthur called his vassals about his throne and said, "I am to be wed in the ancient city of Trinobantes, in the Church of Stephen, upon Candlemas, during the Feast of the Purification of the Blessed Virgin. Now it cannot be that a king is married if his vassals are not. As every fighting Dane and Nord goes forth with his shieldmaiden, and every hero of the Slavs and Poles is accompanied by his guardian vila, so too must every knight of Camelot pledge himself to a lady, to make her the sovereign of his heart, the inspiration for his conduct. Therefore each of you must go forth to find fair brides. Then come all of you to Trinobantes, clad entirely in white, so that we may all be wed together."

All knights but two repaired to private chambers to prepare themselves for travel. Of the two who stood fast by the throne, the first bore a white scar at the left of his throat. He was Balin of Caer Belli, that is, of Baal's Castle, famous from Cornwall to Northumberland. The other was Pellinore, chieftain of the Glassy Isle and possessor of Horn Castle, he that bore a scar identical to Balin's save only that it was on the right of his throat.

These two knights looked one another eye to eye. Although they had been friends and companions, there was suddenly a spark of enmity between them, for what cause they knew not.

"Come now," said Arthur, "have you not ladies to pursue?"

Sir Balin murmured lowly, like the sound of a rolling earthquake, "We have one."

Before he could explain himself, there rode into the midst of the court the Loathly Maid astride a dappled mare and armed with dagger and broadsword. She wore high boots and greaves, a coat of light mail, and over it a sleeveless tabard embroidered front and back with red poppies on a blue-green field. Her hair was caught up in a sparkling net. Her face had much of youth about it, yet was made to seem older by the way she scowled.

The hooves of the mare clattered before the throne, and Arthur was insulted that she would ride into his hall. He had heard of the Loathly Maid prior, and was fascinated by her more than he would care to admit. Her scowling wildness made her homely, but Arthur found himself wondering how she might appear if only she would smile. There was something familiar about her, though he was certain they could never have encountered one another outside of imagination.

When she dismounted, a squire scurried forth to remove the mare from the great hall. Arthur said, "Loathly Maid, why is it you wear armor and bear weapons such as deprive thee of comeliness?"

"Sir King, I am but a messenger, clad for far travel. Do you not recognize my sword?"

Arthur gasped, then felt quickly for his own sword, that leaned beside his throne. "I know you, then," said Arthur. "If only from a dream."

"Perhaps so; or not. This sword of mine is fused to its sheath. As yours cannot be drawn for evil purpose, mine cannot be drawn for good. Here, I will lend it to this squire called Girflet. Boy, take it. Draw the steel."

He tugged at it, making faces and chewing his lip. Those gathered about the court laughed to see him struggle.

The Loathly Maid said, "Give it then to Arthur."

Girflet gave the sword to the king. He looked it over with a shiver, for he would have sworn it was Caliburnus, had not that glorious weapon been ever at his side. He could not draw the blade, so handed it to Pellinore, who likewise struggled.

"Return it to me," said the Loathly Maid, but as Pellinore moved toward her, Balin took two long strides and said, "I will try," taking the sword from Pellinore.

The blade unsheathed easily.

"As you have seen," said the Loathly Maid, "there is one among your vassals sufficiently wicked to draw that steel. If you happen to recall it, Sir King, you do happen to owe me one boon. I require the head of Sir Balin."

Balin bristled. "You Salome!" he hissed.

"But you are no Saint John," said she.

Arthur sat silent in his throne. He knew, indeed, who the Loathly Maid must truly be, and by rights he should bow to her in hard obedience. But there was a voice beckoning from the curtains at his back, from a secret chamber, and Arthur leaned to one side to better listen.

"Send her away," the hoarse voice whispered, so that only the king heard. "If you love Me, and God, and all the things of this World such as I have brought to you, then send her away, for she is the Doom of us, young Pendragon, our Doom."

Arthur gave no indication that his mage had counseled him. He seemed merely to be pensive, and not the least distressed, although his breast was pounding. He said, "Sir Balin is of the privileged circle, and has proven himself many times. Ask something other of me, Loathly Maid. Would you have a castle in Cornwall or southern Wales? Have you foes my captains can bring low? Would you have treasure? I warrant it is true, I owe you much."

"As you have denied me, I will go," she said curtly. When she turned to leave, Balin drew the black steel anew, and laid it against her throat. He said, "As you cannot have my head, you will have me entire; and if you will not have me, then I will have your head."

"Sir Balin!" said Arthur. "Has that black blade charmed you to do evil? You are sworn, and cannot harm a lady."

Balin dragged her by her white throat, bruising her neck in his gauntleted grasp. As he backed to the gate at the far end of the hall, he excused his actions, saying, "But this is no Lady, as you can see by her armor. She is a Knight, so I exempt her from my oath."

When he left the hall, the clatter of hoofs told all the court Sir Balin had ridden away; and Arthur was disturbed to think one of his knights might ravage or behead a maiden. He stood from his throne and strode five steps, his visage clouded with uncertainty of action.

"For love of Me," said the hoarse voice of Merlin. "Let Balin have her. Let them go."

Arthur shook his head, wondering for the first time if there was not some sinister spark in the magery of his old counselor. Only

Arthur heard the voice that spoke into his mind; and he realized he could not in that moment speak any word, for Merlin willed him silent.

Sir Pellinore said, "Allow me, my king, to wrest the black sword from Balin's fist, and restore it to the Loathly Maid, that she may use it to test others. I think her not so hard as she would play, and needs now a champion to save her. Perhaps it is my fate to bring her to your wedding, and be married to her when you wed Gwenhwyvar. Say but one word, and I shall chastise Balin for his misdeed."

Arthur still could not speak. Yet he waved his hand in dismissal, and Pellinore set out to assist the Loathly Maid.

Merlin Ambrosius in a swirl of robes came out from behind the throne. Arthur spoke to him with a petulance unseemly for a king, "How could you ask that I let Balin molest her? Until now, I thought I could deny you nothing because I love you so, and because your counsel was good. Now I see that I am under the compulsion of a sorcerer. What truly is your design?"

"Think not ill of me, young Pendragon. I am a creature, like yourself, in this material world. I live within plots and devices. I love power and treasure. But most of all, I love you, and if I have overstepped propriety this day, it is because I saw the death of me, and the death of you."

Arthur replied, "Until today, you have sown certainty in my bosom. And see how swiftly I rise, assisted by your vision! Now I am to wed a queen whose royal lineage is Trojan and whose estates will treble the breadth of lands I rule. Soon all Britain will bow to me! What was there in the Loathly Maid that tells you your prophecies must change?"

"Prophecies – and machinations," the sorcerer confessed. "What makes them change is a desire I cannot name, let alone suppress. Gleefully would I follow that Loathly Maid to ruin. You recognized her, I know, as the Lady of the Lake, who until this hour I had never met. Yet when I saw her, even so disguised, I felt as though I had known her as of old, and that I owed her far more than simple mortal words can say. I knew at once that I must enter into my final dotage, wherein I will love her to distraction, caring nothing for what you and I have built together, let alone for anything remaining to be built."

There were tears upon the sorcerer's cheeks, and Arthur could not help but forgive him.

Merlin said, "It is best she be destroyed, for otherwise she will weep with mighty queens wailing on all sides of your funeral barge. If Balin kills her, I will grieve. Now that I have seen her, and heard her voice, the best I can hope is to waste away in a quiet place of the forest, surrounded by bards who will sing soothing lies of my greatness. So it is you I seek to save, young Pendragon, and not myself, for I cannot in any case be with you always."

Sir Pellinore, Lord of Horn Castle, forgot at once his purpose of rescuing the Loathly Maid, for Merlin's thought raced forth to make him neglectful of this goal. He recalled, instead, that all the vassals of Arthur's court were sent forth to find worthy damsels, then rally together on Candlemas, in Trinobantes, for the collective wedding.

Pellinore set out, therefore, to find a bride. Within a few days, he came to a castle ruled by young Queen Ettard, who inherited a throne from an enfeebled father. She refused ever to wed, lest power pass out of her hands.

Wintry clouds ringed about Ettard's mountain stronghold. Indeed, the whole of her country seemed to float on cloud. On the parapet of a castle tower was a man playing mournfully upon a bagpipe, with such a look of sadness about him that Pellinore shuddered to see him standing there so straight and strong and full of woe.

Pellinore was received at court. No sooner had he set eyes upon Queen Ettard than he knew he loved her more than his life. He put forth a poetic plea for her hand, naming sundry islands whose inhabitants knew him as King Pelleas. He boasted of the diamond of his realm, the Glassy Isle, where stood the glorious Castle of the Horn of Amalthea, alluding to rare treasures not wholly of this earth. And he begged that she come with him on Candlemas to be wed along with all the vassals that belonged to Arthur, so that the High King's marriage, together with their own, would make the whole land fruitive.

Despite the sincerity in his voice, and the beauty of his ruddy face, there was nevertheless something weird about such an intense and instantaneous affection. Although Ettard thought him irrational, she did not despise him immediately. Many had proposed to her on former occasions, each unable to disguise his obvious designs, gazing not so much at her as at the strength of her vassals and the breadth of her lands. But this knight who presently knelt before her was like a holy fool requiring nothing for himself, while offering all.

For one moment she considered, mayhap, she need not rule alone, but might do well to wed her fortunes to the Lord of the Glassy Isle.

She was swift to suppress such sentimental weakness, suspecting as she did that some witch was playing her a joke, having fed the foolish knight potions of love before sending him, in this bewildered state, to Queen Ettard's fastness. Therefore she spoke to him as though in a rage, and commanded her vassals strip Pellinore of his armor, beat him savagely, and throw him naked from the battlements.

He lay on a slope below the battlements, spread out in winter's brittle scrub. He was unable to move for a long while, not because of any injury, for he had none, but because his heart was broken. Come evening, he roused himself from depths of ennui, and said to himself, "I must eat, to build my strength for tomorrow's encounter with Ettard, fairest of all queens."

A stag wandered into sight. Pellinore leapt upon its shoulder and twisted its head in his arms. With knifeless hands he skinned the beast and, while meat roasted over a pit, sat scraping the skin with a stone, until he had for himself a rude garment.

At dawn, feeling restored and hopeful, he bathed beneath the frigid waterfall, then wrapped the deerskin about him and affixed the antlers to his head. The forelegs of the skin still had bones within, so that a stiff leg hung at each of Pellinore's shoulders, giving him, in silhouette, the look of a four-armed man. In a like manner, he dragged behind him the unboned hindlegs of the stag. And near his buttocks hung the white flag of the stagskin's tail.

Having made himself as presentable as he could – and he did look like a handsome mountain priest of a hunter's mystery cult – he went to the portcullis of Ettard's fastness. When none would open it for him, he raised the portcullis by brute strength, causing damage to the cogs of the wheel, and inducing guards to rush about in confusion.

Once more he stood before Ettard's throne. She saw that he lacked the least bruise from his beating or from the far plunge from the battlements. She was cunningly eager to test the limits of his tremendous strength. Because he loved her greatly, he was willing to submit to all abuse. She berated him for breaking the fastness gate, and charged him with sundry minor crimes of offense before sentencing him harshly. He was bound tightly into his deerskin garment so that he looked like a cocoon of something part stag, part man, that might in the springtime hatch into an even more monstrous being. Then he was tied with a long rope by his feet to the saddle of a horse. One of Ettard's vassals dragged him out from the fortressed castle and down a mountain road.

How he shouted as his body bounced and scraped along! But the words he bellowed were all devoid of complaint; rather, words of adoration echoed against the cliffs and through the valleys so that peasants far and near raised their heads from their plows and wondered whether it be fairies or divinities upon the mountains courting.

When the bounding horse rounded a curve, Pellinore was flung over the high road's ledge, and hung head-down two hundred feet in air. The queen's knight dismounted and peered from the ledge, laughing at the pendulous Pellinore and, with one sweep of the sword, cut him loose.

For several hours he struggled at the base of the cliff amidst bits of broken antler, striving to get out of the stagskin. His fruitless effort was overheard by a knight journeying on a lower road that circumvented the country of Queen Ettard.

It was shy of dusk when the knight climbed onto the crag and unbound Pellinore. The two men looked at one another face to face in mutual surprise.

"I am grateful for my release, Sir Gawain! Good fate that you were passing by!"

"Who has done this terrible thing to you?" asked Gawain, deeply alarmed; and Pellinore told of his love for Queen Ettard, and his willingness to suffer all indignity, if only to see her a few moments every day.

"But this cannot be!" said Gawain. "How I could lash her with my tongue for her unfeeling deeds!"

"Do not think ill of her, I beg you; think, rather, of what high regard I feel."

"Then you must allow me to intercede in your behalf. I will visit this terrible queen who has enticed your heart so cruelly, and beg that she treat you with goodness and reason, giving better consideration to your suit."

Pellinore's highest optimism was restored by Gawain's promise. He said, "Even if you fail to melt her snowy heart to my favor, I will nevertheless be in your debt forever, because you strove sincerely."

When Gawain regained his horse and started for the higher road to Ettard's castle, Pellinore sat alone on a rocky crag as night fell and stars winked score by score into existence. He listened some while to the distant, mournful Piper of the Parapet, until at length Pellinore began to sing of his love for Queen Ettard. From cliff to cliff his song echoed into darkness, and all the countryside heard the tragic rhyme.

At dawn he came again to Ettard's castle, this time clad in a grass mat salvaged from the floor of an abandoned wattle hut; and for his girdle, a frayed rope was hung with bits of broken antler. His hair was wild, and his repulsive garment crawled with lice, but still his face was beautiful as he set his doting gaze upon the immovable queen.

"In that you have come to me like Samson," she said, "you must be seeking your Delilah. Therefore tell me the secret of your invulnerability, that I may finally destroy you."

"As I love you well," said Pellinore, "I can deny you nothing. Take the bejewelled dagger from off your thigh and plunge it just here, into the white spot on the right side of my throat. If you can do so without regret, I will die."

"Come forth, then," she said coldly. He obeyed, going upon one knee. She drew forth the dagger and held it ready to stab his throat. For one long moment she gazed into his innocent eyes. Then she struck swift as an adder. He fell to his side with the blade deep in his neck.

He was tossed from the rear wall of the castle, where it was supposed wolves would clean his bones. He lay quietly all that day and through the night, with only the rotted garment of woven grass to defend him from the cold. His glassy eyes watched the track of the gauzy moon behind the clouds. Before the sun arose, it began to snow, and soon he was dusted over with whiteness. He knew that he was dying. Assuredly Gawain would hear what had happened, and come seeking him; but it would be too late.

The knife in his neck was perturbing. With an effort such as exceeded all his valorous deeds in service of King Arthur, he raised an arm, drew the dagger out of his neck, and kissed the jeweled hilt where Ettard's pretty hand had held it.

An anchorite came down from the higher mountain to look for edible bits of garbage that were commonly thrown over the castle's rear wall. He saw Pellinore and stood by him a long while, wondering if he were living or dead. The anchorite wore a ragged cloth no better suited to the temperature than Pellinore's cloak of grass and snow. And though the hermit was thin to the bone, he was strong even so, and lifted Pellinore onto his back, carrying him upward to a hermit's cell in the face of a cliff.

Elsewhere in Arthur's expanding realm, Sir Balin sought adventure; and his quest was marked by error and darkness. The whole length of his story need not be told, of how he slew the good and avenged those of little merit; inspired the suicides of pure maidens and brave knights; decapitated lovers in their bowers; and in the end slew even his beloved brother, and died miserably beside him. Who is to say that any of it would have happened, had not the Loathly Maid brought him a sword of blackest iron.

Upon that fateful day when first he kidnapped the maiden, she said, as they rode upon the trail, "Sir Balin, you have a good sword at your side, by which you have performed mightily. You do not require this dark sword of mine. So I beseech thee, but just this once, return my sword to me."

"It is a good sword, and I have gained it fairly," said Balin, filled with self-deception. "I will keep it beside my other, and be called the Knight of the Two Swords, until there is someone strong enough to wrest the black sword from me."

"Then know that by your choosing you must slay with that accursed sword one whom you best love, then lie down beside him to die, with heart full of regrets. And the one to wrest the black sword from your stiff dead fingers will be Morgan le Faye, who will make good use of the jeweled sheath, the form of which is the similitude of the scabbard of Caliburnus."

"I will not be frightened by a witch's vision," said Balin, lowering a malignant brow.

The Loathly Maid rode upon the rump of Balin's horse, her back to his. They travelled far together, and through many of his deeds, dark and otherwise, she was there. As days slid by, she seemed not to be offended if he called her My Lady, though as lovers they were chaste; and he counted on her daily for multitudinous assistance.

Never again, after their first meeting, when he pressed his hand around her throat, did he ever think to abuse her, for he was more than a little afraid what she might do. This fear of her came about on the second day out from Arthur's court.

As they rode together on one horse, they came to a sea-green field of poppies. As it was still winter, the vision was unlikely and startling. As if the unseasonable blossoming was an insufficient strangeness, there stood, along both sides of Roman cobbles, thirty lean soldiers at regular intervals, each clad in armor of gleaming jet, looking as though they wore the very Night as protection from the sun. And there was one more knight, smaller than the rest, more elegant, whose armor was alabaster.

The thirty-one knights were so devoid of motion that Balin thought them statues until, as he cantered closer, the thirty in jet turned their heads as with one motion, raised their spears, and stepped into the road facing his direction.

He reined aside his steed and said to the Loathly Maid, "Slide down and wait among the poppies. I will fight these weird knights one by one."

"You will not," said the Loathly Maid at his back. Then she called forth, "Let us pass, for Sir Balin is under my protection."

The thirty knights in jet stood off the road again. The one in alabaster strode forth, leading a dappled mare belonging to the Loathly. Maid. She slid down from Balin's horse and mounted her own. In the same moment, the thirty-one raised their visors, and Balin saw that each had faces of beardless youths – no, they were maidens! – their beauty flawed by the dark round eyes of bitches.

They held their spears aloft so that the Loathly Maid passed underneath the shafts. Balin, full of trepidations, followed humbly. As he and the Loathly Maid neared the forest beyond the red-specked field called Lyll's Meadow, he turned to look behind. He saw no knights by the road, but a white scenting-hound fleeing amidst the poppies, and thirty black bitches in pursuit of some invisible prey.

And Balin's knees were quaking in their greaves.

*   *   *

One evening, not long after Sir Balin slew a knight errant in fair if unnecessarily mortal combat, he and the Loathly Maid were reclining in a pavilion which the freshly deposed knight had pitched alongside a serpentine river. The pleasing sounds of rushing water and evening songbirds eased Balin's mood. He wanted to speak endearments to the Loathly Maid; but he saw she was already sleeping, and thought it best not to rouse her with such backwoods twaddle as must pass for poetry from his lips.

With deep sighs of affection he observed her still body. She frightened people, even as did he, so he thought they were a perfect match. He wanted to take her to the city of Trinobantes on Candlemas, and there be wed to her, even as Arthur would be wed. That day approached, yet Balin had not been able to ask, for fear of her reply.

As he watched her unmoving body, he was gripped by a fear dread that she had died. He wetted his palm and slowly moved his hand before her face, trying to feel a breath, but felt nothing.

In that very moment a terrific vision sent him reeling backward, so that he lay sprawled in a corner of the pavilion with mouth agape. It seemed as though the Loathly Maid burst apart like a chrysalid, and from within her arose a woman whose beauty was exceedingly great, her garment swirling about her as though she stood within a gale.

Yet the Loathly Maid had not moved, had certainly not burst asunder. She merely took a long wakeless breath, as though for her a dream had just then ended, and her sleep grew deeper.

The woman who stood between Balin and the Loathly Maid was no spirit, he was certain; she was as much of flesh as he.

"Who are you, and what, that comes forth from out of my lady?"

"Do you not know me?" said Nimuë.

"Are you the sorceress, Morgan le Faye, come to wrest the black sword from my dead hands?"

Nimuë smiled at that, and pitied Balin his many fears.

"No, I am not the Morrigu, and you are not a ghost. I am the Lady of the Lake that gave you life. This young amazon, who I do perceive you love, is but one of my many selves, such as I have often shed as serpents slough old skins. Yet she is separate from me as well, for serpents do not take up old cloaks again. You have never asked her for her name, so I will tell you it is Lyll, the Lady of Poppies. She has her own history, and will tell it to you, if you ask, and truly care to know all that she has known. You need not be so shy with her, for I leave her at your side for the sake of your illumination. Speak to her warmly, and give up your fear of her powers. While it is true she is not the best part of Me, neither is she entirely the worst. She will love you gladly with encouragement, for at base we demonkind are angels."

"Is she, then, a portion of my awful curse?"

"She is your consolation. You may not have long together. So make all you can of your time, and do everything with grace."

"And you?" asked Balin. "Why have you shed her now?"

"As you are kind enough to wonder, I will tell you only what Lyll by her gift was this moment dreaming. The Lord of Horn Castle has been slain by cruel Queen Ettard, who is another of my sloughed skins. As I desire Pellinore for my husband, I must lead him back from death."

"As you once restored my life," said Balin, remembering.

"Not quite as I made you. But you must forget all that," said Nimuë. "Now sleep, so that when next you see me, you will think it our first meeting."

Nimuë faded like a shadow, like a dream, and sank into the floor of the pavilion as Sir Balin closed his eyes.

"Not long after the Beginning of Days, when first humanity learned to murder, Adam in his grief for Abel separated himself from the Bright Mother. He dwelt for one-hundred twenty-six years with Naamah, on whom he sired a multitude of demons, who dwell yet upon the earth and in the sea, continuing their allegiance to the Mother of Darkness."

Pellinore heard this sermon in an unlit place, from the lips of the sainted anchorite David, bastard son of Nonita, abbess of Ty Gwyn, who some have called Queen of Elves. The voice of David was soft and insinuating, inducing a quiet state so that Pellinore would not move his neck, which David had dressed with healing herbs.

"Darkness is not a fearful thing, but is only Light Unmanifest; for Darkness and Light are each the mother of the other. So it was that Eve, when Adam abandoned her, dwelt in the Cave of Treasure with a serpent, whose name was Emmanuel. And she brought forth a multitude of demonesses, who run in and out between the pretty toes of She Whose Feet Go Down To Sheol, and Whose Head Is In The Stars; for Eve sent her dark daughters into the hollow of the world, beneath the Sea of Reeds, to be wetnursed and schooled by Adam's gloomy paramour. And these demonesses are fair maidens that bear torches in the world below, such as may be seen as stars reflected in the depth of a well."

Now as he learned these mysteries, it seemed to Pellinore that he got up and left the cliffwall cell. He was walking through a forest on a clear night without moon or stars. He came out of the forest onto a little-used road that was overgrown with weeds, and saw thereon, some distance down the way, a maiden holding a firebrand aloft.

In the light of her torch he saw that she was comely, but dressed in sackcloth with ashes on her head. She did not beckon to him, but when she turned her face away and began to walk along the weedy lane, he knew he was meant to follow.

In his current dreamy state, it was difficult to quicken his pace. Yet the road became less difficult as he drew nearer the torchbearer, although once, when he looked behind, he saw that tall briars blocked the path behind him, springing from wherever he set his foot. And he saw, too, caught among the thorns, with a black sword swinging impotently in his left hand, and a bright steel blade in his right, the pathetic spirit of Sir Balin, whose eyes were white and whose armor was like carven stone.

Eventually Pellinore came alongside the torchbearer, and matched his step to hers. He tried to speak, but he was in a soundless place, and could not hear the flutter of the torch, nor any foot tread, nor so little as his own heartbeat or breath. The damsel tarried at a bend and raised one arm to shove aside the writhing vines at the side of the narrow road. Pellinore stepped through the opening, but the maiden did not come after.

Moonlight was restored to the world, as was the sound of wind through branches, though as yet there was no heartbeat or breath within him. He saw Ettard's fastness in the distance, and Saint David's Cliff beyond, with the whole of the countryside made silvery by a planter's moon.

His spirit sought David's cell, knowing he must return to his ailing flesh, or die with all his quests incomplete. He was flying over the castle, drawn toward the high cliff, when he was suddenly overcome by an urge to interrupt his flight. He had to see the beautiful Ettard peaceful in her bed, that his soul might worship hers. Down he flew and down until he peered in at a narrow window with its tinted pane opened, and its draperies parted wide.

He saw Gawain, friend and fellow knight of Arthur's court, upon a fine broad bed, sleeping at the side of Queen Ettard. The wraith of Pellinore stepped through the window into the room. His spirit-heart was leaden. He hung his head, weighted with melancholy. He did not care, in that moment, whether or not he was alive.

Then he looked about the room, that was filled with Queen Ettard's trophies, and saw his own sword hanging on a wall, among many. He pointed his spirit-hand toward his sword and it drifted away from the wall, floating to the bed where it hovered point-down above the throat of Sir Gawain.

Temptation was mighty, but Pellinore would not slay his faithless friend. In the next moment he let the swordpoint hover over Queen Ettard, imagining the blade plunging once, withdrawing, then plunging once again, gouging out her eyes. He despised Ettard with an intensity equal to his former love, for Merlin's spell that had long held him thrall was lifted by tragic revelation.

He slowly changed the position of the sword, which lowered horizontally, until it lay with flatside across the throats of the restful couple, doing them no harm; but upon waking, both would know Pellinore might have slain them.

His spirit flew from the castle straight into the cliff, where Saint David saw the wounded knight's still body lurch into wakefulness. Pellinore felt the bandage at his neck and asked hoarsely, "How long has it been?"

"Many days and nights, my friend, and more than once I thought you dead."

"As I truly would have been," said Pellinore, rising weakly to his knees, "had I succumbed to blind revenge. Even now, a part of me is dead, for I have returned to the world of the living without love, and am bereft."

"Then I commend you, Sir Knight, to the Queen of the World, Our Blessed Virgin Maria Sophia, who knows all things of the light, and all things of the darkness. Let us pray that in days to come, you may plumb these and other mysteries without so grave a portion of pain."

On Candlemas day, the knights gathered in Trinobantes. Their damsels went into the Church of Saint Stephen when the sun was yet showing, but the knights were for some while kept away. They spent the sunlight hours with laughter and field sports, jousting without malice, while all the ravens of England gathered in Trinobantes to watch them play, and caw their raucous approvals.

At evening they took off their armor and clad themselves in bleached linen. They came into the dark, dark church, whose tinted windows had been covered, so that even starlight did not find entry. They could not see, but their mouths were watering from the odors of a waiting meal; and they heard the Bishop of Canterbury as he intoned, "Saint Februaria, Mother of Dispatch! Saint Demetria, Mother of Maiden Death! Queen Maria, Mother of Jesu! Saint Fauna, Mother of the rainsoaked Pan! Come forth with Thy heavenly light to ease our dreadful darkness!"

The knights heard the hollow grinding sound of a sliding grate. The hair of their napes pricked with expectation when up from the crypts beneath the church came Brides in White, one after the other, each bearing a green taper. The Archbishop said, "And when the days of Her purification were fulfilled, She came from out of the darkness, with grain issuing from out of Her Holy Womb, beckoned to the Light of God."

The brides placed their green candles throughout the banquet-set cathedral, while acolytes brought trays of white candles, arranging them everywhere in tiers. Arthur's knights were stunned by the eerie beauty of the thousand scattered lights. And visible on each of ten tables were roasted lambs stuffed with winter apples and partridges, upon beds of crescent cakes, and tankards of wine set all around.

The bishop concluded, "And She came up to Jerusalem, where She held forth a bundle of grain, and said, 'This is My Son, for whom my soul is pierced in seven places. I consent to his death, so that his Flesh may be eaten, and his Blood refresh thy lips.'"

Each of the knights was joined at table by his perfect bride. Balin had his Dame Lyll, who was not so loathly dressed in white. Pellinore was with Nimuë. Sir Gawain took the hand of Dame Ragnall. Sir Kay was with Sgoidamur the Lady of the Bridleless

Mule. Sir Gareth was with Lady Lionessa. Sir Agravaine stood by Lady Laurel. Sir Gaheris smiled beside his Lady Linette. One hundred knights in all, with one hundred damsels; and each bride brought into her marriage lands and castles for husbands to protect and to render into service of their liege lord, King Arthur.

When the Archbishop left off his blessings, and as the expectant gathering awaited the arrival of Arthur and the Giant's Daughter, many embraces were shared between strong men, and many an introduction was given. Old wounds of pride were forgotten, with promise that all the baronies of Britain would be given unity by the weddings of dames and knights of every royal house.

"And you love him, though he stole your sword?" said Pellinore laughing; and Lyll replied, "I am the spirit of the dismal sword, so it was I that Balin captured from the start."

Balin said, "And you, Sir Pellinore, you have won the love of the mysterious Nimuë of the Hidden Country! Has she pledged her secret lands to you, and have you seen them, and are they all beneath the lochs?"

"It was just like this," said Pellinore in famous spirit. "I was dying of a wound, and the herbs of Saint David were insufficient for my cure. But every night in my fever I saw a woman of dream hovering about me in sackcloth, with ashes on her head. I thrashed and raved to David, 'Tell me! Who is she!' as he held me to the floor of the cell and told me there was no one there. Then one morning I awoke from alternating comas and mad ravings knowing I was well, though extremely weak. Right then, who do you think it was that found her way to the hermit's nest? It was the very woman of my dream, though in the dream she was black, and Nimuë is pale. She brought my sword, steed, and armor, which had formerly been stolen and which I'd had no expectation of recovering. I asked how she knew where to find me; she said she was led to me by a poppy's glamor. I knew at once no Dane possessed a greater shieldmaiden, and no Pole a more valiant vila. If ever I have loved another than Nimuë, it was due only to some awful spell best left forgot."

All grew silent when Arthur entered to join the Archbishop at the head of the gathering. He wore the same plain linen as his knights, having added only a crown of willow withes.

The glory of the night belonged to Gwenhwyvar, who entered from the vestry to stand by Arthur. Her glow dimmed the brightness of the candles and her presence illuminated Arthur. Her hair hung down in braided cornrows, woven with sheaves of grain, all golden and bright as an angel's halo. She was exactly as tall as Arthur; and judging by their supernal beauty side by side, they might have been twin divinities born of the same First Thought.

The acolytes moved swiftly and unobtrusively around the edge of the cathedral, drawing the tapestries aside from leaded glass so that tinted portraits, lighted from without by moon and stars, smiled upon the congregation from every angle. Saints, heroes and angels cast blessings with their shining hands, settling peacefulness upon every groom and bride.

Then all were wed as one, with the nation likewise knitted. When the joyous deed was done, Pellinore whispered to Nimuë a thing he thought he must have heard in dream. "Darkness is Light Unmanifest," he said, then: "This night burns brighter in my heart than any sunlit day."

Of the rest of the long night's Lupercalia, no bard has dared to sing, nor scarcely hinted; for hymns were sung to Februaria and Fauna and Demetria and Maria and Brigit of the Two Countenances, as one hundred and one sacred couples went out of the Church of Stephen and scattered to all the farms around Trinobantes.

As they traipsed along merrily in full delight, they sang an ancient hymn that goes, "We are the sons of Benjamin, we are the daughters of Shiloh," knights and their dames in turn. Then all lay down amidst new-sown fields and rutted in the furrows.

And it was seen by many who raised their heads from rutting that a gigantic stag was chased by the edge of the forest. It gave a belling cry and lowered its head to battle thirty sleek black bitches, and one white scenting-hound. Wedged within the antlers was a cross, with the hairless sylvan Merlin on it.

The scenting-hound leapt off the ground to clamp jaws tight upon the throat of the tormented prey. The stag went down and vanished in the midst of black bitches.

The Tor of the Glassy Isle was like the long back of a whale beached amidst swamplands. The sides of the Tor were terraced, and upon the terraces were apple trees in full bloom, having the appearance, from a great distance, of barnacles on the beached whale's hide. The terraces encircled the whole of the great mound in the form of an elaborate maze or cultic causeway patterned upon complicated knotwork, broken in places by passage of long ages, and called by the peasants, from time immemorial, The Roof of the Labyrinth.

Across the generations, the ancient apple trees spread their seed from off the Tor to fill the spaces between the swamps, so that the young forests surrounding the Castle of the Horn constituted a fruit-bearing wilderness. This forest of plenty required no tending, save only that they received the enriching prayers of monks who dwelt by the Church of Our Lady of Apples, established on a site sacred from a time older than myth.

When apples ripened, serfs came in service of King Pelleas, which was the name by which they knew Sir Pellinore of the Round Table. They were allowed to keep a goodly share of the harvest, so that everywhere on the Glassy Isle there were none dissatisfied or willing to revolt.

The Castle of the Horn looked as though it were not made of stone and mortar, but of ivy – a leafy structure of organic parapets and crenelated walls fashioned by shears of a colossal gardener. The highest of the grape-laden greeny towers rivalled the heights of the Apple Tor. And this topiary castle was encircled by a moat thickly covered over with waterlilies in concentric circles of white, pale pink, and yellow.

Nine elfin priestesses arose from out of a secret place within the Tor, to dance around and round the humpy peak, their sweet voices heralding spring. Chief among the Nine was Morganna, who was the warlike Morrigu grown beautiful and tame amidst the flowers. Two of her unearthly followers bore in their slender arms a cornucopia made from the one horn of a fabulous beast, engraved with mystic whorls akin to those which mazed the Tor, and having three stout legs to stand on. This horn, immovable by impure hands, was weightless to the good of heart; and every autumn it was taken under the mound by Morganna's party until, at spring's return, it was restored to the Castle.

Down from the Tor they danced and kicked their heels as three of the Nine played upon flutes, and three slapped tambourines. They followed the winding paths from terrace to terrace, as all the while the Morrigu drew handfuls of flowers from out of the ceaseless fountain that was the Ivory Horn. As the petals were cast to the wind, they were carried merrily across the countryside, adhering to branches that yesterday were bare.

All along their route, they flowered the Glassy Isle, until at last they arrived at the lowered bridge of the ivyed castle. Therein nobles had gathered from near and far for the festive occasion of the Return of the Ivory Horn to the House of King Pelleas and Queen Vivian.

In a large courtyard of the castle, celebratory jousts were in progress. Many valorous companions of the King arrived from their own estates and baronies that they might struggle in the tournament, to please their own fair ladies, and to cast eager eyes upon the Castle's celestial treasures that were laid out annually for public viewing.

Along the ivy-hung galleries overlooking the courtyard observant guests were seated. With them was Pelleas whose crown was draped with flowers and Vivian whose crown was wound about with grape vines. The elfin priestess Morganna went about the tables pouring an endless stream of purple liquor from the Ivory Horn into upheld cups. Her eight companions danced and piped among guests idling throughout the castle.

With a cry half of anguish, half of pleasure, a knight was unseated from his horse. It was Sir Bediver, the Knight With One Hand, who lay laughing at his own defeat; for it had seemed to him no one had done him battle, despite his fall.

In a swirl of refracting light, Bediver's opponent reappeared with steed, having dropped his diaphanous cape from off his shoulders. The champion of the joust was Sir Garlan, Knight of the Magic Cloak. He rode below the galleries, saluting first his queen, then the king who was his brother, and finally his chosen lady, who threw him down a scarf.

Among the knights at table sat Sir Balin, who had come from Northumberland with his Lady Lyll. He had two swords sheathed over his shoulder and was clad in full armor. He stood to challenge Sir Garlan, then descended the stairs from the upper gallery to mount a readied horse.

A squire came forth with shield, but Balin refused it. This made the company grow still and lean attentively across the balustrades, for Balin was too serious. Without a shield he might not be as safely unhorsed.

As Sir Garlan began to raise his cloak of invisibility, Balin said, "Are you too cowardly to fight without magic?"

The audience held its breath. No one had ever before criticized the king's brother.

"Do not be rude and unseemly, Sir Balin, at my brother's feast. I am famous for my cloak; you, for your broad chest as tough as stone and your white eyes as piercing as two swords. You will not make your skin soft for my lance, and I will not throw down my cloak."

So saying, the cloak whirled about Garlan. With a momentary scattering of rainbow flashes, the knight and steed vanished.

Lyll dropped her scarf to Balin, who caught it on a breeze, and tied it about his white eyes, so that he might pursue the encounter without misleading tricks of vision. The young squire handed him a wooden lance, with which Balin rode to a far corner of the yard and took his post, blindly facing the center of the yard.

He kept his horse perfectly still until he heard the clatter of hoofs before him. Then he spurred his steed into that sound. He felt a lance tear through his surcoat and shatter on his armor. His own lance drove hard against a shield with such precision that it was not deflected. He heard Sir Garlan's grunting as he was flung to the packed earth.

When Balin took the scarf from his eyes, he saw the horse rendered visible, with no one on it; but Garlan was still unseen. Balin dismounted and kicked about the dust where he thought Garlan must have fallen.

Sparks flew unexpectedly from Balin's shoulder armor, causing him to turn about and confront – nothing. Before he had fully drawn the iron sword in his left hand, he was stabbed in the hinge of his armor under the arm, though no harm was done to his stone-hard body. Then as his right hand drew the sword of bright steel from across his shoulder, he was struck in the hinge of a legguard with sufficient force that he plunged to one knee.

He stood swiftly, his two broadswords whirling front and back, protecting himself on all sides. When Balin's right-hand sword perchance struck Garlan's unseen weapon, Balin's left-hand sword jabbed instantly into the airy space.

Garlan cried out. Blood appeared upon the cloak of invisibility, a red smear upheld as a feather in a draft. Balin used the flat sides of his two swords to swat again and again that bloody spot, until Garlan submitted, and drew off his cloak begging mercy, clutching his wounded arm.

Balin put boot behind Garlan's leg and shoved him unchivalrously to the ground. Lady Lyll was standing at the edge of the upper gallery. She removed from under her garment the tip of a broken lance and dropped it to Balin, who caught it and with one powerful swift motion pierced Garlan's breastplate and drove the point into his heart.

Knights of Horn Castle swarmed into the courtyard from all sides, horrified by Balin's action, ready to avenge the king's brother. Pelleas stayed their hands, saying, "Stand back from him! His flesh is granite. You could never kill him even were he stripped of armor and bound helplessly before you. Sir Balin! Why have you slain my brother?"

Balin answered, "He used his magic perfidiously when he came upon one of my companions, driving a lance into his back, then rode on, committing further mayhem without semblance of knightly valor. He may have told you his exploits were otherwise, but I saw with these white eyes as the unsuspected lance erupted from the chest of my companion-in-arms. Therefore I have slain the villainous Garlan with the point of the same lance that slew my friend."

Pelleas came down from the gallery, tearing flowers from his crown. He said, "If it is as you say, then there is something of justice in your actions. Nevertheless, you have done it in my castle in a day of joyous revelry. It cannot be forgiven."

"I had no choice, Sir Pellinore!" said Balin with alarm. "He has never been known to fight fairly in an open field. Here, at least, between these courtyard walls, I could hear his every movement."

A squire ran into the courtyard from the armory, bearing the famed spear of Pelleas, that had been, like himself, bathed in the blood of the dragon. "Were I merely Sir Pellinore," he said, "I might have taken this issue differently. But here I am King Pelleas, and cannot pardon such an affront to my people's feastday."

Sir Balin, unused to the necessity of ducking blows, darted awkwardly to one side, and received Pelleas' spear under his arm. His eyes went wide with momentary alarm, jolted by the pain. He rushed forward and struck the Lord of Horn Castle hard against the chest with one sword then the other. The sword of steel shattered; the iron sword rang out and stung Balin's fingers. Pelleas, though without armor, was entirely uninjured.

As Balin fell back, Pelleas' spear swept across his face, drawing blood from a nick on his forehead.

Lady Lyll was no longer in the gallery. She ran through the interior of the castle, encountering no one, as all were pressed to windows overlooking the courtyard. She came to an open room where the castle's treasures were laid out for viewing.

Surrounding a golden table were the Nine Elfin Priestesses, whose charming fay beauty appeared a little wilted. They had stationed their Ivory Horn in a place of honor upon the golden table alongside the Cup and the Spear.

"Let Balin die," said Morganna, tears upon her cheeks. "If you will do so, you will spare him much tragedy and pain."

"I will not," said Lyll. "King Pelleas fights with insufficient honor, knowing as he does how vastly his enchanted spear outranks my husband's pair of swords. I am aware that the spear among these treasures is the equal of Pelleas' Dragon Spear. Do not try to keep me from taking it to Balin and lend fairness to the duel."

The Nine spoke as with one voice, "We cannot keep you from this Spear, dipped in the Blood of the Lamb. It is immovable to anyone not fated by its power."

Morganna continued, "To win the Spear, you must show strength sufficient to gaze into the Well of the World, that is this Stone Chalice, and not be laid low by revelation. As you approach the Golden Table, know that the Spear is Pelleas King of Apples; the Chalice is Queen Vivian the Lady of the Lake; and I am this Horn, Morganna, Queen of Earthly Plenitude and Earthly Wont."

Seemingly the least of the Three Treasures, the Well of the World looked like nothing but a crudely primitive mortar, lacking for a pestle. It may have been as old as the World herself, fashioned from the stuff of the First Creation.

Lyll gazed into terrifying depths. She saw therein, hung in space, the Crown, the Key, the Egg.

Before her alarmed and watchful gaze, the egg burst asunder, flinging far the Crown and Key. Out of the shattered Egg sprang forth the dreadful serpent Plague upon whose tail the Earth depended.

When Lyll raised her head from peering into the dreadful cosmos, her dark hair was shot with streaks of white. She could no longer scowl as the Loathly Maid, for she had obtained an enlightenment that made her holy, and she was wholly beautiful.

She said to Morganna, "You are the World Egg that houses the Dragon, and the Dragon is Nimuë."

"We are the Fate of Arthur," the Nine intoned, and Morganna added, "Upon this golden table, when all other treasures of the world are swept away, I and my sisterhood will lay out Arthur as the Last Treasure of the World, healed of earthly suffering, eternal and undying, but without thought, without motion, hidden in the labyrinth of the blossoming Tor, upon his golden bier. When his time is renewed, he will attend the final battle at the Mountain of Megiddo, where he must choose to fight for Michael, or for Satan, whose natures are intertwined, so that the choosing will never be so clear and certain as first may seem."

Lyll replied, "I care not what happens in the Time of Dissolution, for I and my Lord are alive today, and I wouldst keep it so."

Hearing these unhappy words, the elfin priestesses lowered their faces, and drew dark veils upon their heads.

Dame Lyll took up the Spear of the Lamb's Blood and tossed it expertly through a window. When it struck the ground outside, the earth trembled with warning. Sir Balin dropped his black sword and the broken hilt of steel to take up the Spear of the Lamb as match against the Spear of the Dragon. He parried once then sank the spearpoint into King Pelleas' inner thigh.

Balin could not withdraw the spear. He leapt away unarmed, fearful of the swipe of the Dragon Spear. Pelleas did not continue the dreadful duel. He fell heavily to both knees and laid his spear on the ground at his left. With bloodless hands, he drew the Lamb's Spear from out of his groin, and lay it at his right-hand side. His flushed red face had grown aged. His lion's mane became thin brittle straw beneath a tarnished crown.

He said, "Yours, Sir Balin, is the Dolorous Stroke. You have wounded the Spring, that Spring may smile no more."

Then Pelleas raised palsied hands toward his dour, beloved queen. Nimuë looked on him with pity as she sang, "I gaze on the Lamb that hath been pierced. I weep for Him, as for an only son. There is mournfulness in Avillion, as all the country mourns, knowing that Castle Sangrail, the House of Brave Pellinore, hath fallen into pieces on the ground."

Then she leapt from the gallery and flew upward, up, in the shape of a numinous white raven; and Pelleas lowered his arms and bowed his head, finding himself bereft of all the things by which he knew himself to exist.

The rustling of doom caused Balin to look along the enclosing towers. Ivy swiftly faded from green to yellow, then fell crisp and brown from tendrils rooted destructively in mortar. The earth heaved and rumbled; the castle bucked; towers leaned perilously. Balin shouted helplessly as a beam broke loose above the gallery, striking the Lady of Poppies a mortal blow. Before he had taken two steps toward the place where her shattered body was flung, the first of the toppling towers filled the courtyard with rubble, pressing Balin beneath heavy stones, where he lay weeping and unable to move.

The night full of stars draped herself onto the world without prelude of dusk. Screaming faces withdrew from every window above the courtyard. The remaining towers were tumbling; the whole of the castle was collapsing into itself. These many who arrived as celebrants fled now in stark panic, colliding with one another in buckling, pitch-dark hallways. Blocks of stone and heavy beams of timber came down upon them, crushing mortal flesh into pulp and splintered bone.

Nine only left the castle before the drawbridge fell into the roiling, murky moat. Like pallbearers, eight of the elfin priestesses strode solemnly, carrying the Golden Table upraised to their shoulders. The ninth, Morganna, led them through a night filled with cries from all points of the countryside.

Upon the Golden Table sat the Well of the World and the Ivory Horn of Spring. As the grim procession wound along the road between increasingly fetid swamplands, toward the Apple Tor, blossoms withered prematurely, setting no fruit, scenting the night not with perfume, but mildew and decay.

When the Nine bleak maids reached the foot of the Tor, Morganna with wild hair and fingers like the claws of a falcon lifted the Well of the World from off the table and set it into the ground. It at once became the Chalice Well, a fountain going into the depths of the womb of the Earth. And into the Well she threw the Horn of Spring, where it fell and fell forever, until it reached the stars.

Blight spread swiftly throughout Britain. The trouble was known as far away as Camelot even before the dust had settled around the ruins of Horn Castle. Merlin Ambrosius, awakening on his couch, was chilled to the bone. He went out of Arthur's castle, shifting his shape as he walked along the road.

He came to the shore of the sea, having upon him the form of a barren mule. A barge awaited, and his unshod hooves clattered thereon. There was no mast for sail, but the currents bore the little barge along the coast, upon a route Arthur must someday follow. For three days the mule observed the coastline, that looked all burnt, for every plant and tree was blackened. Already a great number of people were dead of a virulent pox, and widows wailed lamentations from every hill.

On the third day the barge brought the mule to the Glassy Isle. It leapt ashore and plodded into cesspools that until lately were healthy swamps colored with irises and lilies. Then the mule passed through forests of dead trees whose twisted limbs beseeched the deaf of heaven.

Arriving at heaps of rubble covered with tendrils of stiffened vines and rotted grapes, the mule began braying loudly, and kicked angrily at blocks of stone. Small though the mule was, his kicks were mighty, and stones were flung about the landscape, revealing corpse upon rancid corpse.

When Sir Balin was uncovered, he rose at once, and thought how strange it was that a mule should be his savior.

Using a length of timber for a lever, Balin raised stones from off the Maimed King. When Pelleas was freed, he nevertheless lay without movement, staring at the sun, and Balin could not gain any response by speaking or prodding. It passed through his mind to replace the heavy cairn upon the half-living king.

It would be several weeks before Balin heard of the first foul deeds of an insane champion calling himself the Red Knight of the North, whose armor was lacquered crimson and whose roan's trappings were carmine set about with garnets and rubies. The Red Knight was a monster with a festering wound beyond all healing, who went forth in a constant rage of vengeful agony.

And Balin then would know, without wanting to know it, that he should never have raised the stones from off the maimed and moaning Pellinore. But upon the day when a mule brought salvation to Balin, he felt he owed a like deed to another.

He found also Lyll's body. It terrified him to discover she was more beautiful in death than ever he had seen her in life.

He did not know she had seen into the Well of the World, so he thought her peaceful repose proved her preference for the boon companion Death above the ill-fated Balin.

Full of guilty sorrows, he laid his beloved wife across the mule's swayed back and led the beast toward Northumberland.

He was troubled by all that he saw along the way, knowing too well his part in it, though still unable to turn aside from his lamentable destiny. He abandoned the mule at the border of his country, and carried his broken Lady to a poppy field that she had planted soon after they were wed. Here he buried her under a stone table, then sat atop the table a long while moaning the wordless dirge of a hurt animal.

Ambrosius, who knew himself as God, wondered at such powers as had set themselves against him. When, he wondered, had he first blinded himself to the many chinks and breaches in his initially efficacious spells? Where was it that his splendidly woven magicks first began to fail? By whose interference had his overall design transformed against his will?

He lacked the true heart of the quester, and knew not what way to turn, but sought aimlessly in darkness and wild places, seeking an unknown Something he might not recognize even if it spoke.

Of Arthur's further history, he took no part, and did not observe the last unravelling of the dream of Camelot. He was not there to warn Arthur not to spite himself in webs of anger and betrayal. He did not come in time to save the king in the Battle of Camlann. Long before full half the Round Table knights died of morbid quests, and before Queen Morgan preserved her brother upon a golden slab in the cavern beneath Avillion, Ambrosius forgot even that Arthur ever lived, or what he ever hoped to gain by so much sorcery.

He merely wandered gloomy haunts, as mindless as the will o' the wisp. One day he sat atop fallen cedar logs and broken doorways of some extravagant but ruined house, wondering why he, of all divinities, should be denied the key to all mystery. He had thought himself ageless, but now his spine was bent and arthritic; his white beard hung below his bony knees; and he was a most terrible giant hermit feared by all who saw his hoary head raised amidst mountains.

Logs shifted under him, as though they were a heap of thick serpents, but he was not unperched. There came to him from out of a nearby hazel thicket a beautiful young nymph who sat beside him speechless, gazing at him in a tender, wistful manner. After some while, her presence began to annoy him. He tried to set upon her a withering look; but his faded eyes could not focus in her direction.

She said, "Remember, Sylvester, when you feasted only on fruit and herbs, and all beasts were your companions? Now, Ambrosius, you have eaten bloody venison and spurn the berries of the bramble-bush."

As she spoke, there sprouted and matured before him a bush with six branches, hung all about with hazelnuts. Merlin turned his face away; and because of his disdain, the brightness of the bush went out. Where a moment before hazels grew, now there were only branches full of thorns.

"You, my precious Merlin, have becme the Death of Planets," said the nymph, whose seductive intonation increasingly fouled his mood. "You might have been the Lover of the World; but you have refashioned yourself, and now cannot be more than Her deathless sacrifice."

"Destroy me, I care not," said the raspy voice of the old man. "You have taken everything. Why should I alone continue?"

"It was not I that slew the beauty of the world," said the sweet nymph, tempting Merlin with her white shoulder. "Rather, the selfish tyranny of mortals has laid low the earth. That selfishness is manifest in you."

Her words angered him more deeply than weary old age could express. And due to his strengthless anger, he found himself entangled in the thorny bush that was cold as ice.

Arising from out of the ground were stone pillars that surrounded Merlin of the Bramble-bush.

The nymph was weeping copiously as she became a ribboned sheet of water reaching skyward. The deathless soul of the sorcerer heard, from within that celestian fount, the nymph's murmured enticements, "Sylvester, Sylvester, come into my rose-petaled bower." But it was Ambrosius who replied, "Away from me, Harlot," and sank forever beneath the world.

THE CORRUPTION OF PERFECTION

MIKE ASHLEY

There are certain aspects of the Arthurian story that have always fascinated me. One of these is the fact that despite all the heroics of Arthur and the Knights of the Round Table, the legend is pervaded by an inevitable doom, as if there is an inexorable decline to the fate of Arthur and his knights. Elements of this repeat themselves time and again throughout the romances. When James Lowder gave me the opportunity to contribute to The Doom of Camelot, *I thought I would explore this and tie it in to the episode of Sir Urfrey, one of the lesser-known Arthurian knights who also finds himself suffering for his cause.*

Gawain could scarcely believe it was the same Arthur.

The company had travelled hard over the last three days from Camelot into Cornwall and Arthur was no longer young. Yet the king, who only a few days before had been sullen, temperamental, and given to deep bouts of depression, was now happy, buoyant, and chiding Agrivaine for his grimness.

"Just look at this view, Gawain," Arthur called, bringing the company to a halt. They had arrived at the cliffs above a huge bay where the sun turned the water into a sea of stars and the coastline curved its way along into the distant haze. "I played here with Merlin many a time as a boy. In fact I still think of it as Merlin's Bay. Does it have a name, Constantine?"

The fourth member of the company pulled his horse up alongside Arthur. Though Cornwall was Constantine's duchy, he seldom travelled this far south. Still, he did not want to show his ignorance. "I believe the locals now call it Austell Bay after the local holy man."

"I should come this way more often," Arthur remarked. "It is such a beautiful land, so full of wonder. Perhaps we will meet this Austell. I have heard much about him. I wonder if he is related to Merlin."

Gawain looked sideways at Agrivaine, and their eyes met. Both were unsure of the wisdom of this journey, yet the prospect of being reunited with Merlin had clearly rejuvenated Arthur. And who knew what might happen? Maybe Merlin was alive. The king certainly believed that to be true, and strongly enough to bring a royal party to Cornwall's wilds.

As Arthur bid them continue to their destination, Gawain pondered again his uncle's dilemma.

The king had never understood what became of Merlin, and would not accept that his friend and advisor was dead. No one really knew Merlin's fate, though there had been rumours and speculation for years. The king could not believe that Merlin deserted him without good cause. He was certainly used to the old man disappearing on secret missions for months on end, though he'd always returned. Now, Arthur had nearly lost count of the years Merlin had been missing – six? Eight? Ten? It seemed an eternity. In his darker moments, the king was lost without him. No one else had the wisdom and subtlety of vision that Merlin possessed, not even Archbishop Dyfrig.

During the last year, Arthur had become convinced there was a conspiracy against him, or more likely against the queen. First there was the kidnapping of Guinevere by Meleagaunt, and her heroic rescue by Lancelot. Not long before that, the queen had been accused of poisoning Sir Patrise, and of attempting to murder Gawain. There were rumours that Guinevere had been unfaithful, but with whom Arthur never learned; the king thought the gossip to be baseless, but even his most trusted friend, Lancelot, seemed reluctant to remain at court and was forever questing. Was this also part of a conspiracy? Arthur felt surrounded by rumour and did not know who to turn to. Only Merlin would know the truth.

But where was he? Arthur was certain Merlin had fallen victim to one of Morgan's schemes, but Morgan only laughed when confronted, like she always laughed, and revealed nothing. Even Vivienne, with whom Merlin had been infatuated, claimed she had no idea. Arthur had sent knights in search of his old friend, all to no avail. Then plague and famine rampaged across the kingdom, and the Round Table became engrossed in the Quest for the Grail. Memories of Merlin faded into the past.

Except for one strange incident. Some while previous, Gawain and Yvaine had been travelling in the West Country when Gawain fell under the spell of the enchantress Byanne. He was transformed into a dwarf and spent many weeks lost in the Woods of Austell. At one point, he came near a cave and believed he heard the voice of Merlin enquiring about Arthur and Guinevere. The mage revealed that his spirit was trapped and would only be freed when Arthur regained the throne.

When Gawain eventually took on his normal form again and returned to Camelot, he did not tell the king of his experience. First, he was not sure whether it was part of the enchantment or possibly all a dream, and secondly, he did not understand the allusion to regaining the throne. This must mean, he thought, that Arthur would lose the throne at some point, and Gawain did not believe that was something his uncle wanted to hear.

However, one night, when drunk, he told the story to his wife Floriel, who told her brother Brandiles, who told Arthur. Gawain had to claim he had been under an enchantment which prevented him from telling Arthur directly. The king treated this as yet more evidence of the conspiracy against him. He demanded that Gawain lead him to the spot where he had heard Merlin's voice.

Unfortunately, Gawain could not remember the spot. He only knew it was in the woods near the church of the holy man Austell. This seemed to encourage Arthur. Gawain could not think why at the time; as he mused on the subject during the long ride through Cornwall, he realized the site must hold some link with Arthur's youth. The king had been raised in this area by Merlin, and there were doubtless places and connections which meant something only to them.

Gawain still wished they had been accompanied by Yvaine, who might have a better idea of where he had heard Merlin, but Arthur had recently sent the knight on a quest into the North and he was unlikely to return for some months. Instead, Constantine leapt at the chance to ride with Arthur, and since Cornwall was Constantine's duchy, he could hardly be refused. The rest of the quintet was comprised of Agrivaine, who never missed an opportunity like this, and the king's own squire, Kynan.

The joy of the morning turned sombre as they neared Austell's church. About two miles distant resided Austell's close compatriot, Mewan. Unlike Austell, Mewan lived the life of a recluse, and spent much of his time in a cave deep in the woods. He sometimes blocked the cave entrance with large stones; usually, the only betrayal of his presence was if he lit a fire and the smoke drifted out through the vent at the top of the cave.

The path to Austell's church did not pass near Mewan's caves, but once in the woods, Arthur turned from the usual route and set off at great pace, with the others struggling in pursuit. He evidently knew where he was going, and his company could do nothing but follow. Soon the trees became so entangled that they had to dismount. Where they were heading looked at first glance even more impenetrable, but they suddenly broke through into a clearing. Gawain recognized it at once, as if from a dream.

It so happened that for once Mewan was not deep in his cave. He had emerged to gather food, and was sitting outside, plucking some pigeons and preparing a fire, as the company stumbled into the clearing. He had heard them coming for some while, however, and had chosen not to hide. He was watching the knights as they emerged from the thicket.

Gawain was astonished. The holy man looked every inch like Merlin. He was dressed in a humble grey habit, with bare feet, a long, matted beard, and silver-grey hair. His face shone, and his eyes sparkled with an inner depth. Even when he spoke, his voice and his manner were so like Merlin's.

"Welcome, travellers," he said. "You are either lost or come seeking answers."

"Merlin!"

The cry came from Arthur, who had dropped his horse's reins and was staggering forward, arms outstretched, wanting to hug his old friend. Although Mewan remained seated, the king grabbed him by the arms and pulled him erect, revealing a strength he had not shown in years. He clasped Mewan closely, holding him so for a moment. When at length they separated, Gawain could see tears in Arthur's eyes.

Mewan chose not to speak. He simply watched Arthur, with only a token glance at the others.

"Merlin," Arthur cried again. "What's become of you? Why have you not come back to court?"

Only now did Constantine intervene.

"My lord, I fear you are mistaken. This is the holy man, Mewan." He then turned to the hermit. "Mewan, this is your sovereign lord, King Arthur."

Mewan seemed in no way awed by the company. Arthur, for his part, clearly ignored Constantine's words and continued to ask "Merlin" what he had been doing during all those lost years. Mewan finally ceased Arthur's questions with a raise of his hands, bloodstained from the pigeon he had been preparing. The blood caught Arthur's eye and he became transfixed. Meanwhile Mewan at last spoke.

"All who find me are troubled. We may seek our answers from the Lord God and from within ourselves. Please come and pray with me."

Mewan led the company to a small wooden cross nailed to a tree some yards distant. There he knelt in prayer and bid them all to do the same. As Arthur knelt, Gawain was aware that a shaft of sunlight had suddenly pierced the clouds and the canopy of trees, and bathed Mewan in a pool of radiance. Arthur noticed it too, and Gawain saw him tense as he bowed his head in prayer. The knight could only wonder what thoughts were going through his uncle's already tortured mind.

The company remained in prayer for several minutes. Only when Mewan rose did they all do likewise, and return to the cave. As they walked, Arthur caught Gawain's arm and whispered in his ear.

"Did you see the holy aura? Have you seen the blood on Merlin's hands? He has been transfigured. Merlin has been raised for Heaven's duty. No wonder he has not returned to court. He is now in the service of God."

Gawain did not know how to reply. The idea that Merlin would abandon the Old Faith for Christianity seemed impossible. In fact, Gawain had long believed it was Arthur embracing Christianity that had driven the mage from court. Maybe a deep guilt about this had brought the king to believe that Merlin was still alive and would one day embrace the Faith. But Gawain could see that there was no point in giving voice to these thoughts; Arthur was not in the mood to listen.

The king hastened back to sit by Mewan at the cave's entrance. The holy man was pulling together the few pigeons he had plucked.

"I'm afraid I can offer you little by way of food," Mewan apologized. "If you wish to wait, I am sure I could prepare some broth."

It was only then that Arthur seemed to return to some normality. He gestured to his squire, who had remained respectfully at a distance with the horses and bags.

"We have plenty of food, Merlin. You must share ours."

The preparation of a meal broke the spell for a short while. As they ate, though, confusion claimed Arthur again and he returned to his questioning of Mewan.

"Merlin," the king began, "why have you come again to this cave where you taunted me when I was but a child? You have clearly passed through much in these many years, but what has brought you again to this place?"

"My lord Arthur, I do not know how to answer you. You believe that I am Merlin the Enchanter, whom I did once meet, many years ago. But Merlin and I are of different faiths and follow different paths."

For all the holy man protested, Arthur would not accept his denial. "You have always followed your own path, Merlin, and I have never, in all my years, been able to change you from it." Something sounded in the king's voice then – a note of utter weariness. "I need your help more than at any other time," he continued. "My kingdom is crumbling. There are plots against me and against my queen, and without your counsel I do not know which way to turn."

"Have you asked the Lord your God?"

Arthur hung his head.

"There are times when I believe God has forsaken me and my kingdom," he said softly. "Perhaps I transgressed holy authority when I commanded the search for the Grail of Christ. I sought perfection which was not mine to possess, and in doing so I lost the most perfect soul to ever inhabit this earth."

"You lost the soul of Christ?" Mewan asked, knowing full well this was not what Arthur meant.

The king shook his head. "Forgive me, Merlin. I surely did not mean to be sacrilegious. But if you had witnessed the purity of Galahad, you would know you had met a perfect soul. And because of me, Galahad died."

Gawain shifted uneasily at this, and Mewan noticed it.

"Are you sure Galahad died?" the hermit asked. "Or was he taken?"

If the knight intended to answer, he never got the chance. "It is all the same to me," King Arthur sighed. "Galahad's soul passed on, and we were left with a shell."

Mewan paused and seemed to search for an answer in the air before him. At last he noted, in an uplifting tone, "I believe that Galahad saw what no earthly eyes can see and live. If that is so, then his passing was glorious and a matter for celebration, not mourning."

"But so many of my knights suffered in the search for the Grail," Arthur responded. "And the land is still split asunder and ravaged by blight. My search for perfection has led only to corruption."

"Such is the fate of those who strive for something which no human can achieve without the aid of the Lord," the holy man was quick to note. "Remember Icarus who flew too close to heaven and was cast down. Mankind is imperfect because of sin, and there is no way that you can change that, king or no. That was why our Lord Jesus came to earth as a ransom sacrifice."

The company considered this for a time, though the lesson seemed to trouble Arthur the most.

"Tell me, Merlin," he said heavily, "how can I save my kingdom without striving for perfection? What must I do?"

Mewan was quick to answer. "You must look to your heart, my king, and beseech others to do likewise. No one is perfect, and the more perfect they seem, the more dangerous they will be to you. Beware he who betrays perfection, for there is the destiny of your soul."

The king rose to his feet. "Who, Merlin? Galahad was the only perfect soul. He is gone. Surely he can no longer be a threat to my kingdom."

"I cannot help you there, my lord. You will know this seeming perfection when it displays itself before you. And when you recognize it, you must face your fate."

Arthur struggled for words. Gawain could see a range of emotions contorting his face.

"I still cannot understand how perfection can be a danger," the king said. "Surely, Merlin, you of all men have seen the miracle of perfection on earth. Can you not tell me more?"

"I cannot say what Merlin has seen. I can tell you that I have never witnessed true perfection – and do not expect to in this life."

Suddenly Arthur reached for his sword and drew Excalibur from its scabbard. The sword shone and sparkled in the dappled light. Gawain even fancied he saw a shaft of light expand from the blade and cleave through the acrid smoke from the fire, as if banishing anything vile that lurked nearby. Instinctively, with the drawing of Excalibur, both Gawain and Agrivaine reached for their own swords, but the king motioned them to relax.

Arthur turned to the holy man. "You know this sword. Is it not perfection?"

For the first time a look of childlike wonder came over the face of Mewan. He even reached for the sword but Arthur protectively – perhaps even possessively – held it just out of reach.

"I have never seen this blade before," Mewan responded, almost in a whisper. "But I know of it, as do all in your kingdom. It is a sword of beauty, I cannot deny that, but an instrument of death can never be perfection. Also . . ." Mewan hesitated, knowing that what he was going to say next would find little acceptance.

Arthur leaned forward, straining to hear, hoping, waiting for an answer.

Mewan continued slowly, weighing each word with great care. "This sword, as well as the scabbard that you once had but lost, are intended to protect you. Without Excalibur you are vulnerable, but you are human. With the blade you may be invulnerable to physical pain, but you pay the price in spiritual pain. In this way, the sword drains you of your humanity."

"Are you saying I would be better rid of the sword?" the king exclaimed over the shocked gasps of his knights. "You gave Excalibur to me, Merlin. Did you not know then it endangered my soul?" Arthur's voice turned from bewilderment to anger. "Was this a plot from the very start – a plot to damn my soul? Have you been in league with Morgan all along?"

Mewan did not move, but trapped Arthur with his eyes. Moments passed, then the anger fled the king and he slumped slowly back to the ground. He looked again at Excalibur, but now as if it were nothing but useless metal. Mewan spoke, softly and reassuringly.

"Excalibur was, and is, important to you. It gave you strength and allowed you to believe in yourself. Without Excalibur would you have risen to such might and fame? But can anything be perfect that causes its master such anguish, brings him to concentrate more on himself than on his subjects?"

Gawain found himself tensing and was aware that Agrivaine steeled himself, as well. Mewan's words wandered perilously close to treason. Even if the king would not silence the old man, he was not about to let him speak so treacherously against the throne.

Yet it was Constantine, silent all the meal long, who intervened.

"My lord," he interjected calmly, "I believe Mewan has said enough. He can help you no more."

There was no question in Gawain's mind that the hermit's words had not helped Arthur at all; they had, in truth, wounded him far more grievously than might any sword. The king seemed unable to move, unable to stand. It was from that moment on, Gawain noticed, that a melancholy settled over Arthur, a dark mood that haunted them all for many miles on the road.

"We'll stop here."

Gawain looked cautiously at Arthur. These were the first words the king had spoken in several hours, but they were no more encouraging for that. He remained slumped in his saddle, his face as sullen and dour as it had been when they left Mewan's cave.

It was cold and damp up here on the moor, and Gawain had hoped they would have reached shelter farther to the north. But it was growing dark and Tintagel was at least three hours distant.

"Sire, should we not seek to reach the castle, even after nightfall?"

Arthur pulled his horse round and raised his eyes to Gawain. His shoulders slumped with all the weight and responsibility of his years and his crown. This was the Arthur Gawain had grown used to, though the demeanour was all the more troubling for the joy the king had shown just a few hours before.

"I wish to rest." Arthur paused and looked toward the setting sun, already lost behind a haze of dark clouds. He sighed. "And there is something I wish to do."

Arthur urged his horse forward. Gawain started to follow, but the king held up his hand.

"Get Kynan to prepare a camp for the night. I shall be back before it is full dark."

With that, Arthur set off over the brow of a low hill and was soon lost to sight. Despite his uncle's words, Gawain made to follow, but Agrivaine halted him.

"Let him go, brother. He's safe enough here."

"How do you know? You heard Mewan's words."

Agrivaine snorted. "For what they're worth. To me, they were just the ramblings of yet another mad hermit. This is Arthur's country, Gawain. He grew up here. He knows it far better than us."

Gawain remained hesitant. "I still think someone should keep an eye on him."

"His orders were for you to see to camp, Gawain, not me," Constantine offered. "Let me follow him – from a distance."

Without waiting for an answer, Constantine spurred his horse on, but did not follow Arthur directly. Instead, he took a route slightly to the south. Soon he, too, was swallowed up by the terrain. Agrivaine watched him go.

"He's a strange one, that Constantine."

"This is his land as well, Agrivaine. Let him be."

"I'm not sure I trust him. You've seen how he fawns on Arthur. I'm certain he sees himself as the next high king."

"What – Constantine?" Gawain snorted. "He's no high king. Have no fear there, brother. No one would support him."

"Constantine may not think that. We all know Arthur's days are numbered, and there's only one fit to succeed him."

"Our bastard brother Mordred, I suppose."

"And Arthur's son and rightful heir," Agrivaine noted. "Arthur may have disowned him, but the high king's blood flows in Mordred's veins and he can trace his descent from the great Caractacus."

"So do we all, Agrivaine." Gawain started to turn away. "Stop being paranoid, and help me get a fire going. The wind's getting cold."

With bad grace, Agrivaine snatched up some dried bracken. "This expedition was doomed to disaster from the start," he pouted, "and I think it has tipped Arthur over the brink into madness. You saw how he reacted at Mewan's cave."

Gawain withheld his answer until the fire started to take hold. Finally, he wrapped his cloak around him and looked deep into Agrivaine's eyes. "I, too, fear for Arthur's mind. That was why I wanted to follow him. God knows what he intends to do."

Arthur had not gone far. Less than a mile from the camp, but hidden by a crown of trees and tucked just below a ridge, lay the Dozmary Pool. In his youth, Arthur had fought and killed a monster here. With that battle, that victory, Arthur had become a man – at least in his own mind.

The pool had served as the stage for another important moment in Arthur's life, too. Soon after he became king, Arthur returned there with Merlin. That was when he was presented with Excalibur by the Lady of the Lake. He had not returned since that fateful day, though the pool of Dozmary often haunted his dreams.

Now, in the gathering gloom of evening, the pool looked even darker and more secretive than he recalled. Nothing reflected from its abyss-black surface. Even the wind scarcely raised a ripple. It was almost as if the lake mocked him – mocked anyone and everything. Merlin had told him that the dark pool of Dozmary had existed since the dawn of time. As he gazed upon its sinister, impenetrable depths, the king could finally believe that to be true.

Arthur stood at the edge of the lake and stared across the waters. He was still uncertain of his course. Ever since seeing Merlin he'd been full of doubt – if it had even been Merlin at all. The king banished that thought almost as quickly as it formed. He had to believe he'd seen his mentor; otherwise, his whole world would collapse.

Arthur had hoped the meeting with Merlin would provide an answer, but if the mage had offered one, it was not the one the king wanted. Was his whole life a sham, a fabrication dependent upon the power of Excalibur? Had he no authority of his own? The sword had saved his life countless times, but was each rescue won at the cost of his kingdom?

Arthur had pondered this dilemma for hours, ever since leaving Merlin's cave, and the only action to which Merlin's advice pointed was one he hesitated to take. He must return Excalibur from whence it came. Yet the sword had been part of his life –

maybe it had even been his life – for over thirty years. How could he part with it now?

If he cast Excalibur back into the lake, the king knew that he could never retrieve it. The sword would be gone forever. Instead, he might bury it here, at the lake's edge; then he could return for it one day, when he had regained control of his kingdom, of his life. But someone else might find it in the meantime. Would it make them all-powerful? Arthur wondered bitterly.

Once again the king remembered Merlin's words and knelt in prayer. He remained with head bowed for some while, but no inspiration came. Perhaps Merlin was right, he concluded. God would forsake him so long as he clung to the Old Faith. To the sword.

His mind was made up. Before he could hesitate again, Arthur stood, drew Excalibur from its scabbard, and held it high above his head. The bright blade turned as dark as the lake. For a moment, it seemed to Arthur that the blackness of both blade and water threatened to swallow the world. "But you will not swallow me," the king whispered and brought his arm back.

"Are you sure this is what you want?"

Arthur glanced back to find Constantine standing right behind him.

"Leave me, Constantine. This is no concern of yours."

"It is the concern of the whole kingdom, my lord." Constantine's voice was calm and reassuring. For a moment, Arthur almost relaxed his arm. But that urge quickly passed.

"Do not persuade me otherwise. This sword is the source of all my pain and anguish. It has severed my kingdom in two."

"Has it, my lord? Or has it spliced the kingdom together? The sword has protected you, and in that it has certainly protected Logres. Without Excalibur, how will your realm survive?"

Arthur wheeled round to glare at his would-be comforter. "That is precisely the problem. Excalibur rules, not me. Why do you think Morgan tried to rob me of the sword all those years ago? So that I would crumble and falter. If I am to be at peace with God, it must be me that rules, with His grace. I can no longer rely upon this crutch of the Old Faith."

Constantine could see the weakness in Arthur's argument, but was cautious of what to say next for fear of provoking the king. In that hesitation Arthur saw vindication of his words. "You understand now," the king said. "This is the will of God."

"Or the will of Morgan."

Arthur paused again. "What do you mean?"

"How do you know that this – the meeting with the hermit, the doubts assailing you, the conspiracies you perceive – do not form part of another of Morgan's schemes to rid you of the sword?"

Arthur struggled again with his thoughts, not wanting to have to admit how powerless he might be. "How could she plan this, Constantine? She did not send me on my quest for Merlin. She was not there when he told me of the sword's evil."

"I would tend to agree, my lord, and yet I hesitate to underestimate the deviousness of Morgan."

Suddenly Arthur slumped; the energy drained out of him. He stabbed Excalibur into the ground and leaned upon it.

"You have served only to remind me of all of my problems," Arthur sighed. "How can one tell reality from illusion any more in this world? Morgan is not behind every fault, every disaster, every shadow in the world. If I credit her so, I am not fit to rule. Yet she has tried and tested me again and again. Her designs fail, but I must wonder now if I am unknowingly aiding her against me. All the time I cling to the Old Faith by relying upon Excalibur, I am denying God, and that is the one weakness Morgan can still exploit." He looked down at the sword. "Once I am rid of Excalibur, she will have no hold over me."

"Yet has not Morgan tried to gain the sword?"

"To protect it, perhaps," the king suggested, "or to tap its dark power for her own purposes."

"Sire," Constantine said softly, "if I may be so bold, might I suggest you consider this another way?" At Arthur's silence, he continued: "Perhaps Excalibur draws its power from you, not the other way round."

Arthur beckoned Constantine to continue.

"I have no knowledge of such wonders, but it seems to me that you and Excalibur are linked in a special way, that the sword is only powerful in your hands. Has anyone else ever been protected by it?"

Arthur strained to remember. "Gawain used it once to devastating effect, but he is such a powerful knight and a brilliant swordsman he would likely triumph whatever the blade. No, I cannot say with certainty that anyone else has wielded its true power."

A pleased smile flashed across Constantine's lips. "Then might I suggest that Excalibur is not a crutch of the Old Faith at all. The sword reveals its power only in your hands. And if you draw your power from God, then it is God that wields Excalibur. That is the perfection we all glimpse in its working – the touch of the Lord."

This conclusion surprised even Constantine, who marveled a little at the inspired logic of it all. The words had the desired effect upon Arthur, too. The king's eyes visibly brightened, although his brow remained knit with concern.

"It would be so wonderful if you were right, Constantine. It would mean the Lord has recast the Old Faith as a tool, that even Merlin could be a servant of God, even as I had once thought."

"And it would explain, too, why Morgan wants to destroy Excalibur – it is an instrument of God."

Arthur clapped Constantine on his back and sheathed Excalibur. "You have resolved my enigmas, my friend. In that, you've shown that you are wise enough to be high king one day." Smiling still, he started back toward camp.

Constantine untethered his horse and paused, glancing out over the lake. Was that a shimmering he saw on the surface? A white glow in the centre? Perhaps it was merely a trick of the wind and the dying sun. The son of Cador shuddered a little at the mysteries of Dozmary Pool. But even those dark thoughts were soon overcome by the deep glow of pride he felt at Arthur's parting words.

Spurred on by Arthur's newfound vigour, the company returned to Camelot in just two days. Gawain was astonished at the sudden change in the king's character and though pleased, both he and Agrivaine wondered what part Constantine had played in this. Despite their questions, Arthur chose to remain elusive, saying only, "All is well." It left Gawain uneasy. He wondered if the king's transformation were built upon shifting sands.

Events moved fast upon their return. Arthur was determined to reassert his authority and so he sent out messengers to summon kings, lords, and the Round Table to Camelot for a major council. News of the gathering spread throughout the land, luring many who sought help from the court.

So it was that there arrived at Camelot a small procession of a lady with a litter and two horses, accompanied by a demoiselle and a page. The lady asked to see King Arthur, and she and the litter were brought into the keep's great hall. Here Arthur and Guinevere prepared to have audience.

"My lord, I seek your help to cure my son, who lies in this stretcher," the lady began, her voice quiet and quaking with age. "I have a story to tell."

"Pray tell us, my lady," Arthur responded. "But first, what is your name?"

"I am the Lady Philomela from Hungaria. My son is Sir Urfrey of the Mount, a valiant and brave knight who has been the victim of a curse."

A gasp went round the hall, as much at the stricken man's identity as in fear of his curse. Sir Urfrey had vanished early in the days of the Quest for the Grail, and many had pondered his fate. The whole court leaned forward to catch what came next.

"Seven years ago my son was challenged to single combat by the vengeful knight, Sir Alphegus of Iberia. Sir Alphegus was envious of my son's victories in a tournament. And when they finally met on the field, the battle was long and hard, lasting from noon to dusk. My son was triumphant and at length slew Sir Alphegus, but not before he, too, was severely hurt. He received seven wounds – three about his head; three about his body; and one on his left hand. Seeing those injuries, Alphegus's mother thereupon cursed my son that his wounds would not heal until he was touched by the best and most perfect knight in the world."

Lady Philomela bowed her head and concluded mournfully, "We have travelled the world for seven years in search of this most perfect knight, but have not succeeded. We now place ourselves at your mercy, great king."

Gawain started at this reference to a perfect knight, and saw that Arthur's face also betrayed his thoughts. But the king retained his demeanour of authority as he said, "It is indeed a sad story, my lady Philomela. May we see your son?"

Philomela pulled back the curtains from around the litter, and cries of shock and abhorrence went up from the court. There lay Urfrey, unable to move, his body covered in festering wounds. Even to those knights who knew him he was almost unrecognizable, for two sword cuts criss-crossed his face, whilst a third sliced back his scalp. Although his body was wrapped in bandages, blood and pus continually oozed through the dressings.

His left hand was clenched like a claw, the fingers flayed of flesh. The smell of putrefaction filled the air. There was little doubt that Urfrey would have died of his wounds long before, had he not been kept alive by the curse.

Of all those gathered in the great hall, Arthur seemed the most affected by Sir Urfrey's plight. "My lady," he began sorrowfully, "you have done well to survive your travels. If it is within my power to cure your son, it shall be done."

Even as he spoke, Arthur reflected upon Mewan's warning against the knight who betrayed perfection. Here was an opportunity to discover who that might be. Yet it seemed such a cruel twist that a knight pure enough of heart to cure this wretched man might also pose a threat. Still, that alone in the prophecy had been clear.

The king rose from his throne. "If you and your son are ready, my lady, I shall be the first to lay hands upon the wounds and search for any power I may have to heal them. Not that I presume to be the worthiest and best of all my knights, but that it must and should start with me. Let us remove to the tourney field."

Arthur motioned to Archbishop Dyfrig to bless the proceedings. He then ordered that the litter be taken out to the meadow beyond the castle and that Urfrey be laid upon the earth. The whole court bustled out to the field, where Arthur and Guinevere took their seats upon the dais.

Urfrey was prepared, the squires heaving at the smell of the knight's wounds. A golden cushion was placed before him upon which Arthur could kneel. All the knights, dukes, and earls assembled on the meadow. As he looked out over the host, Gawain reckoned there were over a hundred, all waiting for the chance to prove their perfection. Agrivaine stood by his side, and nudged him.

"Little chance any of this rabble will cure that poor sod," he whispered. "If Mewan's prophecy was correct, and Arthur has to beware the perfect knight, the one he has most to worry about is quite a ways off."

Though he did not mention Lancelot's name, Agrivaine's meaning was clear enough to Gawain. "Where is he?"

"Galavanting on some quest or other," Agrivaine smirked. "No doubt he'll be here in due course, or at least before the thing's over. This charade could take days."

"Be quiet, Agrivaine," muttered Gareth, who stood at his brother's shoulder. "This is a momentous occasion. Just imagine if Arthur cures this man."

"Then a dove will surely descend from heaven," Agrivaine mocked, but he was rebuked into silence by several about him.

The king had knelt in prayer before Urfrey, and then raised his hands before him.

"Sir Knight," he began. "I have prayed to the Lord our God to repent on behalf of your pain. Now you must pray and repent."

Urfrey struggled to speak. "My most noble King Arthur, I pray now as I have prayed every hour of my life these last seven years. I am at God's mercy and your command."

Slowly, tentatively, Arthur stretched out his hands and softly touched Urfrey's ruined flesh. It was almost more than Arthur could stand. The smell was repulsive, and as he felt the skin, so blood and pus oozed forth anew. The knight cried out in pain. Finally Arthur withdrew his hands, praying to himself all the while.

The words Constantine had spoken at the Dozmary Pool came to Arthur then. He stood and slowly drew Excalibur from its scabbard. If the sword were God's instrument, as Constantine had suggested, then Urfrey might be cured by it.

The king heard a buzz of apprehension surge through the crowd, followed by an expectant hush. He held the sword high, kissed it, and prayed. The blade sparkled, outshining the sun. Slowly Arthur lowered Excalibur until it touched Urfrey's chest. He closed his eyes and tried to open himself to the power, feel for it flowing through him. There was no doubt that his whole body tingled and the blade seemed to hum.

After what seemed an eternity Arthur opened his eyes. He was horrified to find that the knight was bleeding profusely from all his wounds. The king gasped in amazement. How could this be? God must have abandoned him.

Once again he lowered the sword to Urfrey's chest, but it only seemed to cause the knight greater distress. Arthur had to admit defeat. He resheathed Excalibur and hung his head in shame.

"I am sorry, Urfrey. I am not worthy of you."

Arthur rose, stepped back, and crossed himself. He turned and beckoned to Lord Clarivaus of Northumberland. "Find what you can in your soul for this poor knight."

Distraught, Arthur returned to his seat beside Guinevere. He was aware of the eyes of many upon him and was certain that his court was questioning why their king had not the power to cure Sir Urfrey. For Arthur himself, his failure turned his thoughts back to the mystery of the perfect knight – his secret foe, if the prophecy proved correct.

Until now, Arthur had believed that the only perfect knight in the whole of Christendom had been Galahad, and Galahad was no more. All others on the Grail Quest had failed, even though Bors, Percival, and Lancelot had come close. Might they be his hidden enemy? Since the Quest's end, Percival had retired to a hermitage; surely he could be no threat. Lancelot, certainly the greatest knight in all Christendom, was also the most faithful. Arthur refused to believe that the queen's champion could be his enemy. But what of Bors? Bors, too, had always been loyal, and was the son of one of his oldest allies. Surely Bors would not betray him. But if not Sir Bors, who?

As Arthur pondered, so the ceremony continued. The king had set a precedent with Excalibur, and each of the contenders drew his sword as part of the healing ceremony. But it was all to no avail. Nothing seemed to help the poor knight.

The sun had already climbed past noon, and Arthur realized that if all those assembled were to try to cure Urfrey's wounds, the procession would last well into the night. He beckoned to a page to have rooms prepared for Lady Philomela and her company.

The day wore on, and without success. Arthur, caught up now in pondering the identity of his nemesis, found himself secretly relieved at the failure of those closest to him – first Gawain, then Bedivere and Kay and Lucan. But shame at his own selfishness poisoned even that relief, darkening his mood further.

And still the procession continued. As he approached the injured man, Agrivaine made it clear he found the whole episode distasteful. He went through the ritual in a perfunctory fashion. Bors treated it seriously, and was blatantly upset when he failed, though more for poor Urfrey than for his own imperfection. Constantine, on the other hand, rose to the occasion, making a spectacle out of his prayer and his attempt at healing, even though the smell made him almost visibly sick. When nothing happened, the Duke of Cornwall became distraught. In the end, he collapsed beside Urfrey's body and had to be carried away.

By then it was nearly dusk, and Arthur believed that everyone's stamina had been drained. He held up his hand. "Lady Philomela, this must be as distressing to you and to your son as it is to me and my court. Both you and your son must rest. Join us in feasting tonight. We shall continue tomorrow."

The next morning the court was astir. Word came that Lancelot was on his way back and would arrive by noon. Arthur found his mind in turbulence. Clearly the court saw Lancelot as the last hope for poor Sir Urfrey, and in his heart of hearts Arthur wanted Lancelot to succeed. Yet the king could never believe that his friend was the traitor. Arthur found himself hoping that Lancelot would not cure Urfrey, and then felt guilty for such thoughts. Merlin had been right: wherever there is perfection, corruption lurks near at hand.

The proceedings continued until noon, though no one seemed surprised at the lack of success. All were awaiting the return of Lancelot, and a great cheer arose from the castle battlements as he was espied in the distance. Urfrey's sister, Filloré, cried out to her brother that hope was here at last. Word had already been taken to Lancelot of the events at the castle; as he arrived, he was not surprised to find such a gathering upon the tourney meadow. At the sight of the golden knight, it was as if the whole world sighed with relief.

It was at this moment that Mordred stepped forth to make his attempt at curing Urfrey. In defiant arrogance he marched towards the distraught knight, kicked the golden cushion aside, and pulled a sword from his scabbard.

The gasp from the court was thunderous, as initial astonishment turned to cries and shouts and jeers. For as Mordred stood before the cursed knight, he held aloft what looked like Excalibur. The sword blazed forth light, dazzling the spectators. Its resemblance to the king's blade was so strong that Arthur felt the pommel in his scabbard for reassurance. Then he realized what had happened. He leapt to his feet and cried to Mordred: "Stop! You will kill Sir Urfrey."

Before anyone else could reach Mordred, Lancelot, who had taken in the situation at a moment's glance, galloped across the field. He drew his own sword; it came from his scabbard as if from the very fire in which it was forged. The blade glowed a brilliant gold and, for an instant, both Mordred and Lancelot vanished in the incandescence of their swords.

Mordred turned to face Lancelot as he bore down on him astride his charger. To the surprise of everyone gathered there, Mordred displayed remarkable confidence. He held the sword in both hands and, as Lancelot approached, swung it with all his might. The queen's champion met the stroke with a single blow of his own. The clash of the blades sounded like the heavens rending.

Mordred cried out as if he had been struck by lightning, and the sword flew from his grasp. He was on his knees when Arthur finally reached him. The king picked up the fallen, false Excalibur and held it at Mordred's throat.

"Explain yourself, nephew."

Mordred was capable of a thousand emotions. Although pouting like a small child, he became humble and bewildered all in one. For a while he gasped for breath and then responded, hesitantly.

"I am at a loss to explain it, sire. Until I drew the sword, I had no idea it was Excalibur. See, this is my scabbard. Someone must have placed the sword there."

"And who might that have been?"

"I have no idea."

There was now a small gathering of knights around Arthur and Mordred, including Gawain and Lancelot.

"My lord," Gawain interceded, "I think you might find an answer from Morgan le Fay."

Arthur nodded. "Yes, Morgan would be at the heart of this. Many years ago she created this false Excalibur to confuse and weaken me. It is almost indistinguishable from its cousin, except when the two are close together. Morgan regained the sword long ago; I have not seen it since, but I recognized it instantly. I imagine Morgan must have given it to Mordred—"

"Placed it in my scabbard," Mordred corrected.

Arthur scowled. "Or placed it in his scabbard, hoping to trick him into using it. But this false Excalibur is evil. Had anyone attempted to heal Urfrey with it, he surely would have killed him."

"Or," Gawain offered, "Morgan planned to channel her dark power through the sword to give the appearance of healing – and make the wielder seem to be the most perfect of knights."

"And my worthy successor," Arthur concluded.

Yet the king did not give voice to the full turmoil of his thoughts. Only now was he realizing that the events unfolding were as much a test of Christianity by the Old Faith as they were a search for the perfect knight. And though Mordred could easily be construed now as his hidden enemy, a minion of Morgan's dark ways, his guise of perfection was too flimsy to fulfil the words of the prophecy. There was, however, one other . . .

"Gawain," the king said wearily, "I trust your brother to your keeping. We must attend to the business in hand." As Mordred was led away, Arthur turned to Lancelot, who bowed before his king.

"Lancelot, may it be God's will that it is within your power to cure this poor knight."

"My lord," Lancelot responded, "how can I, a simple knight, possibly succeed where you and these great lords have failed? I cannot presume such power upon me, in the face of God and His holy Son."

"You do not presume, Lancelot, I command you. You are not undertaking this deed on your behalf, but on behalf of myself and the entire Round Table."

Arthur found some relief in what he had just said. Maybe this was the answer – that Lancelot was not to be his nemesis. He was not the perfect knight, but the agent through which the power of all assembled would work.

"But, sire—" Lancelot began. Arthur hushed him and bid him to do his duty.

Lancelot sighed and then prepared himself. First, he approached Archbishop Dyfrig and sought his blessing. He then knelt in prayer before moving to Urfrey and kneeling beside the tortured knight.

"Sir Knight," he said, "I am not worthy of you, but if the Lord God chooses me as the instrument of His power, so be it."

He raised his hands to heaven, uttered a simple prayer, and slowly brought his hands down upon the knight. Never had there been such silence in the court at Camelot. All six score strained forward to see the consequences of Lancelot's action. Even Agrivaine found himself spellbound.

The gasps began from those nearest to Lancelot and Urfrey, and a great wail went up from Philomela and her daughter. "Praise be to God," they wept, sinking to their knees.

Arthur watched, transfixed. There was no doubt. The wounds were healing before his eyes. The flesh was becoming as new. Within moments, Urfrey was himself crying and shouting. Then he jumped into the air, as hearty as he had been seven years past.

The whole court cheered and cried. Then, at Arthur's command, they all bowed in prayer. Arthur declared that there must be feasting and celebration, but even as he spoke a dark cloud came over his face. Lancelot had succeeded where he had failed. Where he *and* Excalibur had failed.

He turned to where Lancelot was slowly rising. The queen's champion bowed to Arthur and to Guinevere, who had joined him at his side. Lancelot's face was streaked with tears, and Arthur watched as Guinevere wiped them away with her handkerchief.

"Lancelot," she said. "You are truly the purest and most perfect of knights. Your name will be remembered for a thousand years."

At that Arthur felt a pain strike through his heart. Somewhere he fancied he heard Morgan laugh. Had God prevailed or had Morgan? Arthur's mind exploded with anguish. Now he realized what had happened: Urfrey's corruption had passed from the cursed knight to the purest knight in the land. That perfection was now despoiled forever.

Arthur looked at Lancelot until his eyes filled with tears and he could see no more.

THE SLEEPER AND THE SEER

H. WARNER MUNN

H.Warner Munn (1903–81) began writing for the legendary Weird
Tales *in 1925 but he was never a prolific writer and the pressure
of other work and family life drew him away from writing until his
retirement in the sixties when the reprinting of his 1939 serial,* King
of the World's Edge, *in paperback revitalized his career. Munn had
a fascination for the Merlin legend, not so much with the Arthurian
connection, but more with its continuity down through history, in
particular how remnants from the old Romano-British world might
live on in later generations.* King of the World's Edge *follows the
journey of Merlin out of Britain with Gwalchmai (Sir Gawain), and
the Roman centurion Ventidius Varro, who narrates the story. They
sail to America, arriving in the land of the Aztecs, where Merlin
is recognized as their god Quetzalcoatl. Munn continued the story
in* The Ship from Atlantis *(1967) – the two volumes later being
published in a single book as* Merlin's Godson *(1976) – and in*
Merlin's Ring *(1974). The following extract comes from the start of*
King of the World's Edge *and is a self-contained episode relating
the events leading up to and just after the battle of Camlann.*

I

Stranger! Know me. I am Ventidius Varro – Roman to the core of
me, though I never have seen that lovely city by the Tiber, nor did
my father before me. He was British born, of a British mother,
and on *his* father's side was possessed of only one quarter of pure
Roman blood. Yet am I Roman, my allegiance is to Rome, and to
her goes my love and my heart's yearning – to that delectable city
which I shall now never see in life!

The story of my family is the tragedy of Britain. When my great-grandfather was called into the troops, my grandfather was a babe in arms. The island was bled white of fighting-men, only skeletons of garrisons remaining, but by the time of my grandfather's entrance into the Legion firm sturdy substance had formed upon these bare bones of organization. One might say that the brains were still Roman, but all the flesh was British.

The Sixth fought the Picts, the Scoti and the Saxons, and although the barbarians had gained a foothold, they were all but dislodged again and were held with their backs to the sea. Then, just as another year might have decided the struggle, Rome called.

Men were needed – Rome itself was in peril – my grandfather followed in his father's footsteps, into mystery, and never returned. None of the levies returned, and his wife, left lorn with young children, my father among them, moved west toward the mountains of Cambria and brought up her brood in Viriconium.

Rome sent us no more governors, no more high officials or low. Our fortresses in the west continued to be held by the decimated Sixth, but the very best men were gone, and I do not know where even their graves may lie.

Then the Jutes, Saxons and Angli, who had occasionally fought beside us as allies against the Picts, turned against us, and my mother fled across the Cambrian border, looking over her shoulder at flaming Viriconium, where my father with other brave men fought and died that Rome might be perpetuated in Britain.

My early childhood was spent in wandering about among the wild Cymri, whose bravery had challenged and broken all the power that Rome could hurl against them, and which now remained the only corner of Britain which was free from the Saxon peril and which, strangely enough, now protected the culture of Rome. And at last I come to my own time and the story you must know.

Among these Cymri dwelt the strange man known to them as Myrdhinn, but to us across the border as Ambrosius; a man of noble aspect and terrifying eye, of flowing white beard and majestic carriage; a man whose very origin is shrouded in mystery.

If the tale is true, Myrdhinn was sired by a demon in the reign of King Vortigern, baptized instantly by Blayse, the mother's confessor, thus becoming a Christian, but retaining the demoniac powers of magic, insight and prophecy. Other have considered him so wise that he could not be even slightly mortal, and maintain that he was born at the age of eighty at a time co-existent with the construction of Earth and has since been growing wiser!

It is more probable, however, that he was a foundling brought up in childhood by Druids who still keep up their ancient practices in Cambria, and taught by them their mystical lore, though he in later life embraced Christianity. Druidism warred in his heart with Christian tenets.

It is well known that the sages of antiquity possessed knowledge lost to us in these times of decadence, and locked fast in Myrdhinn's brain were many secrets, including that of prolonged life.

I am beaten down by years, grizzled, gaunt and almost toothless, yet Myrdhinn in all the time of my acquaintance remained the same as that of my mother's description, when as a young women she first saw him among the hills of Cambria, striding along a lonely glen, hale, rugged and strong, the child Arthur holding his hand and half trotting to keep up with the old man's vigorous pace.

They must then have been going to find his friend. Antor, to whom Myrdhinn delivered Arthur for tuition, and whose diligent care developed the stripling into Arthur, the hoped-for, the undying – Arthur, Imperator, the great Pendragon, dictator – Arthur, save only for treachery's intervention the savior of Britain.

At that time he was about fifteen years older than I who, still a suckling, knew nothing of the stirring events around me. By the time I was growing calluses practicing with sword and spear, Arthur already was leading forays into Saxon land.

Old crippled soldiers of the scattered legion remnants trained the savage youth of Cambria to a fantastic semblance of the iron ranks of Rome. Again the smiths pounded red iron into white blades, again sow and pig★ talked on carroballista and catapult, and at last a ghost of the old Legion marched over the border, with tattered standards, battle-scarred armor, dented shields.

But we marched in full strength! Our metal was bright and polished, our bows strong and arrows sharp (every man an archer,

★ Ratchet and pawl.

whether a member of the cavalry, engineers or simple legionary), and leading us all the glittering eagles gave us courage.

Sixth Legion, Victrix! Hail and farewell! Thy bones make the fields of Britain greener now.

Something of the old imperial spirit came back. Viriconium was captured, lost and held again, and the Cymri streamed over the border, rebuilding all possible of the past glory. On the plain outside the walls scampered the shaggy Cambrian ponies in laughable contrast to the thundering charge of the Roman horse. But the Saxon footmen scattered before the charge, and as time went by we penetrated deeper into hostile country, winning back foot by foot the soil of Britain to be once again free land for us exiles and lovers of Rome.

Here and there we came upon noble steeds and mares in the fertile lowlands, and by the time Arthur's forces were strong enough to meet in pitched battle a superior force of Saxons, three hundred horsemen smashed the shield walls.

The Saxons, streaming away, left us masters of the field in the first great battle to break the invaders' power, and harrying the retreat the cataphracts pursued, hacking them down and wreaking such havoc that from the survivors of the troop Arthur formed his noble band of knights.

Their leather armor, knobbled with bronze, was replaced with plate; stronger horses were bred to carry the extra weight; and as Arthur came victor from field upon field, armies, chieftains, kings thronging to him, naming him amheradawr (or imperator) – the Round Table came into being and held high court in Isca Silurum.

Thus from battle to battle we passed – our glory increasing, our confidence growing, recruits coming in – sneaking by night along hostile shores in coracles of hide and wicker, creeping by the moored Saxon longships – until flaming hilltop beacons farther than the eye could see marked the boundaries of recovered Britain.

Grumbling, growling to ourselves, watching the Legion grow to double strength, we waited for the word to sweep over the Saxon remnant. Then came unexpected help from Armorica – our compatriots across the sea sailing in roundships and galleys to our aid.

Myrdhinn had asked for their help, and nobly they answered.

At that time we had but one warship, the *Prydwen*, a great dromon built as an experiment from a design found in an old book, modeled to be a cruiser which could meet and plow under the enemy galleys. Its like had not been seen in British waters for hundreds of years. Armed with ballistas and arrow engines, driven by oars and sails and with overhanging galleries the better to repel boarders, it towered over the hulking roundships and low galleys, like a proud cock who struts among his family, protector of all.

Already the barbarians were marching upon us, out of Wessex, while at sea a fleet sailed to land forces in our rear.

We met them at Mons Badonicus and spent the day and most of a long moonlight night in killing, while upon the water the allied fleet covered itself with glory.

Armorican, Hibernian and Saxon galleys crashed and flamed to heaven, while among them, ramming, casting firepots, roamed the *Prydwen* in the arrow-sleet, trampling the foe under her forefoot.

Then to us at last came peace, time to live and love and rest – and for some, time to plot treachery.

Myrdhinn had planned for Arthur a marriage with Gwenhyvar, daughter of a noble chieftain, Loadegan of Carmelide; and journeying thither in disguise to see the maid before wooing, Arthur arrived at an opportune time. The walled city of Carmelide was besieged by a wandering foray of savage mountain raiders, but Arthur's armored knights scattered them and drove them far.

Entering the city, Myrdhinn spoke for Arthur, beseeching the hand of Gwenhyvar as a reward to the city's savior.

It was open talk afterward that Myrdhinn had engineered this attack and rescue to bring about his own plans, but I know nothing of the matter, having been far away. I believe him capable of it, for his mind worked in devious ways and he was not a man to do a thing in a simple way if something spectacular could complicate it.

This time, however, if he was at bottom of the matter, his love for a brave show ruined himself, Arthur, Gwenhyvar – and Britain. You see, Gwenhyvar was already in love with a young man named Lanceloc.

Arthur was approaching middle age, Gwenhyvar and Lanceloc much younger. Theirs was the proper union, but how could an ambitious father refuse the great Pendragon, savior of the city?

Laodegan commanded, Gwenhyvar obeyed like a dutiful child, and evil began.

"Forbidden fruit the sweetest of all" – so runs the ancient saw. Others knew what went on in all its seamy detail, but noble Arthur, the soul of bravery and honor, remained in ignorance for years.

Then Agrivain and Medrawd, kinsmen who aspired to be mighty themselves and who thought that could be best done by bringing low those already mighty, came sneaking, telling tales, spewing venom upon all that Arthur held dear, and down crashed our hopes for Britain.

Lanceloc, Agrivain and Medrawd fled into Wessex, fleeing their outraged ruler, taking their kinsmen, their vassals, and their friends.

Here they allied themselves with what remained of Saxon power, sending word overseas that it was safe again for pirates to come and murder, rape and pillage, for Arthur was stricken to the heart and Rome had forgotten her lost colony.

So the Sixth marched and the Saxons marched, and both great armies came toward the fatal field of Camlan – and the end of all glory!

II

It is not for me to describe that tragic calamity to my Emperor, feeling certain that during the passage of these many years the sad events of that cursed day have been so fully described to you that by now you must have a clearer picture of the battle than any I could give. After all, I was but a centurion, nor had I any knowledge of the whole plan of battle. Still, all plans were frustrated by a thick cold fog that shrouded us from the beginning, so that soon we broke up into troops hunting for similar small enemy bands, killing and being killed in many bitter encounters.

Then as the daylight grew more dim, the clash of arms became feebler, and wandering alone, separated from my century, I dismounted from a charger I had previously found running masterless through the slaughter, and now led him along a beach where the waves of an ebbing tide came slowly in, whispering a mournful requiem to all my hopes. The clammy, darkening fog seemed pressing down upon my very soul.

The narrow stand separated the ocean-sea from a small brackish lake at which I mean to water my steed. So I turned to my left, hearing the plash of little waves among the sedges of the salty marsh surrounding the fresher water. There was no other sound, save the occasional croak of a sea bird flying blindly through the mist.

My horse was raising his head from his drink, with a long sigh, when the fog abruptly lifted and gave me a clear view of perhaps a hundred yards. We were standing at the edge of a narrow inlet, and upon its other shore I saw the wreckage of a furious encounter.

Dead men lay in the water and carpeted the sand beyond as far as I could see into the farther haze. But not all there were corpses.

One lay bleeding, partly raised upon an elbow, while bending over him was a ghastly knight. Much of their armor was hacked away and that remaining was dabbled with blood. I recognized the pair.

The dying man was Arthur; the other, with whom he weakly argued, was Sir Bedwyr, one of the most trusted of his knights. I hailed them, but Arthur was too far gone or too absorbed to hear me, though Sir Bedwyr looked across the water and lifted his hand for silence.

Again Arthur commanded and this time Sir Bedwyr agreed, picked up Arthur's great sword, Caliburn, and walked away into the mist. Then the cold gray curtain fell again, and through it I rode around the inlet until the sound of voices halted me.

"This time you did not fail me?" queried Arthur.

"Regretfully I obeyed, my King."

"And what did you see and hear?"

"I threw the sword into the mere, as you commanded, and as it circled flashing, something cried out most dolefully, while up from the mere there raised a long arm in a flowing sleeve of white samite. Caliburn was caught, brandished thrice and drawn under, while from all the mere rose up a various keening of sorrowful voices."

"So Caliburn returns to the hand that gave it, to be held in trust for another who shall succor Britain. Strange that I heard no sound."

"Sadly I say it, my King, but your ears are becoming attuned to other rhythms than those of earth."

"So soon? With my work barely begun?"

With that exclamation his eyes closed. As I approached, I could not tell if Death had touched him or if it was but a swoon.

Sir Bedwyr met me before I reached Arthur, and explained, whispering, the scene I had just witnessed.

"He seems out of his head with despair. His wounds are grievous, but I think not fatal could I only stop the bleeding. I think it is his soul that is dying. He is firmly convinced that the end is come, for himself, for all of us, and for Britain. That is why he bade me cast his great sword into the mere.

"God forgive me! I am a forsworn knight! I have lied to a dying man. You can understand, Centurion? How could I cast it away? The brand has become a symbol to men. With Arthur gone, the scraps of our army will rally only to something they cherish. You know how the rabble need something to follow, a hero, an eagle, a sacred relic. With something to protect or follow they are giants; without it they are only men, afraid of death, afraid of pain. They would fight like demons to keep Arthur's sword out of the hands of the Saxons."

I had dropped upon my knees, examining the deep wounds in side and thigh, but my efforts at stanching were no better than the other's had been, and we worked together while he continued:

"So I cast the jeweled scabbard into the mere and lied! There was no arm in white samite, no wailing, only ripples on the mere and a sea bird's croak!"

"Nor would there have been more had you hurled the sword after the scabbard," I grunted. "Hand me more of that linen shirt."

He smiled sadly.

"Now if he dies, he will die happy in that respect, thinking I obeyed him, and if he lives he will understand I meant it for the best and will forgive me, I hope. Do you think I was right?"

"Unquestionably," I agreed. "With Arthur's sword in our hands we can flee to the hills, gather strength and strike again. If I could only stop this cursed blood!"

His lips had become the color of clay, and I marveled that he still breathed, for it seemed that each faint gasp would be his last.

Hearing the approach of a company, I looking up and clutched my own sword, then relaxed. Robed men, sagely bearded, were about me. Myrdhinn and his Nine Bards had come, and never had I been so glad to see that mysterious person as now.

He wasted no words, but brushing us both away, deftly probed the wounds, pressed at the base of the skull and at two places upon Arthur's back, then motioned for us to stand guard.

"The great Pendragon is departing."

The bards began a sorrowful keening, cut short by the sage.

"Peace! That will not help us. I cannot cure him. Time only can do that, but I can prevent a further sinking while we seek safety."

The groping tendrils of fog swirled thicker about us all as we watched those nimble fingers. Deftly he bound up those dreadful wounds from which the blood no longer pumped, his lips moving in a swift patter of mumbled words. Here was a scrap of Latin or a Cymric phrase, but mostly it was merely a sibilant hissing which belonged to no language of our ken.

And it seemed to us that in the pause between the longer incantations the mist became thicker and thicker yet, while just beyond the circle of our vision there sounded muttered rejoinders, as though Myrdhinn prayed for the life of Arthur and the cold lips of that great host of British dead on Camlan field must supply the responses.

And ever through the mist came the lapping of water on the distant shore. But *was* it distant? The sound seemed closer than it had been.

Once Myrdhinn paused to listen, but went on to complete his charm.

A cold touch lapped my ankles. I was in a puddle of lake water without having realized the fact. I moved closer to the mound upon which the others stood.

"Is he dead?" gasped Sir Bedwyr, and Myrdhinn shook his head.

"He would have been by now, but his breathing has stopped and he will live."

"Stopped his breathing? Then he must die!"

"Not entirely stopped, perhaps," smiled Myrdhinn. "He will breathe possibly once a day, until he has recovered during a long sleep the energy and the blood he has lost. He has been almost drained dry. We will take him to a safe and secret place where I can hide him away until he is recovered and ready to fight again for Britain."

I moved out of the water again. Was I sinking in a marsh? The ground seemed solid.

"How long must he sleep?" Again Sir Bedwyr questioned.

"Longer than you would believe. *Your* bones will be mold and your very tomb forgotten, before Arthur has well begun to sleep! I cannot explain now – hear that clank of arms? Enemies are prowling in the mist! Quick, Varro, help my men to lift him across your saddle. We must flee!"

As I moved to obey, I saw again that I stepped from water to reach higher ground. I looked about me. Unperceived by us, the water of the mere was stealthily rising to surround and cut us off.

Quietly I showed Myrdhinn. His eyes widened. Then he laughed.

"Ah, Bedwyr. It would have been better had you returned Caliburn to the lady who loaned it. My wife, Vivienne, a somewhat grasping person. She may bear us a grudge for cheating her. She held me ensorceled in the wood of Broceliande for some time, I remember very vividly. Come quickly, before the water rises!"

A huge wave came up from the mere and hurled itself along the inlet, swirled about our knees and fell back as though loath to release us.

"Hurry! Hurry!" urged Myrdhinn.

Again we heard the clinking of accouterments, this time much closer, and soon the gruff words of Saxons could be distinguished.

They were hard upon us. Sir Bedwyr looked at me, and I at him. We were the only armed men in the party. With common consent we turned back, but for only a few steps when we again heard the rumble of a monstrous wave breaking upon the lowland we were leaving.

This time other sounds followed – cries of horror, of pain; the screams of tortured men; then groans, and bitter sobbing, awfully intermingled with mumbling, munching sounds, as though in the fog mercifully hidden from us some monstrous thing was feeding.

We stood aghast as Myrdhinn urged us to join the party.

"Come quickly! Tarry not! The mistake will soon be discovered. Let us get far from this evil place."

"What is back there?" I gasped.

"Vivienne's pet, the Avanc. The Worm of the Mere. We have cheated it and her as well. She is probably jealous that I have aided Arthur and she is surely enraged at the loss of Caliburn, which was due her by the terms of the loan.

"Listen, my good wife, and heed!" He called into the fog. "I hold Arthur's sword, and shall now keep it. This to repay for my years of imprisonment in the Ring of Smoky Air.

"Run, for your lives, men, run!"

We ran, beside the trotting horse. For the first few minutes all was still; then the ground surged in waves beneath us like an angry sea. Once, twice, thrice it rolled and threw us from our feet. We picked ourselves up and ran blindly in the fog.

Then somewhere a crash, as though the ocean-sea was hurling itself violently upon the bloody shore, and a long silence, followed by a second mighty roar of waves now mercifully far away. Silence again.

In the fog, just outside our vision, a woman laughed. Long, low and inexpressibly evil! Musically lovely, but oh, so wicked!

Just a laugh, nothing more, but in it was hinted the knowledge of something that we could not then know or guess; something that we should and must know, but which was withheld from us.

We looked at Myrdhinn. He shook his head without speaking.

Something had been done by the Lady of the Lake, to repay insults, to avenge Lanceloc (said to be her kin) and to injure us all, but what it was we did not know.

We went our way again, deeper and deeper inland, on into the fog. And behind us, till we had gone so far we could not hear it, rippled that lovely musical laughter, chilling the blood in our veins.

III

There is no need, my Emperor, to weary you with dry details of all we said and thought and did during the next few days. It is not for that reason I am writing. Briefly, then: We marched for several nights, through hostile country, picking up stragglers as we went, and hiding until we numbered forty men and could march by day. Twice we fought wandering bands of Saxons as we pressed on westward toward Arthur's homeland of Lyonesse, for he had often expressed a wish to be buried in his natal village of Avalon. But as we neared it, we met wild-eyed refugees, fleeing a more dire peril than the sea raiders – the sea itself! For, we learned, on the very eve of that fatal field of Camlan, the fertile and populous province of Lyonesse had sunk beneath the sea!

Yea, sixty villages and towns, each with its church and wealth and people, among them Arthur's own Avalon, lay drowned and nothing remained to mark the spot but a few scattered hilltops, now islands in a sea of yellow muddy waters.

"Vivienne, think you?" I asked Myrdhinn.

He nodded without speaking, but his nine bards, in tones as solemn as a peal of drowned bells, answered, "Aye."

We hurried on through a thick wood and came to a shallow place where the ebbing tide had filled the underbrush with mud, corpses, bodies of horses and cattle, fish with their bellies burst open by the underwater explosions which had accompanied the sinking of the land.

Myrdhinn leading to a goal he had decided upon, we followed: first, the nine bards; then myself and the charger which bore Arthur's body, very yellow and unbreathing, though warm and flexible; then the legionaries, who accepted me as centurion, though only two were from my century, and most of the others were unknown to me.

We passed through the wood and arrived at a great hoar rock, almost a mountain, and up this we climbed and rested. For a long time we looked out over the drowned land murdered by sorcery and spite, watching the tide come in and cut us off from the mainland, while Myrdhinn sat apart, considering the future.

Then, on the ebbing of the tide, we returned to the wood and left the seer alone with the sleeper. We made camp beyond the deathly wood and waited – three days. During all that time a thick black cloud, neither fog nor smoke, hung about the summit of the mount, unmoving in the fiercest wind, and those among as with sharp ears claimed to hear mutterings in an unknown language issuing from the cloud. Likewise, it seemed, they heard various invisible hurrying creatures passing through the air above, speeding toward the mount, conversing as they came.

For myself, I heard none of this, and it was very likely but the stirring of volcanic activity still busy near the sunken province.

Finally Myrdhinn came to us, and the cloud disappeared as had Arthur and the glory and honor of his reign. Where he had been laid with Caliburn, his famed sword, fast in his grip, Myrdhinn would not say, except that he was in a secure spot not to be found by man until the time was come for the waking of him.

Be not concerned for Britain's champion, oh my Emperor, for I have the sure word of Myrdhinn the wise that Arthur shall one day wake! There will be a mighty war in which all the tribes shall engage which possess the tiniest drop of British blood. Then Arthur will wake, make himself known and with Caliburn carry carnage into the lands of Britain's enemies. And war shall be no more and peace shall reign forever over all of Earth!

This, Myrdhinn told us. He told us also that he had writ this in enduring letters of Cymric, Ogham and Latin, about the walls of Arthur's abode, sealing the entrance thereto with a rock cunningly fixed and inscribed:

Here Arthur lies. King once and king to be.

Lest, Emperor (if Britain has by now been reclaimed by Roman legions), they should be tempted to search for and enter this secret place, be warned. Myrdhinn has set watchers there. Arthur cannot and must not be awakened before the appointed time. The watchers will see to that. They are not human, they will not sleep or rest, they do not eat or drink, tire or forget or die! They are there to keep the entrance inviolate. Be warned! They are dangerous and will wait as Myrdhinn commanded, till Arthur wakes, be it one or three thousands of years. I do not know, nor does it concern us. They are there, the Guardians – the Watchers!

The next morning, again we marched, following the coastline westward, and after some time we reached the very end of land, where beyond lay nothing but the boundless ocean. Here on the brink of a high raw cliff stood a monstrous boulder so cleverly poised that the touch of a hand might rock it, but many oxen could not pull it from its place, though bar and pry might dislodge it.

Myrdhinn drew from his robes a bronze plate already prepared and inscribed with an account of what we had done, instructions for entering Arthur's chamber and a warning to the unwary.

Again we left him alone; again we saw the black cloud gather and from a distance saw a marvel hard to explain. The massive and ponderous boulder rose in air to the height of a tall man!

This work, which would have taxed the powers of a Titan, was done noiselessly and with apparent ease. Myrdhinn merely touched it, so far as we could judge, and it rose.

He stooped, put the plate beneath it, and the rocking stone

descended upon it, holding it safe there until such time as Myrdhinn described, upon joining us:

"When the moment is come for Arthur's awaking, the earth will shake, the rocking stone will topple down the cliff and Lyonesse will rise from the sea. Then, according to my vision, men will find my hidden words, will read, understand and obey. Then, when the drowned lands are fertile enough so that apple blossoms blow again in Avalon, in apple blossom time, men will enter his sleeping-chamber, waking him without fear of the watchers, and the era of peace on earth will begin."

You, my Emperor, may think this fantastic, but had you heard the words of the ancient, you could not have doubted. It may occur to you that Myrdhinn was a sorcerer, and it is true that at times he did use sorcery, as will be shown, but he dreaded it mightily. His Christian beliefs warred with his Druidic learning and he had the feeling that he was risking hellfire by the use of Black Magic.

He was an heir to all the lost lore of the ancients, and much of his sorcery was marvelous tricks with quite natural explanations, but the basic facts which made them possible were hidden from the rabble. The world is hoary with years and has forgotten much.

Now, our mission accomplished, we must needs look to our own welfare and so held a council to decide our future, and found that we were of several minds.

Some were for striking deep into the hills and gathering other fugitives about us until we were able to strike again for freedom. Sir Bedwyr proposed this plan and many agreed with him, but I disputed, it seeming wiser to take ship and sail across to Armorica, where we might find kinsmen who would see us on the road to Rome.

Here, I suggested, a punitive expedition might be sent as had been once before from Gaul. Surely, I argued, Britain was too valuable a part of the Empire to be lost – and then Myrdhinn ended the bickering.

"You, Sir Bedwyr, and you, Centurion, think of nothing but the regaining of Britain, but believe me when I tell you this is not possible. The Empire itself is dying; the seat of power is shifting eastward. Britain has been lost for a generation and its only hope of Romano-British domination died when treachery and intrigue brought us to Camlan field. Gaul is going down the same road and soon will be lost forever to Rome.

"Britain belongs now to the strongest and will be dismembered among them. It is for us to flee, not to Rome, whose power is waning, but to another land of which the ancients tell.

"Suppose, now, that there was a land, beyond the western ocean, so far away that it is unknown to the Jutes and Angles, the Saxons and the Norse – known to Rome long ago, but forgotten by all except scholars. Would it not be worth visiting, exploring, conquering perhaps, to furnish for us poor exiles a new home, a new domain into which Rome might send fleets and colonies should the barbarians press too hard? I am certain that there is such a land.

"Firstly, it is said that King Solomon of the Jews obtained precious metals from its mines, brought hence by the men of Tyre. Homer, of the Greeks, speaks of a westerly land beyond the seas, locating, as does Pliny, the Western Ethiopians in this land. Plato tells us of a sunken continent named Atlantis, but this is not the same, for Anaxagoras also tells of a great division of the world beyond this ocean, dry and unsubmerged.

"The historian Theopompus tells us of the Meropians and their continent beyond the western ocean, larger, he says, than all our known world, and Aristotle says that the Carthaginian explorers discovered and settled a part of the southern country, until their Senate decreed that no one should voyage thither, killing all the settlers, lest it no longer remain a secret; for the Carthaginians wished this country to be kept as a refuge for themselves if ever a disaster befell their republic, but lost their shipping in the Punic Wars.

"Statius Sebosius calls this land 'the two Hesperides' and tells us that forty-two days' sailing will bring us there. Could you ask for better proof than all of this?"

"Ridiculous!" snorted Sir Bedwyr. "There is not a vessel in Britain that could be equipped for such a voyage! Far better to recruit, build up strength and have at the Saxons again."

"You are forgetting the *Prydwen*. Arthur's own dromon lies safe at Isca Silurum, if the Saxon dragon-ships have not raided and burned the city. If we find her whole, will you sail with us?"

"Not I," quoth he, stoutly. "I live and die in Britain. What! Should I venture to sea in a ship so weighted down with metal that a puff of breeze might founder her? Let steel kill me, not tin!"

Here he spoke of a novelty, which the Cornish tin miners had conceived. They had sent great stores of this metal, without cost, to Arthur for embellishment of his ship, and the Imperator had sheathed the *Prydwen* with it, from stem to stern, above and below water, knowing it to be protection agains fireballs above and barnacles below. This made the *Prydwen* glitter so handsomely that many called her "The House of Glass."

"Your fears are unfounded. I feel it in my prophetic soul, that I and all who sail with me shall see this land which may indeed prove to be the Isles of the Blest of which you have all heard at your mother's knee. Why not? The wise geographer, Strabo, believed in it. Shall we consider him a romancer? It may indeed be that the Meropians have already sailed eastward and discovered Europe; for Cornelius Nepos, the eminent historian, says that when Q. Metellus Celer was proconsul in Gaul, certain peculiar strangers were sent to him as a gift from the King of the Batavi. They said that they had been driven from their own land, *eastward* over the oceans until they had landed on the coast of Belgica.

"This may have inspired Seneca, one hundred and thirteen years thereafter, to prophesy in his tragedy of Medea, as follows:

"'In later years an age shall come, when the ocean shall relax its bonds, a great continent shall be laid open and new lands revealed. Then Thule shall not be the remotest land known on the earth.'

"Four hundred and fifty years have elapsed since that prediction. If we sail and discover, we cannot now call ourselves the first, because we shall but follow in the footsteps of others who have traveled in less stout vessels than ours.

"Fishers from Armorica, our own kinsfolk, have visited its northern fishing-grounds yearly, in their ridiculous craft, while Maeldune of Hibernia, with seventeen followers, less than a hundred years ago, was blown to sea in flimsy skin currachs, and claimed to have reached a large island where grew marvelous nuts with insides white as snow.

"So you see there are such lands and they can be reached! Moreover, in our own times, Brandon, the monk of Kerry, the same one who recently established the monastery at Clonfert, has been there not once only, but twice! He had no great warship, such as we, but a merchant vessel with strong hides nailed over it, pitched at the seams, and it took him and his people forty days (almost exactly as related by Statius Sebosius) to reach this mysterious country.

"Now who among you will come with me and call yourselves men?"

"There is nothing here for us but a choice between death or slavery and degradation. I say let us all go and find this paradise on earth, this land of Tir-nan-og, this country of Hy Bresail, these Fortunate and Blessed Isles!"

Thus I, carried away with enthusiasm.

Then, indeed, began much arguing pro and con, which in the end resolved itself into a division of our force. Many, fearing monsters of the deep, demons and other fantasies, elected to remain, and choosing Sir Bedwyr as their leader they marched off toward the wild mountains, and whether they died before they reached the safety of the hills or lived henceforward a life of skulking outlawry, I know not.

At a little port we bought skin currachs, and, hugging shore, passed through the muddy waters, left them for cleaner, and in the end we reached Isca Silurum, without seeing a Saxon sail. And mightily glad we were to see the glitter of the *Prydwen*'s sides and the golden glint of Isca's guardian genius, high upon its pillar, for these things told us that we were sailing into a free and friendly province.

So we found it, a little section of free land, bounded by the four cities of Aquae Sulis, Corinium, Glevum and Gobannium – a little island of freedom in a barbarian sea, and we in its one safe port of Isca were loath to leave it for the dreaded Sea of Darkness.

Yet a month later we left it. One hundred fighting-men, besides a full complement of sailors, and thirty Saxons whose strong backs we thought would be useful when winds could not be found. These were prisoners doomed to execution, and we took them to make up a lack of rowers. Better for us if we had let them die by the ax!

So we turned our backs on Britain, never, any of us, to see it more.

MIDWINTER

DAVID SUTTON

The work of David Sutton (b. 1947) is better known to readers of horror and the supernatural rather than fantasy. He is probably best known as an editor, ever since the days of his amateur magazine Shadow *in the late sixties, through his work on* New Writings in Horror and the Supernatural *to his work with Stephen Jones on* Fantasy Tales *and* Dark Voices. *He has been writing short fiction almost as long, some of which has been collected as* Clinically Dead *(2006). Other stories include the Lovecraftian tale "Demoniacal" (*Cthulhu *#3, 1978) and the powerful story of ancient evil, "Those of Rhenea" (*Skeleton Crew, *November 1990). The following story brings us to the later legend of Merlin, long after the death of Arthur, in those dark days when the elder world has collapsed about him.*

The winter was *cold* that year.

I had come to my place during autumn, when the trees were wreathed in a mist that brought to mind harrowing memories. Their branches dripped with sorrowful tears as if they were aware that some great disaster had befallen man. Only the apple trees in the grove were still joyous with fruit and I was able to feast in that sacred place, and lick my wounds.

I arrived with the furs of my raiment torn and stained with dried blood, and I likened myself to the living roedeer that is spiked with spears and struggles in its death throes. My ritual feathers were scalped, my headdress resembling an inexpertly plucked hen. Across my shoulder I clutched my leather satchel, but no longer was there left in it any of the apparatus of my profession.

But the cavern beyond the sacred grove on Hart Fell gave me shelter and the fruits and berries of the forest were my succour.

And winter came . . .

The solstice night was marked by a blizzard that left a deep carpet of glistening snow throughout the spinney, and the pines on the mountain slopes bowed from the pressure of their fresh, thick white coats. The night should have been one for celebration. Ah, those past years, when I played to my audience with tricks and truths, and brought in the new season. There would be feasting and drinking; there would be the sacrifice and magic . . . Now no one visited the hallowed grove of apple trees and I spent that night at the mouth of my cave in sombre mood, transfixed as the crescent moon scooped away silver snow-clouds before it, as if it were a giant's spoon. Although I shivered, I hoped someone would come this way and visit me. Anyone, with whom I might celebrate. They could sit at the fire which burned still within the cave and I would feed them the divine mushrooms and broth and tell them old stories. Even a Christian: yes I would welcome even a disciple of Gildas on that loneliest of nights. For I had not seen a living human soul since the eight month.

By dawn my limbs were ready to crack and my beard was stiff with freezing air. Behind me the fire had died and I too wished to allow myself that luxury. If I sat a little while longer and allowed sleep to overcome me, I might become my spirit self. Then I should fly, fly as the peregrine with its keen eye. Soar as the gull on broad motionless wings, buoyed by currents of air. Streak as the swift and journey to a far country where death might at last claim my soul. Instead an eternity of sour memories left me distraught and wide awake.

As I pondered upon my desires, I became aware of movement among the fruit trees and my mood was disturbed. Yet there was no lumbering human form about to greet me.

Unexpectedly, a stag came and gazed quietly upon me, motionless except for the cloudy tempest from his nostrils. He was a giant, his brown fur shaggy in winter cloak, his antlers convoluted and rearing above the tallest frozen branches of the apple trees. Presently, he passed by. When the wolf followed the stag and gleamed his yellow eye upon me, without fear, yet without malice, I knew not to disregard the omen. He was so large a wolf I thought I might have fitted into his belly with little discomfort. But if he was hungry, it was not for human meat, and the wolf went about his business.

The strange behaviour of the two lords of the forest galvanized me into standing up so that I could warm my limbs with activity, and presently I set off to collect wood to re-light the fire.

The foot-worn track, leading from the glade down the slope of the mountain, was invisible beneath the snow. I was forced to use trees to mark my way, and eventually came to the naked bluff which overlooks the pass between the high peak of Hart Fell and its distant cousin. A hundred feet below me a stream cascaded, deep cut into the rock and overhung with icicles. Beside it a path mimicked its course, but hidden beneath snowdrifts. Further down the pass, in more clement weather, could be seen where the track diverged, one fork leading up here, to the sacred grove.

I stood for a moment and gazed gloomily across the ravine to the distant snow peak. The wind was sharp, carrying with it tiny ice crystals that stung my face. Ice sculpted one massive slope and drew the eye down along its grandeur. And my eye was thus caught by movement deep in the valley.

Seeming no larger than a blackbird at the distance, its clothes flapping as though the bird was injured, someone was laboriously struggling up the valley. He bore a staff with which he prodded the snow before attempting to take a step into what might be a deep crevasse. A wise precaution, even though I knew the route was safe.

I watched for a considerable time as the wanderer strove up the valley towards the higher slopes. I wondered where he was heading with such determination. Stopping for a while, he lay on his stomach before the stream and reached out his hands to cup a drink of water. He took several. The weather was bitingly cold, but the man must have been thirsty with so difficult a task manoeuvring himself through the drifts. My thoughts were on the whole quite idle and so it was a great surprise when I saw the traveller veer away from the stream, which gave him at least guidance, and head up the incline which led to the apple grove. Within minutes he was hidden among trees, but I did not doubt his intention. Unless he were mad and had wandered off the path through the blinding effect of the snow, the man was *intending* to come this way.

The traveller must know of the hallowed glade of the apples in the mountains of Caledonia.

Realizing I had held my breath in astonishment, I exhaled a

cloud of mist, which turned to minute droplets in the wind and was carried off. Hastily I moved away from the crag and began to scour for dead branches. In a while I had a bundle of wood, which I tied together with some strips of leather I had brought with me. I then returned to the cave, staggering under the weight of my burden.

Although in my misery I had allowed my fire to dwindle, I found that there remained an ember, bright under charred timbers. With the few dry twigs that remained I coaxed a flame and hunched shadows of myself were cast familiarly about the walls of the cave. I unstrapped the bundle of wood, and selecting the least sodden pieces, I placed these close to the fire to dry. I busied myself and felt curiously nervous at the thought of welcoming a visitor into my lonely existence.

As I tidied my living quarters and immersed myself in commonplace thoughts, the traveller approached unnoticed. Only when his shadow momentarily screened off half the daylight from the cleft of the cave's narrow opening did I realize he had entered.

I turned.

The being before me was dressed from head to foot in rags. No warming furs covered shoulders or legs or feet. And his head was completely hooded from the weather with simple cloth, its weave impossible to have held at bay the ravening wind.

I shivered in horror for the dreadful torment this traveller must have suffered.

And my visitor shivered too. He was short in stature, though not as diminutive as I, and meagre of bone and muscle. Without a word he dropped to his knees before the fire, which now crackled cheerfully. The traveller stretched out his hands, which were small and quite white with the cold. A skin of ice, which had been welded by the tempest to one side of his garments, now began to fall away and melt on the floor.

I stepped towards the fire, so that the frozen being might see me better, thinking that perhaps he was unaware that I was, at that time, in residence.

"Welcome, stranger." When I spoke, I found my voice hoarse and high of pitch, so long was it since I had uttered a word to any living soul. "Welcome," I repeated, coughing first to clear my throat.

Without speaking, and with one trembling hand, the frozen traveller slowly slid back the soiled hood covering its face; and for the second time that morning I was astonished.

For my uninvited guest was a young woman.

After an hour she wordlessly accepted and drank some of the broth I had heated above the fire. I sat opposite to her and watched her through the flames as she shuddered and shivered away the last lingering chill that must have penetrated to her very soul. Her hunched shoulders visibly relaxed, as did her bent back. Her bone-white fingers clutching the soup bowl regained some of their natural flexibility. I saw all this, but it was her face to which my attention returned. She was noble of feature, with clear, pale skin; beneath heavy eyebrows, large, dark eyes gleamed despondently. Her cheekbones were high and her nose wide, as were her lips. She had her long black hair tied at the back.

She spoke at last, and her voice was pleasing to my ear.

"I am Olwyn," she told me. "And you?"

I hesitated. Though months had elapsed since the awful day, whose events I strove to forget, I paused to give my true name. The guilty are rarely fogotten.

"Lleu," I said, lying. And eager to know the reason for her travail to this neglected region, I continued, "You have obviously tormented yourself to the point of death reaching this place! To make such a pilgrimage in this weather . . .?"

"Were you at the battle of Arderydd?" she asked, ignoring my comments.

Her question stung me more than she could know, but of course I kept my emotions concealed.

"Why do you ask? It was many months ago and most would rather forget . . ."

"*Tell me*," she demanded. Her eyes became fierce with an inner light, but it was not an anger she aimed in my direction.

"Yes. I was," I confessed.

"They say," Olwyn continued, "That king Gwenddolau was a fool to trust the shaman in his dotage."

My heart shook with grief and horror at her words. My king, my patron, had been slain at Arderydd, by his Christianized foe, King Rhydderch. Even so, Gwenddolau's blood was on *my* hands.

"You seem to have much knowledge of the defeat of

Gwenddolau," I said, struggling to maintain a voice measured and without sentiment. "Were you a fighter?"

"No." She spat into the fire and there was a sizzling explosion behind her next words. "My husband was."

I guessed the rest. "He was slain too," I said, thinking that perhaps only now had she succumbed to the need to sojourn to a sacred place, where she might mourn his passing.

"In my arms he died. He lived to tell the battle's tale, lived close to death for three months. Yet he rallied and seemed to recover a little from his wounds, and I rejoiced. But after our love was consummated anew, he faded . . . and never awoke to express his love again. Barely a month has passed since."

"I lament for you in your distress. But it is right that you speak of your husband. I can see that you have remained silent for too long. There will be solace in talking about him." Carefully, I then asked her, "What else did he tell you of Arderydd?"

Olwyn sat for a while, her eyes roving the fire, yellow miniatures of the flames reflected in those melancholy orbs. Wiping the dirty sleeve of her ragged coat across her eyes, to stem the first wellspring of tears, she made to speak, but stopped herself.

She was dwelling upon her husband, but try as I might to deflect my own thoughts to that subject, instead the sound of battle clamoured through my brain. The field of Arderydd, soaked in blood; Liddel Water running with blood; Gwenddolau's fortress hard by . . . splattered with blood . . .

After a while, she said, "They say *he* was a giant. But ancient."

I knew of whom she spoke. Her mind nagged at the failure of the shaman as her tongue might continually prod the iron-taste cavity of a pulled tooth. She wanted reasons, answers, redress.

"Myrddin?" I asked in a voice as innocent as I could muster.

"The same. Seven feet tall, eight maybe. My husband said—"

"Did he see him?" I interrupted, and hoped the speed with which I did so would not arouse in her any suspicion. In any event, it was clear her husband had not clapped eyes on Gwenddolau's shaman. Unless legend had fooled him into shortsightedness!

"My husband said he was a giant. That he carried sorcery like a cloak about him, but he was very old. At the end, how bitter was my man for the faith he placed in him!"

"Yes, he was elderly," I conceded. "Many centuries. And actually wise for it."

"Those long years weakened him." Her voice was waspish, yet she spoke with assurance, as if she knew her words captured the truth. And I was stabbed to the heart with how perceptive indeed they were.

"Perhaps it was not Myrddin's great age that sapped him of his powers. Perhaps it was the Romans and their priests . . . The new faith has made us all weak. Hadrian may have built his wall to protect his empire from the thirteen kings of the north, but still the Christians ventured beyond it, and their miasma has swept aside many of our kind."

Olwyn replied bitterly, "There were heroic stories, of Myrddin. How could a few Christians defeat the one who raised the stones and made them fly? And who nurtured King Arthur to greatness?"

"Those accomplishments were many years ago," I responded angrily. She could not have guessed why, though perhaps she wondered at the harshness of my response.

"What of Myrddin? You seek him too, eh? Else why are you here, living a hermit's life? This was his place, you know it!"

The conversation had moved on. "Do you then seek him also?" I asked.

"To . . . to *kill* . . . perhaps."

Ah, she wished to avenge her husband. How her anguish stained me. The battle of Arderydd had been fought on the pinnacle of my confident predictions, on the promise of the gathering of a spiritual host who, emerging from a supernatural vapour I raised, would take Gwenddolau's forces through to Rhydderch's mere human host . . . and defeat them. But the Celtic spirits failed to materialize and the bodies on the field of Arderydd were those of the army that marched with Gwenddolau. I saw again, in my mind's eye, as the sounds of the dying lay hidden by the fog, the hill behind the fortress rise out of the mist at day's end. The setting sun gleamed on the row of stakes and human skulls I had raised there. And those death's heads glowered down with a vengeful and bloody light upon Arderydd.

And of the druid Myrddin? Should I tell her that I went mad that day? Did she need to know that I had slunk from the field in dishonour? Wounded I might have been, exhausted and scarred from innumerable fights with the enemy, but in disgrace and raving.

"To kill?" My response was sheathed in a haze of self-loathing which, before my eyes, became a wall of congealing blood. "Myrddin is already dead!" Oh how the agony of that desire drove my sad reminiscences to their height.

"*Dead?* How do you know, old man?"

Reply I could not, without admitting the grossness of my deception. Yet, to me, it was a falsehood of little measure, for in myself I *was* surely without life. And if Olwyn murdered me, what satisfaction could she gain for her husband? The satisfaction would, indeed, be all mine.

"His spirit . . . died in the battle."

"You play with words, Lleu," she replied. "Are you Myrddin's servant? Why else are you here, in his cave, if not to await the return of the shaman?"

My voice was lost. I stared at the embers of the fire and the glowing timbers mesmerized me as I sunk deeper and deeper in despair.

"*Old fool!*" Olwyn jumped up, turned on her heel and stormed out of the cave.

I stared at the place where she had sat and realized there were her shoes, which she had removed in order to dry them. A wisp of steam drifted from the sodden fabric as I stood up to follow her.

I found Olwyn on the crag which watched over the valley, her bare feet buried in the snow. Her arms were hugged around her and the wind was visibly bending her towards the cliff's edge. Lunging through the snow I came within spitting distance of the strong-willed woman.

Turning to face me, she said, "*You!* I should have realized at once. *You are Myrddin!*"

I watched as her voice fought against the growing tempest. "I cannot kill you now, though my heart aches for revenge. You are too wretched a creature. You are ugly and a dwarf. My husband must have been bewitched."

And all the rest of those brave fighters too, I added to myself.

Did I see into her mind, or did I guess, that Olwyn, having failed to find the courage to murder me, intended to cast herself from the bluff? She shuffled her feet forwards and the slope of loose snow began to carry her towards the precipice. Her arms spiralled, but not to save herself. Instead they tried to propel her the faster, to bring this day to an end for her forever.

I lunged forwards but stumbled into the snow. As a flurry of snow billowed before my eyes, Olwyn tilted out of sight.

Impotently I raged against the stag and the wolf who had presaged these events. And I called to book the spirits of the dead who had failed to ignite Gwenddolau's men in battle fury, cursing them for deserting their charges. And thereby causing yet one more death this day.

After lying in the snow for a short time I lifted myself up, and followed the footprints of Olwyn to the edge of the crag. Peering down through the howling tempest I saw the stag that had earlier visited me. He was nimbly climbing a narrow ledge of rock that had been laid bare by the wind. Lying across his back, and clinging on with the determination of one who has recently seen death face-to-face, was Olwyn.

The stag reached the top of the bluff and as Olwyn slipped from his hide, he trotted off into the trees. Quickly, but with some difficulty, I carried the half-conscious woman to the cave. As I approached, a wolf – I have no doubt it was the same as I had before seen – came out of the entrance and sloped away.

Once inside and by the fire, I saw the blood and the still warm body of the hare the wolf had left us. That night I roasted it and the hot meat helped revive Olwyn.

"You saved my life," she cried with humility.

Not I, I thought.

"You are truly Lord of the Wild Hunt, Myrddin. If he had seen what happened this day, my husband would surely agree!"

It had been so many years. So many and I had forgotten that the animals of the forest are sometimes bid by my unconscious desires. I knew then that the magic was returned to me.

I gazed upon the woman, conscious of a wonderful certainty beyond her afflicted features. And I knew that the magic of prophecy was also restored to me as a luminous revelation made my eyes bright with tears of joy. The wolf and the stag were an omen of death, *my* death, not long hence, but my *soul* was to be recast nevertheless. And my next utterance was bold with the foreknowledge, and with unrestrained euphoria.

"Eat well and gain strength, Olwyn," I said. "For you are pregnant with your husband's child."

THE DEATH OF NIMUË

ESTHER FRIESNER

Esther Friesner (b. 1951) is known for her humorous novels, which include the Demon series, Here Be Demons *(1988),* Demon Blues *(1989) and* Hooray for Hellywood *(1990), and a wonderful Victorian romp,* Druid's Blood *(1988). Here, though, she gives a more serious and poignant treatment to the final denouement of the relationship between Merlin and Nimuë.*

"Are we there yet, child?" asked the old woman. Her eyes, once blue and bottomless as the waters of the holy lake, were filmed with age. She rested her ringless hand on her guide's slim shoulder, feeling with satisfaction the thick silk of the younger woman's cloak. *By my power,* she said inwardly. *Mine.*

"I think so, Mother," came the reply. She was small, the old woman's daughter, but straight as a poplar, her pearly face framed in a tangle of blue-black curls. Her mother named her Raven; the last-born, the best-loved. "You said it was an oak?"

"An oak, aye. You would not mistake it, once having seen it. Here, take my eyes, child."

The old woman laid her hands across her sightless eyes, then groped for her daughter's face. Obediently the girl tilted back her head to receive her mother's soft fingertips across her eyelids. The old woman felt the thick lashes kiss her hands like frightened butterflies. Sunlight fell greet through the arched branches. The forest was heavy with summer, thick with the earth-smells, the old, familiar calls from root and fruit and flower. Under the moss, hidden in the shadows of a vixen's cub-filled lair, half-dreaming in the murmur of a running stream, the voices sang. *Come away Oh, come away* But the old woman would not listen and the young one could not hear.

"I see it now," said Raven, gently removing her mother's hands. The old woman's skin was papery soft, like the petals of a dying briar rose. Strands of gray hair escaped the loose confinement of her woolen mantle, green as the distant sea. Once, her hair had been a golden net to snare and bind. Now she used other means.

"Then find it, my love. I am tired."

Raven replaced her mother's ringless hand on her shoulder. A stray shaft of sun pierced the leafy canopy to dance and die along the polished length of the old woman's staff. Black and thick, a ring of silver crowned it, and the hand holding it wore a ring whose stone had been wrenched from the living heart of a wave. "Come," said Raven. "We're almost there."

The oak tree stood ageless. Red deer came to drink from a crystal spring welling at its roots. Gray squirrels and their quarrelsome red cousins darted in and out among its branches, and the white ghost eyes of mistletoe glowed faintly from between its leaves. Raven stopped, taking in the tree with her eyes, trying to read its secrets. Patiently the older woman waited. A sigh shook Raven's shoulders. All she could see was a large oak, matching the image her mother's magic had planted in her brain; for Raven, alone, only a tree like many other trees.

"We are here," breathed Nimuë. She released her daughter and began to feel out the terrain with her staff. "Yes, yes, here is the spring – I hear the water bubbling! And here the roots should surge up suddenly, like a giant's knee – ah! So they still do, after all this time. Now come here, my child. Come and tell me, do you see a place where the moss doesn't grow? Look near the roots on the far side of the bole and tell me."

The younger woman looked and found a slab of stone. Wood violets fringed its steely edge, but its surface was bare; nothing dared grow there.

"I see it, Mother. Does it mark – his place? Was it here—?" Raven faltered. Old, old tales told to her in the cradle returned, stories of when her mother was still young and hungering for the power. Remembered firelight danced in Nimuë's eyes as she leaned close to breathe secrets to her child.

"His place, aye, the place where I lured and left him. He was a husk, sucked dry of all magic. I was ripe with it. I could feel it swelling my blood, throbbing beneath my skin. You have many sisters, Raven, but not one of all my brood ever strained so strongly, ever demanded birth so urgently as the magic I drank from that sad old man." She sighed and brushed memories away from her sightless eyes. "I will raise the stone now," she said.

The silver-crowned staff touched the rock almost casually. The older woman murmured words in strange cadence, her rod scraping an answering music from the stone. The violets trembled, and their scent filled Raven's head as the stone yawned back, crushing them, releasing darkness.

"Old man! Come out, old man!" called Nimuë. Echoing blackness replied. "Merlin awake! The sleep I laid on you is done. Come out into the daylight again and take back what I would give you freely."

Raven edged closer to the lip of the pit. Shallow steps cut from the earth itself descended into lightlessness. Drafts of air from below blew strangely dry and warm, without a trace of mold or corruption. Nothing answered Nimuë's call. The women waited.

At last the old woman lost patience. She flailed her staff high overhead and brought it down hard on the tilted stone. Blue-white lightnings arched and crackled.

"*Merlin, come!*" Her summons was a treble shriek. "By every power I or you ever held, I command you!" The lightnings wreathed themselves around her silver head, then plummeted into the crypt, filling it with a momentary flash of starfire.

Raven thought it was a bat. Its wings were gray as ashes, but their leathery shape was more proper to a monstrous butterfly. Wisps of snowy hair trailed its flights as it rose out of the shadows. "Well, Nimuë," its voice creaked, "how long?"

"Long enough," replied the old woman. "Long enough for me to have all I wanted from your magic. Now I return it to you. I release you from the spell of sleeping. Now it is my turn to sleep."

The gray creature chuckled, a musty sound that made Raven feel winter's chill early, even under summer branches. "Ever the same, eh Nimuë? Age cannot change us that much. Still you see no desires beyond your own. But this time, my love, you shall not have them. You cannot force magic back, once drawn off. It is yours, my magic; yours until time's end!" The nightmare wings flapped wide in exultation. Raven cried out, revolted as they caressed her cheek in passing flight.

Nimuë's lips went thin. She clutched her staff with both hands and ground it into the soil. "You will take it back, Merlin," she said fiercely. "I had powers of my own before yours. I can compel—"

"Nothing," answered the thing. "I am beyond your world of spells and conjurings. Only the willing vessel can hold magic to the brim. Oh, I waited long for you, sweet Nimuë! I waited long for one fool enough to desire my powers. Little by little I fed them to you, and you were proud, thinking you tricked a doting old man. But who is the trickster now? Who – seeing the marks of sorcery on your face – will ever believe magic is a prize? Farewell, Nimuë! Rest will never come to your bed." It soared once, then fell like a comet into the dark.

And Nimuë wept by the side of Merlin's tomb. She sat among the violets and wept like a poor, tired old woman. The dark staff lay beside her as her hands caught the tears.

"Mother?" Raven's arms were around her. "Mother, don't cry."

"I will never rest. Never!" wailed the sorceress, pulling away from her daughter's embrace. "He said what I have suspected for many ages. I am the power's slave, now and forever. Who but a fool would ever enter slavery half so willingly as I?"

"Don't cry," said Nimuë's daughter. "You will rest." She stroked her mother's hair. "I will accept the power."

Nimuë's hand fluttered for her child's face. Raven took it and pressed it to her cool lips. "No." The old woman shook her head violently. "Not you."

"Give it to me, Mother. I can bear it. And I will be wise enough, when the time comes, to rid myself of the burden." She held her mother's hand more tightly. "Mother, give me what I was born to have!"

The sorceress's hands broke free to trace the contours of Raven's face, while in her rheumy eyes there seemed to glow a spark of long-lost sight. The squirrels, frightened by the stone slab's strange rising, returned to their branches. At last, Nimuë said only, "Yes," and with a dry kiss she breathed all magic into her daughter's body.

"Now I can go," she said. She left her staff, her green mantle, and her emerald ring in the grass. Her steps were firm as any sighted woman's. She descended the earthen stair with the grace of a queen newly come into her inheritance. Raven watched until the gray head was no more than a lone star, floating down into the heart of the world.

Then the power took her. Ring and staff leaped into her hand like living things, and the blue mantle wrapped itself around her. She screamed with the burning of it, the green balefire now invading her. Merlin was there, branding her inner eye with his image, wresting from a hellspawn the same powers she now controlled and contained. Nimuë was there, still young, still beautiful, drinking the magic greedily from Merlin's body. And the chain of power stretched back, back, each possessor eager to tear it from its former vessel, each eager to add his own measure of ambition to the hoard. Raven's eyes burned. She struck out against the ghosts with her silver-tipped staff, and they scattered. Then she sank down beneath the oak tree.

The grove was quiet.

They came to her there. They came, the small voices. The slab of gray stone drifted softly back into place, the crushed wildflowers bloomed unharmed, and the voices came. She heard them singing, whispering, welcoming, and the fire inside her was gone. A sweetness of cool waters filled her, healed her eyes. The magic stirred inside her; she smiled a waiting mother's smile.

On her hand the ring glowed pure and white as the luster of a unicorn's horn. The staff she took up rivaled it for whiteness. Her black hair gleamed against the filmy blue of her mantle, and in her eyes she held all the mysteries of birth and renewal, life, and creation out of love. She sang, and the voices answered.

Raven knelt on the slab and gently stroked the seamed rock, seeking a face she loved. "Sleep well, Mother," she whispered. "If you – if any before you – had come into the power as I have, you would never have come to see magic as a curse. You saw its shine and wanted it as a child wants every shiny thing it sees. But I heard its music. Farewell."

And the song on her lips was the song of true enchantment as Nimuë's daughter retraced her steps to the sea.

THE KNIGHT OF PALE COUNTENANCE

DARRELL SCHWEITZER

Darrell Schweitzer (b. 1952) is an American writer and critic and the award-winning former editor of Weird Tales. *His books include* We Are All Legends *(1981),* The White Isle *(1990) and* Transients and Other Disquieting Stories *(1992). For this book Darrell tackled the very difficult area of the birth and death of Merlin. One legend relates that Merlin was born an old man and throughout life grew younger until, as a babe, he was reborn again as an old man. Darrell succeeded admirably in translating that into a story. Until the last moment I had planned for this story to open the anthology, but somehow that threw us deep into the mystical legend of Merlin a little too early. So instead here we are in Merlin's final days.*

When the Saxons came to burn the church and school, I had only a moment's warning. I awoke in darkness. The other boys were already shoving one another and shouting in panic, but I kept my head and ran to the scriptorium to save the most precious thing in the world: my book. I shoved it into a bag with a handful of pens and a stoppered jug of ink. It seemed a crazy thing to do, even at the time, considering that this "book" was only a few pages of used parchment onto which I had painstakingly transcribed a passage of Seneca I didn't understand, but Father Bernard had complimented me on my letters and said I would be a fine scribe some day; and the book was *mine*, something I had created, the only beautiful thing I had ever owned and I wasn't going to let it perish.

So I saved it and ran outside into the night. The church was already aflame. I almost tripped, and jumped clumsily over something which I only half recognized as a corpse in a priest's robe. It might even have been Father Bernard. I never knew.

The darkness was filled with screaming, racing figures, Saxons on horseback and on foot, already beginning to round people up; like devils behind the gleaming face-masks of their helmets, laughing as they forced the priests to kneel in a row and chopped off their heads with great war-axes.

Someone had an arm around me, but I wriggled, bit hard, kicked, and was free. I ran across the muddy, half-frozen fields, rattling against old stalks. Only then did I realize how desperately ridiculous was my predicament. I'd saved my book, yes, but it was winter and I might have to run and hide for days and I had no provisions or cloak or even shoes.

The monastery's thatched roof went up with a *whoosh*. I turned to watch, shivering, gasping for cold, hard breath, clutching my bag as sparks spread across the sky like stars.

Someone bumped into me. I screamed and flailed. Then I saw it was a priest. He had blood on his face, but I knew him, Father Caius, our stern teacher of rhetoric. He didn't seem to know me, though. He staggered around in circles.

I caught him by the arm. "Father! It's me, Perry!"

He shook his head. "Peregrinus, we are judged. It is the end of the world!"

"No! We have to get away!"

"We are weighed in the balance and found wanting—"

"Come away! Please!"

I dragged him and he allowed himself to be led. I think we ran for hours, across the empty fields, into the forest which in the terror of that night became as trackless and impenetrable as some forest at the world's edge. We splashed through a frigid stream, then emerged briefly into the open to cross a road. I glanced fearfully one way, then the other, and hauled Father Caius across into the woods on the other side, and the darkness closed around us for what seemed like forever.

"It is the end of the world!" said Father Caius, raving like someone in a deep fever. I supposed it was his wound.

An ancient, crescent moon was rising as we came to the shore of a lake. The water rippled, silver, then dark, then silver again. I pulled Father Caius down to sit on a rock while I tried to tell where he was hurt. I set my book-bag down carefully, then dipped the corner of my sleeve into the water and washed the Father's face.

He brushed me away. "I'm all right."

I dropped to my knees then, trembling violently, resting my face in his lap as if I were a small child, clinging to him. It was a kind of release. Only then could I allow myself to acknowledge how cold and tired I was, how scared. My feet were burning, almost numb. I gasped hoarsely for breath, trying to hold back sobs.

Father Caius held onto my shoulders and rocked gently back and forth, saying nothing.

Then I chanced to look up and gaze along the lake shore. For just an instant, I thought it was a huge, gleaming fish beached there, but, no, it was a man.

"Father, look!"

"God's mercy, we have work to do yet."

We both got up and hurried over to where an armored man lay on his back in the moonlight, only halfway out of the water. His helmet had fallen off and I could see that his face was very pale.

"Is he dead?" I asked.

Father Caius knelt and examined him. "No, but he will be soon."

"Can't we do anything for him?"

"Only convey his soul into the next world."

Suddenly the man's eyes snapped open and he grabbed me by the ankle with surprising strength, so hard it hurt.

"You, boy! You! I have seen you in the magic glass! You are the one who is to hear my tale!"

I struggled but couldn't get loose. I looked to Father Caius. "What's he talking about?"

The priest shook his head. "I don't know. He must be delirious."

"*You must hear my tale!*"

I broke free. The man seemed to have fainted.

"Help me drag him out of the water," said Father Caius, and we two dragged the stranger into the shelter of the trees to hide him in case any Saxons came this way. I ran back into the open once, to recover my bag.

We prayed over the wounded man that night, then slept a little, clinging to him and to one another for warmth. I dreamt of the world going up in flames, and of red and white dragons writhing in those flames, the red devouring the white.

In the morning twilight, the air was a little warmer, but I could still see my breath.

"Father Caius?"

Suddenly the wounded man was awake. He caught me by the arm.

"You, boy. I know you are the one I saw. How old are you?"

"Thirteen . . . I think." In truth I did not know, because I did not remember my birth any more than I remembered my parents, and so was guessing.

"Good enough. You are almost a man, but will live for a long time yet. And you are a learned clerk. You must write my tale in a book so that all men may know it. This is very important."

I gulped and looked down at my bag, which contained, indeed, sufficient materials to write the man's tale. I was terrified then, for I knew some great force was at work, but I didn't know if this was God's doing or the Devil's.

Father Caius stirred beside us. He examined the man's wound again in the light. The warrior's mail-shirt was torn and broken. The whole of the garment underneath was soaked in blood.

"I think you had better confess your sins and be absolved," Father Caius told him, "and forget about telling stories."

But the man rolled away from him, dragging me.

"*No!* It can't *wait!*" he said. Father Caius crossed himself, shocked. The man strained to grab my bag with his free hand, as if he knew what was in it. When I reached for it, he let go of me, and I got it. I opened my precious book in my lap and got out my pens and the jug of ink. I would have to scribble in the margins and between the lines of Seneca, ruining the effect of my calligraphy. So be it.

"Make it *true*," the man said. "Make it *real* and . . ." His head fell back and he uttered a long sigh ". . . and make it beautiful. Please do this for me."

"I'll try."

Father Caius looked on disapprovingly.

The wounded man began to speak rapidly, sometimes incomprehensibly, his tale filled with strange names and turns of language, and I could only approximate, almost guess, sometimes make up what I thought he meant; but he didn't seem to care. If I tried to read something back to him he just went on, his torrent of words like water rushing over rocks. Somehow it felt, and he knew, that the act of writing made it all *true:*

What was his name and what was his quest?
Merlin knew.
And how got he his terrible wound?
Merlin knew that too, but wasn't telling.

Call him the Knight of Pale Countenance. I never knew his name,
but pale he was indeed during those long months, or perhaps years, as
the poison seeped slowly through his body and he knew that he was
dying; yet he could not die, not yet, for Merlin had a task remaining
for him to perform.

In dream or delirium or both, he beheld Merlin, greatest of all
magicians, seated on the stone lip of a pool in some ruined garden,
reaching into the stagnant water to touch the reflection, not of Merlin,
but of the Knight of Pale Countenance.

And the knight cried out at the touch as if he had been branded
with an iron. Merlin, in the dream, jerked back, startled. He raised
his hand, and a huge black bird swooped down to alight on his wrist.
You'd expect a merlin, the kind of falcon after which he is named, but
no, it was a raven, battlefield feaster, harbinger of death. The magician
whispered into the bird's ear, then heaved the creature aloft.

And the Knight of Pale Countenance awoke in his pain, finding
himself on horseback, the raven circling overhead, around and around,
slowly, slowly. Later, it rested on his shoulder and whispered to him
in a human voice of death and the terrors of the grave, but also of the
worldly glory of chivalry, which burned like brilliant fire in the heart.

He could remember that. The fire had not quite gone out, for all his
weariness and pain.

Through hollow lands and bone lands, through thigh-deep, frigid
dust, through forests haunted by crouching, half-remembered, faceless
pagan gods—

"This is all rubbish," said Father Caius suddenly. "It may even
be the Devil's rubbish."

"Father *please . . .*" Somehow I knew it wasn't rubbish at all, but
more true than anything. As the knight's fire burned within his
heart, I had this, as if a fit had come upon me: a story fit, a kind of
prophecy. Yet even then I was still afraid, for this prophecy might
not be from God. The fellow had refused to be shriven, after all.
The Devil's rubbish, gleaming like gold.

"Sometimes my strength comes back to me," the knight said.
"The poison goes to sleep, and I have hope. That is one more
torment I must endure. I seem to awaken as if from a terrible

dream. I rise, like a swimmer far underwater, nearing the surface, not quite able to reach the light. I flare up, the way a candle does, just before it goes out. Write that down, boy. Quickly."

I scribbled in the margin: *As a candle's flame . . .*

The knight laughed softly, as if he'd told a joke. I didn't understand. He continued ". . . and in my flaming moments, I have killed giants by the score, heaping them up like logs, and, oh yes, more than my share of Saxons. But sometimes I hear another's hoofbeats and turn to see death riding by my side on a horse the color of white smoke, and he leans over and whispers to me through lipless teeth, in the friendliest terms, as if we were comrades on a long campaign together. And that damned bird, shrieking—"

Just then a bird *did* shriek somewhere in the branches above us, and I let out a little yelp of abject terror.

Father Caius put his hand on my shoulder and heaved himself to his feet. "This is all lunacy, but if it comforts him, let him have his lunacy. There is no harm or power in words. Now I have things I must do. I'll be back shortly."

The Father departed, leaving the world turned upside down. Nothing made sense. I didn't understand how he could have said such a thing. Sometimes words are all we have. Prayers. *Story.* The story is the world and the world is the story, more powerful than anything. Ask a bard if you don't believe me. *In the beginning was the Word—*

But I didn't have to understand. That wasn't my task. I was there merely to transcribe, to relate the tale with flourish. Let the meaning rise to the surface as it would, like bubbles in a murky pond.

"I was tempted three times," the knight said. "Get that down. *Three times.*"

"Three," I said, scribbling.

"I went mad once, howling in my pain like an animal, cursing God and cursed by him, who caused me to dwell naked among cattle on a hillside, grazing on grass. But the voice of Merlin's raven awakened me—"

I glanced up into the branches once more, in dread. But the breeze merely stirred them, rattling dry leaves.

"What was I saying?" the knight asked.

"You were tempted three times."

"Write this down. Shape it. *Make* it, for that's what you are, the *maker*, if you tell my tale after I am gone—"

In the evening, the Knight of Pale Countenance came to the curving shore of the lake. There he paused to drink, but as he stooped down the blood of his wound poured out, polluting the water until it was dark and smooth like a mirror. He gazed down into the water at his reflection, and at first, saw only his paindrawn face, but then beheld a monstrous serpent lurking in the mud.

The creature stirred. It broke the surface and reared up, as tall as a tower, its flickering tongue like a sword of living fire.

"Will you fight with me, Sir Knight?" The monster's voice cracked like thunder in the gathering darkness.

"Most surely," replied the Knight of Pale Countenance, drawing his sword and taking up his shield, "for I know that you are my enemy, sent by the Devil."

"Is not the serpent one of God's creatures? Doesn't it say in the holy books that the Devil lacks the power to create anything?"

The two of them joined battle for an hour, two hours, three, beneath the brilliant stars, wading in the shallows of the mirrored lake. Sometimes the serpent was a huge warrior clad in scaly armor, wielding a sword of fire, or many burning spears and swords all at once, as if he had a hundred arms.

At the third hour of the night, they paused, the knight leaning on his shield, gasping in pain and exhaustion, the serpent coiling over itself in the mud.

"You still have your courage," said the monster.

"Aye, that," said the knight, "but nothing else."

"And your pride. You have fought impressively. But it is useless. Yield to me. I will make you whole."

"No," said the knight. "Though I am the most wretched of men, I shall not yield."

Merlin's raven circled overhead, the stars winking as it passed in front of them.

The monster reared up once more. The knight raised his sword and shield, and the contest continued until the ancient, crescent moon drifted above the treetops and the serpent-thing paused to look at it. The knight thought he saw an opening and made to strike, but hesitated when the serpent spoke.

"That is false hope. No man may touch the moon, nor slow her journey across the sky. Some things you cannot conquer. Therefore

yield to me. I will allow you to know love. I'll give you happiness. Yield."

But the knight would not yield, and still the two of them fought, the serpent-creature assuming many forms, each more terrible than the last, screaming with all the voices of Hell. But the knight's courage did not fail him, though he recognized it as the courage of desperation, not virtue.

When dawn came, the serpent spoke for a third time.

"Merely yield, and be free of pain. Give it up. Rest."

The knight hesitated then, weeping, and, quick as a whiplash, the serpent wound its coils around his legs, until it rested its huge head at his feet like a faithful dog. He would have yielded then, and fallen asleep, but Merlin's raven cried out, and he snapped awake, and struck off the monster's head.

Father Caius returned. Somewhere he'd found a ragged blanket – it smelled like a horsecloth and probably was – for me to wrap around myself, and more rags, some of them bloody, for me to tie around my feet. Better still, so convenient and unexpected it seemed almost a miracle, he'd found a small, two-wheeled cart, to which a donkey had undoubtedly once been harnessed. Now he could pull it if he had to.

I helped him load the wounded knight into the cart.

Father Caius took the knight's hand in his own and said, "Now, my friend, let me hear your confession before it's too late."

The knight stirred and moaned.

"Will you pray with me?" Father Caius asked. To me he whispered, "Now we shall know. A damned man cannot pray."

The knight folded his hands.

Father Caius began to intone in Latin, but then a huge black bird *did* shriek from a nearby branch and the Knight of Pale Countenance heaved himself up, cursing and raving and weeping. Father Caius and I both drew back in momentary fright. The black bird swirled over our heads.

The knight pointed into empty space. "Can't you see him? *There!* It is Death on his pale horse . . ."

The bird cried out.

But Father Caius invoked the name of Jesu, the conqueror of death, and after a while the bird was gone and the knight rested peacefully.

"His hurt is more than a physical injury, I am sure," the Father said. "His very soul is wounded, by sin."

"Yes. He said he was tempted three times."

"What?"

"In the story—"

Father Caius struck me across the face in sudden, astonishing wrath. "Forget about your stupid story! This is no time for idleness. By rights we ought to abandon this fellow and save ourselves, for he will not pray and that means the Devil owns him."

I began to weep. "Please, Father . . ."

His voice and manner softened. He brushed his hand through my hair. "You are right, Perry. Forgive me. We must not abandon him while he yet lives, for there is still a chance he might be saved, whether he tells preposterous tales or not. That is my duty. I have forgotten it and therefore sinned. Forgive me."

I said nothing.

"Besides," said Father Caius, rapping his knuckles against the side of the cart, "God has provided. Nothing God does is without meaning, if only we can discover it."

I was glad then, less, I will admit, for the prospect of saving the knight's soul than the prospect of hearing the rest of his story.

Overhead, Merlin's raven had returned.

Father Caius insisted that I should get into the cart and he would pull both of us. "Because I am a beast and you are my burden," he said, which was crazy; so I refused, stowed only my bag in the cart, and the two of us dragged the Knight of Pale Countenance along the shore of the lake until we found a path. We followed the path until about midday, when the forest ended and we came to a burned-out farmhouse. We rested there and drank from a well, but went hungry, for we had no provisions. The water tasted of soot. Still the black bird circled overhead. Either Father Caius did not see it or he pretended not to notice it.

Later that afternoon we joined a column of refugees streaming westward along one of the paved, Roman roads. Most were ragged, silent people, a lot of them old women, but there was also a mother who had gone mad. She cradled the black-faced corpse of her baby in her arms, singing to it softly through her tears, as if it were still alive and might wake up.

Father Caius turned away from her. I stared, then looked at the ground as I struggled with the cart.

We marched past a battlefield, strewn with corpses and thick with crows.

"It's all rubbish," Father Caius said. "The Devil's offal. The end of the world."

I looked at him in hopeless terror then, for if he despaired, it had to be the end of the world after all. There was no help anywhere.

The woman kept on singing as we passed more ruined farmhouses and came to a burning town. No one was alive there. The fires were nearly out.

"The Devil's offal," said Father Caius.

I tried to tell myself it was his wound. He was still dazed. I wept for him, and prayed. That cold march seemed to go on forever. The afternoon would not end. Time had stopped.

Then the Knight of Pale Countenance suddenly sat up in the back of the cart, shouting that he knew the answer, that Britain would not only be saved but made glorious. It was all in his tale.

Father Caius pushed him back down into the cart and commanded him to be still. About then, twenty or so British horsemen galloped by, armorless men with painted shields and round, military caps, the *bucellarii* of some rich lord. They paid no attention to us and we ignored them.

The Saxons attacked again just after sundown, horsemen in their demon-masked helmets streaming out of the woods, cleaving their way through the refugees like reapers among wheat. I saw the mad woman's baby hurled through the air. Everyone was screaming and running; and the Saxons circled around and around, laughing, as I climbed into the cart and tried to get out the Pale Knight's sword.

But Father Caius caught hold of me and hauled me to the ground. He looked strange. It took me a moment to realize that the top of his head had been sheared off. He was trying to say something, but blood and brains streamed down over his face, splattering me. He collapsed, dragging me down on top of him in a heap.

Everything has meaning, if only we can find it. In that instant, I could only guess. I called out, not to God, but to Merlin, shouting that the story was in danger, that it should not end like this; and then a miracle happened, a prodigy, maybe the delirium of a dream, *and behold, the Knight of Pale Countenance leapt down from the back of the cart and drew sword. His strength had returned to him, and he struck left and right as the laughing Saxons circled him, as their laughter turned to howls, then thudding silence, as he slew them all, his sword flickering like Jove's terrible lightning.*

When it was over, we two stood alone on the road, but for the corpses, and the Saxons lay in a pile all around him, stacked like logs.

And Merlin's raven dropped down onto the Pale Knight's shoulder, and spoke with the voice of a man.

This is the rest of the tale, how the Knight of Pale Countenance was tempted three times but did not yield. Then the serpent-thing told how it had once been a man, called Sir Vorcilak, a mighty champion until pride had transformed him into a monster.

"Only a genuinely holy man can kill me," he said.

"I am a poor sinner," said the Knight of Pale Countenance.

"That is why I am still alive, though you have cut off my head."

The knight took up the monster's head, which had become human in shape, strong-jawed, with black, curly hair, a thick beard, and dark eyes. He stood on the back of the floating serpent body and drifted far out into the lake. A mist rose. Sir Vorcilak's eyes glowed like lanterns, lighting the way.

In the middle of the lake was an island of glass, revealed as the mist parted, whereon stood a glass castle which gleamed a brilliant white by day, darkened to red in the sunset, and mirrored the stars at night. A lady dwelt in that castle; and she came out to greet the Pale Knight and also Sir Vorcilak, who had been her lover once, but had proven as unworthy as her many other lovers, unable to break the enchantment of this place. Her father, a mighty king, had placed her there long before, that no unworthy man should defile her; and there she dwelt for endless centuries, for the years did not touch her in that castle and time did not pass, and the lives of generations swirled past her like water around a rock.

She greeted Sir Vorcilak and kissed him, then placed his still-living head atop a pillar to guard the isle and warn all who came near that only a true hero could set foot there and come away unwounded.

And she tempted the Knight of Pale Countenance for a fourth time, leading him into her bedchamber, where she showed him two mirrors the size of large books, one hidden beneath a folding cover of horn, the other beneath ivory.

She opened one – but no one who was not there can say which one – and said, "This is the Glass of Seeing, in which the deeds of famous men are revealed, past and to come."

Together they sat before the glass and beheld Troy town newly built, and again Troy when it was burnt; and they saw Brutus the Trojan first reach the shores of Britain and win the isle, hurling giants into the sea one by one. Julius Caesar likewise appeared, and Alexander, and other heroes of great worship.

The knight beheld them with delight, and the lady said to him, "But what are the deeds of men, but strivings to fill the time before they all go down to death, king and poor man alike, lord and slave? All these things are just shadows in my glass. But I have seen you in my glass and brought you into my chamber, because I would have you lie with me and take me for your wife. Then shall you dwell here at my side, always at your ease in my glass castle and crystal garden, where nothing ages or changes or dies and there is no pain. Here you merely watch the world. You are not a part of it. Even your sins do not matter anymore, for where past and future are as one and there is no passage of time, then the time of your sinning has never occurred. You are as free from guilt as you are from fear and sorrow. Tarry with me then, forever."

The Knight of Pale Countenance was greatly tempted. He spoke of his duty, but the lady said merely, "Nay," and laughed as if he had said something ridiculous. He tried to speak again, but she put a finger to his lips and hushed him, as a nursemaid does a small child.

She searched out his wound and touched it with her hands, healing him.

And then, in his weariness, he did lie with her.

Afterwards, he looked into the uncovered glass once more, and saw himself, all his life, and his sins, from beginning to end.

She laughed and snapped the cover shut.

"They're only pictures in a glass," she said. "They don't mean anything, now that we are here."

But he wept, even as Judas wept when he held the silver pieces in his hand, understanding the magnitude of his wrong.

Later, she sang a gentle song to soothe him, to bewitch him; but he sat up angrily in her bed, furious with rage and despair, saying that he had sinned again, unforgivably, even as he had once before. And he rose from the bed, naked. His wound opened, blood pouring over him. Gasping, at the end of his strength, he took up his sword and smashed the Glass of Seeing, then turned to strike off the lady's head.

But she took hold of the blade and turned it gently aside, saying, "Would you murder a damsel who loves you?"

Of course he would not. He struggled to put on his clothing and armor, laboring for a long time in terrible pain. He made to leave.

"But if you will not love me," said she, "I must take another." And she opened the covering of the second glass, just a little way, for it was the Glass of Knowing, wherein the beginning and ending of time itself were contained. To look into it fully would be to see the Earth on the first day of creation, before the waters were parted, and the last day of the world, Judgment; and in both one would inevitably behold the face of God and die at the sight.

But she uncovered the glass only a little way, and one of those demons who would carry off the damned at the Judgment stepped forth into the room and took her in its arms, a giant of living, half-molten iron with a face too brilliant to look upon.

And the knight fled from them, knowing that he had failed in his quest.

The wounded knight and I were alone on the road, surrounded by corpses. He lay back in the cart. It was dawn. Black birds had begun to gather.

I knew that he was truly dying now. He would not rise from the cart again. His blood seeped down over his legs, staining his brazen greaves.

"Please," I said. "You must tell me the rest."

"Write down what you have. Make up the rest. Sometimes not even a story is enough."

"I don't understand."

"Explicate the text, then. You've got an education."

"No, I don't. Not really."

"Then there's nothing for it. Sorry. There's nothing."

I wept again, for a long time, leaning my head against the cart. The day brightened. Once I saw horsemen at the crest of a hill, and I remained very still, clinging to the cart as if draped over it. Whether they were Saxons or not, they must have seen only corpses and didn't come any closer.

Merlin's raven landed on the rim of the cart and said to me, "Ask him about his sin."

I asked, and the knight cursed the bird, swatting at it weakly with one hand, saying that it only wanted to torment him, like twisting a knife in an already fatal wound.

Yet he told me, *how the Knight of Pale Countenance had been brave and true, and loved a lady and was sworn to her. Yet when he was far from her in the midst of the wars, and weary, he rested with another and got a child by her. But the Devil tempted his own lady into cunning despair, and she, through witchcraft, learned of his treason. When he returned home, she greeted him with smiles and prepared a great feast. When he was drowsy with food and drink, she took him into her bed and there stabbed him with a poisoned dagger; but when she saw him bleeding she hurled herself from her window and died, not all at once, but slowly, cursing God, broken on the pavement below.*

In the cart, the Pale Knight seemed to be passing into another delirium, scarcely aware that I was still there. It was well into the afternoon of the second day on the road. I was weak from hunger and from fear, and clung to the edge of the cart, barely able to stand.

"She died," he said. "Went straight to Hell, I suppose. No help for it. Being a knight gets confusing at times."

But I begged him, in the earnest folly of my youth, in all my innocence, to tell me the *true* and proper ending of the tale, how some good might come of all this suffering and Britain might be redeemed.

"Your soul can still be saved. It's never too late." I was beginning to sound like Father Caius, I thought. I wept yet again, at the memory of him. His body lay almost at my feet, with his brains spilled out, gathering flies.

"That too, in the bargain?"

"Yes, that too."

"Then take up your book and write the rest."

Eventually I wrote it all, how the Boy With the Cart found the strength to transport the dying knight back the way he had come, back along the road, past the burning town, the empty farmhouses, and the battlefields; into the dark forest where pagan gods crouched in the shadows beneath the trees, leering and tittering as he went by. But the boy did not tarry. He did not fail in his purpose. He came to the shore of the lake once again. It was midnight. The dark water mirrored the sky. The old moon had just risen.

There, a white mist rose up, and out of the mist came a golden barge with sails of purest silver; and in the barge were maidens clad in gowns the color of the blue morning sky, but their heads were the heads of birds, and they sang sweetly among themselves. They carried the wounded knight into the barge, staining their hands with his blood. They permitted the boy to follow.

Slowly, the barge crossed the lake as the mist parted and the Isle of Glass loomed before them, the castle gleaming like a swarm of brilliant stars. The head of Sir Vorcilak called out from atop its pillar, warning away all who were sinful and unworthy.

I knelt down in the barge and prayed that I would be worthy and that the Knight of Pale Countenance could be redeemed. The bird-women fluttered and chirped like startled sparrows, but they took the knight up in a litter and bore him into the castle.

I followed. We came at last, after many turnings, into the bedchamber of the lady, who was horribly burned from the demon's touch and swollen with the demon's child. Her knight lay down beside her and caressed her and kissed her, hideous as she now was, begging her forgiveness and the forgiveness of all women. While they lay there, she was delivered of her child in a great outpouring of steaming blood.

Merlin the magician stood up at the foot of her bed, his black raven fluttering into his hands, his newly born body man-sized and gnarled, ancient and young at the same time, flames flickering from his fingertips and smoke rising from his mouth and nose as he breathed. Born outside of time, where the years did not pass, it would be his fate to live backward knowing the future as if it were the past, forgetting the past as if it were the unknown future, awesomely powerful at first, youthening, weakening, until he finally ended up under a rock, bound there by a lady who had betrayed him.

He would do much in the meantime. But for good or ill, I wondered. He was a devil's child, after all, born of a woman's despair and a knight's sin.

He stood there glaring at me, his eyes filled with devilish hatred.

But, newly born, ancient and an infant at once, he could not even stand. His limbs spread out in all directions like those of a newborn calf. He fell down into the puddle of his mother's blood. Before he could make any move, I took water from a cup and baptized him, in the name of the Father and of the Son and of the Holy Spirit, and I prayed for his soul, and for the souls of the knight, of both his ladies, and for the whole land of Britain, that the tale might end well at last.

Merlin stood up and wrapped a sheet about himself to cover his nakedness.

Then the weariness of all I had been through overwhelmed me, and I fell down senseless at Merlin's feet. I awoke at dawn by the edge of the lake, lying on my back, clutching my book-bag to my chest. I sat up weakly, feeling light-headed, and saw only trees on the far side of the lake. There was no mist and no Isle of Glass.

"Your tale is preposterous," someone said. "No one will believe a word of it."

I turned, startled and afraid, but also a little indignant.

"It is *true*."

Merlin laughed and helped me to my feet. It was truly the Magician now, clad in a black gown, boots, and a tall cap, leaning on an intricately carven staff which looked like it might come alive at any moment. Its top was shaped like a serpent's head.

"Yes, it is true. But getting people to believe it is something else again."

I didn't understand. He said that didn't matter, yet. He led me a little way along the lake shore and showed me two fresh graves at the forest's edge. I knelt there and prayed for the Knight of Pale Countenance and for the Lady of the Isle of Glass, and resolved to write in my book that those two would whisper their names to one another just before they entered paradise. I, of course, would never know them.

Merlin called a fish out of the water into his hands, and made a fire by snapping his fingers. We two ate, and later he walked with me for a time, speaking many prophecies which he commanded me to write down in a book to be called *The Prophecies of Merlin*; for he knew the beginnings and endings of all stories, even his own. I think he had somehow looked into the Glass of Knowing and survived.

If he knew everything ahead of time, I asked him, couldn't he avoid his doom?

He merely shrugged. "Sorry. There's nothing for it."

He explained that his doom was as necessary as his birth, part of the same pattern. He had seen it all, and, reaching back through time, sending his raven to do his bidding, weaving so many strands together: the knight's sin, his own birth, and my life too, that I might be there to baptize him when he needed it. He had placed the covered two mirrors in the lady's chamber and the cup of water by her bedside. His end grew out of his beginning, as a tree grows out of a seed.

"It's all quite preposterous," he said, "this tale."

But he commanded me to write it down, and many other things also, and I wrote them, naming the names of the heroes to come, and especially of the great king who would make Britain glorious once again. These were my labors as I grew into manhood and journeyed ever eastward, to a place where I would be believed, called Camelot.

THE CASTLE OF KERGLAS

EMILE SOUVESTRE

The tales of Arthur and Merlin became "best sellers" throughout western Europe during the Middle Ages. They soon became inextricably enmeshed with the legends and tales of Brittany where we might claim the real heroic adventures of Arthur and his knights were born, starting with the writings of Chrétien de Troyes in the late twelfth century. It is not unreasonable to say that many of the Breton folk tales owe their origins to some of the same sources as the Arthurian tales. The following story, collected by the French playwright and folklorist Emile Souvestre (1806–54) in Le Foyer Breton *(1844), does not feature Merlin, but it has all the recognizable features of Merlin's world. The hero is Peronnik, a Breton version of Perceval, who was developed by George Moore in his novella* Peronnik the Fool *(1924), which was derived from this story.*

Peronnik was a poor idiot who belonged to nobody, and he would have died of starvation if it had not been for the kindness of the village people, who gave him food whenever he chose to ask for it. And as for a bed, when night came, and he grew sleepy, he looked about for a heap of straw, and making a hole in it, crept in, like a lizard. Idiot though he was, he was never unhappy, but always thanked gratefully those who fed him, and sometimes would stop for a little and sing to them. For he could imitate a lark so well, that no one knew which was Peronnik and which was the bird.

He had been wandering in a forest one day for several hours, and when evening approached, he suddenly felt very hungry. Luckily, just at that place the trees grew thinner, and he could see a small farmhouse a little way off. Peronnik went straight towards it, and found the farmer's wife standing at the door holding in her hands the large bowl out of which her children had eaten their supper.

"I am hungry, will you give me something to eat?" asked the boy.

"If you can find anything here, you are welcome to it," answered she, and, indeed, there was not much left, as everybody's spoon had dipped in. But Peronnik ate what was there with a hearty appetite, and thought that he had never tasted better food.

"It is made of the finest flour and mixed with the richest milk and stirred by the best cook in all the countryside," and though he said it to himself, the woman heard him.

"Poor innocent," she murmured, "he does not know what he is saying, but I will cut him a slice of that new wheaten loaf," and so she did, and Peronnik ate up every crumb, and declared that nobody less than the bishop's baker could have baked it. This flattered the farmer's wife so much that she gave him some butter to spread on it, and Peronnik was still eating it on the doorstep when an armed knight rode up.

"Can you tell me the way to the castle of Kerglas?" asked he.

"To Kerglas? are you *really* going to Kerglas?" cried the woman, turning pale.

"Yes; and in order to get there I have come from a country so far off that it has taken me three months' hard riding to travel as far as this."

"And why do you want to go to Kerglas?" said she.

"I am seeking the basin of gold and the lance of diamonds which are in the castle," he answered. Then Peronnik looked up.

"The basin and the lance are very costly things," he said suddenly.

"More costly and precious than all the crowns in the world," replied the stranger, "for not only will the basin furnish you with the best food that you can dream of, but if you drink of it, it will cure you of any illness however dangerous, and will even bring the dead back to life, if it touches their mouths. As to the diamond lance, that will cut through any stone or metal."

"And to whom do these wonders belong?" asked Peronnik in amazement.

"To a magician named Rogéar who lives in the castle," answered the woman. "Every day he passes along here, mounted on a black mare, with a colt thirteen months old trotting behind. But no one dares to attack him, as he always carries his lance."

"That is true," said the knight, "but there is a spell laid upon him which forbids his using it within the castle of Kerglas. The moment he enters, the basin and lance are put away in a dark cellar which no key but one can open. And *that* is the place where I wish to fight the magician."

"You will never overcome him, Sir Knight," replied the woman, shaking her head. "More than a hundred gentlemen have ridden past this house bent on the same errand, and not one has ever come back."

"I know that, good woman," returned the knight, "but then they did not have, like me, instructions from the hermit of Blavet."

"And what did the hermit tell you?" asked Peronnik.

"He told me that I should have to pass through a wood full of all sorts of enchantments and voices, which would try to frighten me and make me lose my way. Most of those who have gone before me have wandered they know not where, and perished from cold, hunger, or fatigue."

"Well, suppose you get through safely?" said the idiot.

"If I do," continued the knight, "I shall then meet a sort of fairy armed with a needle of fire which burns to ashes all it touches. This dwarf stands guarding an apple-tree, from which I am bound to pluck an apple."

"And next?" inquired Peronnik.

"Next I shall find the flower that laughs, protected by a lion whose mane is formed of vipers. I must pluck that flower, and go on to the lake of the dragons and fight the black man who holds in his hand the iron ball which never misses its mark and returns of its own accord to its master. After that, I enter the valley of pleasure, where some who conquered all the other obstacles have left their bones. If I can win through this, I shall reach a river with only one ford, where a lady in black will be seated. She will mount my horse behind me, and tell me what I am to do next."

He paused, and the woman shook her head.

"You will never be able to do all that," said she, but he bade her remember that these were only matters for men, and galloped away down the path she pointed out.

The farmer's wife sighed and, giving Peronnik some more food, bade him good-night. The idiot rose and was opening the gate which led into the forest when the farmer himself came up.

"I want a boy to tend my cattle," he said abruptly, "as the one I had has run away. Will you stay and do it?" and Peronnik, though he loved his liberty and hated work, recollected the good food he had eaten, and agreed to stop.

At sunrise he collected his herd carefully and led them to the rich pasture which lay along the borders of the forest, cutting himself a hazel wand with which to keep them in order.

His task was not quite so easy as it looked, for the cows had a way of straying into the wood, and by the time he had brought one back another was off. He had gone some distance into the trees, after a naughty black cow which gave him more trouble than all the rest, when he heard the noise of horses' feet, and peeping through the leaves he beheld the giant Rogéar seated on his mare, with the colt trotting behind. Round the giant's neck hung the golden bowl suspended from a chain, and in his hand he grasped the diamond lance, which gleamed like fire. But as soon as he was out of sight the idiot sought in vain for traces of the path he had taken.

This happened not only once but many times, till Peronnik grew so used to him that he never troubled to hide. But on each occasion he saw him the desire to possess the bowl and the lance became stronger.

One evening the boy was sitting alone on the edge of the forest, when a man with a white beard stopped beside him. "Do you want to know the way to Kerglas?" asked the idiot, and the man answered "I know it well."

"You have been there without being killed by the magician?" cried Peronnik.

"Oh! he has nothing to fear from me," replied the white-bearded man, "I am Rogéar's elder brother, the wizard Bryak. When I wish to visit him I always pass this way, and as even I cannot go through the enchanted wood without losing myself, I call the colt to guide me." Stooping down as he spoke he traced three circles on the ground and murmured some words very low, which Peronnik could not hear. Then he added aloud:

> *Colt, free to run and free to eat,*
> *Colt, gallop fast until we meet,*

and instantly the colt appeared, frisking and jumping to the wizard, who threw a halter over his neck and leapt on his back.

Peronnik kept silence at the farm about this adventure, but he understood very well that if he was ever to get to Kerglas he must first catch the colt which knew the way. Unhappily he had not heard the magic words uttered by the wizard, and he could not manage to draw the three circles, so if he was to summon the colt at all he must invent some other means of doing it.

All day long, while he was herding the cows, he thought and thought how he was to call the colt, for he felt sure that once on its back he could overcome the other dangers. Meantime he must be ready in case a chance should come, and he made his preparations at night, when everyone was asleep. Remembering what he had seen the wizard do, he patched up an old halter that was hanging in a corner of the stable, twisted a rope of hemp to catch the colt's feet, and a net such as is used for snaring birds. Next he sewed roughly together some bits of cloth to serve as a pocket, and this he filled with glue and lark's feathers, a string of beads, a whistle of elder wood, and a slice of bread rubbed over with bacon fat. Then he went out to the path down which Rogéar, his mare, and the colt always rode, and crumbled the bread on one side of it.

Punctual to their hour all three appeared, eagerly watched by Peronnik, who lay hid in the bushes close by. Suppose it was useless; suppose the mare, and not the colt, ate the crumbs? Suppose – but no! the mare and her rider went safely by, vanishing round a corner, while the colt, trotting along with its head on the ground, smelt the bread, and began greedily to lick up the pieces. Oh, how good it was! Why had no one ever given it that before, and so absorbed was the little beast, sniffing about after a few more crumbs, that it never heard Peronnik creep up till it felt the halter on its neck and the rope round its feet, and – in another moment – some one on its back.

Going as fast as the hobbles would allow, the colt turned into one of the wildest parts of the forest, while its rider sat trembling at the strange sights he saw. Sometimes the earth seemed to open in front of them and he was looking into a bottomless pit; sometimes the trees burst into flames and he found himself in the midst of a fire; often in the act of crossing a stream the water rose and threatened to sweep him away; and again, at the foot of a mountain, great rocks would roll towards him, as if they would crush him and his colt beneath their weight. To his dying day Peronnik never knew whether these things were real or if he only imagined them, but he pulled down his knitted cap so as to cover his eyes, and trusted the colt to carry him down the right road.

At last the forest was left behind, and they came out on a wide plain where the air blew fresh and strong. The idiot ventured to peep out, and found to his relief that the enchantments seemed to have ended, though a thrill of horror shot through him as he noticed the skeletons of men scattered over the plain, beside the skeletons of their horses. And what were those grey forms trotting away in the distance? Were they – could they be – *wolves*?

But vast though the plain seemed, it did not take long to cross, and very soon the colt entered a sort of shady park in which was standing a single apple-tree, its branches bowed down to the ground with the weight of its fruit. In front was the korigan – the little fairy man – holding in his hand the fiery sword, which reduced to ashes everything it touched. At the sight of Peronnik he uttered a piercing scream, and raised his sword, but without appearing surprised the youth only lifted his cap, though he took care to remain at a little distance.

"Do not be alarmed, my prince," said Peronnik, "I am just on my way to Kerglas, as the noble Rogéar has begged me to come to him on business."

"Begged *you* to come!" repeated the dwarf, "and who, then, are you?"

"I am the new servant he has engaged, as you know very well," answered Peronnik.

"I do not know at all," rejoined the korigan sulkily, "and you may be a robber for all I can tell."

"I am so sorry," replied Peronnik, "but I may be wrong in calling myself a servant, for I am only a bird-catcher. But do not delay me, I pray, for his highness the magician expects me, and, as you see, has lent me his colt so that I may reach the castle all the quicker."

At these words the korigan cast his eyes for the first time on the colt, which he knew to be the one belonging to the magician, and began to think that the young man was speaking the truth. After examining the horse, he studied the rider, who had such an innocent, and indeed vacant, air that he appeared incapable of inventing a story. Still, the dwarf did not feel *quite* sure that all was right, and asked what the magician wanted with a bird-catcher.

"From what he says, he wants one very badly," replied Peronnik, "as he declares that all his grain and all the fruit in his garden at Kerglas are eaten up by the birds."

"And how are you going to stop that, my fine fellow?" inquired the korigan; and Peronnik showed him the snare he had prepared, and remarked that no bird could possibly escape from it.

"That is just what I should like to be sure of," answered the korigan. "My apples are completely eaten up by blackbirds and thrushes. Lay your snare, and if you can manage to catch them, I will let you pass."

"That is a fair bargain," and as he spoke Peronnik jumped down and fastened his colt to a tree; then, stooping, he fixed one end of the net to the trunk of the apple tree, and called to the korigan to hold the other while he took out the pegs. The dwarf did as he was bid, when suddenly Peronnik threw the noose over his neck and drew it close, and the korigan was held as fast as any of the birds he wished to snare.

Shrieking with rage, he tried to undo the cord, but he only pulled the knot tighter. He had put down the sword on the grass, and Peronnik had been careful to fix the net on the other side of the tree, so that it was now easy for him to pluck an apple and to mount his horse, without being hindered by the dwarf, whom he left to his fate.

When they had left the plain behind them, Peronnik and his steed found themselves in a narrow valley in which was a grove of trees, full of all sorts of sweet-smelling things – roses of every colour, yellow broom, pink honeysuckle – while above them all towered a wonderful scarlet pansy whose face bore a strange expression. This was the flower that laughs, and no one who looked at it could help laughing too. Peronnik's heart beat high at the thought that he had reached safely the second trial, and he gazed quite calmly at the lion with the mane of vipers twisting and twirling, who walked up and down in front of the grove.

The young man pulled up and removed his cap, for, idiot though he was, he knew that when you have to do with people greater than yourself, a cap is more useful in the hand than on the head. Then, after wishing all kinds of good fortune to the lion and his family, he inquired if he was on the right road to Kerglas.

"And what is your business at Kerglas?" asked the lion with a growl, and showing his teeth.

"With all respect," answered Peronnik, pretending to be very frightened, "I am the servant of a lady who is a friend of the noble Rogéar and sends him some larks for a pasty."

"Larks?" cried the lion, licking his long whiskers. "Why, it must be a century since I have had any! Have you a large quantity with you?"

"As many as this bag will hold," replied Peronnik, opening, as he spoke, the bag which he had filled with feathers and glue; and to prove what he said, he turned his back on the lion and began to imitate the song of a lark.

"Come," exclaimed the lion, whose mouth watered, "show me the birds! I should like to see if they are fat enough for my master."

"I would do it with pleasure," answered the idiot, "but if I once open the bag they will all fly away."

"Well, open it wide enough for me to look in," said the lion, drawing a little nearer.

Now this was just what Peronnik had been hoping for, so he held the bag while the lion opened it carefully and put his head right inside, so that he might get a good mouthful of larks. But the mass of feathers and glue stuck to him, and before he could pull his head out again Peronnik had drawn tight the cord, and tied it in a knot that no man could untie. Then, quickly gathering the flower that laughs, he rode off as fast as the colt could take him.

The path soon led to the lake of the dragons, which he had to swim across. The colt, who was accustomed to it, plunged into the water without hesitation; but as soon as the dragons caught sight of Peronnik they approached from all parts of the lake in order to devour him.

This time Peronnik did not trouble to take off his cap, but he threw the beads he carried with him into the water, as you throw black corn to a duck, and with each bead that he swallowed a dragon turned on his back and died, so that the idiot reached the other side without further trouble.

The valley guarded by the black man now lay before him, and from afar Peronnik beheld him, chained by one foot to a rock at the entrance, and holding the iron ball which never missed its mark and always returned to its master's hand. In his head the black man had six eyes that were never all shut at once, but kept watch one after the other. At this moment they were all open, and Peronnik knew well that if the black man caught a glimpse of him he would cast his ball. So, hiding the colt behind a thicket of bushes, he crawled along a ditch and crouched close to the very rock to which the black man was chained.

The day was hot, and after a while the man began to grow sleepy. Two of his eyes closed, and Peronnik sang gently. In a moment a third eye shut, and Peronnik sang on. The lid of a fourth eye dropped heavily, and then those of the fifth and the sixth. The black man was asleep altogether.

Then, on tiptoe, the idiot crept back to the colt, which he led over soft moss past the black man into the vale of pleasure, a delicious garden full of fruits that dangled before your mouth, fountains running with wine, and flowers chanting in soft little voices. Further on, tables were spread with food, and girls dancing on the grass called to him to join them.

Peronnik heard, and, scarcely knowing what he did drew the colt into a slower pace. He sniffed greedily the smell of the dishes, and raised his head the better to see the dancers. Another instant and he would have stopped altogether and been lost, like others before him, when suddenly there came to him like a vision the golden bowl and the diamond lance. Drawing his whistle from his pocket, he blew it loudly, so as to drown the sweet sounds about him, and ate what was left of his bread and bacon to still the craving of the magic fruits. His eyes he fixed steadily on the ears of the colt, that he might not see the dancers.

In this way he was able to reach the end of the garden, and at length perceived the castle of Kerglas, with the river between them which had only one ford. Would the lady be there, as the old man had told him? Yes, surely that was she, sitting on a rock, in a black satin dress, and her face the colour of a Moorish woman's. The idiot rode up, and took off his cap more politely than ever, and asked if she did not wish to cross the river.

"I was waiting for you to help me do so," answered she. "Come near, that I may get up behind you."

Peronnik did as she bade him, and by the help of his arm she jumped nimbly on to the back of the colt.

"Do you know how to kill the magician?" asked the lady, as they were crossing the ford.

"I thought that, being a magician, he was immortal, and that no one could kill him" replied Peronnik.

"Persuade him to taste that apple, and he will die, and if that is not enough I will touch him with my finger, for I am the plague," answered she.

"But if I kill him, how am I to get the golden bowl and the diamond lance that are hidden in the cellar without a key?" rejoined Peronnik.

"The flower that laughs opens all doors and lightens all darkness," said the lady; and as she spoke, they reached the further bank, and advanced towards the castle.

In front of the entrance was a sort of tent supported on poles, and under it the giant was sitting, basking in the sun. As soon as he noticed the colt bearing Peronnik and the lady, he lifted his head, and cried in a voice of thunder:

"Why, it is surely the idiot, riding my colt thirteen months old!"

"Greatest of magicians, you are right," answered Peronnik.

"And how did you manage to catch him?" asked the giant.

"By repeating what I learnt from your brother Bryak on the edge of the forest," replied the idiot. "I just said—

> *Colt, free to run and free to eat,*
> *Colt, gallop fast until we meet,*

and it came directly."

"You know my brother, then?" inquired the giant. "Tell me why he sent you here."

"To bring you two gifts which he has just received from the country of the Moors," answered Peronnik: "the apple of delight and the woman of submission. If you eat the apple you will not desire anything else, and if you take the woman as your servant you will never wish for another."

"Well, give me the apple, and bid the woman get down," answered Rogéar.

The idiot obeyed, but at the first taste of the apple the giant staggered, and as the long yellow finger of the woman touched him he fell dead.

Leaving the magician where he lay, Peronnik entered the palace, bearing with him the flower that laughs. Fifty doors flew open before him, and at length he reached a long flight of steps which seemed to lead into the bowels of the earth. Down these he went till he came to a silver door without a bar or key. Then he held up high the flower that laughs, and the door slowly swung back, displaying a deep cavern, which was as bright as day from the shining of the golden bowl and the diamond lance. The idiot hastily ran forward and hung the bowl round his neck from the chain which was attached to it, and took the lance in his hand. As he did so, the ground shook beneath him, and with an awful rumbling the palace disappeared, and Peronnik found himself standing close to the forest where he led the cattle to graze.

Though darkness was coming on, Peronnik never thought of entering the farm, but followed the road which led to the court of the duke of Brittany. As he passed through the town of Vannes he stopped at a tailor's shop, and bought a beautiful costume of brown velvet and a white horse, which he paid for with a handful of gold that he had picked up in the corridor of the castle of Kerglas. Thus he made his way to the city of Nantes, which at that moment was besieged by the French.

A little way off, Peronnik stopped and looked about him. For miles round the country was bare, for the enemy had cut down every tree and burnt every blade of corn; and, idiot though he might be, Peronnik was able to grasp that inside the gates men were dying of famine. He was still gazing with horror, when a trumpeter appeared on the walls, and, after blowing a loud blast, announced that the duke would adopt as his heir the man who could drive the French out of the country.

On the four sides of the city the trumpeter blew his blast, and the last time Peronnik, who had ridden up as close as he might, answered him.

"You need blow no more," said he, "for I myself will free the town from her enemies." And turning to a soldier who came running up, waving his sword, he touched him with the magic lance, and he fell dead on the spot. The men who were following stood still, amazed. Their comrade's armour had not been pierced, of that they were sure, yet he was dead, as if he had been struck to the heart. But before they had time to recover from their astonishment, Peronnik cried out:

"You see how my foes will fare; now behold what I can do for my friends," and, stooping down, he laid the golden bowl against the mouth of the soldier, who sat up as well as ever. Then, jumping his horse across the trench, he entered the gate of the city, which had opened wide enough to receive him.

The news of these marvels quickly spread through the town, and put fresh spirit into the garrison, so that they declared themselves able to fight under the command of the young stranger. And as the bowl restored all the dead Bretons to life, Peronnik soon had an army large enough to drive away the French, and fulfilled his promise of delivering his country.

As to the bowl and the lance, no one knows what became of them, but some say that Bryak the sorcerer managed to steal them again, and that any one who wishes to possess them must seek them as Peronnik did.

OGIER THE DANE

WILLIAM MORRIS

It was not only the influence of Merlin that lived on through the centuries but also that of Morgan le Fay. In later legend and romance Morgan became an increasingly sinister and evil fairy or enchantress, related to Arthur (as half-sister) and bent upon destroying him and the companionship of the Round Table. But in earlier tradition she had a more benevolent side, and was seen as one of the fairy queens of Avalon, a tradition that remained even in later writing when she becomes the queen who bears the body of Arthur away after his death.

The tradition of Morgan as a fairy queen was evident in other tales, not least the medieval story of Ogier the Dane, at the time of King Charlemagne. Ogier (who as Holger is the national hero of Denmark), like Arthur, was spirited away by Morgan to Avalon from where he returned after two hundred years to defend France against invasion.

William Morris (1834–96) had long been enchanted with medieval romances. He included four Arthurian poems in his first collection of verse, The Defence of Guinevere *(1858), and returned to it in his long narrative poem* The Earthly Paradise, *a kind of Nordic* Canterbury Tales, *which he wrote between 1868 and 1870. These stories were later adapted into prose form by Madalen Edgar, in* Stories from the Earthly Paradise *(1919), and it is that version I have reprinted here.*

What nobler vassal had good Charlemaine than Ogier, mightiest of the Danes, and most chivalrous of all knights? For many a generation after he had passed away, minstrels sang of his exploits: how, given as a hostage to the Frankish Emperor, in time he came to bear the Oriflamme against the paynims, fought hand-to-hand with Caraheu, and had slain base Charlot, had not Heaven bade him stay his hand. Denmark was his; he wore the crown of Britain; he stormed the great town of Babylon, waged war in Palestine for the Holy Cross, and ruled in Tyre.

The record of these deeds is a gallant tale, but more wondrous is the story Nicholas the Breton once related of Ogier. He spoke of how Morgan le Fay bore the hero to Avallon, when all his wars seemed ended, and of what came to pass thereafter.

Hearken, and judge of the marvel for yourselves.

The chill air that breathes just before daybreak crept in at the half-opened casements of a room where Death held sway. The fair young Queen of Denmark lay dead; around her head flickered the hallowed tapers that the watchers kept ever burning. The King, grieving sore for his dear wife, had knelt all night long by her bedside in an agony of voiceless despair; while at the far end of the chamber, the nurses bent over the cradle of the new-born prince, from time to time whispering to one another memories of the grace and kindliness of their late mistress.

One of the women had crossed the floor on tiptoe to replace a taper that had burned low in its socket. Her hand was resting on the candle when a sudden tremor passed through her limbs, her eyelids drooped, and she lost all consciousness in a trance that was deep as the Queen's sleep of death. What befell the one nurse befell the others at the same moment. The King also came under the spell; his wan, drawn face relaxed, his eyes closed, and the desolate mourner forgot his woes for a little while in this strange, heavy sleep.

But now the deathlike stillness was broken by the sound of light footsteps on the staircase, muffled in the sweep of long silken robes. Noiselessly the door of the bedchamber swung open, admitting a breath of sweet odour, more fragrant than the scent which was rising to the windows from rose and lily in the gardens below. In the doorway stood a group of fay ladies like a cluster of bright flowers in sunshine. Crowned they were, each with a circlet of gems, and their loose-flowing raiment shone with heavenly hues that seemed to light up the spot where they stood.

One by one they stepped daintily across the room to the infant's cradle, there to whisper over the little Prince of Denmark the promise of a fairy gift. The first to hail him was Gloriande, and the gift she bestowed was courage and steadfastness. "Thou shalt be a true knight," she whispered; "thine honour shall be stainless; and in upholding the right, thou shalt be alike fearless and unwearied."

The second fay advanced, a glorious vision of brightness, her head crowned with blood-red rubies, and a tunic of golden mail upon her breast. "War and strife I promise thee," she said sternly; "throughout thy long life, warfare unending, that so thou mayst win martial fame amongst men, and gain Heaven's blessing by conflict with the paynim."

These words were barely uttered when another of the group raised her voice, and smilingly took up the war-maiden's rede. "To that I add a little gift to sweeten thy labour. I give thee victory in every struggle. Whose thy foe, thou shalt ever be conqueror."

The fourth followed with the gift of courtesy and gentle speech. Then came a grey-eyed fay, with parted lips and a rosy blush overspreading her cheek as she promised the Prince the love of fair women and the power of winning their hearts.

The last to glide to the boy's cradle was the most lovely of the band. She stood a while gazing down on him, then tenderly she whispered: "Ogier, the gift I give thee is mine own love. Not while thou art in the heat of strife, but at the close of thy warfare, thou shalt see me and rejoice in my gift. Till then, Ogier my love, farewell."

Then, softly as they had come, the fairy visitants stole from the palace to the shore, where the waves were breaking in silver ripples on the sand. A moment they paused in silence, their faces turned towards the west; a moment later and they had vanished, leaving the still slumbering palace unwitting of their visit to little Ogier's cradle.

Now as to Ogier's long and honourable life, we must pass it over, strange though that appear when Ogier himself is our hero!

He was, as the world knows, a generous knight, unsurpassed in valour, upright, and greatly beloved by his people. The heathen hordes dreaded to meet him in battle; the evil-doer shuddered beneath his glance. In warfare and in the ruling of his lands he was ever happy; but through the love he bore wife and child, grief no less than joy, fell to his lot. He early lost Bellisande, his sweet wife, and his only child, Baldwin, a winsome bright-eyed lad of great promise, was put to death by the evil-minded Charlot. But even these sorrows did not quench his spirit; bravely he toiled on to a ripe old age, and to the end of his days, Ogier was ever the same stout-hearted warrior.

In the cloudless western sky the sun is sinking softly below the horizon, but over in the east there is an angry look on heaven's face. Great masses of steel-grey cloud, stained red round the edges by the glow of sunset, are lowering above an ocean of tossing waves that change in colour from a glittering silver to green, grey, and sombre black. No wind ruffles the sea this evening, yet the billows, like a great army in rout, are tumbling and surging wildly as though they would dash down the barrier of bare brown rock which rises sharply in their path. This rugged island is the fatal Loadstone Rock, shunned in holy terror by every seaman. On winter nights, when snugly seated by the fireside, the old sailors may tell the strange rumours they have heard of the Rock, but he who nears it, will never return home to tell his own tale. The ship that tries to pass, is drawn to destruction against its magnetic cliffs, and the crew, if not sucked beneath the waters, die ere long of starvation upon its barren heights.

To-night there is a living man upon the Rock. The sun sets upon the wreckage and bleached bones around him, and while the moon rises to throw her cold white light upon the scene, the lonely figure sits undismayed, awaiting sure death. He is an old man, nobly built; his hair is white, his face furrowed by age, but yet his kingly robes – now tarnished by the salt waves – are borne on shoulders quite erect, and his voice is still fresh and vigorous as he speaks his thoughts.

"For a man of my many years, my strength has stood me well. 'Tis seven weeks since our boat was cast on this rock, five days since the last of the crew died with our last crumb of bread between his lips, and still I am alive. If God had not willed me to die here, I had had strength enough to end my days, sword in hand, upon the field of battle. How glorious to have drawn my last breath beneath the banner that waved our challenge to the paynim foe!

"Thou must find thee another leader, Charlemaine, to take my place and drive back these heathen bands from the fair land of

France, for never more shalt thou see me take the field. Ah, never didst thou guess that Ogier's bones would rest upon a lonely sea-girt rock! And yet this death, so different from what he hoped to meet, grieves not thine ancient knight now that he sees it close at hand." And Ogier knelt down to thank God in simple words for thus ordering his end.

As night darkened, he fell into a deep slumber, from which he awoke before dawn; but the darkness that still overhung land and sea was suddenly dispelled by an unlooked for light which broke upon his eyes ere he had been long awake, and which steadily increased in ruddy brightness, while at the same time his ears caught the sound of sweet music.

"This is the dawning," he murmured, "not of an earthly day, but of eternity. Death steals upon me; how pleasant, how gentle its approach!"

Just then he fancied his name was whispered through the air. Taking it to be a summons, he rose and crossed the island towards the east, whence the voice seemed to have come, and from where the light was still streaming.

The music had ceased, and the rays were already growing somewhat dim, yet across the sea, as he raised his eyes eagerly to the east, he could descry a shining palace of gold in the midst of green lawns and shady groves of trees! But even as he gazed upon the scene, the light faded, the palace was lost in the darkness, and sea and sky became alike grey as the night around.

Imagining that the vision and the semblance of music had arisen from his own worldly thoughts, he sat down to turn his mind resolutely towards graver concerns; but the pulse of life beat stronger and stronger in his veins, and after trying for some time to centre his thoughts on approaching death, he gave up the effort, and started instead to climb down the rocky eastern side of his prison, whither he felt drawn in search of further revelations.

It was no easy task to swing himself from ledge to ledge, hanging, sometimes by one hand alone, above the sea which foamed far below. In time, however, he safely reached the base of the rock, where the only foothold was upon the wrecks, which the angry billows dashed ceaselessly to and fro against the fatal magnet cliffs. From one piece of floating timber to another, he leaped out towards the east, until he reached the outermost wreck, where, steadying himself against the rush of the sea and the blinding dash of spray, he stood with his good sword Courtain in his grasp, expectant only of death.

At that moment he heard again a strain of music floating through the air, and a bright speck of light appeared moving on the ocean towards him, rapidly growing in size until he saw it was a gilded boat. His first thought, that this was another wreck to be added to those already drawn to the Rock, was soon disproved, for although unguided by human hand, it steered its course unerringly through the troubled seas and drew up safely by the wreck where Ogier was standing. Believing that, whatever its course, it was intended to bear him from the island, he sheathed his sword Courtain, and stepped into the skiff. There was neither oar nor rudder in the little boat, but oarsman and helmsman were not wanted, for no sooner had the old knight seated himself amongst the cushions in the stern than the skiff shot lightly from the Rock; and he, giving way to overpowering sleep, knew nothing more of his passage.

When he awoke it was to find the boat lying moored in a shaded nook at the edge of a quiet stretch of water. He sprang ashore and, half-alarmed by the rare beauty of the place, drew his sword and murmured a holy prayer; yet as he went forward a step or two, his fears that it might be an unhallowed spot vanished, and he fancied he had come to Paradise. The meadows bore a wealth of gay flowers, the air was soft and birds sang sweetly from blossom-laden trees. The loveliness of the scene, however, was presently dulled to his senses by a new feeling of feebleness. His limbs grew stiff, each step was taken with greater difficulty; his eyes were dim and even his memory was failing, for he could not recall whence he had come, or aught of his past life. His growing weakness he took calmly. It was the hand of death upon him, he supposed, and he was well content to have it so, since he was already in Paradise. Slowly he wandered down a green alley until he reached a wicket-gate opening on the fairest of gardens; then, turning fainter, he staggered to a fountain over which two white-thorns shed their blossoms, while close by sounded the minstrelsy that he had heard faintly on the isle. Here he sank down unconscious, and all his thoughts melted to heavenly dreams. Through these dreams came the murmur of a sweet voice: "Ogier, Ogier, how long thou hast been in coming!"

Fancying himself in heaven, he strove to answer as though he were addressed by his great Master.

"Nay, nay," said the voice, "not yet art thou in Paradise, Ogier. Long may it be ere thou goest on that last journey, now that thou hast reached me, mine own love! Ah! at length the happy day has come when I may give thee again the beauty and freshness of youth, and fit thee to enjoy the love thou didst gain from me even in thy cradle, long years ago."

Life seemed ebbing fast from him as he struggled to shake off the feeling of someone touching his forehead and calling him sweet names. Was it the shade of his young wife (her very name now lost to him) who, years past, had gone to her rest beneath the hawthorns of God's-acre in old St Omer? Was this a troubled dream of things past that haunted him in the shadow of death?

No, it was not so. Once again he swooned, but ere consciousness left him, he felt the soft pressure of a living hand and knew that a ring had been slipped upon his finger.

His eyes opened on the same scene – with what a difference! No longer was his body weak or his mind frail as an old man's. The strength of youth was within him; he was entering on a new life.

At the first glance he thought the garden unchanged, but, as he looked around him a second time, he saw that it now held in its midst a lady whose marvellous beauty enhanced ten times the charm of the scene. So young she seemed that he would have thought her a maiden in her teens, but that her glorious eyes were filled with the wisdom of more than a mortal lifetime. Her raiment matched her loveliness. The finest cloudy veilings fell to her sandals where jewels gleamed against her snowy feet; a ruby shone like a star upon her breast, and her golden locks were wreathed with sweetest rosebuds.

Ogier had sprung to his feet, and as she moved towards him, her eyes seeking his, and her arms outstretched in welcome, he faltered out a question as to where he stood, and in whose presence.

The fair one answered: "Thou hast come to Avallon to dwell with me, Morgan le Fay, whose love was pledged to thee whilst thou wast yet an infant in the Danish palace." She told of how she had visited his cradle with her sister fays those many years ago. "Yet am I young as then, for our youth is eternal; and now that thou art in Avallon, thou shalt be young and changeless too. See, I shall show thee the charm by which thou hast been restored to the strength of early manhood."

She pointed, as she spoke, to a heavy gold ring with curious figures traced upon it, which now encircled one of Ogier's fingers, and told how, when she had placed it there a little while ago, the marks of old age had straightway vanished from his form. "So long as thou wearest it," she said, "death will not touch thee."

At first, overcome by the fay's beauty, he had been enraptured with his new surroundings, but soon a great longing for his old life of warfare upon earth swept over him, and he felt that all before him was dreamlike, dreary and unreal. Morgan read his thoughts, and with a smile linked her hand in his, and drew him toward the castle beyond her gay gardens. "Come, love," she whispered, "our life is fairer than that earthly one for which thou mournest. Thou wilt be happy, aye, radiantly happy, when thou hast forgotten thy stormy past. Bethink thee how thou wouldst even now have been dead, had not I slipped the ring upon thy finger and so kept life within thee. Wilt thou not give me thy love in return for mine already given?"

Across the daisied grass they had passed to a doorway in the castle, round which clustered a group of fair maids singing joyous welcome to Ogier and strewing flowers upon the way. Through long, cool corridors they came at length to a throne placed at the end of a hall, and there, when Morgan had led the hero up the steps, a young girl advanced from the band, and laid at his feet a golden crown. This Morgan placed upon his head, bidding him, in gentle words, forget the world and rise to enjoy the new life in Avallon. At the magic touch of the Crown of Forgetfulness his last regrets vanished; the past was blotted out, and all he knew was that he had now a share in the joys of a wondrous glad and peaceful country. No trouble henceforth met him in Avallon, where base or mischief-making men were unknown; only the noble-hearted (whom men thought dead) were borne like Ogier from earthly seas to these pain-forgetting shores, where all was happiness and content.

A hundred years had passed since the aged Ogier had last been seen upon earth. In those hundred years many a change had befallen the lands in which he had dwelt, and in France, unhappily, these changes had all been for the worse. A cruel, lingering war oppressed her sorely; the heathen foe once more overran the land, besieging cities and laying waste the fertile country.

At the gates of Paris, one spring day, stood crowds of anxious folk pressing round each horseman who rode up to the city walls, and questioning him eagerly of the progress of the foe. Was Harfleur still safe? Did Andelys stand in need of help? And was it true that the Pont de l'Arche had been burnt down? To these and such-like questions each new-comer gave a different answer, and the crowd turned from him impatiently to waylay the next traveller.

Towards sundown a party of three rode up to the gates. Two serving-men followed their master, their eyes fixed on him with doubt and awe, as though striving to determine in what way he differed from other men. He was apparently quite young, for though his face was bronzed, it was still fresh and unfurrowed; his bright golden hair and grey eyes were as a boy's, and the look on his face was radiant as an angel's. In height he far surpassed the men around him, his giant-like form rendering more conspicuous the old-fashioned dress and armour which he wore.

The warders examined his pass, and asked his name and from what city he came. The Ancient Knight, he replied, was the name people gave him in St Omer, the town he had just left. Then, heedless of the questions showered on him, as on all the other wayfarers, he stared pityingly at the sergeants before him.

"Saint Mary!" said he, "if that is all the stature ye reach nowadays, 'tis no wonder the pagans are victorious! When the Hammer-bearer took the field, his men were of a different pattern!"

His words savoured so strangely of bygone times that the group around him ceased their talk, and gazed in wonder at the speaker. A mocking laugh broke the silence. "Charlemaine has risen from the tomb to save our city!" cried a voice in the crowd.

At the name of Charlemaine the horseman started in his saddle, knit his brow and seemed as though he would speak. No words, however, came to his lips, and gathering up the reins with a sigh he rode onwards to the city.

The Ancient Knight was none other than Ogier, and his return from Avallon was on this wise.

One day Morgan le Fay approached him, and told how France was suffering from the onset of fierce tribes whom none could drive back. Would he don his armour and champion the cause of that Christian country, she asked him, if, under a spell, he were borne back to the world which he had left a hundred years ago? So long as he wore the magic ring, he could not suffer death nor lose his youthfulness; and once the pagans were subdued, he would be wafted, as before, to Avallon, his fame immeasurably increased by this new exploit.

To Morgan's proposal Ogier gave willing assent. Beneath her potent spell he fell into a trance during which the mysterious voyage was accomplished, and he awakened to find himself on the Flemish coast; thence journeying to St Omer, the town he knew so well in the old days, he had ridden through the desolated country to join the forces that were mustering in Paris.

His antique dress and old-world talk had roused as much wonder in the country roads as at the gates of Paris, though the simple peasants were less apt to mock at his appearance than were the quick-witted townsmen. But if the French folk thought it strange to see a man of his stamp in their midst, it was stranger for Ogier himself to visit old haunts peopled with a new generation. The memory of Avallon had grown dim, and all his thoughts were given to the world in which he moved again.

Now, the King of France lay besieged by the enemy at Rouen, in dire need of help from his capital. When Ogier entered Paris he learned that the Queen was holding a muster of troops in the square before her palace, and that many knights had gathered to swear fealty, and march, at her orders, to relieve Rouen. Accordingly he made his way to the palace, joined the crowd of soldiers, and awaited his turn to approach the Queen, who, beneath a royal canopy in the open square, was receiving the oaths of fealty from eager lips.

At length his turn came, and he knelt before a handsome woman, tall and dark-haired, whose eyes lit up with surprise and approval as she saw his striking carriage. Then as he rose, the Queen inquired his name and from what country he had come. Once again he replied that men called him the Ancient Knight; as to his home, it was so long since he had left it, to take up his abode in a far country, that he had no recollection of it whatever. That answer made the Queen the more curious to discover the mystery of this old-world young knight, but as there was then no leisure for talk, she bade a page conduct him to the palace, where he should have refreshment, and await her coming. She wished, said she, to appoint him to some command, and to give him his orders that same day.

So Ogier followed the page through a postern gate by which he had often entered the palace in Charlemaine's time. The coat-of-arms above the doorway, which he well remembered looking fresh and gay in those days, was now so faded and weather-stained that the young page paused to point it out to the stranger as a quaint and interesting relic of the past! No wonder Ogier felt as though he were in a dream, and would presently awaken to find himself among the familiar faces of his early days, or perchance alone on the fatal Loadstone Rock!

After a light meal in the hall, he wandered out of doors to the gardens, past merry groups of squires and gay ladies, until, finding a quiet spot beyond the sound of play and laughter, he lay down to rest, and soon lost himself in dreams.

Still slumbering, he was found by the Queen, who, having dispatched her affairs of state in the public square, came through the gardens, accompanied by an elderly dame of honour. Her eyes wandered admiringly over his outstretched form, and with a smile she remarked that the name given to him was ill-suited to such a handsome young knight.

"Ah, my lady," said the dame, shaking her head distrustfully, "I fear there is some dark mystery about him. The squire who took him to the palace says he kept questioning him of men who have been dead these fifty years or more. And look how old a fashion he shows in his armour! God grant he is not a spirit of evil come to lead us into greater trouble! That ring, engraven with strange figures, is doubtful sign of his good faith." And even as the Queen was striving to reassure her, the old dame stooped down, and deftly slipped the ring off his finger.

Instantly his golden hair changed to white, his face grew wrinkled, and, amidst other marks of old age, his breathing became hard and gasping. His eyes half opened, but his lips were too feeble to frame words; he could only move one hand slightly, as if groping for the lost ring.

The Queen grew pale with terror when she saw this change pass over the young and handsome knight. The tears coursed down her cheeks, for she could not endure to see him growing grey and cold, as if the hand of death were already on his heart. Her old attendant, on the contrary, showed neither dismay nor pity. She handed the ring to her mistress, saying that it was indeed a treasure, since the wearer of it would ever remain young. But the Queen would not keep it, tempting prize though it was. To the indignation of the cruel old dame, she knelt over the knight, and whispering, "Ah, wilt not thou think kindly of me if I restore thee this magic ring?" she hastily thrust it upon his finger, in the hope that it might yet be in time to save his life.

As quickly as strength had ebbed, so fast did it flow back to Ogier. In a moment he sprang to his feet, fresh, youthful, and handsome as before, looking around him with dazed eyes, that showed he had newly awakened from dreams and did not understand the reason of the Queen's pallor and her troubled looks. She, hiding her anxiety, smiled, and chided him playfully for sleeping whilst other men were fighting for the cause of France.

"Nay, Queen," said he; "I would far sooner meet thy foemen than be confronted with such dreams of old age and misery as have come to me in my sleep this afternoon."

With a sudden blush that made her look the lovelier in Ogier's eyes, she cried: "Ah, if dreams beset such a mighty man as thou, then it is pardonable that they also visit a frail woman like me! 'Twas but last night I dreamed that enthroned before our people sat a king of France whose face was strange to me; to-day I know it to have been thine."

From the way in which the Queen spoke, Ogier saw that she thought him worthy of every honour, and he, in return, felt deeply grateful for her trust, and longed to prove that it was well placed in him.

Together they walked to the council-room, leaving behind them the dame of honour, who was muttering her disgust at the turn events had taken, and vowing that if ever she had the chance of regaining the ring, she would not again part with it so easily.

Ogier had not long to wait an opportunity of serving in the field. In the council-room, he gave such wise advice, and showed so extraordinary a knowledge of warfare, that he was forthwith appointed to the command of one wing of the newly raised army, which was about to march from Paris to the aid of the King at Rouen.

A proud man was Ogier as he rode forth at the head of his troops next morning, his heart fired with the joy of coming battle and love of the fair Queen, who from her window, watched the passing army, and dropped a wreath of sweet-scented flowers at her champion's feet.

When the army reached Rouen it was met by the news that the King lay slain by an arrow, and that the town and surrounding country were in the hands of the heathen foe. It was not long before Ogier changed the fortunes of the war. He speedily fell upon the enemy, and completely routing them in a great battle, he avenged the King's death and recaptured the city. Then, on his victorious return to Paris, he was welcomed as the saviour of France, and the people, who had now to elect a new monarch, declared, one and all, that the Ancient Knight must succeed to the throne, for he had proved himself be a leader amongst men. For a year he continued to wage war upon the heathen invaders, driving them before him until not one remained within the kingdom of France. So great was his delight in once more being on the field of battle, and so deep his devotion to the Queen, who, after a short widowhood, had now promised to bestow her hand upon him, that amid the pleasures of his new life, Avallon, with its peaceful, uneventful days, faded utterly from his memory.

In due course, when May was again gladdening the land, preparations were made for the coronation of King Charles (the name by which Ogier was known in his new kingdom), and for his marriage, on the same day, with the widowed Queen. Full of joyful thoughts he awoke in the early dawn of that great day. So early it was that the sparrows had scarce begun to twitter in the eaves, and at first the only sound that was heard in his bedchamber was the distant hammering of the woodwrights, who had been busy overnight completing the stagings for the morning's pageant.

Presently, however, a voice ran in his ears: "Ogier! Ogier!" Now, our hero had lost all memory, not only of Avallon, but also of his former days on earth when he was known as Ogier the Dane. The name was strange to him, therefore, and, rising on his elbow, he cried: "Who is here? Why seek ye an Ogier in this room?"

There came a sigh in answer to his questions. "Ogier was once a mighty knight," said the gentle voice, "and many were his gallant deeds when Charlemaine ruled in this land." Then the astonished listener heard the story of his own wonderful prowess and the conquests he had once made. "The Ogier of whom I tell, is none other than thou who to-day callest thyself Charles of France; last year the Ancient Knight was thy title. Ah, Ogier, mine own love, hast thou forgotten that thou camest here only on a short sojourn from the happy land of Avallon? Return, I pray thee; the heathen are swept from France, and thy task is finished. If thou didst linger here, no more fame couldst thou win, and the unending youth that my ring provides for thee, would rouse ill talk amongst mortals. Come, love, take from me the crown which dispels all thought of earthly life, and which will once more bring thee perfect bliss. Dost thou still look on me strangely? Nay, Ogier, this is no empty dream."

By his side stood Morgan le Fay, dazzlingly beautiful, holding in her outstretched hand the crown that had been placed on his head when first he entered the palace of Avallon. At her bidding he now rose as in a dream, put on the kingly robes that had once been Charlemaine's, and seated himself in the royal chair, wearing the golden crown, and holding in his right hand the sceptre of that great conqueror. Then the fairy Morgan drew near, raised the earthly crown from his head, and set in its place her circlet, which brought its wearer the blessed boon of forgetfulness. In a moment the memory of the past months was blotted out; the hero recalled the fair land of Avallon, and knew that it was no creation of his fancy that stood before him, but his own true love, who had come to lead him to those distant shores.

"Oh, love," he faltered, "how came we here? Have I been separated from thee for a while? I dreamed, methinks, of having spent long months toiling and battling upon earth."

Without waiting to answer, she took his hand in hers and drew him gently from the palace. On the threshold they paused, and turned their eyes upon the sleeping city, whose Queen would yet have to seek a new consort to share her throne. Beneath the rising sun the Seine shone like a great stream of molten gold, and very fair lay the misty town along its banks. A moment the pair stood drinking in their last memory of this world – then vanished, and mortals knew Ogier no more. But in far-distant Avallon, he and his fairy bride dwell together in bliss, untouched by age or by the shadow of death.

MERLIN DREAMS IN THE MONDREAM WOOD

CHARLES DE LINT

Charles de Lint (b. 1951) has established a strong reputation in his fantasies drawing upon the roots of British folklore. A Canadian by birth, de Lint is a musician as well as a writer, specializing in folk music, and also operates his own small press called Triskell Press, which published his earliest writings, including the various tales of Cerin Songweaver, a medieval minstrel. Charles's stories are seldom far from the basis of myth and legend, such as Mulengro *(1985) and* Greenmantle *(1988) and his retelling of the fairy tale* Jack, the Giant-Killer *(1987). More recently his work has become darker and sinister taking on the pressures and horrors of American city life, but a thread of the elder world remains. The following story was originally published in the American series* Pulphouse *in 1990. It brings the Merlin legend down to the present day.*

In the heart of the house lay a garden.

In the heart of the garden stood a tree.

In the heart of the tree lived an old man who wore the shape of a red-haired boy with crackernut eyes that seemed as bright as salmon tails glinting up the water.

His was a riddling wisdom, older by far than the ancient oak that housed his body. The green sap was his blood and leaves grew in his hair. In the winter, he slept. In the spring, the moon harped a windsong against his antler tines as the oak's boughs stretched its green buds awake. In the summer, the air was thick with the droning of bees and the scent of the wildflowers that grew in stormy profusion where the fat brown bole became root.

And in the autumn, when the tree loosed its bounty to the ground below, there were hazelnuts lying in among the acorns.

The secrets of a Green Man.

"When I was a kid, I thought it was a forest," Sara said.

She was sitting on the end of her bed, looking out the window over the garden, her guitar on her lap, the quilt bunched up under her knees. Up by the headboard, Julie Simms leaned forward from its carved wood to look over Sara's shoulder at what could be seen of the garden from their vantage point.

"It sure looks big enough," she said.

Sara nodded. Her eyes had taken on a dreamy look.

It was 1969 and they had decided to form a folk band – Sara on guitar, Julie playing recorder, both of them singing. They wanted to change the world with music because that was what was happening. In San Francisco. In London. In Vancouver. So why not in Ottawa?

With their faded bell-bottom jeans and tie-dyed shirts, they looked just like any of the other seventeen-year-olds who hung around the War Memorial downtown, or could be found crowded into coffee houses like Le Hibou and Le Monde on the weekends. Their hair was long – Sara's a cascade of brown ringlets, Julie's a waterfall spill the color of a raven's wing; they wore beads and feather earrings and both eschewed makeup.

"I used to think it spoke to me," Sara said.

"What? The garden?"

"Um-hmm."

"What did it say?"

The dreaminess in Sara's eyes became wistful and she gave Julie a rueful smile.

"I can't remember," she said.

It was three years after her parents had died – when she was nine years old – that Sara Kendell came to live with her Uncle Jamie in his strange rambling house. To an adult perspective, Tamson House was huge: an enormous, sprawling affair of corridors and rooms and towers that took up the whole of a city block; to a child of nine, it simply went on forever.

She could wander down corridor after corridor, poking about in the clutter of rooms that lay spread like a maze from the northwest tower near Bank Street – where her bedroom was located – all the way over to her uncle's study overlooking O'Conner Street on the far side of the house, but mostly she spent her time in the library and in the garden. She liked the library because it was like a museum. There were walls of books, rising two floors high up to a domed ceiling, but there were also dozens of glass display cases scattered about the main floor area, each of which held any number of fascinating objects.

There were insects pinned to velvet and stone artifacts; animal skulls and clay flutes in the shapes of birds; old manuscripts and hand-drawn maps, the parchment yellowing, the ink a faded sepia; Kabuki masks and a miniature Shinto shrine made of ivory and ebony; corn-husk dolls, Japanese *netsuke* and porcelain miniatures; antique jewelry and African beadwork; Kachina dolls and a brass fiddle, half the size of a normal instrument . . .

The cases were so cluttered with interesting things that she could spend a whole day just going through one case and still have something to look at when she went back to it the next day. What interested her most, however, was that her uncle had a story to go with each and every item in the cases. No matter what she brought up to his study – a tiny ivory *netsuke* carved in the shape of a badger crawling out of a teapot, a flat stone with curious scratches on it that looked like Ogham script – he could spin out a tale of its origin that might take them right through the afternoon to suppertime.

That he dreamed up half the stories only made it more entertaining, for then she could try to trip him up in his rambling explanations, or even just try to top his tall tales.

But if she was intellectually precocious, emotionally she still carried scars from her parents' death and the time she'd spent living with her other uncle – her father's brother. For three years Sara had been left in the care of a nanny during the day – amusing herself while the woman smoked cigarettes and watched the soaps – while at night she was put to bed promptly after dinner. It wasn't a normal family life; she could only find that vicariously in the books she devoured with a voracious appetite.

Coming to live with her Uncle Jamie, then, was like constantly being on holiday. He doted on her and on those few occasions when he *was* too busy, she could always find one of the many house guests to spend some time with her.

All that marred her new life in Tamson House were her night fears.

She wasn't frightened of the house itself. Nor of bogies or monsters living in her closet. She knew that shadows were shadows, creaks and groans were only the house settling when the temperature changed. What haunted her nights was waking up from a deep sleep, shuddering uncontrollably, her pajamas stuck to her like a second skin, her heartbeat thundering at twice its normal tempo.

There was no logical explanation for the terror that gripped her – once, sometimes twice a week. It just came, an awful, indescribably panic that left her shivering and unable to sleep for the rest of the night.

It was on the days following such nights that she went into the garden. The greenery and flowerbeds and statuary all combined to soothe her. Invariably, she found herself in the very center of the garden where an ancient oak tree stood on a knoll and overhung a fountain. Lying on the grass sheltered by its boughs, with the soft lullaby of the fountain's water murmuring close at hand, she would find what the night fears had stolen from her the night before.

She would sleep.

And she would dream the most curious dreams.

"The garden has a name, too," she told her uncle when she came in from sleeping under the oak one day.

The house was so big that many of the rooms had been given names just so that they could all be kept straight in their minds.

"It's called the Mondream Wood," she told him.

She took his look of surprise to mean that he didn't understand the word.

"It means that the trees in it dream that they're people," she explained.

He uncle nodded. "'The dream of life among men.' It's a good name. Did you think it up yourself?"

"No. Merlin told me."

"*The* Merlin?" her uncle asked with a smile.

Now it was her turn to look surprised.

"What do you mean, *the* Merlin?" she asked.

Her uncle started to explain, astonished that in all her reading she hadn't come across a reference to Britain's most famous wizard, but then just gave her a copy of Malory's *Le Morte d'Arthur* and, after a moment's consideration, T. H. White's *The Sword in the Stone* as well.

"Did you ever have an imaginary friend when you were a kid?" Sara asked as she finally turned away from the window.

Julie shrugged. "My mom says I did, but I can't remember. Apparently he was a hedgehog the size of a toddler named Whatzit."

"I never did. But I can remember that for a long time I used to wake up in the middle of the night just terrified and then I wouldn't be able to sleep again for the rest of the night. I used to go into the middle of the garden the next day and sleep under that big oak that grows by the fountain."

"How pastoral," Julie said.

Sara grinned. "But the thing is, I used to dream that there was a boy living in that tree and his name was Merlin."

"Go on," Julie scoffed.

"No, really. I mean, I really had these dreams. The boy would just step out of the tree and we'd sit there and talk away the afternoon."

"What did you talk about?"

"I don't remember," Sara said. "Not the details – just the feeling. It was all very magical and . . . healing, I suppose. Jamie said that my having those night fears was just my unconscious mind's way of dealing with the trauma of losing my parents and then having to live with my dad's brother who only wanted my inheritance, not me. I was too young then to know anything about that kind of thing; all I knew was that when I talked to Merlin, I felt better. The night fears started coming less and less often and then finally they went away altogether.

"I think Merlin took them away for me."

"What happened to him?"

"Who?"

"The boy in the tree," Julie said. "Your Merlin. When did you stop dreaming about him?"

"I don't really know. I guess when I stopped waking up terrified, I just stopped sleeping under the tree so I didn't see him anymore. And then I just forgot that he'd ever been there . . ."

Julie shook her head. "You know, you can be a bit of a flake sometimes."

"Thanks a lot. At least I didn't hang around with a giant hedgehog named Whatzit when I was a kid."

"No. You hung out with tree-boy."

Julie started to giggle and then they both broke up. It was a few moments before either of them could catch their breath.

"So what made you think of your tree-boy?" Julie asked.

Another giggle welled up in Julie's throat, but Sara's gaze had drifted back out the window and become all dreamy again.

"I don't know," she said. "I was just looking out at the garden and I suddenly found myself remembering. I wonder what ever happened to him . . .?"

"Jamie gave me some books about a man with the same name as you," she told the red-haired boy the next time she saw him. "And after I read them, I went into the library and found some more. He was quite famous, you know."

"So I'm told," the boy said with a smile.

"But it's all so confusing," Sara went on. "There's all these different stories, supposedly about the same man . . . How are you supposed to know which of them is true?"

"That's what happens when legend and myth meet," the boy said. "Everything gets tangled."

"Was there even a *real* Merlin, do you think? I mean, besides you."

"A great magician who was eventually trapped in a tree?"

Sara nodded.

"I don't think so," the boy said.

"Oh."

Sara didn't even try to hide her disappointment.

"But that's not to say there was never a man named Merlin," the boy added. "He might have been a bard, or a follower of old wisdoms. His enchantments might have been more subtle than the great acts of wizardry ascribed to him in the stories."

"And did he end up in a tree?" Sara asked eagerly. "That would make him like you. I've also read that he got trapped in a cave, but I think a tree's much more interesting, don't you?"

Because her Merlin lived in a tree.

"Perhaps it was in the idea of a tree," the boy said.

Sara blinked in confusion. "What do you mean?"

"The stories seem to be saying that one shouldn't teach, or else the student becomes too knowledgeable and then turns on the teacher. I don't believe that. It's not the passing on of knowledge that would root someone like Merlin."

"Well, then what would?"

"Getting too tangled up in his own quest for understanding. Delving so deeply into the calendaring trees that he lost track of where he left his body until one day he looked around to find that he'd become what he was studying."

"I don't understand."

The red-haired boy smiled. "I know. But I can't speak any more clearly."

"Why not?" Sara asked, her mind still bubbling with the tales of quests and wizards and knights that she'd been reading. "*Were* you enchanted? *Are* you trapped in that oak tree?"

She was full of curiosity and determined to find out all she could, but in that practiced way that the boy had, he artfully turned the conversation onto a different track and she never did get an answer to her questions.

It rained that night, but the next night the skies were clear. The moon hung above the Mondream Wood like a fat ball of golden honey; the stars were so bright and close Sara felt she could just reach up, and pluck one as though it were an apple, hanging in a tree. She had crept from her bedroom in the northwest tower and gone out into the garden, stepping secretly as a thought through the long darkened corridors of the house until she was finally outside.

She was looking for magic.

Dreams were one thing. She knew the difference between what you found in a dream and when you were awake; between a fey red-haired boy who lived in a tree and real boys; between the dream-like enchantments of the books she'd been reading – enchantments that lay thick as acorns under an oak tree – and the real world where magic was a card trick, or a stage magician pulling a rabbit out of a hat on the *Ed Sullivan Show*.

But the books also said that magic came awake in the night. It crept from its secret hidden places – called out by starlight and the moon – and lived until the dawn pinked the eastern skies. She always dreamed of the red-haired boy when she slept under his oak in the middle of the garden. But what if he was more than a dream? What if at night he stepped out of his tree – really and truly, flesh and blood and bone real?

There was only one way to find out.

*   *   *

Sara felt restless after Julie went home. She put away her guitar and then distractedly set about straightening up her room. But for every minute she spent on the task, she spent three just looking out the window at the garden.

I never dream, she thought.

Which couldn't be true. Everything she'd read about sleep had to dream. People just needed to. Dreams were supposed to be the way your subconscious cleared up the day's clutter. So, *ipso facto*, everybody dreamed. She just didn't remember hers.

But I did when I was a kid, she thought. Why did I stop? How could I have fogotten the red-haired boy in the tree?

Merlin.

Dusk fell outside her window to find her sitting on the floor, arms folded on the windowsill, chin resting on her arms as she looked out over the garden. As the twilight deepened, she finally stirred. She gave up the pretense of cleaning up her room. Putting on a jacket, she went downstairs and out into the garden.

Into the Mondream Wood.

Eschewing the paths that patterned the garden, she walked across the dew-wet grass, fingering the damp leaves of the bushes and the low-hanging branches of the trees. The dew made her remember Gregor Penev – an old Bulgarian artist who'd been staying in the house when she was a lot younger. He'd been full of odd little stories and explanations for natural occurrences – much like Jamie was which was probably why Gregor and her uncle had gotten along so well.

"*Zaplakala e gorata*," he'd replied when she'd asked him where dew came from and what it was for. "The forest is crying. It remembers the old heroes who lived under its branches – the heroes and the magicians, all lost and gone now. Robin Hood. Indje Voivode. Myrddin."

Myrddin. That was another name for Merlin. She remembered reading somewhere that Robin Hood was actually a Christianized Merlin, the Anglo version of his name being a variant of his Saxon name of Rof Breocht Woden – the Bright Strength of Wodan. But if you went back far enough, all the names and stories got tangled up in one story. The tales of the historical Robin Hood, like those of the historical Merlin of the Borders, had acquired older mythic elements common to the world as a whole by the time they were written down. The story that their legends were really telling was that of the seasonal hero-king, the May Bride's consort, who with his cloak of leaves and his horns, and all his varying forms, was the secret truth that lay in the heart of every forest.

"But those are European heroes," she remembered telling Gregor. "Why would the trees in our forest be crying for them?"

"All forests are one," Gregor had told her, his features serious for a change. "They are all echoes of the first forest that gave birth to Mystery when the world began."

She hadn't really understood him then, but she was starting to understand him now as she made her way to the fountain at the center of the garden where the old oak tree stood guarding its secrets in the heart of the Mondream Wood. There were two forests for every one you entered. There was the one you walked in, the physical echo, and then there was the one that was connected to all the other forests, with no consideration of distance, or time.

The forest primeval. Remembered through the collective memory of every tree in the same way that people remembered myth – through the collective subconscious that Jung mapped, the shared mystic resonance that lay buried in every human mind. Legend and myth, all tangled in an alphabet of trees, remembered, not always with understanding, but with wonder. With awe.

Which was why the druids' Ogham was also a calendar of trees.

Why Merlin was often considered to be a druid.

Why Robin was the name taken by the leaders of witch covens.

Why the Green Man had antlers – because a stag's tines are like the branches of a tree.

Why so many of the early avatars were hung from a tree. Osiris. Balder. Dionysus. Christ.

Sara stood in the heart of the Mondream Wood and looked up at the old oak tree. The moon lay behind its branches, mysteriously close. The air was filled with an electric charge, as though a storm was approaching, but there wasn't a cloud in the sky.

"Now I remember what happened that night," Sara said softly.

Sara grew to be a small woman, but at nine years old she was just a tiny waif – no bigger than a minute, as Jamie liked to say. With her diminutive size she could slip soundlessly through thickets that would allow no egress for an adult. And that was how she went.

She was a curly-haired gamine, ghosting through the hawthorn hedge that bordered the main path. Whispering across the small glade guarded by the statue of a little horned man that Jamie said was Favonius, but she privately thought of as Peter Pan, though he bore no resemblance to the pictures in her Barrie book. Tiptoeing through the wildflower garden, a regular gallimaufry of flowering plants, both common and exotic. And then she was near the fountain. She could see Merlin's oak, looming up above the rest of the garden like the lordly tree it was.

And she could hear voices.

She crept nearer, a small shadow hidden in deeper patches cast by the fat yellow moon.

"—never a matter of choice," a man's voice was saying. "The lines of our lives are laid out straight as a dodman's leys, from event to event. You chose your road."

She couldn't see the speaker, but the timbre of his voice was deep and resonating, like a deep bell. She couldn't recognize it, but she did recognize Merlin's when he replied to the stranger.

"When I chose my road, there was no road. There was only the trackless wood; the hills, lying crest to crest like low-backed waves; the glens where the harps were first imagined and later strung. Ca'canny, she told me when I came into the Wood. I thought go gentle meant go easy, not go fey; that the oak guarded the Borders, marked its boundaries. I never guessed it was a door."

"All knowledge is a door," the stranger replied. "You knew that."

"In theory," Merlin replied.

"You meddled."

"I was born to meddle. That was the part I had to play."

"But when your part was done," the stranger said, "you continued to meddle."

"It's in my nature, Father. Why else was I chosen?"

There was a long silence then. Sara had an itch on her nose but she didn't dare move a hand to scratch it. She mulled over what she'd overheard, trying to understand.

It was all so confusing. From what they were saying it seemed that her Merlin *was* the Merlin in the stories. But if that was true, then why did he look like a boy her own age? How could he even still be alive? Living in a tree in Jamie's garden and talking to his father . . .

"I'm tired," Merlin said. "And this is an old argument, Father. The winters are too short. I barely step into a dream and then it's spring again. I need a longer rest. I've earned a longer rest. The Summer Stars call to me."

"Love bound you," the stranger said.

"An oak bound me. I never knew she was a tree."

"You knew. But you preferred to ignore what you knew because you had to riddle it all. The salmon wisdom of the hazel wasn't enough. You had to partake of the fruit of every tree."

"I've learned from my error," Merlin said. "Now set me free, Father."

"I can't. Only love can unbind you."

"I can't be found, I can't be seen," Merlin said. "What they remember of me is so tangled up in Romance, that no one can find the man behind the tales. Who is there to love me?"

Sara pushed her way out of the thicket where she'd been hiding and stepped into the moonlight.

"There's me," she began, but then her voice died in her throat.

There was no red-haired boy standing by the tree. Instead, she found an old man with the red-haired boy's eyes. And a stag. The stag turned its antlered head toward her and regarded her with a gaze that sent shivers scurrying up and down her spine. For a long moment its gaze held hers, then it turned, its flank flashing red in the moonlight, and the darkness swallowed it.

Sara shivered. She wrapped her arms around herself, but she could not escape the chill.

The stag . . .

That was impossible. The garden had always been strange, seeming so much larger than its acreage would allow, but there couldn't possibly be a deer living in it without her having seen it before. Except . . . What about a boy becoming an old man overnight? A boy who really and truly did live in a tree?

"Sara," the old man said.

It was Merlin's voice. Merlin's eyes. Her Merlin grown into an old man.

"You . . . you're old," she said.

"Older than you could imagine."

"But—"

"I came to you as you'd be most likely to welcome me."

"Oh."

"Did you mean what you said?" he asked.

Memories flooded Sara. She remembered a hundred afternoons of warm companionship. All those hours of quiet conversation and games. The peace that came from her night fears. If she said yes, then he'd go away. She'd lose her friend. And the night fears . . . Who'd be there to make the terrors go away? Only he had been able to help her. Not Jamie nor anyone else who lived in the house, though they'd all tried.

"You'll go away . . . won't you?" she said.

He nodded. An old man's nod. But the eyes were still young. Young and old, wise and silly, all at the same time. Her red-haired boy's eyes.

"I'll go away," he replied. "And you won't remember me."

"I won't forget," Sara said. "I would never forget."

"You won't have a choice," Merlin said. "Your memories of me would come with me when I go."

"They'd be . . . gone forever . . .?"

That was worse than losing a friend. That was like the friend had never been there in the first place.

"Forever," Merlin said. "Unless . . ."

His voice trailed off, his gaze turned inward.

"Unless what?" Sara asked finally.

"I could try to send them back to you when I reach the other side of the river."

Sara blinked with confusion. "What do you mean? The other side of what river?"

"The Region of the Summer Stars lies across the water that marks the boundary between what is and what has been. It's a long journey to that place. Sometimes it takes many lifetimes."

They were both quiet then. Sara studied the man that her friend had become. The gaze he returned her was mild. There were no demands in it. There was only regret. The sorrow of parting. A fondness that asked for nothing in return.

Sara stepped closer to him, hesitated a moment longer, then hugged him.

"I do love you, Merlin," she said. "I can't say I don't when I do."

She felt his arms around her, the dry touch of his lips on her brow.

"Go gentle," he said. "But beware the calendaring of the trees."

And then he was gone.

One moment they were embracing and the next her arms only held air. She let them fall limply to her sides. The weight of an awful sorrow bowed her head. Her throat grew thick, her chest tight. She swayed where she stood, tears streaming from her eyes.

The pain felt like it would never go away.

But the next thing she knew she was waking in her bed in the northwest tower and it was the following morning. She woke from a dreamless sleep, clear-eyed and smiling. She didn't know it, but her memories of Merlin were gone.

But so were her night fears.

The older Sara, still not a woman, but old enough to understand more of the story now, fingered a damp leaf and looked up into the spreading canopy of the oak above her.

Could any of that really have happened? she wondered.

The electric charge she'd felt in the air when she'd approached the old oak was gone. That pregnant sense of something about to happen had faded. She was left with the moon, hanging lower now, the stars still bright, the garden quiet. It was all magical, to be sure, but natural magic – not supernatural.

She sighed and kicked at the autumn debris that lay thick about the base of the old tree. Browned leaves, broad and brittle. And acorns. Hundreds of acorns. Fred the gardener would be collecting them soon for his compost – at least those that the black squirrels didn't hoard away against the winter. She went down on one knee and picked up a handful of them, letting them spill out of her hand.

Something different about one of them caught her eye as it fell and she plucked it up from the ground. It was a small brown ovoid shape, an incongruity in the crowded midst of all the capped acorns. She held it up to her eye. Even in the moonlight she could see what it was.

A hazelnut.

Salmon wisdom locked in a seed.

Had she regained her memories, memories returned to her now from a place where the Summer Stars always shone, or had she just had a dream in the Mondream Wood where as a child she'd thought that the trees dreamed they were people?

Smiling, she pocketed the nut, then slowly made her way back into the house.

THE DRAGON LINE

MICHAEL SWANWICK

With this story we reach the present. Michael Swanwick (b. 1950) is a multi-award winning author of many science fiction and fantasy novels and stories including Vacuum Flowers *(1987),* Stations of the Tide *(1991),* The Iron Dragon's Daughter *(1994) and* Tales of Old Earth *(2000). He has long been fascinated with revisiting legends and ancient tales, reworking them for the modern day and in the process not only testing their significance but exploring and comparing our values with the old. He told me that this story was "a particular favourite".*

Driving by the mall in King of Prussia that night, I noticed that between the sky and earth where the horizon used to be is now a jagged-edged region, spangled with bright industrial lights. For a long yearning instant, before the car topped the rise and I had to switch lanes or else be shunted onto the expressway, I wished I could enter that dark zone, dissolve into its airless mystery and cold ethereal beauty. But of course that was impossible: Faerie is no more. It can be glimpsed, but no longer grasped.

At the light, Shikra shoved the mirror up under my nose, and held the cut-down fraction of a McDonald's straw while I did up a line. A winter flurry of tinkling white powder stung through my head to freeze up at the base of the skull, and the light changed, and off we went. "Burn that rubber, Boss-man," Shikra laughed. She drew up her knees, balancing the mirror before her chin, and snorted the rest for herself.

There was an opening to the left, and I switched lanes, injecting the Jaguar like a virus into the stream of traffic, looped around, and was headed back toward Germantown. A swirling white pattern of flat crystals grew in my left eye, until it filled my vision. I was only seeing out of the right now. I closed the left and rubbed it, bringing tears, but still the hallucination hovered, floating within the orb of vision. I sniffed, bringing up my mouth to one side. Beside me, Shikra had her butterfly knife out and was chopping more coke.

"Hey, enough of that, okay? We've got work to do."

Shikra turned an angry face my way. Then she hit the window controls and threw the mirror, powder and all, into the wind. Three grams of purest Peruvian offered to the Goddess.

"Happy now, shithead?" Her eyes and teeth flashed, all sinister smile in mulatto skin, and for a second she was beautiful, this petite teenaged monstrosity, in the same way that a copperhead can be beautiful, or a wasp, even as it injects the poison under your skin. I felt a flash of desire and of tender, paternal love, and then we were at the Chemical Road turnoff, and I drifted the Jag through three lanes of traffic to make the turn. Shikra was laughing and excited, and I was too.

It was going to be a dangerous night.

Applied Standard Technologies stood away from the road, a compound of low, sprawling buildings afloat on oceanic lawns. The guard waved us through and I drove up to the Lab B lot. There were few cars there; one had British plates. I looked at that one for a long moment, then stepped out onto the tarmac desert. The sky was close, stained a dull red by reflected halogen lights. Suspended between vastnesses, I was touched by a cool breeze, and shivered. How fine, I thought, to be alive.

I followed Shikra in. She was dressed all in denim, jeans faded to white in little crescents at the creases of her buttocks, trade beads clicking softly in her cornrowed hair. The guards at the desk rose in alarm at the sight of her, eased back down as they saw she was mine.

Miss Lytton was waiting. She stubbed out a half-smoked cigarette, strode briskly forward. "He speaks modern English?" I asked as she handed us our visitors' badges. "You've brought him completely up to date on our history and technology?" I didn't want to have to deal with culture shock. I'd been present when my people had dug him, groggy and corpse-blue, sticky with white chrysalid fluids, from his cave almost a year ago.

Since then, I'd been travelling, hoping I could somehow pull it all together without him.

"You'll be pleased." Miss Lytton was a lean, nervous woman, all tweed and elbows. She glanced curiously at Shikra, but was too disciplined to ask questions. "He was a quick study – especially keen on the sciences." She led us down a long corridor to an unmanned security station, slid a plastic card into the lockslot.

"You showed him around Britain? The slums, the mines, the factories?"

"Yes." Anticipating me, she said, "He didn't seem at all perturbed. He asked quite intelligent questions."

I nodded, not listening. The first set of doors sighed open, and we stepped forward. Surveillance cameras telemetered our images to the front desk for reconfirmation. The doors behind us closed, and those before us began to cycle open. "Well, let's go see."

The airlock opened into the secure lab, a vast, overlit room filled with white enamelled fermentation tanks, incubators, autoclaves, refrigerators, workbenches and enough glass plumbing for any four dairies. An ultrafuge whined softly. I had no clear idea what they did here. To me AST was just another blind cell in the maze of interlocking directorships that sheltered me from public view. The corporate labyrinth was my home now, a secure medium in which to change documentation, shift money and create new cover personalities on need. Perhaps other ancient survivals lurked within the catacombs, mermen and skinchangers, prodigies of all sorts, old Grendel himself; there was no way of telling.

"Wait here," I told Shikra. The lab manager's office was set halfway up the far wall, with wide glass windows overlooking the floor. Miss Lytton and I climbed the concrete and metal stairs. I opened the door.

He sat, flanked by two very expensive private security operatives, in a chrome swivel chair, and the air itself felt warped out of shape by the force of his presence. The trim white beard and charcoal grey Savile Row pinstripe were petty distractions from a face as wide and solemn and cruel as the moon. I shut my eyes and still it floated before me, wise with corruption. There was a metallic taste on my tongue.

"Get out," I said to Miss Lytton, the guards.

"Sir, I—"

I shot her a look, and she backed away. Then the old man spoke, and once again I heard that wonderful voice of his, like a subway train rumbling underfoot. "Yes, Amy, allow us to talk in privacy, please."

When we were alone, the old man and I looked at each other for a long time, unblinking. Finally, I rocked back on my heels. "Well," I said. After all these centuries, I was at a loss for words. "Well, well, well."

He said nothing.

"Merlin," I said, putting a name to it.

"Mordred," he replied, and the silence closed around us again.

The silence could have gone on forever for all of me; I wanted to see how the old wizard would handle it. Eventually he realized this, and slowly stood, like a thunderhead rising up in the western sky. Bushy, expressive eyebrows clashed together. "Arthur dead, and you alive! Alas, who can trust this world?"

"Yeah, yeah, I've read Malory too."

Suddenly his left hand gripped my wrist and squeezed. Merlin leaned forward, and his face loomed up in my sight, ruthless grey eyes growing enormous as the pain washed up my arm. He seemed a natural force then, like the sun or wind, and I tumbled away before it.

I was on a nightswept field, leaning on my sword, surrounded by my dead. The veins in my forehead hammered. My ears ached with the confusion of noises, of dying horses and men. It had been butchery, a battle in the modern style in which both sides had fought until all were dead. This was the end of all causes: I stood empty on Salisbury Plain, too disheartened even to weep.

Then I saw Arthur mounted on a black horse. His face all horror and madness, he lowered his spear and charged. I raised my sword and ran to meet him.

He caught me below the shield and drove his spear through my body. The world tilted and I was thrown up into a sky as black as well water. Choking, I fell deep between the stars where the shadows were aswim with all manner of serpents, dragons and wild beasts. The creatures struggled forward to seize my limbs in their talons and claws. In wonder I realized I was about to die.

Then the wheel turned and set me down again. I forced myself up the spear, unmindful of pain. Two-handed, I swung my sword through the side of Arthur's helmet and felt it bite through bone into the brain beneath.

My sword fell from nerveless fingers, and Arthur dropped his spear. His horse reared and we fell apart. In that last instant our eyes met and in his wondering hurt and innocence I saw, as if staring into an obsidian mirror, the perfect image of myself.

"So," Merlin said, and released my hand. "He is truly dead, then. Even Arthur could not have survived the breaching of his skull."

I was horrified and elated: he could still wield power, even in this dim and disenchanted age. The danger he might have killed me out of hand was small price to pay for such knowledge. But I masked my feelings.

"That's just about enough!" I cried. "You forget yourself, old man. I am still the Pen-dragon, *Dux Bellorum Britanniarum* and King of all Britain and Amorica and as such your liege lord!"

That got to him. These medieval types were all heavy on rightful authority. He lowered his head on those bullish shoulders and grumbled, "I had no right, perhaps. And yet how was I to know that? The histories all said Arthur might yet live. Were it so, my duty lay with him, and the restoration of Camelot." There was still a look, a humour, in his eye I did not trust, as if he found our confrontation essentially comic.

"You and your damned Camelot! Your bloody holy and ideal court!" The memories were unexpectedly fresh, and they hurt as only betrayed love can. For I really had loved Camelot when I first came to court, an adolescent true believer in the new myth of the Round Table, of Christian chivalry and glorious quests. Arthur could have sent me after the Grail itself, I was that innocent.

But a castle is too narrow and straight a space for illusions. It holds no secrets. The queen, praised for her virtue by one and all, was a harlot. The king's best friend, a public paragon of chastity, was betraying him. And everyone knew! There was the heart and exemplar of it all. Those same poetasters who wrote sonnets to the purity of Lodegreaunce's daughter smirked and gossiped behind their hands. It was Hypocrisy Hall, ruled over by the smiling and genial Good King Cuckold. He knew all, but so long as no one dared speak it aloud, he did not care. And those few who were neither fools nor lackeys, those who spoke openly of what all knew, were exiled or killed. For telling the truth! That was Merlin's holy and Christian court of Camelot.

Down below, Shikra prowled the crooked aisles dividing the workbenches, prying open a fermenter to take a peek, rifling through desk drawers, elaborately bored. She had that kind of rough, destructive energy that demands she be doing something at all times.

The king's bastard is like his jester, powerless but immune from criticism. I trafficked with the high and low of the land, tinsmiths and river-gods alike, and I knew their minds. Arthur was hated by his own people. He kept the land in ruin with his constant wars. Taxes went to support the extravagant adventures of his knights. He was expanding his rule, croft by shire, a kingdom here, a chunk of Normandy there, questing after Merlin's dream of a Paneuropean Empire. All built on the blood of the peasantry; they were just war fodder to him.

I was all but screaming in Merlin's face. Below, Shikra drifted closer, straining to hear. "That's why I seized the throne while he was off warring in France – to give the land a taste of peace; as a novelty, if nothing else. To clear away the hypocrisy and cant, to open the windows and let a little fresh air in. The people had prayed for release. When Arthur returned, it was my banner they rallied around. And do you know what the real beauty of it was? It was over a year before he learned he'd been overthrown."

Merlin shook his head. "You are so like your father! He too was an idealist – I know you find that hard to appreciate – a man who burned for the Right. We should have acknowledged your claim to succession."

"You haven't been listening!"

"You have a complaint against us. No one denies that. But, Mordred, you must understand that we didn't know you were the king's son. Arthur was . . . not very fertile. He had slept with your mother only once. We thought she was trying to blackmail him." He sighed piously. "Had we only known, it all could have been different."

I was suddenly embarrassed for him. What he called my complaint was the old and ugly story of my birth. Fearing the proof of his adultery – Morgawse was nominally his sister, and incest had both religious and dynastic consequences – Arthur had ordered all noble babies born that feast of Beltaine brought to court, and then had them placed in an unmanned boat and set adrift. Days later, a peasant had found the boat run aground with six small corpses. Only I, with my unhuman vigour, survived. But, typical of him, Merlin missed the horror of the story – that six innocents were sacrificed to hide the nature of Arthur's crime – and saw it only as a denial of my rights of kinship. The sense of futility and resignation that is my curse descended once again. Without understanding between us, we could never make common cause.

"Forget it," I said. "Let's go get a drink."

I picked up 476 to the Schuylkill. Shikra hung over the back seat, fascinated, confused, and aroused by the near-subliminal scent of murder and magic that clung to us both. "You haven't introduced me to your young friend." Merlin turned and offered his hand. She didn't take it.

"Shikra, this is Merlin of the Order of Ambrose, enchanter and master politician." I found an opening to the right, went up on the shoulder to take advantage of it, and slammed back all the way left, leaving half a dozen citizens leaning on their horns. "I want you to be ready to kill him at an instant's notice. If I act strange – dazed or in any way unlike myself – slit his throat immediately. He's capable of seizing control of my mind, and yours too if you hesitate."

"How 'bout that," Shikra said.

Merlin scoffed genially. "What lies are you telling this child?"

"The first time I met her, I asked Shikra to cut off one of my fingers." I held up my little finger for him to see, fresh and pink, not quite grown to full size. "She knows there are strange things astir, and they don't impress her."

"Hum." Merlin stared out at the car lights whipping toward us. We were on the expressway now, concrete crashguards close enough to brush fingertips against. He tried again. "In my first life, I greatly wished to speak with an African, but I had duties that kept me from travelling. It was one of the delights of the modern world to find I could meet your people everywhere, and learn from them." Shikra made that bug-eyed face the young make when the old condescend; I saw it in the rear-view mirror.

"I don't have to ask what you've been doing while I was . . . asleep," Merlin said after a while. That wild undercurrent of humour was back in his voice. "You've been fighting the same old battles, eh?"

My mind wasn't wholly on our conversation. I was thinking of the *bons hommes* of Languedoc, the gentle people today remembered (by those few who do remember) as the Albegensians. In the heart of the thirteenth century, they had reinvented Christianity, leading lives of poverty and chastity. They offered me hope, at a time when I had none. We told no lies, held no wealth, hurt neither man nor animal – we did not even eat cheese. We did not resist our enemies, nor obey them either, we had no leaders and we thought ourselves safe in our poverty. But Innocent III sent his dogs to level our cities, and on their ashes raised the Inquisition. My sweet, harmless comrades were tortured, mutilated, burnt alive. History is a laboratory in which we learn that nothing works, or ever can. "Yes."

"Why?" Merlin asked. And chuckled to himself when I did not answer.

The Top of Centre Square was your typical bar with a view, a narrow box of a room with mirrored walls and gold foil insets in the ceiling to illusion it larger, and flacid jazz oozing from hidden speakers. "The stools in the centre, by the window," I told the hostess, and tipped her accordingly. She cleared some businessmen out of our seats and dispatched a waitress to take our orders.

"Boodles martini, very dry, straight up with a twist," I said.

"Single malt Scotch. Warm."

"I'd like a Shirley Temple, please." Shikra smiled so sweetly that the waitress frowned, then raised one cheek from her stool and scratched. If the woman hadn't fled it might have gotten ugly.

Our drinks arrived. "Here's to progress," Merlin said, toasting the urban landscape. Silent traffic clogged the far below streets with red and white beads of light. Over City Hall the buildings sprawled electric-bright from Queen Village up to the Northern Liberties. Tugs and barges crawled slowly upriver. Beyond, Camden crowded light upon light. Floating above the terrestrial galaxy, I felt the old urge to throw myself down. If only there were angels to bear me up.

"I had a hand in the founding of this city."

"Did you?"

"Yes, the City of Brotherly Love. Will Penn was a Quaker, see, and they believed religious toleration would lead to secular harmony. Very radical for the times. I forget how many times he was thrown in jail for such beliefs before he came into money and had the chance to put them into practice. The Society of Friends not only brought their own people in from England and Wales, but also Episcopalians, Baptists, Scotch-Irish Presbyterians, all kinds of crazy German sects – the city became a haven for the outcasts of all the other religious colonies." How had I gotten started on this? I was suddenly cold with dread. "The Friends formed the social elite. Their idea was that by example and by civil works, they could create a pacifistic society, one in which all men followed their best impulses. All their grand ideals were grounded in a pragmatic set of laws, too; they didn't rely on goodwill alone. And you know, for a Utopian scheme it was pretty successful. Most of them don't last a decade. But . . ." I was rambling, wandering further and further away from the point. I felt helpless. How could I make him understand how thoroughly the facts had betrayed the dream? "Shikra was born here."

"Ahhh." He smiled knowingly.

Then all the centuries of futility and failure, of striving for first a victory and then a peace I knew was not there to be found, collapsed down upon me like a massive barbiturate crash, and I felt the darkness descend to sink its claws in my shoulders. "Merlin, the world is dying."

He didn't look concerned. "Oh?"

"Listen, did my people teach you anything about cybernetics? Feedback mechanisms? Well, never mind. The earth—" I gestured as if holding it cupped in my palm—" is like a living creature. Some say that it is a living creature, the only one, and all life, ourselves included, only component parts. Forget I said that. The important thing is that the earth creates and maintains a delicate balance of gases, temperatures and pressures that all life relies on for survival. If this balance were not maintained, the whole system would cycle out of control and . . . well, die. Us along with it." His eyes were unreadable, dark with fossil prejudices. I needed another drink. "I'm not explaining this very well."

"I follow you better than you think."

"Good. Now, you know about pollution? Okay, well now it seems that there's some that may not be reversible. You see what that means? A delicate little wisp of the atmosphere is being eaten away, and not replaced. Radiation intake increases. Meanwhile, atmospheric pollutants prevent reradiation of greater and greater amounts of infrared; total heat absorption goes up. The forests begin to die. Each bit of damage influences the whole, and leads to more damage. Earth is not balancing the new influences. Everything is cycling out of control, like a cancer.

"Merlin, I'm on the ropes. I've tried everything I can think of, and I've failed. The political obstacles to getting anything done are beyond belief. The world is dying, and I can't save it."

He looked at me as if I were crazy.

I drained my drink. "'Scuse me," I said. "Got to hit up in the men's room."

In the john I got out the snuffbox and fed myself some sense of wonder. I heard a thrill of distant flutes as it iced my head with artificial calm, and I straightened slightly as the vultures on my shoulders stirred and then flapped away. They would be back, I knew. They always were.

I returned, furious with buzzing energy. Merlin was talking quietly to Shikra, a hand on her knee. "Let's go," I said. "This place is getting old."

We took Passayunk Avenue west, deep into the refineries, heading for no place in particular. A kid in an old Trans Am, painted flat black inside and out, rebel flag flying from the antenna, tried to pass me on the right. I floored the accelerator, held my nose ahead of his, and forced him into the exit lane. Brakes screaming, he drifted away. Asshole. We were surrounded by the great tanks and cracking towers now. To one side, I could make out six smoky flames, waste gases being burnt off in gouts a dozen feet long.

"Pull in there!" Merlin said abruptly, gripping my shoulder and pointing. "Up ahead, where the gate is."

"Getty Gas isn't going to let us wander around in their refinery farm."

"Let me take care of that." The wizard put his forefingers together, twisted his mouth and bit through his tongue; I heard his teeth snap together. He drew his fingertips apart – it seemed to take all his strength – and the air grew tense. Carefully, he folded open his hands, and then spat blood into the palms. The blood glowed of its own light, and began to bubble and boil. Shikra leaned almost into its steam, grimacing with excitement. When the blood was gone, Merlin closed his hands again and said, "It is done."

The car was suddenly very silent. The traffic about us made no noise; the wheels spun soundlessly on the pavement. The light shifted to a melange of purples and reds, colour dopplering away from the centre of the spectrum. I felt a pervasive queasiness, as if we were moving at enormous speeds in an unperceived direction. My inner ear spun when I turned my head. "This is the wizard's world," Merlin said. "It is from here that we draw our power. There's our turn."

I had to lock brakes and spin the car about to keep from overshooting the gate. But the guards in their little hut, though they were looking straight at us, didn't notice. We drove by them, into a busy tangle of streets and accessways servicing the refineries and storage tanks. There was a nineteenth-century factory town hidden at the foot of the structures, brick warehouses and utility buildings ensnarled in metal, as if caught midway in a transformation from City to Machine. Pipes big enough to stand in looped over the road in sets of three or eight, nightmare vines that detoured over and around the worn brick buildings. A fat indigo moon shone through the clouds.

"Left." We passed an old metre house with gables, arched windows and brickwork ornate enough for a Balkan railroad station. Workmen were unloading reels of electric cable on the loading dock, forklifting them inside. "Right." Down a narrow granite block road we drove by a gothic-looking storage tank as large as a cathedral and buttressed by exterior struts with diamond-shaped cutouts. These were among the oldest structures in Point Breeze, left over from the early days of massive construction, when the industrialists weren't quite sure what they had hold of, but suspected it might be God. "Stop," Merlin commanded, and I pulled over by the earth-and-cinder containment dike. We got out of the car, doors slamming silently behind us. The road was gritty underfoot. The rich smell of hydrocarbons saturated the air. Nothing grew here, not so much as a weed. I nudged a dead pigeon with the toe of my shoe.

"Hey, what's this shit?" Shikra pointed at a glimmering grey line running down the middle of the road, cool as ice in its feverish surround. I looked at Merlin's face. The skin was flushed and I could see through it to a manically detailed lacework of tiny veins. When he blinked, his eyes peered madly through translucent flesh.

"It's the track of the groundstar," Merlin said. "In China, or so your paperbacks tell me, such lines are called *lung mei*, the path of the dragon."

The name he gave the track of slugsilver light reminded me that all of Merlin's order called themselves Children of the Sky. When I was a child an Ambrosian had told me that such lines interlaced all lands, and that an ancient race had raised stones and cairns on their interstices, each one dedicated to a specific star (and held to stand directly beneath that star) and positioned in perfect scale to one another, so that all of Europe formed a continent-wide map of the sky in reverse.

"Son of lies," Merlin said. "The time has come for there to be truth between us. We are not natural allies, and your cause is not mine." He gestured up at the tank to one side, the clusters of cracking towers, bright and phallic to the other. "Here is the triumph of my Collegium. Are you blind to the beauty of such artifice? This is the living and true symbol of Mankind victorious, and Nature lying helpless and broken at his feet – would you give it up? Would you have us again at the mercy of wolves and tempests, slaves to fear and that which walks the night?"

"For the love of pity, Merlin. If the earth dies, then mankind dies too!"

"I am not afraid of death," Merlin said. "And if I do not fear mine, why should I dread that of others?" I said nothing. "But do you really think there will be no survivors? I believe the race will continue beyond the death of lands and oceans, in closed and perfect cities or on worlds built by art alone. It has taken the wit and skill of billions to create the technologies that can free us from dependence on earth. Let us then thank the billions, not throw away their good work."

"Very few of those billions would survive," I said miserably, knowing that this would not move him. "A very small elite, at best."

The old devil laughed. "So. We understand each other better now. I had dreams too, before you conspired to have me sealed in a cave. But our aims are not incompatible; my ascendancy does not

require that the world die. I will save it, if that is what you wish."
He shrugged as he said it as if promising an inconsequential, a
trifle.

"And in return?"

His brows met like thunderstorms coming together; his eyes
were glints of frozen lightning beneath. The man was pure
theatre. "Mordred, the time has come for you to serve. Arthur
served me for the love of righteousness; but you are a patricide
and cannot be trusted. You must be bound to me, my will your
will, my desires yours, your very thoughts owned and controlled.
You must become my familiar."

I closed my eyes, lowered my head. "Done."

He owned me now.

We walked the granite block roadway towards the line of cool
silver. Under a triple arch of sullen crimson pipes, Merlin abruptly
turned to Shikra and asked, "Are you bleeding?"

"Say what?"

"Setting an egg," I explained. She looked blank. What the hell
did the kids say nowadays? "On the rag. That time of month."

She snorted. "No." And, "You afraid to say the word
menstruation? Carl Jung would've had fun with you."

"Come." Merlin stepped on the dragon track, and I followed,
Shikra after me. The instant my feet touched the silver path, I
felt a compulsion to walk, as if the track were moving my legs
beneath me. "We must stand in the heart of the groundstar to
empower the binding ceremony." Far, far ahead, I could see a
second line cross ours; they met not in a cross but in a circle.
"There are requirements: We must approach the place of power
on foot, and speaking only the truth. For this reason I ask that
you and your bodyguard say as little as possible. Follow, and I will
speak of the genesis of kings.

"I remember – listen carefully, for this is important – a stormy
night long ago, when a son was born to Uther, then King and
bearer of the dragon pennant. The mother was Igraine, wife to
the Duke of Tintagel, Uther's chief rival and a man who, if the
truth be told, had a better claim to the crown than Uther himself.
Uther begot the child on Igraine while the duke was yet alive,
then killed the duke, married the mother, and named that son
Arthur. It was a clever piece of statecraft, for Arthur thus had a

twofold claim to the throne, that of his true and also his nominal father. He was a good politician, Uther, and no mistake.

"Those were rough and unsteady times, and I convinced the king his son would be safest raised anonymously in a holding distant from the strife of civil war. We agreed he should be raised by Ector, a minor knight and very distant relation. Letters passed back and forth. Oaths were sworn. And on a night, the babe was wrapped in cloth of gold and taken by two lords and two ladies outside of the castle, where I waited disguised as a beggar. I accepted the child, turned and walked into the woods.

"And once out of sight of the castle, I strangled the brat."

I cried aloud in horror.

"I buried him in the loam, and that was the end of Uther's line. Some way farther in was a woodcutter's hut, and there were horses waiting there, and the wetnurse I had hired for my own child."

"What was the kid's name?" Shikra asked.

"I called him Arthur," Merlin said. "It seemed expedient. I took him to a priest who baptized him, and thence to Sir Ector, whose wife suckled him. And in time my son became king, and had a child whose name was Mordred, and in time this child killed his own father. I have told this story to no man or woman before this night. You are my grandson, Mordred, and this is the only reason I have not killed you outright."

We had arrived. One by one we entered the circle of light.

It was like stepping into a blast furnace. Enormous energies shot up through my body, and filled my lungs with cool, painless flame. My eyes overflowed with light: I looked down and the ground was a devious tangle of silver lines, like a printed circuit multiplied by a kaleidoscope. Shikra and the wizard stood at the other two corners of an equilateral triangle, burning bright as gods. Outside our closed circle, the purples and crimsons had dissolved into a blackness so deep it stirred uneasily, as if great shapes were acrawl in it.

Merlin raised his arms. Was he to my right or left? I could not tell, for his figure shimmered, shifting sometimes into Shikra's, sometimes into my own, leaving me staring at her breasts, my eyes. He made an extraordinary noise, a groan that rose and fell in strong but unmetred cadence. It wasn't until he came to the antiphon that I realized he was chanting plainsong. It was a crude form of music – the Gregorian was codified slightly after his day – but one that brought back a rush of memories, of ceremonies performed to the beat of wolfskin drums, and of the last night of boyhood before my mother initiated me into the adult mysteries.

He stopped. "In this ritual, we must each give up a portion of our identities. Are you prepared for that?" He was matter-of-fact, not at all disturbed by our unnatural environment, the consummate technocrat of the occult.

"Yes," I said.

"Once the bargain is sealed, you will not be able to go against its terms. Your hands will not obey you if you try, your eyes will not see that which offends me, your ears will not hear the words of others, your body will rebel against you. Do you understand?"

"Yes." Shikra was swaying slightly in the uprushing power, humming to herself. It would be easy to lose oneself in that psychic blast of force.

"You will be more tightly bound than slave ever was. There will be no hope of freedom from your obligation, not ever. Only death will release you. Do you understand?"

"Yes."

The old man resumed his chant. I felt as if the back of my skull were melting and my brain softening and yeasting out into the filthy air. Merlin's words sounded louder now, booming within my bones. I licked my lips, and smelled the rotting flesh of his cynicism permeating my hindbrain. Sweat stung down my sides on millipede feet. He stopped.

"I will need blood," said Merlin. "Hand me your knife, child." Shikra looked my way, and I nodded. Her eyes were vague, half-mesmerized. One hand rose. The knife materialized in it. She waved it before her, fascinated by the coloured trails it left behind, the way it pricked sparks from the air, crackling transient energies that rolled along the blade and leapt away to die, then held it out to Merlin.

Numbed by the strength of the man's will, I was too late realizing what he intended. Merlin stepped forward to accept the knife. Then he took her chin in hand and pushed it back, exposing her long, smooth neck.

"Hey!" I lunged forward, and the light rose up blindingly. Merlin chopped the knife high, swung it down in a flattening curve. Sparks stung through ionized air. The knife giggled and sang.

I was too late. The groundstar fought me, warping up underfoot in a narrowing cone that asymptotically fined down to a slim line yearning infinitely outward toward its unseen patron star. I flung out an arm and saw it foreshorten before me, my body flattening, ribs splaying out in extended fans to either side, stretching tautly vectored membranes made of less than nothing. Lofted up, hesitating, I hung timeless a nanosecond above the conflict and knew it was hopeless, that I could never cross that unreachable centre. Beyond our faint circle of warmth and life, the outer darkness was in motion, mouths opening in the void.

But before the knife could taste Shikra's throat, she intercepted it with an outthrust hand. The blade transfixed her palm, and she yanked down, jerking it free of Merlin's grip. Faster than eye could follow, she had the knife in her good hand and – the keen thrill of her smile! – stabbed low into his groin.

The wizard roared in an ecstasy of rage. I felt the skirling agony of the knife as it pierced him. He tried to seize the girl, but she danced back from him. Blood rose like serpents from their wounds, twisting upward and swept away by unseen currents of power. The darkness stooped and banked, air bulging inward, and for an instant I held all the cold formless shapes in my mind and I screamed in terror. Merlin looked up and stumbled backward, breaking the circle.

And all was normal.

We stood in the shadow of an oil tank, under normal evening light, the sound of traffic on Passayunk a gentle background surf. The groundstar had disappeared, and the dragon lines with it. Merlin was clutching his manhood, blood oozing between his fingers. When he straightened, he did so slowly, painfully.

Warily, Shikra eased up from her fighter's crouch. By degrees she relaxed, then hid away her weapon. I took out my handkerchief and bound up her hand. It wasn't a serious wound; already the flesh was closing.

For a miracle, the snuffbox was intact. I crushed a crumb on the back of a thumbnail, did it up. A muscle in my lower back was trembling. I'd been up days too long. Shikra shook her head when I offered her some, but Merlin extended a hand and I gave him the box. He took a healthy snort and shuddered.

"I wish you'd told me what you intended," I said. "We could have worked something out. Something else out."

"I am unmade," Merlin groaned. "Your hireling has destroyed me as a wizard."

It was as a politician that he was needed, but I didn't point that out. "Oh come on, a little wound like that. It's already stopped bleeding."

"No," Shikra said. "You told me that a magician's power is grounded in his mental somatype, remember? So a wound to his generative organs renders him impotent on symbolic and magical levels as well. That's why I tried to lop his balls off." She winced and stuck her injured hand under its opposite arm. "Shit, this sucker stings!"

Merlin stared. He'd caught me out in an evil he'd not thought me capable of. "You've taught this . . . chit the inner mysteries of my tradition? In the name of all that the amber rose represents, why?"

"Because she's my daughter, you dumbfuck!"

Shocked, Merlin said, "When—"

Shikra put an arm around my waist, laid her head on my shoulder, smiled. "She's seventeen," I said. "But I only found out a year ago."

We drove unchallenged through the main gate, and headed back into town. Then I remembered there was nothing there for me anymore, cut across the median strip and headed out for the airport. Time to go somewhere. I snapped on the radio, tuned it to XPN and turned up the volume. Wagner's valkyries soared and swooped low over my soul, dead meat cast down for their judgment.

Merlin was just charming the pants off his great-granddaughter. It shamed reason how he made her blush, so soon after trying to slice her open. "—make you Empress," he was saying.

"Shit, I'm not political. I'm some kind of anarchist, if anything."

"You'll outgrow that," he said. "Tell me, sweet child, this dream of your father's – do you share it?"

"Well, I ain't here for the food."

"Then we'll save your world for you." He laughed that enormously confident laugh of his that says that nothing is impossible, not if you have the skills and the cunning and the will to use them. "The three of us together."

Listening to their cheery prattle, I felt so vile and corrupt. The world is sick beyond salvation; I've seen the projections. People aren't going to give up their cars and factories, their VCRs and Styrofoam-packaged hamburgers. No one, not Merlin himself, can pull off that kind of miracle. But I said nothing. When I die and am called to account, I will not be found wanting. "Mordred did his devoir" – even Malory gave me that. I did everything but dig up Merlin, and then I did that too. Because even if the world can't be saved, we have to try. We have to try.

I floored the accelerator.

For the sake of the children, we must act as if there is hope, though we know there is not. We are under an obligation to do our mortal best, and will not be freed from that obligation while we yet live. We will never be freed until that day when heaven, like some vast and unimaginable mall, opens her legs to receive us all.